THE REPUBLIC OF THIEVES

BOOK THREE *of the*
Gentleman Bastard Sequence

THE REPUBLIC OF THIEVES

Book Three *of the*
Gentleman Bastard Sequence

SCOTT LYNCH

GOLLANCZ
LONDON

The right of Scott Lynch to be identified as the author of
this work has been asserted by him in accordance with the
Copyright, Designs and Patents Act 1988.

First published in Great Britain in 2013 by Gollancz
An imprint of the Orion Publishing Group
Orion House, 5 Upper St Martin's Lane, London WC2H 9EA
An Hachette UK Company

A CIP catalogue record for this book is
available from the British Library.

ISBN 978 0 575 07701 0 (Cased)
ISBN 978 0 575 08447 6 (Export Trade Paperback)

1 3 5 7 9 10 8 6 4 2

Typeset by Input Data Services Ltd, Bridgwater, Somerset

Printed and bound by CPI Group (UK) Ltd, Croydon, CR0 4YY

The Orion Publishing Group's policy is to use papers that
are natural, renewable and recyclable products and made
from wood grown in sustainable forests. The logging and
manufacturing processes are expected to conform to the
environmental regulations of the country of origin.

www.scottlynch.us
www.orionbooks.co.uk
www.gollancz.co.uk

For Jason McCray,
one man who in his time
has played many parts

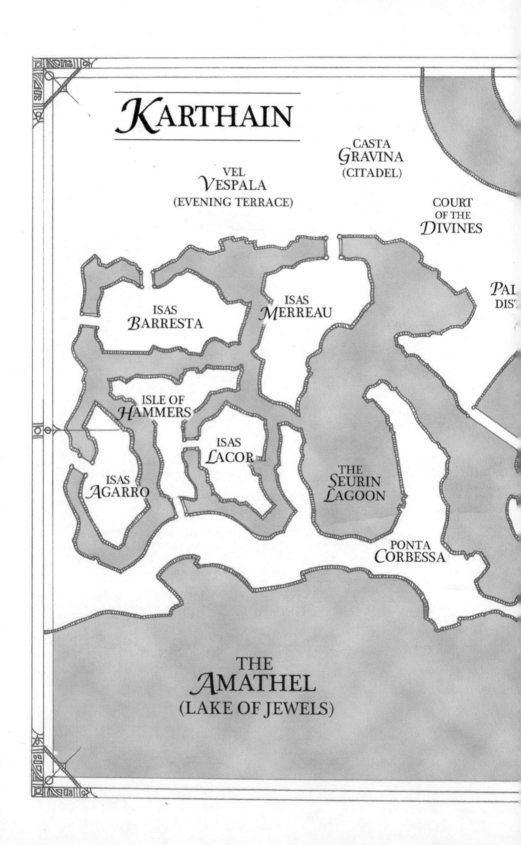

KARTHAIN

CASTA
GRAVINA
(CITADEL)

VEL
VESPALA
(EVENING TERRACE)

COURT
OF THE
DIVINES

ISAS
MERREAU

PAI
DIS

ISAS
BARRESTA

ISLE OF
HAMMERS

ISAS
LACOR

ISAS
AGARRO

THE
SEURIN
LAGOON

PONTA
CORBESSA

THE
AMATHEL
(LAKE OF JEWELS)

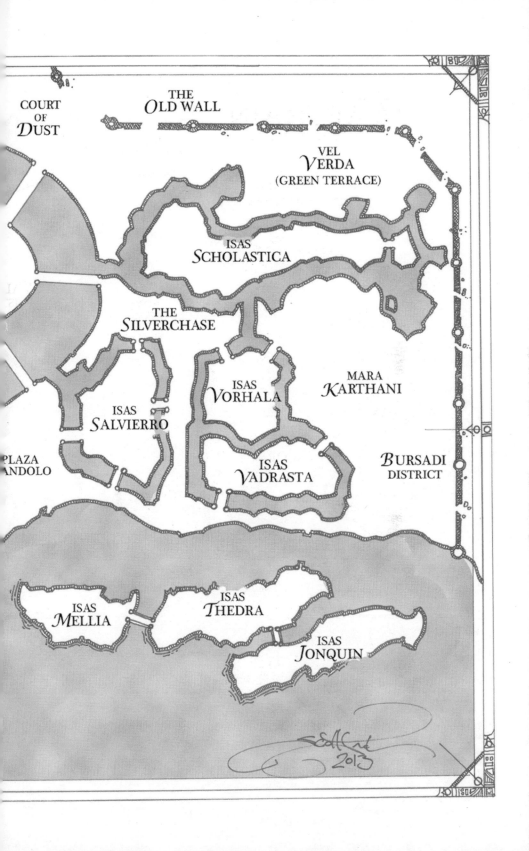

COURT
OF
DUST

THE
OLD WALL

VEL
VERDA
(GREEN TERRACE)

ISAS
SCHOLASTICA

THE
SILVERCHASE

ISAS
VORHALA

MARA
KARTHANI

ISAS
SALVIERRO

PLAZA
ANDOLO

ISAS
VADRASTA

BURSADI
DISTRICT

ISAS
MELLIA

ISAS
THEDRA

ISAS
JONQUIN

PROLOGUE
The Minder

I

Place ten dozen hungry orphan thieves in a dank burrow of vaults and tunnels beneath what used to be a graveyard, put them under the supervision of one partly crippled old man, and you will soon find that governing them becomes a delicate business.

The Thiefmaker, skulking eminence of the orphan kingdom beneath Shades' Hill in old Camorr, was not yet so decrepit that any of his grimy little wards could hope to stand alone against him. Nonetheless, he was alert to the doom that lurked in the clutching hands and wolfish impulses of a mob – a mob that he, through his training, was striving to make more predatory still with each passing day. The veneer of order that his life depended on was insubstantial as damp paper at the best of times.

His presence itself could enforce absolute obedience in a certain radius, of course. Wherever his voice could carry and his own senses seize upon misbehaviour, his orphans were tame. But to keep his ragged company in line when he was drunk or asleep or hobbling around the city on business, it was essential that he make them eager partners in their own subjugation.

He moulded most of the biggest, oldest boys and girls in Shades' Hill into a sort of honour guard, granting them shoddy privileges and stray scraps of near-respect. More importantly, he worked hard to keep every single one of them in constant deadly terror of himself. No failure was ever met with anything but pain or the promise of pain, and the seriously insubordinate had a way of vanishing. Nobody had any illusions that they had gone to a better place.

So he ensured that his chosen few, steeped in fear, had no outlet save to vent their frustrations (and thus enforce equivalent fear) upon the next oldest and largest set of children. These in turn would oppress the next weakest class of victim. Step by step the misery was shared out, and the Thiefmaker's authority would cascade like a geological pressure out to the meekest edges of his orphan mass.

It was an admirable system, considered in itself, unless of course you happened to be part of that outer edge – the small, the eccentric, the friendless. In their case, life in Shades' Hill was like a boot to the face at every hour of every day.

Locke Lamora was five or six or seven years old. Nobody knew for certain, or cared to know. He was unusually small, undeniably eccentric, and perpetually friendless. Even when he shuffled along inside a great smelly mass of orphans, one among dozens, he walked alone and he damn well knew it.

2

Meeting time. A bad time under the Hill. The shifting stream of orphans surrounded Locke like an unfamiliar forest, concealing trouble everywhere.

The first rule to surviving in this state was to avoid attention. As the murmuring army of orphans headed toward the great vault at the centre of Shades' Hill, where the Thiefmaker had called them, Locke flicked his glance left and right. The trick was to spot known bullies at a safe distance without making actual eye contact (nothing worse, the mistake of mistakes) and then, ever so casually, move to place neutral children between himself and each threat until it passed.

The second rule was to avoid responding when the first rule proved insufficient, as it too often did.

The crowd parted behind him. Like all prey animals, Locke had a honed instinct for approaching harm. He had enough time to wince preemptively, and then came the blow, sharp and hard, right between his shoulder blades. Locke smacked into the tunnel wall and barely managed to stay on his feet.

Familiar laughter followed the blow. It was Gregor Foss, years older and two stone heavier, as far beyond Locke's powers of reprisal as the duke of Camorr.

'Gods, Lamora, what a weak and clumsy little cuss you are.' Gregor put a hand on the back of Locke's head and pushed him along, still in full contact with the moist dirt wall, until his forehead bounced painfully off one of the old wooden tunnel supports. 'Got no strength to stay on your own feet. Hell, if you tried to bugger a cockroach, the roach'd spin you round and do you up the ass instead.'

Everyone nearby laughed, a few from genuine amusement, the rest from fear of being seen not laughing. Locke kept stumbling forward, seething but silent, as though it were a perfectly natural state of affairs to have a face covered with dirt and a throbbing bump on the forehead. Gregor shoved him once more, but without vigour, then snorted and pushed ahead through the crowd.

Play dead. Pretend not to care. That was the way to keep a few moments of humiliation from becoming hours or days of pain; to keep bruises from becoming broken bones or worse.

The river of orphans was flowing to a rare grand gathering, nearly all the Hill, and in the main vault the air was already heavier and staler than usual. The Thiefmaker sat in his high-backed chair, his head barely visible above the press of children, while his oldest subjects carved paths through the crowd to take their accustomed places near him. Locke sought a far wall and pressed up against it, doing his best impression of a shadow. There, with the welcome comfort of a guarded back, he touched his forehead and indulged in a momentary pout. His fingers were slippery with blood when he took them away.

After a few moments, the influx of orphans trickled to a halt, and the Thiefmaker cleared his throat.

It was a Penance Day in the seventy-seventh Year of Sendovani, a hanging day, and outside the dingy caves below Shades' Hill the duke of Camorr's people were knotting nooses under a bright spring sky.

3

'It's a lamentable business,' said the Thiefmaker. 'That's what it is. To have some of our own brothers and sisters snatched into the unforgiving arms of the duke's justice. Damned deplorable that they were slackards enough to get caught! Alas. As I have always been at pains to remind you, loves, ours is a delicate trade, not at all appreciated by those we practise upon.'

Locke wiped the dirt from his face. It was likely that his tunic sleeve deposited more grime than it removed, but the ritual of putting himself in order was calming. While he tended to himself the master of the Hill spoke on.

'Sad day, my loves, a proper tragedy. But when the milk's gone bad you might as well look forward to cheese, hmm? Oh yes! Opportunity!

It's unseasonal fine hanging weather out there. That means crowds with spending purses, and their eyes are going to be fixed on the *spectacle*, aren't they?'

With two crooked fingers (broken of old, and badly healed) he did a pantomime of a man stepping off an edge and plunging forward. At the end of the plunge the fingers kicked spasmodically and some of the older children giggled. Someone in the middle of the orphan army sobbed, but the Thiefmaker paid them no heed.

'You're all going out to watch the hangings in groups,' he said. 'Let this put fear into your hearts, loves! Indiscretion, clumsiness, want of confidence – today you'll see their only possible reward. To live the life the gods have given you, you must clutch wisely, then run. Run like the hounds of hell on a sinner's scent! That's how we dodge the noose. Today you'll have a last look at some friends who could not.

'And before you return,' he said, lowering his voice, 'each of you will do them one better. Fetch back a nice bit of coin or flash, at all hazards. Empty hands get empty bellies.'

'Has we gots to?'

The voice was a desperate whine. Locke identified the source as Tam, a fresh catch, a lowest-of-the-low teaser who'd barely begun to learn the Shades' Hill life. He must have been the one sobbing, too.

'Tam, my lamb, you *gots* to do nothing,' said the Thiefmaker in a voice like mouldy velvet. He reached out and sifted through the crowd of orphans, parting them like dirty stalks of wheat until his hand rested on Tam's shaven scalp. 'But then, neither do I if you don't work, right? By all means, remove yourself from this grand excursion. A limitless supply of cold graveyard dirt awaits you for supper.'

'But … can't I, like, do something else?'

'Why, you could polish my good silver tea service, if only I had one.' The Thiefmaker knelt, vanishing briefly from Locke's sight. 'Tam, this is the job I got, so it's the job you're gonna do, right? Good lad. Stout lad. Why the little rivers from the eyes? Is it just 'cause there's the hangings involved?'

'They – they was our friends.'

'Which means only—'

'Tam, you little piss-rag, stuff your whining up your stupid ass!'

The Thiefmaker whirled, and the new speaker recoiled from a slap to the side of his head. There was a ripple in the close-packed orphans as the unfortunate target stumbled backward and was returned to his feet by shoves from his tittering friends. Locke couldn't suppress a smile. It always warmed his heart to see a bullying oldster knocked around.

'Veslin,' said the Thiefmaker with dangerous good cheer, 'do you enjoy being interrupted?'

'N-no … no, sir.'

'How pleased I am to find us of a like mind on the subject.'

'Of … course. Apologies, sir.'

The Thiefmaker's eyes returned to Tam, and his smile, which had evaporated like steam in sunlight a moment before, leapt back into place.

'As I was saying about our friends, our lamented friends. It's a shame. But isn't it a grand show they're putting on for us as they dangle? A ripe plum of a crowd they're summoning up? What sort of friends would we be if we refused to work such an opportunity? Good ones? Bold ones?'

'No, sir,' mumbled Tam.

'Indeed. Neither good nor bold. So we're going to seize this chance, right? And we're going to do them the honour of not looking away when they drop, aren't we?'

'If … if you say so, sir.'

'I do say so.' The Thiefmaker gave Tam a perfunctory pat on the shoulder. 'Get to it. Drops start at high noon; the Masters of the Ropes are the only punctual creatures in this bloody city. Be late to your places and you'll have to work ten times as hard, I promise you. Minders! Call your teasers and clutchers. Keep our fresher brothers and sisters on short leashes.'

As the orphans dispersed and the older children called the names of their assigned partners and subordinates, the Thiefmaker dragged Veslin over to one of the enclosure's dirt walls for a private word.

Locke snickered, and wondered who he'd be partnered with for the day's adventure. Outside the Hill there were pockets to be picked, tricks to be played, bold larceny to be done. Though he realized his sheer enthusiasm for theft was part of what had made him a curiosity and an outcast, he had no more self-restraint in that regard than he had wings on his back.

This half-life of abuse beneath Shades' Hill was just something he had to endure between those bright moments when he could be at work, heart pounding, running fast and hard for safety with someone else's valuables clutched in his hands. As far as his five or six or seven years had taught him, ripping people off was the greatest feeling in the whole world, and the only real freedom he had.

4

'Think you can improve upon my leadership now, boy?' Despite his limited grip, the Thiefmaker still had the arms of a grown man, and he pinned Veslin against the dirt wall like a carpenter about to nail up a decoration. 'Think I need your wit and wisdom when I'm talking out loud?'

'No, your honour! Forgive me!'

'Veslin, jewel, don't I always?' With a falsely casual gesture, the Thiefmaker brushed aside one lapel of his threadbare coat and revealed the handle of the butcher's cleaver he kept hanging from his belt. The faintest hint of blade gleamed in the darkness behind it. 'I forgive. I remind. Are you reminded, boy? *Most thoroughly* reminded?'

'Indeed, sir, yes. Please …'

'Marvellous.' The Thiefmaker released Veslin, and allowed his coat to fall over his weapon once again. 'What a happy conclusion for us both, then.'

'Thank you, sir. Sorry. It's just … Tam's been whining all gods-damned morning. He's never seen anyone get the rope.'

'Once upon a time it was new to us all,' sighed the Thiefmaker. 'Let the boy cry, so long as he plucks a purse. If he won't, hunger's a marvellous instructor. Still, I'm putting him and a couple of other problems into a group for special oversight.'

'Problems?'

'Tam, for his delicacy. And No-Teeth.'

'Gods,' said Veslin.

'Yes, yes, the speck-brained little turd is so dim he couldn't shit in his hands if they were stitched to his asshole. Nonetheless, him. Tam. And one more.'

The Thiefmaker cast a significant glance at a far corner, where a sullen little boy leaned with his arms folded across his chest, watching other orphans form their assigned packs.

'Lamora,' whispered Veslin.

'Special oversight.' The Thiefmaker chewed nervously at the nails

6

of his left hand. 'There's good money to be squeezed out of that one, if he's got someone keeping him sensible and discreet.'

'He nearly burnt up half the bloody city, sir.'

'Only the Narrows, which mightn't have been missed. And he took hard punishment for that without a flinch. I consider the matter closed. What he needs is a responsible sort to keep him in check.'

Veslin was unable to conceal his expression of disgust, and the Thiefmaker smirked.

'Not you, lad. I need you and your little ape Gregor on distraction detail. Someone else gets made, you cover for 'em. And get back to me straightaway if anyone gets taken.'

'Grateful, sir, very grateful.'

'You should be. Sobbing Tam … witless No-Teeth … and one of hell's own devils in knee-breeches. I need a bright candle to watch that crew. Go wake me up one of the Windows bunch.'

'Oh.' Veslin bit his cheek. The Windows crew, so-called because they specialized in traditional burglary, were the true elite among the orphans of Shades' Hill. They were spared most chores, habitually worked in darkness, and were allowed to sleep well past noon. 'They won't like that.'

'I don't give a damn what they like. They don't have a job this evening anyway. Get me a sharp one.' The Thiefmaker spat out a gnawed crescent of dirty fingernail and wiped his fingers on his coat. 'Hell, fetch me Sabetha.'

5

'Lamora!'

The summons came at last, and from the Thiefmaker himself. Locke padded warily across the dirt floor to where the master of the Hill sat whispering instructions to a taller child whose back was turned to Locke.

Waiting before the Thiefmaker were two other boys. One was Tam. The other was No-Teeth, a hapless twit whose beatings at the hands of older children had eventually given him his nickname. A sense of foreboding scuttled into Locke's gut.

'Here we are, then,' said the Thiefmaker. 'Three bold and likely lads. You'll be working together on a special detail, under special authority. Meet your minder.'

The taller child turned.

She was dirty, as they all were, and though it was hard to tell by the pale silver light of the vault's alchemical lanterns, she looked a little tired. She wore scuffed brown breeches, a long baggy tunic that at some distant remove had been white, and a leather flat cap over a tight kerchief, so that not a strand of her hair was visible.

Yet she was undeniably a *she*. For the first time in Locke's life some unpractised animal sense crept dimly to life to alert him to this fact. The Hill was full of girls, but never before had Locke dwelt on the thought of *a* girl. He sucked in a breath and realized that he could feel a nervous tingling at the tips of his fingers.

She had the advantage of at least a year and a good half-foot on him, and even tired she had that unfeigned natural poise which, in certain girls, makes young boys feel like something on the order of an insect beneath a heel. Locke had neither the eloquence nor the experience to grapple with the situation in anything resembling those terms. All he knew was that near her, of all the girls he'd seen in Shades' Hill, he felt touched by something mysterious and much vaster than himself.

He felt like jumping up and down. He felt like throwing up.

Suddenly he resented the presence of Tam and No-Teeth, resented the implication of the word 'minder,' and yearned to be doing something, anything, to impress this girl. His cheeks burned at the thought of how the bump on his forehead must look, and at being teamed up with two useless, sobbing clods.

'This is Beth,' said the Thiefmaker. 'She's got your keeping today, lads. Take what she says as though it came from me. Steady hands, level heads. No slacking and no gods-damned capers. Last thing we need is you getting *ambitious*.' It was impossible to miss the icy glance the Thiefmaker spared for Locke as he uttered this last part.

'Thank you very much, sir,' said Beth with nothing resembling actual gratitude. She pushed Tam and No-Teeth toward one of the vault exits. 'You two, wait at the entrance. I need to have a private word with your friend here.'

Locke was startled. A word with him? Had she guessed that he knew his way around clutching and teasing, that he was nothing like the other two? Beth glanced around, then put her hands on his shoulders and knelt. Some nervous animal in Locke's guts turned somersaults as her gaze came level with his. The old compunction about refusing eye contact was not merely set aside, but vaporized from his mind.

Two things happened then.

First, he fell in love – though it would be years before he realized what the feeling was called and how thoroughly it was going to complicate his life.

Second, *she* spoke directly to him for the first time, and he would remember her words with a clarity that would jar his heart long after the other incidents of that time had faded to a haze of half-truths in his memory:

'You're the Lamora boy, right?'

He nodded eagerly.

'Well, look here, you little shit. I've heard all about you, so just shut your mouth and keep those reckless hands in your pockets. I swear to all the gods, if you give me one hint of trouble, I will heave you off a bridge and it will *look* like a bloody accident.'

6

It was an unwelcome thing, to suddenly feel half an inch tall.

Locke dazedly followed Beth, Tam, and No-Teeth out of the darkness of the Shades' Hill vaults and into the late-morning sunshine. His eyes stung, and the daylight was only part of it. What had he done (and who had told her about it?) to earn the scorn of the one person he now wanted to impress more than any other in the world?

Pondering, his thoughts wandered uneasily to his surroundings. Out here in the ever-changing open there was so much to see, so much to hear. His survival instincts gradually took hold. The back of his mind was all for Beth, but he forced his eyes to the present situation.

Camorr today was bright and busy, making the most of its reprieve from the hard grey rains of spring. Windows were thrown open. The more prosperous crowds had moulted, shedding their oilcloaks and cowls in favour of summery dress. The poor stayed wrapped in the same reek-soaked dross they wore in all seasons. Like the Shades' Hill crowd, they had to keep their clothes on their backs or risk losing them to rag-pickers.

As the four orphans crossed the canal bridge from Shades' Hill to the Narrows (it was a source of mingled pride and incredulity to Locke that the Thiefmaker was so convinced that one little scheme of his could have burnt this *whole* neighbourhood down), Locke saw at least three boats of corpse-fishers using hooks to pluck bloated bodies from under wharves and dock pilings. Those would sometimes go ignored for days in cool, foul weather.

Beth led the three boys through the Narrows, dodging up stone stairs and across rickety wooden foot-bridges, avoiding the most cramped and twisted alleys where drunks, stray dogs, and less obvious dangers were sure to lurk. Tam and Locke stayed right behind her, but No-Teeth was constantly veering off or slowing down. By the time they left the Narrows and crossed to the overgrown garden passages of the Mara Camorrazza, the city's ancient strolling park, Beth was dragging No-Teeth by his collar.

'Damn your pimple of a brain,' she said. 'Keep to my heels and quit making trouble!'

'Not making trouble,' muttered No-Teeth.

'You want to cock this up and go hungry tonight? You want to give some brute like Veslin an excuse to pry out any teeth he hasn't got to yet?'

'Nooooooo.' No-Teeth stretched the word out with a bored yawn, looked around as though noticing the world for the first time, then jerked free of Beth's grip. 'I want to wear your hat,' he said, pointing at her leather cap.

Locke swallowed nervously. He'd seen No-Teeth pitch these sudden, unreasonable fits before. There was something not quite right in the boy's head. He frequently suffered for calling attention to himself inside the Hill, where distinctiveness without strength meant pain.

'You can't,' said Beth. 'Mind yourself.'

'I want to. I want to!' No-Teeth actually stomped the ground and balled his fists. 'I promise I'll behave. Give me your hat!'

'You'll behave because I say so!'

No-Teeth's response was to lunge and snatch the leather cap off Beth's head. He yanked it so hard that her kerchief came as well, and an untidy spray of reddish-brown curls tumbled to her shoulders. Locke's jaw fell.

There was something so indefinably lovely, so *right*, about seeing that hair free in the sunlight that he momentarily forgot that his enchantment was expressly one-way, and that this was anything but convenient for their task. As Locke stared he noticed that only the lower portion of her hair was actually brown. Above the ears it was rusty red.

She'd had it coloured once, and it had grown out since.

Beth was even faster than No-Teeth once her shock wore off, and before he could do anything with her cap it was back in her hands. She slapped him viciously across the face with it.

'Ow!'

Not placated, she hit him again, and he cringed backward. Locke recovered his wits and assumed the vacant expression used inside the Hill by the uninvolved when someone nearby was getting thrashed.

'Stop! Stop!' No-Teeth sobbed.

'If you *ever* touch this cap again,' Beth whispered, shaking him by his collar, 'I swear to Aza Guilla who numbers the dead that I will deliver you straight to her. You *stupid* little ass!'

'I promise! I promise!'

She released him with a scowl, and with a few deft movements made her red curls vanish again beneath the tightly drawn kerchief. When the leather cap came down to seal them in, Locke felt a pang of disappointment.

'You're lucky nobody else saw,' said Beth, shoving No-Teeth forward. 'Gods love you, you little slug, you're just lucky nobody else saw. Quick, now. At my heel, you two.'

Locke and Tam followed her without a word, as close as nervous ducklings fixed on a mother's tail feathers.

Locke shook with excitement. He'd been horrified at the incompetence of his assigned partners, but now he wondered if their problems could do anything but make him look better in Beth's eyes. Oh yes. Let them whine, let them throw fits, let them go home with nothing in their hands. Hell, let them tip off the city watch and get chased through the streets to the sounds of whistles and baying dogs. She'd have to prefer anything to that, including him.

7

They emerged at last from the Mara Camorrazza into a whirl of noise and confusion.

It was indeed unseasonably fine hanging weather, and the normally dreary neighbourhood around the Old Citadel, the duke's seat of justice, bustled like a carnival. Common folk were thick on the cobblestones, while here and there the carriages of the wealthy rattled through the mess with hired guards trotting alongside passing out threats and shoves as they went. In some ways, Locke already knew, the world outside the Hill was much like the world within.

The four orphans formed a human chain to thread their way through the tumult. Locke held fast to Tam, who clung in turn to Beth. She was so unwilling to lose sight of No-Teeth that she thrust him before them all like a battering ram. From his perspective Locke glimpsed few adult faces; the world became an endless procession of belts, bellies, coattails and carriage wheels. They made their way west by equal parts luck and perseverance, toward the Via Justica, the canal that had been used for hangings for half a thousand years.

At the edge of the canal embankment a low stone wall prevented a direct plunge to the water seven or eight feet below. This barrier was crumbling but still solid enough for children to sit upon. Beth never once loosened her grip on No-Teeth as she helped Locke and Tam up out of the press of the crowd. Locke scrambled to sit next to Beth, but it was Tam that squeezed up against her, leaving Locke no means to move him without causing a scene. He tried to conceal his annoyance by adopting a purposeful expression and looking around.

From here, at least, Locke had a better view of the affair. There were crowds on both sides of the canal and vendors hawking bread, sausages, ale, and souvenirs from boats. They used baskets attached to poles to collect their coins and deliver goods to those standing above.

Locke could make out groups of small shapes dodging through the forest of coats and legs – fellow Shades' Hill orphans at work. He could also see the dark yellow jackets of the city watch, moving through the crowd in squads with shields slung over their backs. Disaster was possible if these opposing elements met and mixed like bad alchemy, but as yet there were no shouts, no watch-whistles, no signs of anything amiss.

Traffic had been stopped over the Black Bridge. The lamps that dotted the looming stone arch were covered with black shrouds, and a small crowd of priests, prisoners, guards, and ducal officials stood behind the execution platform that jutted from the bridge's side. Two boats of yellowjackets had anchored in the canal on either side of the bridge to keep the water beneath the dropping prisoners clear.

'Don't we has to do our business?' said No-Teeth. 'Don't we has to get a purse, or a ring, or something—'

Beth, who'd taken her hands off him for all of half a minute, now seized him again and whispered harshly, 'Keep your mouth shut about that while we're in the crowd. Mouth shut! We're going to sit here and be mindful. We'll work after the hanging.'

Tam shuddered and looked more miserable than ever. Locke sighed, confused and impatient. It was sad that some of their Shades' Hill fellows had to hang, but then it was sad they'd been caught by the yellow-jackets in the first place. People died everywhere in Camorr, in alleys and canals and public houses, in fires, in plagues that scythed down whole neighbourhoods. Tam was an orphan too; hadn't he realized all this? Dying seemed nearly as ordinary to Locke as eating supper or making water, and he was unable to make himself feel bad that it was happening to anyone he'd barely known.

As for that, it looked to be happening soon. A steady drumbeat rose from the bridge, echoing off water and stone, and gradually the excited murmur of the crowds dropped off. Not even divine services could make Camorri so respectfully attentive as a public neck-snapping.

'Loyal citizens of Camorr! Now comes noon, this seventeenth instant, this month of Tirastim in our seventy-seventh Year of Send-ovani.' These words were shouted from atop the Black Bridge by a huge-bellied herald in sable plumage. 'These felons have been found guilty of capital crimes against the law and customs of Camorr. By the authority of his grace, Duke Nicovante, and by the seals of his honourable magistrates of the Red Chamber, they are here brought to receive justice.'

There was movement beside him on the bridge. Seven prisoners were hauled forward, each by a pair of scarlet-hooded constables. Locke saw that Tam was anxiously biting his knuckles. Beth's arm appeared around Tam's shoulder, and Locke ground his teeth together. He was doing his job, behaving, refusing to make a spectacle of himself, and *Tam* was the one that received Beth's tenderness?

'You get used to it, Tam,' Beth said softly. 'Honour them, now. Brace up.'

On the bridge platform the Masters of the Ropes tightened nooses around the necks of the condemned. The hanging ropes were about as long as each prisoner was tall, and lashed to ringbolts just behind each prisoner's feet. There were no clever mechanisms in the hanging platform, no fancy tricks. This wasn't Tal Verrar. Here in the east, prisoners were simply heaved over the edge.

'Jerevin Tavasti,' shouted the herald, consulting a parchment. 'Arson, conspiracy to receive stolen goods, assault upon a duke's officer! Malina Contada, counterfeiting and attendant misuse of His Grace the Duke's name and image. Caio Vespasi, burglary, malicious mummery, arson, and horse theft! Lorio Vespasi, conspiracy to receive stolen goods.'

So much for the adults; the herald moved on to the three children. Tam sobbed, and Beth whispered, 'Shhhh, now.' Locke noted that Beth was coldly calm, and he tried to imitate her air of disinterest. Eyes just so, chin up, mouth just shy of a frown. Surely, if she glanced at him during the ceremony, she'd notice and approve …

'Mariabella, no surname,' yelled the herald. 'Theft and wanton disobedience! Zilda, no surname. Theft and wanton disobedience!'

The Masters were tying extra weights to the legs of this last trio of prisoners, since their own slight bodies might not provide for a swift enough conclusion at the ends of their plunges.

'Lars, no surname. Theft and wanton disobedience.'

'Zilda was kind to me,' whispered Tam, his voice breaking.

'The gods know it,' said Beth. 'Hush now.'

'For crimes of the body you shall suffer death of the body,' continued the herald. 'You will be suspended above running water and hanged there by the necks until dead, your unquiet spirits to be carried forth upon the water to the Iron Sea, where they may do no further harm to any soul or habitation of the duke's domain. May the gods receive your souls mercifully, in good time.' The herald lowered his scroll and faced the prisoners. 'In the duke's name I give you justice.'

Drums rolled. One of the Masters of the Ropes drew a sword, in case any of the prisoners fought their handlers. Locke had seen a hanging before, and he knew the condemned only got one chance at whatever dignity was left to them.

Today the drops ran smooth. The drumroll crashed to silence. Each pair of hooded yellowjackets stepped forward and shoved their prisoner off the edge of the hanging platform.

Tam flinched away, as Locke had thought he might, but even he was unprepared for No-Teeth's reaction when the seven ropes jerked taut with snapping noises that might have been hemp, or necks, or both.

'Ahhhhhhh! Ahhhhhhhhhhhhh! AHHHHHHHHHHHHHHHH-HHHHHHHHHH!'

Each scream was longer and louder than the last. Beth clamped a hand over No-Teeth's mouth and struggled with him. Over the water, four large bodies and three smaller ones swung like pendulums in arcs that quickly grew smaller and smaller.

Locke's heart pounded. Everyone nearby had to be staring at them. He heard chuckling and disapproving comments. The more attention they drew to themselves, the harder it would be to go about their real business.

'Shhh,' said Beth, straining to keep No-Teeth under control. 'Quiet, damn you. Quiet!'

'What's the matter, girl?'

Locke was dismayed to see that a pair of yellowjackets had parted the crowd just behind them. Gods, that was worse than anything! What if they were prowling for Shades' Hill orphans? What if they asked hard questions? He curbed an impulse to leap for the water below and froze in place, eyes wide.

Beth kept an arm locked over No-Teeth's face yet managed to somehow squirm around and bow her head to the constables.

'My little brother,' she gasped out, 'he's never seen a hanging before. We don't mean to cause a fuss. I've shut him up.'

No-Teeth ceased his struggles, but he began to sob. The yellowjacket who'd spoken, a middle-aged man with a face full of scars, looked down at him with distaste.

'You four come here alone?'

'Mother sent us,' said Beth. 'Wanted the boys to see a hanging. See the rewards of idleness and bad company.'

'A right-thinking woman. Nothing like a good hanging to scare the mischief out of a sprat.' The man frowned. 'Why ain't she here with you?'

'Oh, she loves a hanging, does Mother,' said Beth. Then, lowering her voice to a whisper: 'But, um, she's got the flux. Bad. All day she's been sitting on her—'

'Ah. Well then.' The yellowjacket coughed. 'Gods send her good health. You'd best not bring *this* one back to a Penance Day ceremony for a while.'

'I agree, sir.' Beth bowed again. 'Mother'll scratch his hide for this.'

'On your way then, girl. Don't need no more of a scene.'

'Of course, sir.'

The constables moved away into the crowd, which was itself coming back to life. Beth slid off the stone wall, rather gracelessly, because No-Teeth and Tam came with her. The former was still held tightly, and the latter refused to let go of her other arm. He hadn't cried out like No-Teeth, but Locke saw that his eyes brimmed with tears and he was even more pale-looking than before. Locke ran his tongue around the inside of his mouth, which had gone dry under the scrutiny of the yellowjackets.

'Come now,' said Beth. 'Away from here. We've seen all there is to see.'

8

Another passage through the forest of coats, legs, and bellies. Locke, feeling excitement rise again, gently clung to the back of Beth's tunic to avoid losing her, and he was both pleased and disappointed when she didn't react at all. Beth led them back into the green shadows of the Mara Camorrazza, where quiet solitude reigned not forty yards from a crowd of hundreds, and once they were safely ensconced in a concealed nook she pushed Tam and No-Teeth to the ground.

'What if another bunch from the Hill saw that? Gods!'

'Sorry,' moaned No-Teeth. 'But they … but they … they got kill—'

'People die when they get hanged. It's why they hang them!' Beth wrung the front of her tunic with both hands, then took a deep breath. 'Recover yourselves. Now. Each of you must lift a purse, or something, before we go back.'

No-Teeth broke into a new fit of sobs, rolled over on his side, and chewed his knuckles. Tam, sounding more weary than Locke would have imagined possible, said, 'I can't, Beth. I'm sorry. I'll get caught. I just can't.'

'You'll go without supper tonight.'

'Fine,' said Tam. 'Take me back, please.'

'Damn it.' Beth rubbed her eyes. 'I need to bring you back with something to show for it or I'll be in just as much trouble as you, understand?'

'You're in Windows,' muttered Tam. 'You got no worries.'

'If only,' said Beth. 'You two need to pull yourselves together—'

'I can't, I can't, I can't!'

Locke sensed a glorious opportunity. Beth had saved them from trouble on the embankment, and here was an ideal moment for him to do the same. Smiling at the thought of her reaction, he stood as tall as he could manage and cleared his throat.

'Tam, don't be a louse,' said Beth, completely ignoring Locke. 'You *will* clutch something, or work a tease so someone else can clutch. I'll not give you another choice—'

'Excuse me,' said Locke, hesitantly.

'What do you want?'

'They can each have one of mine,' said Locke.

'What?' Beth turned to him. 'What are you talking about?'

From under his tunic, Locke produced two leather purses and a fine silk handkerchief, only mildly stained.

'Three pieces,' he said. 'Three of us. Just say we all clutched one and we can go home now.'

'Where in all the *hells* did you—'

'In the crowd,' said Locke. 'You had No-Teeth … you were paying so much attention to him, you must not have seen.'

'I didn't tell you to lift anything yet!'

'Well, you didn't tell me not to.'

'But that's—'

'I can't put them back,' said Locke, far more petulantly than he'd intended.

'Don't snap at me! Oh, for the gods' sake, don't sulk,' said Beth. She knelt and put her hands on Locke's shoulders, and at her touch and close regard he found himself suddenly trembling uncontrollably. 'What is it? What's the matter?'

'Nothing,' said Locke. 'Nothing.'

'Gods, what a strange little boy you are.' She glanced again at Tam and No-Teeth. 'A pack of disasters, the three of you. Two that won't work. One that works without orders. I suppose we've got no choice.'

Beth took the purses and the handkerchief from Locke. Her fingers brushed his, and he trembled. Beth's eyes narrowed.

'Hit your head earlier?'

'Yes.'

'Who pushed you?'

'I just fell.'

'Of *course* you did.'

'Honest!'

'Seems to be troubling you. Or maybe you're ill. You're shaking.'

'I'm … I'm fine.'

'Have it your way.' Beth closed her eyes and massaged them with her fingertips. 'I guess you've saved me a hell of a lot of trouble. Do you want me to … look, is there someone bothering you that you want to stop?'

Locke was startled. An older child, *this* older child, of all people, and a member of Windows, was offering him protection? Could she do that? Could she put Veslin and Gregor in their place?

No. Locke forced his eyes away from Beth's utterly fascinating face to bring himself back down to earth. There would always be other Veslins, other Gregors. And what if they resented him all the more for her interference? She was Windows; he was Streets. Their days and nights were reversed. He'd never seen her before today; what sort of protection could he possibly get from her? He would keep playing dead. Avoid calling attention to himself. Rule one, and rule two. As always.

'I just fell,' he said. 'I'm fine.'

'Well,' she replied, a little coldly. 'As you wish.'

Locke opened and closed his mouth a few times, trying desperately to imagine something he might say to charm this alien creature. Too late. She turned away and heaved Tam and No-Teeth to their feet.

'I don't believe it,' she said, 'but you two idiots owe your supper to the arsonist of the Narrows here. Do you understand just how much hell we'll all catch if you ever breathe a word of this to anyone?'

'I do,' said Tam.

'I'd be very put out to catch any at all,' Beth continued. 'Any at all! You hear me, No-Teeth?'

The poor wretch nodded, then sucked his knuckles again.

'Back to the Hill, then.' Beth tugged at her kerchief and adjusted her cap. 'I'll keep the things and pass them to the master myself. Not a word about this. To *anyone*.'

She kept her now-customary grip on No-Teeth all the way back to the graveyard. Tam dogged her heels, looking exhausted but relieved. Locke followed at the rear, scheming to the fullest extent of his totally inadequate experience. What had he said or done wrong? What had he misjudged? Why wasn't she delighted with him for saving her so much trouble?

She said nothing to him for the rest of the trip home. Then, before he could find an excuse to speak to her again once there, she was gone, vanished into the tunnels that led to the private domain of the Windows crew, where he could not follow.

He sulked that night, eating little of the supper his nimble fingers had earned, fuming not at Beth but at himself for somehow driving her away.

9

Days passed, longer days than any Locke had ever known, now that he had something to preoccupy him beyond the brief excitement of daily crimes and the constant chores of survival.

Beth would not leave his thoughts. He dreamed of her, and how the hair spilling out from beneath her cap had caught the light filtering down through the interlaced greenery of the Mara Camorrazza. Strangely, in his dreams, that hair was purely red from edge to root, untouched by dye or disguise. The price for these visions was that he would wake to cold, hard disappointment and lie there in the dark, wrestling with mysterious emotions that had never troubled him before.

He would have to see her again. Somehow.

At first he nurtured a hope that his relegation to a crew of troublemakers might be permanent, that Beth might be their minder on an ongoing basis. Unfortunately, the Thiefmaker seemed to have no such plans. Locke slowly realized that if he was ever going to get another chance to impress her, he'd have to stick his neck out.

It was hard to break the routines he'd established for himself, to say nothing of those expected of someone in his lowly position. Yet he began to wander more often throughout the vaults and tunnels of his home, anxious for a glimpse of Beth, exposing himself to abuse and ridicule from bored older children. He played dead. He didn't react. Rule one and rule two. It almost felt good, earning bruises for a genuine purpose.

The lesser orphans of Streets (that is, nearly all of them) slept en masse on the floor of crèche-like side vaults, several dozen to a room. When his dreams woke him at night Locke would now try to stay awake, to strain his ears to hear past the murmuring and rustling of those around him, to detect the coming and going of the Windows crew on their secretive errands.

Before he'd always slept securely in the heart of his snoring fellows, or against a nice comforting wall. Now he risked positions at the outer edge of the huddled mass, where he could catch glimpses of people in the tunnels. Every shadow that passed and every step he heard might be hers, after all.

His successes were few. He saw her at evening meals several times, but she never spoke to him. Indeed, if she noticed him at all, she did a superb job of not showing it. And for Locke to try and speak to her on his own initiative, with her surrounded by her Windows friends, and they by the older bullies from Streets ... no presumption could have been more fatal. So he did his feeble best to skulk and spy on her, relishing the fluttering of his stomach whenever he caught so much as a half-second glimpse. Those glimpses and those sensations paid for many days of frustrated longing.

More days, more weeks passed in the hazy forever now of childhood time. Those bright brief moments he'd spent in Beth's presence, actually speaking to her and being spoken to, were polished and re-polished in Locke's memory until his very life might have begun on that day.

At some point that spring, Tam died. Locke heard the mutterings. The boy was caught trying to lift a purse, and his would-be victim smashed his skull with a walking stick. This sort of thing wasn't uncommon. If the man had witnesses to the attempted theft he'd probably lose a finger on his weaker hand. If nobody backed his story, he'd hang. Camorr was civilized, after all; there were acceptable and unacceptable times for killing children.

No-Teeth went soon after that, crushed under a wagon wheel in broad daylight. Locke wondered if it wasn't all for the best. He and Tam had been miserable in the Hill, and maybe the gods could find something better to do with them. It wasn't Locke's concern anyway. He had his own obsession to pursue.

A few days after No-Teeth got it, Locke came home from a long, wet afternoon of work in the North Corner district, casing and robbing vendor stalls at the well-to-do markets there. He shook the rain from his makeshift cloak, which was the same awful-smelling scrap of leather that served him as a blanket each night. Then he went to meet the crowd of oldsters, led by Veslin and Gregor, who shook down the smaller children each day as they came in with their takings.

Usually they spent most of their energy taunting and threatening Locke's fellows, but today they were talking excitedly about something else. Locke caught snatches of the conversation as he waited his turn to be abused.

'… right unhappy he is about it … one of the big earners.'

'I know she was, and didn't she put on airs about it, too.'

'But that's all Windows for you, eh? Ain't they all like that? Well here's something they won't like. Proves they's as mortal as we is. They fuck up just the same.'

'Been a right messy month. That poor sod what got the busted head … that little shit we used to kick the chompers out of … now her.'

Locke felt a cold tautness in his guts.

'Who?' he said.

Veslin paused in mid-sentence and stared at Locke, as though startled that the little creatures of Streets had the power of speech.

'Who what, you little ass-tickler?'

'Who are you talking about?'

'Wouldn't you like to fucking know.'

'WHO?'

Locke's hands had formed themselves into fists of their own accord, and his heart pounded as he yelled again at the top of his lungs, 'WHO?'

Veslin only had to kick him once to knock him down. Locke saw it coming, saw the bully's foot rising toward his face, growing impossibly in size, and still he couldn't avoid it. Floor and ceiling reversed themselves, and when Locke could see again, he was on his back with Veslin's heel on his chest. Warm coppery blood was trickling down the back of his throat.

'Where does he get off, talking to us like that?' said Veslin mildly.

'Dunno. Fuckin' sad, it is,' said Gregor.

'Please,' said Locke. 'Tell me—'

'Tell you what? What right you got to know anything?' Veslin knelt on Locke's chest, rifled through his clothes, and came up with the things he'd managed to clutch that day. Two purses, a silver necklace, a handkerchief, and some wooden tubes of Jereshti cosmetics. 'Know what, Gregor? I don't think I remember Lamora here coming home with anything tonight.'

'Nor me, Ves.'

'Yeah. How's that for sad, you little piss-pants? You want dinner, you can eat your own shit.'

Locke was too used to the sort of laughter that now rose in the tunnel to pay any attention to it. He tried to get up and was kicked in the throat for his trouble.

'I just want to know,' he gasped, 'what happened—'

'Why do you care?'

'Please … please …'

'Well, if you're gonna be civil about it.' Veslin dropped Locke's takings into a dirty cloth sack. 'Windows had themselves a bad night.'

'Cocked up proper, they did,' said Gregor.

'Got pinched hitting a big house. Not all of 'em got clear. Lost one in a canal.'

'Who?'

'Beth. Drowned, she did.'

'You're lying,' whispered Locke. 'YOU'RE LYING!'

Veslin kicked him in the side of his stomach and Locke writhed. 'Who says … who says she's—'

'I fuckin' say.'

'Who told you?'

'I got a letter from the duke, you fuckin' half-wit. The master, that's who! Beth drowned last night. She ain't coming back to the Hill. You sweet on her or something? That's a laugh.'

'Go to hell,' whispered Locke. 'You go to—'

Veslin cut him off with another hard kick to the exact same spot.

'Gregor,' he said, 'we got a real problem here. This one ain't right in the head. Forgot what he can and can't say to the likes of us.'

'I got just the thing for it, Ves.' Gregor kicked Locke between the legs. Locke's mouth opened, but nothing came out except a dry hiss of agony.

'Give it to the little shit-smear.' Veslin grinned as he and Gregor began to work Locke over with hard kicks, carefully aimed. 'You like that, Lamora? You like what you get, you put on airs with us?'

Only the Thiefmaker's proscription of outright murder among his orphans saved Locke's life. No doubt the boys would have pulped him if their own necks wouldn't have been the price of their amusement, and as it was they nearly went too far.

It was two days before Locke could move well enough to work again, and in that interval, lacking friends to tend him, he was tormented by hunger and thirst. But he took no satisfaction in his recovery, and no joy in his return to work.

He was back to playing dead, back to hiding in corners, back to rule one and rule two. He was all alone in the Hill once again.

I

HER SHADOW

'I CANNOT tell you now;
When the wind's drive and whirl
Blow me along no longer,
And the wind's a whisper at last—
Maybe I'll tell you then
some other time.'

—*Carl Sandburg* from 'The Great Hunt'

CHAPTER ONE
Things Get Worse

I

Weak sunlight against his eyelids drew him out of sleep. The brightness intruded, grew, made him blink groggily. A window was open, letting in mild afternoon air and a freshwater smell. Not Camorr. Sound of waves lapping against a sand beach. Not Camorr at all.

He was tangled in his sheets again, lightheaded. The roof of his mouth felt like sun-dried leather. Chapped lips peeled apart as he croaked, 'What are you …'

'Shhhh. I didn't mean to wake you. The room needed some air.' A dark blur on the left, more or less Jean's height. The floor creaked as the shape moved about. Soft rustle of fabric, snap of a coin purse, clink of metal. Locke pushed himself up on his elbows, prepared for the dizziness. It came on punctually.

'I was dreaming about her,' he muttered. 'The times that we … when we first met.'

'Her?'

'Her. You know.'

'Ah. The canonical *her*.' Jean knelt beside the bed and held out a cup of water, which Locke took in his shaking left hand and sipped at gratefully. The world was slowly coming into focus.

'So vivid,' said Locke. 'Thought I could touch her. Tell her … how sorry I am.'

'That's the best you can manage? Dreaming of a woman like *that*, and all you can think to do with your time is apologize?'

'Hardly under my control—'

'They're your dreams. Take the reins.'

'I was just a little boy, for the gods' sakes.'

'If she pops up again move it forward ten or fifteen years. I want to see some blushing and stammering next time you wake up.'

'Going somewhere?'

'Out for a bit. Making my rounds.'

'Jean, there's no point. Quit torturing yourself.'

'Finished?' Jean took the empty cup from him.

'Not nearly. I—'

'Won't be gone long.' Jean set the cup on the table and gave the lapels of his coat a perfunctory brushing as he moved to the door. 'Get some more rest.'

'You don't bloody listen to reason, do you?'

'You know what they say about imitation and flattery.'

The door slid shut and Jean was gone, out into the streets of Lashain.

2

Lashain was famous as a city where anything could be bought and anything could be left behind. By the grace of the *regio*, the city's highest and thinnest order of nobility (where a title that could be traced back more than two generations qualified one for the old guard), just about anyone with cash in hand and enough of a pulse to maintain semiconsciousness could have their blood transmuted to a reasonable facsimile of blue.

From every corner of the Therin world they came – merchants and criminals, mercenary captains and pirates, gamblers and adventurers and exiles. As commoners they entered the chrysalis of a counting-house, shed vast quantities of precious metal, and as newborn peers of Lashain they emerged into daylight. The *regio* minted demibarons, barons, viscounts, counts, and even the occasional marquis, with styles largely of their own invention. Honours were taken from a list and cost extra; 'Defender of the Twelvefold Faith' was quite popular. There were also half a dozen meaningless orders of knighthood that looked marvellous on a coat lapel.

Because of the novelty of this purchased respectability to those who brokered it for themselves, Lashain was the most violently manners-conscious city Jean Tannen had ever visited. Lacking centuries of aristocratic descent to assure them of their worth, the neophytes of Lashain overcompensated with ceremony. Their rules of precedence were like alchemical formulae, and dinner parties killed more of them each year than fevers and accidents combined. It seemed that little could be more thrilling for those who'd just bought their family names than to risk them (not to mention their mortal flesh) over minor insults.

The record, as far as Jean had heard, was three days from counting-house to duelling green to funeral cart. The *regio*, of course, offered no refunds to relations of the deceased.

As a result of this nonsense, it was difficult for those without titles, regardless of the colour of their coin, to gain ready access to the city's best physikers. They were made such status symbols by their noble clients that they rarely had to scamper after gold from other sources.

The taste of autumn was in the cool wind blowing off the Amathel, the Lake of Jewels – the freshwater sea that rolled to the horizon north of Lashain. Jean was conservatively dressed by local standards, in a brown velvet frock coat and silks worth no more than, say, three months' wages for an average tradesman. This marked him instantly as someone's man and suited his current task. No gentleman of consequence did his own waiting at a physiker's garden gate.

Scholar Erkemar Zodesti was regarded as the finest physiker in Lashain, a prodigy with the bone saw and the alchemist's crucible. He'd also shown complete disinterest, for three days straight, in Jean's requests for a consultation.

Today Jean once again approached the iron-barred gate at the rear of Zodesti's garden, from behind which an elderly servant peered at him with reptilian insolence. In Jean's outstretched hand was a parchment envelope and a square of white card, just like the three days previous. Jean was getting testy.

The servant reached between the bars without a word and took everything Jean offered. The envelope, containing the customary gratuity of (far too many) silver coins, vanished into the servant's coat. The old man read or pretended to read the white card, raised his eyebrows at Jean, and walked away.

The card said exactly what it always did – *Contempla va cora frata eminenza*. 'Consider the request of an eminent friend,' in the Throne Therin that was the polite affectation for this sort of gesture. Rather than giving an aristocrat's name, this message meant that someone powerful wished to pay anonymously to have someone else examined. This was a common means of bringing wealth to bear on the problem of, say, a pregnant mistress, without directly compromising the identity of anyone important.

Jean passed the long minutes of his wait by examining the physiker's house. It was a good solid place, about the size of a smaller Alcegrante mansion back in Camorr. Newer, though, and done up in a mock Tal

Verrar style that laboured to proclaim the importance of its inhabitants. The roof was tiled with slats of volcanic glass, and the windows bordered with decorative carvings that would have better suited a temple.

From the heart of the garden itself, closed off from view by a ten-foot stone wall, Jean could hear the sounds of a lively party. Clinking glasses, shrieks of laughter, and behind it all the hum of a nine-stringed viol and a few other instruments.

'I regret to inform your master that the scholar is presently unable to accommodate his request for a consultation.' The servant reappeared behind the iron gate with empty hands. The envelope, a token of earnestness, was of course gone. Whether into the hands of Zodesti or this servant, Jean couldn't say.

'Perhaps you might tell me when it would be more convenient for the scholar to receive my master's petition,' said Jean, 'the middle of the afternoon for half a week now being obviously unsuitable.'

'I couldn't say.' The servant yawned. 'The scholar is consumed with work.'

'With work.' Jean fumed as the sound of applause drifted from the garden party. 'Indeed. My master has a case which requires the greatest possible skill and discretion—'

'Your master could rely upon the scholar's discretion at all times,' said the servant. 'Unfortunately, his skill is urgently required elsewhere at the moment.'

'Gods damn you, man!' Jean's self-control evaporated. 'This is important!'

'I will not be spoken to in a vulgar fashion. Good day.'

Jean considered reaching through the iron bars and seizing the old man by the throat, but that would have been counter-productive. He wore no fighting leathers under his finery, and his decorative shoes would be worse than bare feet in a scuffle. Despite the pair of hatchets tucked away under his coat, he wasn't equipped to storm even a garden party by choice.

'The scholar risks giving offence to a citizen of considerable importance,' growled Jean.

'The scholar *is* giving offence, you simple fellow.' The old man chuckled. 'I tell you plainly, he has little interest in the sort of business arranged in this fashion. I don't believe a single citizen of quality is so unfamiliar with the scholar that they need fear to be received by the front door.'

'I'll call again tomorrow,' said Jean, straining to keep his composure. 'Perhaps I might name a sum that will penetrate even your master's indifference.'

'You are to be commended for your persistence, if not for your perception. Tomorrow you must do as your master bids. For now, I have already said good day.'

'Good day,' growled Jean. 'May the gods cherish the house wherein such kindness dwells.' He bowed stiffly and left.

There was nothing else to be done at the moment, in this gods-damned city where even throwing envelopes of coins was no guarantee of attracting attention to a problem.

As he stomped back to his hired carriage, Jean cursed Maxilan Stragos for the thousandth time. The bastard had lied about so much. Why, in the end, had the damned poison been the one thing he'd chosen to tell the truth about?

3

Home for the time being was a rented suite in the Villa Suvela, an un-adorned but scrupulously clean rooming house favoured by travellers who came to Lashain to take the waters of the Amathel. Those waters were said to cure rheumatism, though Jean had yet to see a bather emerge leaping and dancing. The rooming house overlooked a black sand beach on the city's northeast shore, and the other lodgers kept to themselves.

'The bastard,' said Jean as he threw open the door to the suite's inner apartment. 'The motherless Lashani reptile. The greedy son of a piss-bucket and a bad fart.'

'My keen grasp of subtle nuance tells me you might be frustrated,' said Locke. He was sitting up, and he looked fully awake.

'We've been snobbed off again,' said Jean, frowning. Despite the fresh air from the window the inner apartment still smelled of old sweat and fresh blood. 'Zodesti won't come. Not today, at least.'

'To hell with him then, Jean.'

'He's the only physiker of repute I haven't got to yet. Some of the others were difficult, but he's being impossible.'

'I've been pinched and bled by every gods-damned lunatic in this city who ever shoved a bolus down a throat,' said Locke. 'One more hardly signifies.'

'He's the best.' Jean flung his coat over a chair, set his hatchets down, and removed a bottle of blue wine from a cabinet. 'An alchemical expert. A real smirking rat-fucker, too.'

'It's all for the good, then,' said Locke. 'What would the neighbours say if I consulted a man who screws rodents?'

'We need his opinion.'

'I'm tired of being a medical curiosity,' said Locke. 'If he won't come, he won't come.'

'I'll call again tomorrow.' Jean poured two half-glasses of wine and watered them until they were a pleasant afternoon-sky colour. 'I'll have the self-important prick here one way or another.'

'What would you do, break his fingers if he won't consult? Might make things ticklish for me. Especially if he wants to cut something off.'

'He might find a solution.'

'Oh, for the gods' sake.' Locke's frustrated sigh turned into a cough. 'There is no solution.'

'Trust me. Tomorrow is going to be one of my unusually persuasive days.'

'As I see it, it's cost us only a few pieces of gold to discover how unfashionable we are. Most social failures incur far greater expense, I should think.'

'Somewhere out there,' said Jean, 'must be an illness that makes its sufferers meek, mild, and agreeable. I'll find it someday, and see that you get the worst possible case.'

'I'm sure I was born immune. Speaking of agreeable, will that wine be arriving in my hands any time this year?'

Locke had seemed alert enough, but his voice was slurring, and weaker than it had been even the day before. Jean approached the bed uneasily, wineglasses held out like a peace offering to some unfamiliar and potentially dangerous creature.

Locke had been in this condition before, too thin and too pale, with weeks of beard on his cheeks. Only this time there was no obvious wound to tend, no cuts to bandage. Just Maxilan Stragos' insidious legacy doing its silent work. Locke's sheets were spotted with blood and with the dark stains of fever-sweat. His eyes gleamed in bruised sockets.

Jean pored over a pile of medical texts each night, and still he didn't have adequate words for what was happening to Locke. He was being unknit from the inside; his veins and sinews were coming apart. Blood seeped out of him as though by some demonic whim. One hour he might cough it up, the next it would come from his eyes or nose.

'Gods damn it,' Jean whispered as Locke reached for the wineglass. Locke's left hand was red with blood, as though his fingers had been dipped in it. 'What's this?'

'Nothing unusual,' Locke chuckled. 'It started up while you were gone … from under my nails. Here, I can hold the glass with my other one—'

'Were you trying to hide it from me? Who else changes your gods-damned sheets?'

Jean set the glasses down and moved to the table beneath the window, which held stacks of linen towels, a water jug and a washing bowl. The bowl's water was rusty with old blood.

'It doesn't hurt, Jean,' muttered Locke.

Ignoring him, Jean picked up the bowl. The window overlooked the villa's interior courtyard, which was fortunately deserted. Jean heaved the old bloody water out the window, refilled the bowl from the jug, and dipped a linen cloth into it.

'Hand,' said Jean. Locke sulkily complied, and Jean moulded the wet cloth around his fingers. It turned pink. 'Keep it elevated for a while.'

'I know it looks bad, but it's really not that much blood.'

'You've little left to lose!'

'I'm also in want of wine.'

Jean fetched their glasses again and carefully placed one in Locke's right hand. Locke's shakes didn't seem too bad for the moment, which was pleasing. He'd had difficulty holding things lately.

'A toast,' said Locke. 'To alchemists. May they all be stricken with the screaming fire-shits.' He sipped his wine. 'Or strangled in bed. Whatever's most convenient. I'm not picky.'

At his next sip, he coughed, and a ruby-coloured droplet spiralled down into his wine, leaving a purplish tail as it dissolved.

'Gods,' said Jean. He gulped the rest of his own wine and set the glass aside. 'I'm going out to fetch Malcor.'

'Jean, I don't need another damned dog-leech at the moment. He's been here six or seven times already. Why—'

'Something might have changed. Something might be different.'

Jean grabbed his coat. 'Maybe he can help the bleeding. Maybe he'll finally find some clue—'

'There is no *clue*, Jean. There's no antidote that's going to spring from Malcor or Kepira or Zodesti or any boil-lancing fraud in this whole tedious shitsack of a city.'

'I'll be back soon.'

'Dammit, Jean, save the money!' Locke coughed again, and nearly dropped his wine. 'It's only common sense, you brick-skulled tub! You obstinate—'

'I'll be back soon.'

'... obstinate, uh, something ... something ... biting and witty and thoroughly convincing! Hey, if you leave now, you'll miss me being thoroughly convincing! Damn it.'

Whatever Locke might have said next, Jean closed the door on it. The sky outside was now banded in twilight colours, orange at the horizons giving way to silver and then purple in the deep bowl of the heavens. Purple like the colour of blood dissolving in blue wine.

A low grey wall sliding in to the north, from out of the Amathel, seemed to promise an oncoming storm. That suited Jean just fine.

4

Six weeks had passed since they'd left the little port of Vel Virazzo in a forty-foot yacht, fresh from a series of more or less total disasters that had left them with a fraction of the vast sum they'd hoped to recoup for two years invested in a complex scheme.

As he walked out into the streets of Lashain, Jean ran his fingers over a lock of curly dark hair, tightly bound with leather cords. This he always kept in a coat pocket or tucked into his belt. Of all the things he'd lost recently, the money was the least of his concerns.

Locke and Jean had discussed sailing east, back toward Tamalek and Espara ... back toward Camorr. But most of the world they'd known there was swept away, and most of their old friends were dead. Instead they'd gone west. North and west.

Following the coast, straining their lubberly skills to the utmost, they had skirted Tal Verrar, swept past the blackened remains of once-luxurious Salon Corbeau, and discussed making far north for Balinel, in the Kingdom of the Seven Marrows. Both of them spoke Vadran well enough to do just about anything while they sought some new criminal opportunity.

They left the sea and headed inland, up the wide River Cavendria, which was Eldren-tamed and fit for oceangoing vessels. The Cavendria flowed west from the Amathel, Lake of Jewels, the inland sea that separated the ancient sister-cities of Karthain and Lashain. Locke and Jean had once hoped to buy their way into the ranks of Lashain's nobility. Their revised plan had merely been to weigh their boat down with stores for the voyage up to Balinel.

Locke's symptoms revealed themselves the day they entered the Cavendria estuary.

At first it had been nothing more than bouts of dizziness and blurred vision, but as the days passed and they slowly tacked against the current, he began bleeding from his nose and mouth. By the time they reached Lashain, he could no longer laugh away or hide his increasing weakness. Instead of taking on stores, they'd rented rooms, and against Locke's protests Jean began to spend nearly every coin they had in pursuit of comforts and cures.

From Lashain's underworld, which was tolerably colourful if nowhere near the size of Camorr's, he'd consulted every poisoner and black alchemist he could bribe. All had shaken their heads and expressed professional admiration for what had been done to Locke; the substance in question was beyond their power to counteract. Locke had been made to drink a hundred different purgatives, teas, and elixirs, each seemingly more vile and expensive than the last, each ultimately useless.

After that, Jean had dressed well and started calling on accredited physikers. Locke was explained away as a 'confidential servant' of someone wealthy, which could have meant anything from secret lover to private assassin. The physikers too had expressed regret and fascination in equal measure. Most had refused to attempt cures, instead offering palliatives to ease Locke's pain. Jean fully grasped the meaning of this, but paid no heed to their pessimism. He simply showed each to the door, paid their exorbitant fees, and went after the next physiker on his list.

The money hadn't lasted. After a few days, Jean had sold their boat (along with the resident cat, essential for good luck at sea), and was happy to get half of what they'd paid for it.

Now even those funds were running thin, and Erkemar Zodesti was

35

just about the only physiker in Lashain who had yet to tell Jean that Locke's condition was hopeless.

5

'No new symptoms,' said Malcor, a round old man with a grey beard that curled out from his chin like an oncoming thunderhead. Malcor was a dog-leech, a street physiker with no formal training or license, but of all his kind available in Lashain he was the most frequently sober. 'Merely a new expression of familiar symptoms. Take heart.'

'Not likely,' said Locke. 'But thanks for the hand job.'

Malcor had poulticed the tips of Locke's fingers with a mixture of corn meal and honey, then tied dry linen bandages around the fingers, turning Locke's left hand into a padded lump of uselessness.

'Heh. Well, the gods love a man who laughs at hardship.'

'Hardship is boring as all hell. Gotta find laughs if you can't stay drunk,' said Locke.

'So the bleeding is nothing new? Nothing worse than before?' asked Jean.

'A new inconvenience, yes.' Malcor hesitated, then shrugged. 'As for the total loss to his body's sanguine humours ... I can't say. A close examination of his water could, perhaps—'

'You want a bowl full of piss,' said Locke, 'you can uncork your private reserve. I've given quite enough since I came here.'

'Well then.' Malcor's knees creaked like rusty hinges as he stood up. 'If I won't scry your piss, I won't scry your piss. I can, however, leave you with a pill that should bring you excellent relief for twelve to twenty-four hours, and perhaps encourage your depleted humours to rekindle—'

'Splendid,' said Locke. 'Will it be the one composed primarily of chalk, this time? Or the one made of sugar? I'd prefer sugar.'

'Look ... I say, look here!' Malcor's seamy old face grew red. 'I might not have Collegium robes, but when I go to the gods they'll know that I gave an honest damn about lending ease to my patients!'

'Peace, old man.' Locke coughed and rubbed his eyes with his unbandaged hand. 'I know you mean the best. But spare me your placebo.'

'Have your friend remove your bandages in a few hours,' said Malcor testily, shrugging back into a worn frock coat that was spattered with dark stains. 'If you drink, drink sparingly. Water your wine.'

'Rest assured my friend here waters my wine like a virgin princess' nervous chaperone.'

'I'm sorry,' said Jean, as he showed Malcor outside. 'He's difficult when he's ill.'

'He's got two or three days,' said the old man.

'You can't be—'

'Yes, I can. The bleeding is worse. His enervation is more pronounced. His humours are terminally imbalanced, and I'm certain an examination of his water would show blood. I tried to hearten him, but your friend is obviously undeceived.'

'But—'

'As should you be.'

'There must be someone who can do something!'

'The gods.'

'If I could convince Zodesti—'

'Zodesti?' Malcor laughed. 'What a waste of a gift in that one. Zodesti treats only two ailments, wealth and prominence. He'll never condescend to do so much as take your friend's pulse.'

'So you've no other clues? No other suggestions?'

'Summon priests. While he's still lucid.' Jean scowled, and the aged dog-leech took him gently by the shoulders. 'I can't name the poison that's killing your friend. But the one that's killing you is called hope.'

'Thank you for your time,' growled Jean. He shook several silver coins out of his purse. 'If I should have further need of these marvellous insights—'

'A single *duvesta* will be quite adequate,' said Malcor. 'And despite your mood now, know that I'll come whenever you require. Your friend's discomfort is more likely to wax than wane before the end.'

The sun was gone, and the roofs and towers of the city were coming alive with specks of fire against the deepening night. As he watched Malcor vanish down the street, Jean wanted more than anything to have someone to hit.

6

'Fair day to you,' said Jean, approaching the garden gate again. It was the second hour of the afternoon, the next day, and the sky overhead was a boiling mess of grey. The rain had yet to fall, but it was coming, certain and soon. 'I'm here for my usual petition.'

'How completely unexpected,' said the old man behind the iron bars.

'Is it a convenient time?' From inside the garden, Jean could hear laughter again, along with a series of echoing smacks, as though something were being thrown against a stone wall. 'Or is the scholar consumed—'

'By work. Stranger, has the conversation we had yesterday fled your memory?'

'I must beg you, sir.' Jean put as much passionate sincerity as he could into his voice. 'A good man lies dying, in desperate need of aid. Did your master not take oath as a physiker of the Collegium?'

'His oaths are no business of yours. And many good men lie dying, in desperate want of aid, in Lashain and Karthain and every other place in the world. Do you see the scholar saddling his horse to seek them out?'

'Please.' Jean shook a fresh envelope, jingling the coins within. 'At least carry the message, for the love of all the gods.'

Wearing half a scowl and half a smirk, the servant reached through the bars. Jean dropped the envelope, seized the man by the collar, and slammed him hard against the gate. An instant later Jean flourished a knife in his free hand.

It was a push-dagger, the sort wielded with a thrusting fist rather than a fencer's grip. The blade seated against Jean's knuckles was half a foot long and curved like an animal's claw.

'There's only one use for a knife like this,' whispered Jean. 'You see it? You try to call out or pull away, and you'll be wearing your belly-fat for an apron. Open the gate.'

'You'll die for this,' hissed the servant. 'They'll skin you and boil you in salt water.'

'And what a consolation that will be for you, eh?' Jean prodded him in the stomach with his knife. 'Open the gate or I'll take the keys from your corpse.'

With a shaking hand, the old man opened the gate. Jean threw it aside, grabbed the servant again, and turned him around. The knife was now at the small of the man's back.

'Take me to your master. Stay composed. Tell him that an important case has come up and that he *will* want to hear my offer.'

'The scholar is in the garden. But you're mad. … He has friends in the highest places … urk!'

Jean poked him again with the blade, urging him forward.

38

'Of course,' said Jean. 'But do you have any friends closer than my knife?'

At the heart of the garden, a short, solid man of about thirty-five was sharing a hearty laugh with a woman who had yet to see twenty. Both of them wore light breeches, silk shirts, and padded leather gloves. That explained the rhythmic noise from before. They'd been using a cleared section of stone wall for *pursava*, the 'partner chase,' an aristocratic cousin of handball.

'Sir, madam, a thousand pardons,' said the servant at another poke from Jean. Jean stood half a pace behind the man, where neither Zodesti nor his guest could see the true means of his entry into the garden. 'A very urgent matter, sir.'

'Urgent?' Zodesti had a mop of black curls, now slick with sweat, and the remains of an upper-class Verrari accent. 'Who does this fellow come to speak for?'

'An eminent friend,' said Jean. 'In the usual fashion. It would not be appropriate to discuss these matters in front of your young—'

'By the gods, I'll say what's appropriate or not in my own garden! This fellow has some cheek, Loran. You know my preferences. This had better be in earnest.'

'Dire earnest, sir.'

'Let him leave his particulars. If I find them suitable he may call again after dinner.'

'Now would be better,' said Jean, 'for everyone.'

'Who in all the hells do you think you are? Shit on your dire earnest! Loran, throw this—'

'Refusal noted and cordially declined.' Jean shoved Loran to the turf. Half a second later he was upon Zodesti, with a meaty forearm wrapped around the physiker's throat and his blade held up so the young woman could see it. 'Cry out for help and I will use this, madam. I would hate to have an injury to the scholar resting upon your conscience.'

'I … I …' she said.

'Babble all you like, so long as you don't scream. As for *you*—' Jean squeezed the man's windpipe to demonstrate his strength, and the physiker gasped. 'I've tried to be civil. I would have paid well. But now I'll teach you a new way of doing business. Do you have a kit you would bring to a case of poisoning? Materials you'd need for a consultation?'

'Yes,' choked Zodesti. 'In my study.'

'We're going to calmly walk into your house, all of us. On your feet, Loran. You have a carriage and driver on the grounds, Scholar?'

'Yes,' said Zodesti.

'Inside, then, as though nothing is amiss. If any of you give me any trouble, by the gods, I'll start practising throat surgery.'

<h1 style="text-align:center">7</h1>

The ticklish part was getting them all into Zodesti's study, past the curious eyes of a cook and a kitchen-boy. But none of Jean's hostages caused a scene, and soon enough the study door was between them and any interference. Jean shot the bolt, smiled, and said, 'Loran, would you—'

At that moment, the old man found the courage for a last desperate struggle. Foul as his temper was, Jean didn't truly have the heart to stab the poor idiot, and smashed the edge of his knife hand into Loran's jaw instead. The servant hit the floor senseless. Zodesti darted to a desk in the corner and had a drawer open before Jean collared him and flung him down beside Loran. Jean glanced into the drawer and laughed.

'Going to fight me off with a letter-opener? Take a seat, both of you.' Jean indicated a pair of armchairs against the rear wall. While Zodesti and his companion sat there, wide-eyed as pupils awaiting punishment from a tutor, Jean cut down one of the drapes that hung beside the study's shuttered window. He slashed it into strips and tossed them to Zodesti.

'I don't quite understand—'

'Your young friend offers a problem,' said Jean. 'Meaning no particular offence to you, madam, but one hostage is difficult enough to handle, let alone two. Particularly when they're clumsy amateur hostages, unused to their roles and expectations. So we'll leave you in that fine big closet over there, where you won't be found too late *or* too soon.'

'How dare you,' said the young woman. 'I'll have you know that my uncle is—'

'Time is precious and my knife is sharp,' said Jean. 'When some servant finally opens that closet, do they find you alive or dead?'

'Alive,' she gulped.

'Gag her, Scholar,' said Jean. 'Then tie some good, firm knots. I'll check them myself when you're done. After she's secure, do the same for old Loran.'

As Zodesti worked to tie up his *pursava* partner (if that was indeed the limit of their partnership), Jean tore down another drape and cut it into more strips. His eyes wandered to the room's glass-fronted cabinets. They contained a collection of books, glass vessels, herbal samples, alchemical powders, and bizarre surgical instruments. Jean was heartened; if Zodesti's esoterica reflected his actual ability, he might just have an answer after all.

8

'This will do,' said Jean.

'Michel,' said Zodesti, leaning out the window on his side of the carriage, 'pull up here.'

The carriage rattled to a halt, and the driver hopped down to open the door. Jean, knife half-concealed by the wide cuff of his coat, gestured for Zodesti to step out first. The scholar did, carrying a leather bag and a bundle of clothing.

A light rain had begun to fall, for which Jean was grateful. It would drive bystanders from the streets, and the overcast sky gave the city the look of twilight rather than midafternoon. A kidnapper could ask for no more.

Jean had ordered the halt about two blocks from the Villa Suvela, in front of an alley that would lead there by twists and turns with a dozen other possible destinations branching off along the way.

'The scholar will require several hours,' said Jean, passing a folded slip of parchment to the driver. 'Wait at this address until we meet you again.'

The address on the parchment was a coffeehouse in Lashain's mercantile district, a half-mile distant. The driver frowned.

'Is this well with you, sir? You'll miss dinner—'

'It's fine, Michel,' said Zodesti with a hint of exasperation. 'Just follow directions.'

'Of course, sir.'

Once the carriage had clattered down the street, Jean pulled Zodesti into the alley and said, 'You may live through this yet. Get dressed as we discussed.'

The pile of clothing included a battered hat and a rain-stained cloak, both belonging to Loran, who was a fair match in size for his master. Zodesti threw the cloak on, and Jean pulled a strip of slashed drapery from his pocket.

'What the hell is this, now?' said Zodesti.

'Did you really imagine I'd go to all this trouble and let you see where I'm taking you? I thought you'd prefer blindfolded to unconscious.'

Zodesti stood still as Jean blindfolded him, pulled up the cloak's hood, and pushed the hat down on top of it. It was a good effect. From more than a few feet away, the blindfold would be concealed by the hat or lost in the shadows of the hood.

From Zodesti's medical bag, Jean withdrew a bottle of wine. He pulled the cork (Jean had found the bottle in Zodesti's study, half empty), splashed some on the physiker, poured the rest on the ground, and pressed the empty bottle into Zodesti's right hand. From the smell that wafted up around them, Jean guessed he'd just wasted a very valuable *kameleona*.

'Now,' said Jean, 'you're my drunk friend, being escorted to safety. Keep your head down.' Jean pressed Zodesti's bag into the physiker's left hand. 'I've got my arms around you to keep you from stumbling, and my knife closer than you'd like.'

'You'll boil alive for this, you son of a bitch.'

'Let's keep my mother out of this. Mind your feet.'

It took about ten minutes for them to stumble to the rooming house together. There were no complications. The few people out in the rain had better things to pay attention to than a pair of drunks, it seemed.

Once safely inside their suite, Jean locked the front doors, shoved Zodesti into a chair, and said, 'Now we're well away from anyone else. If you try to escape, or raise your voice, or call attention to yourself in *any* way, I'll hurt you. Badly.'

'Stop threatening me and show me your damned patient.'

'In a moment.' Jean opened the doors to the inner apartment, saw that Locke was awake, and quickly gestured in their private sign language:

Don't use any names.

'What am I,' muttered Locke, 'an idiot? I knew he wasn't coming back here of his own free will.'

'How—'

'You wore your fighting boots and left your dress shoes by the wardrobe. And all of your weapons are missing.'

42

'Ah.' Jean tore off Zodesti's blindfold and disguise. 'Make yourself comfortable and get to work.'

The physiker hefted his satchel and, sparing a hateful glance for Jean, moved to Locke's bedside. He stared at Locke for a few moments, then pulled a wooden chair over and sat down.

'I smell wine,' said Locke. '*Kameleona*, I think. I don't suppose you've brought any with you?'

'Only what your friend bathed me with,' said Zodesti. He snapped his fingers a few times in front of Locke's eyes, then took his pulse from both wrists. 'My, you are in a sad state. You believe you've been poisoned?'

'No,' said Locke with a cough. 'I fell down some fucking stairs. What's it look like?'

'Can't you ever be polite to any of your physikers?' said Jean.

'*You're* the one who bloody well kidnapped him.'

'Since I appear to have no choice,' said Zodesti, 'I'm going to give you a thorough examination. This may cause some discomfort, but don't complain. I won't be listening.'

Zodesti's first examination took a quarter of an hour. Ignoring Locke's grumbling, he poked and prodded at his joints and limbs, working from the top of his arms to his feet.

'You're losing sensation in your extremities,' said Zodesti at last.

'How the hell can you tell?'

'I just stuck a lancet into each of your large toes.'

'You poked holes in my feet?'

'I'm adding teardrops to a river, given the blood you're losing elsewhere.' Zodesti fumbled in his bag, removed a silk case, and from this extracted a pair of optics with oversized lenses. Wearing them, he pulled Locke's lips back and examined his gums and teeth.

'Ahm naht a fckhng horth,' said Locke.

'Quiet.' Zodesti held the clean portion of one of Locke's discarded bandages to his gums for several seconds, pulled it away, and frowned at it.

'Your gums are seeping blood. And I see your fingernails are trim,' said Zodesti.

'What of it?'

'Were they trimmed on a Penance Day?'

'How the hell should I remember?'

'Trimming the nails on any day but a Penance Day weakens the

43

blood. Tell me, when you were first taken with your symptoms, did you think to swallow an amethyst?'

'Why would I have had one close at hand?'

'Your pig-ignorance of basic medicine is your own misfortune. You sound like an easterner, though, so I can't say I'm surprised.'

The rest of the physiker's work took an hour, with Zodesti performing increasingly esoteric tests and Jean hovering behind him, alert for any sign of treachery. Finally, Zodesti sighed and rose to his feet, wiping his bloody hands on Locke's sheets.

'You have the unfortunate distinction,' said Zodesti, 'of being poisoned by a substance beyond my experience. Given the fact that I have a Master's Ring in alchemy from the Therin Collegium—'

'Gods damn your jewelry,' said Jean. 'Can you *do* anything?'

'In the early stages of the poisoning, who could have said? But now...' Zodesti shrugged.

'You maggot!' Jean grabbed Zodesti by his lapels, whirled, and slammed him against the wall beside Locke's bed. 'You arrogant little fraud! You're the best this city has? DO SOMETHING!'

'I can't,' said Zodesti with a new firmness in his voice. 'Think whatever you like, do whatever you like. He is beyond my powers of intervention. I daresay that puts him beyond anyone's.'

'Let him go,' said Locke.

'There must be something—'

'Let him go!' Locke retched, spat up more blood, and broke into a coughing fit. Jean released Zodesti, and the physiker slid away, glaring.

'Shortly after the poison was administered,' said the physiker, 'I could have tried a purgative. Or filled his stomach with milk and parchment pulp. Or bled him to thin out the venom. But this thing has been with him for too long now.

'Even with known poisons,' he continued, returning his instruments to his bag, 'there comes a point where the harm to organs or humours cannot be reversed. Antidotes don't restore dead flesh. And with this, an unknown poison? His blood is pouring out of him. I can't just put it back.'

'Gods damn it,' whispered Jean.

'The question is no longer *if* but *when*,' said Zodesti. 'Look, you ugly bastard, despite the way you brought me into this mess, I've given him my full and fair attention.'

'I see.' Jean slowly walked over to the linen table, took up a clay cup, and filled it with water from the jug. 'Do you have anything with you that can bring about a strong sleep? In case his pain should worsen?'

'Of course.' Zodesti removed a small paper pouch from his bag. 'Have him take this in water or wine and he won't be able to keep his eyes open.'

'Now wait just a damn minute,' said Locke.

'Give it here,' said Jean. He took the packet, poured its contents into the water, and shook the cup several times. 'How long will it last?'

'Hours.'

'Good.' Jean passed the cup to Zodesti and gestured at it with a dagger. 'Drink up.'

'What?'

'I don't want you running off to the first constable you can find as soon as I dump you on the street.'

'Don't think I would be so foolish as to try and run from you—'

'Don't think I give a damn. Drink the whole thing or I'll break your arms.'

Zodesti quickly gulped the contents of the cup. 'How I'm going to laugh when they catch you, you son of a bitch.' He tossed the cup down carelessly on Locke's bed and sat with his back against the wall. 'All the justices of Lashain are my patients. Your friend's too sick to run. If he's still alive when they catch you they'll draw and quarter him just to give you something to watch while you wait for your own exe … execution. …'

A few seconds later his head rolled forward and he began snoring.

'Think he's pretending?' said Locke.

Jean shoved the tip of his dagger into the calf of Zodesti's out-stretched right leg. The physiker didn't stir.

'I hate to say that I told you so,' said Locke, settling back against his cushions and folding his hands in front of him. 'Wait, no I don't. I could use a bottle of wine, and don't add any water this—'

'I'll get Malcor,' said Jean. 'I'll have him stay the night. Constant attention.'

'Damn it, Jean, wake up.' Locke coughed and pounded on his chest. 'What a reversal this is, eh? I wanted to die in Vel Virazzo and you pulled me back to my senses. Now I really am dying and you're bereft of yours.'

'There's—'

'No more physikers, Jean. No more alchemists, no more dog-leeches.

No more rocks to pry up looking for miracles.'

'How can you just lie there like a fish washed up on shore, with no fight at all?'

'I suppose I could flop around a bit, if you thought it would help.'

'The Grey King sliced you like a veal cutlet and you came back from that, twice as aggravating as ever.'

'Sword cuts. If they don't turn green, you can expect to heal. It's the nature of things. With black alchemy, who the hell knows?'

'I'll give you wine, but I want you to take it with two parts water, like Malcor said. And I want you to eat tonight, everything you can. Keep your strength up—'

'I'll eat, but only to give the wine some ballast. There's no other point to it, Jean. There's no cure forthcoming.'

'If you can't be cured, you'll have to endure. Outlast it, until it breaks like a fever.'

'The poison's more likely to last than I am.' Locke coughed and dabbed at his mouth with one of his sheets. 'Jean, you've called down some trouble by stealing this little weasel out of his house. Surely you can see that.'

'I was very careful.'

'You know better! He'll remember your face, and Lashain's not so very big. Look, take the money that's left. Take it and get out of town tonight. You can slip into a dozen trades at will, you speak four languages, you'll be wealthy again in—'

'Incomprehensible babble.' Jean sat on the edge of the bed and gently pushed Locke's sweat-slick hair out of his eyes. 'I don't understand a word you're saying.'

'Jean, I know you. You'll kill half a city block when your blood's up, but you'll *never* slit the throat of a sleeping man who's done us no real harm. That means constables will kick our doors down sooner or later. Please don't be here when they do.'

'You brought this upon yourself when you cheated that antidote into my glass. The consequences are yours to—'

'Like hell. You would have robbed me of that choice, too! Gods, all this manoeuvring for moral advantage! You'd think we were married.' Locke coughed and arched his back. 'The gods must truly have it in for you, to make you my nurse,' he said quietly. 'Not once but twice, now.'

'Hell, they made me your nurse when I was ten years old. You can

46

knock down kingdoms on a whim. What you need is someone to make sure you don't get hit by a carriage when you cross the street.'

'That's all over now, though. And it might have been kinder for you if I had been hit by a carriage—'

'You see this?' Jean took the tightly bound lock of dark, curly hair out of his coat pocket and held it up. 'You see this, you bloody bastard? You know where it came from. I'm done losing. Do you fucking hear me? I am *done* losing. Spare me your precious self-pity, because this isn't a stage and I didn't pay two coppers to cry my eyes out over anyone's death speech. You don't fucking get one, understand? I don't care if you cough up buckets of blood. Buckets I can carry. I don't care if you howl like a dog for months. You're going to eat and drink and keep fighting.'

'Well,' said Locke after a few moments had passed in silence. He smiled wryly. 'If you are going to be an intractable son of a bitch, why don't you uncork that wine so we can start with the part about drinking?'

9

Jean left Zodesti in an alley about three blocks west of the Villa Suvela, taking care to conceal him well and cover his bag with trash. He wouldn't be at all pleased when he awoke, but at least he'd be alive.

Locke's condition changed little that night; he slept in fits and starts, sipped wine, grudgingly chewed cold beef and soft bread, and continued bleeding. Jean fell asleep sitting up and managed to spill ale over a useless treatise on poisons. Most of their nights had been like this, recently.

The rain kept up well into the next night, enfolding the city in murk. Just before the unseen sundown Jean went out to fetch fresh supplies. There was a merchants' inn not ten minutes from the Villa Suvela that was used to dealing in necessities at odd hours.

When Jean came back, the front door was completely unmarked. He had no reason to suspect that anything was amiss, until he glanced down in the entry and saw the great mess of water that had recently been brought across the threshold.

Movement on both sides – too many attackers, too prepared. A basket of food and wine was no weapon at all. Jean went down under

47

a press of bodies. With desperate strength he smashed a nose, kicked a foot, tried to claw out the space he needed to pull and use his hatchets—

'Enough,' said a commanding voice. Jean looked up. The door to the inner apartment was open, and there were men standing over Locke's bed.

'No!' Jean yelled, ceasing his fight. Four men seized him and dragged him into the inner room, where he counted at least five more visible opponents. One of them grabbed a towel from the linens table and held it up to his bleeding nose.

'I'm sorry,' said Locke, hoarsely. 'They came right after you left—'

'Quiet.' The speaker was a rugged man about Locke and Jean's age, with a brawler's scarred jaw and a nose that looked like it had been used to break a hard fall. His hair was scraped down to stubble, and he wore quality fighting leathers under a long black coat. Had Jean been thinking straight, he would have realized that the consequences of Zodesti's abduction might come back to them from directions other than the Lashani constabulary. 'How's your head, Leone?'

'Broge my fuggin node,' said the man holding a towel to his face.

'Builds character.' The man in the black coat picked up a chair, set it down in front of Jean, then kicked him in the stomach, good and fast, barely giving him time to flinch before the pain hit. Jean groaned, and the four men holding him bore down on him with all of their weight, lest he try anything stupid.

'Wait,' coughed Locke. 'Please—'

'If I have to say "quiet" again,' said the black-coated man, 'I'll cut your fucking tongue out and pin it to the wall. Now shut up.' He sat down in the chair and smiled. 'My name is Cortessa.'

'Whispers,' said Jean. This was much worse than the constabulary. Whispers Cortessa was a top power in the Lashani underworld.

'So they call me. I presume you're Andolini.'

That was the name Jean had given when renting their rooms, and he nodded.

'If it's real I'm the king of the Seven Marrows,' said Cortessa. 'But nobody cares. Can you tell me why I'm here?'

'You ran out of sheep to fuck and went looking for some action?'

'Gods, I love Camorri. Constitutionally incapable of doing things the easy way.' Cortessa slapped Jean hard enough to make his eyes water. 'Try again. Why am I here?'

'You heard,' Jean gasped, 'that we'd finally discovered the cure for being born with a face like a stray dog's ass.'

'No. If that were true you would have used it.' Cortessa's next blow was no slap, but a back-handed bruise-maker. Jean blinked as the room swam around him.

'Now, I would *love* to sit here and paint the floor with your blood. Leone would probably love it even more. But I think I can save us all a lot of time.' Cortessa beckoned, and one of the men standing over Locke's bed lifted a club. 'What does your friend lose first? A knee? A few toes? I can be creative.'

'*No*. Please.' Jean would have bent his head to Cortessa's feet if he hadn't been restrained. 'I'm the one you want. I won't waste any more of your time. Please.'

'You're the one I want, suddenly? Why would I want you?'

'Something about a physiker, I'd guess.'

'There we are. That wasn't so hard after all.' Cortessa cracked his knuckles. 'What did you think might happen when someone like Zodesti came home from the shit you pulled yesterday?'

'Certainly would have been nice if he'd never said anything at all.'

'Don't be simple. Now, I know you're a friend of the friends. I hear things. When you first came to Lashain you knew your business. Kept the peace, made your gifts, *behaved*. You clearly understand how things work in our world. So do you think Zodesti ran up and down the streets, screaming that he'd been stolen away like a child? Or do you think he sent a few private messages to people who know people?'

'Shit,' said Jean.

'Yeah. So, I got the job and I thought to myself … wasn't there a big man looking for alchemists and dog-leeches just last week? What might they have to say about him? Oh? A bad poisoning? A man bleeding to death in bed at the Villa Suvela?' Cortessa spread his arms and smiled beatifically. 'Some problems just solve themselves.'

'How can I make amends?' said Jean.

'You can't.' Cortessa stood up, laughing.

'Please don't do anything to my friend. He had nothing to do with the physiker. Do whatever you like with me. I'll cooperate. Just—'

'My, you've gone from hard to soft, big man. You'll cooperate? Of course you'll fucking cooperate, you've got four of my men sitting on you.'

'There's money,' said Jean. 'Money, or I could work for you—'

'You've got nothing I want,' said Cortessa. 'And that's your problem. But I have a serious problem of my own.'

'Oh?'

'Ordinarily, this is the part where we'd make soup out of your balls and watch you drink it. Ordinarily. But we have what you might call a *conflict of interest*. On the one hand, you're an outlander and you touched a Lashani with all the right friends. That says we fucking kill you.

'On the other hand, it's plain you are or were some sort of connected man in Camorr. Big Barsavi might not be with us anymore, gods rest his crooked soul, but nobody in their right mind wants to fuck with the capas. You could be somebody's cousin. Who knows? A year or two from now, maybe someone comes looking for you. Asks around town. Whoops! Someone tells them to look on the bottom of the lake. And who gets sent back to Camorr in a box to pay the debt? Yours truly. That says we *don't* fucking kill you.'

'Like I said, I have some money,' said Jean. 'If that can help.'

'It's not your money anymore. But what does help is that your friend here is already dying … and from the looks of it, he'll be pretty damn glad to go.'

'Look, if you'll just let him stay, he needs rest—'

'I know. That's why I'm kicking your asses out of Lashain.' Cortessa waved his hands at his people. 'Strip the place. All the food, all the wine. Blankets, bandages, money. Take the wood out of the fireplace. Throw the water out of the jug. Pass word to the innkeeper that these two fucks are under the interdict.'

'Please,' said Jean. 'Please—'

'Shut up. You can keep your clothes and your weapons. I won't send you out completely naked. But I want you gone. By sunrise, you're out of the city or Zodesti gets to cut your ears off himself. Your friend can find somewhere else to die.' Cortessa gave Locke a pat on the leg. 'Think fondly of me in hell, you poor bastard.'

'You might not be long in getting there yourself,' said Locke. 'I'll have a big hug waiting for you.'

Cortessa's people ransacked the suite. They carefully piled Jean's weapons on the floor; everything else was taken or smashed. Locke was left on the empty bed in his bloodstained breeches and tunic. Jean's private purse and the one that had contained their general funds were both emptied. A few moments later, one of

Cortessa's men stuffed the empty purses into his pockets as well.

'Oh,' said Cortessa to Jean as the tumult was winding down, 'one thing more. Leone gets a minute alone with you in the corner. For his nose.'

'Bleth you, bothss,' muttered Leone, gingerly poking at the swollen bruises that had spread to his lips.

'And you get to take it, outlander. Lift so much as a finger and I'll have your friend gutted.' Cortessa patted Jean on the cheek and turned to leave. 'Sunrise. Get the fuck out of Lashain. Or our next conversation takes place in Scholar Zodesti's cellar.'

10

'Jean,' whispered Locke as soon as the last of Cortessa's bruisers had left. 'Jean! Are you alright?'

'I'm fine.' Jean was huddled where the linens table had been before Cortessa's men removed it. Leone had been straightforward but enthusiastic, and Jean felt as though he'd been thrown down a rocky hillside. 'I'm just … enjoying the floor. It was kind enough to catch me when I fell.'

'Jean, listen. I took some of the money when we got here on the boat. … I hid it. Loosened a floorboard under the bed.'

'I know you did. I unloosened it. Took it back.'

'You eel! I wanted you to have something to get away with when you—'

'I knew you'd try it, Locke. There weren't many hiding places available within stumbling distance of the bed.'

'Argh!'

'Argh, yourself.' Jean heaved himself over on his back and stared at the ceiling, breathing shallowly. Nothing felt broken, but his ribs and everything attached to them were lined up to file complaints. 'Give me a few minutes. I'll go out and find some blankets for you. I can get a cart. Maybe a boat. Get you out of here somehow, before the dawn. We've got a lot of darkness to use.'

'Jean, you'll be watched until you leave. They're not going to let you—' Locke coughed several times. '—steal anything big. And I'm not going to let you carry me.'

'Not let me carry you? What are you going to fend me off with, sarcasm?'

'You should have had a few thousand solari to work with, Jean. Could have gone anywhere … done anything with it.'

'I did exactly what I wanted to do with it. Now, you go with me. Or I stay here to die with you.'

'There's no reasoning with you.'

'You're such a paragon of compromise yourself. Pig-brained gods-damned egotist.'

'This isn't a fair contest. You have more energy for big words than I do.' Locke laughed. 'Gods, look at us. Can you believe they even took our firewood?'

'Very little surprises me these days.' Jean slowly stood up, wincing all the way. 'So, inventory. No money. Clothes on our backs. Mostly *my* back. Some weapons. No firewood. Since I doubt we'll be allowed to lift anything in the city, looks like I'll have to do some highway work.'

'How do you plan on halting carriages?'

'I'll throw you in the road and hope they stop.'

'Criminal genius. Will they be stopping out of heartfelt sympathy?'

'Revulsion, more likely.'

There was a knock at the front door.

Locke and Jean glanced at one another uneasily, and Jean picked up a dagger from the small pile of weapons that had been left to him.

'Maybe they're back for the bed,' said Locke.

'Why would *they* bother knocking?'

Jean kept most of his body behind the door as he opened it, and he tucked the dagger just out of sight behind his back.

It wasn't Cortessa, or a dog-leech, or even the master of the Villa Suvela, as Jean had expected. It was a woman, dressed in a richly embroidered oilcloak streaming with water. She held an alchemical globe in her hands, and by its pale light Jean could see that she was not young.

Jean scanned the curb behind her. No carriage, no litter, no escort of any sort – just misty darkness and the patter of the rain. A local? A fellow guest of the Villa Suvela?

'I, uh … can I be of assistance, madam?'

'I believe we can be of assistance to one another. If I might come in?' She had a soft and lovely voice, with something very close to a Lashani accent. Close, but not exact.

'We are … that is, I'm sorry, but we have some difficulty at the moment. My friend is ill.'

'I know they took your furniture.'

'You do?'

'And I know that you and your friend didn't have much else to begin with.'

'Madam, you seem to have me at a disadvantage.'

'And you seem to have me out in the rain.'

'Um.' Jean shuffled the dagger and made it vanish up his tunic sleeve. 'Well, my friend, as I said, is gravely ill. You should be aware—'

'I don't mind.' She entered the instant Jean's resolution wavered, and gracefully got out of the way as he closed the door behind her. 'After all, poison is only contagious at dinner parties.'

'How the hell ... are you a physiker?'

'Hardly.'

'Are you with Cortessa?'

The woman only laughed at that, and threw back the hood of her oilcloak. She was about fifty, the well-tended sort of fifty that only wealth could make possible, and her hair was the colour of dry autumn wheat with currents of silver at the temples. She had a squarish face, with disconcertingly wide, dark eyes.

'Here, take this.' She tossed the alchemical globe to Jean, who caught it by reflex. 'I know they took your lights, too.'

'Um, thank you, but—'

'My, my.' The woman unclasped her cloak and spun it off her shoulders as she strolled into the inner apartment. Her coat and skirts were richly brocaded with silver threads, and puffs of silver lace from beneath her cuffs half-covered her hands. She glanced at Locke. 'Ill would seem to be an understatement.'

'Forgive me for not getting up,' said Locke. 'And for not offering you a seat. And not being dressed. And for not ... giving a damn.'

'Down to the last dregs of your charm, I see.'

'Down to the last dregs of my everything. Who are you, then?'

The woman shook out her oilcloak, then threw it over Locke like a blanket.

'Th-thank you.'

'It's difficult to have a serious conversation with someone whose dignity is compromised, Locke.'

The next sound in the room was that of Jean slamming home the bolt on the front door. In an instant he returned to the inner apartment, knife in hand. He tossed the light-globe onto the bed, where

Locke prevented it from bouncing onto the floor.

'In faith,' said Jean, 'my patience for mysterious shit went out that door with the money and the furniture. So you explain how you know that name, and I won't have to feel guilty for—'

'I doubt you'd survive what would happen if you acted on that impulse, Jean Tannen. I know your pride wouldn't. Put your blade away.'

'Like hell!'

'Poor Gentlemen Bastards,' said the woman softly. 'So far from home. But always in our sight.'

'*No*,' said Jean in a disbelieving whisper.

'Oh, gods,' said Locke. He coughed and closed his eyes. 'It's *you*. I suspected you'd kick our door down sooner or later.'

'You sound disappointed.' The woman frowned. 'As though you'd just failed to avoid an awkward social call. Would you really find death preferable to a little conversation, Locke?'

'Little conversations with Bondsmagi never end well.'

'You're the reason we're here,' growled Jean. 'You and your games in Tal Verrar. Your damned letters!'

'Not entirely,' said the woman.

'You didn't scare us in the Night Market.' Jean's grip tightened on the hilt of his blade, and the pain of his recent beating was entirely forgotten. 'You don't fucking scare us now!'

'Then you don't know us at all.'

'I think I do. And I don't give a damn about your gods-damned *rules*!'

He was already in motion, and her back was to him. She had no chance to speak or gesture with her hands; his left arm went around her neck and he slammed the dagger home as hard as he could, directly between her shoulder blades.

II

The woman's flesh was warm and solid beneath Jean's arm one moment, and in the next his blade bit empty air.

Jean had faced many fast opponents in his life, but never one that dissolved instantly at his touch. That wasn't human speed; it was sorcery.

His chance was gone.

He inhaled sharply, and a cold shudder ran down his back, the old familiar sensation of a misstep made and a blow about to fall. His pulse beat like a drum inside his skull, and he waited for the pain of whatever reprisal was coming—

'Oh yes,' said their visitor mildly from somewhere behind him. 'That would have been very clever of me, Jean Tannen. Leaving myself at the mercy of a strong man and his grudges.'

Jean turned slowly, and saw that the woman was now standing about six feet to his left, by the window where the linens table had once been.

'I hold your true name like a caged bird,' she said. 'Your hands and eyes will deceive you if you try to harm me.'

'Gods,' said Jean, suddenly overcome by a vast sense of weary frustration. 'Must you play with your food?' He sat down on the edge of Locke's bed and threw his knife at the floor, where it stuck quivering in the wood. 'Just kill me like a fucking normal person. I won't be your toy.'

'What will you be?'

'I'll stand still and be boring. Get it over with.'

'Why do you keep assuming I'm here to kill you?'

'If not kill, then something worse.'

'I have no intention of murdering either of you. Ever.' The woman folded her hands in front of her chest. 'What more proof do you need than the fact that you're still alive? Could you have stopped me?'

'You're not gods,' said Locke, weakly. 'You might have us at your mercy, but we've had one of you at ours before.'

'Is that meant to be some poor cousin to a threat? A reminder that you just happened to be present when the Falconer's terrible judgment finally got the best of him?'

'How is dear Falconer these days?' asked Locke.

'Well kept. In Karthain.' The woman sighed. 'As he was when agents of Camorr brought him home. Witless and comatose.'

'He didn't seem to react well to pain,' said Jean.

'And you imagine it was your torture that drove him mad?'

'Can't have been our conversation,' said Locke.

'His real problem is self-inflicted. You see, we can deaden our minds to any suffering of the flesh. But that art requires caution. It's extremely dangerous to use it in haste.'

'I'm delighted to hear that,' said Locke. 'You're saying that when he tried to escape the pain—'

'His mind gaoled itself, in a haze of his own making,' said the woman. 'And so we've been unable to correct his condition.'

55

'Marvellous,' said Locke. 'I don't really care how or why it happened, I'm still glad that it did. In fact I encourage the rest of you to use that power in haste.'

'You do many of us an injustice,' said the woman.

'Bitch, if I had the power I'd pull your heart out of your chest and use it for a handball,' said Locke, coughing. 'I'd do it to all of you. You people kill anyone you like and fuck with the lives of those that treat you fairly for it.'

'Despising us must be rather like staring into a mirror, then.'

'I despise you,' said Locke, straining to heave himself up, 'for Calo and Galdo, and for Bug, and for Nazca and Ezri, and for all the time we … wasted in …Tal Verrar.' Red-faced and shuddering, he fell back to the empty bed.

'You're murderers and thieves,' said the woman. 'You leave a trail of confusion and outrage wherever you go. You've brought down at least one government, and prevented the destruction of another for sentimental reasons. Can you really keep a straight face when you damn us for doing as we please?'

'We can,' said Jean. 'And I can take the matter of Ezri very personally.'

'Would you even have met the woman if we hadn't intervened in your affairs? Would you have gone to sea?'

'That's not for any of us to say—'

'So we own your misfortunes entirely, yet receive no credit for happier accidents.'

'I—'

'We've interfered here and there, Jean, but you're flattering yourself if you imagine that we've drawn such an intricate design around you. The woman died in battle, and we had nothing to do with that. I'm sorry for your loss.'

'Are you *capable* of feeling sorry for anything?'

The woman came toward Jean, reaching out with her left hand, and it took every ounce of his self-control not to fling himself away. He rose to his feet and stared fiercely down at her as she set warm fingers gently against his cheek.

'Time is precious,' she said. 'I lift my ban upon you, Jean Tannen. This is my real flesh against yours. I *might* be able to stop you if you try to harm me, but now the matter is much less certain. So what will you do? Must we fight now, or can we talk?'

Jean shook; the urge to take her at her word, to smash her down, was rising hot and red within him. He would have to strike as fast as he ever had in his life, as hard as muscle and sinew could allow. Break her skull, throttle her, bear her down beneath his full weight, and pray to the gods he did enough damage to postpone whatever word or gesture she would utter in return.

They stood there for a long, tense moment, perfectly still, with her dark eyes meeting his unblinkingly. Then his right hand darted up and closed around her left wrist, savagely tight. He could feel thin bones under thin skin, and he knew that one good sharp twist—

The woman flinched. Real fear shone out from the depths of those eyes, the briefest flash before her vast self-possession rolled in again like resurging waters to drown her human weakness. But it had been there, genuine as the flesh beneath his fingers. Jean loosened his grip, closed his eyes, and exhaled slowly.

'I'll be damned,' he said. 'I don't think you're lying.'

'This is very important,' she whispered.

Jean kept his right hand where it was, and reached up with his left to push back the silver lace that sprouted from her jacket cuff. Black rings were tattooed around her wrist, precise lines on pale skin.

'Five rings,' said Locke. 'All I ever heard was that more is better. Just how many can one of you people have, anyway?'

'This many,' said the woman with a hint of a smirk.

Jean released her arm and took a step back. She held her left hand up beside her head and stroked the tattoos gently with the fingers of her other hand. The blackness became silver, rippling silver, as though she wore bracelets of liquid moonlight.

As he stared at the eerie glow, Jean felt a cold itch behind his eyes, and a hard pressure against the fingertips of his right hand. Reeling, he saw images flash in his mind – fold upon fold of pale silk, needles punching in and out of delicate lace, the rough edge of a cloth unravelling into threads – the pressure on his fingers was an actual needle, moving up and down, in an endless steady dance across the cloth ...

'Oh,' he muttered, putting a hand to his forehead as the sensations receded. 'What the hell was that?'

'Me,' said the woman. 'In a manner of speaking. Have you ever recalled someone by the scent of their tobacco, or a perfume, or the feel of their skin? Deep memories without words?'

'Yeah,' said Locke, massaging his temples. Jean guessed that he'd somehow shared the brief vision.

'In my society, we speak mind to mind. We … announce ourselves using such impressions. We construct images of certain memories or passions. We call them *sigils*.' She hitched her laced sleeve back up over her wrist, where the black rings had entirely lost their ghostly gleam, and smiled. 'Now that I've shared mine with you, you're less likely to jump out of your skin if I ever need to speak mind to mind, rather than voice to ear.'

'What the hell are you?' said Jean.

'There are four of us,' said the woman. 'In an ideal world, the wisest and most powerful of the fifth-circles. If nothing else, we do get to live in the biggest houses.'

'You rule the Bondsmagi,' said Locke, incredulously.

'Rule is too strong a term. We do occasionally manage to avert total chaos.'

'You have a name?'

'Patience.'

'What, you have some rule against telling us now?'

'No, it's what I'm called. Patience.'

'No shit? Your peers must think pretty highly of you.'

'It doesn't mean anything, any more than a girl named Violet needs to be purple. It's a title. Archedama Patience. So, have we decided that nobody's going to be murdering anyone here?'

'I suppose that depends on what you want to talk about,' said Jean.

'The pair of you,' said Patience. 'I've been minding your business for some time now. Starting with the fragments I could pull out of the Falconer's memories. Our agents retrieved his possessions from Camorr after he was … crippled. Among them a knife formerly belonging to one of the Anatolius sisters.'

'A knife with my blood on it,' said Jean.

'From that we had your trail easily enough.'

'And from that you fucked up our lives.'

'I need you to understand,' said Patience, 'just how *little* you understand. I saved your lives in Tal Verrar.'

'Funny, I don't recall seeing you there,' said Jean.

'The Falconer has friends,' said Patience. 'Cohorts, followers, tools. For all of his flaws he was very popular. You saw their parlour tricks in the Night Market, but that was all I permitted. Without my intervention, they would have killed you.'

'You can call that mess "parlour tricks,"' said Jean. 'That interference in Tal Verrar still made a hell of a problem for us.'

'Better than death, surely,' said Patience. 'And kinder by far than I might have been, given the circumstances.'

'Circumstances?'

'The Falconer was arrogant, vicious, misguided. He was acting in obedience to a contract, which we consider a sacred obligation, but I won't deny that he amplified the brutality of the affair beyond what was called for.'

'He was going to help turn hundreds of people into empty shells. Into gods-damned furniture. That wasn't brutal enough?' said Jean.

'They were part of the contract. You and your friends were not.'

'Well, if this is some sort of apology, go to hell,' said Locke, cough-ing. 'I don't care what a humane old witch you think you are, and I don't care how or why the Falconer went wrong in the head. If I'd had more time I would have used every second of it to bleed him. All he got was the thinnest shred of what he really deserved.'

'That's more true than you know, Locke. Oh, so much truer than you know.' Patience folded her hands together and sighed. 'And no one comprehends it quite as well as I do. After all, the Falconer is my son.'

The Undrowned Girl

I

The world broadened for Locke Lamora in the summer of the seventy-seventh year of Sendovani, the summer after Beth vanished, the summer he was sold out of the Thiefmaker's care and into that of Father Chains, the famous Eyeless Priest at the Temple of Perelandro. Suddenly his old worries and pains were gone, though they were replaced by a fresh set of bafflements on a daily basis.

'And what if a priest or priestess of another order should walk by?' asked Chains, adjusting the hooded white robe the Sanza twins had just thrown over Locke's head.

'I make the sign of our, um, joined service.' Locke enfolded his left hand within his right and bowed his head until it nearly touched his thumbs. 'And I don't speak unless spoken to.'

'Good. And if you cross paths with an initiate of another order?'

'I give the blessing for troubles to stay behind them.' Locke held out his right hand, palm up, and swept it up as though he was pushing something over his left shoulder.

'And?'

'Um, I greet if greeted … and say nothing otherwise?'

'What if you meet an initiate of Perelandro?'

'Always greet?'

'You missed something.'

'Um. Oh yeah. Sign of joined service. Always greet. Speak, ah, cordially with initiates and shut my mouth for anyone, um, higher.'

'What about the alternate signals for when it's raining on a Penance Day?' said one of the Sanza twins.

'Um …' Locke coughed nervously into his hands. 'I don't … I'm not sure …'

'There *is* no alternate signal for when it's raining on a Penance Day. Or any other day,' muttered Chains. 'Well, now you look the part. And I think we can trust you with exterior ritual. Not bad for four days

60

of learning. Most initiates get a few months before they're trusted to count above ten without taking their shoes off.'

Chains stood and adjusted his own white robe. He and his boys were in the sanctuary of the Temple of Perelandro, a dank cave of a room that proclaimed not only the humility of Perelandro's followers but their apparent indifference to the smell of mildew.

'Now then,' said Chains, 'twit dexter and twit sinister – fetch my namesakes.'

Calo and Galdo scrambled to the wall where their master's purely ceremonial fetters lay, joined to a huge iron bolt in the stone. They raced one another to drag the chains across the floor and snap the manacles on the big man.

'Aha,' said the first to finish, 'you're slower than an underwater fart!'

'Funny,' said the second. 'Hey, what's that on your chin?'

'Huh?'

'Looks like a fist!'

In an instant the space in front of Locke was filled with a mad whirl of Sanza limbs, and for the hundredth time in his few days as Chains' ward, Locke lost track of which brother was which. The twins giggled madly as they wrestled with one another, then howled in unison as Chains reached out with calm precision and caught them each by an ear.

'You two savants,' he said, 'can go put your own robes on, and carry the kettle out after Locke and I take our places.'

'You said we weren't going to sit the steps today!' said one of the brothers.

'You're not. I'm just not in the mood to carry the kettle. After you bring it out, you can go downstairs and mind your chores.'

'Chores?'

'Remember those customs papers I said I was forging up last night? They weren't customs papers, they were arithmetic problems. A couple pages for each of you. There's charcoal, ink, and parchment in the kitchen. Show your work.'

'Awwwwwwwwwwwwwwww.' The sound of simultaneously disappointed Sanza brothers was curiously tuneful. Locke had already heard the twins practising their singing voices, which were quite good, and by accident or design they often harmonized.

'Now, get the door, Locke.' Chains tied on the last and most important part of his costume: the blindfold precisely adjusted to suggest his total helplessness while still allowing him to avoid tripping over the hem of his robe. 'The sun is up, and all that money out there won't steal itself.'

Locke worked the mechanism concealed behind one of the room's mouldering tapestries, and there was a faint rumble within the temple walls. A vertical line of burning gold appeared on the eastern wall as the doors creaked apart, and the sanctuary was quickly flooded with warm morning light. Chains held out a hand, and Locke ran over to take it.

'Ready?'

'If you say I am,' whispered Locke.

Hand in hand, the imaginary Eyeless Priest and his newest imaginary initiate walked out of their imaginary stone prison, into a morning heat so fierce that Locke could smell it baking up from the city's stones and taste it on his tongue.

For the first of a thousand times, they went out together to rob passersby, as surely as if they were muggers, armed with nothing more than a few words and an empty copper kettle.

2

In his first few months with Father Chains, Locke began to unlearn the city of Camorr he'd once known and discover something entirely different in its place. As a Shades' Hill boy, he'd known daylight in flashes, exploring the upper world and then running back to the graveyard's familiar darkness like a diver surfacing before his breath ran out. The Hill was full of dangers, but they were *known* dangers, while the city above was full of infinite mysteries.

Now the sun, which had once seemed to him like a great eye burning down in judgment, did nothing but make his head warm as he sat the temple steps in his little white robe. A happier boy might have been bored by the long hours of begging, but Locke had learned patience in the surest way possible – by hiding for his own survival. Spending half a night hugging the same shadow was nothing extraordinary to him, and he luxuriated in the idea of lazing around while people actually brought money to him.

He studied the rhythms of daily life in the Temple District. When nobody was near enough to eavesdrop, Chains would quietly answer Locke's questions, and slowly the great mass of Camorri revealed themselves to him. What had once been a sea of mystifying details resolved bit by bit until Locke could identify the priests of the twelve orders, sort the very rich from the merely wealthy, and make a dozen other useful distinctions.

It still made his heart jump to see a patrol of yellowjackets walking past the temple steps, but their polite indifference was a pure delight. Some of them even *saluted*. It amazed Locke that the thin cotton robe he wore could provide him with such armour against a power that had previously seemed so arbitrary and absolute.

Constables. *Saluting* him! Gods above.

Inside the temple, down in the secret burrow that lay beneath its façade of poverty, further transmutations were under way. Locke ate well for the first time ever, sampling all the cuisines of Camorr under Chains' enthusiastic direction. Although he started as an inept hindrance to the more experienced Sanzas, he quickly learned how to shake weevils out of flour, how to slice meats, and how to tell a filleting knife from an eel-fork.

'Bless us all,' said Chains one night, patting Locke on the belly. 'You're not the ragged little corpse that came to us all those weeks ago. Food and sunlight have worked an act of necromancy. You're still small, but now you look like you could stand up to a moderate breeze.'

'Excellent,' said one of the Sanzas. 'Soon he'll be fat, and we can butcher him like all the others for a Penance Day roast.'

'What my brother means to say,' said the other twin, 'is that all the others died of purely natural causes, and you have nothing to fear from us. Now have some more bread.'

Life in the care of Father Chains offered Locke more comfort than Shades' Hill ever had. He had plenty to eat, new clothes, and a cot of his own to sleep on. Nothing more dangerous than the attempted pranks of the Sanza twins menaced him each night. Yet strangely enough Locke would never have called this new life easier than the one he'd left.

Within days of his arrival he'd been trained as an 'initiate of Perelandro,' and the lessons only grew more intense from there. Chains was nothing like the Thiefmaker – he didn't allow Calo and Galdo to actually terrorize Locke, and he didn't punish failure by pulling out a butcher's cleaver. But Chains could be disappointed. Oh, yes. On the steps of the temple he could marshal his mysterious powers to sway passersby, to plead logically or sermonize furiously until they parted with hard-earned coins, and in his tutelage he focused those same powers on Locke until it seemed that Chains' disappointment was a rebuke worse than a beating.

It was a strange new set of affairs, to be sure. Locke feared what Chains might do if provoked (the leather pouch Locke was forced to wear around his neck, with the shark's tooth inside, was an inescapable reminder), but he didn't actually fear Chains himself. The big bearded man seemed so genuinely pleased when Locke got his lessons right, seemed to give off waves of approval that warmed like sunlight. With his two extremes of mood, sharp disappointment and bright satisfaction, Chains drove all of his boys on through their constant tests.

There were the obvious matters of Locke's daily training – he learned to cook, to dress, to keep himself reasonably clean. He learned more about the order of Perelandro and his fictional place within it. He learned about the meanings of flags on carriages and coats of arms on guards' tabards, about the history of the Temple District, about its landmarks.

Most difficult of all, at first, he learned to read and write. Two hours a day were spent at this, before and after sitting the steps. He began with fragmentary knowledge of the thirty letters of the Therin alphabet, and he could do simple sums when he had counters in front of him, like coins. But Chains had him reciting and scribing his letters until they danced in his dreams, and from there he moved to puzzling out small words, then bigger ones, then full sentences.

Chains began leaving written instructions for him each morning, and Locke wasn't allowed to break his fast until he'd deciphered them. Around the time short paragraphs ceased to be his match in a battle of wits, Locke found himself up against arithmetic with slates and chalk. Arriving at the answers in his head was no longer sufficient.

'Twenty-six less twelve,' said Chains one night in early autumn. It was an unusually pleasant time in Camorr, with warm days and mild nights that neither drenched nor scalded the city. Chains was absorbed in a game of Catch-the-Duke against Galdo, alternately moving his pieces and giving mathematical problems to Locke. The three of them sat at the kitchen table, beneath the golden light of Chains' fabulous alchemical chandelier, while Calo sat on a nearby counter plucking at a sad little instrument called a road-man's harp.

'Um …' Locke scribbled on his slate, being careful to show his work properly. 'Fourteen.'

'Well done,' said Chains. 'Add twenty-one and thirteen.'

'Now go forth,' said Galdo, pushing one of his pieces along the squares of the game board. 'Go forth and die for King Galdo.'

'Sooner rather than later,' said Chains, countering the move immediately.

'Since you two are at war,' said Calo, 'how do you like this?'

He began to pluck a tune on his simplified harp, and in a soft, high voice he sang:

'From fair old Camorr to far Godsgate Hill,
Three thousand bold men marched to war.
A full hundred score are lying there still,
In red soil they claimed for Camorr.'

Galdo cleared his throat as he fiddled with his pieces on the board, and when his twin continued he joined in. Barely a heartbeat passed before the Sanzas found their eerie, note-perfect harmony:

'From fair old Camorr to far Godsgate Hill,
Went a duke who would not be a slave.
His Grace in his grave is lying there still,
In red soil he claimed for the brave.

'From fair old Camorr to far Godsgate Hill,
Is a hundred hard leagues overland.
But our host slain of old is lying there still,
In soil made red by their stand!'

'Commendable playing,' muttered Chains, 'wasted on a nothing of a song shat out by soft-handed fops to justify an old man's folly.'

'Everyone sings it in the taverns,' said Calo.

'They're supposed to. It's artless doggerel meant to dress up the stink of a pointless slaughter. But I was briefly a part of those three thousand men, and nearly everyone I knew in those days is *lying there still*. Kindly sing something more cheerful.'

Calo bit the inside of his cheek, retuned his harp, and then began again:

'Said the reeve to the maid who was fresh to the farm
'Let me show you the beasts of the yard!'

Here's a cow that gives milk, and a pig that's for ham
Here's a cur and a goat and a lamb;
Here's a horse tall and proud, and a well-trained old hawk,
But the thing you should see is this excellent cock!'

'Where could you possibly have learned that?' shouted Chains. Calo broke up in a fit of giggles, but Galdo picked up the song with a dead-pan expression on his face:

'Oh, some cocks rise early and some cocks stand tall,
But the cock now in question works hardest of all!
And they say hard's a virtue, in a cock's line of work
So what say you, lovely, will you give it a—'

There was the unmistakable echoing slam of the burrow's secret entrance, in the Elderglass-lined tunnel beside the kitchen, being thrown shut by someone who didn't care that they were overheard. Chains rolled to his feet. Calo and Galdo ran behind him, putting themselves in easy reach of the kitchen's knives. Locke stood up on his chair, arithmetic slate held up like a shield.

The instant he saw who it was coming around the corner, the slate slipped from his fingers and clattered against the floor.

'My dear,' cried Chains, 'you've come back to us early!'

She was, if anything, taller even than Locke remembered, and her hair was well-dyed a uniform shade of light brown. But it *was* her. It was undeniably Beth.

3

'You can't be here,' said Locke. 'You're dead!'

'I certainly can be here. I live here.' Beth dropped the brown leather bag she was carrying and unbound her hair, letting it fall to her shoulders. 'Who might you be?'

'I … um … you don't know?'

'Should I?'

Locke's astonishment merged with a sour disappointment. While the gears of his mind turned furiously to conjure a reply, she studied him. Her eyes widened.

'Oh, gods. The Lamora boy, isn't it?'

'Yes,' said Chains.

'Bought him as well, have you?'

'I've paid more for some of my lunches, but yes, I've taken him from your old master.' Chains ruffled Beth's hair with fatherly affection, and she kissed the back of hand.

'But you were dead,' insisted Locke. 'They said you'd drowned!'

'Yeah,' she said, mildly.

'But why?'

'Our Sabetha has a complicated past,' said Chains. 'When I took her out of Shades' Hill, I arranged a bit of theatre to cover the trail.'

Beth. Sabetha. They'd mentioned *Sabetha* at least a dozen times since he'd come to live here. Locke suddenly felt like an idiot for not connecting the two names before ... but then, he'd thought she was dead, hadn't he? Beneath his astonishment, his embarrassment, his frustration, a warmth was rising in the pit of his stomach. Beth was alive ... and she lived *here*!

'Well, where have ... where did you go?' Locke asked.

'For training,' said Sabetha.

'And how was it?' asked Chains.

'Mistress Sibella said that I wasn't as vulgar and clumsy as most of the Camorri she teaches.'

'So you ... are, um—' said Locke.

'High praise, coming from that gilded prune,' said Chains, ignoring Locke. 'Let's see if she was on the mark. Galdo, take Sabetha's side for a four-step. *Complar entant.*'

'Must I?'

'Good question. Must I continue feeding you?'

Galdo hurried out from behind Chains and gave Sabetha a bow so exaggerated his nose nearly brushed the floor. 'Enchanted, demoiselle. May I beg the pleasure of a dance? My patron won't feed me anymore if I don't pretend to enjoy this crap.'

'What a bold little monkey you are,' said the girl. The two of them moved into the widest clear area of the room, between the table and the counters.

'Calo,' said Chains, 'if you would.'

'Yes, yes, I have it.' Calo fiddled with his harp for a moment before he began to pluck out a fast, rhythmic tune, more complex than the ditties he'd been playing before.

Galdo and Sabetha moved in unison, slowly at first but gaining confidence and speed as the tune went on. Locke watched, baffled but fascinated, as they danced in a manner that was more controlled than anything he'd ever seen in a tavern or a back alley. The key to the dance seemed to be that they would strike the ground with their heels forcefully, four taps between each major movement of the arms. They joined hands, twirled, unjoined, switched places, and all the while kept up a near-perfect rhythm with their feet.

'It's popular with the swells,' said Chains, and Locke realized he was speaking for his benefit. 'All the dancers form a circle, and the dancing master calls out partners. The chosen couple dances in the main, in the centre of everything, and if they screw it up, well … penalties. Teasing. Romantic frustration, I would imagine.'

Locke was only half-listening, his eyes and thoughts lost in the dance. In Galdo he recognized the nervous quickness of a fellow orphan, the grace born of need that separated the living in Shades' Hill from the likes of No-Teeth. Yet Sabetha had that and something more; not just speed but fluidity. Her knees and elbows seemed to vanish as she danced, and to Locke's eyes she became all curves, whirls, effort-less circles. Her cheeks turned red with exertion, and the golden glow of the chandelier lightened her brown hair until Locke, hypnotized, could almost imagine it red as well …

Chains clapped three times, ending the dance if not Locke's spell. If Sabetha knew she was being stared at she was either too polite or too disdainful to stare back.

'I can see that's a fountain of gold I didn't shit out in vain,' said Chains. 'Well done, girl. Even having Galdo for a partner didn't seem to hold you back.'

'Does it ever?' Sabetha smiled, still acting as though Locke wasn't in the room, and drifted back toward the table where Galdo and Chains had been playing their game. She glanced over the board for a few seconds, then said, 'You're doomed, Sanza.'

'In a donkey's dick I am!'

'Actually, I've got him in three moves,' said Chains, settling back down into his chair with a smile. 'But I was going to spin it out for a while longer.'

While Galdo fretted over his position on the board, he and Calo and Sabetha fell into an animated conversation with Chains on subjects of which Locke was ignorant – dances, noble customs, people he'd never heard of, cities that were only names to him. Chains grew more and more boisterous until, after a few minutes, he gestured to Calo.

'Fetch us down something sweet,' he said. 'We'll have a toast to Sabetha's return.'

'Lashani Black Sherry? I've always wanted to try it.' Calo opened a cabinet and carefully withdrew a greenish glass bottle that was full of something ink-dark. 'Gods, it looks so disgusting!'

'Spoken like the midwife who delivered the pair of you,' said Chains. 'Bring glasses for all of us, and for the toasting.'

The four children gathered around the table while Chains arranged the glasses and opened the bottle. Locke strategically placed the Sanzas between himself and Sabetha, giving him a better angle to continue staring at her. Chains then filled a glass to the brim with the sherry, which rippled black and gold in the chandelier light.

'This glass for the patron and protector, the Crooked Warden, our Father of Necessary Pretexts.' Chains carefully pushed the glass aside from the others. 'Tonight he gives us the return of our friend, his servant Sabetha.' Chains raised his left hand to his lips and blew into his palm. 'My words. My breath. These things bind my promise. A hundred gold pieces, duly stolen from honest men and women, to be cast into the sea in the dark of the Orphan's Moon. We are grateful for Sabetha's safety.'

The Orphan's Moon, Locke knew, came once a year, in late winter, when the world's largest two moons were in their dark phases together. At the Midsummer-mark, commoners who knew their dates of birth legally turned a year older. The Orphan's Moon meant the same thing for those, like him, whose precise ages were mysteries.

Now Chains filled glasses and passed them out. Locke was surprised to see that while the other children received quarter-glasses of the alarmingly dark sherry, his own was mostly full. Chains grinned at him and raised his glass.

'Deep pockets poorly guarded,' he said.

'Watchmen asleep at their posts,' said Sabetha.

'The city to nurture us and the night to hide us,' said Calo.

'Friends to help spend the loot!' As soon as Galdo finished the toast Locke had already heard many times since coming to the Gentlemen Bastards, five glasses went up to five sets of lips. Locke kept both hands on his for fear of spilling it.

The black sherry hit Locke's throat with a blast of sweet flavours – cream, honey, raspberries, and many others he had no hope of naming.

Warm prickly vapours seemed to slide up into his nose and waft behind his eyes, until it felt like he was being tickled from inside his own skull by dozens of feathers at once. Knowing how ill-mannered it would be to make a mess of a solemn toast, he bent every ounce of his will to gulping the full glass down.

'Waugh,' he said as soon as he was finished. It was a cross between a polite cough and the last gasp of a dying bird. He pounded on his chest. 'Waugh, waugh, waugggggh!'

'Concur,' said Galdo in a harsh whisper. 'Love it.'

'All the outward virtues of liquid shit,' said Chains, musing on his empty glass, 'and a taste like pure joy pissed out by happy angels. Mind you, it doesn't signify in the world at large. Don't drink anything else that looks like this unless you want a swift release from mortal concerns.'

'I wonder,' said Locke, 'don't they ever make wine-coloured wine in other cities?' He stared down into his own glass, which, like the fingers holding it, was beginning to blur around the edges.

'Some things are much more interesting when alchemists get their hands on them,' said Chains. 'Your head, for example. Black sherry is renowned for kicking like a mule.'

'Yesh, renowned,' said Locke, grinning stupidly. His belly was warm, his head seemed not to weigh an ounce, and his intentions were disconnected from his actual movements by a heartbeat interval. He was aware that, if not already drunk, he was headed for it like a dart thrown at a wall.

'Now, Locke,' said Chains, his voice seeming to come from a distance, 'I've a few things to discuss with these three. Perhaps you'd like to get to bed early tonight.'

A sharp pang pierced the bubble of warm contentment that had all but swallowed him. Go to bed early? Leave the company of Sabetha, whose blurry loveliness he was fixating on, barely managing to grudge himself the time required to blink every now and then?

'Um,' he said. 'Wha?'

'It wasn't a request, Locke,' said Chains gently. 'You've a busy evening tomorrow, I can assure you, and you need all the sleep you can get.'

'Tomorrow?'

'You'll see.' Chains rose, moved around the table, and carefully took Locke's empty glass from his hand. Locke looked down in surprise, having forgotten that he'd been holding it. 'Off you go.'

A tiny part of Locke's mind, the cold wariness that had been his sentry in Shades' Hill, realized Chains had long planned to send him, happily befuddled, to an early rest. Even through his wine-induced haze, that stung. He'd been feeling more and more at home, but no sooner had Sabetha walked through the door than it was Streets and Windows all over again, and he was packed off to some dark corner without the privileges enjoyed by the older children.

'I,' he muttered, taking his eyes of Sabetha for the first time in several minutes, but directing his voice at her. 'I will. But ... I'm g-glad you're here.' He felt the urge to say something else, something weighty and witty that would turn that beautiful head of hers and fix her attention to him, a mirror of his own. But even drunk he knew he was more likely to pull rubies out of his ass than he was to speak as older people spoke, with words that were somehow careful and powerful and right. 'Sabetha,' he half mumbled.

'Thanks,' she said, looking at the table.

'I mean, I knew ... you knew I meant you, Sabetha ... sorry. I just ... I'm glad you're not drowned, you know.'

More than anything, at that moment, he just wanted to hear her say his name, call him anything but 'him' or 'the Lamora Boy.' Acknowledge his existence ... their partnership in Chains' gang ... gods, he would exile himself to bed early every night if he could just hear his name come out from between those thin lips of hers.

'Good night,' she said.

4

Locke woke the next day feeling as though the contents of his skull had been popped out and replaced upside-down.

'Here,' said one of the Sanzas, who happened to be sitting next to Locke's cot with a book on his lap. The Sanza (Locke, muddled as he was, could not quite identify which one) passed over a wooden cup of water. It was lukewarm but clean, and Locke gulped it down without delicacy, marvelling at how parched he felt.

'What time is it?' he croaked when he was finished.

'Must be past noon.'

'Noon? But ... my chores ...'

'No real work today.' The Sanza stretched and yawned. 'No arithmetic. No Catch-the-Duke. No languages. No dancing.'

'No sitting the steps,' yelled the other Sanza from the next room. 'No swordplay. No knots and ropes. No coins.'

'No music,' said the Sanza with the book. 'No manners. No history. No bloody heraldry.'

'What are we doing, then?'

'Calo and I are to make sure you can stand up straight,' said the Sanza with the book. 'Nail you to a plank if we have to.'

'And when that's done, you're to do all the dishes.'

'Sabetha ...' Locke rubbed his eyes and rolled off his cot. 'She's really one of us?'

'Course she is,' said the Sanza with the book.

'Is she ... here right now?'

'Nah. Out with Chains. Looking into things for tonight.'

'What's tonight?'

'Dunno. All's we know is the afternoon, and the afternoon, far as you're concerned, is dishes.'

<h1 style="text-align:center">5</h1>

Though energetic enough when set a task, Calo and Galdo were virtuosos of laziness when left to their own devices. Between subtle interference and overt clowning, they managed to stretch the half-hour Locke would ordinarily have needed to tend the dishes into nearly three hours. By the time the secret door to the temple above banged shut behind the returning Father Chains, Locke's fingers were wrinkled and bleached from the alchemical polish he'd been using on the silver.

'Ah,' said Chains. 'Good, good. You look more or less among the living. Feeling spry?'

'I suppose,' said Locke.

'We've a job tonight. Housebreaking. Windows work, and most of it on your little shoulders.' Chains patted his broad belly and smirked. 'I parted ways with climbing and scampering some time ago.'

'Windows work?' said Locke, the drudgery of his long afternoon in the kitchen instantly forgotten. 'I ... I'd love to. But I thought you, um, didn't do that sort of thing.'

'For its own sake, not usually. But I need to find some things out about you, Locke.'

'Oh, good.' Locke felt his excitement cool slightly. 'Another test. When do they stop?'

'When you're buried, my boy.' Chains knelt and gave Locke a friendly squeeze on the back of his neck. 'When you're under the dirt and colder than a fish's tits. That's when it stops. Now listen.

'I've got a tip from a friend at Meraggio's.' Chains bustled about the kitchen, snatching up chalk and one of the slates the children used for their lessons. He sketched on it rapidly. 'Seems a certain olive merchant is looking to marry his useless son to a noble wife. To sweeten the deal sufficiently, he'll need to put his family splendids back into circulation.'

'What's that mean?' said Locke.

'Means he needs to sell his jewels and things,' said Calo.

'Sharp lad. About an hour ago, the merchant's man left the counting-house with a lot of nice old things in a bag. He's staying at a townhouse in the Razona; just him and two guards. The old man and a bigger retinue are coming in from his estate tomorrow. So tonight we have a bit of an opportunity.'

'Why us?' Locke's excitement was tempered with genuine puzzlement. 'If he's only got two guards, anyone who wanted to could go in there with a gang.'

'Never in life,' said Chains, chuckling. 'Barsavi won't have it. The Razona's a quiet district where doors don't get kicked in. That's the Peace. Anybody breaks it, they're liable to have their precious bits cut off and stitched to their eyeballs. So instead of sending in brutes through the door, we send a quiet type through the window.'

Chains turned the slate toward Calo, Galdo, and Locke. The top half was taken up by a rough diagram of houses and their surrounding streets and alleys. Beneath that was a sketch of a necklace, with large ovoid shapes dangling from a thick central collar. Chains tapped one of his fingers against this sketch.

'One piece,' he said. 'That's all we're after. One from twenty or so, and they won't have time to put up much of a fuss about it. A gold necklace with nine hanging emeralds. Pop out the stones, send them nine different directions, and melt down the gold. Untraceable profit.'

'How do we do it?' asked Locke.

'Well, that's half the fun.' Chains scratched at his chin. 'You said yourself, it's a test. You'll be working with Sabetha, since she's had more experience at this sort of thing. Calo and Galdo will be your top-eyes; that is, watching the area to cover your ass. I'll be on the ground nearby, but I won't be directly involved. My crooked little wonders get to sort the rest out for themselves.'

Locke's heart raced. Test or not, a chance to work together with Sabetha, on something exciting? The gods loved him!

'Where is she now?'

'Here.' Chains pointed to a square sketched on the upper portion of the slate. 'On the Via Selaine. Four-storey house with a rooftop garden. That's our target. She'll be nearby until dark; at first moonrise she'll meet you in this alley.' Chains ran his finger up and down a set of chalk lines, blurring them. 'Once the Sanzas are in position to keep an eye on the street, the rest is up to you and Sabetha.'

'That's it, then?'

'That's it. And remember, I want one emerald necklace. I don't need two, or the deed to the townhouse, or the bloody crown jewels of Camorr. Tonight's definitely a night for you to underachieve.'

6

Full Camorri night at last, after a twilight spent nervously fidgeting in an alley, waiting for Sabetha to make contact. Now Locke was with her, up on the roof of the house next door to their target, crouched among the old wooden frames and empty pots of a long-untended garden. It was just past second moonrise, and the wide-open sky was on fire with stars, ten thousand flickering white eyes staring down at Locke, as though eager to see him get to work.

Three feet away, a low dark shape against the stone parapet, lay Sabetha. Her only words to him at their meeting had been 'Shut up, keep close, and stay quiet.' He'd done that, following her up the alley wall of the house they now sat upon, using windowsills and deep decorative carvings to haul himself up with little effort. Since then his urge to speak with her had been overruled by his terror of annoying her, and so he fancied that he'd done a fine imitation of a corpse from the moment they'd arrived. When she finally did speak, her soft voice actually startled him.

'I think they've gone to sleep at last.'

'Wh-what? Who?'

'The three old women who live here.' Sabetha set her head against the stones of the rooftop and listened for several moments. 'They sleep on the second floor, but it never hurts to be careful.'

'Oh. Of course.'

'Never worked a roof before. Isn't that the case, boy?' Sabetha moved slightly, and so quietly that Locke couldn't hear a single ruffle of her dark tunic and trousers. She peeked over the parapet for no more than the span of a few heartbeats, then crouched back down.

'I, um, no. Not like this.'

'Well, think you can confine yourself to stealing just what we've been sent for? Or should I have the yellowjackets rouse out bucket-lines in case you burn the Razona down?'

'I – I'll do whatever you say. I'll be careful.'

'Whatever I say?' Her face was in silvery-grey shadow, but her eyes caught the starlight as she turned to him, so he could see them clearly. 'You mean it?'

'Oh, yes.' Locke nodded several times. 'On my heart. Come hell or Eldren-fire.'

'Good. You might not fuck this up, then.' She gestured toward the parapet. 'Move slow. Raise up just high enough to get your eyes over the edge. Take a good look.'

Locke peeked out over the southern parapet of the townhouse; their target house with its thick rooftop garden was to his right, and four storeys below him was a clean stretch of cobbled road washed with moonlight. The Razona seemed a gentle, quiet place – no drunks sprawled in gutters, no tavern doors banging constantly open and closed, no yellowjackets moving in squads with truncheons drawn and shields out. Dozens of alchemical globes burned at street level, behind windows and above doors, like bunches of fiery fruit. Only the alleys and rooftops seemed wrapped in anything like real darkness.

'You see Calo and Galdo?' asked Sabetha.

'No.'

'Good. That means they're where they should be. If something goes wrong – if a squad of yellowjackets shows up in the street, let's say – those two will start hollering "The master wants more wine, the master wants more wine."'

'What then?'

'They run, and we do likewise.' Sabetha crawled over beside him, and Locke felt his breath catch in his throat. Her next words were spoken into his ear. 'First rule of roof work is, know how you're getting down. Do you?'

'Um, same way we came?'

'Too slow. Too risky. Climbing down at speed is more dangerous than going up, especially at night.' She pointed to a thin grey line in the middle of the roof, a line that Locke's eyes followed to a mess of pots and broken trellises. 'I anchored that line when I came up. Demi-silk, should get us down to five feet off the ground. If we need to run, throw it over the edge, slide down as fast as you can, and leave it behind. Got it?'

'Got it.'

'Now, look across here.' She nudged his head up above the parapet again, and pointed at an alley across the street. 'That's the escape route. You'll have to cross the road, but one of the Sanzas should be in cover there watching for you. Chains is another block or two past that. If it all goes to hell, find a Sanza. Understand?'

'Yeah. But what if we don't get caught?'

'Same plan, boy. We just do it slower. Ready?'

'Sure. Whenever you say. How do we, um, get across?'

'Fire plank.' Sabetha crawled toward the parapet facing their target house, beckoning for him to follow. She gently tapped a long wooden board that rested snug against the stone wall. 'In case the place burns up beneath you, you swing it across to the neighbours and hope they like you.'

Working quietly and slowly, the two children lifted the fifteen-foot plank to the edge of the parapet and swivelled it out over the alley, Sabetha guiding it while Locke put his full weight on the inner edge. He felt uneasily like a catapult stone about to fly if the other end should fall, but after a few chancy moments Sabetha had the far end of the plank settled on the parapet of their target house. She hopped gracefully atop it, then got down on her hands and knees.

'One at a time,' she whispered. 'Stay low and don't hurry.'

Across she went, while Locke's heart raced with the familiar excitement of a crime about to get under way. The farm-field smell of the Hangman's Wind filled the air, and a warm breeze caught at Locke's hair. To the northeast loomed the impossibly tall shadows of the Five Towers, with their crowns of silver and gold lanterns, warm artificial constellations mingling with the cold and real stars.

Now came Locke's turn. The board would have been unnervingly narrow for an adult, but someone Locke's size could turn around on it without bothering to stand up. He went over with ease, rolled off the edge of the plank, and crouched amid the wet smells of a living garden.

Dark boughs of leaves rustled above him, and he almost jumped when Sabetha reached out of the shadows and grabbed him by the shoulder.

'No noise,' she whispered. 'I'll go in after the necklace. You watch the roof. Make sure the plank stays where we need it.'

'Wh-what if something happens?'

'Pound the floor three times. If something happens that you can see before I do, won't be anything for us to do but flee anyway. Don't ever use my name if you call out.'

'I won't. Good … um, good luck—'

But she was already gone, and a moment later he heard a faint set of clicks. Somewhere in the garden, Sabetha was picking a lock. A moment later she had it, and the hinges of a door creaked ever so faintly.

Locke stood guard at the plank for many long minutes, constantly glancing around, although he admitted to himself that a dozen grown men could have been hiding in the darkness of the vines and leaves around him. Occasionally he popped above the parapet and glanced back across the narrow bridge. The other rooftop remained reassuringly empty.

Locke was just settling back down from his fourth or fifth peek across the way when he heard a commotion beneath his feet. He knelt down and placed one ear against the warm stone; it was a murmur. One person talking, then another. A rising chorus of adult voices. Then the shouting began.

'Oh, shit,' Locke whispered.

There was a series of thumps from the direction Sabetha had gone, then the loud bang of a door being thrown open. She flew out of the shadows at him, grabbed him by the arms, and heaved him onto the plank.

'Go, go, go,' she said, breathlessly. 'Fast as you can.'

'What's wrong?'

'Just go, gods damn it! I'll steady the plank.'

Locke scuttled across the fifteen feet to safety as fast as he'd ever moved in his life, so fast that he tumbled off the parapet on arrival and tucked into an ungainly roll to avoid landing teeth-first. He popped up, head spinning, and whirled back toward Sabetha.

'Come on,' he cried. 'Come on!'

'The rope,' she hissed. 'Get down the fucking rope!'

'I'll s-steady the plank for you now.' Locke clamped his hands onto it, gritted his teeth, and braced himself, knowing with some part of his mind just how ridiculous a display of such feeble strength must look. Why was she not coming?

'THE ROPE,' she yelled. 'GO!'

Locke looked up just in time to see tall dark shapes burst out of the garden behind her. Adults. Their arms were reaching for her, but she wasn't trying to escape; she wasn't even turning toward them. Instead her hands were on the plank, and she was—

'No,' Locke screamed. 'NO!'

Sabetha was seized from behind and hoisted into the air, but as she went up she managed to swivel her end of the plank just off the parapet and push it into empty space. Locke felt the terrible sensation of that weight tipping and plummeting into the alley, far too much for him to hold back. His end of the plank leapt up and cracked against his chin, knocking him backward, and as he was landing on his posterior he heard the echoing crash of the plank hitting the ground four storeys below.

'GO,' yelled Sabetha one more time. Her shout ended in a muffled cry, and Locke spat blood as he clambered back to his feet.

'The other roof!' A new voice, a man. 'Get down to the street!'

Locke wanted to stay, to keep Sabetha in sight, to do something for her, but his feet, ever faster than his wits, were already carrying him away. He snatched at the rope as he stumbled along, threw it over the opposite parapet, and without hesitation flung himself over the edge. The stones flew past, and the pressure of the rope against his palm rapidly grew into a hot, searing pain. He yowled and let go of the rope just as he reached the bottom, all but flinging himself the last five feet to land gracelessly in a heap.

Nothing seemed broken. His chin ached, his palms felt as though they'd been skinned with a dull axe, and his head was still spinning, but at least nothing seemed broken. He stumbled into a run. As his bare feet slapped against the cobbles of the road the door to the target house burst open, revealing two men outlined in golden light. An instant later they were after him with a shout.

Locke sprinted into the darkness of the alley, willing his legs to rise and fall like water-engine pistons. He knew that he would need every inch of the lead he already had if he hoped to escape. Vague black shapes loomed out of the shadows like something from a nightmare, only transforming into normal objects as he ran past – empty barrels, piles of refuse, broken wagons.

Behind him came the slap-slap-slap of booted feet. Locke sucked in his breath in short, sharp gasps and prayed he wouldn't run across a broken pot or bottle. Bare feet were better for climbing, but in a dead run someone with shoes had every advantage. The men were getting closer—

Something slammed into Locke so forcefully that his first thought was that he'd struck a wall. His breath exploded out of him, and his next impression was a confused sense of movement. Someone grabbed him by his tunic and threw him down; someone else leapt out of the darkness and sprinted in the direction he'd been headed. Someone about his size or a little bigger …

'Shhhh,' whispered one of the Sanzas, directly into his ear. 'Play dead.'

Locke was lying with his cheek against wet stone, staring at a narrow opening into a brick-walled passage. He realized he'd been yanked into a smaller alley branching off the one he'd tried to escape down. The Sanza restraining him pulled something heavy, damp, and fetid down around them, leaving only the thinnest space exposed for them to see out of. A split second later Locke's two pursuers pounded past, huffing and swearing. They continued after the shape that had taken Locke's place and didn't spare a glance for the two boys huddled under cover a few feet away.

'Calo will give 'em a good chase, then get back to us once they're slipped,' said the Sanza after a few seconds.

'Galdo,' said Locke. 'They got her. They got Beth.'

'We know.' Galdo pushed aside their camouflage. It looked like an ancient leather coat, gnawed by animals and covered in every possible foulness an alley could cultivate. 'When we heard the shouting we ran for it and got in position to grab you. Quick and quiet now.'

Galdo hoisted Locke to his feet, turned, and padded down the branch alley.

'They got her,' repeated Locke, suddenly aware that his cheeks were hot with tears. 'They got her, we have to do something, we have to—'

'I bloody well know.' Galdo seized him by the hand and pulled him along. 'Chains will tell us what to do. Come on.'

As Sabetha had promised, Chains wasn't far. Galdo pulled Locke west, toward the docks, to the rows of cheaper warehouses beside the canal that marked the farthest boundary of the Razona. Chains was waiting there, in plain clothes and a long brown coat, inside an empty warehouse that smelled of rot and camphor. When the two boys stumbled in the door, Chains shook a weak light from an alchemical globe and hurried over to them.

'It went wrong,' said Galdo.

'They got her,' said Locke, not caring that he was bawling. 'They got her, I'm sorry, they just, they just got her.' Locke threw himself at Father Chains, and the man, without hesitation, scooped him up and held him, patting his back until his racking sobs quieted down.

'There, boy, there,' said Chains. 'You're with us now. All's well. Who got her? Can you tell me?'

'I don't know … men in the house.'

'Not yellowjackets?'

'I don't … I don't think so. I'm sorry, I couldn't … I tried to think of something, but—'

'There was nothing you could have done,' said Chains firmly. He set Locke down and used a coat sleeve to dry his cheeks. 'You managed to get away, and that was enough.'

'We didn't g-get … the necklace—'

'Fuck the necklace.' Chains turned to the Sanza who'd brought Locke in. 'Where's Galdo?'

'I'm Galdo.'

'Where's—'

'Calo's ditching a couple of men that chased us.'

'What kind of men? Uniforms? Weapons?'

'I don't think they were mustard. They might've been with the old guy you wanted us to rob.'

'Hell's flaming shits.' Chains grabbed up his walking stick (an affectation for his disguise, but a fine way to have a weapon close at hand), then produced a dagger in a leather sheath that he tossed to Galdo. 'Stay here. Douse the light and hide yourselves. Try not to stab Calo if he returns before I do.'

'Where are you going?' asked Locke.

'To find out who we're dealing with.'

Chains went out the door with a speed that put the lie to his frequent claims of advancing infirmity. Galdo picked up the tiny alchemical light and tossed it to Locke, who concealed it within his closed hands. Alone in the darkness, the two boys settled down to wait for whatever came next.

Chains returned a brief fraction of an hour later, with an ashen-faced Calo in tow. Locke uncovered the light as they entered the warehouse and ran toward them.

'Where is she?' he asked.

Chains stared at the three boys and sighed. 'I need the smallest,' he said quietly.

'Me?'

'Of course you, Locke.' Chains reached out and grabbed both Sanza brothers. He knelt beside them and whispered instructions that were too brief and quiet for Locke to catch. Calo and Galdo seemed to recoil.

'Gods damn it, boys,' said Chains. 'You know we've got no choice. Get back home. Stay together.'

They ran out of the warehouse without another word. Chains rose and turned to Locke.

'Come,' he said. 'Time is no friend of ours this evening.'

'Where are we going?' Locke scampered to keep up.

'Not far. A house a block north of where you were.'

'Is it … should we really be going back that way?'

'Perfectly safe now that you're with me.' True to his word, Chains had turned east, on a street rather than an alley, and was walking briskly toward the neighbourhood Locke had just fled.

'Who's got her? The yellowjackets?'

'No. They'd have taken her to a watch station, not a private residence.'

'The, um, men we tried to rob?'

'No. Worse than that.' Locke couldn't see Chains' face, but he imagined that he could hear his scowl in every word he spoke. 'Agents of the duke. His secret police. Commanded by the man with no name.'

'No name?'

'They call him the Spider. His people get work that's too delicate for the yellowjackets. They're spies, assassins, false-facers. Dangerous folk, as dangerous as any of the Right People.'

'Why were they at the house?'

'Bad luck is much too comforting a possibility. I believe my information about the necklace was a poisoned tip.'

'But then … holy shit, but that means we have an informer!'

'It is a vile sin for *that word* to come lightly off the lips of our kind.' Chains whirled, and Locke stumbled backward in surprise. Chains' face was grimmer than Locke had ever seen it, and he waved a finger to emphasize his words. 'It's the worst thing one Right Person can say or think of another. Before you accuse, you'd damn well better *know*. Drop that word carelessly and you'd best be armed, understand?'

'Y-yes. Sorry.'

'My man at Meraggio's is solid.' Chains turned, and with Locke at his heels hurried down the street again. 'My *children* are beyond reproach, all of you.'

'I didn't mean—'

'I know. That means the information itself was bait for a trap. They probably didn't even know who'd bite. They set a line and waited for a fish.'

'Why would they care?'

'It's in their interest,' grumbled Chains. 'Thieves with contacts at Meraggio's, thieves willing to work in a nice quiet place like the Razona … that sort of person merits scrutiny. Or stepping on.'

Locke held onto Chains' sleeve as they threaded their way back into the quality neighbourhoods, where the peace and calm seemed utterly surreal to Locke, given the disturbance he and Sabetha had raised so recently. At last Chains guided Locke into the low, well-kept gardens behind a row of three-storey homes. He pointed to the next house over, and the two of them crouched behind a crumbling stone wall to observe the scene.

Half-visible past the edge of the house was a carriage without livery, guarded by at least two men. The lights in the house were on, but all the windows, save one, were covered by curtains behind thick mosaic glass. The lone exception was on the rear wall, where an orange glow was coming from under a second-storey window that had been cracked open.

'Is she in there?' whispered Locke.

'She is. That open window.'

'How do we get her out?'

'We don't.'

'But … we're here … you brought me here—'

'Locke.' Chains set a hand on Locke's right shoulder. 'She's tied down in that room up there. They have four men inside and two out front with the carriage. Duke's men, above every law. You and I can't fight them.'

'Then why did you bring me here?'

Chains reached inside his tunic, snapped the cord that held a small object around his neck, and held the object out to Locke. It was a glass vial, about the size of Locke's smallest finger.

'Take this,' Chains said. 'You're small enough to climb the vines on that back wall, reach the window, and then—'

'*No.*' The realization of what that vial meant made Locke want to throw up. 'No, no, no!'

'Listen, boy, listen! Time is wasting. We can't get her out. They'll start asking her questions soon. You know how they do that? Hot irons. Knives. When they're finished they'll know everything about you, me, Calo, Galdo. What we do and where we work. We'll never be safe in Camorr again, and our own kind will be as hot for our blood as the duke's people.'

'No, she's clever, she'll—'

'We're not made of iron, boy.' Chains grabbed Locke's right hand, squeezed it firmly, and placed the warm glass vial against his palm. 'We're flesh and blood, and if they hurt us long enough we'll say anything they want us to say.'

Chains gently bent Locke's fingers in over the vial, then lifted his own hands away slowly.

'She'll know what to do,' he said.

'I can't,' said Locke, fresh tears starting down his cheeks. 'I can't. Please.'

'Then they'll torture her,' said Chains quietly. 'You know she'll fight them as long as she can. So they'll do it for hours. Maybe days. They'll break her bones. They'll peel her skin. And you're the *only one* who can get up to that window. You ... trip over your tongue around her. You like her, don't you?'

'Yes,' said Locke, staring into the darkness, trying desperately to think of anything bolder, cleverer, braver than climbing to that window and handing a beautiful girl a vial with which she would kill herself.

He had nothing.

'Not fair,' he sobbed. 'Not fair, not fair.'

'We can't get her out, Locke.' The gentleness and sorrow in Chains' voice caught Locke's attention in a way that scolding or commanding could not have. 'What happens now is up to you. If you can't get to her, she'll live. For a while. And she'll be in hell. But if you can get to that window ... if you can just pass the vial to her ...'

Locke nodded, and hated himself for nodding.

'Brave lad,' whispered Chains. 'Don't wait. Go. Fast and quiet as a breeze.'

It was no great feat to steal across thirty feet of dark garden, to find hand and footholds in the lush vines at the rear of the house, to scuttle upward. But the moments it took felt like hours, and by the time Locke was poised beside the second-storey window he was shaking so badly that he was sure anyone in the house could hear it.

By the grace of the Crooked Warden there were no shouts of alarm, no windows slamming open, no armed men charging into the garden. Ever so carefully, he set his eyes level with the two-inch gap at the bottom of the open window, and moved his head to the right just far enough to peek into the room.

Locke swallowed a sob when he saw Sabetha, seated in a heavy, high-backed chair, facing away from him. Beside her, some sort of cabinet – No. It was a man in a long black coat, a huge man. Locke ducked back out of sight. Gods, Chains was right about at least one thing. They couldn't fight a brute like that, with or without a house full of other men to aid him.

'I'm not an enemy, you know.' The man had a deep, precise voice with the barest hint of a strange accent. 'We want so little from you. You must realize that your friends can't save you. Not from us.'

There was a long silence. The man sighed.

'You might think that we couldn't do the things I suggested earlier. Not to a pretty little girl. But you're as good as hung now. Makes it easy on the conscience. Sooner or later, you'll talk. Even if you have to talk through your screams.

'I'll, ah, leave you alone for a bit. Let you think. But think hard, girl. We're only patient as long as we have orders to be.'

There was a slamming sound, a heavy door being shut, and then a slight metallic clank; the man had turned a key behind him.

Now it was time. Time to slip into the room, pass the vial over, and escape as quickly as possible. And then Sabetha would kill herself, and Locke would … would …

'Fuck this,' he whispered to himself.

Locke pushed at the window, widening the opening at its bottom. Windows that slid up and down were a relatively new and expensive development in Camorr, so rare that even Locke knew they were special. Whatever mechanism raised and lowered this one was well-oiled, and it rose with little resistance. Sabetha turned her head toward the noise as Locke slid over the windowsill and flopped inside. Her eyes were wide with surprise.

'Hi,' whispered Locke, less dramatically than he might have hoped. He stood up from the inch-deep carpet and examined Sabetha's chair. His heart sank. It was glossy hardwood, taller than the window, and likely weighed more than he did. Furthermore, while Sabetha's arms were free, she was shackled at the ankles.

'What are you doing?' she hissed.

'Getting you out,' Locke whispered. He glanced around the room, pondering anxiously. They were in a library, but the shelves and scroll-cases were bare. Not a single book in sight. No sharp objects, no levers, no tools. He examined the door, hoping for some sort of interior lock or bar he could throw, and was disappointed there as well.

'I can't get out of this chair,' said Sabetha, her voice low and urgent. 'They could be back any moment. What's that you're holding?'

Locke suddenly remembered the vial he was clutching tightly in his right hand. Before he could think of anything else to do he moved it behind his back like a fool.

'It's nothing,' he said.

'I know why Chains sent you up here.' Sabetha closed her eyes as she spoke. 'It's okay. He and I talked about it before. It's—'

'No. I'll think of something. Help me.'

'It's going to be all right. Give it to me.'

'I can't.' Locke held up his hands, pleading. 'Help me get you out of that chair.'

'Locke,' said Sabetha, and the sound of her speaking his name at last was like a hammer-blow to his heart. 'You swore to do what I said. Come hell or Eldren-fire. Did you mean it?'

'Yes,' he whispered. 'But you'll die.'

'There's no other way.' She held out one of her hands.

'No.' He rubbed at his eyes, feeling tears starting again.

'Then what are you loyal to, Locke?'

A coldness gnawed at the pit of Locke's stomach. Every failure he'd experienced in his few short years, every time he'd been caught or foiled, every time he'd ever made a mistake, been punished, gone hungry – all those moments churned up and relived at once couldn't have equalled the bitter weight of the defeat that settled in his gut now.

He placed the glass vial in her hand, and for a moment their fingers met, warmth against warmth. She gave his hand a little squeeze, and Locke gasped, letting the vial out of his grip. Her fingers curled around it, and now there was no taking it back.

'Go,' she whispered.

He stared at her, unable to believe he'd actually done it, and then finally turned away. It was just three steps to the window, but his feet felt distant and numb. He braced one hand on the windowsill, more to steady himself than to escape.

A loud click echoed in the room, and the door began to swing open.

Locke heaved himself over the sill, scrambled to plant his feet in the vines that clung to the house's brick exterior, and prayed to drop down fast enough to escape notice, or at least get a head start—

'Locke, wait!' came a deep and familiar voice.

Locke clung precariously to the windowsill and strained to lift his head enough to glance back into the room. The door was wide open, and standing there was Father Chains.

'No,' whispered Locke, suddenly realizing what the whole point of the night's exercise really was. But that meant – That meant Sabetha wouldn't have to—

He was so startled he lost his grip, and with a sharp cry he fell backward into the air above the darkened garden.

8

'Told you he wasn't dead.' It was one of the Sanzas, his voice coming out of the darkness. 'Like a physiker, I am. Ought to charge you a fee for my opinion.'

'Sure.' The other Sanza now, speaking close to Locke's right ear. 'Hope you like getting paid in kicks to the head.'

Locke opened his eyes and found himself on a table in a well-lit room, a room that had the same strange lack of opulence as the library Sabetha had been chained up in. There was the table and a few chairs, but no tapestries, no decorations, no sense that anyone actually lived here. Locke winced, took a deep breath, and sat bolt upright. His back and his head ached dully.

'Easy, boy.' Chains was at his side in an instant. 'You took quite a tumble. If only you weren't so damnably quick on your feet, I might have convinced—'

Chains reached out to gently push him back down, and Locke swatted his hands away.

'You *lied*,' he growled.

'Forgive me,' said Chains, very softly. 'There was still one thing we needed to know about you, Locke.'

'You lied!' The depth of Locke's rage came as a shock; he couldn't remember feeling anything like it even for tormentors like Gregor and Veslin – and he'd killed them, hadn't he? 'None of it was real!'

'Be reasonable,' said Chains. 'It's a bit risky to stage a kidnapping using actual agents of the duke.'

'No,' said Locke. 'It was wrong. It was wrong! It wasn't like they really would have done! I might have got her out!'

'You can't fight grown men,' said Chains. 'You did the very best you could in a bad situation.'

'IT WAS WRONG!' Locke forced himself to concentrate, to articulate what his gut was telling him. 'They would ... real guards might have done differently. Not chained her down. This was all made for me. All made so I had no choice!'

'Yes,' said Chains. 'It was a game you couldn't win. A situation that finds us all, sooner or later.'

'No,' said Locke, feeling his anger warm him from his head to his toes. 'It was all wrong!'

'He did it to us too, once,' said Calo, grabbing his right arm. 'Gods, we wanted to die, it was so bad.'

'He did it to *all* of us,' said Sabetha, and Locke whirled at the sound of her voice. She was standing in a corner, arms folded, studying him with a combination of interest and unease. 'He's right. We had to know if you could do it.'

'And you did superbly,' said Chains. 'You did better than we could have—'

'It wasn't fair,' shouted Locke. 'It wasn't a fair test! There was no way to win!'

'That's life,' said Chains. 'That's your one sure inheritance as flesh and blood. Nobody wins all the time, Locke.'

Locke shook himself free from Calo's grasp and stood on the table, so that he actually had to look down to meet Chains eye to eye.

Gods, he'd thought Sabetha was gone once, and he'd rejoiced to find her alive. Then he'd been sent to *kill* her. That was the rage, he realized, burning like a coal behind his heart. For a few terrible minutes Chains had made him believe that he would have to lose her all over again. Narrowed his world to one awful choice and made him feel helpless.

'I will never lose again.' He nodded slowly to himself, as though his words were the long-sought solution to some mathematical puzzle. Then he shouted at the top of his lungs, not caring if he was heard across the length and breadth of the Razona.

'Do you hear me? I WILL NEVER LOSE AGAIN!'

CHAPTER TWO

The Business

I

'Merciful gods,' said Locke. To Jean's eyes, he seemed genuinely taken aback. 'Your actual flesh-and-blood son? By, ah, traditional means?'

'I certainly didn't brew him in a cauldron.'

'Well, come now,' said Locke, 'as though we'd know one way or the other—'

'There are no means *but* traditional means for such an undertaking.'

'Damn,' said Locke. 'And I thought this was an awkward conversation before.'

'The Falconer's heart is still beating. You've nothing to fear from me.'

'You expect us to believe that?' said Jean. His defensive instincts, sharpened over years of alternating triumphs and disasters, came hotly to life. Even if Patience chose to pose no immediate threat, surely wheels were turning somewhere inside her mind. 'His friends would have killed us, but you can just wave the whole mess off with a sad smile?'

'You two didn't get along,' said Locke.

'Very mildly put,' said Patience. She looked down at her feet, a gesture that struck Jean as totally outside her usual character. 'Even before he earned his first ring … the Falconer was my antagonist in all philosophies, magical or otherwise. If our positions were reversed he certainly wouldn't feel bound to vengeance on my account.'

Now Patience slowly raised her head until her dark eyes met Jean's, and he was able to really study them for the first time. Certain people had what Jean privately thought of as *archer's eyes* – a steady coolness, a detached precision. People with eyes like that could sort the world around them into targets, pick their first shot before those nearby even knew the time for talk had passed. Eyes like that had killers behind them, and Patience for-fucking-sure had a pair.

'He and I live with the consequences of the decisions we made before

89

he took the contract in Camorr,' she said, her voice firm. 'Whether or not I choose to explain those decisions is my business.'

'Fair enough,' said Jean, taking an instinctive half-step back and raising his hands.

'Indeed. Take it easy.' Locke stifled a cough. 'Well, you could murder us, yet supposedly you don't want to. Your son pickled his own mind, but you say you don't really give a shit. So what's the story, Patience? Why are you in Lashain, lending me your cloak?'

'I've come to offer the two of you a job.'

'A job?' Locke laughed, then broke into more painful-sounding coughs. 'A *job*? I hope you need someone to line a casket for you, you poor Karthani witch, because that's the only job I'm presently qualified for.'

'Until you finally lose the strength for sarcasm, Locke, I wouldn't hire any mourners.'

'I'm on my way.' Locke pounded on his chest a few times. 'Believe me, I've ducked out of paying this bill before, but this time I'm pretty sure the house is going to make me settle. You should have tried, I don't know, *not fucking revealing my plans to the gods-damned Archon of Tal Verrar so he could fucking well poison me*! Maybe then my schedule for the immediate future would be a tad more ... open.'

'I can remove the poison from your body.'

Nobody spoke for several seconds. Jean was dumbstruck, Locke merely scowled, and Patience let the words hang in the empty air without further adornment. The timbers of the roof creaked faintly at the touch of the wind.

'Bullshit,' Locke muttered at last.

'You keep presuming that my powers are infinite where they concern your discomfort. Why not credit me with an equivalent capacity to render aid?' Patience folded her arms. 'Surely some of the black alchemists you consulted must have passed on hints ...'

'I'm not talking about your damned sorcery. I mean, I see the *game* now. It's bullshit. Act one, those Lashani bastards trash the place. Act two, a mysterious saviour appears out of the night, and we buy whatever you're selling. You arranged this whole mess.'

'I had nothing to do with Cortessa. Jean brought the Lashani down on your heads when he mishandled the physiker yesterday.'

'What an eminently reasonable excuse! Good gods, woman, who the hell do you think you're *talking* to here?' Locke erupted into a coughing fit, and just as quickly brought it under control by evident force of will. 'I ought to know a setup when it lands right on top of my head!'

'Locke, calm down.' Jean felt his heartbeat all the way to the base of his throat. 'Think about this for a moment.' It had to be a trick, a plan, a scheme of some sort, but by all the gods, what was that against the total certainty of death? Jean sent a silent plea to the Crooked Warden to give Locke just a few moments of lucid reason.

'I have no money,' said Locke. 'No resources. No treasure. And I'm too sick now to even stand up. That leaves me just one single thing you can still take.'

'We need to consider—'

'You want my name, don't you?' Locke's voice was hoarse and teasing. He sounded triumphant at having something to fuel a real argument; evidently the god of thieves had no common sense available for lending at the moment. 'You knock everything out from under me, then show up at the last minute, waving a reprieve. And all you'd need is my real name, right? Oh, you want leverage, that's for sure. You haven't forgiven *anyone* for what happened to the Falconer.'

'You're dying,' said Patience. 'Do you really think I'd take these pains just to turn the screws on you? Gods be gracious, how much more pressure could I possibly apply?'

'I believe you'd do anything, if you wanted your hooks in me bad enough.' Locke wiped his lips with the back of his hand, and Jean could see that his spit was blood-tinged. 'I know a thing or two about revenge, and you have powers I can only dream of. So I must believe you'd do *anything*.'

'Why bother when I could have your real name any time I wanted it?'

'Now that's so much arrogant bull—'

'It would simply be a question,' Patience continued, 'of how long you could watch Jean Tannen suffer before you would beg for the privilege of telling me.'

'You're no different than the Falconer,' said Locke. 'Same fucking—'

'Locke,' said Jean, very loudly.

'—attitude toward ... yeah?'

'Kindly *shut the hell up*,' said Jean, enunciating every word as though teaching the phrase to a small child for the first time. Locke's slack-jawed stare was gratifying.

'She's right,' continued Jean, unable to keep a growing excitement out of his voice. 'If your true name was all she wanted, why *not* torture me? I'm compromised, I'm bloody helpless. It would be quick and simple. So why aren't I screaming right now?'

'Because if these people were any good at "quick and simple" the Falconer would have killed us back in Camorr.'

'No, dammit. Think harder.'

'Because you have such a sweet and innocent face?'

'Because if she doesn't want your real name the easy way—'

'Then she has some other motive. Sweet dancing donkey shit, Jean!' Locke rolled back toward Patience, but closed his eyes and rubbed at them. 'She wants me to stick my own head in the noose, of my own free will. Get it? She wants me to step off the cliff. Cut my own wrists so she can gloat … humiliate—' Locke broke into another severe coughing fit, and Jean sat down on the bed and pounded gently on his back. The rhythmic movement did nothing good for Jean's collection of fresh aches and bruises, but it calmed Locke rapidly.

'What we're discussing,' said Patience, 'is *employment*, not compulsion. Credit me with enough wit to recall the fate of Luciano Anatolius and Maxilan Stragos. Coercing you two never seems to work. We're willing to trade service for service.'

'Patience,' said Jean, 'can you really get rid of this poison? Can you do it without using his real name?'

'If we hurry, yes.'

'If you're lying,' said Jean, 'if you're leaving anything out, I'll try to kill you again. Understand? I'll give it everything I have, even if it forces you slay me on the spot.'

Patience nodded.

'Then let's talk business.'

'Let's not,' snarled Locke. 'Let's show this bitch to the door and refuse to be puppets.'

'Shut up.' Jean pushed firmly down on Locke's shoulders, foiling his attempt to roll out of bed. 'Tell us about this job.'

Locke drew in a rasping breath to spew some more damn fool craziness. Jean, with the reflexes that kept him alive when blades were drawn, clamped a hand over Locke's mouth before he could speak and pushed his head back down against his pillow. 'I can't agree to anything on Locke's behalf, but I want us to hear your proposal. Tell us what the job is.'

'It's political,' said Patience.

'Mmmmph mmph,' said Locke, struggling in vain against Jean's arm. 'Mmmph fckhnnng fmmmph!'

'He wants to hear more,' said Jean. 'He says he's very excited to hear the whole thing.'

2

'I need an election adjusted.'

'How adjusted?'

'As a cautious estimate?' Patience turned to the window and stared out into the rain. 'I need it rigged from top to bottom.'

'Government affairs are a bit beyond our experience,' said Jean.

'Nonsense. You'll feel right at home. What is government but theft by consent? You'll be moving in a society of kindred spirits.'

'What sort of election are we supposed to be mucking about with here?'

'Every five years,' said Patience, 'the citizens of Karthain elect an assembly, the Konseil. Nineteen representatives for nineteen city districts. This dignified mess runs the city, and I need a majority of their seats to go to the faction of my preference.'

'This is what you want us for?' Locke finally slipped Jean's hand aside and managed to speak. 'My dead ass! With your powers, you'd have to be out of your gods-damned minds to settle for anything Jean and I could pull off! You could wiggle your fingers and make them elect cats and dogs, for fuck's sake.'

'No,' said Patience. 'In public, the magi stand completely aloof from the government of the city. In private, we are forbidden to use any of our arts. Not on the poorest citizen of Karthain, not for a single vote.'

'You won't use your sorcery on the people of Karthain?' said Jean. 'Not at all?'

'Oh, Karthain is our city, through and through. We've adjusted everything to suit our needs, and that includes the inhabitants. It's this contest we can't touch. The election itself.'

'Seems awkward as all hell. Why the limitation?'

'You've seen some of our arts. You opposed the Falconer. You survived Tal Verrar.'

'In a manner of speaking,' muttered Locke.

'Imagine a society of men and women where those powers are

93

universal,' said Patience. 'Imagine … sitting down to dinner with four hundred people, each of whom has a loaded crossbow set beside their wineglass. Some very strict rules will have to be enforced if anyone wants to live long enough to see the last course.'

'I think I get it,' said Jean. 'You have some sort of rule about not shitting where you eat?'

'Magi must *never* work magic against one another,' said Patience. 'We're as human as you are, as complicated, as insecure, as driven to argument. The only difference is that any one of us, out of the mildest irritation, could make someone evapourate into smoke with a gesture.

'We don't duel,' she continued. 'We don't so much as *tease* one another with our arts. We forcefully separate ourselves from any situation where our crossed purposes might tempt us to do so.'

'Situations like this election,' said Jean.

'Yes. We do need to control the Konseil, one way or another. Once the election is over, the new government becomes a general tool. We adjust its members by consensual design. But during the contest itself, when our blood is up, we need to keep our arts entirely out of the situation. We need to be pure spectators.'

Patience raised both of her hands, palms up, as though presenting two invisible objects for weighing.

'There are two major factions among my people. Two major parties in Karthani politics. We battle by proxy. Each side is allowed to choose agents. Enterprising individuals, never magi. We set them loose to fight on our behalf. In the past we've favoured orators, political organizers, demagogues. This time, I've convinced my people to hire someone with a more unusual portfolio of achievement.'

'Why?' said Jean.

'Some people play handball,' said Patience, smiling. 'Some people play Catch-the-Duke. This is our sport. The election diverts much of the frustration our factions come to feel for one another, and brings prestige to the side that backs the winner. It's become a highly anticipated tradition.'

'I've imagined you people must run the show in Karthain,' said Locke. 'I just never would have suspected this. What a joke on all the poor saps lining up to vote every five years.'

'They get an orderly city regardless of the winner,' said Patience. 'In Karthain, nobody empties the treasury and vanishes. Nobody holds grand masques every night while the streets fill with night soil and dead animals. We see to that.'

'Would a city of puppets really give a damn if you didn't?' said Locke, wheezing. He cleared his throat. 'You want us to work fraud in the service of order and public sanitation. What a thought!'

'Isn't theft theft? Aren't lies lies? Isn't this exactly the sort of opportunity you'd spend years chasing if it was your own idea? Besides, the job serves you as much as anyone. Accepting it will save your life.'

'How long would you need us?' said Locke.

'The election is in six weeks.'

'What about resources? Clothes, money, lodging—'

'We have complete identities prepared for you, all possible comforts, and a large pool of funds to dispose of on business.'

'Only business?' said Locke.

'You'll be treated luxuriously for six weeks. What more could you want?'

'Perelandro's balls, a little incentive to win would be nice.'

'Incentive? Life itself isn't sufficient? You'll be well-dressed, you'll recover your health, and you'll be in a greatly improved position from which to resume your … career. If you win, our gratitude might easily extend so far as comfortable transportation to the city of your choice.'

'And if we lose?'

'You can't expect us to reward failure. You'll still be free to leave, but you'll do it on foot.'

'I can only speak for myself,' said Locke, and Jean's heart sank. 'I meant what I said. I have no idea what your full powers are. I don't trust you. I don't trust this situation, and I have no reasonable chance to catch you if you're lying. If you're not sincere, this is a trap, and if you are sincere it's some kind of bizarre pity-fuck.'

'And all the years you might have had coming? All the things you have yet to do?'

'Spare me. You're not *my* mother. If Jean will take the job, you won't find a better man anywhere. He can do anything I could, and he's better at keeping himself in one piece. Thanks for coming all this way to entertain me, but leave me alone.'

'Hold on—' Jean began.

'I'm disappointed,' said Patience. 'I would have thought you had at least one more thing to live for. Can you honestly say you've never hoped for any chance of a reunion with Sabetha, somewhere out there in the—'

'You go *fuck yourself*,' snarled Locke. 'I don't care what you think you know. That's one subject you don't get to presume anything about.'

'As you like.' Patience flexed her right hand and Jean noticed the gleam of silver thread woven between the fingers. 'It seems I've wasted our time. Shall I expect you in Karthain when your friend is dead, Jean?'

'Hold!' said Jean. 'Patience, please, give us time to talk. In private.'

Patience nodded curtly and moved the knuckles of her right hand. Light shifted on the silvery gleam of her cat's cradle. Jean blinked, and in that instant thread and woman alike vanished into thin air.

'Great,' said Jean. 'Fucking magnificent. I think you've finally managed to *really* piss her off.'

'Nice to know I still have the knack,' said Locke.

'Are you really, truly out of your gods-damned mind? She could save your life.'

'She could do a lot of things.'

'Take the chance, Locke.'

'She's up to something.'

'What a *revelation*! What an amazing deduction! I'm sorry, remind me again what your other options are?'

'She wants something from *me*, damn it, more than she's letting on! But she's already got everything she can take from you, right? You said it yourself. If she's out to get you, she'll get you. But if she does right by you, then you'll be in a strong position to move on.'

'It works that way for both of us.'

'I won't be that witch's toy,' said Locke. 'Not for all the money in Karthain. She's not *human*. None of them are.'

Jean glared coldly at Locke. He lay under Patience's cloak, his wild aspect incongruous next to the fine oilcloth. A cornered animal, preparing to die, huddled under delicate material worth several years of a skilled labourer's life. The whites of his eyes were turning pink.

'Patience was right,' Jean said quietly. 'She has wasted our time. You'll die choking on your own blood. Today, tomorrow. Doesn't matter. And you'll be so *happy* with yourself. Because somehow dying has become an achievement.'

'Jean, wait—'

'Wait, wait, *wait*.' The resentments and frustrations of the past few weeks seemed to boil up as Jean spoke. The old familiar temper, snapping like a rope frayed down to a single strand, the rage like a hot pressure under his skin, pulsing from his skull to his fingertips. Only it was worse than usual, because there was nothing he could hit. Zodesti, Cortessa – Jean would have snapped their bones like badly fired pottery. Patience, even – he would have gone for her throat, dared her sorcery. But with Locke he was limited to words, so he weighted them with scorn and let fly. 'What the hell have I done but wait? Wait on the boat to see if you got sick. Wait here, week after week, watching you get worse. Day and night, chasing any hope this fucking city could offer, while you—'

'Jean, I am telling you, every instinct I have says this is a setup.'

'No shit. And since we *know* they mean to use us, why can't we use them as well, for everything we can get out of the deal?'

'Give me up, Jean. Let me go and their fun vanishes. Then they'll have that much less reason to play you false.'

'Oh, marvellous. Fucking masterful. You'll be dead and they'll be *inconvenienced*. Maybe even *mildly disappointed*. What a worthy trade! Like slashing your throat just before your opponent can take a piece in Catch-the-Duke.'

'But—'

'Shut it. Just shut it. You know, when you're healthy, you'll laugh the gods right in their faces. But when you're convalescing, sweet hell, you are a *miserable* bastard.'

'I've always admitted—'

'No. You've never admitted *this*. You don't stand still, Locke. I played along in Tal Verrar when we talked about retiring on our money, but that was bullshit and we both knew it. You don't retire. You don't even take holidays. You move from scheme to scheme, jumping around like a spider on a hot skillet. And when you're *forced* to stand still, when you don't have a thousand things going on to keep you distracted from your own thoughts, you *actually want to die*. I see that now. I'm so godsdamned slow and stupid I see it for the first time!'

'What the hell are you talking about?'

'You and I, in the boat, after we torched the glass burrow. After we killed Bug's murderer. Do you remember what we talked about? What you were like? And Vel Virazzo. You tried to finish the Grey King's work by drowning yourself in wine. Now this. You're not just cranky when you're ill, Locke, you have the ... look, it's called *Endliktgelaben*. It's a High Vadran word. I learned about it when I was studying as an initiate of Aza Guilla. It means, ah, death-love, death-desire. It's hard to translate. It means you have moods where you *absolutely want to destroy yourself*. Not as some self-pitying idle notion, either. As a certainty!'

'For Perelandro's sake, Jean, I wouldn't want this if I had a fucking choice!'

'You don't want it up *here*,' said Jean, pointing to his own head. 'You want it somewhere deeper, so deep you can't recognize it. You think you've got some logical, noble excuse for showing Patience the door. But it's really that darkness inside, trying to fuck you over once and for all. Something has you so scared you're seeing everything backwards.'

'What is it, then? If you're so smart, what is it?'

'I don't know. Maybe Patience can read thoughts like a book, but I sure as hell can't. However, I can tell you what the hell *I'm* scared of – being *alone*. Being the very last one of us standing, all because you're a selfish, stubborn coward.'

'Not fair,' wheezed Locke.

'No, it isn't. A lot of good people have died to bring you this far. You keep this shit up and you'll be seeing them soon. What are you going to tell Calo and Galdo and Bug? Chains? Nazca?' Jean leaned over and all but whispered his next words down at Locke. 'What are you going to tell the woman I loved? The woman who *burned* so you could have the slightest chance in hell of even being here in the first place?'

All the faint colour left in Locke's face had drained out; he moved his lips but seemed unable to convince any words to get that far past his throat.

'If I can get up and live with that every gods-damned day, then so can *you*, you son of a bitch.' Jean stepped away from the bed. 'I'll be outside. Make your choice.'

'Jean ... call her back.'

'Are you just humouring me?

'No. Please. Call Patience back.'

'Are you ashamed?'

'Yes! Yes, how couldn't I be, you ass?'

'And you'll do it? Whatever it takes, whatever Patience requires to keep you alive?'

'Get her back in the room. Get her back! By the gods, I need her to fix me so I can punch your guts into soup.'

'That's the spirit. Patience!' Jean yelled, turning toward the apartment's door. 'Patience! Are you—'

'Of course.'

Jean whirled. She was already in the room, standing behind him.

'I didn't say I was going far,' she said, cutting off his question before it was spoken. 'You'll both do it?'

'Yes, we'll—'

'There are going to be some conditions,' interrupted Locke.

'Dammit, Locke,' said Jean.

'Trust me.' Locke coughed and shifted his gaze from Jean to Patience. 'First, I want it clear that our obligation to you begins and ends with this election. That's our side of the bargain in full. No hidden surprises. No snake-bite double-dealing bondsmage bullshit.'

'I beg your pardon?' said Patience.

'You heard me.' Locke's voice was still hoarse, but to Jean it seemed infused with genuine strength. Or anger, which was as good for the time being. 'I don't want one of you people popping out of my ass five years from now and implying that I'm still on the hook for having my life spared. I want to hear it from you, right to our faces. Once this is done, we don't owe you *shit*.'

'What a high art you've made of insolence,' said Patience. 'If that's the game you feel you have to play, so be it. Service for service and a clean severance, just as I said.'

'Good. I want another privilege, too.'

'Our side of the bargain is already exceptionally generous.'

'Who do you think you're haggling with, a fucking pie vendor? If you'd rather lose your election—'

'State your request.'

'Answers. I want the answer to any question I ask, when I ask, to the best of your ability. I don't want you to wave your hands and give me any bullshit about how great and terrible and incomprehensible everything is.'

'What questions?'

'Anything. Magic, Karthain, yourself, Falconer. Anything that comes to mind. I'm tired of the gods-damned shadow dance you people call conversation. If I'm going to work for you, I want you to explain some things.'

Patience considered this for some time.

'I have a private life and a professional life,' she said at last. 'I may be prepared to discuss the latter. If you fail to respect the former, you will earn … consequences.'

'Good enough.' Locke wiped his mouth on his tunic sleeve, adding new blood to old stains. 'Okay, Jean, do you still want the job?'

'Yes.'

'Good,' said Locke. 'I do too. You've hired us, Patience. Now do your thing. Get this shit out of me.'

'I can't work here,' said Patience. 'We'll need to move, and quickly. A ship is waiting at the docks to take us across the Amathel; everything I need is on board.'

'Alright,' said Jean. 'I'll go out and call a—'

Patience snapped her fingers, and the outer door fell open. A carriage was waiting on the street outside, its yellow lamps glowing softly in the drizzle, its quartet of horses standing in silent readiness.

'Aren't you theatrical as hell,' said Locke.

'We've lost enough time taming your pride, Locke. We need every moment we can steal back if you're going to survive what comes next.'

'Hold it,' said Jean, 'What do you mean, "survive what comes next"?'

'It's partly my fault. I waited to approach you. I should have done it before you had a chance to start kidnapping physikers. Now Locke's condition is worse than precarious, and this would be hard enough for someone in perfect health.'

'But you—'

'Stand down, Jean, it's the same hard sell we use,' said Locke. 'Astonishing promises first, important disclaimers second. Just get on with it, Patience. Do your worst. I'm pissed off enough to take any sorcery you can throw at me.'

'Jean must have said something very interesting to shame you into finding your courage again.' Patience clapped her hands, and two tall men strode in through the front door. They wore broad-brimmed hats and long black leather coats, and carried a folding litter between them. 'Keep that shame burning if you want to live.'

Patience touched Locke briefly on the forehead, and then she beckoned her coachmen over to roll him onto the litter. Jean watched warily but let them handle the work alone, as they seemed steady and careful enough.

'The only thing I can promise with absolute certainty,' said Patience as she watched this delicate process, 'is that what I need to do when we reach the ship will be one of the worst things that's ever happened to you.'

The Boy Who Chased Red Dresses

I

'You're still angry with me,' said Chains.

It wasn't a question. Locke's attitude would have been plain to someone with the empathy of a shithouse brick.

A day had passed since the affair of Sabetha's 'capture,' and while Locke had rapidly shrugged off the effects of his fall into the garden, he'd been snappish and sullen since returning to the Temple of Perelandro. He'd flat-out refused to help prepare dinner or eat it, and after a brief, awkward attempt at a meal Chains had finally dragged him up to the temple roof.

They sat there now, under the dying aura of Falselight, the hour when every visible inch of Elderglass in Camorr threw off enough supernatural radiance to bring on a second sunset. Every bridge and avenue and tower was limned in eerie light, and beneath the steel-blue sky the city was a dark tapestry knit with ten thousand glowing stitches.

The parapets of the temple's untended rooftop garden shielded Locke and Chains from prying eyes. They sat a few paces apart amidst the shards of broken pottery, staring at one another. Chains was taking unusually frequent drags on his sheaf of rolled tobacco, the red embers flaring with each indrawn breath.

'Look at me,' he muttered. 'You've got me smoking the Anacasti Black. My holiday blend. Of course you're still angry with me. You're about seven years old and your view of the world is *this wide*.' Chains held up the thumb and the forefinger of his left hand, and the distance between them was not generous. This, at last, drew Locke out of his silence.

'What happened wasn't fair!'

'Fair? You mean to claim with a straight face that you buy into that heresy, my boy?' Chains took a last long puff on his dying cigar and flicked the remnants into the darkness. 'Everyone in Catchfire dropped dead except for you and your fellow wolf cubs. In Shades'

Hill, you avoided death for at *least* two grandiose mistakes that would have got a grown man's balls peeled like grapes, and you still want to talk about—'

'No,' said Locke, his look of self-righteous annoyance instantly changing to one of startled embarrassment, as though he'd been accused of wetting his breeches. 'No, no, I didn't say *those* things were fair. I know *life's* not fair. But I thought … I thought … you were.'

'Ah,' said Chains, 'well, now. I've always thought of myself as fair to a fault. Look, what are you more upset about, the fact that I lied about what had to happen to Sabetha or the fact that the contest I rigged wasn't, ah, as open to improvisation as you might have wished?'

'I don't know. Both! All of it!'

'Locke, you may be too young for formal rhetoric, but you've got to at least try to pick your problems apart and explain them piece by piece. Now, here's another important question. Are you comfortable at this temple?'

'Yes!'

'You eat well and sleep soundly. Your clothes are clean, you have many diversions, and you even get to bathe every week.'

'Yes. Yes, I like it a lot, it's all worth having to bathe, even!'

'Hmmm,' said Chains. 'You live long enough for your stones to drop, then tell me if bathing is really such a hardship when the young women around you have bosoms that are more than theoretical.'

'What? When my *what*?'

'Never mind. That subject will be sufficiently confusing in its own good time. So, you like it here. You're comfortable, you're protected. Have I behaved badly? Treated you as you were treated in Shades' Hill?'

'Well, no … no, not like that at all.'

'Yet none of that buys me any consideration in the matter of last night? Not one speck of trust? One tiny instant of the benefit of the doubt?'

'I, uh, well, it's not … uh, crap.' Locke made a desperate grab for eloquence and came up with empty hands as usual. 'I don't mean … it's not that I don't appreciate—'

'Easy, Locke, easy. Just because you've been uncouth doesn't mean you might not have a point. But hear me now – this is a small home we live in. The temple might seem marvellous compared to living and sleeping in heaps of dozens, but believe me – walls squeeze the people who live inside them, sooner or later.'

'They don't bother me,' said Locke quickly.

'It's not so much the walls, though, Locke, it's the *people*. This will be your home for many years to come, gods willing, and you and Sabetha and the Sanzas are going to be as close as family. You'll strike sparks off one another. I can't have you shoving your thumb up your ass and doing your best impression of a brick wall every time you get annoyed. Crooked Warden help us, we've got to be ready and willing to talk, or we're all going to wake up with cut throats sooner or later.'

'I'm … I'm sorry.'

'Don't hang your head like a kicked puppy. Just keep it in mind. If you're going to live here, staying civil is as much a duty as sitting the steps or washing dishes. Now, while I bask in the glow of another moral sermon delivered with the precision of a master fencer, hold your applause and let's get back to last night. You're upset because the situation was contrived to give you only one real means of resolving it, short of curling up into a little ball and crying yourself into a stupor.'

'Yes! It wasn't like it would have been, if they'd been real guards. If they weren't, you know, watching for me.'

'You're right. If those men had been real agents of the duke, some of them might have been incompetent, or open to bribery, and they might not have taken their duty to guard a little girl very seriously. Correct?'

'Uh, yes.'

'Of course, if they'd been real agents of the duke, they might also have taken her somewhere truly impregnable, like the Palace of Patience. And instead of six there might have been twelve, or twenty, or the entire Nightglass company, prowling the streets looking to have an urgent personal conversation with *you*.' Chains leaned forward and poked Locke's forehead. 'That's how luck works, lad. You can bitch all you like about how things could have been more favourable for you, but rest assured things can *always be worse*. Always. Understood?'

'I think so,' said Locke, with the neutral tone of a student gingerly accepting a master's assurances on something far beyond personal verification, like the number of angels that could play handball on the edge of a rose petal.

'Well, if I can even get you thinking about it, that's a victory of sorts, at your age. No offence.' Chains cracked his knuckles before continuing. 'You, after all, have publicly vowed to never lose again, which is about as likely as me learning to crap gold bars on command.'

'But—'

'Let it be. I know your temperament, lad, and I'm too wise to try and give it more than a few sharp nudges at a time. So, the other thing. You're upset that I lied about what needed to be done with Sabetha.'

'Well, yeah.'

'You feel something for her.'

'I … I don't, um …'

'Quit it. This is important. You *do* feel something for her. There's more to this than a little wounded pride. Can you tell me about it?'

Slowly, grudgingly, feeling as though he might be about to get up and run away, Locke somehow found the will to give Chains the barest sketch of his first encounter with Sabetha, and of her later disappearance.

'Hells,' said Chains quietly when the tale was finished. The sky and the city beneath it had darkened while Locke had stumbled through his explanation. 'I can see why you snapped, having that rug pulled out from under you twice. Forgive me, Locke, I honestly didn't know you'd grown feelings for her in Shades' Hill.'

'It's okay,' mumbled Locke.

'You have a crush, I think.'

'Do I?' Locke had a vague idea of what that word meant, and somehow it didn't seem right. It didn't seem *enough*.

'It's not meant to belittle your feelings, lad. A crush can come on hot and sharp like an illness. I know exactly what it's like. Years to go before your body will even be ready for, ah, what comes between men and women, but a crush doesn't care. It's got a power all its own. That's the bad news.'

'What's the good news?'

'Crushes fade. Sure as you and I are sitting here now. They're like sparks thrown from a fire – hot and bright for a moment, then gone.'

Locke frowned, not at all sure he wanted to be released from his feelings for Sabetha. They were a bundle of mysteries, and every attempt to unravel them in his own mind seemed to send a pleasant warm shiver to every nerve in his body.

'Heh. You don't believe me, or you don't want to. Fair enough. But you're going to be living with Sabetha day in and day out any time one of you isn't away for training. My guess is, she'll be like a sister to you in a few years. Familiarity has a way of filing the sharp edges off our feelings for other people. You'll see.'

2

Time passed, days and months chaining together into years, and Jean Tannen joined the Gentlemen Bastards. In the summer of the seventy-seventh Year of Perelandro, two years after Jean's arrival, a rare dry spell came over the city-state of Camorr, and the Angevine ran ten feet below its usual height. The canals went grey and turgid, thickening like blood in the veins of a ripening corpse.

Canal trees, those glorious affectations that usually roamed and twirled on the city's currents with their long float-threaded roots drinking the filth around them, now bobbed in sullen masses, confined to the river and the Floating Market. Their silk-bright leaves dulled and their branches drooped; their roots hung slack in the water like the tentacles of dead sea-monsters. Day after day the Temple District was shrouded in layers of smoke, as every denomination burned anything that came to mind in sacrifices pleading for a hard, cleansing rain that wouldn't come.

In the Cauldron and the Dregs, where the lowest of the low slept ten to a room in windowless houses, the usual steady flow of murders became a torrent. The Duke's corpse-hunters, paid as they were by the head, whistled while they fished putrefying former citizens out of barrels and cesspits. The city's professional criminals, more conscientious than its impulsive killers, did their part for Camorr's air by throwing the remains of their victims into the harbour by night, where the predators of the Iron Sea quietly made the offerings vanish.

In this atmosphere, in the hot summer evening heavy with smoke and the stink of a hundred distinct putrefactions, the temple roof was out of the question for meetings, so Father Chains let his five young wards gather in the dank coolness of the glass burrow's kitchen. Their recent meals, by Chains' orders, had been lukewarm affairs, with anything cooked brought in from stalls near the Floating Market.

They had come together that week, as a complete set, for the first time in half a year. Chains' interwoven programmes of training had taken on the complexity of an acrobat's plate-spinning act as his young wards were shuffled back and forth between apprenticeships in assorted temples and trades, learning their habits, jargon, rituals, and trivia. These excursions were arranged by the Eyeless Priest via a re-markable network of contacts, extending well beyond Camorr and the criminal fraternity, and they were largely paid for out of the small fortune that the citizens of Camorr had charitably donated over the years.

Time had begun to work its more obvious changes on the young Gentlemen Bastards. Calo and Galdo were dealing with a growth spurt that had given their usual grace a humbling dose of awkwardness, and their voices were starting to veer wildly. Jean Tannen was still on the cherubic side, but his shoulders were broadening, and from scuffles like the Half-Crown War he had acquired the confident air of someone well versed in the art of introducing faces to cobblestones.

Given these evident signs of physical progress around him, Locke was secretly displeased with his own condition. His voice had yet to drop, and while he was larger than he'd ever been, all this did was maintain him in the same ratio as before, a medium child surrounded on all sides by the taller and the wider. And while he knew the other boys depended upon him to be the heart and brains of their combined operations, it was a cold comfort whenever Sabetha came home.

Sabetha (who, if she objected to being the only Gentle-lady Bastard, had never said so out loud) was freshly returned from weeks of immersive training as a court scrivener's apprentice, and bore new signs of physical progress herself. She was still taller than Locke, and the natural colour of her tightly plaited hair remained hidden by a brown alchemical wash. But her slender figure seemed to be pressing outward, ever so slightly, against the front of her thin chemise, and her movements around the glass burrow had revealed the hints of other emerging curves to Locke's vigilant eyes.

Her natural poise had grown in direct proportion to her years, and while Locke held firm sway over the three other boys, she was a separate power, neither belittling his status in the gang nor overtly acknowledging it. There was a seriousness to her that Locke found deeply compelling, possibly because it was unique among the five of them. She had embarked upon a sort of miniature adulthood and skipped the wild facetiousness that defined, for example, the Sanzas. It seemed to Locke that she was more eager than the rest of them to get to wherever their training was taking them.

'Young lady,' said Father Chains as he entered the kitchen, 'and young gentlemen, such as you are. Thank you for your prompt attention to my summons, a courtesy which I shall now repay by setting you on a path to frustration and acrimony. I have decided that you five do not fight amongst yourselves nearly enough.'

'Begging your pardon,' said Sabetha, 'but if you'll look more closely at Calo and Galdo you'll see that's not the case.'

'Ah, that's merely communication,' said Chains. 'Just as you and I speak by forming words, the natural, private discourse of the Sanza twins appears to consist entirely of farts and savage beatings. What I want is all five of you facing off against one another.'

'You want us to start … hitting each other?' said Locke.

'Oh, I volunteer to hit Sabetha,' said Calo, 'and I volunteer to be hit by Locke!'

'I would also volunteer to be hit by Locke,' said Galdo.

'Quiet, you turnip-brained alley apes,' said Chains. 'I don't want you boxing with one another. Not necessarily. No, I've given you all a great many tasks that have pitted you against the world, as individuals and as a group, and for the most part you've trounced my expectations. I think the time has come to pry you out of your comfortable little union and see how you fare in competition against one another.'

'What sort of competition?' said Jean.

'Highly amusing competition,' said Chains, raising his eyebrows. 'From the perspective of the old man who gets to sit back and watch. It's been three or four years of steady training for most of you, and I want to see what happens when each of you tries to pit your zest for criminal enterprise against an opponent with a similar education.'

'So, uh, just to be clear,' said Calo, 'none of us are going to be fighting Jean?'

'Not unless you're inconceivably stupid.'

'Right,' said Calo. 'What's the plan?'

'I'm going to keep you all here for the rest of the summer,' said Chains. 'A break from your apprenticeships. We can enjoy the marvellous weather together, and you can chase each other across the city. Starting with—' He lifted a finger and pointed it at Locke. 'You. Aaaaaaand …' He slowly shifted his finger until it was pointed at Sabetha. 'You!'

'Um, meaning what, exactly?' said Locke. Butterflies instantly came to life in his stomach, and the little bastards were heavily armed.

'A bit of elementary stalking and evasion, on Coin-Kisser's Row. Tomorrow at noon.'

'Surrounded by hundreds of people,' said Sabetha coolly.

'Quite right, my dear. It's easy enough to follow someone when you've got the whole night to hide in. I think you're ready for something less forgiving. You'll begin at the very southern end of Coin-Kisser's Row, carrying a handbag with an open top. Inside the bag will be four small rolls of silk, each a different colour. Easily visible from ten or twenty feet away. You'll take a leisurely stroll up the full length of the district.

'Somewhere in your wake will be Locke, wearing a jacket with a certain number of brass buttons, also easily counted from a fairly narrow distance. The game is simple. Locke wins if he can tell me the colours of the silk. Sabetha wins if she crosses the Goldenreach Bridge from Coin-Kisser's Row to Twosilver Green without revealing the colours. She can *also* win if Locke is clumsy enough for her to count the number of buttons on his coat. Each of you wishing to report to me will have only one chance to be accurate, so you can't simply keep guessing until you get it right.'

'Hold on,' said Locke. 'I get one way to win and she gets two?'

'Perhaps you can try burning down the Goldenreach Bridge,' Sabetha said sweetly.

'Yes, she gets two,' said Chains, 'and fortunately for Camorr, the bridge is made of stone. Sabetha has a package to guard, and must, as I have said, move at a *leisurely* pace, with dignity. No running or climbing. Locke, you'll be expected to cause no scenes, but your freedom of movement will be less restricted.'

'Ah.'

'You're not to physically touch one another. You may not simply cover up the silk or the buttons. You may not have your opponent harmed or restrained in any fashion. And neither of you may call upon any of the other Gentlemen Bastards for help.'

'Where do we get to be, then?' said Galdo.

'Safely at home,' said Chains, 'sitting the steps in my place.'

'Oh, balls to that, we want to see what happens!'

'One thing the contest does not need,' said Chains, 'is a chorus of gawkers stumbling along for the duration. I'll be nearby, watching everything, and I promise to give you a very lively account upon my return. Now—' He produced two small leather bags and tossed them to Locke and Sabetha. 'Your operating funds.'

Locke opened his bag and counted ten silver Solons.

'You've got all night to think about what you're doing,' said Chains.

'You may come and go as you please. Don't feel compelled to buy any-thing, but if you do, the coins I've given you are your absolute limit.'

'What's this all for?' said Locke.

'To put you on the spot, and thereby—'

'I think,' said Sabetha, 'he meant to ask, what's in it for the winner?'

'Ah,' said Chains. 'Of course. Well, other than acquiring a vast sense of personal satisfaction, the winner will hand their dinner chores over to the loser for three nights. How's that?'

Locke watched Sabetha, and when she nodded once, he did the same. The girl already seemed to be lost in thought, and Locke felt a touch of apprehension beneath his rising excitement. He had every confidence in his own skills, as they had fetched him everything from coin-purses to corpses without much difficulty, but the full extent of Sabetha's abilities was unknown to him. Her absences from the temple had been lengthier than those of any of the boys, and out there in the wider world she could have learned an infinite variety of nasty surprises.

3

Sabetha excused herself a few minutes later and vanished into the night, off to make whatever arrangements she thought were necessary. Locke followed in haste, throwing on the white robes of an initiate of Perelandro, but by the time he reached the hot, smoky air of the Temple District's central plaza, she had long since vanished into the shadows. Might she be waiting out there, watching, hoping to follow *him* and learn what he was up to? The thought gave him a brief pause, but the unhappy fact was that he had no concrete plans at all, so it really didn't matter whether or not she dogged his heels all night.

Lacking any better ideas, he decided to tour Coin-Kisser's Row and refresh his memory of the district's landmarks.

He hurried along with a brisk step, fingers interlaced within the sleeves of his robe, pondering. He trusted his clerical guise to shield him from inconvenience and harm (for he was keeping to better neigh-bourhoods), and so he remained caught up in the whirl of his own thoughts as his feet carried him down the full length of Coin-Kisser's Row, then back up again.

The great counting houses were shuttered for the night, the bars and coffee shops all but empty, and the reeking canal had little of its usual drunken pleasure traffic. Locke stared at the monuments, the bridges, and the long deserted plazas, but no fresh inspiration fell out of the sky. When he returned home, somewhat discouraged, Sabetha had not yet returned.

He fell asleep still waiting to hear her come back down the glass tunnel from the temple above.

4

Coin-Kisser's Row at noon lay sweltering beneath the molten bronze sun, but the upper classes of Camorr had fortunes and appearances to maintain. The empty plazas of the previous night had become a lively pageant of overdressed crowds, which Locke and Sabetha now prepared to join.

'I give you the field,' said Chains, 'upon which you two shall fight your mighty battle, wherein one shall stand tall, and the other shall end up with the dishes.' Chains was ascending the unforgiving heights of fashion in a black velvet coat and pearl-studded doublet, with three silver-buckled belts taut against his belly. He wore a broad-brimmed black hat over a curly brown wig, and he had enough sweat running down his face to refill at least one of the city's canals.

Locke was dressed far more comfortably, in a simple white doublet, black breeches, and respectable shoes. Chains was holding Locke's jacket, with its telltale number of buttons, until Sabetha was sent on her way. For her part, Sabetha wore a linen dress and a simple jacket, both of a darkish red that was nearly the colour of cinnamon. Her hair and face were concealed beneath a four-cornered hat with hanging grey veils – a fashion that had come rapidly back into vogue in the heat and foulness of recent weeks. Chains had carefully studied and approved these clothes. Locke and Sabetha could pass for servants dressed moderately, or rich children dressed lazily, and would be able to pursue their game without suspicion or interference so long as they behaved.

'Well, daylight's burning,' said Chains, kneeling and pulling the two children toward him. 'Are you ready?'

'Of course,' said Sabetha. Locke merely nodded.

'Young lady first,' said Chains. 'Twenty-second head start, then uncover your satchel as we discussed. I'll be moving along in the crowd beside you, looming over your performance like a merciless god.

Cheating will be dealt with in a thoroughly memorable fashion. Go, go, go.'

Chains held fast to Locke's upper right arm as Sabetha moved off into the crowd. After a few moments, Chains spun Locke around, lifted his arms, and slipped the coat onto him. Locke ran his fingers up and down the right lapel, counting six buttons.

'I stretch forth my arm and cast you into the air.' Chains gave Locke a little shove. 'Now hunt, and let's see whether you're a hawk or a parakeet.'

Locke allowed the push to carry him into the flow of the crowd. His initial position seemed good. Sabetha was about thirty yards away, headed north, and her cinnamon dress was hard to miss. Furthermore, Locke couldn't help but notice that the patrons of Coin-Kisser's Row formed an ideal crowd for this sort of work, tending to move together in small, self-aware clusters rather than as a more sprawling chaos. He would be chasing Sabetha down narrow avenues that would temporarily open and close around her, and even if she made good time she wasn't likely to be able to hide in the blink of an eye.

Still, Locke was as uneasy as he was excited, feeling much more parakeet than hawk. He had no plan beyond trusting to skill and circumstance, while Sabetha could have arranged anything … Or had she merely snuck off into the night for a few empty hours to make him *think* that she could have arranged anything? 'Gah,' he muttered in disgust, at least wise enough to recognize the danger of second-guessing himself into a panic before she even made her move.

The first few minutes of the chase were uneventful, though tense. Locke managed to close the distance by a few strides, no mean feat considering Sabetha's longer legs. As he moved, the peculiar chatter of the Row enfolded him on all sides. Men and women blathered about trade syndicates, ships departing or expected back, interest rates, scandals, weather. It wasn't all that different from the conversation of one of the lower districts, in fact, save for more references to things like compound interest rates. There was no shortage of talk about handball and who was fucking whom.

Locke hurried on through the din. If Sabetha noticed him creeping up on her, she didn't speed up. Perhaps she couldn't, not while staying 'dignified,' though she did sidestep here and there, gradually moving herself farther and farther away from the canal side of the district and closer to the steps of the countinghouses, on Locke's left.

Locke could see her satchel from time to time, hanging casually from her right shoulder, and it seemed that with perfectly innocent little gestures she was managing to keep it mostly forward of her right hip, conveniently out of sight. Was that the game, then? Without using his arms or hands to directly conceal his row of brass buttons, Locke began making sure that his various twists and turns in the crowd were always made with his left shoulder turned forward.

If Chains (occasionally visible as a large lurking shape somewhere to Locke's right) had any objection to this sort of mild rules-bending, he wasn't yet leaping out of the crowd to end the contest. Squinting, Locke spared a few seconds to glance around for unexpected hazards, then returned his gaze to Sabetha just in time to catch her causing a commotion.

With smooth falseness that was readily apparent to Locke's practised eye, Sabetha 'tripped' into a huge merchant, rebounding lightly off the massive silk-clad hemispheres of his posterior. As the man whirled around Sabetha was already turning in profile to Locke – curtseying in apology, concealing her satchel on the far side of her body, and no doubt peering straight at Locke from under her veils. Forewarned, he turned in unison with her, the other way, giving her a fine view of his buttonless left side as he pretended to scan to his right for something terribly important. Perfect stalemate.

Locke was just too far away to hear what Sabetha said to the fat merchant, but her words brought rapid satisfaction, and she was hurrying off to the north again before he'd even finished turning back to his own business. Locke followed instantly, flush with much more than the day's stifling heat. He realized they'd covered nearly half the southern district of Coin-Kisser's Row; a quarter of the field was already used up. Even worse, he realized that Sabetha was indulging him if she even bothered trying to count his buttons. All she really had to do was keep him stymied until she could dash across the final bridge to Twosilver Green.

She continued veering to the left, closer and closer to a tall countinghouse, a many-gabled structure fronted by square columns carved with dozens of different representations of round-bellied Gandolo, Filler of Vaults, god of commerce. Sabetha moved up the building's steps and ducked behind one of those pillars.

Another trap to try and eyeball his jacket? Tautly alert, carefully keeping his precious buttons turned away from Sabetha's last known position, he hurried toward the pillars. Might she be attempting to reach the inside of the countinghouse? No, there she was—

Two of her! Two identical figures in cinnamon-coloured dresses and long dark veils, with little bags slung over their right shoulders, stepped back out into the sunlight.

'She *couldn't* have,' Locke whispered. Yet clearly she had. During the night, while he'd been fretting up and down the dark streets, she'd arranged help and a set of matching costumes. Sabetha and her double strolled away from the carvings of the fat god, headed north toward the Bridge of the Seven Lanterns, the halfway point of their little contest. For all the opportunities he'd already seized in his short life to dwell upon Sabetha's every feature, both of the girls looked exactly alike to him.

'Tricky,' said Locke under his breath. There had to be some difference, if he could only spot it. The bags were probably his best chance; surely they would be the hardest elements of the costumes to synchronize.

'Blood for rain!' boomed a deep voice as Locke reentered the crowd. Bearing down on him came a procession of men in black-and-grey robes. Their mantles bore emblems of crossed hammers and trowels, marking them as divines of Morgante, the City Father, the god of order, hierarchies, and harsh consequences. While none of the Therin gods were ever called enemies, Morgante and his followers were undeniably the least hospitable to the semi-heresy of the Nameless Thirteenth. Morgante ruled executioners, constables, and judges, and no thief would willingly set foot in one of his temples.

The black-robed procession, a dozen strong, was pushing along an open-topped wagon holding an iron cage. A slender man was chained upright inside it, his body covered with wet red gouges. Behind the cage stood a priest holding a wooden switch topped with a claw-like blade about the size of a finger.

'Blood for rain!' hollered the leader of the priests once again, and initiates behind him held baskets out to the passing crowd. It was a mobile sacrifice, then. For every coin tossed into a basket, the caged prisoner would receive another painful but carefully measured slash. That man would be a resident of the Palace of Patience, worming his way out of something harsh (judicial amputation, most likely) by offering his body up for this cruel use. Locke had no further thoughts to spare the poor fellow, for the two girls in dark red dresses were vanishing around the far left side of the procession. He ducked wide around the opposite side, just in case another ambush was in the offing.

The girls weren't troubling themselves; they were headed straight for the Bridge of Seven Lanterns, and were close enough that Locke dared not close the gap. While the bridge was wide enough for two wagons to pass without grinding wheel-rims, it was narrow indeed compared to the plaza, with nowhere to duck and dodge if the girls tried anything clever. Locke matched their pace and trailed them like a kite, fading back to a distance of about thirty yards. Halfway to the end of the contest, and he hadn't actually gained a foot!

The Bridge of Seven Lanterns was plain solid stone, no unnerving toy left over from the long-vanished Eldren. Its parapets were low, and as Locke moved step by step up the gentle arch he was offered a fine view of dozens of boats moving sluggishly on the canal below – a view he ignored, focused as he was on the slender red shapes of his two rivals. There was no wagon traffic at the moment, and while Locke watched, the dress-wearers separated, moving to opposite sides of the bridge. There they paused, each one turning her body as though she were gazing out over the water.

'Hell shit damn,' muttered Locke, trying for the first time in his life to emulate the lengthy chains of profanity woven by the few adult role models he'd ever had. 'Pissing shit monkeys.' What was the game now? Stall him indefinitely and let the sun cook them all? Looking for inspiration, he glanced around, and then back the way he'd come.

A *third* girl in a cinnamon-red dress and grey veil was walking straight toward him, not twenty yards behind, just at the point where the cobbles of the plaza met the bridge embankment. Locke's stomach performed a flip that would have been the highlight of any court acrobat's career.

He turned away from the newcomer, trying not to look too startled. Crooked Warden, he'd been stupid not to check the whole area where Sabetha had picked up her first decoy. And now, yes, his eyes weren't merely playing tricks – the two girls in front of him were slowly, calmly, demurely edging in his direction. He was trapped on a bridge at the centre of a collapsing triangle of red dresses. Unless he ran like mad, which would signal to Chains and Sabetha alike that he'd broken character and given up, one of the girls would surely manage to count his buttons.

Sweet gods, Sabetha had outwitted him before he'd even woken up that morning.

'Not done yet,' he muttered, desperately scanning the area for any distraction he could seize. 'Not yet, not *yet*.' His vague frustration had flared up into a sweat-soaked terror of losing – no, not merely losing, but failing by such an astounding degree in his first contest against a girl he would have swallowed hot iron nails to impress. This wouldn't just embarrass him, it would convince Sabetha that he was a little boy of no account. *Forever.*

As it happened, it wasn't fresh and subtle inspiration that saved him – it was his old teaser's reflexes, the unsociably crude methods he'd used to create street incidents back in his Shades' Hill days. Barely realizing what he was doing, he flung himself down on his knees against the nearest parapet, with his brass buttons scant inches from the stone. With every ounce of energy he possessed, he pretended to throw up.

'Hooouk,' he coughed, a minor prelude to a disgusting symphony, 'hggggk ... hoooo-gggghhhhkkk ... HNNNNNN-BLAAAAAARGH!' The noises were fine, as convincing as he'd ever conjured, and he pushed hard against the parapet with one shaking arm. That was always a great touch; adults fell hard for it. Those that were repulsed would back off an extra three feet, and those that were sympathetic would all but tremble.

He stole quick glances around while he moaned, shuddered, and retched. Adult passersby were swinging wide around him, in the typical fashion of the rich and busy; there was no profit in attending to someone else's sick servant or messenger boy. As for his red-dressed nemeses, they had all halted, wavering like veiled apparitions. Approaching him now would be suspicious and dangerous, while standing there like statues would rapidly invite needless attention. Locke wondered what they would do, knowing he had merely succeeded in restoring a stalemate, but that was certainly better than letting their trap snap him up.

'Just keep retching,' he whispered, and did so. As far as plans went, it was perhaps the worst he'd ever conceived, but now it was up to someone else to make the next move.

'What goes?' A woman's voice, brimming with authority. 'Explain yourself, boy.'

That someone else was, as it turned out, wearing the mustard-coloured jacket of the city watch.

'Lost your grip on breakfast, eh?' The guardswoman nudged Locke with the tip of a boot. 'Look, just move along and be sick at the end of the bridge.'

'Help me,' whispered Locke.

'Can't stand on your own?' The woman's leather fighting harness creaked as she crouched beside him, and her belt-slung baton tapped the ground. 'Give it a minute—'

'I'm not really sick!' Locke beckoned to her with one hand, concealing the gesture from everyone else with his body. 'Bend down, please. I'm in danger.'

'What the hell are you on about?' She looked wary, but did come closer.

'Don't react. Don't hold this up.' In an instant, Locke had his little purse of silver coins, thus far unspent, transferred from his right hand to her left. He pushed the woman's fingers gently closed over the bag. 'That's ten solons. My master is a rich man. Help me, and he'll know your name.'

'Gods be gracious,' the woman whispered. Locke knew that bag of silver represented several months of her pay. Would she bend for it? 'What's going on?'

'I'm in danger,' Locke muttered. 'I'm being followed. A man wants the messages I carry for my master. Back on the plaza south of here, he tried to grab me twice.'

'I'll take you to my watch station, then.'

'No, there's no need. Just get me to the north side of this bridge. Pick me up and carry me, like I'm being arrested. If he sees that, he won't wait around. He'll go tell his masters the watch has me, and once we've gone a little way, you can just let me go.'

'Let you go?'

'Sure, just set me down, let me off with a warning, talk to me sternly.'

'That'd look damned irregular.'

'You're the watch. You can do what you like and nobody's going to say anything!'

'I still don't know. ...'

'Look, you're not breaking any law. You're just lending me a hand.' Locke knew he nearly had her. She had already taken his coin; now it was a matter of notching the promised reward up a bit. 'Get me off this bridge and my master will double what I've given you. Easily.'

The guardswoman seemed to consider this for a few seconds, then rose from her crouch and seized him by the back of his jacket. 'You're not sick,' she yelled. 'You're just making a gods-damned scene!'

'No, please,' cried Locke, praying that he was, in fact, witnessing a purchased performance and not a sudden change of heart. The guardswoman lifted him, tucked him under her left arm, and marched north. Some of the well-dressed onlookers chuckled, but they all moved out of the way as Locke's improvised transportation carried him away from the scene of his near-humiliation.

He kicked and struggled to keep up his end of the presumed deception. Some of his squirming was only too real, as the woman's baton handle kept jabbing him in the ribs, spoiling what was an otherwise surprisingly comfortable ride. At least he was being carried with his all-important buttons facing the guardswoman's side.

Locke scanned his tilted field of vision and saw, to his delight, that the two red dresses in front of him had darted far to the left and were keeping their distance from him and his temporarily tame yellowjacket. Would Sabetha believe he'd really been seized against his will? Probably not, but now she'd have to sort out a new plan of attack with her accomplices, whoever they were.

His own plans were developing speedily as he pretended to fight back against his captor. Once he'd got well ahead of the girls, he could cut off their progress to the final choke point, Goldenreach Bridge. And while his ultimate position there would find him once again outnumbered three to one, at least he would have more time to play spot-the-real-Sabetha.

Kicking, snarling, and shaking his fists, Locke was carried at last down the opposite side of the bridge, onto the northern plaza. Here the real powers of Coin-Kisser's Row were situated, houses like Meraggio's and Bonaduretta's, whose webs of coin and credit reached out across the continent.

'Don't make me knock your teeth in,' his guardswoman growled down at him as a particularly large group of onlookers moved past. Locke could have applauded her theatrical sense; yellowjacket or not, the woman had good instincts. Now, all they had to do was find a decent spot to set him down, and he was as good as—

'Oh, Constable, Constable, *please* wait!' Locke heard the soft sound of running feet even before he heard Sabetha's voice, and he squirmed madly, trying to spot her before she arrived. Too late – she was at the guardswoman's other side, veil flipped back over her four-cornered hat. She was holding out a small dark pouch in her right hand. 'You dropped this, Constable!'

'Dropped what?' The woman turned to face Sabetha, swinging Locke into position to look directly at her. Her cheeks were flushed red and, inexplicably, she was letting her open satchel just hang there. Locke stared open-mouthed at the four tidy little rolls of silk tucked therein – red, green, black, and blue.

'You must be mistaken, girl.'

'Not at all. I saw it myself. I'm *sure* this is yours.' Sabetha pressed the little pouch into the constable's free hand, precisely as Locke had just moments earlier, and in so doing she moved closer and lowered her voice. 'That's four solons. Please, please let my little brother go.'

'What?' The constable sounded thoroughly mystified, but Locke noticed that she slipped the pouch into her coat with smooth reflexes. He was beginning to suspect that this yellowjacket had some prior experience with making offerings disappear.

'I'm sure he didn't mean to cause a scene,' said Sabetha, letting a note of desperate worry break into her voice. 'He's not supposed to be out on his own. He's not quite right in the head.'

'Hey,' said Locke, suddenly realizing that knowledge of the silk colours wouldn't mean much if he let the situation spin further out of his control. What the hell was Sabetha doing? 'Wait just a minute—'

'He's a *total* idiot,' Sabetha whispered, squeezing the constable's free hand. 'It's just not safe for him to be out without an escort! He makes up storeys, you see. Please … let me take him home.'

'I don't … I just … now, look here—'

One or more wheels was clearly about to fly off the previously smooth-running engine of the guardswoman's thought processes, and Locke cringed. Suddenly a wide, dark shape insinuated itself between Locke's constable and the cinnamon-red figure of Sabetha, gently pushing the girl aside.

'Ahhhhhhhhhh, Madam Constable, I am so utterly delighted to see that you've retrieved the two parcels I misplaced,' said Chains. 'You are a jewel of efficiency, excellent woman, a gift from the heavens. I beg leave to shake your hand.'

For the third time in the span of a few minutes, a tiny parcel of coins slipped into the palm of the now utterly dumbstruck watchwoman. This exchange was faster and smoother by far than either of those effected by the children; Locke only saw it because he was being held in just the right position to catch a tiny glimpse of something dark nestled in Chains' hand.

'Um … well, sir, I …'

Chains leaned over and whispered a few quick sentences in her ear. Even before he finished, the woman gently lowered Locke to the ground. Not knowing what else to do, he moved over to stand beside Sabetha, adopting a much-practised facial expression meant to radiate absolute harmlessness.

'Ahhh,' said the constable. Chains' new offering joined the previous two inside her coat.

'Indeed,' said Chains, beaming. 'Blessings of the Twelve, and fair rains follow you, dear Constable. These two will trouble you no further.'

Chains gave a cheery wave (which was just as cheerfully returned by the guardswoman), then turned and pushed Locke and Sabetha toward the east bank of the plaza, where stairs led down to a wide landing for the hiring of passenger boats.

'What happened to your little accomplices?' whispered Chains.

'Told them to get lost when I went after that yellowjacket,' said Sabetha.

'Good. Now, shut up and behave while I get us a boat. We'd best be anywhere but here.'

All of the nearby gondolas were departing or passing by, save for one bobbing at the quay, about to be boarded by a middle-aged man of business who was fishing in a coin purse. Chains stepped smoothly past him and gave the pole-man a peculiar sort of wave.

'I say,' said Chains, 'sorry to be late. We're in such a desperate hurry to reach a friend of a friend, and I just knew that this would be the right sort of boat.'

'The rightest sort of right, sir.' The pole-man was young and skinny, tanned brown as horse droppings, and he wore a sandy-coloured beard down to the middle of his stained blue tunic. Charms of silver and ivory were woven into that beard, so many that the man actually chimed as he moved his head about. 'Sir, I'm apologetic as hell, but this is the gentleman I've been waiting for.'

'Waiting for?' The man looked up from his coin-counting, startled. 'But you only just pulled up!'

'Nonetheless, I got a previous engagement, and this is it. Now, I do beg pardon—'

'No, no, this is my boat!'

'It pains me to correct you,' said Chains, rendering his appropriation of the gondola final by ushering Sabetha into it. 'Nonetheless, I must point out that the boat is actually the property of the young man with the pole.'

'Which it is, already and unfortunately, at this time engaged,' said that man.

'Why … you brazen, disrespectful little pack of dockside shits! I was here first! Don't you dare take that boat, boy!'

Locke had been following Sabetha, and the middle-aged man reached down and grabbed him by the front of his jacket. Equally swiftly, Chains backhanded the man so hard that he immediately let go and stumbled back two paces, nearly falling into the canal.

'Touch either of my children again,' said Chains in a tone of voice unlike anything Locke had ever heard, 'and I'll break you into so many fucking pieces not a whore in the city will *ever* be able to figure out which wrinkled scrap to suck.'

'Dog,' yelled the man of business, holding a hand up to his bleeding lips. 'Fucking scoundrel! I'll have your name, sir, your name and a place where my man can find you. I'll have you out for this, just you—'

Chains threw an arm around the man's neck. Wrenching the unfortunate fellow toward him, Chains whispered harshly into his ear – again, just a few sentences. Chains then shoved him away, and Locke was astonished to see how pale the man's face had become.

'I … uh, I … understand,' said the man. He seemed to be having difficulty making his voice work properly. 'My, uh, apologies, deepest apologies. I'll just—'

'Get the hell out of here.'

'Quite!'

The man took Chains' advice, with haste, and Chains helped Locke into the boat. Locke sat on a bench at the bow directly beside Sabetha, feeling a warmth in his cheeks that had nothing to do with the sun when his leg brushed hers. As Chains settled onto the bench in front of the two children, the pole-man nudged the gondola away from the quay stones and out into the calm, slimy water of the canal.

At that moment, Locke was as much in awe of Chains as he was of his proximity to Sabetha. Charming yellowjackets, commandeering boats, and making wealthy men piss themselves – all of that, bribes notwithstanding, with just a few whispered words here and there. Who and what did Chains know? What was his actual place in Capa Barsa-vi's hierarchy?

'Where to?' said the pole-man.

'Temple District, Venaportha's landing,' said Chains.

'What's your outfit?'

'Gentlemen Bastards.'

'Right, heard of you. Seem to be doing well for yourselves, mixing with the quality.'

'We do well enough. You one of Gap-Tooth's lads?'

'Spot on, brother. Call ourselves the Clever Enoughs, out of the west Narrows. Some of us have what you'd call gainful employment, spotting likely marks on the canals. Business ain't but shit lately.'

'Here's a picture of the duke for a smooth ride.' Chains slapped a gold tyrin down on the bench behind him.

'I'll drink your health tonight, friend, no fuckin' lie.'

Chains let the pole-man get on with his work, and turned back to Locke and Sabetha, leaning close to them. He folded his hands and said quietly, 'Now, what the hell did I just see on Coin-Kisser's Row? Can either of you translate the fuck-wittery into some sort of vaguely logical account?'

'He's got six buttons,' said Sabetha.

'Redgreenblack*blue*,' spat Locke.

'Oh no,' said Chains. 'Contest's over. I declare a tie. No slithering to victory on a technicality.'

'Well, I had to try,' said Sabetha.

'That might have been the lesson,' muttered Locke.

'It's not over until it's really, really over,' said Sabetha. 'Or something. You know.'

'My prize students,' sighed Chains. 'Sometimes a contest to chase one another up and down a crowded plaza really *is* just a contest to chase one another up and down a crowded plaza. Let's start with you, Locke. What was your plan?'

'Uhhh …'

'You know, believe it or not, "the gods will provide" is not a fucking plan, lad. You've got one hell of a talent for improvisation, but when that lets you down it lets you down *hard*. You've got to have a next move in mind, like in Catch-the-Duke. Remember how you managed that affair with the corpse? I *know* you can do better than you just did.'

'But—'

'Sabetha's turn. Near as I could tell, you had him. You were the one in the rear, the one that came out after he chased the first two north, right?'

'Yeah,' said Sabetha, warily.

'Where'd you get the decoys?'

'Girls I used to know in Windows. They're seconds in a couple of the bigger gangs now. We lifted the dresses and went over the plan last night.'

'Ah,' said Chains. 'There's that charming notion I was just discussing, Locke. A *stratagem*. What did your friends have in their bags?'

'Coloured wool,' said Sabetha. 'Best we could do.'

'Not bad. Yet all you could manage was a tie with young Master Planless here. You had him in a fine bind, and then ... what, exactly?'

'Well, he pretended to be sick. Then that yellowjacket came along and collared him, and I ... I thought it was more important than anything else to go after him and get him loose.'

'Get me loose?' Locke sputtered in surprise. 'What do you mean, get me loose? I passed that woman ten solons to get her to pick me up and carry me north!'

'I thought she'd grabbed you for real!' Sabetha's soft brown eyes darkened, and the colour rose in her cheeks. 'You little ass, I thought I was *rescuing* you!'

'But ... why?'

'There was nothing on the ground when I followed behind you!' Sabetha pulled her hat and veil off, and angrily yanked out the lacquered pins in her hair. 'I didn't see any sick-up on the bridge, so I thought that had tipped the yellowjacket to the fact that you were bullshitting!'

'You thought I got collared for real because I *threw up wrong*?'

'I know what sort of mess you could make back when you were a street teaser.' Sabetha shook her hair out – alchemically adjusted or not, it was a sight that made Locke's heart punch the front of his rib cage. 'I didn't see any mess like that, so I assumed you got pinched! I gave that woman all the money I had left!'

'Look, I might have ... I might have stuck my finger down my throat when I was *little*, but ... I'm not gonna do that *all* the time!'

'That's not the point!' Sabetha folded her arms and looked away. They were moving east now, across the long curving canal north of the Videnza, and in the distance beyond Sabetha Locke could see the dark, blocky shape of the Palace of Patience rising above slate roofs. 'You knew you were losing, you had no plan, so you pitched a fit and made a mess of everything! You weren't even trying to win; you were just *sloppy*. And *I* was sloppy to fall for it!'

'I was afraid this might happen, sooner or later,' said Chains in a musing tone of voice. 'I've been thinking that we need a more elaborate sort of sign language, more than what we flash back and forth with the other Right People. Some sort of private code, so we can keep one another on the same page when we're running a scheme.'

'No, Sabetha, look,' said Locke, hardly hearing Chains. 'You weren't sloppy, you were brilliant, you deserved to win—'

'That's right,' she said. 'But you didn't lose, so I *didn't* win.'

'Look, I concede. I give it to you. I'll do all your kitchen chores for three days, just like—'

'I don't want a damned *concession*! I won't take your pity as a coin.'

'It's not … it's not pity, honest! I just … you thought you were really rescuing me, I owe you! I *want* your chores, it would be a pleasure. It would be my, my *privilege*.'

She didn't turn back toward him, but she stared at him out of the corner of her eye for a long, silent moment. Chains said nothing; he had gone still as a stone.

'Sloppy idiot,' Sabetha muttered at last. 'You're trying to be charming. Well, I do not choose to be charmed by you, Locke Lamora.'

She shuffled herself on the bench and gripped the gunwale of the gondola with both hands, so that her back was completely toward him.

'Not today, at any rate,' she said softly.

Sabetha's anger stung Locke like a swallowed wasp, but that pain was subsumed by a warmer, more powerful sensation that seemed to swell his skull until he was sure it was about to crack like an egg.

For all her seeming indifference, for all her impenetrability and frustration, she'd cared enough about him to throw the contest aside the instant she'd thought he was in real danger.

Across the rest of that seemingly endless, miserably hot summer of the seventy-seventh Year of Perelandro, he clung to that realization like a talisman.

INTERSECT (I)
Fuel

In the no-time no-space of thought, conspiracy could have no witnesses. The old man's mind reached out across one hundred and twenty miles of air and water. Child's play for the wearer of four rings. His counterpart answered immediately.

It's done, then?

The Camorri have accepted her terms. As I told you they would.

We never doubted. It's not as though she wants for persuasiveness.

We're moving now.

Is Lamora that ill?

The Archedama put this off too long. A genuine mistake.

And not her first. If Lamora dies?

Your exemplar would crush Tannen alone. He's formidable, but he already carries a weight of mourning.

Could you not ... assist Lamora to an early exit?

I told you I won't go that far. Not right under her eyes! My life still means something to me.

Of course, brother. It was an unworthy suggestion. Forgive me.

Besides, she didn't choose Lamora just to boil your blood. There's something about him you don't understand yet.

Why are you dropping hints instead of information?

I can't risk letting this loose. Not this. Be assured, this is deeper than the five-year game, and Patience means for you to know it all soon enough.

Now THAT worries me.

It shouldn't. Just play the game. If we manage to save Lamora, your exemplar will have a busy six weeks.

Our reception is already prepared.

Good. Look after yourself, then. We'll be in Karthain tomorrow, whatever happens.

From start to finish, the conversation spanned three heartbeats.

CHAPTER THREE
Blood And Breath And Water

I

The sky above the harbour of Lashain was capped with writhing clouds the colour of coal slime, sealing off any speck of light from stars or moons. Jean remained at Locke's side as Patience's attendants carried his cot down from the carriage and through the soft spattering rain, toward the docks and a dozen anchored ships whose yards creaked and swayed in the wind.

While there were Lashani guards and functionaries of various sorts milling about, none of them seemed to want anything to do with the business of the procession around Locke. They carried him to the edge of a stone pier, where a longboat waited with a red lamp hung at its bow.

Patience's attendants set the cot down across the middle of several rowing benches, then took up oars. Jean sat at Locke's feet, while Patience settled alone at the bow. Beyond her Jean could see low black waves like shudders in the water. To Jean, who had grown accustomed to the smell of salt water and its residues, there seemed something strangely lacking in the fresher odours of the Amathel.

Their destination was a brig floating a few hundred yards out, at the northern mouth of the harbour. Its stern lanterns cast a silvery light across the name painted above its great cabin windows, *Sky-Reacher*. From what Jean could see of her she looked like a newer vessel. As they came under her lee Jean saw men and women rigging a crane with a sling at the ship's waist.

'Ahhh,' said Locke weakly. 'The indignity. Patience, can't you just float me up there or something?'

'I could bend my will to a lot of mundane tricks.' She glanced back without smiling. 'I think you'd rather have me rested for what's going to happen.'

The crane's harness was a simple loop of reinforced leather, with a few strands of rope hanging loose. Using these, Jean lashed Locke into the harness, then waved to the people above. Hanging like a puppet, Locke rose out of the boat, knocked against the side of the brig once or twice, and was hauled safely into the ship's waist by several pairs of hands.

Jean pulled himself up the boarding net and arrived on deck as Locke was being untied. Jean nudged Patience's people aside, pulled Locke out of the harness himself, and held him up while the harness went back down for Patience. Jean took a moment to examine the *Sky-Reacher*.

His first impressions from the water were reinforced. She was a young ship, sweet-smelling and tautly rigged. But he saw very few people on deck – just four, all working the crane. Also, it was an unnaturally silent vessel. The noises of wind and water and wood were all there, but the human elements, the scuttling and coughing and murmuring and snoring belowdecks, were missing.

'Thank you,' said Patience as the harness brought her up to the deck. She stepped lightly out of the leather loop and patted Locke on the shoulder. 'Easy part's done. We'll be down to business soon.'

Her attendants came up the side, unpacked the folding cot once more, and helped Jean settle Locke into it.

'Make for open water,' said Patience. 'Take our guests to the great cabin.'

'The boat, Archedama?' The speaker was a stout grey-bearded man wearing an oilcloak with the hood down, evidently content to let the rain slide off his bald head. His right eye socket was a disquieting mass of scar tissue and shadowed hollow.

'Leave it,' said Patience. 'I've cut things rather fine.'

'Far be it from me to remind the Archedama that I suggested as much last night, and the night—'

'Yes, Coldmarrow,' said Patience, 'far be it from you.'

'Your most voluntary abject, madam.' The man turned, cleared his throat, and bellowed, 'Put us out! North-northeast, keep her steady!'

'North-northeast, keep her steady, aye,' said a bored-sounding woman who detached herself from the group breaking down the crane.

'Are we going to take on more crew?' said Jean.

'What ever for?' said Patience.

'Well, it's just … the wind's out of the north-northeast. You're going to be tacking like mad to make headway, and as near as I can see, you've only got seven or eight people to work the ship. That's barely enough to mind her in harbour—'

'Tacking,' said the man called Coldmarrow, 'what a quaint notion. Help us get your friend into the stern cabin, Camorri.'

Jean did so. *Sky-Reacher*'s aft compartment wasn't flush with the main deck; Locke had to be carried down a narrow passage with treacherous steps. Whatever the ship had been constructed for, it wasn't the easy movement of invalids.

The cabin was about the same size as the one Locke and Jean had possessed on the *Red Messenger*, but far less cluttered – no weapons hung on the bulkheads, no charts or clothes were strewn about, no cushions or hammocks. A table formed from planks laid over sea-chests was in the centre of the room, lit by soft yellow lanterns. The shutters were thrown tight over the stern windows. Most strikingly, the place had a deeply unlived-in smell, an aroma of cinnamon and cedar oils and other things people threw into wardrobes to drive out staleness.

While Jean helped Locke onto the table, Coldmarrow somehow produced a blanket of thin grey wool and handed it over. Jean wiped the rain from Locke's face, then covered him up.

'Better,' whispered Locke, 'moderately, mildly, wretchedly better. And ... what the—'

A small dark shape detached itself from the shadows in a corner of the cabin, padded forward, and leapt up onto Locke's chest.

'Gods, Jean, I'm hallucinating,' said Locke. 'I'm actually hallucinating.'

'No, you're not.' Jean stroked the silky black cat that was supposed to be long gone from their lives. Regal was exactly as Jean remembered, down to the white spot at his throat. 'I see the little bastard too.'

'He can't be here,' muttered Locke. The cat circled his head, purring loudly. 'It's impossible.'

'What a myopic view you have on the splendours of coincidence,' said Patience, coming down the steps. 'It was one of my agents that purchased your old yacht. It lay briefly alongside the *Sky-Reacher* a few weeks ago, and this little miscreant took the opportunity to change residences.'

'I don't get it,' said Locke, gently tugging at the scruff of Regal's neck. 'I never even liked cats all that much.'

'Surely you realize,' said Patience, 'that cats are no great respecters of human opinion.'

'Kin to Bondsmagi, perhaps?' said Jean. 'So what do we do now?'

'Now,' said Patience, 'we speak plainly. What's going to happen, Jean, will be hard for you to watch. Possibly too hard. Some … ungifted cannot bear close proximity to our workings. If you wish to go into the middle deck, you'll find hammocks and other accommodations—'

'I'm staying,' said Jean. 'For the whole damn thing. That's not negotiable.'

'Be resolved, then, but hear me. No matter what happens, or seems to happen, you *cannot* interfere. You *cannot* interrupt. It could be fatal, and not just for Locke.'

'I'll behave,' said Jean. 'I'll bite my damn knuckles off if I have to.'

'Forgive me for reminding you that I know the nature of your temper—'

'Look,' said Jean, 'if I get out of hand, just speak my gods-damned name and *make* me calm down. I know you can do it.'

'It may come to that,' said Patience. 'So long as you know what to expect if you cause trouble. Speaking of which, remove our little friend and take him forward.'

'Off you go, kid.' Jean plucked Regal up before the cat realized he'd been targeted for transportation. The smooth bundle of fur yawned and nestled into the crook of Jean's right elbow.

Jean carried his passenger to the main deck, where he was surprised to find the vessel already moving under topsails, although he'd heard no shouting or struggling from above to get them down. He ran up the stairs leading to the quarterdeck, from which he could see the rain-blurred lights of Lashain already dwindling behind the dark shapes bobbing in her harbour. The boat they'd abandoned was barely visible, a tiny silhouetted slat on the waves.

The woman who'd been at the crane was now at the helm, just abaft the mainmast where it marked the forward boundary of the quarter-deck. Her face was only half-visible within the hood of her cloak, but she seemed lost in thought, and Jean was startled to see that she wasn't actually touching the wheel. Her left hand was raised and slightly cupped, and from time to time she would spread her fingers and move it forward, as though pushing some unseen object.

Lightning broke overhead, and by the sudden flash Jean could see the other members of the crew scattered across the deck, also cloaked and hooded, standing at silent attention with their hands similarly raised.

As thunder rolled across the Amathel, Jean walked over to stand beside the woman at the wheel.

'Excuse me,' he said, 'can you talk? What's our current heading?'

'North ... northeast,' said the woman dreamily, not moving to face him when she spoke. 'Straight on for Karthain.'

'But that's dead into the wind!'

'We're using ... a private wind.'

'Fuck me sideways,' Jean muttered. 'I, uh, I need somewhere to stow this cat.'

'Main deck hatch ... to the middle hold.'

Jean carried his fuzzy comrade to the ship's waist and found an access hatch, which he slid open. A narrow ladder led six or seven feet down to a dimly lit space, where Jean could see straw on the floor and pallets of some soft material.

'Perelandro's balls, little guy,' whispered Jean, 'what ever gave me the idea I could get the best of people who make their own fucking weather?'

'Mrrrrwwwww,' said the cat.

'You're right. I am desperate. And stupid.' Jean let Regal go, and the cat landed lightly on a pallet in the semi-darkness below. 'Keep your head down, puss. I think shit's about to break weird all over the place.'

2

'Close the door firmly,' said Coldmarrow when Jean returned.

'Bolt it?'

'No. Just keep the weather out where it belongs.'

Patience was pouring pale yellow liquid from a leather skin into a clay cup as Jean came down the steps.

'Well, Jean,' said Locke, 'if nothing else, at least I get a drink before I go.'

'What's that?' said Jean.

'Several somethings for the pain,' said Patience.

'So Locke's going to sleep through this?'

'Oh no,' said Patience. 'No, he won't be able to sleep an instant, I'm afraid.'

She held the cup to Locke's lips, and with her assistance he managed to gulp the contents down.

'Agggggh,' he said, shaking his head. 'Tastes like a dead fishmonger's piss, siphoned out of his guts a week after the funeral.'

'It *is* a rather functional concoction,' allowed Patience. 'Now relax. You'll feel it take hold swiftly.'

'Ohhh,' sighed Locke, 'you're not wrong.'

Coldmarrow set a bucket of water beside the table. He then pulled Locke's tunic off, exposing the pale skin and old scars of his upper body. It was obvious that vigour had fled from every slack strand of muscle. Coldmarrow dampened a cloth and carefully cleaned Locke's chest, arms, and face. Patience folded and resettled the grey blanket over his lower half.

'Now,' said Patience, 'certain requirements.' She retrieved an ornamented witchwood box from a corner of the cabin. At a wave from her hand, it unlocked itself and slid open, revealing nested trays of small objects, rather like a physiker's kit.

Patience took a slim silver knife out of the box. With this, she sliced off several lengths of Locke's damp hair, and placed them in a clay bowl held out by Coldmarrow. As the bearded man moved, his sleeves fell back far enough for Jean to see that he had four rings on his left wrist.

'Just a few deductions,' said Patience. 'The outermost flourishes. Surely he could use the trimming.'

Coldmarrow held another bowl under Locke's right hand as Patience whittled slivers from his nails. Locke murmured, rolled his head back, and sighed.

'Blood, too,' said Patience, 'what little he can spare.' She pricked two of Locke's fingers with the blade, eliciting no response from him. Jean, however, grew more and more anxious as Coldmarrow collected red drops in a third bowl.

'I hope you're not planning to keep any of that, after this ... thing is finished,' said Jean.

'Jean, please,' said Patience. 'He'll be lucky to be alive after this *thing* is finished.'

'We won't do anything untoward,' said Coldmarrow. 'Your friend is a valuable asset.'

'Is he now?' growled Jean. 'An asset? An asset's something you can put on a shelf or write down on a ledger, you spooky bastard. Don't talk about him like—'

'Jean,' said Patience sharply. 'Command yourself or be commanded.'

'Hey, I'm calm. Placid as pipe-smoke,' said Jean, folding his arms.

'Just look at how placid I can be. What's that you're doing now?'

'The last thing I need,' said Patience, 'is a wisp of breath.' She held a ceramic jar at Locke's mouth for some time, then capped it and set it aside.

'Fascinating, I'm sure,' said Locke groggily. 'Now get this shit *out* of me.'

'I can't just will it so,' said Patience. 'Life is far more easily destroyed than mended. Magic doesn't change that. In fact, you shouldn't think of this as a healing at all.'

'Well, what the hell is it?' said Jean.

'Misdirection,' said Patience. 'Imagine the poison as a spark smouldering in wood. If the spark becomes flame, Locke dies. We need to make it expend itself somewhere else, *destroy* something else. Once that power is drawn from it, the spark goes out.'

Jean watched uneasily for the next quarter of an hour as Patience and Coldmarrow used a strange-smelling black ink to paint an intricate network of lines across Locke's face and arms and chest. Although Locke muttered from time to time, he didn't appear to be in any greater discomfort than before.

While the ink dried, Coldmarrow fetched a tall iron candelabrum, which he set between the table and the shuttered stern windows. Patience produced three white candles from her box.

'Wax tapers, made in Camorr,' she said. 'Along with an iron candlestand, also from Camorr. All of it stolen, to establish a more powerful sympathy with your unfortunate friend.'

She rolled one candle back and forth in her hands, and its surface blurred and shimmered. Coldmarrow used Patience's silver knife to transfer Locke's blood and hair and nail-trimmings to the surface of the wax. There, rather than running messily down the sides as Jean would have expected, the 'certain requirements' vanished smoothly into the candle.

'Effigy, I name you,' said Patience. 'Blood-bearer, I create you. Shadow of a soul, deceiving vessel, I give you the flesh of a living man and not his heart-name. You are him, and not him.'

She placed the taper in the candelabrum. Then she and Coldmarrow repeated the process exactly with the two remaining candles.

'Now,' said Patience softly, 'you must be still.'

'I'm not exactly fuckin' dancing,' said Locke.

Coldmarrow picked up a coil of rope. He and Patience used this to bind Locke to the table by a dozen loops of cord between his waist and his ankles.

'One thing,' said Locke as they finished. 'Before you begin, I'd like a moment alone with Jean. We're … adherents of a god you might not want to be associated with.'

'We can respect your mysteries,' said Patience. 'But don't dawdle, and don't disturb *any* of the preparations.'

She and Coldmarrow withdrew from the cabin, closing the door behind them, and Jean knelt at Locke's side.

'That slop Patience gave me made things fuzzy for a moment, but I think I've got some wits back,' said Locke, 'So – have I ever looked more ridiculous?'

'Have you ever looked *not* ridiculous?'

'Fuck you,' said Locke, smiling. 'That end-likt-ge-whatever—'

'*Endliktgelaben.*'

'Yeah, that *Endliktgelaben* shit you brought up … were you just trying to piss me off, or were you serious?'

'Well … I *was* trying to piss you off.' Jean grimaced. 'But did I mean it? I suppose. Am I right about it? I don't know. I really hope not. But you are one gods-damned *miserable* brat when you decide to feel guilty about everything. I'd like that read into the record.'

'I have to tell you, Jean … I don't really want to die. Maybe that makes me some kind of chickenshit. I meant what I said about the magi; I'd sooner piss in their faces than take gold from their hands, but all the same, I don't want to die … I don't!'

'Easy there,' said Jean. 'Easy. All you have to do to prove it is *not* die.'

'Give me your left hand.'

The two of them touched hands, palm to palm. Locke cleared his throat.

'Crooked Warden,' he said, 'Unnamed Thirteenth, your servant calls. I know I'm a man of so many faults that listing them here would only detain us.' Locke coughed and wiped fresh blood from his mouth. 'But I meant what I said … I don't want to die, not without a real fight, not like this. So if you could just find it in your heart to tip that scale for me one more time – Hell, if not for me, do it for Jean. Maybe his credit's better than mine.'

'This we pray with hopeful hearts,' said Jean. He rose to his feet again. 'Still scared?'

'Shitless.'

'Less chance you'll make a mess on the table, then.'

'Bastard.' Locke closed his eyes. 'Call them back. Let's get on with this.'

3

Jean watched, moments later, as Patience and Coldmarrow took up positions on either side of Locke.

'Unlock the dreamsteel,' said Patience.

Coldmarrow reached down the front of his tunic and pulled out a silvery pendant on a chain. At his whisper of command, pendant and chain alike turned to brightly rippling liquid, which ran in a stream down his fingers, coalescing in a ball that quivered in his cupped hand.

'Quicksilver?' said Jean.

'Hardly,' said Patience. 'Quicksilver poisons the wits of those who handle it. Dreamsteel is something of ours. It shapes itself to our thoughts, and it's harmless as water … mostly.'

The magi spread their arms over the table. Slender threads of dreamsteel sprouted from the shimmering mass in Coldmarrow's hand and slid forward, falling through the gaps between his fingers. They landed on Locke's chest, not with careless splashing but with uncanny solidity. Though the stuff ran like water, the flow was slow and dreamlike.

The thin silvery streams conformed to the black lines painted across Locke's upper body. Steadily, sinuously, the threads of liquid metal crept across the design, into every curve and whorl. When at last the delicate work was complete and the final speck of dreamsteel fell from Coldmarrow's hand, every line on Locke's skin had been precisely covered with a minuscule layer of rippling silver.

'This will feel rather strange,' said Patience.

She and Coldmarrow clenched their fists, and instantly the complex tracery of dreamsteel leapt up in a thousand places, exploding off Locke's skin. Locke arched his back, only to be pressed gently back down by the hands of the magi. The dreamsteel settled as a forest of needles.

Like the victim of a mauling by some metallic porcupine, Locke now had countless hair-thin silver shafts embedded bloodlessly in his skin, running along the painted lines.

'Cold,' said Locke. 'That's awfully damn cold!'

'The dreamsteel is where it needs to be,' said Patience. She picked up the jar she had used to catch Locke's exhaled breath and approached the candelabrum.

'Effigy, I kindle you,' she said, opening the jar and wafting it past the three candles. 'Breath-sharer, I give you the wind of a living man but not his heart-name. You are him, and not him.'

She gestured with her right hand, and the wicks of the three candles burst into flickering white flame.

She then resumed her place at Locke's side. She and Coldmarrow put their right hands together, fingertip to fingertip, over Locke's chest. The silver thread that Patience had used earlier reappeared, and by deft movements Jean could barely follow the two magi bound their hands together in a cat's cradle. Jean shuddered, remembering that the Falconer had wielded a silver thread of his own.

Patience and Coldmarrow then placed their free hands on Locke's arms.

'Whatever happens now, Locke,' said Patience, 'remember your shame and anger. Stay angry with *me*, if you must. Hate me and my son and all the magi of Karthain with everything you've got, or you won't live to get up off this table.'

'Quit trying to scare me,' said Locke. 'I'll see you when this is over.'

'Crooked Warden,' murmured Jean to himself, 'you've heard Locke's plea, now hear mine. Gandolo, Wealth-Father, I was born to merchants and beg to be remembered. Venaportha, Lady With Two Faces, surely you've had some fun with us before. Give us a smile now. Perelandro, forgiving and merciful, we might not have served you truly, but we put your name on every set of lips in Camorr.

'Aza Guilla,' he whispered, feeling a nervous trickle of sweat slide down his forehead, 'Lady Most Kind, I peeked up your skirts a little, but you know my heart was in the right place. Please have urgent business elsewhere tonight.'

There was an itch at the back of Jean's neck; the same eerie sensation he had felt before in the presence of the Falconer, and when the magi had tormented him and Locke in the Night Market of Tal Verrar. Patience and Coldmarrow were deep in concentration.

'Ah,' gasped Locke. 'Ah!'

A metallic taste grew in Jean's mouth, and he gagged, only to discover that his throat had gone dry. The top of his mouth felt as raspy as paper. What had happened to his spit?

'Hells,' said Locke, arching his back. 'Oh, this is … this is worse than cold …'

The timbers of the cabin bulkheads creaked, as though the ship were being tossed about, though all of Jean's senses told him the *Sky-Reacher* was plodding along as slowly and smoothly as ever. Then the rattling began, faintly at first, but soon the yellow alchemical lanterns were shaking and the shadows in the room wobbled.

Locke moaned. Patience and Coldmarrow leaned forward, keeping his arms pinned, while their joined hands intricately wove and unwove the silver thread. The sight would have been mesmerizing in calm circumstances, but Jean was far from calm. His stomach roiled as though he had eaten rotten oysters and they were clamouring for release.

'Dammit,' Jean whispered, and bit on his knuckles just as he'd promised. The pain helped drive back the rising tide of nausea, but the atmosphere of the room was growing stranger. The lanterns rattled now like kettles on a high boil, and the white flames of the candles flared and danced to an unfelt breeze.

Locke moaned again, louder than before, and the thousand silvery points of light embedded in his upper body made eerie art as he strained at his ropes.

There was a sizzling sound, then a whip-like crack. The alchemical lanterns shattered, spraying glass across the cabin along with puffs of sulphurous-smelling vapour. Jean flinched, and the Bondsmagi reeled as lantern fragments rattled onto the floor around them.

'I've been poisoned a lot,' muttered Locke, for no apparent reason.

'Help,' hissed Coldmarrow in a strained voice.

'How? What do you need?' Jean was caught in another shuddering wave of nausea, and he clung to a bulkhead.

'Not … you.'

The cabin door burst open. One of the attendants who had carried Locke on the cot stomped down the stairs, discarding his wet cloak as he came. He put his hands against Coldmarrow's back and settled his feet as though bracing the old man against a physical force. Shadows reeled wildly around the cabin as the candle flames whirled, and Jean's nausea grew; he went down to his knees.

There was an uncanny vibration in the air, in the deck, in the bulkheads, in Jean's bones. It felt as though he were leaning against a massive clockwork machine with all of its gears turning. Behind his eyes, the vibration grew past annoyance to pain. Jean imagined a maddened insect trapped inside his skull, biting and scrabbling and beating its wings against whatever it found in there. That was too much; bludgeoned by awful sensations, he tilted his head forward and threw up on the deck.

A thin dark line appeared beside the vomit as he finished – blood from his nose. He coughed out a string of profanities along with the acidic taste of his last meal, and though he couldn't find the strength to heave himself to his feet, he did manage to tilt his head back far enough to see what happened next.

'This is your death, effigy. You are him,' cried Patience, her voice cracking, 'and not him!'

There was a sound like marrow bones cracking, and the three candle flames surged into conflagrations large enough to swallow Jean's hands. Then the flames turned *black* – black as the depths of night, an unnatural hue that caused actual pain to behold. Jean flinched away from the sight, his eyes gushing hot tears. The light of the black fires was pallid grey, and it washed the cabin with the tint of stagnant graveyard water.

Another shudder passed through the timbers of the ship, and the young Bondsmage at Coldmarrow's back suddenly reeled away from the table, blood pouring from his nose. As he toppled, the woman who'd been on the quarterdeck came through the door, hands up to shield her eyes from the unearthly glare. She stumbled against a bulkhead but kept her feet, and began to chant rapidly in a harsh unknown language.

Who the hell is steering the ship? thought Jean, as the sickly grey light pulsed with a speed to match his own heartbeat and the very air seemed to thicken with a fever heat.

'Take this death. You are him,' gasped Coldmarrow, 'and not him! *This death is yours!*'

There was a sound like nails on slate, and then Locke's moans turned to screams – the loudest, longest screams Jean had ever heard.

4

Pain was nothing new to Locke, but pain was an inadequate term for what happened when the two Bondsmagi pressed him down and squeezed him between their sorceries.

The room around him became a whirl of confusion – white light, rippling air. His eyes blurred with tears until even the faces of Patience and Coldmarrow bled at the edges like melting wax. Something shattered, and hot needles stung his scalp and forehead. He saw a strange swirl of yellow vapours, then gasped and moaned as the silver needles in his upper body suddenly came alive with heat, driving away all concern for his surroundings. It felt like a thousand coal-red flecks of ash were being driven into his pores.

Stabbed, he thought, clenching his teeth and swallowing a scream. *This is nothing. I've been stabbed before. Stabbed in the shoulder. In the wrist. In the arm. Cut, smashed, clubbed, kicked … drowned … nearly drowned. Poisoned.*

He cast his memory back across the long catalogue of injuries, realizing with some deeper and still vaguely sensible part of his mind that counting inflictions of pain to take his mind off the infliction of pain was both very stupid and very funny.

'I've been poisoned a lot,' he said to himself, shuddering in a paroxysm born of the struggle between laughter and the hot-needle pain.

There was noise after that, the voices of the Bondsmagi, and Jean – then creaking, moaning, slamming, banging. It all went hazy while Locke fought for self-control. Then, after an unguessable interval, a voice penetrated his misery at last, and was more than a voice. It was a thought, shaped by Patience, whose touch he now instinctively recognized in the word-shapes that thrust themselves to the centre of his awareness:

'You are *him* … and not him!'

Beneath the hornet-stings of the dreamsteel needles, something moved inside Locke, some pressure in his guts. The quality of the light and the air around him changed; the white glow of the candles turned black. Like a snake, the force inside him uncoiled and slid upward, under his ribs, behind his lungs, against his pulsating heart.

'F-fuck,' he tried to say, so profoundly disquieted that no air moved past his lips. Then the thing inside him surged, frothed, *ate* – like tar heated instantly to a boil, scalding the surface of every organ and cavity between his nose and his groin. All of those never-thought-of crevices of the body, suddenly alive in his mind, and suddenly limned in pure volcanic agony.

Stop oh please oh please stop just let the pain end, he thought, so far gone that his previous resolution was forgotten beneath sheer animal pleading. *Stop the pain stop the pain—*

'You are him … and not him!' The thought-voice was a weak echo above the cresting tide of internal fire. Coldmarrow? Patience? Locke could no longer tell. His arms and legs were numb, dissolving into meaningless sensory fog beyond the hot core of his agony. The Bondsmagi and everything beyond them faded into haze. The table seemed to fall away beneath him; blackness rose like the coming of sleep. His eyelids fluttered shut, and at last the blessed numbness spread to his stomach and chest and arms, smothering the hell that had erupted there.

Let that be it. I don't want to die, but gods, just let that be the last of the pain.

The outside world had gone silent, but there was still some noise in the darkness – his own noise. The faint throb of a heartbeat. The dry shudder of breath. Surely, if he were dead, all that business would have ended. There was a pressure on his chest. A sensation of weight – someone was pushing down on his heart, and the touch felt cold. Surprised at the amount of will it required, Locke forced his eyes partly open.

The hand above his heart was Bug's, and the eyes staring down from the dead boy's face were solid black.

'There is no *last of the pain*,' said Bug. 'It always hurts. Always.'

Locke opened his mouth to scream, but no sound moved past his lips – just a barely perceptible dry hissing. He strained to move, but his limbs were lead. Even his neck refused to obey his commands.

This can't be real, Locke tried to say, and the unspoken words echoed in his head.

'What's real?' Bug's skin was pale and strangely loose, as though the flesh behind it had collapsed inward. The curls had come out of his hair, and it hung limp and lifeless above his dead black eyes. A crossbow quarrel, crusted with dry blood, was still buried in his throat. The cabin was dark and empty; Bug seemed to be crouching above him, but the only weight Locke could feel was the cold pressure of the hand above his heart.

You're not really here!

'We're *both* here.' Bug fiddled with the quarrel as though it were an annoying neck-cloth. 'You know why I'm still around? When you die, your sins are engraved on your *eyes*. Look closely.'

Unable to help himself, Locke stared up into the awful dark spheres, and saw that their blackness was not quite unbroken. It had a rough and layered quality, as though made up of a countless number of tiny black lines of script, all running together into a solid mass.

'I can't see the way out of this place,' said Bug softly. 'Can't find the way to what's next.'

You were twelve fucking years old. How many sins could you have—

'Sins of omission. Sins of my teachers and my friends.' The chilling weight above Locke's heart pressed down harder.

That's bullshit, I know better, I'm a divine of the Crooked Warden!

'How's that working out for you?' Bug wiped at the trails of blood running down his neck, and the blood came away on his pale finger-tips as a brown powder. 'Doesn't seem to have done either of us much good.'

I'm a priest, I'd know how this works, this isn't how it's supposed to be! I'm a priest of the Unnamed Thirteenth!

'Well … I could tell you how far you'll get trusting people when you don't even know their real name.' Again the pressure on Locke's chest grew.

I'm dreaming. I'm dreaming. It's just a dream.

'You're dreaming. You're dying. Maybe they're the same thing.' The corners of Bug's mouth twitched up briefly in a weak attempt at a smile. The sort of smile, thought Locke, that you give someone when you can see they're in deep shit.

'Well, you've made all your decisions. Nothing left for you to do but see which one of us is right.'

Wait, wait, don't—

The pain in Locke's chest flared again, spreading sharply outward from his heart, and this time it was cold, deathly cold, an unbearable icy pressure that squeezed him like a vice. Darkness swept in behind it, and Locke's awareness broke against it like a ship heaved onto rocks.

INTERLUDE
Orphan's Moon

I

They let him out of the darkness at last, and cool air touched his skin after an hour of stuffy helplessness.

It had been a rough trip to the site of the ritual, wherever it was. The men carrying him hadn't had much difficulty with his relatively slight weight, but it seemed they'd gone down many stairs and through narrow, curving passages. Around and around in the dark he'd been hauled, listening to the grunts and whispers of the adults, and to the sound of his own breathing inside the scratchy wool sack that covered his head.

At last that hood was drawn away. Locke blinked in the dimness of a high barrel-vaulted room, faintly lit by pale globes tucked away in sconces. The walls and pillars were stone, and here and there Locke could see decorative paintings flaking with age. Water trickled some-where nearby, but that was hardly unusual for a structure in lower Camorr. What was significant was that this was a human place, all blocks and mortar, without a shred of visible Elderglass.

Locke was on his back in the middle of the vaulted room, on a low slab. His hands and feet weren't tied, but his freedom of movement was sharply curtailed when a man knelt and put a knife to his throat. Locke could feel the edge of the blade against his skin, and knew instantly that it was the not-fooling-around sort of edge.

'You are bound and compelled to silence in all ways, at all times, from now until the weighing of your soul, concerning what we do here this night,' said the man.

'I am bound and compelled,' said Locke.

'Who binds and compels you?'

'I bind and compel myself,' said Locke.

'To break this binding is to be condemned to die.'

'I would gladly be condemned for my failure.'

'Who would condemn you?'

'I would condemn myself.' Locke reached up with his right hand and placed it over the man's knuckles. The stranger withdrew his hand, leaving Locke holding the knife at his own throat.

'Rise, little brother,' said the man.

Locke obeyed, and passed the knife back to the man, a long-haired, muscular *garrista* Locke knew by sight but not by name. The world Capa Barsavi ruled was a big place.

'Why have you come here tonight?'

'To be a thief among thieves,' said Locke.

'Then learn our sign.' The man held up his left hand, fingers slightly spread, and Locke mirrored the gesture, pressing his palm firmly against the *garrista*'s. 'Left hand to left hand, skin to skin, will tell your brothers and sisters that you do not come holding weapons, that you do not shun their touch, that you do not place yourself above them. Go and wait.'

Locke bowed and moved into the shadow of a pillar. There was enough space, he calculated, for a few hundred people to fit down here. At the moment, there were just a few men and women visible. He'd been brought in early, it seemed, as one of the very first of the postulants to take the oath of secrecy. He watched, feeling the churn of excitement in his stomach, as more boys and girls were carried into the room, stripped of their hoods, and given the treatment he'd received. Calo ... Galdo ... Jean ... one by one they joined him and watched the ongoing procession. Locke's companions were uncharacteristically silent and serious. In fact, he'd have gone so far as to say that both Sanzas were actually nervous. He didn't blame them.

The next hood yanked from a postulant's head revealed Sabetha. Her lovely false-brown curls tumbled out in a cloud, and Locke bit the insides of his cheeks as the knife touched her throat. She took the oaths quickly and calmly, in a voice that had grown a shade huskier in the last season. She spared him a glance as she walked over to join the Gentlemen Bastards, and he hoped for a few seconds that she might choose to stand beside him. However, Calo and Galdo moved apart, offering her a place between them, and she accepted. Locke bit the insides of his cheeks again.

Together, the five of them watched more adults enter and more children about their own age pass under the oath-taking blade. There were some familiar faces in that stream.

First came Tesso Volanti from the Half-Crowns, with his night-black mane of oiled hair. He held Locke's crew in high esteem despite (or probably because of) the fact that Jean Tannen had given him a thunderous ass-kicking a few summers previously. Then came Fat Saulus and Fatter Saulus from the Falselight Cutters ... Whoreson Dominaldo ... Amelie the Clutcher, who'd stolen enough to buy an apprenticeship with the Guilded Lilies ... a couple of boys and girls that must have come out of the Thiefmaker's burrow around the time Locke had ... and then, the very last initiate to have her hood yanked back, Nazca Belonna Jenavais Angeliza Barsavi, youngest child and only daughter of the absolute ruler of Camorr's underworld.

After Nazca finished reciting her oaths, she removed a pair of optics from a leather pouch and slid them onto her nose. While nobody in their right mind would have laughed at her for doing so, Locke suspected that Nazca would have been unafraid to wear them in public even if she hadn't been the Capa's daughter.

Locke could see her older brothers, Pachero and Anjais, standing in the ranks of the older initiates, but her place was with the neophytes. Smiling, she walked over to Locke and gently pushed him out of his spot against the pillar.

'Hello, Lamora,' she whispered. 'I need to stand next to an ugly little boy to make myself look better.'

She certainly did *not*, thought Locke. An inch taller than him, Nazca was much like Sabetha these days, closer to woman than girl. For some reason, she also had a soft spot for the Gentlemen Bastards. Locke had begun to suspect that the 'little favours' Father Chains had once done for Capa Barsavi were not as little as he'd let on, and that Nazca was privy to at least some of the story. Not that she ever spoke of it.

'Good to see you here in the cheap seats with us, Nazca,' said Sabetha as she gracefully nudged Jean out of his position behind Locke. Locke's spine tingled.

'No such thing on a night like this,' said Nazca. 'Just thieves among thieves.'

'Women among boys,' said Sabetha with an exaggerated sigh.

'Pearls among swine,' said Nazca, and the two of them giggled. Locke's cheeks burned.

It was early winter in the seventy-seventh year of Aza Guilla, the month of Marinel, the time of the empty sky. It was the night called the Orphan's Moon, when Locke and all of his kind became, by ancient Therin custom, one year older.

It was the one night per year on which young thieves were fully initiated into the mysteries of the Crooked Warden, somewhere in the dark and crumbling depths of old Camorr.

It was, by Chains' best guess, the night of Locke's thirteenth birthday.

2

The day's activities had started with the procurement of an appropriate offering.

'Let's toss the cake on that fellow right there,' said Jean. It was high afternoon, and he and Locke lay in wait in an alley just off the Avenue of Five Saints in the upper-class Fountain Bend district.

'He seems the type,' agreed Locke. He hefted the all-important package into his arms – a cube of flax-paper wrapped around a wooden frame, with a sturdy wooden base, the whole thing about two and a half feet on a side. 'Where you coming from?'

'His right.'

'Let's make his acquaintance.'

They went in opposite directions – Jean directly east onto the avenue, and Locke to the western end of the alley, so he could head north on the parallel Avenue of the Laurels and swing around the long way to intercept the chosen target.

The Fountain Bend was a nest of the quality; one could tell merely by counting the number of servants on the streets, and noting the character of the yellowjackets taking relaxed strolls around the gardens and avenues. Their harnesses were perfectly oiled, their boots shined, their coats and hats unweathered. Postings to an area like this came only to watch-folk with connections, and once they had the posting they took pains to make themselves decorative as well as functional, lest they be reassigned somewhere much livelier.

Winter in Camorr could be pleasant when the sky wasn't pissing like an old man who'd lost command of his bladder. Today warm sun and cool breeze hit the skin at the same time, and it was easy to forget the thousand and one ways the city had of choking, stifling, reeking, and sweating. Locke hurried north for two blocks, then veered right, onto the Boulevard of the Emerald Footfall. Dressed as he was, in servant's clothing, it was perfectly acceptable for him to scamper along with his awkward cargo at an undignified pace.

When the boulevard met the Avenue of Five Saints, Locke turned right again and immediately spotted his quarry. Locke had beaten him to the intersection by fifty yards, and so had plenty of time to slow down and get his act sorted. No more rushing about – on this street, he became the picture of caution, a dutiful young servant minding a delicate package at a sensible speed. Forty yards ... thirty yards ... and there was Jean, coming up behind the target.

At twenty yards, Locke veered slightly, making it clear that there could be no possible collision if he and the stranger continued on their present courses. Ten yards ... Jean was nearly at the man's elbow.

At five yards, Jean bumped into the target from behind, sending him sprawling in just the right direction, with just enough momentum, to smack squarely into Locke's flax-paper package. Locke ensured that the fragile cube was snapped and crushed instantly, along with the fifteen pounds of spice cake and icing it contained. Much of it hit the cobbles with a sound like meat hitting a butcher's counter, and the rest of it hit Locke, who artfully fell directly onto his ass.

'Oh gods,' he cried. 'You've ruined me!'

'Why, I, I've – I don't ... damn!' sputtered the target, jumping back from the splattered cake and checking his clothing. He was a well-fed, round-shouldered sort in respectable dress, with a smooth leather ink-guard on his right jacket cuff that told of life lived behind a desk. 'I was struck from behind!'

'Indeed you were,' said Jean, who was as well-dressed as the target, and as wide despite a threefold difference in age. Jean was carrying a half-dozen scroll cases. 'I stumbled into you entirely by accident, sir, and I apologize. But the two of us together have smashed this poor servant's cake.'

'Well, the fault is hardly mine.' The target carefully brushed a few stray pieces of icing off his breeches. 'I was merely caught in the middle. Come now, boy, come now. It's nothing to cry about.'

'Oh, but it is, sir,' said Locke, sniffling as artfully as he ever had in his Shades' Hill days. 'My master will have my skin for book-bindings!'

'Chin up, boy. Everyone takes a few lashes now and again. Are your hands clean?' The target held a hand out, grudgingly, and helped Locke back to his feet. 'It's only the merest cake.'

'It's not just any cake,' sobbed Locke. 'It's my master's birthday confection, ordered a month in advance. It's a crown-cake from Zakasta's. All kinds of alchemy and spices.'

'Zakasta's,' said Jean with an admirable impression of awe. 'Damn! This is awful luck.'

'That's my pay for a year,' burbled Locke. 'I don't get to claim a man's wages for two more to come. He'll have it out of my hide *and* my pocket.'

'Let's not be hasty,' said Jean soothingly. 'We can't get you a new cake, but we can at least give your master his crown back.'

'What do you mean, "we"?' The target rounded on Jean. 'Who the devil are you to speak for me, boy?'

'Jothar Tathis,' said Jean, 'solicitor's apprentice.'

'Oh? Which solicitor?'

'Mistress Donatella Viricona,' said Jean with the hint of a smile. 'Of Meraggio's.'

'Ahhhh,' said the target, as though Jean had just pointed a loaded crossbow directly at his privates. Mistress Viricona was one of Camorr's best-known litigators, a woman who served as the voice of several powerful noble families. Anyone who slung parchment for a living was bound to know her legend. 'I see … but—'

'We owe this poor boy a crown,' said Jean. 'Come, we can split the sum. I might have stumbled into you, but you certainly could have avoided him if you'd been more careful.'

Locke suppressed a grin that would have reached his temples if it hadn't been checked.

'But—'

'Here, I carry enough as pocket-money.' Jean held out two gold tyrins on his right palm. 'Surely it's no hardship for you, either.'

'But—'

'What are you, a *Verrari*? Are you that much of a scrub that two tyrins is an *imposition* for you? If so, at least give me your name so I can let my mistress know who wouldn't—'

'Fine,' said the man, holding his hands up toward Jean. 'Fine! We'll pay for the damn cake. Half and half.' He passed a pair of gold tyrins over to Locke, and watched as Jean did the same.

'Th-thank you, sirs,' said Locke with a quavering voice. 'I'll catch some hell for this, but not nearly what I would have had coming.'

'It's only reasonable,' said Jean. 'Gods go with you, both of you.'

'Yes, yes,' said the older man, scowling. 'Be more careful next time you're hauling a cake around, boy.' He hurried on his way without another word.

'Guilt is such a beautiful thing,' sighed Locke as he scooped up the toppled mess of the boxed cake – a horrid conglomeration of old flour, sawdust, and white plaster worth about a hundredth of what the unfortunate mark had handed over. 'That's a solid tyrin apiece for tonight.'

'Think Chains will be pleased?'

'Let's hope it's the Benefactor that ends up pleased,' said Locke with a grin. 'I'll just clear this mess up and find someplace to dump it so the yellowjackets don't break my skull. Back home?'

'Yeah, roundabout way,' said Jean. 'See you in half an hour.'

3

'So then this fellow backs off like Jean's started juggling live scorpions,' said Locke, just over half an hour later. 'And Jean starts calling him a scrub, and a Verrari, and all kinds of things, and the poor bastard just handed over two gold coins like that.'

Locke snapped his fingers, and the Sanza twins applauded politely. Calo and Galdo sat side by side atop the table in the glass burrow's kitchen, disdaining the use of anything so commonplace as chairs.

'And that's your offering?' said Calo. 'A tyrin apiece?'

'It's a fair sum,' said Jean. 'And we thought we put some effort into it. Artistic merit and all that.'

'Took us two hours to make the cake,' said Locke. 'And you should have seen the acting. We could have been on stage. That man's heart melted into a puddle, I was so sad and forlorn.'

'So it wasn't acting at all, then,' said Galdo.

'Polish my dagger for me, Sanza,' said Locke, making an elaborate hand gesture that Camorri only used in public when they absolutely wanted to start a fight.

'Sure, I'll get the smallest rag in the kitchen while you draw me a map to where it's been hiding all these years.'

'Oh, be fair,' said Calo. 'We can spot it easily enough whenever Sabetha's in the room!'

'Like now?' said Sabetha as she appeared from around the corner of the burrow's entrance tunnel.

The fact that Locke didn't die instantly may be taken as proof that a human male can survive having every last warm drop of blood within his body rush instantly to the vicinity of his cheeks.

Sabetha had been exerting herself. Her face was flushed, several strands of her tightly queued hair had fallen out of place, and the open neckline of her cream-coloured tunic revealed a sheen of sweat on her skin. Locke's eyes would ordinarily have been fixed on her as though connected to the aforementioned tunic by invisible threads, but he pretended that something terribly important had just appeared in the empty far corner of the kitchen.

'And where do you two get off teasing Locke?' said Sabetha. 'If either of you have any hair on your stones yet, you've been putting it there with a paintbrush.'

'You wound us deeply,' said Calo. 'And good taste prevents us from being able to respond in kind.'

'However,' said Galdo, 'if you were to ask around certain Guilded Lilies, you'd discover that your—'

'You've been visiting the Guilded Lilies?' said Jean.

'Ahhh,' said Calo with a cough, 'that is to say, *were* we to visit the, ah, Guilded Lilies, hypothetically—'

'Hypothetically,' said Galdo. 'Excellent word. Hypothetically.'

'Oh, I don't know. It's just like you two to make someone else do all the work, isn't it?' Sabetha rolled her eyes. 'So what's your offering, then?'

'Red wine,' said Calo. 'Two dozen bottles. We borrowed them from that half-blind old bastard just off Ropelayer's Way.'

'I went in dressed like a swell,' said Galdo, 'and while I kept him busy around the shop, Calo was in and out the rear window, quiet as a spider.'

'It was too easy,' said Calo. 'That poor fellow couldn't tell a dog's ass from a douche bucket if you gave him three tries.'

'Anyhow, Chains said they could be used for the toasting after the ceremony,' said Galdo. 'Since the point is to get rid of the offerings anyway.'

'Nice,' said Jean, scratching at the faint dark fuzz on his heavy chin. 'What have you been up to, Sabetha?'

'Yeah, what's your offering?' said the twins in unison.

'It's taken me most of the day,' said Sabetha, 'and it hasn't been easy, but I liked the look of *these*.' She brought three polished witchwood truncheons out from behind her back. One of them was new, one was moderately dented, and one looked as though it had been used to crack skulls for as long as any of the younger Gentlemen Bastards had been alive.

'Oh, you're kidding,' said Galdo.

'No, you're *fucking* kidding,' said Calo.

'Your eyes do *not* deceive you,' said Sabetha, twirling the batons by their straps. 'Several of Camorr's famously vigilant city watchmen have indeed misplaced their convincing sticks.'

'Oh, gods,' said Locke, his guts roiling with a tangled mess of admiration and consternation. His self-satisfaction at squeezing half a crown out of the poor slob in the Fountain Bend vanished. 'That's ... that's a bloody work of art!'

'Why thank you,' said Sabetha, giving a mock bow to the room. 'I have to admit, I only got two of them off belts. Third one was lying around in a watch station. I figured I had no business turning down that sort of temptation.'

'But why didn't you tell us what you were doing?' said Locke. 'Chasing the watch on your own—'

'Have you always told everyone else what *you're* up to?' said Sabetha.

'But you could have used some top-eyes, or a distraction just in case,' said Locke.

'Well, you were busy. I saw you and Jean baking your little cake.'

'You're showing off,' said Calo. 'Hoping to make an impression?'

'You think there'll be a choosing,' said Galdo, slyly.

'Chains said there's a chance every year,' said Sabetha. 'Might as well stand out. Haven't you two ever thought about it?'

'The full priesthood?' Calo stuck out his tongue. 'Not our style. Don't get us wrong, we love the Crooked Warden, but the two of us ...'

'Just because we like to drink doesn't mean we want to run the tavern,' finished Calo.

'What about you, Jean?' said Sabetha.

'Interesting question.' Jean took his optics off and wiped them against a tunic sleeve as he spoke. 'I'd be surprised if the Crooked Warden wanted someone like me as a divine. My parents took oath to Gandolo. I like to think I'm welcome where the gods have put me, but I don't believe I'm meant for anything like a priesthood.'

'And you, Locke?' Sabetha asked quietly.

'I, uh, guess I haven't really thought about it.' That was a lie. Locke had always been fascinated by the hints Chains dropped about the secretive structure of the Crooked Warden's priesthood, but he wasn't sure what Sabetha wanted to hear from him. 'I, ah, take it you have?'

'I have.' There was that smile of hers, a smile that was like the sun coming out from behind a cloud. 'I want it. I want to know what Chains smirks about all the time. And I want to *win* it. I want to be the best—'

She was interrupted by an echoing clang from the entrance tunnel. That could only be Chains returning to the burrow from the various preparations the night would require. He rounded the corner and smiled when he saw them all gathered.

'Good, good,' he muttered. 'Sanzas, the wine is being carried in by some people who'll be less busy than yourselves. Everyone else, I trust you have your offerings?' He looked pleased at the nods he received. Locke caught the twinkle of unusual excitement in his eyes despite the dark circles beneath them. 'Excellent. Then let's have some dinner before we leave.'

'Will we need to dress up or bathe for this?' asked Sabetha.

'Oh no, my dear, no. Ours is a pragmatic sort of temple. Besides, it's no use in trying to prettify yourselves, since you're going to have sacks thrown over your heads. Try to act surprised. That's the only little secret I'll be giving away in advance.'

4

A hush ran through the assembled thieves as several men and women, using a collapsible wooden frame, hung curtains over the door the postulants had been carried through. Other than a few vents in the ceiling, that door was the only entrance to the room Locke could see. Guards took up positions by the curtains – serious bruisers in long leather coats, with cudgels and axes ready. Chains had explained that their purpose was to ensure the privacy of the ritual. Other guards would be out there somewhere, an entire network, lurking along every route an outsider could use to spy upon or disrupt the Orphan's Moon rites.

There were about ten dozen people in the vault. That was a scant fraction of the people in Camorr whose lives were supposed to be ruled by the god with the hidden name, but that, according to Chains, was the nature of devotion. It was easy to mutter prayers and curses in the heat of the moment, and less convenient to skulk around in the middle of nowhere on the one night a year the dedicated actually came together.

'This is the temple of the church without temples,' said a woman in a hooded grey cloak as she stepped into the middle of the vaulted chamber. 'This is the ceremony of the order without ceremonies.'

'Father of our fortunes, we consecrate this hall to your purpose; to be joined to your grace and to receive your mysteries.' This was Chains, his voice rich and resonant. He took his place by the woman's side, wearing a similar robe. 'We are thieves among thieves; our lot is shared. We are keepers of signs and passwords, here without malice or guile.'

'This is our calling and our craft, which you from love have given us.' The third speaker was the *garrista* who'd sworn the postulants to secrecy, now robed in grey. 'Father of Shadows, who teaches us to take what we would dare to take, receive our devotions.'

'You have taught us that good fortune may be seized and shared,' said the female priest.

'*Thieves prosper,*' chanted the crowd.

'You have taught us the virtue and the necessity of our arts,' said Father Chains.

'*The rich remember.*'

'You have given us the darkness to be our shield,' said the third priest. 'And taught us the blessing of fellowship.'

'*We are thieves among thieves.*'

'Blessed are the quick and the daring,' said Chains, moving to the front of the hall, where a block of stone had been covered with a black silk drape. 'Blessed are the patient and the watchful. Blessed is the one who aids a thief, hides a thief, revenges a thief, and remembers a thief, for they shall inherit the night.'

'*Inherit the night,*' chanted the crowd solemnly.

'We are gathered in peace, in the eyes of our Benefactor, the Thirteenth Prince of Earth and Heaven, whose name is guarded.' The female priest spoke now, and took a place by Chains' left hand. 'This is the night he claims for his remembrance, the Orphan's Moon.'

'Are there any among us who would swear a solemn covenant with this temple, and take the oath of joining?' said the third priest.

This was the crucial moment. Any thief, anyone even remotely connected to an unlawful existence, was welcome in this company, so long as they took the oath of secrecy. But those taking the next step, the oath of joining, would proclaim their choice of the Unnamed Thirteenth as their heavenly patron. They would certainly not be turning their backs on the other gods of the Therin pantheon, but to their patron they would owe their deepest prayers and best offerings for as long as they lived. Even children studying to become priests didn't take formal oaths of joining until their early teens, and many people never took them at all, preferring to cultivate a loose devotion to all gods rather than a more formal obligation to one.

Nazca was the first to step forward, and behind her in a self-conscious rush came everyone else. Once the postulants had arranged themselves with as much dignity as they could manage, Chains held up his hands.

'This decision, once made, cannot be unmade. The gods are jealous of promises and *will not* suffer this oath to be cast aside. Be therefore sober and solemnly resolved, or stand aside. There is no shame in not being ready at this time.'

None of the postulants backed down. Chains clapped three times, and the sound echoed around the vault.

'Hail the Crooked Warden,' said the three priests in unison.

'STOP!'

A new voice boomed from the back of the chamber, and from behind the crowd of watchers came a trio of men in black robes and masks, followed by a woman in a red dress. They stormed down the aisle in the centre of the vault, shoving the postulants aside, and formed a line between them and the altar.

'STOP AT ONCE!' The speaker was a man whose mask was a stylized bronze sun, with carved rays spreading from a sinister, unsmiling face. He seized Oretta, a scar-covered girl with a reputation as a knife fighter, and dragged her forward. 'The Sun commands you now! I burn away shadows, banish night, make your sins plain! Honest men rise as I rise, and sleep as I set! I am lord and father of all propriety. Who are you to defy me?'

'A thief among thieves,' said Oretta.

'Take my curse. The night shall be your day, the pale moons your sun.'

'I take your curse as a blessing of my heavenly patron,' said Oretta.

'Does this one speak for you all?'

'*She does*,' yelled the crowd of postulants. The Sun threw Oretta to the ground, not gently, and turned his back on them all.

'Now hear the words of Justice,' said the woman in the red dress, which was short and slashed. She wore a velvet mask like those used by the duke's magistrates to conceal their identities. Justice pulled Nazca forward by her shoulders and forced her to kneel. 'All things I weigh, but gold counts dearest, and you have none. All names I read, but those with titles please me best, and you descend from common dirt. Who are you to defy me?'

'A thief among thieves,' said Nazca.

'Take my curse. All who serve me shall be vigilant to your faults, blind to your virtues, and deaf to your pleading.'

'I take your curse as a blessing of my heavenly patron,' said Nazca.

'Does this one speak for you all?'

'*She does!*'

Justice flung Nazca into the crowd and turned her back.

'I am the Hired Man,' said a man in a brown leather mask. A shield and truncheon were slung over the back of his robe. He grabbed Jean. 'I bar every door, I guard every wall. I wear the leash of better men. I fill the gutters with your blood to earn my bread. Your cries are my music. Who are you to defy me?'

'A thief among thieves,' said Jean.

'Take my curse. I shall hound you by sun or stars. I shall use you and incite you to betray your brothers and sisters.'

'I take your curse as a blessing of my heavenly patron,' said Jean.

'Do you?' The man shook Jean fiercely. 'Does this one speak for you all?'

'*He does!*'

The Hired Man released Jean, laughed, and turned his back. Locke nudged several other postulants aside to be the first to help Jean back to his feet.

'I am Judgment,' said the last of the newcomers, a man whose black mask was without ornament. He wielded a hangman's noose. With this, he caught Tesso Volanti around the neck and yanked him forward. The boy grimaced, clutched at the rope, and fought for balance. 'Hear me well. I am mercy refused. I am expedience. I am a signature on a piece of parchment. And that is how you die – by clerks, by stamps, by seals in wax. I am *cheap*, I am *easy*, I am *always hungry*. Who are you to defy me?'

'A thief among thieves,' gasped Tesso.

'And will they all hang with you, for fellowship, and split death into equal shares like loot?'

'I am not caught yet,' growled the boy.

'Take my curse. I shall *wait* for you.'

'I take your curse as a blessing of my heavenly patron,' said Tesso.

'Does this fool speak for you all?'

'*He does!*'

'You were all born to hang.' The man released Tesso from his noose and turned away. Volanti stumbled backward and was caught by Calo and Galdo.

'Depart, phantoms!' shouted Chains. 'Go with empty hands! Tell your masters how slight a dread we bear for thee, and how deep a scorn!'

The four costumed antagonists marched back down the aisle, until they vanished from Locke's sight somewhere behind the crowd near the chamber door.

'Now face your oath,' said Chains.

The female priest set a leather-bound book on the altar, and the male priest set a metal basin next to it. Chains pointed at Locke. Tense with excitement, Locke stepped up to the altar.

'What are you called?'

'Locke Lamora.'

'Are you a true and willing servant of our thirteenth god, whose name is guarded?'

'I am.'

'Do you consecrate thought, word, and deed to his service, from now until the weighing of your soul?'

'I do.'

'Will you seal this oath with blood?'

'I will seal it with blood on a token of my craft.'

Chains handed Locke a ceremonial blade of blackened steel.

'What is the token?'

'A coin of gold, stolen with my own hands,' said Locke. He used the knife to prick his left thumb, then squeezed blood onto the gold tyrin he'd scored from the cake business. He set the coin in the basin and passed the blade back to Chains.

'This is the law of men,' said Chains, pointing at the leather-bound tome, 'which tells you that you must not steal. What is this law to you?'

'Words on paper,' said Locke.

'You renounce and spurn this law?'

'With all my soul.' Locke leaned forward and spat on the book.

'May the shadows know you for their own, brother.' Chains touched a cool, gleaming coin to Locke's forehead. 'I bless you with silver, which is the light of moons and stars.'

'I bless you with the dust of cobblestones, on which you tread,' said the female priest, brushing a streak of grime onto Locke's right cheek.

'I bless you with the waters of Camorr, which bring the wealth you hope to steal,' said the third priest, touching wet fingers to Locke's left cheek.

And so it was done – the oath of joining, without a fumble or a missed cadence. Warm with pride, Locke rejoined the other boys and girls, though he stood just a few feet apart from them.

The ritual continued. Nazca next, then Jean, then Tesso, then Sabetha. There was a general murmur of appreciation when she revealed her offering of stolen truncheons. After that, things went smoothly until one of the Sanzas was beckoned forth, and they stepped up to the altar together.

'One at a time, boys,' said Chains.

'We're doing it together,' said Calo.

'We figure the Crooked Warden wouldn't want us any other way,' said Calo. The twins joined hands.

'Well then!' Chains grinned. 'It's your problem if he doesn't, lads. What are you called?'

'Calo Giacomo Petruzzo Sanza.'

'Galdo Castellano Molitani Sanza.'

'Are you true and willing servants of our Thirteenth God, whose name is guarded?'

'We are!'

'Do you consecrate thought, word, and deed to his service, from now until the weighing of your souls?'

'We do!'

Once the Sanzas were finished, the remaining postulants took their oaths without further complication. Chains addressed the assembly while his fellow priests carried away the offering-filled basin. They would give its contents to the dark waters of the Iron Sea later that night.

'One thing, then, remains. The possibility of a choosing. We priests of the Crooked Warden are few in number, and few are called to join our ranks. Consider carefully whether you would offer yourselves for the third and final oath, the oath of service. Let those who would not desire this join their fellows at the sides of the chamber. Let those who would stand for choosing remain where they are.'

The crowd of postulants cleared out rapidly. Some hesitated, but most had looks of perfect contentment on their faces, including Jean and the Sanzas. Locke pondered silently … *did* he truly want this? Did it feel right? Weren't there supposed to be signs, omens, some sort of guidance one way or another? Maybe it would be best just to step aside—

He suddenly realized that the only person still standing on the floor beside him was Sabetha.

There was no hesitation in *her* manner – arms folded, chin slightly up, she stood as though ready to physically fight anyone who questioned her feelings. She was staring sideways at Locke, expectantly.

Was this the sign? What would she think of him if he turned away from this chance? The thought of failing to match Sabetha's courage while standing right in front of her was like a knife in his guts. He squared his shoulders and nodded at Chains.

'Two bold souls,' said Chains quietly. 'Kneel and bow your heads in silence. We three shall pray for guidance.'

Locke went down to his knees, folded his hands, and closed his eyes. *Crooked Warden, don't let me make some sort of awful mistake in front of Sabetha*, he thought; then realized that praying on the matter of his own problems at a moment like this might well be blasphemous. *Shit*, was his next thought, and that of course was even worse.

He struggled to keep his mind respectfully blank, and listened to the murmur of adult voices. Chains and his peers conferred privately for some time. At last Locke heard footsteps approaching.

'One will be chosen,' said the female priest, 'and must answer directly. The chance, if refused, will never be offered again.'

'Small things guide us in this,' said the long-haired *garrista*. 'Signs from the past. The evidence of your deeds. Subtle omens.'

'But the Benefactor doesn't make difficult decisions for us,' said the woman. 'We pray that our choice will serve his interests, and thus our own.'

'Locke Lamora,' said Father Chains softly, setting his hands on Locke's shoulders. 'You are called to the service of the thirteenth Prince of Earth and Heaven, whose name is guarded. How do you answer his call?'

Wide-eyed with shock, Locke glanced at Chains, and then at Sabetha. 'I …' he whispered, then cleared his throat and spoke more clearly. 'I … I must. I do.'

Cheers broke out in the vault, but the look on Sabetha's face at that instant cut coldly through Locke's excitement. It was a look he knew only too well, a look he'd practised himself – the game face, the perfect blank, a neutral mask meant to hide hotter emotions.

Given her earlier attitude, Locke had no difficulty guessing what those hotter emotions must be.

CHAPTER FOUR
Across The Amathel

I

Everything that was wrong came to a crescendo at once: Locke's screams, Jean's crippling vertigo, and the surging black candle flames, filling the cabin with their ghastly grave-water un-light.

There was a bone-rattling vibration in the hot air, a sensation that something vast and unseen was rushing past at high speed. Then the black flames died, casting the room into real darkness. Locke's screams trailed off into hoarse sobs.

Jean's strength failed. Pressed down by nausea that felt like a weighted harness, he tumbled forward, and his chin hit the deck hard enough to bring back memories of his less successful alley brawls. He resolved to rest for just a handful of heartbeats; heartbeats became breaths became minutes.

Another of Patience's cohorts pushed the cabin door open at last and came down the steps with a lantern. By that wobbling yellow light, Jean was able to take in the scene.

Patience and Coldmarrow were still standing, still conscious, but clutching one another for support. The two younger Bondsmagi were on the floor, though whether alive or dead Jean couldn't muster the will to care.

'Archedama!' said the newcomer with the lantern.

Patience brushed the woman off with a shaky wave.

Jean rose to one knee, groaning. The nausea was still like ten hangovers wrapped around a boot to the head, but the thought that Patience was upright stung his pride enough to lend him strength. He blinked, still feeling a prickly inflammation at the edges of his eyes, and coughed. The candelabrum was charred black and wreathed in vile-smelling smoke. The woman with the lantern flung the stern windows open, and blessedly fresh lake air displaced some of the miasma.

Another few moments passed, and Jean finally stumbled to his feet.

Standing beside Coldmarrow, he clung to the table and shook Locke's left arm.

Locke moaned and arched his back, to Jean's immense relief. The ink and dreamsteel ran off Locke's pale skin in a hundred black-and-silver rivulets, forming a complete mess, but at least he was breathing. Jean noticed that Locke's fingers were curled tightly in against his palms, and he carefully eased them apart.

'Did it work?' Jean muttered. When neither of the magi responded, Jean touched Patience on the shoulder. 'Patience, can you—'

'It was close,' she said. She opened her eyes slowly, wincing. 'Stragos' alchemist knew his business.'

'But Locke's all right?'

'Of course he's not *all right*.' She extricated herself from the silver thread that bound her to Coldmarrow. 'Look at him. All we can promise is that he's no longer poisoned.'

Jean's nausea subsided as the night breeze filled the room. He wiped some of the silvery-black detritus from under Locke's chin and felt the fluttering pulse in his neck.

'Jean,' Locke whispered. 'You look like hell.'

'Well, you look like you lost a fight with a drunken ink merchant!'

'Jean,' said Locke, more sharply. He seized Jean's left forearm. 'Jean, gods, this is real. Oh, gods, I thought … I saw—'

'Easy now,' said Jean. 'You're safe.'

'I …' Locke's eyes lost their focus, and his head sank.

'Damnation,' muttered Patience. She wiped more of the black-and-silver mess from Locke's face and touched his forehead. 'He's so far gone.'

'What's wrong now?' said Jean.

'What you and I just endured,' said Patience, 'was a fraction of the shock he had to bear. His body is strained to its mortal limits.'

'So what do you do about it? More magic?'

'My arts can't heal. He needs nourishment. He needs to be stuffed with food until he can't hold another scrap. We've made arrangements.'

Coldmarrow groaned, but nodded and staggered out of the cabin.

He returned carrying a tray. This bore a stack of towels, a pitcher of water, and several plates heaped with food. He set the tray on the table just above Locke's head, then cleaned Locke's face and chest with the towels. Jean took a pinch of baked meat from the tray, pulled Locke's chin down, and stuffed it into his mouth.

'Come now,' said Jean. 'No falling asleep.'

'Mmmmph,' Locke mumbled. He moved his jaw a few times, started to chew, and opened his eyes once more. 'Whhhgh hgggh fgggh igh hhhhgh,' he muttered. 'Hgggh.'

'Swallow,' said Jean.

'Mmmmph.' Locke obeyed, then gestured for the water.

Jean eased Locke onto his elbows and held the pitcher to his lips. Coldmarrow continued to wipe the ink and dreamsteel away, but Locke took no notice. He gulped water in undignified slurps until the pitcher was empty.

'More,' said Locke, turning his attention to the food. The mage with the lantern set it down, took the pitcher, and hurried out.

The stuff on the tray was simple fare – baked ham, rough dark bread, some sort of rice with gravy. Locke attacked it as if it were the first food the gods had ever conjured on earth. Jean held a plate for him while Locke pushed the bread around with shaking hands, scooped everything else into his mouth, and barely paused to chew. By the time the water pitcher returned, he was on his second plate.

'Mmmm,' he mumbled, and a number of other monosyllables of limited philosophical utility. His eyes were bright, but they had a dazed look. His awareness seemed to have narrowed to the plate and pitcher. Coldmarrow finished cleaning him off, and Patience stretched a hand out above his legs. The rope that had bound him to the table unknotted itself and leapt into her grasp, coiling itself neatly.

The first tray of food – enough to feed four or five hungry people – was soon gone. When the attending mage brought a second, Locke attacked it without slowing. Patience watched him alertly. Coldmarrow, meanwhile, tended to the young magi who had collapsed during the ritual.

'They alive?' said Jean, at last finding a residue of courtesy if nothing more. 'What happened to them?'

'Ever tried to lift a weight that was too heavy?' Coldmarrow brushed his fingers against the forehead of the unconscious young woman. 'They'll be fine, and wiser for the experience. Young minds are brittle. Oldsters, now, we've had some disappointments. We've set aside the notion that we're the centre of the universe, so our minds bend with strain instead of meeting it head-on.'

Coldmarrow's knees popped as he stood.

'There,' he said, 'on top of all our other services this evening, some philosophy.'

'Jean,' Locke muttered, 'Jean, where the hell … what am I doing?'

'Trying to fill a hole,' said Patience.

'Well, was I …? I seem to have lost myself just now. I feel gods-damned strange.'

Jean put a hand on Locke's shoulder and frowned. 'You're getting warmer,' he said. He set his palm against Locke's forehead and felt a fever-heat.

'Certainly doesn't feel like it on my side of things,' said Locke. Shivering, he reached for the blanket on his legs. Jean grabbed it for him and draped it across his shoulders.

'You back to your senses, then?' asked Jean.

'Am I? You tell me. I just … I've never felt so hungry. Ever. Hell, I'd still be eating, but I think I'm out of room. I don't know what came over me.'

'It will come over you again,' said Patience.

'Oh, lovely. Well, this may be a stupid question,' said Locke, 'but did it work?'

'If it hadn't, you'd have died twenty minutes ago,' said Patience.

'So it's out of me,' muttered Locke, staring down at his hands. 'Gods. What a mess. I feel … I don't know. Other than the hundred tons I just shoved into my stomach, I can't tell if I'm actually feeling any better.'

'Well, *I'm* sure as hell feeling better,' said Jean.

'I'm cold. Hands and feet are numb. Feels like I've aged a hundred years.' Locke slid off the table, drawing the blanket more tightly around himself. 'I think I can stand up, though!'

He demonstrated the questionable optimism of this pronouncement by falling on his face.

'Damn,' he muttered as Jean picked him up. 'Sure you can't do anything about this, Patience?'

'Master Lamora, you full-blooded ingrate, haven't I worked enough miracles on your behalf for one night?'

'Purely as a business investment,' said Locke. 'But I suppose I should thank you nonetheless.'

'Yes, nonetheless. As for your strength, everything now falls to nature. You need food and rest, like any other convalescent.'

'Well,' said Locke, 'uh, if it's no trouble, I'd like to speak alone with Jean.'

'Shall I have the cabin cleared?'

'No.' Locke stared at the unconscious young magi for a moment. 'No, let your apprentices or whatever sleep off their hangovers. A walk on deck will do me some good.'

'They do have *names*,' said Patience. 'You'll be working for us; you might as well accept that. They're called—'

'Stop,' said Locke. 'I'm bloody grateful for what you've done here, but you're not hauling me to Karthain to be anyone's friend. Forgive me if I don't feel cordial.'

'I suppose I should take your restoration to boorishness as a credit to my arts,' said Patience with a sigh. 'I'll give instructions to have more food and water set out for you.'

'I doubt I could eat another bite,' said Locke.

'Oh, wait a few minutes,' said Patience. 'I've been with child. Rely on my assurance that you'll be ruled by your belly for some time to come.'

2

'I tell you, Jean, he was there. He was there looking down at me, closer than you are right now.'

Locke and Jean leaned against the *Sky-Reacher*'s taffrail, watching the soft play of the ghost-lights that gave the Lake of Jewels its name. They gleamed in the black depths, specks of cold ruby fire and soft diamond white, like submerged stars, far out of human reach. Their nature was unknown. Some said they were the souls of the thousand mutineers drowned by the mad emperor Orixanos. Others swore they must be Eldren treasures. In Lashain, Jean had even read a pamphlet in which a Therin Collegium scholar argued that the lights were glowing fish, imbued with the alchemical traces that had spilled into the lake in the decades since the perfection of light-globes.

Whatever they were, they were a pretty enough distraction, rippling faintly beneath the ship's wake. Smears of grey at the horizon hinted the approach of dawn, but a low ceiling of dark clouds still occluded the sky.

Locke was shaky and feverish, wearing his blanket like a shawl. In between sentences, he munched nervously at a piece of dried ship's biscuit from the small pile he carried wrapped in a towel.

'Given what was happening to you, Locke, I think the safest bet by far would be that you imagined it.'

'He spoke to me in his own voice,' said Locke, shuddering. Jean gave him a friendly squeeze on the shoulder, but Locke went on. 'And his eyes … his eyes … did you ever hear anything like that, at the temples you entered? About a person's sins being engraved on their eyes?'

'No,' said Jean, 'but then, you'd know more inner ritual of at least one temple than I would. Is it treading on any of your vows to ask if you—'

'No, no,' said Locke. 'It's nothing I ever learned in the order of the Thirteenth.'

'Then you did imagine the whole mess.'

'Why the hell would I imagine something like that?'

'Because you're a gods-damned guilt-obsessed idiot?'

'Easy for you to be glib.'

'I'm not. Look, do you really think the life beyond life is such a farce that people wander around in spirit with their bodies mutilated? You think souls have two eyes in their heads? Or *need* them?'

'We see certain truths manifested in limited forms for our own apprehension,' said Locke. 'We don't see the life after life as it truly is, because in our eyes it conforms to our mechanics of nature.'

'Straight out of elementary theology, just as I learned it. Several times,' said Jean. 'Anyway, since when are you a connoisseur of revelation? Have you ever, at any point in your life since you became a priest, been struck by the light of heavenly clarity, by dreams and visions, by omens, or anything that made you quake in your breeches and say, "Holy shit, the gods have spoken!"'

'You *know* I would have told you if I had,' said Locke. 'Besides, that's not how things work, not as we're taught in our order.'

'You think any sect isn't told the exact same thing, Locke? Or do you honestly believe that there's a temple of divines out there somewhere constantly getting thumped on the head by bolts of white-hot truth while the rest of you are left to stumble around on intuition?'

'Broadening the discussion, aren't you?'

'Not at all. After so many years, so many scrapes, so much blood, why would you suddenly start having true revelations from beyond the grave *now*?'

'I can't know. I can't presume to speak for the gods.'

'But that's precisely what you're doing. Listen, if you walk into a whorehouse and find yourself getting sucked off, it's because you put some money on the counter, not because the gods transported a pair of lips to your cock.'

'That's … a really incredible metaphor, Jean, but I think I could use some help translating it.'

'What I'm saying is, we have a duty to accept on faith, but *also* a duty to weigh and judge. Once you insist that some mundane thing was actually the miraculous hand of the gods, why not treat everything that way? When you start finding messages from the heavens in your breakfast sausages, you've thrown aside your responsibility to use your head. If the gods *wanted* credulous idiots for priests, why wouldn't they make you that way when you were chosen?'

'This didn't happen while I was eating breakfast, for fuck's sake.'

'Yeah, it happened while you were *this far* from death.' Jean held up his thumb and forefinger, squeezed tightly together. 'Sick, exhausted, drugged, and under the tender care of our favourite people in the world. I'd find it strange if you *didn't* have a nightmare or two.'

'It was so vivid, though. And he was so—'

'You said he was cold and vengeful. Does that sound like Bug? And do you really think he'd still be there, wherever you imagined him, hovering around years after he died just to frighten you for half a minute?'

Locke stuffed more biscuit into his mouth and chewed agitatedly.

'I *refuse* to believe,' said Jean, 'that we live in a world where the Lady of the Long Silence would let a boy's spirit wander unquiet for years in order to scare someone else! Bug's long gone, Locke. It was just a nightmare.'

'I sure as hell hope so,' said Locke.

'Worry about something else,' said Jean. 'I mean it, now. The magi came through on their end of our deal. We'll be expected to make ourselves useful next.'

'Some convalescence,' said Locke.

'I am glad as hell to see you up and moping on your own two feet again. I need you, brother. Not lying in bed, useless as a piece of pickled dogshit.'

'I'm gonna remember all of this tender sympathy next time you're ill,' said Locke.

'I tenderly and sympathetically didn't heave you off a cliff.'

'Fair enough,' said Locke. He turned around and glanced across the lantern-lit reaches of the deck. 'You know, I think my wits might be less congealed. I've just noticed that there's nobody in charge of this ship.'

Jean glanced around. None of the magi were visible anywhere else on deck. The ship's wheel was still, as though restrained by ghostly pressure.

'Gods,' said Jean. 'Who the hell's doing that?'

'I am,' said Patience, appearing at their side. She held a steaming mug of tea and gazed out across the jewel-dotted depths.

'Gah!' Locke slid away from her. 'My nerves are scraped raw. Must you do that?'

Patience sipped her tea with an air of satisfaction.

'Have it your way,' said Locke. 'What happened to all of your little acolytes?'

'Everyone's shaken from the ritual. I've sent them down for some rest.'

'You're not shaken?'

'Nearly to pieces,' she said.

'Yet you're moving this ship against the wind. Alone. While talking to us.'

'I am. Nonetheless, I'd wager that you're still going to misplace your tone of respect whenever you speak to me.'

'Lady, you knew I was poison when you picked me up,' said Locke.

'And how are you now?'

'Tired. Damned tired. Feels like someone poured sand in my joints. But there's nothing eating at my insides … not like before. I'm hungry as all hell, but it's not … *evil*. Not anymore.'

'And your wits?'

'They'll serve,' said Locke. 'Besides, Jean's here to catch me when I fall.'

'I've had the great cabin cleaned for you. There's a wardrobe with a set of slops. They'll keep you warm until we reach Karthain and throw you to the tailors.'

'We can't wait,' said Locke. 'Patience, are we in any danger of running aground or something if we ask you a few questions?'

'There's nothing to run aground on for a hundred miles yet. But are you sure you don't want to rest?'

'I'll collapse soon enough. I can feel it. I don't want to waste another lucid moment if I can help it,' said Locke. 'You remember what you promised us in Lashain? Answers, I mean.'

'Of course,' she said. 'So long as you recall the limitation I set.'

'I'll try not to get too personal.'

'Good,' said Patience. 'Then I'll try not to waste a great deal of effort by setting you on fire if my temper runs short.'

3

'Why do you people serve?' said Locke. 'Why take contracts? Why *Bonds*magi?'

'Why work on a fishing boat?' Patience breathed the steam from her tea. 'Why stomp grapes into wine? Why steal from gullible nobles?'

'You need money that badly?'

'As a tool, certainly. Its application is simple and universally effective.'

'And that's it?'

'Isn't that good enough for your own life?'

'It just seems—'

'It seems,' said Patience, 'that what you really want to ask is why we care about money at all when we could take anything we please.'

'Yes,' said Locke.

'What makes you think we would behave like that?'

'Despite your sudden interest in my welfare, you're scheming, skull-fucking bastards,' said Locke, 'and your consciences are shrivelled like an old man's balls. Start with Therim Pel. You did burn an entire city off the map.'

'Any few hundred people sufficiently motivated could have destroyed Therim Pel. Sorcery wasn't the only means that would have sufficed.'

'Easy for you to say,' said Locke. 'Let's allow that maybe all you theoretically needed was some gardening tools and a little creativity; what you actually did was *rain fire from the fucking sky*. If your lot couldn't rule the world with *that* …'

'Are you smarter than a pig, Locke?'

'On occasion,' said Locke. 'There are contrary opinions.'

'Are you more dangerous than a cow? A chicken? A sheep?'

'Let's be generous and say yes.'

'Then why don't you go to the nearest farm, put a crown on your head, and proclaim yourself emperor of the animals?'

'Uh … because—'

'The thought of doing anything so ridiculous never crossed your mind?'

'I suppose.'

'Yet you wouldn't deny that you have the power to do it, any time you like, with *no* chance of meaningful resistance from your new subjects?'

'Ahhh—'

'Still not an attractive proposition, is it?' said Patience.

'So that's really it?' said Jean. 'Any half-witted bandit living on bird shit in the hinterlands would make himself emperor if he could, but you people, who actually *can* do it at will, are such paragons of reason—'

'Why sit in a farmyard with a crown on your head when you can buy all the ham you like down at the market?'

'You've banished ambition completely?' said Jean.

'We're ambitious to the bone, Jean. Our training doesn't give the meek room to *breathe*. However, most of us find it starkly ludicrous that the height of all possible ambition, to the ungifted, must be to drape oneself in crowns and robes.'

'Most?' said Locke.

'Most,' said Patience. 'I did mention that we've had a schism over the years. You might not be surprised to hear that it concerns *you*.' She crooked two fingers on her left hand at Locke and Jean. 'The ungifted. What to do with you. Keep to ourselves or put the world on its knees? Nobility would no longer be a matter of patents and lineages. It would be a self-evident question of sorcerous skill. You would be enslaved without restraint to a power you could never possess, not with all the time or money or learning in the world. Would you *like* to live in such an empire?'

'Of course not,' said Locke.

'Well, I have no desire to build it. Our arts have given us perfect independence. Our wealth has made that freedom luxurious. *Most* of us recognize this.'

'You keep using that word,' said Locke. '"Most."'

'There *are* exceptionalists within our ranks. Mages that look upon your kind as ready-made abjects. They've always been a minority, held firmly in check by those of us with a more conservative and practical philosophy, but they have never been so few as to be laughed off. These are the two factions I spoke of earlier. The exceptionalists tend to be young, gifted, and aggressive. My son was popular with them, before you crossed his path in Camorr.'

'Great,' said Locke. 'So those assholes that came and paid us a visit in Tal Verrar, on *your* sufferance, don't even have to leave the comforts of home for another go at us! Brilliant.'

'I gave them that outlet to leaven their frustration,' said Patience. 'If I had commanded absolute safety for you, they would have disobeyed and murdered you. After that, I would have had no answer to their insubordination short of civil war. The peace of my society balances at all times on points like this. You two are just the most recent splinter under everyone's nails.'

'What will your insubordinate friends do when we get to Karthain? Give us hugs, buy us beer, pat us on our heads?' said Jean.

'They won't trouble you,' said Patience. 'You're part of the five-year game now, protected by its rules. If they harm you outright, they call down harsh retribution. However, if their chosen agents outmanoeuvre you, then they steal a *significant* amount of prestige from my faction. They need you to be pieces on the board as much as I do.'

'What if we win?' said Jean. 'What will they do afterward?'

'If you do manage to win, you can naturally expect the goodwill of myself and my friends to shelter under.'

'So we're working for the kind-hearted, moral side of your little guild, is that what we should understand?' said Locke.

'Kind-hearted? Don't be ridiculous,' said Patience. 'But you're a fool if you can't believe that we've spent a great deal of time reflecting on the moral questions of our unique position. The fact that you're even here, alive and well, testifies to that reflection.'

'And yet you hire yourselves out to overthrow kingdoms and kill people.'

'We do,' said Patience. 'Human beings are afflicted with short memories. They need to be reminded that they have valid reasons for holding us in awe. That's why, after very careful consideration, we still allow magi to accept black contracts.'

'Define "careful consideration,"' said Locke.

'Any request for services involving death or kidnapping is scrutinized,' said Patience. 'Black work needs to be authorized by a majority of my peers. Even once that's done, there needs to be at least one mage willing to accept the task.'

Patience cupped her left hand, and a silver light flashed behind her fingers. 'You curious men,' she said. 'I offer you the answers to damn near anything, secrets thousands of people have died trying to uncover, and you want to learn how we go about paying our bills.'

'We're not done pestering you,' said Locke. 'What are you doing there?'

'Remembering.' The silver glow faded, and a slender spike of dreamsteel appeared, cradled against the first two fingers of her hand. 'You're bold enough in your questions. Are you bold enough for a direct answer?'

'What's the proposal?' said Locke, nibbling half-consciously at a biscuit.

'Walk in my memories. See through my eyes. I'll show you something relevant, if you've got the strength to handle it.'

Locke swallowed in a hurry. 'Is this going to be as much fun as the last ritual?'

'Magic's not for the timid. I won't offer again.'

'What do I do?'

'Lean forward.'

Locke did so, and Patience held the silver spike toward his face. It narrowed, twisted, and poured itself through the air, directly into Locke's left eye.

He gasped. The biscuits tumbled from his hand as the dreamsteel spread in a pool across his eye, turning it into a rippling mirror. A moment later droplets of silver appeared in his right eye, thickening and spreading.

'What the hell?' Jean was torn between the urge to slap Patience aside and the sternness of her earlier warning not to interfere with her sorcery.

'Jean … wait …' whispered Locke. He stood transfixed, tied to Patience's hand by a silver strand, his eyes gleaming. The trance lasted perhaps fifteen seconds, and then the dreamsteel withdrew. Locke wobbled and clutched the taffrail, blinking furiously.

'Holy hells,' he said. 'What a sensation.'

'What happened?' said Jean.

'She was … I don't know, exactly. But I think you'll want to see this.'

Patience turned to Jean, extending the hand with the silver needle. Jean leaned forward and fought to avoid flinching as the narrow silver point came toward him. It brushed his open eye like a breath of cold air, and the world around him changed.

4

Footsteps echoing on marble. Faint murmur of conversation in an unknown language. No, not a murmur. Not a noise at all. A soft tickle of thoughts from a dozen strangers, brushing against an awareness that Jean hadn't previously known he'd possessed. A flutter like moth wings against the front of his mind. The sensation is frightening. He tries to halt, is startled to discover that the vapourous mass of his body refuses his commands.

Ah, but these aren't your memories. The voice of Patience, inside his head. *You're a passenger. Try to relax, and it will grow easier soon enough.*

'I don't weigh anything,' Jean says. The words come from his lips like the weakest half-exhalation of a man with dead stones for lungs. Squeezing them out takes every ounce of will he can muster.

It's my body you're wearing. I'm leaving some things hazy for your peace of mind. You're here for a study in culture, not anatomy.

Warm light on his face, falling from above. His thoughts are buoyed from below by a sensation of power, a cloud of ghostly whispers he can't seem to grab meaningful hold of. He rides atop these like a boat bobbing on a deep ocean.

My mind. My deeper memories, which are quite irrelevant, thank you. Concentrate. I'll make you privy to my strongest, most deliberate thoughts from the moments I'm revealing.

Jean tries to relax, tries to open himself to this experience, and the impressions tumble in, piece by piece, faster and faster. He is struck by a disorienting jumble of information – names, places, descriptions, and, threaded through it all, the thoughts and sigils of many other magi:

Isas Scholastica

Isle of Scholars
—Archedama, it's not like you to keep us waiting—
(private citadel of the magi of Karthain)
—is it because—
… feeling of resigned annoyance …
—Falconer—
(damn that obvious and inevitable question)
… sound of footsteps on smooth marble …
—can well understand—
His presence has nothing to do with my tardiness.
—would feel the same in your place—
As if I'd hide from my duties because of him.
(gods above, did I earn five rings by being meek?)
There is a plain wooden door before Jean, the door to the Sky

169

Chamber, the seat of what passes for government among the magi of Karthain. The door will not open by touch. Anyone attempting to turn the handle will stand dumbfounded as their hand fails again and again to find it, plainly visible though it is. Jean feels a flutter of power as he/ Patience sends his/her sigil against the door. At this invisible caress, the door falls open.

        —pardon, did not mean to offend—

… the warm air of the Sky Chamber, already packed with …

      I will not take the wall to my own son!

      —no need to get annoyed, I was merely—

        … there he sits, waiting.

    (watching, watching, like his damned bird)

The Sky Chamber is a vault of illusion that would make the artificers of Tal Verrar weak-kneed with envy. It is the first object of free-standing, honest-to-the-gods sorcery that Jean has ever seen. The room is circular, fifty yards in diameter, and Jean knows from Patience's penumbra of knowledge that the domed ceiling is actually twenty feet beneath the ground. Nonetheless, across the great glass sweep of that dome is a counterfeit sky, like a painting brought to life, perfect in every detail. It shows a stately early evening, with the sun hidden away behind gold-rimmed clouds.

The magi await Patience in high-backed chairs, arranged in rising tiers like the Congress of Lords from the old empire – a congress long since banished to ashes by the men and women who emulate them. They wear identical hooded robes, a soft dark red, the colour of roses in shadow. This is their ceremonial dress. Grey or brown robes might have been more neutral, more restful, but the progenitors of the order didn't *want* their inheritors to grow too restful in their deliberations.

One man sits in the foremost rank of chairs, directly across from Jean/Patience as the door slides shut behind him/her. Perched on one robed arm, statue-still, is a hawk that Jean recognizes instantly. He has looked directly into its cold, deadly eyes before, as well as those of its master.

(watching, watching, like his damned bird)

A bombardment of questions and greetings and sigils comes on like a crashing wave, then steadily fades. Order is called for, and relative silence descends, a relief to Jean. And then:

Mother.

The greeting comes a moment too late to be polite. It is sharp and clear as only the thoughts of a blood relative can be. Behind it is an emotional grace note, artfully subdued – the wide bright sky, a sensation of soaring, a feeling of wind against the face. The absolute freedom of high flight.

The sigil of the Falconer.

Speaker, she/Jean replies.

Must we be such prisoners of formality, Mother?

This is a formal occasion.

Surely we're alone in our thoughts.

You and I are never alone.

And yet we're never together. How is it we can both mean the exact same thing by those statements?

Don't wax clever with me, Speaker. Now isn't the time for your games.

– This is as much your game as it is mine – *I WILL NOT BE INTERRUPTED.*

There is strength behind that last thought, a pulse of mental muscle the younger mage cannot yet match. A vulgar way to punctuate a conversation, but the Falconer takes the point. He bows his head a fraction of a degree, and Vestris, his scorpion hawk, does the same.

At the centre of the Sky Chamber is a reflecting pool of dreamsteel, its surface a perfect unrippled mirror. Four chairs surround it; three are occupied. The magi have little care for the ungifted custom of setting the highest-ranked to gaze upon their inferiors. When so much business is transacted in thought, physical directions begin to lose even symbolic meaning.

Jean/Patience takes the open seat, and reaches out to the other three arch-magi. It's as easy as joining flesh-and-blood hands. Archedons and archedamas pool energies, crafting a joined sigil, an ideogram that fills the room for an instant with the thought-shape of four names:

—Patience-Providence—

—Foresight-Temperance—

The names are meaningless, traditional, having nothing to do with the personal qualities of their holders. The fused sigil proclaims the commencement of formal business. The light in the chamber dims in response; the early evening sky is replaced by a bowl of predawn violet with a warm line of tawny gold at the horizon. Archedon Temperance, seniormost of the four, sends forth:

—We return to the matter of the black contract proposed by Luciano Anatolius of Camorr—

There is a twist, a wrench in Jean's perceptions. Patience, the here-and-now Patience, adjusts her memories, shifts them to a context he can better understand. The thought-voices of the magi take on the quality of speech.

'We remain divided on whether or not the consequences of this proposal exceed the allowances of our guiding Mandates – first, the question of self-harm. Second, the question of common detriment.'

Temperance is a lean man of seventy, with brown skin the texture of wind-whipped tree bark. His hair is grey, and his clouding eyes are milky agates in deep, dark sockets. Yet his mind remains vigourous; he has worn five rings for half his life.

'With respect, Archedon, I would call on the assembly to also consider the question of higher morality.' This from a pale woman in the first row of seats. Her left arm is missing, and a fold of robe hangs pinned at that shoulder like a mantle. She stands, and with her other hand sweeps her hood back, revealing thin blonde hair woven tightly under a silver mesh cap. This gesture is the privilege of a Speaker, announcing her intention to take the floor and attempt to influence the current discussion.

Jean knows this woman from Patience's subtle whispers – *Navigator*, three rings, born on a Vadran trading ship and brought to Karthain as a child. Her private obsession is the study of the sea, and she is closely identified with Patience's allies.

'Speaker,' says Jean/Patience, 'you know full well that no proposed contract need be proven against *anything* broader than our own Mandates.'

Patience gets this out quickly, to create an impression of neutrality that is not entirely honest and to stress the obvious before someone with a more belligerent outlook can seize the chance to make a fiercer denunciation.

'Of course,' says Navigator. 'I have no desire to challenge the law provided by our founders in all their formidable sagacity. I am not suggesting that we test the proposed contract on my terms, but that we have an obligation to test ourselves.'

'Speaker, the distinction is meaningless.' Foresight speaks now, youngest of the arch-magi, barely forty. She and the Falconer are associates. She is also the most aggressive of the five-ring magi, her will as hard as Elderglass. 'We are divided on questions of clear and binding law. Why do you muddle this deliberation with nebulous philosophy?'

'The point is hardly nebulous, Archedama. It bears directly upon the first Mandate, the question of self-harm. The sheer scope of the slaughter this Anatolius proposes risks some diminishment of ourselves if we agree to it. We are discussing the single greatest bloodbath in the history of our black contracts.'

'Speaker, you exaggerate,' says Foresight. 'Anatolius has been clear concerning his plans for the nobility of Camorr. Few, if any, would actually be killed.'

'Candidly, Archedama, you surprise me with your dissembling. Surely we are not such children as to delude ourselves that someone reduced to the state of a living garden decoration by Wraithstone poisoning has *not*, by any practical measure, been murdered!'

There is a brightening in the artificial sky as the sun peeks above the horizon. Regardless of the justice of Navigator's argument, the assembly approves of the manner in which she's making it. The ceiling responds to the mental prodding of the magi in attendance. The sun literally shines on those that capture general approval, and visibly sets on those that stumble in their arguments.

'Sister Speaker,' says the Falconer, rising calmly and pushing his own hood back. Jean feels another chill at the uncovering of his familiar features – the receding hairline, the bright dangerous eyes and easy air of command. 'You've never been coy about the fact that you oppose black contracts on general principle, have you?'

Jean draws knowledge from Patience's whispers. There are about half-a-dozen Speakers at any time, popular and forthright magi, chosen by secret ballots. They have no power to make or contravene laws, but they do have the right to intrude on Sky Chamber discussions and indirectly represent the interests of their supporters.

'Brother Speaker, I'm not aware of having been coy about anything.'

'What, then, is the full compass of your objection? Is it all higher morality?'

'Wouldn't that be sufficient? Isn't the question of whether we might be found wanting at the weighing of our souls an *adequate* basis for restraint?'

'Is it your only basis?'

'No. I also put forth the question of our dignity! How can we not do it an injury when we reduce ourselves to paid assassins for the ungifted?'

'Is that not the very credo by which we work? *Incipa veila armatos de* – "we become instruments,"' says Falconer. 'To serve the client's design, we make ourselves tools. Sometimes that makes us weapons of murder.'

'Indeed, a murder weapon is a tool. But not all tools are murder weapons.'

'When our prospective clients want us to find lost relatives or summon rain, do we not take the contracts? Such is the condition of the world, however, that they tend to want our assistance in matters which are regrettably more *sanguine*.'

'We are not helpless in the choosing of the contracts proposed to—'

'Sister Speaker, your pardon. I interrupt because I fear that we are prolonging this discussion unnecessarily. Allow me to lay your points to rest, so that we may return to cutting our previous knot. You say it's the scope of this particular contract that earns your strenuous objection. How do you suggest that we scale it down to a more agreeably moral operation?'

'Scale it down? The whole enterprise is so bloodthirsty and reckless that I can hardly conceive of how we might mitigate it by sparing a few victims among the crowd.'

'How many would we have to spare for such mitigation as would please you?'

'You know as well as I, Brother Speaker, that this is not a question of simple arithmetic.'

'Isn't it? You've listened to proposals for many black contracts over the years, contracts involving the removal of individuals, gangs, even families. You might have objected in principle, but you never made any attempt to have them disallowed.'

'A contract for a single murder, while an undignified thing in itself, is at least more precise than the wholesale destruction of an entire city-state's rulers!'

'I see. Can we agree, then, on a point at which "precise" becomes "wholesale"? How many removals tip the balance? Are fifteen corpses moral, but sixteen excessive? Or seventeen? Or twenty-nine? Surely we must be able to compromise. The low triple digits, perhaps?'

'You are deliberately reducing my argument past the point of absurdity!'

'Wrong, Sister Speaker. I take your points very seriously. They have been treated seriously in our laws and customs for centuries! And they have been treated thus: *Incipa veila armatos de*! We become instruments. Instruments do not judge!'

The Falconer spreads his arms. Vestris flaps her wings, hops to his left shoulder, and settles back into comfortable stillness.

'That has been our way for centuries, precisely because of situations like this. *Precisely* because we are not gods, and we are not wise enough to sift the worthy from the unworthy before we take action on behalf of our clients!'

Jean has to admire the Falconer's cheek – appealing to humility in defence of an argument that magi should be free to slaughter without remorse!

'It is madness to try,' continues the Falconer. 'It leads to sophistry and self-righteousness. Our founders were correct to leave us so few Mandates by which to weigh the proposals we receive. *Will we harm ourselves?* This we can answer! *Will we harm the wider world*, to the point that our interests may be damaged? This we can answer! But are the men and women we might remove penitent before the gods? Are they good parents to their children? Are they sweet-tempered? Do they give alms to beggars, and if so, does this compel us to stay our hands? How can we possibly begin to answer such questions?

'We make ourselves instruments! Anyone we kill *as* instruments, we deliver to a judgment infinitely wiser than our own. If the removal be a sin, it weighs upon the client who commands it, not those who act under the bond of obedience!'

'Well put, Speaker.' Archedama Foresight is unable to suppress a smile; the sun has risen while Falconer has made his arguments, and the chamber is flush with a soft golden glow. 'I call to my fellow arch-magi for binding. We have no time for the diversion of philosophy. The subject of a specific contract divided us this morning. It divides us now. One way or another, we should end that division, working firmly within the context of the *law*.'

'Agreed,' says Temperance. 'Binding.'

'Reluctantly agreed,' says Providence. 'Binding.'

Jean/Patience feels a warm glow of gratitude. Providence has bent a point of etiquette, speaking his judgment before that of the more senior Patience, but in so doing he has confirmed the verdict, three out of four. Patience, whatever her actual thoughts on the subject, is now free to conceal them and do a small kindness to Navigator.

'Abstain,' Jean/Patience says.

175

'Binding,' says Foresight.

'Bound, then,' says Temperance. 'All further discussion outside the Mandates is set aside.'

Navigator pulls her hood up, bows, and sits. The assembly is restored to its previous stalemate. Providence has refused to sanction the proposed contract, while Foresight has endorsed it. Temperance and Patience have yet to express their opinions.

'You have more for us, Speaker?' Temperance directs his question at the Falconer, who remains standing.

'I do,' says the young man, 'if I don't strain your *patience* in continuing.'

Jean is struck by the ambiguity of his insight into this affair. Is it possible to make puns in thought-speech? Was that the Falconer's design? Or is Patience, in translation, highlighting nuances her son didn't intend? Whatever the truth, none of the arch-magi take exception.

'I bear no particular love for the people of Camorr. Neither do I bear them any particular ill-will,' says the Falconer. 'The proposed contract is drastic, yes. It will require deftness and discretion, and the removal of many people. It will have consequences, but I would argue that none of them are relevant to us.

'Let us look to the first Mandate, the question of self-harm. Do we have any particular attachment to the current rulers of Camorr? No. Do we have any properties or investments in the city we can't protect? No! Do we invite trouble for Karthain by causing upheaval two thousand miles away? Please … as if our presence here couldn't protect the interests of Karthain, even were Camorr two miles down the road!'

'You talk of investments.' Archedon Providence speaks now, a disarmingly mild man about Patience's age, a staunch ally of hers. 'Anatolius casts a wide net with this scheme. Any feast at Raven's Reach will command the presence of the city's money, including Meraggio himself. We *do* maintain accounts at his house, and others.'

'I've researched them,' says Falconer. 'But do these people run countinghouses or trade syndicates by themselves? Any one of them will have family, advisors, lieutenants. Capable and ambitious inheritors. The money in the vaults won't go anywhere. The letters of credit won't vanish. The organizations will continue operating under new authorities. At least that's my conclusion. Do you find it to be in error, Archedon?'

'Not necessarily.'

'Nor I,' says Foresight. 'Our few ties to Camorr are secure, our obligations to it nonexistent. Who can name a single concrete injury we would do ourselves if we accepted the Anatolius contract?'

The chamber is silent.

'I trust we may consider the first Mandate dispensed with,' says the Falconer. 'Let's give due airing to the second. What Anatolius proposes – and offers to pay a fair, which is to say, exorbitant price for – is that we *engineer an opportunity* for him to work his revenge against the nobility of Camorr and against its foremost criminal family. Now, I am merely being exact. I'm not attempting to disguise the magnitude of his intentions.

'With our aid, Anatolius will likely succeed, and hundreds of the most powerful men and women in Camorr will be Gentled. Our sister Navigator is correct to point out the foolishness of dancing around this point. These men and women will never again have a single meaningful thought. They won't be able to wipe the filth from their own asses. Their fate will be tantamount to murder.

'I would certainly not wish that on anyone I knew or cared for, but then, we are here to consider, as the Archedama put it, the concrete injuries of our actions, not to hone our sympathy for distant persons. We must measure whether the disruption this would inflict could be so widespread as to compromise our own interests, and our freedom of action.'

'Forgive my suspicion,' says Jean/Patience, 'that the Speaker has come to this assembly well-armed with conclusions to aid us in that measurement.'

'Archedama, I would be a poor advocate indeed if I dared to speak extemporaneously on such a crucial matter. I've given this contract a great deal of thought since it was first proposed.'

'If it were carried out,' says Archedama Foresight, 'what would happen to Camorr?'

'I think it impossible,' says Falconer, 'that literally every noble in Camorr could be caught in this trap. There must inevitably be those too ill to attend, those out of favour at court, and those travelling abroad. There will also be those that leave too early or arrive too late. Dozens of them are sure to survive. Anatolius understands this. His point is made regardless.

'Camorr possesses a standing army of several companies, along with a rather infamous constabulary. At the end of the night, the survivors would retain a disciplined force to keep the peace.'

'That's what they'd be used for, then?' Archedon Providence adopts a tone of mock surprise. 'Certainly not to settle old scores? Camorri are so famous for their deep sense of restraint where lingering grudges are concerned.'

'I'm not trying to be fatuous, Archedon,' says the Falconer, 'or unduly optimistic. But our information – and our information is better than the duke of Camorr's – is that the duke's standing forces are reasonably loyal to the throne and to Camorr itself. Of course there'd be blood on the walls. Doors kicked in, alley fights, that personal Camorri touch. Yet I think it likely the army and constabulary would stand aside from these affairs until the strongest survivors restored a legitimate chain of command.'

'Are you seriously arguing,' says Providence, 'that Camorr would, after a few knife-fights in the dark, suffer no further instability from the sudden and rather horrific subtraction of several hundred nobles?'

'Of course not. Archedon, you do me a rhetorical injustice. Camorr will lose much – its present ambitions, its particular relations with other city-states, its high culture. If Anatolius has his way, he'll wipe out most of the old dogs who won the Thousand Days and put down the Mad Count's rebellion.

'Camorr will be severely tested. Tal Verrar, we must assume, will poke every visible wound. But will Camorr collapse? Will there be riots in the streets? Will its soldiers throw down their pikes and run to the wilds? Gods be gracious, no. And will it lash out? At whom? Anatolius intends to make it generally known, if his plan is successful, that what took place was an act of vengeance by Camorri, upon Camorri. There'll be no foreign phantoms to chase.'

'They will try,' says Temperance, musingly. 'And they'll hunt Anatolius to the ends of creation. Assassins will be lined up at the city gates for work.'

'I agree,' says Falconer. 'But that would be Anatolius' problem, and he's eager to have it. He knows how to reach our agents if he wishes to discuss the price of making himself vanish.'

There is a good-humoured murmur from around the chamber. The sun has climbed higher; the warm golden glow is steady.

'I believe the chaos unleashed by Anatolius' plan would be brief, local, and easily contained,' says Falconer. 'It is, of course, the place of the arch-magi to determine whether or not I've been convincing. But I would say one thing more – a decision here is only the first requirement for a contract to be placed into action. It must also have a mage willing to become its instrument. I am no hypocrite! If the arch-magi allow it, I would be the first to request the honour of the assignment.'

Jean feels a strange flare of emotion from somewhere below the surface of the memories he rides. It isn't anger, or even surprise. Rather … satisfaction? Anticipation? The hint of feeling vanishes quickly, pushed back behind the curtains of Patience's mental stage.

'Are there any further arguments to be made,' says Temperance, 'against the Anatolius proposal, on the basis of the second Mandate?'

Silence around the room.

'We call the question.' Temperance raises his left hand, a gesture that allows his sleeve to fall back just far enough to reveal his five rings. 'Have these arguments changed the opinions already offered by my peers?'

'I still can't deem it acceptable,' says Providence.

'I can,' says Foresight.

'Then the time has come for Patience and myself to make our declarations.' Temperance broods before continuing. 'I agree that this is a proposal without precedent. I agree that it seems a singular and sinister thing, and I am no enemy of black contracts. But our custom compels a duty to fact, not to vague impressions. I find no valid reason in law to disqualify the proposal.'

A critical moment. Temperance has handed Patience the most meaningful decision of the entire assembly. If she refuses the proposal, agents of the Bondsmagi will politely inform Luciano Anatolius that his proposition has not been found convenient. If she allows the proposal, the Falconer will go to Camorr to work an act of butchery.

'I share the qualms of the honourable Navigator, and our esteemed Archedon Providence,' Jean/Patience says at last. 'I also share the Archedon Temperance's respect for the strictness of our Mandates. I too lack any valid reason to disallow the contract.'

Jean is chilled to the core of his vapourous body as he feels this statement come from his/Patience's lips. Of all the curious privileges he has ever been granted in life, surely this is among the most awful – the chance to speak the words that sent the Falconer to Camorr, to slaughter the Barsavi family, to cause the deaths of Calo and Galdo and Bug, to come within a hair's width of killing himself and Locke.

'The proposal is accepted,' says Temperance. 'I think it no small justice that the task should be yours, Falconer. We know you have

179

the stomach for black contracts. Now we'll see if your subtlety is any match for your enthusiasm.'

The Falconer has been handed a double-edged opportunity, a chance to crown his relatively early success with a contract unlike any other. A chance to fail spectacularly if he lacks the nerve to pull it off.

'This assembly is adjourned,' says Temperance. Jean's perception shifts again; in mid-sentence, the sound of the eldest archedon's voice transmutes to the sensation of thoughts. Patience has returned to her natural perspective.

Like a theatre audience with no applause, the magi rise and begin to file out of the Sky Chamber. A hundred private discussions continue, but there is no need to form conversational knots and clusters when they are taking place in the swift silence of thought.

The other arch-magi rise to leave, but Jean/Patience lingers, staring at the pool of dreamsteel in the middle of the chamber. He/she can feel the Falconer's eyes from across the room.

I must admit, I wasn't expecting you to make that allowance, Mother.

If you're no hypocrite, neither am I.

Jean/Patience waves a hand across the surface of the dreamsteel; currents of warmth pulse up and down the ghostly fingers. The silvery metal ripples birth slender shapes. The sculpting takes a few moments, and is far from perfect, but soon enough Jean/Patience has beckoned the dreamsteel into a caricature of the Camorr skyline, with the Five Towers looming over islands studded with smaller buildings.

Having no excuse to forbid this isn't the same as condoning it.

Frame it as you like.

Is there any point to my offering a piece of advice?

If it's truly advice, I'll be surprised.

Don't go to Camorr. This contract isn't just complex, it's dangerous.

I thought as much. Dangerous? I don't recall my name being on Luciano Anatolius' list of enemies.

Not merely dangerous for the ungifted. Dangerous for you.

Oh, Mother. I hardly know whether your game is too deep or too shallow for me. Is this your legendary prescience again? Curious how you seem to cite it whenever you have an obvious reason to slow me down.

The Falconer stretches forth a hand, and the Five Towers sink. In seconds the liquid-sculpture buildings dissolve back into their primordial silver ooze. The dreamsteel quivers, then becomes mirror-smooth once again. The Falconer grins.

Someday, Speaker, you may have cause to regret the intensity of your self-regard.

Yes, well, perhaps we can continue to explore your rather thorough catalog of my faults when I return from Camorr. Until then—

I doubt we'll ever have the opportunity. Farewell, Falconer.

Farewell, Mother. Rest assured I do look forward to enjoying the last word, whenever it comes.

He turns toward the door. As he walks away, Vestris cocks her head slightly, stares with cold hunter's eyes, and makes the slightest squawk. The bird's equivalent of a disdainful laugh.

The Falconer departs on his mission to Camorr two days later. When he returns, months will have passed, and he will be in no condition to enjoy any words at all.

5

'Gods above,' whispered Jean as the deck of the *Sky-Reacher* became real beneath his feet again. His eyes felt as though he'd been staring into a bitter wind. It was a deep relief to find himself back in the familiar shape and mass of his own body. 'That was insane.'

'The first time isn't easy. You bore it well enough.'

'You people do that often?' asked Jean.

'I wouldn't go so far as "often."'

'You can just pass your memories back and forth,' said Locke, shaking his head. 'Like an old jacket.'

'Not quite. The technique requires preparation and conscious guidance. I couldn't simply give you the sum total of my memories. Or teach you to speak Vadran with a touch.'

'*Ka spras Vadrani anhalt.*'

'Yes, I know you do.'

'Falconer,' muttered Jean, rubbing his eyes. 'Falconer! Patience, you could have stopped him. You were *inclined* to stop him!'

'I was,' said Patience. She stared out at the Amathel, the cooling dregs of her tea forgotten.

'But the Falconer was one of your exceptionalists, right?' said Locke. 'Along with what's-her-name, Foresight. And here you had a contract, a mission, to go and really fuck things up, Therim Pel style. If he'd actually pulled it off – and he came gods-damned close, let me tell you – isn't that just the sort of thing that would have given more prestige to his faction?'

'Absolutely.'

'And you let him go anyway.'

'I thought of abstaining, until he announced his willingness to take the contract. No, his *intention* of taking the contract. Once he'd done so, I realized that he wouldn't be coming back safely from Camorr.'

'What, you had some sort of premonition?'

'After a fashion. It's one of my talents.'

'Patience,' said Locke, 'I *would* like to ask you something deeply personal. Not to antagonize you. I ask because your son helped kill four close friends of mine, and I want to know … I guess …'

'You want to know why we don't get along.'

'Yes.'

'He hated me.' Patience wrung her hands together. 'Still does, behind the fog of his madness. He hates me as much as he did when we parted that day in the Sky Chamber.'

'Why?'

'It's simple. And yet … rather hard to explain. The first thing you should understand is how we choose our names.'

'Falconer, Navigator, Coldmarrow, etcetera,' said Jean.

'Yes. We call them *grey names*, because they're mist. They're insubstantial. Every mage chooses a grey name when their first ring is tattooed on their wrist. Coldmarrow, for example, chose his in memory of his northern heritage.'

'What were you, before you were Patience?' said Jean.

'I called myself *Seamstress*.' She smiled faintly. 'Not all grey names are grandiose. Now, there's another sort of name. We call it the red name, the name that lives in the blood, the true name which can never be shed.'

'Like mine,' muttered Jean.

'Just so. The second thing you need to understand is that magical talent has no relation to heredity. It doesn't breed true. Many decades of regrettable interference in the private lives of magi made this abundantly clear.'

'What do you do,' said Jean, 'with, ah, "ungifted" children when you have them?'

'Cherish them and raise them, you imbecile. Most of them end up working for us, in Karthain and elsewhere. What did you think we'd do, burn them on a pyre?'

'Forget I asked.'

'And gifted children?' said Locke. 'Where do they come from, if they're not home-grown?'

'A trained mage can sense an unschooled talent,' said Patience. 'We usually catch them very young. They're brought to Karthain and raised in our unique community. Sometimes their original memories are suppressed for their own comfort.'

'But not Falconer,' said Locke. 'You said he was your flesh-and-blood son.'

'Yes.'

'And for him to have the power ... how rare is that?'

'He was the fifth in four hundred years.'

'Was his father a mage?'

'A master gardener,' said Patience softly. 'He drowned on the Amathel six months after our son was born.'

'I'm sorry.'

'Of course you're not.' Patience moved her fingers slightly and her tea mug disappeared. 'I suppose I might have gone mad, if not for the Falconer. He was my solace. We became so close, that little boy and I. We explored his talents together. Ultimately, though, for magi to be born of magi is more curse than blessing.'

'Why?' said Jean.

'You've been Jean Tannen all your life. It's what your mother and father called you when you were learning how to speak. It's engraved on your soul. Your friend here also has a red name, but, to his great good fortune, he stumbled into a grey name for himself at an early age. He calls himself Locke Lamora, but deep down inside, when he thinks of himself, he thinks something else.'

Locke smiled thinly and nibbled a biscuit.

'The very first identity that we accept and recognize as *us*, that's what becomes the red name. When we grow from the raw instincts of infancy and discover that we exist, conscious and separate from the things around us. Most of us acquire red names from what our parents whisper to us, over and over, until we learn to repeat it in our own thoughts.'

'Huh,' said Locke. An instant later, he spat crumbs. 'Holy shit. You know the Falconer's true name because you gave it to him!'

'I tried to avoid it,' said Patience. 'Oh, I tried. But I was lying to myself. You can't love a baby and not give him a name. If my husband had lived, he would have given Falconer a secret name. That was the procedure … other magi might have intervened, would have if I hadn't deceived them. I wasn't thinking straight. I needed that private bond with my boy so desperately … and, inevitably, I named him.'

'He resented you for it,' said Jean.

'A mage's deepest secret,' said Patience. 'Never shared, not between masters and students, closest friends, even husbands and wives. A mage who learns another mage's true name wields absolute power over them. My son has bitterly resented me since the moment he realized what I held over him, whether or not I ever chose to use it.'

'Crooked Warden,' said Locke. 'I guess I should be able to find it in my heart to have some sympathy for the poor bastard. But I can't. I sure as hell wish you'd had a normal son.'

'I think I've said enough for the time being.' Patience moved away from the taffrail and turned her back to Locke and Jean. 'You two rest. We can dispose of any further questions when you awake.'

'I could sleep,' admitted Locke. 'For seven or eight years, I think. Have someone kick the door in at the end of the month if I'm not out yet. And Patience … I guess … I am sorry for—'

'You're a curious man, Master Lamora. You bite on reflex, and then your conscience bites you. Have you ever wondered where you might have acquired such contradictory strains of character?'

'I don't repent anything I said, Patience, but I do occasionally re-member to try and be civil after the fact.'

'As you said, I'm not dragging you to Karthain to be anyone's friend. Least of all mine. Go take some rest. We'll talk after.'

6

Jean hadn't realized just how exhausted the long night had left him, and after settling into his hammock he tumbled into the sort of sleep that squashed awareness as thoroughly as a few hundred pounds of bricks dropped on the head.

He woke, groggy and disoriented, to the smell of baked meat and crisp lake air. Locke was sitting at a smaller version of the makeshift table on which he'd been subjected to the cleansing ritual, hard at work on another small mountain of ship's fare.

'Nnngh.' Jean rolled to his feet and heard his joints creak and pop. His bruises from the encounter with Cortessa would smart for a few days, but bruises were bruises. He'd had them before. 'What's the time?'

'Fifth hour of the afternoon,' said Locke around a mouthful of food. 'We should be in Karthain just before dawn, they say.'

Jean yawned, rubbed his eyes, and considered the scene. Locke was dressed in loose clean slops, evidently chosen from an open chest of clothing set against the bulkhead behind him.

'How do you feel, Locke?'

'Bloody hungry.' He wiped his lips against the back of his hand and took a swig of water. 'This is worse than Vel Virazzo. Wherever we go, I seem to get thinner and thinner.'

'I'd have thought you'd still be sleeping.'

'I had a will for it, but my stomach wouldn't be put off. You, if you'll forgive me, look like a man desperately in search of coffee.'

'I don't smell any. Suppose you drank it all?'

'Come now, even I'm not that much of a scoundrel. Never was any aboard. Seems Patience is big on tea.'

'Damn. Tea's no good for waking up civilized.'

'What's boiling in that muddled brain of yours?'

'I suppose I'm bemused.' Jean took one of the two empty chairs at the table, picked up a knife, and used it to slide some ham onto a slab of bread. 'And dizzy. Our Lady of the Five Rings has spun our situation well beyond anything I expected.'

'That she has. You think it's odd from where *you're* sitting!'

'It is.' Jean ate, and studied Locke. He'd cleaned up, shaved, and pulled the lengthening mass of his hair into a short tail. The removal of his beard made the marks of his convalescence plain. He was pale, looking far more Vadran than Therin for a change, and the creases at the edges of his mouth were graven a bit deeper, the lines beneath his eyes more pronounced. Some invisible sculptor had been at work the past few weeks, carving the first real hints of age into the face Jean had known for nearly twenty years. 'Where on the gods' fair earth are you putting all that food, Locke?'

'If I knew that I'd be a physiker.'

Jean took another look around the cabin. A copper tub had been set near the stern windows, and beside it a pile of towels and oil bottles.

'Wondering about the tub?' said Locke. 'Water's fresh – they replaced it after I was done. They don't expect us to go diving in the lake to make ourselves presentable.'

There was a knock at the cabin door. Jean glanced at Locke, and Locke nodded.

'Come,' yelled Jean.

'I knew you were awake,' said Patience. She came down the steps, made a casual gesture, and the door shut itself behind her. She settled into the third chair and folded her hands in her lap. 'Are we proving ourselves adequate hosts?'

'We seem to be well-kept,' said Jean with a yawn, 'excepting a barbaric absence of coffee.'

'Endure for another day, Master Tannen, and you'll have all the foul black misuse of water you can drink.'

'What happened to the last person you hired to rig this little game of yours, Patience?' said Jean.

'Straight to business, eh?' said Locke.

'I don't mind,' said Patience. 'It's why I'm here. But what do you mean?'

'You do this every five years,' said Jean. 'You choose to work through agents that can't be Bondsmagi. So what happened to the last set you hired? Where are they? Can we speak to them?'

'Ah. You're wondering whether we tied weights around their ankles and threw them into the lake when it was over.'

'Something like that.'

'In some cases, we traded services. In others we offered payments. All of our former exemplars, regardless of compensation, left our service freely and in good health.'

'So, you ruthlessly protect every aspect of your privacy for centuries, but every few years you pick a special friend, answer any questions they might have, show them your fuckin' *memories*, begging your pardon, and then you just send them off when you're finished, with a cheerful wave?'

'None of our previous exemplars ever crippled a Bondsmage, Jean. None of them was ever shown what you were. But you needn't flatter yourself that you've been made privy to some shattering secret that can only be preserved by the most extreme measures. When this is over, we expect confidentiality for the rest of your lives. And if that courtesy isn't granted, you both know that we'll never have *any* difficulty tracking at least one of you down.'

'I guess that works,' said Jean sourly. 'So who took the ribbon, last time you did this?'

'You're being entrusted with a winning tradition,' said Patience. 'Though two victories in a row doesn't quite make a dynasty, it's a good basis from which to expect a third. Now, we will discuss your work in Karthain, but I made an unusual promise to get you both here. I would have it fulfilled for good and all. Have you any further questions about my people, about our arts?'

'Ask now or forever bite our tongues?' said Locke.

'I offered a brief opportunity, not a scholarly treatise.'

'As it happens,' said Locke, 'I do have one last thing I want a real answer to. Jean asked about the contracts you take. He asked *why*, and you gave us *why not*? But I don't think that cuts to the heart of things. I can't imagine that you people actually need the money after four hundred years. Am I wrong?'

'No. I could touch sums, at an hour's notice, that would buy a city-state,' said Patience.

'So why are you still mercenaries? Why build your world around it? Why do you call yourselves Bondsmagi without flinching? Why "*Incipa veila armatos de*"?'

'Ahhh,' said Patience. 'This is a deeper draught than you might wish to take.'

'Let me be the judge.'

'As you will. When did the Vadrans start raiding the northern coasts, where the Kingdom of the Marrows is now?'

'What the hell does *that* have to do with anything?'

'Indulge me. When did they first come down from that miserable waste of theirs, whatever their word for it—'

'Krystalvasen,' said Jean. 'The Glass Land.'

'About eight hundred years ago,' said Locke. 'So I was taught.'

'And how long since the Therin people moved onto this continent, from across the Iron Sea?'

'Two thousand years, maybe,' said Locke.

'Eight hundred years of Vadran history,' said Patience. 'Two thousand for the Therin. The Syresti and the Golden Brethren are older still. Let's generously give them three thousand years. Now … what if I told you that we had reason to believe that some of the Eldren ruins on this continent were built more than twenty thousand years ago? Perhaps even thirty thousand?'

'That's pretty damned wild,' said Locke. 'How can you—'

'We have means,' said Patience with a dismissive wave. 'They're not important. What's important is this – no one in recorded history has ever made credible claim of meeting the Eldren. Whatever they were, they vanished *so long ago* that our ancestors didn't leave us any storeys about meeting them in the flesh. By the time we took their empty cities, only the gods could know how long they'd been deserted.

'Now, one glance at these cities tells us they were masters of a sorcery that makes ours look like an idiot's card tricks by comparison. They built miracles, and built them to last for hundreds of centuries. The Eldren *meant* to tend their garden here for a very, very long time.'

'What made them leave?' said Locke.

'I used to scare myself as a kid by thinking about this,' said Jean.

'You can scare yourself now by thinking about it,' said Patience. 'Indeed, Locke, what made them leave? There are two possibilities. Either something wiped them out, or something frightened them so badly that they abandoned all their cities and treasures in their haste to be gone.'

'Leave the *world*?' said Locke. 'Where would they go?'

'We don't have the faintest speck of an idea,' said Patience. 'But regardless of how their marvellous cities were emptied in advance of our tenancy, it happened. Something out there *made* it happen. We have to assume that *something* could return.'

'Gah,' said Locke, putting his head in his hands. 'Patience, you're a regular bundle of smiles, you know that?'

'I warned you this might not be cheering.'

'This world and all its souls are the sovereign estate of the Thirteen,' said Locke. 'They rule it, protect it, and tend the mechanisms of nature. Hell, maybe they were the ones that kicked the Eldren out.'

'Strange, then, that they wouldn't mention it to us explicitly,' said Patience.

'Patience, let me reveal something from personal experience,' said Locke. 'The gods tell us what we *need* to know, but when you start asking about things you really just *want* to know, you'd best expect long pauses in the conversation.'

'Inconvenient,' said Patience. 'Of course it's possible that the gods are keeping mum about what happened to the Eldren. Or they couldn't act to stop it … or wouldn't. We've spent centuries arguing these possibilities. The only sensible assumption is that we've got to take care on our own behalf.'

'How?' said Locke.

'The use of sorcery in a long-term fashion, in a grand and concerted manner, with many magi working together, leaves an indelible imprint upon the world. Persons and forces sensitive to magic can detect this phenomenon, just as you can look at a river and tell which direction it's flowing, and put your hand in the water to tell how fast and warm it is. Great workings are like burning beacons on a clear dark night. Somewhere out in the darkness, we must assume, are things it would be in our best interest not to signal.

'That's why we maintain only a handful of places like the Sky Chamber, and prefer not to spend our time building fifty-storey towers out of glass. We suspect the Eldren paid for their lack of subtlety. They made themselves obvious to some power they didn't necessarily need to cross paths with.'

'Did my ... did the ritual you used to get rid of that poison—'

'Oh, hardly. It *was* a significant piece of work. Any mage within twenty miles would have felt it, but what I'm talking about requires a great deal more time and trouble. And that, at last, is why we've made our contracts such a focus of our lives. Working toward the diverging goals of thousands upon thousands of others over the years dissipates the magical consequences of concentrating our power.

'Think of us as a few hundred tiny flames, crackling in the night. By sparking randomly, at different times, in different directions, we avoid the danger of flaring together into one vast and visible conflagration.'

'I congratulate you,' said Locke. 'My mind has been thoroughly bent. But I think I sort of understand. Your little guild ... if what you're saying is true, you didn't band together just to keep the peace or any bullshit like that. This Eldren thing really spooks you.'

'Yes,' she said. 'The court magicians of the last few years of the Therin Throne were out of control. Circles of pure ambition, working to undermine one another. They wouldn't heed reason. The founders of our order brought their concerns to Emperor Talathri and were laughed off. But we knew the truth of the matter. If human sorcery is to exist at all, it must be quiet and disciplined, or we risk firsthand knowledge of the fate of the Eldren.'

'Pardon my limited understanding of your powers,' said Jean, 'but what you did to Therim Pel was anything but quiet.'

'Or disciplined,' said Patience. 'Yes, it was precisely the sort of focused, grand-scale will-working we can't afford. But on that one occasion, it was a necessary risk. The imperial seat, its infrastructure, its archives – all the heritable trappings of power *had* to be obliterated. Without Therim Pel, any would-be restorer of the empire found the easy path to legitimacy swept away. We needed that security in our early years.'

'While you hunted down any magician that wouldn't join you,' said Locke.

'Without mercy,' said Patience. 'You're right not to think of us as altruists. Certainly we can be hard. But perhaps you'll grant now that our motivations are, if not philanthropic, at least … complicated.'

Locke merely grunted and spooned porridge into his mouth.

'Have I satisfied you on this matter?'

Locke nodded and swallowed. 'I'm afraid that if you tell me any more I'll never be able to sleep in a dark room again.'

'Shall we talk about our business in Karthain?' said Jean, sensing that he and Locke were both in the mood for a less disquieting subject.

'The five-year game,' said Patience. 'Are the two of you ready for details?'

'My fighting spirit's back in residence,' said Locke. 'I've been stuck in bed for weeks. Turn me loose with a list of laws you want broken.'

'Are you sure you don't want any tea, Jean?' said Patience.

'No,' said Jean. 'Not for breaking fast. I wouldn't say no to red wine, though. Good rugged paint-stripping stuff. Plonk with sand in it. That's a good planning wine.'

'I'll see to it.'

'So,' said Locke, 'we work for your faction. I presume that's you, Coldmarrow, Navigator, all you high-minded types who only slaughter people when they've been naughty little children. What about your fellow five-ringers? Where do they stand?'

'Providence and Temperance will be cheering for you. Foresight, as I'm sure will be no surprise, will be hoping for you to slip and break your neck.'

'Foresight and Falconer's lot, that's the other team? Just two sides, no splinter factions, no lurking surprises?' said Locke.

'We only have enough major disagreements to supply two factions, I'm afraid.'

The door slipped open, and Coldmarrow entered with a tray. He set down an open bottle of red wine, several glasses, and Patience's mug from the previous night. He then handed Patience two scrolls and withdrew as soundlessly as he'd come.

Patience took her tea mug in hand. There was a sizzling noise, and a cloud of steam wafted from the cup. Jean poured two glasses of wine and set one in front of Locke. He took a swig from his own. It tasted like something out of a tanning vat.

'Ah,' he said, 'demonic ass-wash. Just the thing.'

'I'm not sure we meant that for drinking,' said Patience. 'Possibly for repelling boarders.'

'Smells adequate to the task,' said Locke, adding water to his glass.

'Now, these,' said Patience, pushing the scrolls toward Locke and Jean with her free hand, 'would be you.'

Jean picked up his scroll, snapped the seal, and found that it was actually several tightly rolled documents. He scanned them and saw Lashani letters of transit.

'For … Tavrin Callas!' He scowled.

'An old and comfortable piece of clothing, I should think,' said Patience with a smirk.

Beneath the letters of transit, which were a reasonably common means for travellers to prove themselves something less than total vagabonds, there was a letter of credit at one Tivoli's countinghouse, for the sum of three thousand Karthani ducats. If he wanted to lay claim to that money, of course, he'd have to accept his old alias one more time.

'Cheer up, Jean,' said Locke. 'I'm Sebastian Lazari, it seems. Never heard of the fellow.'

'I apologize if the selection of your own false faces is part of the savour for you,' said Patience. 'We needed to set up those accounts and put other things into motion before we fetched you out of Lashain.'

'This is swell,' said Locke. 'Don't think we can't start working with this, now that my nerves are more settled, but I hope this isn't the fullness of our suckle on the golden teat.'

'Those are merely your setting-up funds, to get you through your first few days. Tivoli will put you in control of your working treasury. One hundred thousand ducats, same as your opposition. A goodly sum for graft and other needs, but not so much that you can simply drench Karthain in money and win without being clever.'

'And, uh, if we set aside a little for afterward?' said Locke.

'We encourage you to spend these funds down to the last copper on the election itself,' said Patience, 'since anything left over when the results are confirmed will disappear, as though by magic. Clear?'

'Frustratingly damn clear,' said Locke.

'How does this election work, at the most basic level?' said Jean.

'There are fourteen districts in the city, and five representing the rural manors. Nineteen seats on the ruling Konseil. Each political party stands one candidate per seat, and designates a line of seconds in case the primary candidate is embroiled in scandal or otherwise distracted. That tends to happen with curious frequency.'

'No shit,' said Locke. 'What are these political parties?'

'Two major interests dominate Karthain. On one hand there's the Deep Roots party, old aristocracy. They've all been legally debased out of their titles, but the money and connections are still there. On the other side you've got the Black Iris party – artisans, younger merchants. Old money versus new, let's say.'

'Who are we taking care of?' said Jean.

'You've got the Deep Roots.'

'How? I mean, what are we to these people?'

'Lashani consultants, hired to direct the campaign behind the scenes. Your power will be more or less absolute.'

'Who's told these people to listen to us?'

'They've been *adjusted*, Jean. They'll defer enthusiastically to you, at least where the election is concerned. We've prepared them for your arrival.'

'Gods.'

'It's nothing you don't try to do with raw charm and fancy storeys. We just work faster.'

'We've got six weeks, is that right?' said Locke.

'Yes.' Patience sipped at her tea. 'The formal commencement of electoral hostilities is the night after tomorrow.'

'And this Deep Roots party,' said Locke, 'you said they've won the last two elections?'

'Oh, no,' said Patience.

'You did,' said Jean. 'You said we were being entrusted with a winning tradition!'

'Ah. Pardon. I meant that *my* faction of magi has backed the winning party of ungifted twice in a row. It's a matter of chance, you see, which party either side gets. The Deep Roots have been rather lacklustre these past ten years, but during those years fortune gave us the Black Iris. Now, alas—'

'Gods' immaculate piss,' muttered Locke.

'What are the limits on our behaviour?' said Jean.

'As far as the ungifted are concerned, not many. You'll be working with people eager to help you break every election law ever scribed, so long as you don't do anything bloody or vulgar.'

'No violence?' said Locke.

'Brawls are a natural consequence of enthusiasm,' said Patience. 'Everyone loves to hear about a good fistfight. But keep it at fists. No weapons, no corpses. You can knock a few Karthani about, and make whatever threats you like, but you *cannot* kill anyone. Nor can you kidnap any citizen of Karthain, or physically remove them from the city. Those rules are enforced by my people. I should think the reasons are obvious.'

'Right. You're not paying us to assassinate the entire Black Iris bunch and ride off into the sunset.'

'Your own situation is more ambiguous,' said Patience. 'You two, and your counterpart controlling the Black Iris, should expect anything, including kidnapping. Guard your own backs. Only outright murder is forbidden in your respect.'

'Well, that's cheery,' said Locke. 'About this counterpart, what do we get to know?'

'You know quite a bit already.'

'What do you mean?'

'It's uncomfortable news,' said Patience, 'but we've learned that at least one person within the ranks of my faction is passing information to Archedama Foresight.'

'Well, that's bloody careless of you!'

'We're working on the situation. At any rate, Foresight and her associates learned of my intention to hire you several weeks ago. They acquired a direct countermeasure.'

'Meaning what?'

'You and Jean have a unique background in deception, disguise, and manipulation. You're a rare breed. In fact, there's only one other person left in the world with intimate knowledge of your methods and training—'

Locke shot to his feet as though his chair were a crossbow and the trigger had been pulled. His glass flew, spilling watered wine across the tabletop.

'No,' he said. 'No. You're fucking kidding. No.'

'Yes,' said Patience. 'My rivals have hired your old friend Sabetha Belacoros to be their exemplar. She's been in Karthain for several days now, making her preparations. It's a fair bet that she's laying surprises for the two of you as we speak.'

II

CROSS-PURPOSES

When the rose's flash to the sunset
Reels to the rack and the twist,
And the rose is a red bygone,
When the face I love is going
And the gate to the end shall clang,
And it's no use to beckon or say, 'So long'—
Maybe I'll tell you then
some other time.

—*Carl Sandburg* from 'The Great Hunt'

Striking Sparks

I

It was cool and dark in the Elderglass burrow of the Gentlemen Bastards, and far quieter than usual, when Locke awoke with the certain knowledge that someone was staring at him. He caught his breath for an instant, then mimicked the deep, slow breathing of sleep. He squinted and scanned the grey darkness of the room, wondering where everyone was.

Down the hall from the kitchen there were four rooms, or, more appropriately, four cells. They had dark curtains for doors. One belonged to Chains, another to Sabetha, the third to the Sanzas, and the fourth to Locke and Jean. Jean should have been on his cot against the opposite wall, just past their little shelf of books and scrolls, but there was no sound from that direction.

Locke listened, straining to hear over the thudding of his pulse. There was a whisper of bare skin against the floor, and a flutter of cloth. He sat up, left hand outstretched, only to find another warm set of fingers entwined around his, and a palm in the middle of his chest pushing him back down.

'Shhhh,' said Sabetha, sliding onto the cot.

'Wha … where is everyone?'

'Gone for the moment,' she whispered into his ear. Her breath was warm against his cheek. 'We don't have much time, but we do have some.'

She took his hands and guided them to the smooth, taut muscles of her stomach. Then she slid them upwards until he was cupping her breasts – she'd come into the room without a tunic.

One thing the bodies of sixteen-year-old boys (and that was more or less what Locke was) don't do is respond mildly to provocation. In an instant he was achingly hard against the thin fabric of his breeches, and he exhaled in mingled shock and delight. Sabetha brushed aside his blanket and slid her left hand down between his legs. Locke arched his back and uttered a noise that was far from dignified. Luckily, Sabetha giggled, seeming to find it endearing.

'Mmmm,' she whispered. 'I do feel appreciated.' She pressed down firmly but gently and began to squeeze him to the rhythm of their breathing, which was growing steadily louder. At the same time, she slid his other hand down from her breast, down her stomach, down to her legs. She was wearing a linen breechclout, the sort that could be undone with just a tug in the right place. She pressed his hand between her thighs, against the intriguing heat just behind the fabric. He caressed her there, and for a few incredible moments they were completely caught up in this half-sharing, half-duel, their responses to one another becoming less controlled with every ragged breath, and it was delicious suspense to wonder who would snap first.

'You're driving me mad,' he whispered. The heat from her skin was so intense he imagined he could see it as a ghost-image in the dark. She leaned forward, and her breath tickled his cheeks again; he drew in the scents of her hair and sweat and perfume and laughed with pleasure.

'Why are we still wearing clothes?' she said, and they rolled apart to amend the situation, fumbling, struggling, giggling. Only now the soft heat of her skin was fading, and the grey shadows of the room loomed more deeply around them, and then Locke was kicking out, spasming in a full-body reflex as she slipped from his grasp like a breath of wind.

That cruellest of landlords, cold morning reality, finished evicting the warm fantasy that had briefly taken up residence in his skull. Muttering and swearing, Locke fought against his tangled blanket, felt his cot tipping away from the wall, and failed in every particular to brace himself for his meeting with the floor. There are three distinct points of impact no romantically excited teenage boy ever hopes to slam against a hard surface. Locke managed to land on all three.

His outflung right hand failed to do anything useful, but it did snatch the opaque cover from his cot-side alchemical globe, bathing the cell in soft golden light for him to gasp and writhe by. A carelessly stacked pile of books toppled loudly to the floor, then took several similar piles with it in a fratricidal cascade.

'Gods below,' muttered Jean, rolling away from the light. Jean was definitely in his proper place, and their cell was once again the cluttered mess of daily life rather than the dark private stage of Locke's dream.

'Arrrrrrrrrrgh,' said Locke. It didn't help much, so he tried again. 'Arrrrrrrrrrr—'

'You know,' said Jean, yawning irritably, 'you should burn some offerings in thanks for the fact that you don't actually talk in your sleep.'

'... rrrrrgh. What the hell do you mean?'

'Sabetha's got really sharp ears.'

'Nnngh.'

'I mean, it's pretty gods-damned obvious you're not dreaming about calligraphy over there.'

There was a loud knock on the wall just outside their cell, and then the curtain was swept aside to reveal Calo Sanza, long hair hanging in his eyes, working his way into a pair of breeches.

'Good morning, sunshines! What's with all the noise?'

'Someone took a tumble,' muttered Jean.

'What's so hard about sleeping on a cot like a normal person, ya fuckin' spastic dog?'

'Kiss my ass, Sanza,' Locke gasped.

'Heyyyyyyyyy EVERYBODY!' Calo pounded on the wall as he shouted. 'I know we've got half an hour yet to sleep, but Locke thinks we should all be up right now! Find your happy faces, Gentlefucker Bastards, it's a bright new day and we get to start it EARLY!'

'Calo, what the hell is wrong with you?' hollered Sabetha, somewhere down the hall.

Locke put his forehead against the floor and moaned. It was the height of the endless steaming summer of the seventy-eighth Year of Preva, Lady of the Red Madness, and everything was absolutely screwed up to hell.

2

Sabetha darted in, parried Locke's attempt at a guard, and smacked the outside of his left knee with her chestnut wood baton.

'Ow,' he said, hopping up and down while the sting faded. Locke wiped his forehead, lined up again in the duellist's stance, and touched the tip of his baton to Sabetha's. They were using the sanctuary of the Temple of Perelandro as a practice room, under Jean's watchful eye.

'High diamond, low square,' said Jean. 'Go!'

This was more an exercise in speed and precision than actual fighting technique. They slammed their batons together in the patterns demanded by Jean, and after the final contact they were free to swipe at one another, scoring touches against arms or legs.

Clack! Clack! Clack! The sound of their batons echoed across the stone-walled chamber.

Clack! Clack! Clack!

Clack! Clack! Thump!

'Yeow,' said Locke, shaking his left wrist, where a fresh red welt was rising.

'You're faster than this, Locke.' Sabetha returned to her starting position. 'Something distracting you this morning?'

Sabetha wore a loose white tunic and black silk knee-breeches that left nothing about her lithely-muscled legs to the imagination. Her cheeks were flushed, her hair pulled tightly back with linen cord. If she'd heard anything specific about the disturbance he'd kicked off to start the day, at least she wasn't saying much.

'More than one something?' she said. 'Any of them attached to me?'

So much for the lukewarm comfort of uncertainty.

'You know *I'm* attached to you,' said Locke, trying to sound cheerful as they touched batons again.

'Or might like to be, hmmm?'

'Middle square,' yelled Jean, 'middle square, middle diamond! Go!'

They wove their pattern of strikes and counter-strikes, rattling their batons off one another until the end of the sequence, when Sabetha flicked Locke's weapon down and smacked a painful crease into his right bicep. Sabetha's only commentary on this victory was to idly twirl her baton while Locke rubbed at his arm.

'Hold it,' said Jean. 'We'll try a new exercise. Locke, stand there with your hands at your sides. Sabetha, you just hit him until you get tired. Be sure to concentrate on his head so he won't feel anything.'

'Very funny.' Locke lined up again. 'I'm ready for another.'

He was nothing of the sort. At the end of the next pattern, Sabetha slapped him on the right bicep again. And again, following the pattern after that, with precision that was obviously deliberate.

'You know, most days you can at least manage to hit back,' she said. 'Want to give it up as a bad job?'

'Of course not,' said Locke, trying to be subtle about wiping the nascent tears from the corners of his eyes. 'Barely getting started.'

'Have it your way.' She lined up again, and Locke couldn't miss the coldness of her poise. Ah, gods. When Sabetha felt she was being trifled with, she had a way of radiating the same calm, chilly regard that Locke imagined might pass from executioner to condemned victim. He knew all too well what it meant to be the object of that regard.

'High diamond,' said Jean warily, apprehending the change in Sabetha's mood. 'Middle square, low cross. Go.'

They flew through the patterns with furious speed, Sabetha setting the pace and Locke straining to match her. The instant the last stroke of the formal exercise was made, Locke flew into a guard position that would have deflected any blow aimed at his much-abused right bicep. Sabetha, however, was actually aiming for a point just above his heart, and the hotly stinging slap nearly knocked him over.

'Gods above,' said Jean, stepping between them. 'You know the rules, Sabetha. No cuts at anything but arms or legs.'

'Are there rules in a tavern brawl or an alley fight?'

'This isn't a damned alley fight. It's just an exercise for building vigour!'

'Doesn't seem to be working for one of us.'

'What's gotten into you?'

'What's gotten into *you*, Jean? Are you going to stand in front of him for the rest of his life?'

'Hey, hey,' said Locke, stepping around Jean and attempting to hide a considerable amount of pain behind a disingenuous smile. 'All's well, Jean.'

'All's not well,' said Jean. 'Someone is taking this far too seriously.'

'Stand aside, Jean,' said Sabetha. 'If he wants to stick his hand in a fire, he can learn to pull it out himself.'

'*He* is right here, thank you very much, and *he* is fine,' said Locke. 'It's fine, Jean. Let's have another pattern.'

'Sabetha needs to calm down.'

'Aren't I calm?' said Sabetha. 'Locke can have quarter any time he asks for it.'

'I don't choose to yield just yet,' said Locke, with what he hoped was a charming, devil-may-care sort of grin. Sabetha's countenance only darkened in response. 'However, if you're concerned about me, you can back off to any degree you prefer.'

'Oh, no.' Sabetha was anything but calm. 'No, no, no. I don't withdraw. *You* yield! Deliberately. Or we keep going until you can't stand up.'

'That might take a while,' said Locke. 'Let's see if you have the patience—'

'Damn it, when will you learn that refusing to admit you've lost isn't the same as winning?'

'Sort of depends on how long one keeps refusing, doesn't it?'

Sabetha scowled, an expression that cut Locke more deeply than any baton-lash. Staring fixedly at him, she took her baton in both hands, snapped it over her knee, and bounced the pieces off the floor.

'Forgive me, *gentlemen,*' she said. 'I seem to be unable to conform to the intended spirit of this exercise.'

She turned and left. When she'd vanished into the rear hall of the temple, Locke let out a dejected sigh.

'Gods,' he said. 'What the hell is going on between us? What happened, just now?'

'She has a cruel streak, that one,' said Jean.

'No more than any of us!' said Locke, more hotly than he might have intended. 'Well, we've got some ... philosophical differences, to be sure.'

'She's a perfectionist.' Jean picked up the broken halves of Sabetha's baton. 'And you're a real idiot from time to time.'

'What did I do, besides fail to be a master baton duellist?' Locke massaged some of the tender reminders Sabetha had left him of her superior technique. 'I didn't train with Don Maranzalla.'

'Neither did she.'

'Well, come on, how does that make me an idiot?'

'You're no Sanza,' said Jean, 'but you can certainly be one sharp stab in the ass. Look, you'd have stood here and let her slap you into paste just for the sake of being in the same room with her. I know it. You know it. *She* knows it.'

'Well, uh—'

'It's not *endearing*, Locke. You don't court a girl by inviting her to abuse you from sunrise to sunset.'

'Really? That sounds an awful lot like courtship in every story I've ever read—'

'I mean literally abused, as in getting pounded into bird shit with a wooden stick. It's not charming or impressive. It just makes you look silly.'

'Well, she doesn't like it when I beat her at anything. She's certainly not going to respect me if I give up! So just what the hell *can* I do?'

'No idea. Maybe I see some things clearer than you because I'm not bloody infatuated, but what to actually do with the pair of you, gods know.'

'You're a deep well of reassurance.'

'On the bright side,' said Jean, 'I'm sure you're higher in her esteem right now than the Sanzas.'

'Sweet gods, that's sickly praise.' Locke leaned against a wall and stretched. 'Speaking of Sanzas, did you see Chains' face when we woke him up this morning?'

'I wish I hadn't. He's going to break those two over his knee like Sabetha's stick.'

'Where do you think he stomped off to?'

'No idea. I've never seen him leave angry before the sun was even up.'

'What in all the hells is going on with us?' said Locke. 'This whole summer has been one long exercise in getting everything wrong.'

'Chains muttered to me a few nights ago,' said Jean, fiddling with the broken baton. 'Something about awkward years. Said he might have to do something about us being all pent up together.'

'Hope that doesn't mean more apprenticeships. I'm really not in the mood to go and learn another temple's rituals and then pretend to kill myself.'

'No idea what it means, but—'

'Hey, you two!' Galdo Sanza appeared out of the rear corridor, the spitting image of Calo, save for the fact that his skull was shaven clean of every last speck of hair. 'Tubby and the training dummy! Chains is back, wants us in the kitchen with a quickness. And what'd you do to Sabetha this time?'

'I exist,' said Locke. 'Some days that's enough.'

'You should make some friends at the Guilded Lilies, mate,' said Galdo. 'Why fall on your face trying to tame a horse when you can have a dozen that are already saddled?'

'So now you like to fuck horses,' said Jean. 'Bravo, baldy.'

'Laugh all you will, we're in demand over there,' said Galdo. 'Favourite guests. Command performances.'

'I'm sure you're popular,' said Jean with a yawn. 'Who doesn't like getting paid for fast, easy work?'

'I'll say a prayer for you next time I'm having it with two at once,' said Galdo. 'Maybe the gods will hear me and let your stones drop.

But, seriously, Chains came in the river entrance, and I think we're all about to die.'

'Well, hurrah,' said Locke. 'When the weather's like this, who honestly wants to live?'

3

The Father Chains waiting in the glass burrow's kitchen wasn't wearing any of his usual guises or props. No canes or staves to lean on, no robes, no look of sly benevolence on that craggy, bearded face. He was dressed to be out and about in the city, heavily sweated with exertion, and all the furrows in his forehead seemed to meet in an ominous valley above his fierce dark eyes. Locke was unsettled; he'd rarely seen Chains glower like that at an enemy or a stranger, let alone at his apprentices.

Locke noticed that everyone else was keeping a certain instinctive distance from Chains. Sabetha sat on a counter, well away from anyone, arms folded. The Sanzas sat near one another more out of old habit than present warmth. Their appearances were divergent; Calo with his long, oiled, well-tended tresses and Galdo scraped smooth as a prize-fighter. The twins shared no jokes, no gestures, no small talk.

'I suppose it's only fair to begin,' said Chains, 'by apologizing for having failed you all.'

'Um,' said Locke, stepping forward, 'how have you failed us, exactly?'

'My mentorship. My responsibility to not allow our happy home to turn into a seething pit of mutual aggravation ... which it has.' Chains coughed, as though he'd irritated his throat merely by bringing such words out. 'I thought I might ease up on the regimen of previous summers. Fewer lessons, fewer errands, fewer tests. I hoped that without constraints, you might blossom. Instead you've rooted yourselves deep without flowering.'

'Hold on,' said Calo, 'it hasn't been such an unwelcome break, has it? And we've been training. Jean's seen to it that we've kept up with battering one another about.'

'That's hardly your principal form of exercise these days,' said Chains. 'I've heard things from the Lilies. You two spend more time in bed than invalids. Certainly more than you spend planning or practising our work.'

'So we haven't run a game on anyone for a few weeks,' said Calo. 'Is the fuckin' Eldren-fire falling? Who gives a damn if we take some ease?

What should we be doing, sir, learning more Vadran? More dances? A seventeenth way to hold knives and forks?'

'You snot-nosed grand duke of insolence,' said Chains, growing louder with each word, 'you ignorant, wet-eared, copper-chasing shit-barge puppy! Do you have any idea what you've been given? What you've worked for? What you *are*?'

'What I am is tired of being yelled at—'

'Ten years under my roof,' said Chains, looming over Calo like an ambulatory mountain, suffused with moral indignation, 'ten years under my protection, eating at my table, nurtured by my hand and coin. Have I beaten you, buggered you, put you out in the rain?'

'No,' said Calo, cringing. 'No, of course not—'

'Then you can stand one gods-damned rebuke without flapping your jaw.'

'Of course,' said Calo, most meekly. 'Sorry.'

'You're educated thieves,' said Chains. 'No matter how you might think it profits you to feign otherwise, you are *not ordinary*. You can pass for servants, farmers, merchants, nobles; you have the poise and manners for any station. If I hadn't let you grow so callow, you might realize what an unprecedented personal freedom you all possess.'

Locke reflexively opened his mouth to deliver some smooth assuagement, but the merest half-second flick of Chains' glare was more than enough to keep him mute.

'What do you think this is all *for*?' said Chains. 'What do you suppose it's all been in aid of? So you can laze around and work the occasional petty theft? Drink and whore and dice with the other Right People until you get called out or hung? Have you *seen* what happens to our kind? How many of your bright-eyed little chums will live to see twenty-five? If they scrape thirty they're gods-damned elders. You think they have money tucked away? Villas in the country? Thieves may prosper night by night, but there's nothing for them when the lean times come, do you understand?'

'But there's *garristas*,' said Galdo, 'and the Capa, and a lot of older types at the Floating Grave—'

'Indeed,' said Chains. 'Capas and *garristas* don't go hungry, because they can take scraps from the mouths of their brothers and sisters. And how do you suppose you get to grow old in the Capa's service? You guard his doors with an alley-piece, like a constable on the beat. You watch your friends hang, and die in the gutters, and get called up for teeth lessons because they said the wrong thing in their cups or held back a few silvers one fucking time. You put your head down and shut up, forever. That's what earns you some grey hair.

'No justice,' he continued sourly. 'No true fellowship. Vows in darkness, that's all, valid until the first time someone goes hungry or needs a few coins. Why do you think I've raised you to wink at the Secret Peace? We're like a sick dog that gnaws its own entrails, the Right People are. But *you've* got a chance to live in real trust and fellowship, to be thieves as the gods intended, scourging the swells and living true to yourselves. I'll be damned before I'll let you forget what a gift you've been given in one another.'

No smart remark ever made could stand before the gale of this sort of chastisement. Locke noted that he wasn't the only one with a sudden overwhelming compulsion to stare at the floor.

'And so, I need to apologize for my own failure.' Chains drew a folded letter from his coat. 'For allowing us to reach this pretty state of affairs, falling out with one another and forgetting ourselves. It's a bad time for all of you. You're confused bundles of nerves and passion, cooped up down here where you can do maximum damage to your mutual regard. You've certainly been disagreeable company for me. I've decided I need a vacation.'

'Well then,' said Jean, 'where will you be going?'

'Going? Drinking, I suppose. Perhaps I'll go see old Maranzalla. And I've a mind to hunt down some chamber music. But forgive me if I've been unclear. I require a vacation from all of you, but I'm not leaving Camorr. You five will be making a journey to Espara. I've arranged work there to keep you busy for several months.'

'Espara?' said Locke.

'Yes. Isn't it exciting?' The room was quiet. 'I thought that might be your response. Look, I tucked a pin into my jacket for this very moment.'

Chains drew a silver pin from one of his lapels and tossed it into the air. It hit the floor with the faintest chiming clatter.

'One of those expressions I've always wanted to put to the test,' said Chains. 'But seriously, you're out. All of you. Evicted. There's a wagon caravan leaving from the Cenza Gate on Duke's Day. You've got two days to make yourselves part of it. After that, it's a week and a half to Espara.'

'But,' said Calo, 'what if we don't want to go to bloody Espara?'

'Then leave, and don't come back to this temple,' said Chains. 'Forfeit everything. In fact, leave Camorr. I won't want to see you again, anywhere.'

'What's in Espara that's so important?' said Sabetha.

'Your partnership. It's past time it was put to a real test, far beyond my reach. Take all your years of training and make something of them. False-face together, rely upon one another, and come back alive. Prove that we haven't been wasting our time down here. Prove it to me … and prove it to yourselves.'

Chains held up the folded letter.

'You're going to Espara to enjoy a career on the stage.'

4

'After my soldiering ended,' continued Chains, 'and before I came back to Camorr, I indulged in several vices, not the least of which was acting. I fell in with a troupe in Espara run by the single unluckiest thick-skulled son of a bitch that ever crawled out of a womb. Jasmer Moncraine. I saved his life by design and he saved mine by accident. We've kept in touch across the years.'

'Oh gods,' said Sabetha, 'you're sending us in payment of a debt!'

'No, no. Jasmer and I are square. The favour is mutual. I need the five of you occupied elsewhere. Jasmer has desperate need of players, and an equally desperate need to avoid paying them.'

'So it *is* questionable circumstances, then.'

'Oh, never doubt. I get the impression from his letters that he's one mistake away from being chained up for debt. I'd appreciate you preventing that. He wants to do Lucarno's *Republic of Thieves*. Your story will be that you're a band of up-and-coming thespians from Camorr; I sent a letter ahead of you telling him how to play the angles right. The rest is entirely up to you.'

'Do you have a copy of the letter for us?' said Locke.

'Nah.'

'Well, then, what should we do about—'

Chains tossed a jingling bag at Locke's head. Locke barely managed to pluck it out of the air before it struck his nose.

'Oh, look, a bag of money. That's all the help you'll be getting from me, my boy.'

'But … aliases, travel arrangements—'

'Your problem, not mine.'

'We don't know anything about the stage!'

'You know about costumes, makeup, elocution, and deportment. Everything else, you can learn once you get there.'

'But—'

'Look,' said Chains. 'I don't want to spend the rest of the day interrupting your questions, so I'm going to temporarily forget how to make words come out of my mouth. I'll be nursing a chilled bottle of Vadran white over at the Tumblehome until further notice. Remember the caravan. Two days. You can be part of it, or you can leave the Gentlemen Bastards. Your time is henceforth your own.'

He left the kitchen in a state of extreme self-satisfaction. A few moments later, Locke heard the creak and slam of the burrow's concealed river-side exit. Locke and his cohorts traded a sincere set of bewildered looks.

'Well, this is a fist-fuck and a flaming oil bath,' said Calo.

'Is there anyone here,' said Locke quietly, 'who'd rather leave the gang than go to Espara?'

'There'd better *not* be,' said Galdo.

'The billiard ball's right for once,' said Calo. 'It's not as though I'm enthusiastic about this, but anyone who wants to leave can do it headfirst off the temple roof.'

'Good,' said Locke. 'Then we need to talk. Get some ink and parchment.'

'Count the money,' said Sabetha.

'I'll fetch some wine,' said Jean. 'Strong wine.'

5

They were far from comfortable together. The Sanzas sat on opposite sides of the table, and Sabetha leaned against a chair pushed away from everyone else. Yet they all seemed to grasp the urgency of their situation; over the course of two bottles of Verrari lemon wine they hashed out mostly civil arguments and scratched up lists of supplies and responsibilities.

'Right, then,' said Locke when his glass was empty and his note-pages full. 'Sabetha will try to scare up any portions of *The Republic of Thieves* from the shops and scribes, so we can all have a look at it on the road.'

'I've got some other Lucarno plays I'll pack,' said Jean. 'And some Mercallor Mentezzo dross I'm not so fond of, but we should all study them and pick up some lines.'

'Jean and I will find a wagon and get us in with a caravan master,' said Locke. He passed one of his lists over to Galdo. 'The Sanzas will pack the common goods and supplies.'

'We need aliases,' said Sabetha. 'We can smooth out our storeys on the way, but we should have our game names ready to use.'

'Who do you want to be, then?' said Jean.

'Hmmmm. Call me ... Verena. Verena Gallante.'

'Lucaza,' said Locke. 'I'll be Lucaza ... de Barra.'

'Must you?' said Sabetha.

'Must I what?'

'You always have to choose an alias that starts with "L," and Jean nearly always goes for a "J."'

'Keeps things simple,' said Jean. 'And now, just because you've said that, I'll be ... Jovanno. Hell, Locke and I can be first cousins. I'll be Jovanno de Barra.'

'False names are fun,' said Calo. 'Call me Beefwit Smallcock.'

'These are aliases, not biographical sketches,' said Galdo.

'Fine then,' said Calo. 'Lend me a hand. There's a masculine form of Sabetha, isn't there?'

'Sabazzo,' said Galdo, snapping his fingers.

'Yeah, Sabazzo. I'll be Sabazzo.'

'Like *hell* you will,' said Sabetha.

'Hey, I know,' said Galdo. 'I'll be Jean. You can call yourself Locke.'

'You two will crap splinters for a month after I make you eat this table,' said Jean.

'Well, if you put it like that,' said Calo. 'Why don't we use our middle names? I'll be Giacomo, and you can be Castellano.'

'Might work,' said Galdo grudgingly. 'Need a last name.'

'*Asino!*' said Calo. 'It's Throne Therin for "donkey."'

'Gods lend me strength,' said Sabetha.

6

'Master de Barra,' said Anatoly Vireska two nights later, looking up with a smile that put every gap in his teeth on display, like archery ports in a crumbling fortress wall. The rangy, middle-aged Vadran caravan master gave the Gentlemen Bastards' wagon a friendly thump as Jean brought their team of four horses to a halt. 'And company. You picked a good time to show up.'

'I've seen this place when it's busy.' Locke glanced backward at the Millfalls District and the Street of Seven Wheels, which lay under the strange particoloured haze of fading Falselight. Traffic on the cobbled road itself was sparse, since few business travellers came or went from the Cenza Gate as darkness was falling. 'Figured we might get a jump on the chaos.'

'Just so. Pull up anywhere in the commons beneath the wall. Now, if you want more than half-assed shelter, there's the Andrazi stable down the lane to the right, and the Umbolo stable just yonder, the one with all the mules. Andrazi tips me a few coppers a week to point people her way, but I wouldn't take the money if I didn't think her place was the better bargain, hey?'

'Duly noted,' said Jean.

'Want me to send a boy around to help with your horses? I could have my outfitter check your packing, too.'

'I'm sure we're fine, thanks,' said Locke.

'Glad to hear it. Just so we're clear, though, my guards don't stand to duty until we line up all our ducklings tomorrow morning. As long as we're behind walls, your security is your own business. Given that you're bedding down twenty yards from a watch barracks, I wouldn't lose any sleep over it.'

'Nor shall we.' Jean waved farewell, and convinced the horses to take them into the shadow of Camorr's walls. Rickety overhanging panels topped about a hundred yards worth of barren common space in the lee of the wall, where those unwilling or unable to pay for service at the commercial stables could pull in. Sabetha, Calo, and Galdo piled out of the back of the open-topped wagon as it rolled to a stop.

'One quarter of a mile down, a mere two hundred to go,' said Locke. The humid air was heavy with the smells of old hay, animal sweat, and droppings. Other travellers were lighting lanterns, laying out bedrolls, and starting cooking fires; there were at least a dozen wagon parties stopped beside the wall. Locke wondered idly how many of them were bound for Espara as part of Vireska's caravan.

'Let's get you fixed up for the night, boys.' Jean hopped down from the wagon and gave a reassuring pat to the flank of the nearest cart-horse. Jean had spent several months in the role of a teamster's apprentice two years earlier, and had assumed responsibility for driving and tending their animals without complaint. The team represented a significant portion of the money Chains had given them, but could be resold in Espara to flesh out their temporarily thinned finances.

'Sweep beneath the wagon, would you, Giacomo?' said Galdo. 'Don't want turds for pillows.'

'Sweep it your fuckin' self, *Castellano*,' said Calo. 'Nobody put you in charge.'

'Mind yourself,' whispered Sabetha, grabbing Calo by the arm. 'We've got ten days on the road ahead of us. Do they have to be a miserable trial for no good reason?'

'I'm not his damn valet,' said Calo.

'That's right.' Locke stepped between the Sanzas, thinking quickly. 'None of us are. We'll share sweeping duties, all of us. Calo starts tonight—'

'I'm Giacomo.'

'Right, sorry. Giacomo starts tonight. Other brother when we stop tomorrow. I'll take the night after that, and so on. A fair rotation. Good enough?'

'I can live with it,' muttered Calo. 'I'm not afraid to get my hands dirty. Just won't have him putting on airs.'

Locke ground his teeth together. The Sanzas had spent the last several months steadily discarding their old habits of synchronicity in action and appearance. They took pains to distinguish themselves from one another, and their differences in grooming were the merest outward flourishes of the phenomenon. Locke would never have begrudged the twins an individualistic phase, but their timing was awkward as hell, and their ongoing spats were like fresh wood heaped on an already rising fire.

'Look,' said Locke, realizing that the gang's mechanisms of fellowship needed oiling rather badly, 'with so many taverns close at hand, I don't see any need for us to torture ourselves with boiled beef and bag water. I'll fetch us something more pleasing.'

'We have the coin for that sort of luxury?' said Sabetha.

'I might have cut a purse or two while I was out this morning. Just for the sake of, ah, financial flexibility.' Locke shuffled his feet and cleared his throat. 'You want to come with?'

'You need me to?'

'Well ... I'd like you to.'

'Hmmm.'

She stared at him for a few seconds, during which Locke experienced the curious sensation of his heart apparently sinking several inches deeper into his chest. Then she shrugged.

'I suppose.'

They left Jean with the horses, Galdo watching their supplies, and Calo gingerly cleaning the ground beneath the wagon. There was a well-lit tavern at the end of the lane beside the wall, just past the Andrazi stable, and by unspoken mutual consent they headed toward it in the gathering darkness. Locke stole a glance at Sabetha as they walked.

Her tightly-bound hair was further packed beneath a close-fitting linen cap, and all of her clothing was long and loose, disguising her curves. It was the sort of dress a prudent, mild, and unassertive young woman would choose for the road, and as such it suited Sabetha not at all. Still, she wore it as well as anyone could, as far as Locke's eyes were concerned.

'I was, ah, hoping I could talk to you,' he said.

'Easily done,' said Sabetha. 'Open your mouth and let words come out.'

'I – Look, can you not … can you please not be glib with me?'

'Requesting miracles now, are we?' Sabetha looked down and kicked a stone out of her path. 'Look, I'm sorry. Contemplating ten days stuck together on the road. And the brothers being … you know. The whole thing has me feeling like a hedgehog, rolled up with my spikes out. Can't help myself.'

'Oh, a hedgehog is absolutely the *last* thing I would ever compare you to,' said Locke with a laugh.

'Interesting,' said Sabetha, 'that I mention my own feelings, and you seem to think that what I'm after is reassurance concerning your perceptions.'

'But …' Locke felt another knot in his chest. Conversations with Sabetha always seemed to call his attention to malfunctioning internal mysteries he hadn't previously known he possessed. 'Look, come on, do you have to *dissect* everything I say, pin it up like an anatomist and sift through it?'

'First I'm too glib, now I'm cutting too fine. Surely you should be pleased to be receiving such close attention to what you're actually saying?'

'You know,' said Locke, feeling his hands shake nervously with the thought of what he was about to put in the open, 'you *know* that when I'm around you I find it very easy to shove my foot into my mouth. Sometimes both feet. And you do see it.'

'Mmmmm,' she said.

'More than that. You make use of the advantage.'

'I do.' She looked at him strangely. 'You fancy me.'

'That,' said Locke, feeling thunderstruck, 'that is … really … not how I would have …'

'Not as grand in plain speech as it is up here?' She tapped her forehead.

'Sabetha, I … I value your good opinion more than anything in the world. It kills me not to have it. It kills me not to know *whether* I have it. We've lived together all these years, and still there's this fog between us. I don't know what I did to put it there, but I would throw myself under a cart to lift it, believe me.'

'Why do you assume it's something *you've* done, and something you can undo at will? I'm not some arithmetic problem just waiting for you to show your work properly, Locke. Did you ever think that I might … gods, you've got me stumbling now. That I might be actively contributing to this … to our awkwardness?'

'Actively contributing?'

'Yes, as though I might have warm-blooded motives of my own, being as I'm not an oil painting, or some other decorative object of desire—'

'Do you like me?' said Locke, shocked at himself for blurting the question out. It was an invitation to have his heart laid out and smashed on an anvil, and there were a thousand things she could say that would do the hammer's work. 'At all? Do I ever please you with my company? Am I at least preferable to an empty room?'

'There are times when the empty room is a sore temptation.'

'But—'

'Of course I *like* you,' she said, raising her hands as though to touch him reassuringly. She didn't complete the gesture. 'You can be clever, and enterprising, and charming, though rarely all three at once. And … I do sometimes admire you, if it helps you to hear it.'

'It means everything to hear it,' he said, feeling the tightness in his chest turn to buoyant warmth. 'It's worth a thousand embarrassments, just to hear it. Because … because I feel the same way. About you.'

'You don't feel the same way about me,' she said.

'Oh, but I do,' he said. 'Without qualifying remarks, even.'

'That's—'

'Hey there!'

A polished club came down on Locke's shoulder, a gentle tap, yet impossible to ignore. The club was attached to a heavyset man in the leather harness and mustard-yellow coat of the city watch, attended by a younger comrade carrying a lantern on a pole.

'You're in the middle of a lane,' said the big yellowjacket, 'not a bloody drawing-room. Move it elsewhere.'

'Oh, of course, sir,' said Locke in one of his better respectable-citizen voices (this constable, not being agitated, didn't require the use of Locke's very best). He and Sabetha moved off the lane and into the shadows beneath the wall, where fireflies sketched pale green arcs against the darkness.

'No one thinks of anyone else without *qualifying remarks*,' said Sabetha. 'I love Chains dearly, and still he and I have ... disappointed one another. I'll always be fond of the Sanzas, but right now I wish they'd go away for a year. And you—'

'I've frustrated you, I know.'

'And I've returned the favour.' She did touch him now, gently, on his upper left arm, and it took most of his self-control not to jump out of his shoes. 'Nobody admires anyone else without qualification. If they do they're after an image, not a person.'

'Well,' said Locke, 'in that case, I harbour a great many resentments, reservations, and suspicions about you. Does that please you better?'

'You're trying to be charming again,' she said softly, 'but I choose not to be charmed, Locke Lamora. Not with things as they stand.'

'Can I make amends for whatever I've done to frustrate you?'

'That's ... complicated.'

'I like to think that I take hints as well as anyone,' said Locke. 'Why not throw some at my head?'

'Going to be a lot of time to kill between here and Espara, I suppose.'

'Can we ... speak again tomorrow night? After we've stopped?'

'The gentleman requests the favour of a personal engagement, tomorrow evening?'

'At the lady's pleasure, before the dancing and iced wine, immediately following the grand sweep beneath the wagon for stray horseshit.'

'I may consent.'

'Then life is worth living.'

'Don't be a dunce,' she said. 'We should do our business at the tavern and get back before the Sanzas try to sneak off to the Guilded Lilies one last time.'

They came away from the tavern with cold boiled chicken, olives, black bread, and two skins of yellow wine with a flavour somewhere between turpentine and wasp piss. Simple as it was, the meal was ducal indulgence compared to the salted meat and hardtack waiting in crates on the back of their wagon. They ate in silence, distracted by the sight of the Five Towers shining in the oncoming night, and by hungry insects.

Jean volunteered to sit first watch (no Camorri ever born, least of all one who'd made it out of Shades' Hill, would blithely trust to providence even in the literal shadow of a city watch barracks). After acknowledging this noble sacrifice, the other four curled up beneath the wagon, sweaty and mosquito-plagued, to bed down.

It occurred to Locke that this was technically the first time he and Sabetha had ever slept together in any sense of the term, even if they were separated by nothing less than a complete pair of Sanza twins.

'We crawl before we walk,' he sighed to himself. 'We walk before we run.'

'Hey,' whispered Galdo, who was curled against his back, 'you don't fart in your sleep, do you?'

'How would you be able to detect a fart over your natural odour, Sanza?'

'For shame,' said Galdo. 'There's no Sanzas here, remember? I'm an Asino.'

'Oh yes,' said Locke with a yawn. 'Yes, you certainly are.'

Chapter Five
The Five-Year Game: Starting Position

'Sabetha's in Karthain,' said Locke.

'She could hardly do the job from elsewhere,' said Patience.

'Sabetha. My Sabetha—'

'I marvel at such a confident assertion of possession.'

'*Our* Sabetha, then. *The* Sabetha. How do you people know so gods-damned much about my life? How did you find her?'

'I didn't,' said Patience. 'Nor do I know how it was done. All I know is that her instructions and resources will mirror your own.'

'Except she has a head start,' said Jean, easing Locke back into his chair. The expression on Locke's face was that of a prize fighter who'd just received a proper thunderbolt to the chin.

'And she's working alone,' said Patience, 'whereas you two have one another. So one might hope that her positional advantage will be purely temporary. Or is she really that much of a tiger, to set you both quaking?'

'I'm not quaking,' said Locke quietly. 'It's just ... so gods-damned unexpected.'

'You've always hoped for a reunion, haven't you?'

'On my own terms,' said Locke. 'Does she know that it's us she's up against? Did she know before she took the job?'

'Yes,' said Patience.

'Your opposition, they didn't do anything to her?'

'As far as I'm aware, she required no compulsion.'

'This is hard to take,' said Locke. 'Gentlemen Bastards, well, we trained against one another, and we've quarrelled, obviously, but we've never, ah, never actually opposed one another, not for real.'

'Given that she's completely removed herself from your company for so many years now,' said Patience, 'how can you believe that she still considers herself part of your gang?'

'*Thank you* for that, Patience,' growled Jean. 'Do you have anything else for us? If not, I think we need to—'

'Yes, I'm sure you do. The cabin is yours.'

She withdrew. Locke put his head in his hands and sighed.

'I don't expect life to make sense,' he said after a few moments, 'but it would certainly be pleasant if it would stop kicking us in the balls.'

'Don't you want to see her again?'

'Of course I want to see her again!' said Locke. 'I *always* meant to find her. I meant to do it in Camorr; I meant to do it after we'd made a big score in Tal Verrar. I just – You know how it's all gone. She's not going to be impressed.'

'Maybe she *wants* to see you,' said Jean. 'Maybe she leapt at the chance when the Bondsmagi approached her. Maybe she'd already tried to hunt us down.'

'Gods, what if she did? I wonder what she made of the mess we left behind in Camorr. I just can't believe … working against her. Those *bastards!*'

'Hey, we're just supposed to fix an election,' said Jean. 'Nobody's going to hurt her, least of all us.'

'I hope,' said Locke, brightening. 'I hope … damn, I have no idea what to hope.' He spent a few minutes nibbling at his food in a nervous daze, while Jean sipped his warm red plonk.

'I do know this,' Locke said at last. 'On the business side of things, we're already in the shit.'

'Up to our elbows,' said Jean.

'Given a choice, I would have grudged her a ten-minute head start, let alone a few days.'

'Makes me think back to when Chains used to play you two off one another,' said Jean. 'All those arguments … all those stalemates. Then more arguments.'

'Don't think I don't remember.' Locke tapped a piece of biscuit distractedly against the table. 'Well, hell. It's been five years. Maybe she's learned to lose gracefully. Maybe she's out of practice.'

'Maybe trained monkeys will climb out of my ass and pour me a glass of Austershalin brandy,' said Jean.

2

Dawn over the Amathel, the next morning. A hazy golden-orange ribbon rose from the eastern horizon, and the calm dark waters mirrored the cobalt sky. A dozen fishing boats were moving past the *Sky-Reacher* in a swarm, their triangular white wakes giving the small craft the appearance of arrowheads passing in dreamlike slow motion. Karthain itself was coming up to larboard, not half a mile away.

From the quarterdeck, Jean could see the clean white terraces of the city, bulwarked with thick rows of olive and cypress and witchwood trees, misted with a silver morning fog that gave him an unexpected pang for Camorr. A blocky stone lighthouse dominated the city's waterfront, though at the moment its great golden lanterns were banked down so that their glow was no more than a warm aura crowning the tower.

Locke leaned against the taffrail, staring at the approaching city, eating cold beef and hard white cheese he'd piled awkwardly into his right hand. Locke had paced the great cabin most of the night, unable or unwilling to sleep, settling into his hammock only to rest his unsteady legs.

'How do you feel?' Patience, wrapped in a long coat and shawl, chose not to appear out of thin air, but approached them on foot.

'Ill-used,' said Locke.

'At least you're alive to feel that way.'

'No need to drop hints. You'll get your command performance out of us, never worry about that.'

'I wasn't worried,' she said sweetly. 'Here comes our dock detail.'

'Dock detail?' Jean glanced past Patience and saw a long, low double-banked boat rowed by twenty people approaching behind the last of the fishing boats.

'To bring the *Sky-Reacher* in,' said Patience, 'and mind her lines and sails and other tedious articles.'

'Not in the mood to wiggle your fingers and square everything away?' said Locke.

'One of the few things that we agree upon, exceptionalists and conservatives alike, is that our arts don't exist for the sake of swabbing decks.'

The dock detail came aboard at the ship's waist, a very ordinary-looking pack of sailors. Patience beckoned for Locke and Jean to follow her as two of the newcomers took the wheel.

'I do assume you're carrying your hatchets, Jean? And all of the documents I gave you?'

'Of course.'

'Then you shouldn't mind going ashore immediately.'

She led them to the *Sky-Reacher*'s larboard waist, where Jean could see four sailors still waiting in the boat. It was an easy trip down the boarding net, just seven or eight feet. Even Locke made it without mishap, and then Patience, who evidently required a hoist only when gravity wasn't on her side.

'Some of your people are waiting on the pier,' she said as she settled onto a rowing bench. 'They're all sensible of the urgency of the situation.'

'Our people?' said Locke.

'As of now, they're entirely *your* people. The arrangement of their affairs is in your hands.'

'And they'll just do as we say? To what extent?'

'To a *reasonable* extent, Locke. Nobody will fling themselves into the lake at your whim, but you two are now the de facto heads of the Deep Roots party's election apparatus. Functionaries will take your orders. Candidates will kiss your boots.'

The sailors pushed them away from the *Sky-Reacher* and pulled for the lantern-lit waterfront.

'This is the Ponta Corbessa,' said Patience, gesturing ahead. 'The city wharf. I take it neither of you knows much about this place?'

'Our former plan was to avoid Karthain, uh, *forever*,' said Jean.

'Your new associates will acquaint you with everything. Give it a few days and you'll be very comfortable, I'm sure.'

'Hrm,' said Locke.

'Speaking of comfort, there is one last thing I should mention.'

'And that is?' said Locke.

'You will of course be free to communicate with Sabetha in whatever fashion she allows, but collusion will not be acceptable. You are opponents. You will oppose and be opposed, without quarter. We're paying you to see a contest. Disappoint us in that regard and I can assure you, not getting paid will be the least of your worries.'

'Give the threats a rest,' said Locke. 'You'll get your gods-damned contest.'

The longboat drew up against a stone quay. Jean clambered out of the boat and heaved Locke up after him, then grudgingly offered his arm to Patience. She took it with a nod.

They were in the shadow of the lighthouse now, on a stretch of cobbled waterfront backed by warehouses and shuttered shops. A sparse forest of masts rose behind the buildings – probably some sort of lagoon, Jean thought, where ships could rest in safety. The area was strangely deserted, save for a small group of people standing beside a carriage.

'Patience, said Jean, 'what should we— Ah, hell!'

Patience had vanished. The sailors in the longboat pushed off without a word and headed back toward the *Sky-Reacher*.

'Bitch knows how to make an exit,' said Locke. He popped the last of his meat and cheese into his mouth and wiped his hands on his tunic.

'Excuse me!' A heavyset young man in a grey brocade coat broke from the group at the carriage. 'You must be Masters Callas and Lazari!'

'We must,' said Jean, flashing a friendly smile. 'Pray give us a moment.'

'Oh,' said the man, who possessed the true Karthani accent, which was something like the speech of a Lashani after a few strong drinks. 'Of course.'

'Now,' said Jean quietly, turning to Locke, 'who are we?'

'A pair of rats about to stick their noses into a big fucking trap.'

'Characters, you git. Lazari and Callas. We should settle the particulars before we start talking to people.'

'Ah, right.' Locke scratched his chin. 'We've got no time to practise Karthani accents, so to hell with hiding that we're from out of town.'

'Less work suits me,' said Jean.

'Good. Then we need to decide who's the iron fist and who's the velvet glove.'

'Sounds like something you should be hiring a couple of strumpets to help you with.'

'I'd hit you if I thought it would do any good, Jean. You know what I mean.'

'Right. Let's be obvious. Me brute, you weasel.'

'Agreed. You brute, me charming mastermind. But there's no sense in setting things too taut before we even know who we're dealing with. Be a brute that plays nice until provoked.'

'So we're not actually playing characters at all, then?'

'Well, hell.' Locke cracked his knuckles and shrugged. 'It's one less detail for us to muck up. Anyway, Patience said these people would eat out of our hands. Let's put that to the test.'

'Now then,' said Jean, turning back to the heavyset young man. 'Start talking again.'

'I'm delighted to see you alive and well, gentlemen!' The stranger came closer, and Jean noted his round, ruddy features, the look of a man eager to please and be pleased. And yet his eyes, behind slender optics, were shrewd and measuring. His hair had failed to retain any sort of hold on the areas forward of his ears, but he had a thick and well-tended plait that hung, black as a raven's wing, to the small of his back. 'When we heard about the wreck, we were distraught. The Amathel is lately so mild, it's hard to credit—'

'Wreck,' said Locke. '*Ah*, yes, the wreck! Yes. The terrible, convenient wreck. What else could compel us to be here without decent clothing or purses? Well, I'm afraid everything happened in such a terrible rush, but I'm told that we survived.'

'Ha! Splendid. Fear nothing, gentlemen, I'm here to mend your situation in every particular. My name is Nikoros.'

'Sebastian Lazari.' Locke extended his hand. Nikoros shook it with a look of surprise on his face.

'Tavrin Callas,' said Jean. Nikoros' grip was dry and firm.

'Well, I say, thank you, gentlemen, thank you! What an unexpected mark of confidence. I take it very kindly.'

'Mark of confidence?' said Locke. 'Forgive us, Nikoros. We're new to Karthain. I'm not sure we understand what we've done.'

'Oh,' said Nikoros. 'Damned stupid of me. I apologize. It's just that … well, you'll probably think us such a pack of credulous ninnies, but I assure you … it's tradition. Here in Karthain we're close, *extremely* close, with our given names. On account of, you know, the Presence.'

It was easy enough for Jean to hear the capital 'P' as Nikoros pronounced the word.

'You mean,' he said, 'the Bonds—'

'Yes, the magi of the Isas Scholastica. When we speak of "the Presence," well – we're just being polite. We're quite used to them, really. They're not the objects of, ah, curiosity they might be elsewhere. In fact, I can assure you they look almost like ordinary people. You'd be amazed!'

'I don't doubt it,' said Locke. 'Well, this is useful stuff. I take it we should withhold our given names when we're introduced to Karthani?'

'Well, yes. It's the hoariest old superstition, but it's been our custom since the fall of the old Throne. Most of us use birth-order titles or nicknames. I'm called Nikoros Via Lupa, since my office is on the Avenue of the Wolves. But plain Nikoros suits as well.'

'We're obliged to you,' said Jean. 'Now, what is it that you do, exactly?'

'I'm a trade insurer. Ships and caravans. But, ah, more relevantly, I'm on the Deep Roots party standing committee. I'm sort of a shepherd for party business.'

'You have real authority over party affairs?'

'Oh, quite. Funds and operations, with some latitude. But, ah, when it comes to that, gentlemen, my most important duty is to carry out your instructions. Once I've helped you settle in, of course.'

'And you understand the nature of our employment,' said Locke. 'The *real* nature of it, that is.'

'Oh, oh, quite.' Nikoros tapped the side of his nose with a finger several times and smiled. 'Those of us at the top understand that half the fight is, well, unconventional. We're all for it! After all, the Black Iris are out to do the same to us. We think they might even bring in specialists like yourselves.'

'Be assured they have,' said Locke. 'How long have you been involved with all this?'

'Party business, you mean? Oh, ten years or so. It's the biggest thing going, socially. More fun than billiards. I worked with our, ah, specialist last election. We pulled off nine seats, and nearly won! We have such hopes, this time around.'

'Well,' said Jean, 'the sooner we're settled in, the sooner we can nourish those hopes.'

'Right! To the carriage. We'll get you two wrapped up in something more suitable.' He beckoned, and a slender blonde woman in a black velvet jacket met them halfway as they moved toward the carriage. 'Allow me to present Seconddaughter Morenna, Morenna Clothiers.'

'Your servant.' She curtsied, and a brass-weighted measuring line appeared in her hands as swiftly as an assassin's knife. 'It seems you have a sartorial emergency.'

'Yes,' said Locke. 'Circumstance has flung us down and danced upon us.'

'Clothes first,' said Nikoros as he hustled Locke and Jean into the enclosed carriage box, 'then we'll see to your funds.' Morenna came last. Nikoros drew the door shut and pounded on the underside of the carriage roof. As it rattled off, Morenna seized the collar of Locke's slop jacket and pulled him firmly to a hunched-over standing position.

'I beg your deepest pardon,' she muttered, plying her measuring line around his neck and shoulders. 'We usually keep a fellow on hand at the shop to take the measurements of our gentlemen customers, but he's taken ill. I assure you that I make these intrusions as impersonally as a physiker.'

'It would never occur to me to be offended,' said Locke in a dazed voice.

'Marvellous. If you'll excuse me, sir, we'll just need to have your jacket off.' She somehow managed to fold, wrench, and twirl Locke within the confined space, removing his jacket at last and causing a small rain of twice-baked ship's biscuits to patter around the carriage interior. 'Oh my, I had no idea—'

'Not your fault,' said Locke with an embarrassed cough. 'I, uh, like to feed birds.'

Under his arms, around his chest, along the outside of his legs – Morenna took measurements from Locke with the speed of a fencer scoring touches. Soon it was Jean's turn.

'Same thing, sir,' she muttered while she fussed with his coat.

'There's no need – If you'll give me a moment—' said Jean, but it was too late.

'Heavens,' said Morenna as she pulled his hatchets out of their make-shift hiding place at the small of his back. 'These have seen some use.'

'I've had to settle the occasional misunderstanding.'

'Do you prefer to carry them tucked away like this under a coat or jacket?'

'There's nowhere better.'

'Then I can show you several rigs that could be stitched into your coats. We've got leather harness, cloth straps, metal rings, all reliable and discreet. Tuck a whole arsenal into your breeches and waistcoats, if you like.'

'You're my new favourite tailor,' said Jean, contentedly submitting to the darting play of the measuring line while the carriage rolled along.

3

Their journey took about ten minutes, while the sun rose and painted the walls and alleys around them with warm light. Jean took advantage of his window seat to form several impressions of Karthain along the way.

The first was that it was a city of tiered heights. As they moved inward from the waterfront, past the ship-filled lagoon, he saw that the more northerly sections of the city rose, hills and terraces alike, to a sort of plateau that must have been several hundred feet above the Ponta Corbessa. Nothing so extreme as Tal Verrar's precipitous drops, but it did seem as though the gods or the Eldren had tilted the city about forty-five degrees toward the water after originally laying it out.

Furthermore, it seemed to be an unusually well-tended place. Perhaps Nikoros had chosen a route that would best flatter his city? Whatever the case, Jean couldn't fail to note the swept streets, the clean white stone of the newer houses, the neatly trimmed trees, the smooth bubbling of every fountain and waterfall, or the decorative enamel mosaics on the cable cars sliding between the taller buildings.

Most striking was the character of the city's Elderglass. Its bridges over the wide Karvanu (which poured down five separate white-foaming falls before it reached the heart of the city) were not solid arches, but rather suspension bridges made of thousands of panels of milky black Elderglass, connected by countless finger-thick lengths of glass cable to supporting towers like spindly caricatures of human temple spires.

The first bridge they crossed had a disconcerting amount of sway and bounce – just a few inches of give, to be sure, but any bounce at all was of immediate interest to someone high over water in a carriage.

'Never fear,' said Nikoros, noticing the matching expressions on Locke and Jean's faces. 'You'll be used to this in no time. It's Elderglass! Nothing we do could so much as fray a cable.'

Jean stared at the other huge bridges spanning the Karvanu. They looked like the work of mad giant spiders, or harps designed for hands the size of palaces. He also noticed, for the first time, a strangely tuneful humming and creaking that he assumed was the music of the cables.

'Welcome to the Isas Salvierro,' said Nikoros when the carriage halted a few minutes later, blessedly back on unyielding stone. 'A business district, one of the pumping hearts of the city. My office is just north of here.'

The small group bustled out of the carriage and into Morenna Clothiers, where they found a wide shop floor surrounded by a raised second-floor gallery. Seconddaughter Morenna locked the door behind them.

'These aren't our usual hours,' she said. 'You're an emergency case.'

There was a strong smell of coffee wafting throughout the shop, and Jean's mouth watered. The walls of the lower room were layered with bolts of cloth in a hundred different colours and textures, while several wooden racks of coats and jackets had been brought out into the middle of the floor.

'Allow me to introduce Firstdaughter Morenna,' said Seconddaughter, pointing to a taller, heavier blonde woman on the upper level, who was pulling a gleaming metallic thread from a rattling clockwork spindle. 'And of course our darling Thirddaughter.'

The youngest of the tailoring sisters was as petite as Seconddaughter, though her hair was a shade darker and she alone of the three wore optics. She was absorbed in trimming some unknown velvet bundle with a pair of blackened-iron shears, and she gave the merest nod in greeting.

'Thimbles on, girls, it's time for battle,' said Seconddaughter.

'My,' said Firstdaughter, who stepped away from her machine and descended to the first floor. 'Shipwreck, was it? You gentlemen look like you've been in the wars. Is Lashain having some sort of difficulty?'

'Lashain is its old charming self, madam,' said Locke. 'Our misfortune was personal.'

'You've come to the right place. We adore a challenge. And we adorn the challenged! Second, have you taken their measurements?'

'Everything I could in decency.' Seconddaughter snatched up a slate, and with a squeaky piece of chalk scribed two columns of numbers on it. She threw the slate to Firstdaughter. 'Save for breeches inseams. Could you be a dear?'

Firstdaughter conjured a measuring line in her free hand and advanced on Locke and Jean without hesitation. 'Now, gentlemen, our male apprentice is out sick, so you'll need to bear my scrutiny a moment. Take heart, there's many a wife that won't give her husband this sort of attention for love or money.' Chuckling, she took rapid and mostly professional measurements from crotch to ankles on both men, then added some squiggles to the bottom of the slate.

'I assume that we're replacing an entire wardrobe?' said Thirddaughter, setting her velvet down.

'Yes,' said Locke. 'These fine dishrags represent the sum of our current wardrobe.'

'You've the sound of an easterner,' said Thirddaughter. 'Will you want the style to which you're accustomed, or something more—'

'Local,' said Jean. 'Absolutely local. Fit us out like natives.'

'It will take several days,' said Seconddaughter, holding a swatch of something brown up to Jean's neck and frowning, 'to deliver all the bespoke work, you understand, and that's with us chugging along like water-engines. But while we're arranging that, we can set you up with something respectable enough.'

'We don't do boots, though,' said Firstdaughter, stripping Jean's jacket and sending his hatchets clattering to the floor. 'Oh, dear. Will you be wanting somewhere to tuck those?'

'Absolutely,' said Jean.

'We've got a thousand ways,' said First. She picked up the Wicked Sisters and set them respectfully on a table. 'But as I was saying, Nikoros, we haven't turned cobblers in the last few hours. Have you kept that in mind?'

'Of course,' said Nikoros. 'This is but the first stop. I'll have them set up like royalty before lunch.'

The next half hour was a furious storm of fittings, removals, tests, measurements, remeasurements, suggestions, counter-suggestions, and sisterly arguments as Locke and Jean were gradually peeled out of their slops and reskinned as fair approximations of gentlemen. The creamy silk shirts were a little too big, the vests and breeches taken in or let out with some haste. Locke's long coat hung loose and Jean's was tight across the chest. Still, it was a drastic improvement, at least from the ankles up. Now they could set foot in a countinghouse without provoking the guards into raising weapons.

Once the immediate transmutation was accomplished, the three women took notes for a more expansive wardrobe – evening coats, morning jackets, formal and informal waistcoats, breeches in half a dozen styles, velvet doublets, fitted silk shirts, and all the trimmings.

'Now, you said you'd be doing more, ah, entertaining, as it were,' said Thirddaughter to Locke. 'So I gather you'll need a slightly wider selection of coats than your friend Master Callas.'

'Entirely correct,' said Jean, rolling his arms around and enjoying his restoration to a state of elegance, tight coat or no. 'Besides, I'm the careful one. I can make do with less. Give my friend a bit more of your attention.'

'As you will,' said Thirddaughter, gently but firmly grabbing Jean by his left cuff. A long dangling thread had caught her attention; she had her shears out with a graceful twirl and snipped it in the blink of an eye. 'There. Squared away. I believe, then, we'll start with seven coats for Master Lazari, and give you four.'

'We'll send them to your inn as we finish them,' said Firstdaughter, tallying figures on a new slate. These figures had nothing to do with Locke and Jean's measurements. She passed the slate to Nikoros, and when he nodded curtly her pleasure was readily apparent.

'Lovely,' said Locke. 'Except we don't know where we're staying just yet.'

'The Deep Roots party does,' said Nikoros with a half-bow. 'You're in our bosom now, sirs. You'll want for nothing. Now, might I beg you to come along, just a few steps up the lane? Those bare feet will never do for lunch or dinner.'

4

The next two hours of the morning were spent, as Nikoros had prophesied, scuttling up and down the streets of the Isas Salvierro in pursuit of boots, shoes, jewelry, and every last detail that would help Locke and Jean pass as men of real account. Several of the shops involved had not yet opened for regular business, but the force of Nikoros' connections and pocketbook unlocked every door.

As their list of immediate needs grew shorter, Jean noticed that Locke was spending more and more time eyeballing the alleys, windows, and rooftops around them.

Behaviour very obvious, he signalled.

Threat gods-damned serious, was the reply.

And despite himself, despite personal experience that one of the least intelligent things to do, when you fear being spied upon, is to crane your head in all directions and advertise your suspicion, Jean did just that. As the carriage rattled toward Tivoli's countinghouse, he stole fretful glances out his window.

Sabetha. Gods below, he couldn't imagine a more troublesome foe. Not only had he and Locke set foot in a city where their presence was expected, she knew precisely how they worked. That was true in reverse, to some extent, but all the same he felt like they were just leaving the starting mark in a race that had been going on without them for some time.

'Think she'll hit us early?' said Jean.

'She's hitting us as we speak,' muttered Locke. 'We just don't know where yet.'

'Gentlemen,' said Nikoros, who was working to keep the pile of parcels on the seat next to him from toppling onto the compartment floor at every turn, 'what's troubling you?'

'Our opposition,' said Locke. 'The Black Iris people. Is there a woman that you know of, a new woman, only recently arrived?'

'The redheaded woman, you mean?' said Nikoros. 'Is she important?'

'She—' Locke seemed to think better of whatever he was about to say. 'She's our problem. Don't tell anyone we asked, but keep your ears open.'

'We haven't identified her yet,' said Nikoros. 'She's not Karthani.'

'No,' said Locke. 'She's not. Do you have any idea where she is?'

'I could show you a few coffeehouses and taverns run by Black Iris members. Not to mention the Sign of the Black Iris itself. They got their name from that place. If I had to guess, I'd look for her there.'

'I'll want a list of all those places,' said Locke. 'Get me the name of every business, every inn, every hole in the wall connected with the Iris people. Write them down. I'll have paper sent out to you while we're in Tivoli's.'

'I fancy I can give you something useful off the top of my head. Do you want something more complete, later? I have membership lists, property lists …'

'I'll want it all,' said Locke. 'Make copies. Do you have a scribe you trust, really trust?'

'I have a bonded scrivener I've used forever,' said Nikoros. 'He votes Deep Roots.'

'Have the poor bastard cancel his life for a day or two,' said Locke. 'Pay him whatever he asks. I assume you can tug on the party's purse strings at will?'

'Well, yes—'

'Good, because that teat is about to be milked. Have your scribe copy everything important. Everything. Anything election-related goes to us. Anything personal goes to your countinghouse vault.'

'But, why—'

'For the next month and a half, I expect you to behave as though your office is in danger of burning down at any moment.'

'But surely they wouldn't …'

'Nothing is off the table. Nothing! Got it?'

'If you insist.'

'Maybe we'll have a meeting with the opposition sooner or later,' said Locke. 'Set some rules. Until then, a bad accident is a near-certainty. I know if I could get at someone like you on the Black Iris side, turn their papers into ash, I'd be sorely tempted.'

'I can give you names—'

'Write them down,' said Locke. 'Write them all down. You're going to be tasting ink with your lunch, I'm afraid.'

5

Tivoli's countinghouse was a classic of its type, a perfect cross between inviting extravagance and blatant intimidation.

Locke admired the building. The narrow windows, like fortress embrasures, were girded with iron bars, and the shelves beneath the windows were cement blocks studded with broken glass. The exterior walls (all four of them, for the three-storey building stood alone on a hard-packed dirt courtyard) were painted with well-executed frescoes of fat, infinitely content Gandolo blessing account books, scales, and stacks of coin. The alchemical resin used to protect these images from the weather gave the walls a faint gleam, and Locke knew from personal experience it also made them devilishly hard to climb.

The interior smelled of mellow incense. Golden lanterns hung in niches, casting a warm, inviting light except where pillars and drapes contrived to create equally inviting pools of shadow. To either side behind the main doors, guards sat on stools in gated alcoves, and a quick glance up confirmed that there was a tastefully concealed portcullis ready to be dropped, if not by the guards or bankers then by hidden watchers behind the walls.

There was no chance of robbing such a place on a whim, nor with anything less than a dozen armed and ready types, and even that was more likely to earn a bloodbath than a fortune. The shrine-like inviolability of houses like this was actually as necessary to those in the criminal line as it was to any honest citizen. There was no point in stealing well or wisely if the loot couldn't be stashed somewhere safe.

'I see Nikoros in the carriage outside,' said a woman who emerged from behind a painted screen. She was about forty, dark-skinned, with chestnut hair bound beneath a black silk skullcap. Her right eye was clouded, and she wore a pair of optics from which the corresponding lens had been removed. 'You must be the political gentlemen.'

'Callas and Lazari,' said Jean.

'Singular Tivoli, gentlemen. Your servant.'

'Singular?' said Locke.

'More elegant than "Only Tivoli," I find, and far more sociable than "Solitary Tivoli." You have some documents?'

Locke handed over the papers they'd been given by Patience. Tivoli barely glanced at them before she nodded.

'Private credit for three thousand each,' she said. 'Scratched these up myself a few days ago. Do you want to draw any of it?'

'Yes,' said Jean. 'Can you give us fifty apiece?'

That was adequate pocket money, thought Locke. Half a pound of Karthani ducats each. He turned the sum into Camorri crowns in his head, and idly reflected on what it could get him: a small company of mercenaries for several months, half-a-dozen outstanding horses, twice as many adequate ones, plain food and lodging for years … not that he'd have any reason to buy such far-fetched things. Yet it would certainly procure an excellent dinner. His stomach rumbled at the thought.

'Might I offer you gentlemen some refreshment while the matter is tended to?' Tivoli glanced at Locke. Were her ears that sharp? 'Dark ale? Wine? Pastries?'

'Yes,' said Locke, resenting his weakness but unable to master it. 'Yes, anything solid, that would be ne … nice.' Gods above, he'd almost said 'necessary'.

'Also,' said Jean, 'could we trouble you to have paper, ink, and quills sent out to our carriage? Nikoros has some scribbling to do.'

Tivoli settled Locke and Jean in one of the alcoves, on chairs that would have been at home in the suite of false furniture they'd given to Requin. An attendant brought a tray of flaky brown pastries in the western style, filled with cheese and minced mushrooms. They were the richest thing Locke had eaten in weeks. Jean and Tivoli took small cups of dark ale, and watched in joint bemusement as Locke removed the pastries from existence, rank by rank.

'I'm sorry,' he said around a mouthful of food. 'I've been ill. My stomach might as well have been locked up on another continent.' He knew he was being less than polite, but the alternative was to gnaw on more ship's biscuit, which he had transferred to an inner pocket of his new coat.

'Think nothing of it,' said Tivoli. 'Manners that would keep you starving are no manners worth respecting. Shall I call for more?'

Locke nodded, and in moments the surviving pastries received reinforcements. These were followed by an attendant carrying a wooden board with a neatly gridded surface, on which low stacks of gold and silver coins had been set out. Jean divided this money into two new leather purses while Locke continued eating.

'Now,' said Tivoli, 'I trust there's little more to say about your personal funds. The other matter we need to touch upon is a certain sum left in my care with strict instructions that it remain unrecorded. Before we discuss its handling, I must ask that you make absolutely no reference to my name in connection with this sum, at any time, save in the utmost privacy between yourselves. Certainly never in writing.'

'I assure you, madam, that in all matters of discretion not involving food, we make etiquette tutors look like slobbering barbarians,' said Jean.

'Excellent,' she said, rising from her chair. 'Then let me acquaint you with the hundred thousand ducats I'm not holding on your behalf.'

6

The unrecorded sum lay in a windowless cell off an underground hallway guarded by clockwork doors that must have weighed half a ton apiece. A stack of iron-bound chests was set against an interior wall, and Tivoli pushed one open to reveal gleaming contents.

'About seven hundred and fifty pounds of gold,' she said. 'I can turn a fair percentage of it into silver without much notice, whenever you require.'

'I … yes, that may indeed be necessary before we're finished,' said Locke. He felt a strange tug at his heart. He'd taken the vast fortune of the Gentlemen Bastards for granted for so long, and now here was another, set out for his disposal, as though the first had never been lost.

'Is there anyone besides yourselves,' said Tivoli, 'that you would wish to have access to these funds?'

'Absolutely not,' said Jean.

'And that's never to be countermanded,' added Locke. '*Ever.* No one else will come on our behalf. Anyone who says otherwise will be lying. Any evidence they produce should be torn up and stuffed down their breeches.'

'We have, from long practise, developed many efficient means of dealing with mischief-makers,' said Tivoli.

'May my associate and I speak privately?' said Locke.

'Of course.' Tivoli stepped out of the cell and pushed the door half-closed. 'This door will open from your side at just a touch of the silver lever. Take as long as you require.'

When the door had clattered all the way shut, Jean closed the open chest and sat upon it. 'Your guts doing tumbling exercises like mine?'

'I'd never have credited it,' said Locke, running his fingers over the cool wood of another strongbox. 'All those years we spent stealing bigger and bigger sums. The money was like a painted backdrop for me. Now that we've had a couple fortunes yanked out from under us, though ...'

'Yeah,' said Jean. 'It seems dearer, somehow. This Tivoli – how far do you suppose we can trust her?'

'I think we can afford to assume the best in her case,' said Locke. 'Patience sent us here. Probably means that Sabetha can't touch our funds at their source, and that hers are equally beyond our reach. This is ammunition for the game. You'd want it kept safe for proper use if you were the magi, wouldn't you?'

'You've saved me some explaining.' The voice was deep, cultured, with a languid Karthani accent, and it came from right behind Locke. He whirled.

A man leaned against the door, about Locke's age and height, wearing a long coat the colour of dried rose petals. His hair and short beard were icy blond. Gloves, breeches, boots, and neck-scarf were all black, without ornament.

'Gods,' said Locke, regaining control of himself. 'I would have opened the door for a knock.'

'I didn't choose to wait,' said the man.

'Well, I don't need to ask to see the rings on *your* wrist,' said Locke. 'Who are you, then? With Patience, or against?'

'With. I've come for a private word on behalf of all of us you stand to disappoint.'

'We've been at work in your interest for about four hours now,' said Locke. 'Surely you could wait a day or two before coming it the total asshole? What do you think, Jean?'

'Jean is occupied,' said the stranger.

Locke turned to see Jean with his eyes unfocused and mouth slightly open. Save for the faint rise and fall of his chest, he might have been a well-dressed statue.

'Gods' truth,' said Locke, turning back to the stranger. 'I don't care who you are, I am tired of talking to you fucking people under circumstances like—'

Before he finished his sentence, he threw a punch. Without betraying any surprise or concern, the mage caught Locke's fist in one of his gloved hands and struck back, straight to Locke's midsection. The strength bled from his legs and he went down gasping. The mage retained his hold on Locke's hand and used it to wrench him around, until he was on his knees facing away from his antagonist.

'Just breathe through the pain,' said the mage, casually. 'Even for you, that was arrogant. You're no threat to anyone in your condition.'

'T-t-Tivoli,' Locke gasped. 'Tivoli!'

'Grow up.' The mage knelt behind him, put his left hand on Locke's jaw, and set the other in a choking hold. Locke kicked and struggled, but the man effortlessly maintained control of Locke's head and tightened the grip. 'She can't hear you, either.'

'Patience,' hissed Locke. 'Patience … will … nggghk …'

'This conversation is never going to be any concern of hers. She isn't hovering over you like a little cloud. She has people like *me* to do that for her.'

'Ngggh … ygggh … fghkingggh … bastarrrgh!'

'Yes,' said the mage, loosening his choke at last. Locke coughed and sucked air into his burning lungs. 'Yes, I do want for manners, don't I? And you're such a gentle saint-like fellow yourself. Are you ready to listen?'

Locke, relieved to be breathing again and deeply ashamed of his weakened state, said nothing.

'The message is this,' continued the mage, taking silence for acquiescence. 'We want the contest to be genuine. We want to see you *work* for six weeks. If you make peace with that woman and contrive some sort of dumb-show—'

'Patience already warned me,' coughed Locke. 'Gods above, you must've known that, you tedious piece of shit!'

'It's one thing to be told, it's another thing to understand. You've got a real entanglement with the woman on the other side. We'd have to be idiots not to allow that you might be tempted.'

'I've already promised—'

'Your promises aren't worth a dead man's spit, Camorri. So here's something tangible. Make any arrangement with your redheaded friend to fix this contest, in either direction, and we'll kill her.'

'You son of a— You can't—'

'Of course we can. Just as soon as the election is over. We'll take our time while you watch.'

'The other mages—'

'You think they give a damn about her? The Falconer's friends? They hired her to vex *you*. Once the five-year game is over, they'll be no protection.'

Locke attempted to stumble to his feet, and after a moment the mage yanked him up by the back of his coat. Locke turned, glared, and made a show of dusting himself off.

'It's no use giving me the evil eye, Lamora. Take the warning to heart. You should be flattered that we understand how useless half-measures are with you.'

'Flattered,' said Locke. 'Oh, yeah. *Flattered.* That's exactly the word that was on the tip of my tongue. Thanks.'

'The woman is a hostage to your good behaviour. You don't get another reminder. And don't bother telling Patience about this, either. You'd suffer for it.'

'That all?'

'That's all the conversation I have in me, friend.'

'Then wake Jean up.'

'He'll stop daydreaming once I've gone.'

'Too chickenshit to say this sort of thing in front of him?'

'Hasn't it occurred to you,' said the mage, 'that the *last* thing your partner needs is another one of my kind proving just how helpless he is while he's awake to bear the disgrace?'

'I ...'

'I'm not without my sympathies, Lamora. They just don't necessarily reside with *you*. Now mind the job we hired you for.'

With a wave of his hand he was gone. Locke swung his arms around the empty air where the mage had been standing, then patted the nearby wall, then checked to make sure the door was still tightly closed. He gave a grunt of disgusted resignation and massaged his neck.

'Locke? Did you say something?'

Jean was back on his feet, looking hale.

'Uh, no Jean, I'm sorry. I just ... uh, coughed.'

'Are you all right?' Jean peered at him over the rims of his optics. 'You're sweating like mad. Did something happen?'

'It's just ... nothing.' Gods above, the red-coated bastard was right. Jean didn't need another reminder of how casually the magi could make a puppet of him. With Locke barely started on the path to recovery, he needed all of Jean's confidence and energy, without distraction. 'I'm sure it's just all this walking about. I'll get used to it again soon enough.'

'Well, then, let's have Nikoros take us to our lodgings,' said Jean. 'We've got clothes; we're in funds. Let's see to your comfort before we start the good fight on behalf of Patience and her cohorts.'

'Right,' said Locke, reaching for the lever that would open the cell door. 'Last people in the world I'd want to disappoint.'

7

'Nikoros, who the hell votes in this place, anyway?' asked Locke as the carriage bobbed and weaved its way across one of the Elderglass suspension bridges, headed northwest for somewhere Nikoros had called the Palanta District.

'Well, there's, uh, three ways to earn the right. You can show title to property worth at least sixty ducats. You can serve in the constabulary for twenty-five years. Or you can be enfranchised for a lump sum of one hundred and fifty, at any time except the actual day of an election.'

'Hmmm,' said Locke. 'Sounds like an eminently corruptible process. That might be useful. So how many people in Karthain, and how many can vote?'

'About seventy thousand in the city,' said Nikoros, who was sitting awkwardly indeed, protecting the stack of parcels with one hand and gently waving a still-drying sheet of parchment with the other. 'Five thousand with voting rights, more or less. I'll have more precise figures as the election goes on.'

'That's what, about two hundred and fifty voters per Konseil seat?' said Jean. 'Or am I wrong?'

'Close enough. You're allowed to choose one of the two final candidates in whatever district you live in. Ballots are in writing and you've got to be able to sign your name, too.'

'So, as far as voting goes, we're not really looking at one big fight, but nineteen smaller ones.'

'Indeed. I, ah, if I may, I believe this list is dry—'

Jean took it. He scanned the columns of chicken-scratch handwriting (no wonder Nikoros had a longstanding relationship with a trustworthy scribe), a short list of businesses, and a longer list of names. 'These people make the Black Iris party tick?'

'Our counterparts, yes. They call themselves the Trust. We always refer to ourselves as the Committee.'

'When can we meet this Committee?' said Jean.

'Well, actually, I had hoped you wouldn't mind a bit of a get-together this evening. Just the Committee and select Deep Roots supporters—'

'How many?'

'Not above a hundred and fifty.'

'Gods below,' said Locke. 'I suppose we'll have to do it sooner or later, though. Where did you want to hold this mess?'

'At your lodgings. Josten's Comprehensive Accommodations. I'm eager for you to see it. It's the best place in the city, our temple for Deep Roots affairs.'

A temple it could have been, given its size. They pulled up before Josten's just as the sun was reaching its mild zenith in a sky that was gradually greying over with clouds. Porters scrambled from the building's shaded front entrance and took packages under Nikoros' direction. Jean hopped out of the carriage before Locke did, and studied the structure.

It was a sprawling, gabled, three-storey affair with at least nine visible chimneys and several dozen windows. A dozen carriages could have lined up before it with room to spare.

'Hell of an inn,' said Locke as his shoes hit the cobbles.

'Not just an inn,' said Nikoros. 'A fine dining establishment, a complete bar, a coffeehouse. Paradise on earth for merchants and traders with party sympathies. A quarter of the city's commerce gets hashed out here.'

The interior lived up to Nikoros' enthusiasm. At least five dozen men and women drank and conversed at long tables amidst solid, darkly varnished wooden pillars. An entire clothier's shop worth of hats and coats hung from nearly every surface, and waiters in black jackets and breeches bustled about with the haste of siege engineers preparing an attack. To Jean's eye the place looked like Meraggio's turned inside-out, with the dining and drinking made a centrepiece of business affairs rather than a concealed luxury.

'Up there,' said Nikoros, gesturing toward raised galleries with polished brass rails, 'you'll find the reserved sections. One for the biggest syndicates, the ones I write for. Another for the scribes and solicitors; they pay the house a ransom to stay close to the action. And there's a gallery for Deep Roots business.'

Jean sensed a number of eyes upon him, and although Nikoros drew waves and nods from onlookers, it was obvious that the two Gentlemen Bastards had become objects of curiosity merely by walking in with him. Jean sighed inwardly, thinking that a back-door entrance might have been wiser, but the die was cast. If Sabetha hadn't already known they were loose on the streets of Karthain, it was inconceivable that at least one person here wasn't in her employ, watching for their arrival.

Behind the well-furnished bar on the far side of the room was a tall black man, thin as a hat rack, wearing a more expensive version of the waiter's uniform under a billowing white cravat and leather apron. The instant he caught sight of Nikoros, he set down the ledger he was reading and crossed the room, dodging waiters.

'Welcome, sirs, welcome, to Josten's Comprehensive, the Hall Inclusive!' The man bowed at the waist before Locke and Jean. 'Diligence Josten, gentlemen, master of the house. You're expected. How can I make your life easier?'

'I'd do public murder for a cup of coffee,' said Jean.

'You've come to the only house in Karthain with coffee worth murdering for. We have seven distinct blends, from the aromatic Syresti dry to the thick—'

'I'll take the kind I don't have to think about.'

'The very best kind of all.' Josten snapped his fingers, and a nearby waiter hurried off. 'Now, your rooms. They're in the west wing, second floor, a pair of joined suites, and I'll have your things—'

'Yes, yes,' said Locke. 'Forgive me, I require a moment.' He grabbed Jean and Nikoros by their lapels and dragged them into a private huddle.

'This innkeeper,' whispered Locke, 'how far can we trust him, Nikoros?'

'He's been Deep Roots since this place was three bricks and some postholes in the mud. Gods above, Lazari, he's as likely to turn as I am.'

'What makes you think we trust you?'

'I ... I—'

'Take a breath, I'm kidding.' Locke patted Nikoros on the back and smiled. 'If you're wrong, of course, we're buggered as all hell. Josten! My dear fellow. Yes, have our junk sent to our rooms, I'm sure they're perfect, with just the right number of walls and ceilings. I'll count them later. You know why we're here?'

'Why, to help us kick the Black Iris in the teeth for a change. And to enjoy your coffee.'

A waiter appeared at Jean's side, offering a steaming mug on a brass tray. Jean took it and swallowed half of it in one gulp, shuddering with pleasure as the heat cascaded down his battle-hardened gullet.

'Oh yes,' he said. 'That's the stuff. Sweet liquid death. With just a hint of ginger.'

'Okanti beans,' said Josten. 'My family once grew them on the home islands, before we came north.'

'Feeling human again?' said Locke.

'This brew could make a dead eunuch piss lightning,' said Jean. He tossed back the second half of the cup. 'You want to go up and rest?'

'Gods, no,' said Locke. 'Time is precious, security's nonexistent, and our collective ass is hanging in the wind just begging a certain some-one to put an arrow right between the cheeks. Josten, I've got to make cruel use of you, I'm afraid.'

'Name any requirement. I'll meet it eye to eye.'

'Good man, but you'll learn soon enough not to say that sort of thing to me until I've finished speaking. And then you'll probably learn not to say nice things at all. Your waiters, porters, and the like, have you hired any new ones in the last week?'

'Five or six.'

'Get their names on paper. Get that paper to Master Callas here.' Locke jerked a thumb at Jean. 'Instruct your most trusted employees to watch your newest hirelings at all times. Don't *do* anything, but get full reports of their activities. On paper.'

'And get that paper to Master Callas?'

'Right you are. Next, consider every door in the entire structure that you routinely keep locked. Excepting the guest rooms, of course. Have all the locks changed, every last one. Do it tomorrow, during business hours. Nikoros will reimburse you from party funds.'

'I—' said Nikoros.

'Nikoros, your job this afternoon is to say *yes* to anything that comes out of my mouth. The more you rehearse this, the sooner it'll become a smooth mechanical process allowing no time for painful reflection. Can you practise for me?'

'Yes.'

'You're a natural. Anyway, Josten, get locksmiths down here tomorrow even if you have to promise them a month's pay. Make sure your fresh hirelings don't get new keys. Arrange to make it look like the locksmiths have simply run out. Tell them they'll get theirs in a few days. We'll see if any of them do anything interesting as a result. Clear so far?'

Josten nodded and tapped his right temple with one finger.

'Next, get a metalsmith to bang up some simple neck chains for all of your employees. Dignified but cheap. Gilded iron, nothing anyone would want to pawn. This is important. We don't want some enterprising spy throwing together an outfit to mimic one of your waiters so they can lurk about. Anyone on duty wears a chain. Anyone working without a chain gets hauled in back for an impolite conversation. *Nobody* takes their chain with them when they leave, or they're fired. Got it? Chains get handed in to you and your most trusted associates, and donned again when it's time to start a new shift.

'Once you've seen to that, announce to all of your employees that you're doubling their wages until the day after the election. Nikoros will reimburse you out of party funds.'

'Er … yes,' said Nikoros.

'Mention also,' said Locke, 'the importance of preserving a secure house during the election, and that anyone reporting *anything* genuinely unusual or out of place will be compensated for their trouble. If a spider farts in a wine cellar, I want you to hear about it.'

Josten's eyes had widened, but he nodded as before.

'What else …? Physical security! We need brutes. Say half a dozen. Reliable types, patient, ready for a scrap but not slobbering to start one. No idiots. And some women we can blend in with the crowd. Handy things, pretty girls with knives under their skirts. Where can we get some?'

'The Court of Dust,' said Nikoros. 'The caravan staging and receiving posts. There's always guards for hire. Not exactly Collegium scholars, mind you.'

'Just so long as they don't suck their thumbs in polite company,' said Locke. 'See to it tomorrow, Nikoros, and take Master Callas with you. He can sort cream from crap. Clean up the new recruits, get them decent clothes, and put them up here for the duration. Pay for the rooms out of party funds. Also – make it clear that anyone brought on as muscle answers directly to me or Callas. They take *no* orders from anyone else without our permission.'

'Uh, sure,' said Nikoros.

'Now, Nikoros, you have an office full of papers to preserve. Run off and get your scribe working. Take the steps we discussed earlier. What time are you parading us around?'

'Ninth hour of the evening.'

'Good, good, *shit*. Wait. Will everyone in attendance know that Callas and I are running the show?'

'No, no, only the members of the Committee. We did hire you, remember.'

'Ah,' said Locke. 'That's fine. You carry on with getting the hell out of here, and we'll see you tonight.'

Nikoros nodded, shook hands with Josten, and went out the front door.

'What else …?' Locke turned back to Josten. 'Rooms. Yes. The rooms adjacent to our suite, and across from it, are not to be let. Keep them vacant. Have Nikoros pay you the full six weeks' rent for them out of party funds. But give the keys for the empty rooms to me, right?'

'Easily done.'

Jean studied Locke carefully. This rapid transition to a state of wide-eyed energetic scheming was something he'd seen many times before. However, there was a nervous, feverish quality to Locke's mood that made Jean bite his lip with concern.

'What else …?'

'Luncheon, perhaps?' Jean interrupted as gracefully as he could. 'Food, wine, coffee? A few minutes to sit down and catch your breath in private?'

'Food, yes. Coffee and wine are a ghastly mix. One or the other, I don't care which. Not both.'

'As for food, sir—,' said Josten.

'Put anything on my plate short of a live scorpion and I'll eat it. And … and …' Locke snapped his fingers. 'I know what I've forgotten! Josten, have you had any new customers in the past few days? *Particularly* new customers, never seen before, ones that spend a great deal of time sitting around?'

'Well, now that you mention it … Don't stare at them, but on your

240

right, far side of the room, the third table from the rear wall, under the painting of the lady with the exceptional boso … necklace.'

'I see,' said Locke. 'Yes, that is an extraordinary place to hang a necklace. Three men?'

'First started coming three days ago. They eat and drink, more than enough to keep their spot. But they keep it for hours at a time, and they come and go in shifts, sometimes. There's a fourth fellow not there right now.'

'Do they have rooms?'

'No. And they don't do business with the regular crowd. Sometimes they play cards, but mostly … well, I don't know what they do. Nothing offensive.'

'Would you call them gentlemen? In their manner of dress, in their self-regard?'

'Well, they're not penniless. But I wouldn't go so far as gentlemen.'

'Hirelings,' said Locke, removing some of the more obvious pieces of jewelry Nikoros had secured for him and stuffing them into a coat pocket. 'Valets. Professional men of convenience, unless I miss my guess. I'm a little overdressed for this, but I think I can compensate by toning down my manners.'

'Overdressed for what?' said Jean.

'Insulting complete strangers,' said Locke, loosening his neck-cloth. 'Got to mind the delicate social nuances when you inform some poor fellow that he's a dumb motherfucker.'

8

'Hang on,' said Jean. 'If you're looking to start a fight, I'm—'

'I thought about that,' said Locke. 'You're likely to scare them. I need them to feel insulted and *not* threatened. That makes it my job.'

'Well, would you like me to intervene before you get your teeth punched out, or is that part of your scheme?'

'If I'm right,' said Locke, 'you won't need to. If I'm wrong, I grant you full license to indulge in an "I told you so" when I'm conscious again, with an option for a "you stupid bastard" if you choose.'

'I'll claim that privilege.' The quick-moving waiter appeared with a second cup of coffee for Jean. He seized it and slapped a pair of copper coins down in its place. The waiter bowed.

'Josten,' said Locke, 'if it turns out I'm about to do something knavish to honest customers, we'll compensate you.'

'Going to be a damned interesting six weeks,' muttered Josten.

Locke took a deep breath, cracked his knuckles, and walked over to the table at which the three strangers sat. Jean stayed some distance behind, minding his cup of coffee. His presence there was a comfort, familiar as a shadow.

'Good afternoon,' said Locke. 'Lazari is my name. I trust I'm intruding.'

'I'm sorry,' said the man closest to Locke, 'but we were—'

'I'm afraid I don't care,' said Locke. He slid into an unclaimed chair and appraised the strangers: young, clean, well-groomed, not quite expensively dressed. They were sharing a bottle of white wine and a pitcher of water.

'We were having a private discussion!' said the man on Locke's right.

'Ah, but I'm here to do you two a service.' Locke gestured at the two men sitting across from him. 'Concerning the fellow I'm sitting next to. Word around the bar is that he can only get it up when he's on top of another fellow he's taken by force or subterfuge.'

'What the hell is this?' hissed the man on the right.

'Phrased less delicately,' said Locke, 'if you continue to associate with this well-known deceiver, he's going to tie you down, do you somewhere very untidy until you bleed, and not bother to untie you after.'

'This is *unseemly*,' said one of the men across the table. 'Unseemly, and if you don't withdraw immediately—'

'I'd be more worried about your friend not withdrawing immediately,' said Locke. 'He's not known for being quick.'

'What's the meaning of this infantile interruption?' The man on Locke's right pounded on the table, just strongly enough to rattle the bottle and glasses.

'Good gods,' said Locke, pretending to notice the wine for the first time, 'you thoroughly artless fuck-stains didn't actually *drink* any of that, did you?'

He swept his hat off and used it to knock the wineglasses of the men across from him into their laps.

'You bastard!' said one.

'Why I … I …' sputtered the other.

'But then, maybe it's not drugged after all.' Locke grabbed the bottle and took a long swig. 'Wouldn't need to be, for Karthani. Milk-sucking pants-pissers could get drunk off the smell of an empty bottle!'

'I'll ... fetch the landlord!' said the man across from him on the left, retrieving his empty glass from his lap.

'Frightening,' said Locke. 'Savage as a kitten on a tit. Say, did you ever hear the one about the rich Karthani and the Karthani who knew who his mother was? Shit, wait, I said *Karthani*, didn't I? Told the damn thing wrong.'

'Leave,' said the man on his right. 'Leave! Now!'

'Hey, how does a Karthani find out his wife is having her monthly flow? He crawls into his son's bed and the boy's cock is already wet. Ha! Oh, have you heard the one about the Karthani who claimed he could count to five—'

The man on Locke's right pushed his chair away from the table and stood up. Locke grabbed him by the lapel. The man halted, glowering. Locke didn't have the strength to drag him back down if he decided to fight, but the crucial insult of the uninvited touch was already given.

'Where are you off to?' said Locke. 'I haven't finished my sensitive cultural exchange.'

'Remove your hand from my coat, you obnoxious—'

'Or else what?'

'We take this to the master of the house.'

'I *am* the master of the house,' said Locke. 'And you already know it. You've been sent here to watch for my coming. See the hefty gentleman ten yards behind me? He's the other one you're looking for. Take a long, careful look, children. I don't doubt that your mistress expects a detailed report.'

The man jerked away.

'Come now,' said Locke reasonably, taking another swig from the wine bottle. 'No men with any quantity of self-respect could have borne the abuse I've just given you. If you were gentlemen you'd have called me out, and if you were roughs you'd have punched me in the teeth. The fact is, you've been paid a tidy sum to sit here spying on me, and you were all confused as hell about what to do when I pissed on your dignity.'

The two men across the table started to rise, and Locke gestured sharply for them to remain seated.

'Don't do anything stupid *now*, sirs. There's no retrieving your situation. Lift one finger in an unkind act, and I guarantee it'll take six

243

months for your bones to knit. I'll also have fifty witnesses swearing you had it coming.'

'What do you want with us?' muttered the man on the right.

'Haul your pathetic carcasses out the door. Be quick and polite. If I ever see you within shouting distance of Josten's again, you'll wake up in an alley with all your teeth shoved up your ass. That goes for your absent friend, too.'

Locke put his hat back on, stood up, and strolled casually away. He spared a smile for Jean, who raised his coffee cup in salute – the scrape of chairs against the floor behind him told Locke that the men were departing in haste. He and Jean watched them leave.

'You really are a vulgar little cuss when the spirit moves you,' said Jean.

'I've got worse,' said Locke. 'Stored on some high shelf in my mind like an alchemist's poisons. Got most of it from Calo and Galdo.'

'Well, you were venomous enough for our obvious friends.'

'Yes. Obvious. A fine thing to chase out the conspicuous spies. Now all we have to worry about is the capable ones.'

9

Locke destroyed an excellent luncheon for six – Jean contented himself with a small corner of the feast, and came away grateful for not losing any limbs – then dozed fitfully in their suite of rooms, alternating naps in a lounging chair with episodes of furious pacing.

As the sun set and the tiny fragments of sky visible around the window curtains turned black, men from Morenna's delivered the beginnings of the promised wardrobe. Locke and Jean examined the new coats, vests, and breeches for concealed needles or alchemical dusts before hanging them in the massive rosewood armoires provided with the rooms.

At the eighth hour of the evening maids and porters appeared with tubs of steaming water. Locke tested each tub with a finger and, when his flesh didn't peel from his bones, allowed that they might just be safe for their intended use.

By the time Nikoros knocked forty minutes later, the two Gentlemen Bastards were cleaned up and comfortably ensconced in clothes that fit perfectly.

'Gentlemen,' said Nikoros, who had substantially upgraded his own clothes, 'I've brought you some useful things, I hope.'

He passed a leather portfolio to Locke, who flipped it open and found at least a hundred pages inside. Some were covered with dense scribbling that was surely Nikoros', others with flawless script that surely wasn't.

'Deep Roots party financial reports,' said Nikoros. 'Important membership lists, plans and minutes from the last election, lists of properties and agents, matching lists for what we know of the Black Iris, copies of the city election laws—'

'Splendid,' said Locke. 'And you took all the steps I discussed earlier?'

'My scribe's still working, but everything else is seen to. If the earth should open up and swallow my offices, I swear I won't be losing anything irreplaceable.'

'Good,' said Locke. 'Want a drink? We've got a liquor cabi— No, wait, I haven't examined the bottles yet, sorry.'

'I'm sure anything provided by Josten is perfectly safe,' said Nikoros, raising his eyebrows.

'It's not Josten's faithfulness I worry about.'

'Well, let me assure you that we don't throw parties in Karthain for the purpose of staying dry.' He reached inside his coat and drew out two ornate silver lapel badges attached to green ribbons; an identical ornament was on his own left breast, though his was gold. 'As for that, I mustn't forget your colours.'

'The official Deep Roots plumage?' said Jean, extending a hand for his pin.

'Yes. For the party tonight, Committee members wear gold pins, Konseil members wear jade, privileged others wear silver. These will mark you as men to respect, but not men who need to be followed around and remarked upon, if you don't wish it.'

'Good,' said Locke, decorating his lapel. 'Now that we're properly garnished, let's serve ourselves up to the family.'

10

The entire character of Josten's main room had changed for the evening. The number of attendants at the street doors had doubled, and their uniforms were far more impressive. Dark green banners hung from the rafters and down the varnished pillars. Carriages could be heard coming and going constantly, and Locke caught a glimpse of several more attendants outside, holding their hands up to a party of well-dressed men without green ribbons. Clearly the party was a closed affair … Were the men on the pavement legitimately uninformed late diners, or some sort of opposition mischief? There was no time to investigate.

A string quintet was bowing away pleasantly in one of the upper galleries, and all the visible fireplaces had huge kettles for tea and coffee bubbling before them. Curtained tables held thousands of glass bottles, and enough decanters, flutes, pitchers, and tumblers to blind every eye in the city with the force of their reflected light. Locke blinked several times and turned his attention to the men and women flowing into the room.

'This is already well more than a hundred and fifty,' he said.

'These things happen,' said Nikoros, giggling energetically as though at some private joke. 'We plan with s-such restraint, but there's so many people we can't afford to offend!'

Locke peered at him. Nikoros had changed, somehow, in the few minutes between their room and the party. He was sweating profusely, his cheeks were flushed, his eyes darted around like little creatures trapped behind glass panes. Yet he wasn't nervous; he was beatific. *Gods!*

Their straight-arrow trade insurer, their liaison to the Deep Roots upper crust, was a taker of Akkadris dust. Locke smelled the sharp pine-like odour of the stuff. Damn! Akkadris, Muse-of-Fire, the poet killer. Liquor soothed and loosened wits, but dust did the opposite, lighting fires in the mind until the dusthead shook with excitement for no discernible reason. It was an expensive and incrementally suicidal habit.

'Nikoros,' said Locke, grabbing one of his lapels, 'you and I need to have a very frank discussion about—'

'Via Lupa! Via Lupa, dear boy!' A ponderous old man with a face like a seamed pink pudding bore down on them, witchwood cane tapping the floor excitedly. The man's white eyebrows fluttered like wisps of smoke, and his lapel badge was polished jade. 'Nikoros of the wolves, so-called for his profit margins. Ha!'

'G-good evening, Your Honour!' Nikoros used the interruption to extricate himself from Locke's grasp. 'Oh! Gentlemen, may I present Firstson Epitalus, Konseil member for Isas Thedra for forty-five years. Some would call him the, ah, f-figurehead on our political vessel.'

'So I'm a figurehead, am I? A helpless woman splashing about without the good sense to cover my tits? Do I need to send a friend along to require an explanation of that remark, young fellow?'

'Leave the poor boy alone, First. It's quite clear that you *do* have the good sense to cover your tits.' A lean, grizzled woman took Epitalus by the arm in a friendly fashion. She looked a lived-in sixty to Locke, though she had lively eyes and a mischievous smile. She, too, wore a jade badge, and as she and Epitalus burst into laughter Nikoros joined in nervously, louder than either of them.

'And allow me to also present ... ah—'

It was only a momentary lapse, but the woman seized upon it eagerly.

'Oh, say the name, Nikoros, it won't burn your tongue.'

'Ahem. Yes, ahem: Damned Superstition Dexa, Konseil member for Isas Mellia and head, ah, head of the Deep Roots Committee.'

'Damned Superstition?' said Locke, smiling despite himself.

'Which it is,' said Dexa, 'though you'll note I play firmly by the rules anyway. Hypocrisy and caution are such affectionate cousins.'

'Your Honours,' said Nikoros, 'please, please allow me the p-pleasure of introducing Masters Lazari and Callas.'

Bows, handshakes, nods, and endearments were exchanged with the speed of a melee, and once all the appropriate strokes had been made, Their Honours immediately relapsed into informality.

'So you're the gentlemen that we've discussed so often recently,' said Dexa. 'I understand you smoked some vipers out of our midst this very afternoon.'

'Hardly vipers, Your Honour. Just a few turds our opposition threw into the road to see if we were minding our feet,' said Locke.

'Well, keep it up,' said Epitalus. 'We have such confidence in you, my lads, such confidence.'

Locke nodded, and felt a flutter in his guts. These people certainly hadn't read a single note on the fictional exploits of Lazari and Callas. Their warmth and enthusiasm had been installed by the spells of the Bondsmagi. Would it last forever, or dissolve like some passing fancy once the election was over? Could it dissolve *before* then, by accident? An unnerving thought.

Nikoros managed to herd their little group toward the gleaming mountains of liquor. While his heart-to-heart with Nikoros had been postponed by the circumstances, Locke did feel more comfortable once he'd secured a drink. A glass in the hand seemed as much a uniform requirement as a green ribbon on the chest for this affair.

Epitalus and Dexa soon went off to tend to the business of being important. Nikoros whirled Locke and Jean around the room several times, making introductions, pointing out prodigies and curiosities, Committee members, friends, cousins, cousins of friends, and friends of cousins.

Locke had once been used to mingling with the aristocracy of Camorr, and while the upper crust of Karthain lacked for nothing in terms of wit and pomp, there seemed to be a distinct difference in character that ran deeper than mere variations of habit between east and west. It took half an hour of conversation for him to finally apprehend the nature of the contrast – the Karthani gentry lacked the martial quality that was omnipresent in the well-to-do of most other city-states.

There were no obvious battle scars, no missing arms within pinned-up jacket sleeves, no men and women with the measured step of old campaigners or the swagger of equestrians. Locke recalled that the army of Karthain had been disbanded when the magi took up their residence. For four centuries, the ominous Presence had been the city's sole (and entirely sufficient) protection against outside interference.

Introductions and pleasantries continued. 'Now, who's that fellow over there?' said Locke, sipping at his second Austershalin brandy and water. 'The one with the odd little hat.'

'The natty-hatted gentleman? Damn … his name escapes me at the moment.' Nikoros took a generous gulp of wine as though it might help; whatever aid it rendered was not instantaneous. 'Sorry. But I do know his particular friend, the one at his shoulder. One of our district organizers. Firstson Cholmond. Always claims to be writing a book.'

'What sort?' said Jean.

'History. A grand historical study of the city of Karthain.'

'Gods grant him a paralyzing carriage accident,' said Jean.

'I sympathize. Most historians have always struck me as perpetrators of tedium,' said Nikoros. 'He swears that his book is different. Still—'

Whatever Nikoros might have said next was lost in a general uproar. Firstson Epitalus had ascended to one of the upper galleries, and he was waving for something resembling order from the crowd, which had by now soaked up a good fraction of its own weight in liquor.

'Good evening, good evening, good evening!' yelled Epitalus. 'Good evening!' And then, as though anyone in the audience might conceivably remain unenlightened as to the quality or time of day: 'Good *evening!*'

The string quintet ceased its humming and twanging, and the general acclamation sank to a tipsy murmur.

'Welcome, dear hearts and cavaliers, devoted friends, to the seventy-ninth season of elections in our Republic of Karthain! Take a moment, I pray, to reflect with pity on how few of us remain who can remember the first ...'

Good-natured laughter rippled across the crowd.

'Even those of you still moist behind the ears should be able to recall our heroic efforts of five years past, which, despite furious opposition, preserved our strong minority of nine seats on the Konseil!'

Curiously raucous cheers echoed across the hall for some time. Locke winced. Strong minority? Was he missing out on some bit of Karthani drollery, or were they really that incapable of admitting they'd lost?

'And so, surely, the burden of defending their old gains rests heavily on our foes, and must render them eminently vulnerable to what's coming their way this time!'

This was answered with full-throated yells, the clinking of glasses, applause, and the sound of at least one thin-blooded reveller succumbing to the influence of complimentary liquor. Fortunately, his tumble from a balcony was interrupted by a crowd of soft-bodied folks, who were deep enough in their cups to take no offence at his sudden arrival. Waiters discreetly removed the poor fellow while Epitalus went on.

'Might I beg you, therefore, to raise a glass in toast to our dear opposition, the overconfident lads and lasses across the city? What shall we wish them, eh? Confusion? Frustration?'

'They're already confused,' yelled Damned Superstition Dexa from somewhere near the front of the crowd, 'so let it be frustration!'

'*Frustration to the Black Iris*,' boomed Epitalus, raising his glass. The cry was echoed from every corner of the crowd, and then with one vast gulp several hundred people were in pressing need of a refill. Waiters wielding bottles in both hands waded into the fray. When Epitalus had received a fresh supply of wine, he raised his glass again.

'Karthain! Gods bless our great jewel of the west!'

This toast, too, was echoed enthusiastically, but in its wake Locke witnessed something curious. A fair number of the people around him touched their left hands to their eyes, bowed their heads, and whispered, '*Bless the Presence.*'

'Gods grant us all the blessing of a long-awaited victory,' said

Epitalus, 'as they have granted me the Honour of your very kind attention. I'll not detain you a moment longer! We have plenty of work to do in the coming six weeks, but tonight is for pleasure, and I must insist that you all pursue it vigourously!'

Epitalus descended from the elevated gallery to a round of applause that shook the rafters. The musicians started up again.

'What do you think of the old boy?' said Jean.

'He's got a strangely sunny view of ten years of defeat,' said Locke, 'but if I get killed in the next six weeks, I want him to speak at my funeral.'

'Not to piss on the good cheer,' said Jean in a much lower voice, 'but did you notice that our friend Nikoros—'

'Yeah,' sighed Locke. 'We'll straighten him out later.'

The mass of well-dressed Firstsons, Secondsons, Thirddaughters, and the like returned to its previous knots of conversation and besieged the silver platters of food which were now being uncovered at the back of the hall. Performance alchemists in bright silk costumes emerged from the kitchens, some to mix drinks, others already juggling heatless fire or conjuring glowing steam in rainbows of colour.

'My compliments, Nikoros,' said Locke. 'Your party seems to be a smashing success. Something tells me we're not going to be getting any bloody work done before noon tomorrow, though.'

'Oh, Josten's your man for that,' said Nikoros. 'He, ah, he mixes a hangover remedy that'll knock the f-fumes right out of your brain! Alchemy ain't in it. So I think we can help ourselves to another glass or two with a clear—'

It was then that Locke noticed a new murmur from the crowd near the main doors, not the low purr of drunken contentment, but a spreading signal of unease. Men and women with green ribbons parted like clouds before a rising sun, and out of the gap came a stout, curly-haired man in a pale blue coat and matching four-cornered hat. He carried a polished wooden staff about three feet long, topped with a silver figurine of a rampant lion. A tipstaff if Locke had ever seen one.

'Herald Vidalos,' said Nikoros warmly, 'D-dear fellow, have you come at a fine time! You must, must take a little something against the chill! Help yourself.'

'Deepest regrets, Nikoros.' The man called Vidalos had a curiously gentle voice, and it was obvious that he was in some discomfort. 'I'm afraid I've come on the business of the Magistrates' Court.'

'Oh?' Nikoros stiffened. 'Well, ah, perhaps I can, I can help you keep it discreet. Who do you need to see?'

'Diligence Josten.'

By now a wide circle of the floor had cleared around Vidalos. Josten pushed his way through the crowd and stepped into the open.

'What news, Vidalos?'

'Nothing that gives me any pleasure.' Vidalos touched his staff gently to Josten's left shoulder. 'Diligence Josten, I serve you before witnesses with a warrant from the Magistrates' Court of Karthain.'

He withdrew the staff and handed the innkeeper a scroll sealed inside a case. While Josten broke the seal and unrolled the contents, Locke casually moved to stand beside him.

'What's the trouble?' he whispered.

'By the Ten fucking Holy Names,' said Josten, running his eyes down the neat, numerous paragraphs on the scroll. 'This can't be right. All of my fees are properly paid—'

'Your license for the dispensation of ardent spirits is in arrears,' said Vidalos. 'There's no record at the Magistrates' Court of the fee having been received for this year.'

'But ... but I did pay it. I certainly did!'

'Josten, sir, I desire to believe you with all my soul, but it's my charge to execute this warrant, and execute it I must, or it's my hide they'll have off on Penance Day.'

'Well, we can settle the business about the records later,' said Josten. 'Just tell me what I owe and I'll pay it right now.'

'I'm *forbidden* to take fees or penalties in hand, sir,' said Vidalos. 'As you well know. You'll have to go to the next Public Proceedings at the Magistrates' Court.'

'But ... that's three days from now. Until then—'

'Until then,' said Vidalos quietly, 'I'm afraid I'm going to have to disperse this party. After that it's your choice, whether we seal your doors or remove your liquor. It's only a few days, sir.'

'Only a few days?' hissed Josten, incredulous.

'Oh, Sabetha,' Locke muttered to himself. 'You gods-damned artist. Hello to you, too.'

INTERLUDE
Bastards Abroad

I

They were forty miles beyond the border of greater Camorr, on the third morning of their journey, when they passed the first corpse swaying beneath the arching branch of a roadside tree.

'Oh, look,' said Calo, who sat beside Jean at the front of the wagon. 'All the comforts of home.'

'It's what we do with bandits when there's a spare noose about,' said Anatoly Vireska, who was walking beside them munching on a late breakfast of dried figs. Their wagon led the caravan. 'There's one every mile or two. If the noose is occupied, or it ain't convenient, we just open their throats and shove 'em off the road.'

'Are there really that many bandits?' said Sabetha. She sat atop the wagon with her feet propped on the snoring form of Galdo, who'd kept the predawn watch. 'Beg pardon. It's just that there doesn't seem to be anyone actually lurking about.' She sounded bored.

'Well, there's good and bad times,' said the caravan master. 'Summer like this we might see one once a month. Our friend here, we strung him up about that long ago. Been quiet since.

'But when a harvest goes bad, gods help us, they're in the woods thick as bird shit. And after a war, it's mercenaries and deserters raising hell. I double the guard. And I double my fees, heh.'

Locke wasn't sure he agreed that there was nothing lurking. The countryside had the haunted quality he remembered from the months he'd once spent learning the rudiments of farm life. All those nights he'd lain awake listening to the alien sound of rustling leaves, yearning for the familiar clamour of carriage wheels, footsteps on stone, boats on water.

The old imperial road had been built well, but it was starting to crumble now in these remote places between the major powers. The empty garrison forts, silent as mausoleums, were vanishing behind misty groves of cypress and witchwood, and the little towns that had grown around them were reduced to moss-covered ruins and lines in the dirt.

Locke walked along beside the wagon on the side opposite Vireska, trying to keep his eyes on their surroundings and away from Sabetha. She'd discarded her rather matronly hood, and her hair fluttered in the warm breeze.

She hadn't kept their 'appointment' the second evening. In fact, she'd barely spoken to him at all, remaining absorbed in the plays she'd packed and deflecting all attempts at conversation as adroitly as she'd parried his baton strokes.

The caravan, six wagons total, trundled along in the rising morning heat. At noon they passed through a thicket like a dark tunnel. A temporarily empty noose swung from one of the high dark branches, a forlorn pendulum.

'You know, it was novel at first,' said Calo, 'but I'm starting to think the place could use a more cheerful sort of distance marker.'

'Bandits would tear down proper signposts,' said Vireska, 'but they're all afraid to touch the nooses. They say that when you don't hang someone over running water, the rope holds the unquiet soul. Awful bad luck to touch it unless you're giving it a new victim.'

'Hmm,' said Calo. 'If I was stuck out here jumping wagon trains in the middle of shit-sucking nowhere, I'd assume my luck was already as bad as it gets.'

2

They halted for the night in the village of Tresanconne, a hamlet of about two hundred souls built on three marsh-moated hills, protected by stockades of sharpened logs. It was the only kind of settlement that could flourish out here, according to Vireska – too big for bandits to overrun, but too remote to make it worthwhile for parties of soldiers from Camorr to pay it a visit for 'road upkeep taxes.'

No rural idyll, this. The villagers were sullen and suspicious, more appreciative of outside goods than the outsiders who brought them. Still, the rough hilltop lot they provided for caravans was preferable to any bed awaiting them out in the lightless damps of the wilderness.

Locke took his turn sweeping beneath the wagon while Jean saw to the horses. The Sanza twins, grudgingly accepting one another's proximity, wandered off to survey the village. Sabetha remained atop the wagon, guarding their possessions. Locke needed just a few minutes to ensure that the space in which they would set their bedrolls was no embarrassment to civilization, and then it occurred to him that they were more or less alone.

'I, ah, I regret not having a chance to speak to you last night,' he said.

'Oh? Was it any real loss to either of us?'

'You had— Well, I don't suppose you did promise. You'd said you'd consider it, at least.'

'That's right, I didn't promise.'

'Well ... damn. You're obviously in a mood.'

'Am I?' There was danger in her tone. 'Am I really? Why should that be exceptional? A boy may be as disagreeable as he pleases, but when a girl refuses to crap sunshine on command the world mutters darkly about her *moods*.'

'I only meant it by way of, uh, well, nothing, really. It was just a conversational note. Look, it's really damned ... odd ... having to look for ploys to speak with you, as though we were complete strangers!'

'If I'm in a mood,' said Sabetha after a moment of reflective silence, 'it's because this journey is unfolding more or less as I had foreseen. Tedium, bumpy roads, and biting insects.'

'Ah,' said Locke. 'Do I count as part of the tedium or one of the biting insects?'

'If I didn't know any better,' she said softly, 'I'd swear the horseshit-sweeper was attempting to be charming.'

'You might as well assume,' said Locke, not sure whether he was feeling bold or merely willing himself to feel bold, 'that I'm always attempting to be charming where you're concerned.'

'Now that's risky.' Sabetha rolled sideways and jumped down beside him. 'That sort of directness compels a response, but what's it to be? Do I encourage you in this sort of talk or do I stop you cold?'

She took a step forward, hands on hips, and despite himself Locke leaned backward, bracing against the wagon at the last second to avoid a fall that would have been, perhaps, the most graceless thing ever accomplished in the history of Therin civilization.

'I get a vote?' he said meekly.

'If it's not to be encouragement, can you accept being stopped cold?' She raised one finger and touched his chin. It was neither invitation nor chastisement. 'The Sanzas might be driving us all crazy at the moment, but I will say this on their behalf … when their advances were made and refused, they never brought the subject up again.'

'Calo and Galdo made a *pass* at you?'

'Certainly not at the same time,' she said. 'Why so surprised? Surely you've noticed that you're not the only hot-blooded young idiot with fully functional bits and pieces in our little gang.'

'Yes, but they—'

'They understand that my feelings for them lie somewhere between sisterly affection and saintly tolerance. And while I sometimes imagine that they would hump trees if they thought nobody was around to see it, they've respected my wishes absolutely. Could you handle disappointment so well?'

'If I'm to be disappointed,' said Locke, heart pounding, 'I really wish you would cut the prelude and just disappoint me, already.'

'Oooh, there's some fire at last.' Sabetha folded her arms beneath her breasts and edged closer to him. 'Tell me, how do you even know for sure that I don't fancy *girls*?'

'I—' Locke was lucky to spit the one syllable out before the power of coherent speech ran up a white flag and deserted him. Gods above…

'You never even thought about that, did you?' she said, her voice a sly whisper.

'Well, hells … is that … I mean to say, do you—'

'Fancy oysters or snails? What a damned awkward thing to be unsure of, for someone in your position. Oh … oh, for Perelandro's sake, you look like you're about to be executed.' She bent over and whispered in his right ear. 'I happen to like snails *very well*, thank you.'

'Ahhh,' he said, feeling the earth grow solid beneath his feet again. 'I've never … never been so pleased at such a comparison before.'

'It's a champion among metaphors,' she said with the faintest smile. 'So very apt.'

'And now that you've had your sport with me, do I join Calo and Galdo in their exclusive little club?'

'They're still my friends.' She sounded genuinely hurt. 'My oath-brothers. That's nothing to scorn, especially for a … a would-be priest of your order.'

'Sabetha, I *do* fancy you. It scares the hell out of me to admit it, but I say it plainly, as you did the other night. Only I don't say it casually. I have … I have admired you since the instant we met, do you understand, the very instant, that day we went out from Shades' Hill to see the hangings. Do you remember?'

'Of course,' she whispered. 'The strange little boy who wouldn't leave Streets. What a sad trial you were. But what was there to *admire*, Locke? We were dusty, starving little creatures. You couldn't have been six. What feelings were there to *have*?'

'I only know they were there. When I heard that you'd drowned I felt as though my heart had been stepped on.'

'I'm sorry for that. It was necessary.' She glanced away from him for a long moment before continuing. 'I think you look upon our past in the light of your present feelings and imagine some glow that is ... more *reflection* than substance.'

'Sabetha, I don't remember my own father. And other than a *single* memory of ... of sewing needles, my mother is as much a mystery. I don't remember where I was born, or the Catchfire plague, or how I survived it, or *anything* that I did before the Thiefmaker bought me from the city watch!'

'Locke—'

'Listen! It's all gone! But the moments I've spent with you, whether you knew I was there or not – *they're* still with me, smouldering like coals. I can touch them and feel the heat.'

'You've been reading too many of Jean's romances. What basis for comparison have you ever had, Locke? You and I have been together all these years ... why wouldn't you evolve some sort of fixation? It's only ... perfectly natural ... expected familiarity—'

'Who are you trying to convince?' On the attack now, he played her game, took a step forward. 'That doesn't sound like it's meant for my benefit. You're trying to talk *yourself* out of confiding in me! Why—'

His voice had grown louder with every word, and she startled him by slapping a hand over his mouth.

'You are turning something quite personal into a speech for the whole camp,' she said in her flawless Vadran.

'Sorry,' he whispered in the same language. 'Look, this isn't some damn fixation, Sabetha. If I could just – somehow let you see yourself through *my* eyes. I guarantee your feet would never touch the ground again.'

'There's magic that might have some useful applications,' she said, wistfully, 'if you were to pull that off. And if I were to ... choose to be charmed just now.'

'Well, if not now, then—'

'I told you my feelings for you are complicated. Everything concerning you is *complicated*, and by that I don't mean that I'm confused or muddle-headed or, or … frightened. I mean that there are actual, genuine circumstances *about* us and *around* us that make this difficult. There are obstacles, damn it.'

'Then tell me about them. Tell me anything I can do—'

'Are we speaking Vadran now?' said Calo, from his previously silent perch in Sabetha's vacated place atop the wagon.

'Oh, Sanza, damn your eyes,' hissed Sabetha. 'I just about jumped out of my bloody skin.'

'Now that's praise,' said Galdo, who rolled out from beneath the wagon. 'You're not easy to take unawares. You must have really had your head—'

'—shoved up your ass,' said Calo.

'Are you two back in your usual rhythm, then?' said Locke crossly.

'Nah,' said Galdo. 'Just curious, is all.'

'How sharp is your Vadran?' said Locke.

'Mine Vadran is great sharp,' said Calo in that tongue, exaggeratedly mangling each word. 'Perfect like without flaws, am the clever Sanza I being.'

'I think the two of us are bit rusty, though,' said Galdo, 'so if you could just repeat all the parts we missed—'

'Get used to gaps in your comprehension,' said Sabetha. 'The rest of us certainly have.'

'Village not worth your attention?' said Locke with a sigh.

'Just the opposite,' said Galdo. 'We thought we'd fetch a few pieces of silver. Some of these smelly hillside mudfuckers are playing cards at what passes for their tavern.'

'Shouldn't take much of the old Camorr flash to dazzle 'em,' said Calo, making a small rock appear and disappear from the palm of his hand. 'Could roll off in the morning owning half this bloody place.'

'I don't think that's wise,' said Sabetha.

'What are they gonna do,' said Galdo, 'declare war? Look, if we come back in a few months and find out that a hundred swamp country yokels have knocked over the Five Towers, we'll write a sincere apology.'

'And we only need a few coins anyway,' said Calo, throwing back the

tarp over their supplies. 'To buy in. After that, we'll be taking donations, not giving 'em.'

'Hold on,' said Locke. 'Since when are you two criminals?'

'Since ...' Calo squinted and pretended to calculate. 'Sometime between first leaving Mother and hitting the ground between her legs, I
imagine.'

'Head first,' added Galdo.

'I know the *Sanzas* are as crooked as a snake in a clockwork
snake-bending machine,' said Locke, 'but the *Asino* brothers are actors,
not cardsharps.'

'You know how actors make a living between engagements?' said
Calo. 'Believe me, some of them are flash fucking cardsharps. I learned
some of my best stuff from—'

'What I mean,' said Locke, 'is that we should all just be actors, and
only actors. I've been thinking about this. No games of opportunity on
the way. No more picked pockets. We should draw a line between the
people we are in Camorr and the people we are in Espara. When we go
home, anyone thinking to follow us back to our real lives should find
nothing. No hints, no trail.'

'Seems ... sensible,' said Galdo.

'And it starts here,' said Locke. 'It means we don't do anything to
make ourselves memorable. You really think your yokel friends will
simply let you clean them out and send us on our merry way tomorrow morning? Someone's going to get *cut*, Sanzas. Everyone in
this village will be after your skins, and our guards won't save you.
They have to work this route week in and week out. They need these
people.'

'He's right,' said Calo. 'I knew it was a dumb fuckin' plan, you bald
degenerate.'

'It was *your* idea, you greedy turd-polisher!'

'Well, at any rate,' said Calo to Locke. 'We ain't following through
on it.'

'Then why not start boiling dinner? Or better yet, if you really want
to drop a coin in the village, see if you can hunt down some meat that
doesn't come in the form of a brick.'

The Sanzas received this suggestion with enthusiasm, and vanished
once again down the winding track to what passed for Tresanconne's
high street. Locke and Sabetha faced one another in their absence, and
Locke detected a sudden coolness in her demeanour.

'That right there,' she said, 'would be one of the obstacles I mentioned.'

'What?'

'You really didn't notice?'

'Notice *what*? What am I meant to realize?'

'Think about it,' she said. She crossed her arms again, this time with her shoulders hunched forward. A protective, unwelcoming gesture. 'I'm serious. I'll give you a moment. Think about it.'

'Think about *what*?'

'Years ago,' said Sabetha, 'I was the oldest child in a small gang. I was sent away by my master to train in dancing and manners. When I returned, I found that a younger child had taken my place.'

'But – I hardly—'

'Calo and Galdo, who once treated me as a goddess on earth, had transferred their allegiance to the small newcomer. In time, he got himself a third ally, another boy.'

'That is purest— Why, Jean is devoted to you, as a friend.'

'But not as a *particular* friend,' she said. 'Not as he is to you.'

'Is that your obstacle?' Locke felt as though a heavy object had just spun out of the darkness and cracked him on the head. 'My friendship with Jean? Does it make you jealous?'

'You listen about as well as you observe,' said Sabetha. 'Haven't you ever noticed that suggestions from me are treated as suggestions, while suggestions from you are taken as a sacred warrant? Even if those suggestions are *identical*?'

'I think you're being very unfair,' said Locke weakly.

'You saw it just now! I couldn't dissuade the Sanzas from drinking arsenic on the strength of mere common sense, but they trip over themselves to take your directions. This is *your* gang, Locke – it has been since you arrived, and with Chains' blessing. You've been shaped and groomed as *garrista* for when he's gone. And as ... well, as a priest. His replacement.'

'But I ... I had no notion, or intention—'

'Of course not. You haven't really questioned *anything* since your arrival. You've assumed a position of primacy, which is easy to take for granted ... until you're quietly shuffled out of it. After that, I find the matter never quite leaves one's thoughts.'

'But – I have been worked and tested as sorely as you,' said Locke, fighting to keep his voice down. 'As sorely as anyone! Do you remember how long it took me to pay *this* off?' He reached down the front of his tunic and pulled out his shark's tooth, ensconced in its little leather bag. 'Gods above, I could have a city house and a carriage for the money I poured into this damn thing. And I served as many apprenticeships as—'

'I'm not talking about your *training*, Locke, I know what Chains has done to us all. I'm talking about the way you accepted everything as you accept your own skin. Something natural and undeserving of reflection. Well, let me assure you that the only woman in a house of men has frequent cause for reflection.'

'This is a complete surprise to me,' said Locke.

'I know,' she said softly. 'That's a problem.'

She stared up at the sky, where one of the moons was emerging from behind a low haze of clouds, and Locke had no idea how to begin responding to her.

'A week to go,' she said at last. 'A long, slow week of all the pleasures I named earlier. We're going to be tired, sore, smelly, and bitten half to death by the time we reach Espara. I would ... I want to talk to you again, Locke, but I can't bring myself to make it a subject of hopeful anticipation night after night under these circumstances. Neither of us will be at our best.'

'And this merits our best,' he said grudgingly.

'I think it does. So can we keep it simple while we're travelling? Eyes on the ground, asses in our seats, and all of these ... matters tabled until a later date?'

'You think it's fair to dump this in my lap and then request a conversational truce?'

'I don't think it's fair at all,' she said. 'Just necessary.'

'Well, then. If nothing else, it seems I'll have a lot of time to ruminate on an explanation for you—'

'An explanation? You think what I want out of you is some sort of *defence*? Surely you can see that I've explained you already. What comes next is—'

'Yes?'

'I won't say. I think I need *you* to tell *me*.'

'All you have to do is—'

'No,' she said sharply. 'I've told you everything you need to know to figure out what comes next. If my words really are like smouldering coals, Locke, then let these ones smoulder. Sift them, and bring me an answer sometime after we reach Espara. Bring me a *good* answer.'

<h1 style="text-align:center">3</h1>

Espara, formerly a seat of prestige only one step below Therim Pel itself, had descended from its imperial years the way some men and women descend into middle-aged lethargy, discarding the vigour and ambition of youth like a suit of clothes that can no longer be wriggled into.

Locke caught his first glimpse of the place just after noon on the tenth day, when the caravan turned the bend between two ruin-studded hills and entered the familiar, irregular green-and-brown whorls of a farming landscape. On the southern horizon lay the faint shapes of towers under curling grey smears of smoke.

'Espara,' said Anatoly Vireska. 'Right where I left it. No more stops for rest, my young friends. Before the sun sets you'll be in the city looking for your actor fellows.'

'Well done, caravan master,' said Locke, who had the reins while Jean was snoring gently under the tarp at the rear of the wagon. 'Not what I'd call a scenic tour, but you've brought us through without a scratch.'

'When the crop of bandits is thin, it's a restful little walk. Now it's back to dodging carriages, breathing smoke, and paying rent for the beds you sleep in, eh?'

'Gods be praised,' said Locke.

'City creatures are the strangest of all,' said Vireska with a friendly shake of his head. He moved off to visit the rest of the wagons.

All the Gentlemen Bastards, more or less as footsore, ass-sore, un-washed, and drained of blood as Sabetha had predicted, had given up on walking this morning. Calo and Galdo leaned against each other, watching the landscape roll by at its strolling pace, while Sabetha was absorbed in the copy of *The Republic of Thieves* she'd picked up before they'd left Camorr.

'Is the play any good?' said Galdo.

'I think so,' said Sabetha, 'except the final act has been torn out of this folio, and half the pages have stains blotting out some of the lines. I keep imagining that every scene ends with the characters hurling cups of coffee at one another.'

'Sounds like my kind of play,' said Calo.

'Are there any decent roles?' said Galdo.

'They're all decent,' said Sabetha. 'Better than decent. I think they're very romantic. We should have names like this, like all the heroes in these plays, all the famous bandits and sorcerers and emperors.'

'Most people could give half a dry shit for having an emperor's name,' said Galdo. 'It's the wealth and power they'd want.'

'What I mean,' said Sabetha, 'is that we should have aliases like out of the old storeys. Big, grand titles like the Ten Honest Turncoats, you know? Red Jessa, the Duke of Knaves. Amadine, the Queen of Shadows.'

'I think Verena Gallante's a fine alias,' said Locke.

'No, I mean *big* and *important*, and *uncommon*. Not something you get called to your face. The sort of alias that people whisper when something unbelievable happens. "Oh, gods, this can only be the work of the Duke of Knaves!"'

'Heavens,' said Galdo in a deep, dramatic voice, 'only one man living could have squeezed forth such a gleaming brown jewel – this is the work of Squatting Calo, the Midnight Shitter!'

'You two want for imagination,' said Sabetha.

'Not at all,' said Galdo. 'The lower the enterprise, the hotter the fire of our invention burns.'

'Are you going a bit stir-crazy, Sabetha?' said Locke, secretly pleased to hear the energy in her voice after so many days of brooding tedium.

'Maybe I am. I've been stuck in this wagon counting Sanza farts for a week; maybe I'm due a little flight of fancy. I mean, wouldn't it be grand, to have a legend that grew while you were alive to enjoy it? To sit in a tavern and hear all the people around you speaking of what you'd done, with no notion that you were among them as flesh and blood?'

'I can sit in a tavern and be ignored any time I please,' muttered Calo.

'I want to see the Kingdom of the Marrows someday,' said Sabetha. 'Game my way from city to city … on the arms of nobles, emptying their pockets as I go, charming them witless. I'd be like a force of nature. They'd come up with some elegant title for their shared affliction. 'It was *her* … it was … it was the *Rose*.'

Sabetha rolled this off her tongue, obviously savouring it.

'The *Rose of the Marrows*, they'll say. "The Rose of the Marrows has been my ruin!" And they'll tear their hair out explaining everything to their wives and bankers, while I ride on to the next city.'

'Are we all going to need stupid nicknames, then?' said Calo. 'We could be … the Shrubs of the North.'

'The Weeds of Vintila,' said Galdo.

'And if you're a rose,' said Calo, 'Locke's going to need something as well.'

'He can be a tulip,' said Galdo. 'Delicate little tulip.'

'Nah, if she's the rose, he can be her thorn.' Calo snapped his fingers. 'The *Thorn of Camorr*! Now that's got some shine to it!'

'That's the dumbest fucking thing I've ever heard,' said Locke.

'We can do it as soon as we get home,' said Calo. 'Disguise ourselves. Drop hints in bars. Tell storeys here and there. Give us a month and everyone will be talking about the Thorn of Camorr. Even the ones that don't know shit will just tell more lies, so they can sound like they're clued in on the latest.'

'If you ever do anything like that,' said Locke, 'I swear to all the gods, I will murder you.'

4

Just after the fourth hour of the afternoon, with the faintest warm drizzle sweating out of the greying sky, their wagon rolled through the mud beneath the stone arch of the Jalaan River Gate on the east side of Espara. Jean was back at the reins, and he bade their horses to halt for a squad of armed men in cloaks.

'What goes, Vireska?' said the evident leader, one of those graceful hulking types, the sort that gave every impression of being able to dance a minuet despite possession of a belly fit for carving into ham steaks. 'We could set a water-clock by you. Dull trip, eh?'

'Just the way it ought to be,' said the caravan master as he shook hands with the watchman. The gratuity that instantly vanished into the heavy fellow's pocket was generous; Vireska had discussed it back in Camorr and collected an equal portion from each wagon owner. 'Now, when you're poking through everything, watch-sergeant, just be especially delicate with the drugs and the hidden weapons, eh?'

'I promise not to keep you more than ten hours this time,' laughed the big Esparan. His men made an extremely cursory examination of the wagons, clearly more for the benefit of anyone watching than for the enforcement of the city's customs laws.

'Welcome,' said one of the guards to Sabetha, who'd once again donned all her more modest clothing. 'First time in Espara?'

'Actually, yes,' she said.

'Might we help you find anything?' said the big watch-sergeant, edging in next to his man.

'Oh, that would be so *very* kind of you,' she said, bubbling with girlish charm. Locke bit his tongue to stifle a snicker. 'We're looking for a man called Jasmer Moncraine. The Moncraine Company, the actors.'

'Why?' said the watch-sergeant. 'You creditors?'

All the men behind him burst into laughter.

'Ah, no,' she said. 'We're players, from Camorr, come to join his troupe.'

'They got theatres in Camorr, miss?' said one of the guards. 'I thought you was all more about, like, sharks bitin' women in half.'

'I'd like to see that,' mumbled another watchman.

'There *is* an awful lot of that where we come from,' said Sabetha. 'In fact, we spend more time touring than at home. Moncraine's engaging us for the rest of the summer.'

'Well,' said the watch-sergeant, 'In that case, best of luck. You can find some of the Moncraine Company at, uh, what's that place with the olive tree torn out of its courtyard?'

'Gloriano's Rooms,' said another guard.

'Right, right. Gloriano's,' said the sergeant. 'Look, you follow this lane straight down to the Temple of Venaportha, and just past it turn left, hear? Take that lane across the river, you're in a place we call Solace Hill. Gloriano's Rooms would be on your right. If you find gravestones on three sides, you've gone too far.'

'We're obliged to you,' said Locke, while nursing a faint premonition that that might not, in the grand scheme of things, turn out to be entirely true.

They parted company with Vireska's caravan and made their way into Espara, keeping to the watch-sergeant's directions. It seemed to Locke that they all perked up considerably at finding themselves back in the familiar world of high stone walls, rain-dampened smoke, junk-strewn alleys, and people crammed elbow-to-elbow on the dry portions of the boulevards.

'Three cheers for a proper ale,' said Galdo wistfully. 'In a proper tavern, that doesn't have a fucking palisade built round it to keep out the bloody bog monster.'

'I think this is Solace Hill,' said Jean, as they entered a neighbourhood that seemed to regress further from prosperity with every turn of the wagon wheels. The buildings grew lower, the windows became dirtier, and the lights grew fewer. 'Look, that's a graveyard, this Gloriano's has to be close.'

They found it not a block down, the best-lit structure for some distance in any direction, though the illumination was perhaps unwise given the things it revealed about the condition of walls and roofs. A pair of city watchmen, looking soaked behind the misty glow of their lanterns, were standing in the turn to the inn-yard and impeding the passage of the Gentlemen Bastards' wagon.

'Is there a problem, Constables?' called Jean.

'You don't actually mean to turn in here?' said one of the men warily, as though he suspected himself the butt of a joke.

'I think we do,' said Jean.

'But this is the way to Gloriano's inn-yard,' said the constable, even more warily.

'Pleased to hear it.'

'You delivering something?'

'Just ourselves,' said Jean.

'Gods above, you mean it,' said the constable. 'I could tell you ain't from here, even if I never heard your voice.' He and his companion stepped out of the way with exaggerated courtesy and walked on, shaking their heads.

Locke first heard the shouting as Jean brought them in under a sloping canvas awning that was more holes than fabric, next to a dark stable that contained only one horse. The animal looked at them as though in hope of rescue.

'What the hells is that noise?' said Sabetha.

It wasn't any sort of row that Locke recognized. Fisticuffs, theft, murder, domestic quarrel – all of those things had familiar rhythms and notes, sounds he could have identified in a second. This was something stranger, and it seemed to be coming from just around the right-hand corner of the building.

'Jean, Sabetha, come quietly with me,' he said. 'Sanzas, mind the horses. If they have any brains they might try to bolt.'

It didn't occur to him until his boots hit the mud that he'd again done precisely what Sabetha had railed against: presumed leadership without hesitation. But damn it, this wasn't a time for putting his life under a magnifying lens; it was a time for making sure they weren't all about to be murdered.

'I shall break you, joint by joint,' bellowed a man with a deep, attention-seizing voice, 'and drink your screams like a fine wine, and burn in brighter ecstasy with every ... fading ... whimper from your coward's throat!'

'Holy shit,' said Locke. 'No, wait. That's ... that's from a play.'

'*Catalinus, Last Prince of Amor Peth*,' whispered Jean.

Side by side, Locke, Jean, and Sabetha moved carefully around the corner. They found themselves facing a courtyard, the interior of three double-storeyed wings of the inn, with a vast ugly hole in the middle where something had been torn out of the ground.

A man and a woman sat off to one side, out of the light, watching a third man, who stood on the edge of the muddy hole with a bottle in either hand. This man was a prodigious physical specimen, surpassing Father Chains in girth and breadth, with a rain-slick crown of white hair pasted down around his creased face. He wore a loose grey robe and nothing else.

'I shall grind your bones to *powder*,' he hollered, transfixing the three Gentlemen Bastards with his gleaming eyes. 'And with that dust I'll make cement for paving stones, and for a hundred years to come you'll have no rest beneath the crush of strange wheels and the tramp of strange boots! Drunkards will make their unclean water upon you, and I shall laugh to think of it, Catalinus! I shall laugh until I die, and *I* shall die whole in body, wholly revenged upon thee!'

He flung forth his arms, perhaps intentionally, perhaps at random, and when he seemed to realize that he still held bottles in his hands he drank from them.

'Excuse me,' said Locke. Thunder rumbled overhead. The rain grew heavier. 'We're, ah, looking for the Moncraine Company.'

'Moncraine,' yelled the white-haired man, dropping one of his bottles and waving his arms to keep his balance at the edge of the hole. 'Moncraine!'

'Are you Jasmer Moncraine?' said Jean.

'I, Jasmer Moncraine?' The man leapt down into the hole, which was about thigh-deep, raising a dark splash of water. He scrambled up the other side and came toward them, now thoroughly be-mucked from the waist down. 'I am Sylvanus Olivios Andrassus, the greatest actor in a thousand miles, in a thousand *years*! Jasmer Moncraine wishes … on his best day … that he was worth a single drop … OF MY PISS!'

Sylvanus Olivios Andrassus shambled forward, and put his empty hand on Jean's shoulder. 'Stupid boy,' he said. 'I need you to let me have … five royals … just until Penance Day. Oh, gods …'

He went down to one knee and threw up. Jean's reflexes were sharp enough to save everything except one of his shoes.

'Fuck *me*!' said Jean.

'Oh no, I assure you, that is quite out of the question,' said Sylvanus. He attempted several times to stumble back to his feet, then once again noticed the remaining bottle in his hand, and began to suckle at it contentedly.

'Look, sorry about this,' said the woman who'd been watching as she emerged from the shadows. She was tall, dark-skinned, and wearing a shawl over her hair. Her fellow spectator was a thin young Therin man just a few years older than the Gentlemen Bastards. 'Sylvanus has what you might call rare ambition in the field of self-degradation.'

'Are you the Moncraine Company?' said Locke.

'Who wants to know?' said the woman hesitantly.

'I'm Lucaza de Barra,' said Locke. 'This is my cousin, Jovanno de Barra. And this is our friend Verena Gallante.' When this elicited no response, Locke cleared his throat. 'We're Moncraine's new players. The ones from Camorr.'

'Oh, sweet gods above,' said the woman. 'You're real.'

'Yeah,' said Locke. 'And, uh, wet and confused.'

'We thought— Well, look, we didn't think you *existed*. We thought Moncraine was making you up!'

'Took ten slow days in a wagon to get here,' said Jean. 'Let me assure you, nobody made us up.'

'I'm Jenora,' said the woman. 'And this is Alondo—'

'Alondo Razi,' said the young man. 'Weren't there supposed to be more of you?'

'The Asino brothers are minding the wagon, back around the corner,' said Locke. 'So, we're flesh and blood. I guess the next question is, does Jasmer Moncraine exist?'

'Moncraine,' muttered Sylvanus. 'Wouldn't shit on his head to give him … shade from the sun.'

'Moncraine,' said Jenora, 'is why Sylvanus is … um … making a clean break from sobriety at the moment.'

'Moncraine's in the Weeping Tower,' said Alondo.

'What's that?' said Jean.

'The most secure prison in Espara. It's Countess' Dragoons on the doors, not city watch.'

'Aw, hell's blistered balls,' said Locke. 'He already got taken up for debt?'

'Debt?' said Jenora. 'No, he never got the chance to be hauled in for all that mess. He decked some pissant lordling across the jaw this morning. He's up for assaulting someone of noble blood.'

CHAPTER SIX
The Five-Year Game: Change Of Venue

I

'Fourthson Vidalos,' said Josten. 'Would that your parents had stopped at their third! How many nights have you spent leaning against my bar, eh? How many times have I brought you in out of the rain for a glass? You two-faced son of a—'

'For the gods' sakes,' said Vidalos, 'Do you think I wanted this? It's my duty!'

'In front of half the Konseil and the entire Deep Roots—'

'Josten,' said Locke, stepping between the innkeeper and Vidalos, 'let's talk. Herald, how do you do? I'm Lazari, an advisor.'

'Whose advisor?'

'Everyone's advisor. I'm a solicitor from Lashain, retained in a broad capacity. I require a moment in private with Master Josten, to discuss his options.'

'I don't see that he has any,' said Vidalos.

'Do you have orders to refuse us a few minutes for reflection?' said Locke.

'Of course not.'

'Then I'll thank you not to enforce orders you haven't been given.' Locke put an arm firmly around Josten's shoulders, turned the sputtering innkeeper away from the herald, and whispered, 'Josten, one thing. Are you absolutely certain your license is truly paid up?'

'I have a signed receipt in my papers. I could fetch it now and shove it up this powder-blue pimp's ass! Until tonight, I would've called the bastard a good friend, on my honour. I never would've thought—'

'Don't think,' said Locke. 'I'm paid to do that for you. Herald Vidalos isn't your enemy. It's whoever summoned him to work and gave him a warrant that *somehow* urgently needed to be served at half past the tenth hour of the evening, do you follow?'

'Ah,' said Josten. '*Ahhhhhhh.*'

'We shouldn't abuse the poor bastard whose boots are on the

269

pavement,' said Locke. 'Our troubles come from higher offices. Niko-ros, get over here! Look at this seal and signature.'

'Capability Peralis,' said Nikoros. Sweat ran down his forehead in glistening lines. 'Second clerk, Magistrates' Court. I've heard of her.'

'She wouldn't need an actual magistrate to sign this?' said Locke.

'No,' said Nikoros, 'magistrates only sign off on, uh, arrests.'

'And this,' said Locke, 'is just a little sting in the ass. Is she Black Iris? Or any of her superiors?'

'Not according to my lists,' said Nikoros. 'Most of the people at the court make a point of not, uh, not declaring for either party.'

'Well, someone got her to perform a favour.' Locke suddenly became aware that most of the party, rank on tipsy rank, were watching closely to see if their mountain of fine liquor was really to be severed from them on the word of a single nervous functionary. 'I don't suppose Konseil members can just order Vidalos to make himself scarce?'

'Magistrates are, ah, co-equal with the Konseil,' said Nikoros. 'Their heralds don't have t-to take orders from anyone else.'

'Well, our drunk friends are going to hang this poor bastard from the rafters if I let this go through.' Locke turned back to Herald Vida-los, grinning broadly. 'Everything seems to be perfectly in order!'

'It gives me little satisfaction,' said Vidalos.

'I'd have thought you'd be happy,' said Locke, 'since there's abso-lutely no need for you to shut down the party.'

'Having delivered the warrant,' said Vidalos, 'it pains me to report that I'm bound to carry out my directions therein; I have to observe that Master Josten has ended this affair and sealed his doors to new customers.'

'Begging your pardon, but you're not allowed to do anything of the sort,' said Locke. 'That's *premature restraint of trade*, which is forbidden under the Articles of Karthain. Whoever signed this warrant should have known that Josten is entitled, by law, to verification of these charges before a magistrate—'

'But—'

'Prior to interruption of commerce!' continued Locke. 'Look, this is fairly basic stuff from that amendment business about, what – twenty years ago.'

'I ... really?' Vidalos' face lost some of its plum colour. 'Are you quite sure? I'm not entirely familiar with that. And I have served a number of similar—'

'I'm fully bonded for practise in Karthain. Imposition of penalty without proper verification of these charges would expose you to censure for negligence, the penalties for which could be ... well, of course *you* know what they could be. Let's not dwell on them.'

'Um ...,' said Vidalos. 'Uh, of course.'

'So, you've served your warrant in front of the most credible body of witnesses the city could hope to produce. I accept the warrant on Josten's behalf and formally request a magistrate's verification of its charges. Since we can't possibly have that until at least tomorrow morning, the party must continue.'

'Ha! That's served you out,' shouted someone within the crowd. 'Shuffle off, tipstaff!'

'None of *that*!' yelled Locke. 'For shame! This man is a good friend to this house, given the awful task of serving this warrant against his will. And did he flinch? No! Obedient to duty, he stepped into the lion's den!'

'Hear him,' cried Firstson Epitalus. Whether he realized the stupidity of needlessly making an enemy of Vidalos or merely wished his own voice to ring loudest in any acclamation, Locke blessed him. 'Karthain should be proud to have such an honest and fearless fellow in its service!'

People immediately followed Epitalus' lead. Catcalls that had barely started up were replaced with a rising swell of applause.

'I regret my harsh words,' said Diligence Josten, propelled toward Vidalos by a subtle elbow from Locke, and fully taking the hint. 'Give me your pardon, and have a glass with us.'

'Oh, but ...' Vidalos seemed pleased, relieved, and embarrassed all at once. 'I'm on duty—'

'Surely not,' said Josten. 'The warrant is served, so your duties are finished.'

'Well, if you put it that way—'

Josten and several accomplices enfolded the herald into the crowd and shuffled him toward the liquor supply.

'Oh, thank the gods,' muttered Nikoros. 'I had no idea you'd picked up such a knowledge of Karthani law, Lazari.'

'I haven't,' said Locke. 'When the sky's falling, I take shelter under bullshit. Someone's going to figure that out soon enough tomorrow.'

'Then there's no such statute?'

'Fake as a man with three cocks.'

'Really? Damn! It sounded so r-reasonable. Lying to an officer of the court is an offence they could—'

'That's not worth worrying about. If pressed I'll use the never-fail universal apology.'

'What's the n-never-fail universal apology?'

'"I was badly misinformed, I deeply regret the error, go fuck yourself with this bag of money." But it shouldn't come to that. First thing tomorrow, we need to reach this Capability Peralis. If Josten's papers are magically found to have been "misplaced", then the whole affair dries up before it can call further attention to itself.'

'And if she won't roll over for us?' said Jean, who'd been hovering nearby.

'We get someone else. First Clerk, maybe, or an actual magistrate. We're buying ourselves a little corner of the Magistrates' Court tomorrow, come hell or Eldren-fire. When do the courts open?'

'Ninth hour of the morning.'

'Be outside our door at eight.'

'Oh, uh—'

'At *eight*,' said Locke, reducing his voice to a cold whisper. 'So don't stuff any more of that shit down your throat tonight.'

'Oh, I, uh, I don't have any idea what you—'

'Yes. *You do.* I don't care if you're totally out of your head on Akkadris, I'll put a damn leash around your neck and drag you by it. We're all going together to put this fire out before it spreads.'

2

'Nikoros,' muttered Locke, bleary-eyed and fog-brained, as he swung the apartment door open in response to a frenzied pounding. 'What the hell are you about, man? It can't be anywhere near eight yet.'

'It's just after five.' Nikoros looked as though he'd been bootstomped by a gang of hangover fairies. His hair was undone, his clothes haphazard, and the bags under his eyes could have been used for coin pouches. 'They've got my office, Lazari. Just like you said.'

'What?' Locke blinked the glue from his eyes and ushered Nikoros inside. 'Someone burned your office down?'

'No, it's not arson.' Nikoros nodded to Jean, who'd come in through the connecting door from his side of the suite. Jean wore a black silk dressing gown and was carrying his hatchets casually in his right hand.

'The Master Ratfinder's office cordoned off my whole bloody building for a suckle-spider infestation. Sheer luck I wasn't there when they showed up, otherwise I'd be getting an alchemical bath in quarantine.'

'Your scribe?'

'He dodged them too. Almost everything was copied or removed in time, but now they'll be fumigating with brimstone for three days. Can't use the place until they're done.'

'I don't suppose you'd ever seen so much as one hair on a suckle-spider's ass?'

'The building's two years old! Clean as an infant's soul.'

'Another how-do-you-do from our friends across town. How many people work for this ratfinder?'

'A dozen or so. Alchemists, sewer-stalkers, corpse-hunters. They handle all things pestilent and sanitary.'

'How are they regarded?'

'Master Bilezzo's a hero! Hells, I mostly think so, too. Keeps the city damned clean, compared to a lot of other places. Forty years without a plague in Karthain, not even cholera. People notice that sort of thing.'

'This is touchy, then,' said Jean. 'We can't be heavy-handed dealing with this or it'll snap right back at us. Sa ... someone in the opposition keeps choosing delicate instruments to poke us with.'

'We need some delicate instruments of our own,' said Locke. 'We're not going to have any time to deal with the election if we have to run around pissing on these distractions.'

'Do you think you can get my office back?'

'Hmmm.' Locke scratched his stubble. 'No. Look, Nikoros, no offence, but if we've got you and your files, we don't need your office. Let them smoke it out. Our job as far as this Master Bilezzo is concerned is to make sure Josten's isn't closed down for similar treatment.'

'Very well,' said Nikoros. 'But I, uh, my rooms – I suppose I'll have to board here for a few days.'

'That might not be a bad thing. This place is our castle, and the siege has started. Speaking of which, after we deal with the Magistrates' Court, get me some actual solicitors. Trustworthy sorts. I presume the party has a few?'

'Of course.'

'Have them join the menagerie here, in the best suites Josten has left. Next time someone walks in with writs or warrants or gods know what, I want real paper-pushers on hand to spin authentic nonsense.'

'We seem to be off to a bad start,' said Nikoros.

'We are.'

'And I must apologize … for my, uh, you know. It's just an occasional thing, you understand. Keeps me working through the long nights. I can … stop, if you—'

'Do. Throw that shit away. We need you steady and reliable. Dust-heads are neither.'

'I'm not a dusthead—'

'Save it. I've seen more dustheads, gazers, pissers, burners, and stonelickers than you can imagine. I've even crawled into a bottle myself, once or twice. Don't try to placate me; just do us all a favour and stay off it. Get pickled on booze like an ordinary Deep Roots man.'

'I can … as you say. I can do it.'

'And don't sweat our situation. By tonight, we'll be walled in with brutes and solicitors, most of the locks will be changed, Josten will secure his staff. … You'll feel better once our basic defences are in place. Now get a room, get what sleep you can. Master Callas and I will fetch you at eight. And hey. Tell whoever's on duty we want enough coffee to kill a horse.'

When the coffee came a few minutes later, the maid delivering it wore a gleaming brass chain around her neck.

'That was quick work on Josten's part,' said Jean, pouring two steam-ing cups. 'The chains, I mean. You don't believe it'll keep out real mis-chief, though? Wouldn't stop either of us, I should think.'

'It's not meant to,' said Locke. 'It's a simple obstacle for the witless and unlucky. The less time we have to waste on idiots, the more we can devote to everything else Sabetha does.'

3

It was a cool, mist-haunted morning. Water trickled down every window, and the pavements were slick. A few minutes before eight, Locke and Jean hustled Nikoros, who looked as though sleep had been scarce, into a carriage. Locke gnawed indelicately at half a loaf of bread stuffed with cold meat from the party. This breakfast was disposed of by the time they made their first stop of the morning, at Tivoli's, to reinforce the coins in their purses with a few hundred comrades.

Next, they rattled north to the Casta Gravina, the old citadel of

Karthain, whose interior walls and gates had been knocked down years before to make more room for a government that didn't have to fear anything so mundane as a hostile army at its doorstep. The plazas and gardens were so beautifully laid out that the fog might have been just one more decoration, artfully conjured and shaped by crews of over-ambitious groundskeepers.

'Magistrates' Court,' said Nikoros, leading the way out of the carriage. 'I know the place. If you want to make any money in my business, you'll end up party or witness in your share of lawsuits.'

Locke and Jean followed him across a circular plaza, into the clammy silver mist that opened a few paces ahead of them and swallowed their carriage an equal distance behind. The fog echoed faintly with the sounds of the city coming to life – doors opening, horses and wheels clattering, people shouting to one another.

'Clerks' office is just over here,' said Nikoros.

'OOF!' A woman came out of the fog to Locke's left before he could react. She collided with Locke, steadied herself against him, and was then snatched away rather ignominiously by Jean.

'Gods above!' she cried. The voice was creaky, middle-aged, Karthani.

'It's fine, Master Callas, it's fine,' said Locke. He patted his purse and papers, verifying their undisturbed state. The collision might or might not be innocent, but the woman seemed to be no pickpocket.

'A thousand apologies. You startled us, madam,' said Jean, releasing the woman. She was a few inches shorter than Locke, broad and heavy, dressed in a dull but expensive fashion. Her grey-dusted brown hair was pinned up under an elegant four-cornered cap, and her face was lined with whatever cares had chased her through life. Locke prayed silently that they hadn't just upset one of the very clerks they might want to suborn.

'It's you who startled me, looming out of the fog like a pack of highwaymen!'

'I wouldn't call it looming, madam. Some of us simply aren't built for looming,' said Locke.

'You, perhaps not, but I could plant your big friend in the street to shade the roof of my house.' She readjusted her coat with a sharp tug and went on her way, scowling. 'Good day, oafs.'

'Nikoros,' said Jean, 'was that anyone important?'

'Never seen her before.'

'Well, let's get inside before we trip over someone we can't afford to offend,' said Locke.

The office of the clerks wasn't particularly large, but it was comfortably appointed. The purgatory of quiet halls and empty chairs outside the clerical chambers looked like a decent place to fall asleep in. Capability Peralis, a round and attractive woman on the kinder side of forty, was scratching away at papers behind her desk when Locke, Jean, and Nikoros entered her chamber.

'I'm sorry,' she said, irritably tossing thick dark ringlets out of her eyes as she looked up. 'No appointments before half ten. Where's the hall secretary?'

'The secretary has been taken advantage of by my excessive natural and financial charms,' said Locke, who'd been charming to the tune of a month's salary. 'I'm sure you can sympathize.'

Locke settled smoothly into one of the chairs before Peralis' desk, and Jean casually drew the door shut. Nikoros stood off to one side and pretended to admire the walls.

'I've no idea who you think you are, sir—'

'Last night,' said Locke, 'a warrant was signed and sent out from this office, a warrant concerning Josten's Comprehensive Accommodations.'

'If you're Josten's counsel, you know bloody well when Public Proceedings are held!'

'What I know,' said Locke, 'is that some miracle caused the records for the payment of Josten's ardent spirits license, which is perfectly sound, to be misplaced. I'd like that miracle reversed. I do understand that miracles are expensive.'

Sighing inwardly at the artlessness of this approach (there was no time to waste on subtlety), Locke swept a hand across the desktop, leaving a comet-like trail of gold coins.

'Is that meant to impress me?' said Peralis softly, fiercely. Oh, her version of Offended Honest Public Functionary deserved applause! 'Attempted bribery of a civic official. You'll shed your boldness when you're chained to an interrogation cell wall.'

'Good *gods*, that's lovely,' said Locke. 'I'm really sorry that I simply don't have time to play this game with you. That's your annual salary right there on the desktop. I propose to give you six more payments just like it, one per week until this election is over. All I ask is that no further complications to Deep Roots party business be specially conjured by you or your staff. Nothing more.'

'Well,' she said, dropping her façade of outrage, 'what if another benefactor is willing to provide additional funds in a contrary direction?'

'Notify us,' said Locke. 'We'll match anything you're offered. I don't even want you to take action against that other benefactor; merely refrain from taking action against us. Make up excuses. Imply that you're under scrutiny, that further accommodations are temporarily impossible. Surely you can see it's a sweet arrangement where you're concerned.'

'It's not without its temptations,' she mused.

'Quit being coy. Just say yes and earn a fortune.'

'Well, then – yes.'

'I have your word this warrant concerning Josten is a misunderstanding, and the record in question is going to be found, by the happiest happenstance, as soon as I leave this office?'

'You may safely consider the matter settled.'

'Good. If it remains settled next week, I'll call again with more decorations for your desk. Now, if you'll excuse us, we have a tight schedule of pushing boulders up hills.'

'You know,' said Nikoros quietly as they left the Second Clerk's office, 'not to criticize, but if no particular tact is required in these matters, I've a hundred Deep Roots men and women who can make these calls in their official capacities—'

'No,' said Locke. 'When it comes to just laying out money, leave our official friends out of it. Save them for areas in which their authority is needed. There's no point in blunting our tools in the wrong applications.'

'Well,' said Nikoros, 'you're damned impossible to argue with, Master Lazari.'

'Not impossible,' said Jean placidly. 'About as intractable as a tortoise with its ass on fire, though.'

'If we're going to catch up to the opposition,' said Locke, 'we've got to step boldly at every—'

'There he is! *There's the man who stole my purse!*' cried a familiar voice as Locke emerged once again onto the fog-shrouded plaza.

The middle-aged woman stood there, flanked by two men in pale blue coats reminiscent of the one worn by Vidalos. These men wore studded leather vests beneath them, however, and had clubs hanging from their belts.

Gods. So it hadn't been an innocent collision after all.

277

'Your pardon, sir,' said one of the guards, stepping forward, 'but I must ask to see your pockets.'

'A black silk purse,' said the woman, 'with the initials "G.B." in red in one of the corners. Seven ducats in it. Or at least there were!'

Locke patted himself down hurriedly. Yes, there *was* a slender new weight in the lower left inside pocket of his rather excellent new coat. He hadn't noticed the addition; he'd been so satisfied with verifying that nothing had been removed. Stupid, clumsy, amateurish—

'I say,' he sputtered, 'this is an intolerable accusation! How dare you, madam, how dare you! And how dare you, sir, suggest that a gentleman might be turned upside-down and shaken like a common cutpurse!'

'Be reasonable, sir,' said the guard. 'The lady has a precise description of what was taken, and surely proving that you don't have it is worth a moment of your time—'

'It is a liberty beyond comprehension! This is Karthain, not the lawless wilds!' Into his furious gesticulations, Locke worked a number of quick hand signals for Jean's benefit. 'I take great ... I take the most ... I take take take ... arrrrrggggggggh!'

Locke spasmed and sputtered. His eyes rolled back in his head, and he stumbled forward moaning, clutching at the approaching guard. Alarmed, the man reached for his club. While Nikoros watched in mute bewilderment, Jean sprang between Locke and the guard.

'For pity's sake!' Jean hissed. 'Don't pull that cudgel, he's having a fit!'

'Nnnnngggggggggghhhhh,' said Locke, spraying flecks of spittle and waving his head about furiously.

'He's cursed,' said the other guard, making a gesture against evil with both of his hands. 'He's got a spirit influence on him!'

'He's not cursed, you damned simpleton, it's an illness,' said Jean. 'Whenever his emotions run high, there's a chance he'll have a fit, and I daresay *you*, madam, have brought him to this state!'

In a manner that seemed perfectly accidental and natural (Jean's interference was nothing less than expert), Locke broke away from Jean and the guard. Lurching like a marionette whose puppeteer was dying of some convulsive poison, he tumbled sobbing against the woman, who shrieked and pushed him away. Locke wound up on his back with Jean crouching protectively over him as he babbled, twitched, and kicked at the air.

'Stand back,' said Jean. 'Give him some air. The fit will pass. In a moment he'll be calm.'

Locke, taking the hint, gradually reduced the severity of his symptoms until he was only gently shuddering and mumbling.

'If you really must render such low treatment to a gentleman,' said Jean, 'I suggest you examine his pockets now, while he's not entirely himself.'

The guard Locke had initially stumbled against knelt down beside him and, carefully, as though Locke might leap back up at any moment, went through Locke's coat.

'Private papers and a purse not matching your description,' he said, standing up. 'Madam, I'm afraid it's just not there.'

'He must have discarded it inside,' she cried. 'Search the building!'

'Now this is *beyond* all propriety,' said Jean. 'My friend is a gentleman and a solicitor, and you insult him with these ridiculous accusations!'

'He's a pickpocket,' said the woman. 'He ran into me to steal my purse!'

'This man is a *convulsive*,' Jean bellowed. 'He has fits half a dozen times a day! What the hell kind of pickpocket do you think he'd make? Twitching and trembling and falling over? Gods!'

'Madam,' said the guard standing over Locke, 'he doesn't have your purse, and you must admit a gentleman with, ah, twitching fever hardly seems a likely cutpurse.'

'Check his friend,' she said. 'Check the big one.'

'I'll gladly hand my coat over,' said Jean, slowly and coldly, pretending to come to a realization. 'Yet I must insist that *you* do the same, madam.'

'Me?'

'Yes,' said Jean. 'I understand what's going on now. I marvel that I didn't grasp it before. There is a pickpocket at work, sirs, but one wearing a lady's dress rather than a gentleman's breeches.'

'You foreign slime!' shouted the woman.

'Constables, no doubt you've been in the company of this woman since she approached you with her complaint. I'd check, if I were you, to make sure of your own purses.'

The guards patted themselves down, and the one standing over Locke gasped.

'My coin bag!' he said. 'It was right here in my belt!'

'You may examine me at length,' said Jean, extending his arms with his empty palms up. 'But I must insist that your more fruitful course of action would be to examine my accuser.'

The guard nearest the woman put a hand on her shoulder, mumbled apologies, and gingerly sifted her coat pockets while she screeched and struggled. After a moment, he held up a small leather coin bag and a black silk purse.

'Stitched with the initials "G.B. "!' he said.

'But it was missing!' she cried. 'It was nowhere to be found!'

'What about my coin bag, eh?' The first guard snatched the leather purse from his partner and shook it at her. 'What's this doing in your pocket?'

'I'm bloody confused,' muttered the other guard.

'You're meant to be,' said Jean. 'Forgive me for saying so. I've seen this act before. Our harmless-looking friend here has been plucking purses. Clearly she meant to frame *my* friend for her deeds, even while plying her trade on you, sirs. Thus, when you and any other victims discovered your light pockets, you'd have a culprit already in hand, ready to soak up all the blame. I can only imagine she tried and failed to plant her purse on my friend. Perhaps age is catching up with you, madam?'

'Lying bastard,' she shouted, trying and failing to fight off the firm grip of a guard. 'Lying, thieving, pocket-picking foreigner!'

'Right, you,' said the first guard, taking her other arm. 'I don't like being taken advantage of. Gentlemen, would you like to come inside with us and register your complaint as well?'

'Actually,' said Jean, 'I'd like to get my friend home, if not to a physiker. I daresay this woman's in enough trouble for having lifted your purse. I can be content with that.'

'And if you should need anything else from us,' said Nikoros, handing one of the guards a small white card, 'I'm Nikoros Via Lupa, Isas Salvierro. These men are my guests.'

'Very good, sir,' said the first guard, pocketing Nikoros' card. 'Sorry for the trouble. I hope the gentleman recovers.'

'Time and fresh lake air,' said Jean, swinging Locke up and supporting him under his right arm.

'Time's the one thing he doesn't have,' yelled the woman as the guards dragged her toward the court offices. 'And you two know it! *You know it!* Be seeing you, gentlemen!'

Once all three men were safely ensconced in their carriage and it was clattering away down the street, Locke returned to life and burst out laughing. 'Thank you, Nikoros,' he said, wiping flecks of spittle from his chin. 'That last note of respectability at the end was just what the scene needed to bring everything back down to earth.'

'I bloody well rejoice to hear it,' said Nikoros, 'but what the hell just happened?'

'That woman slipped a purse into my coat when she stumbled into me. Obviously she meant to get me snared for pickpocketing,' said Locke. 'I checked to see if anything was missing, but like a dolt I didn't think to feel around for unexpected gifts. She nearly had me.'

'Who was she?'

'No idea,' said Locke. 'She works for our counterpart, obviously. And she's a jewel … Anyone who can live to that age charming coats for a living knows their business. We'll see her again.'

'She'll be in a cold dark cell.'

'Oh, she'll slip those idiots in about five minutes,' said Jean. 'There'll be arrangements. Trust us.'

'I'm ashamed to admit that I actually thought for a moment that you, uh, were genuinely ill, Lazari,' said Nikoros.

'We didn't have any time to warn you. Pitching a fit's a crude bit of theatre, but it's surprising how often it works.'

'How did you guess she'd lifted that guard's purse?'

'I didn't guess,' said Locke with an indulgent chuckle. 'I borrowed it when I stumbled against him.'

'Then he passed it on to our lady friend, along with her own purse, when he stumbled against her,' said Jean.

'Gods above,' said Nikoros.

'And *don't* think she didn't realize it,' added Jean. 'But there's only so many ways you can arrange to bump tits with strangers before it starts to look fishy.'

'Ain't we clever?' said Locke, idly examining his own pockets again. 'And I'm pretty sure I still have … everything. *Holy hells!*'

There was a folded piece of parchment, sealed with wax, in his left inner pocket. He drew it out and stared at it.

'This wasn't in my pocket when I came out the door,' he said. 'She … she stuck me with it while I was slipping her the two purses!'

Jean gave a low whistle as Locke popped the seal and flipped the parchment open in haste. He read the contents aloud:

Msrs Lazari and Callas

Sirs—

I trust you will excuse the unorthodox means by which this letter finds its way into your hands. Karthani post-masters, enterprising as they are, rarely deliver directly to the interior pocket of a gentleman's coat. I present my compliments, and desire that you should call upon me at the seventh hour of this evening, at the Sign of the Black Iris, in the Vel Vespala.

Your most affectionate servant—

'*Verena Gallante,*' said Locke in a harsh whisper. His heart seemed to expand and fill his entire chest with its beating. 'She wants to … she wants to see … oh, gods—'

He looked out the window, craning his neck furiously to see behind them, into the swirling silvery fog, where of course there was nothing meaningful to be found.

'What is it?' said Nikoros.

'That was no middle-aged stranger,' said Locke. 'That was *her*.'

'Who?'

'The opposition,' said Locke, settling back into his seat, feeling dazed. 'Our counterpart. The woman we spoke of.'

'Verena Gallante?'

'It seems that's her present alias.'

'Oh my,' said Jean. 'The initials on the silk purse … now that was cheeky.'

'Only if we weren't too dense to notice it right away,' said Locke.

'I fail to see how "Verena Gallante" yields "G.B",' said Nikoros.

'A private matter,' said Locke. 'I have … we have a history with this woman.'

'What must we do now?' said Nikoros.

'Now,' said Locke, 'you can direct our driver to wherever this Master Ratfinder keeps his office, and after we've persuaded him to quit being a nuisance, you and Master Callas can go scrounge up the brutes we discussed yesterday.'

'And what about you?'

'I, well …' said Locke, running one hand over his stubble, 'I'll need to go find a barber.'

4

Their unannounced appointment with Master Ratfinder Bilezzo took less time than their protracted encounter at the court offices. After the initial exchange of greetings and the sudden appearance of a pile of ducats on Bilezzo's desk, it rapidly became clear to Locke and Jean that Bilezzo was a fatuous, contrary, self-satisfied fellow who was deeply amused at the chance to have a bit of harmless mischief with his far-ranging civic powers.

The two Gentlemen Bastards decided to correct his attitude in a traditional Camorri fashion. Locke doubled the amount of his proposed bribe while Jean picked Bilezzo up by his lapels, scraped the ceiling with his head, and cheerfully offered to nail his tongue to the back of a carriage and whip the horses around the city.

No middle-aged civil servant in a comfortable position could easily refuse such entreaties, and they parted with a mutually satisfactory arrangement. Bilezzo's men would continue (for appearance's sake) to carry out the pointless fumigation of Nikoros' building, Locke would conjure piles of gold to ensure it didn't happen again, or anywhere else of value to the Deep Roots party, and Jean would spare Bilezzo the unwanted carriage ride.

Nikoros came away from the meeting having learned several new words, as well as some novel hyphenations of familiar ones, and a fascinating twist to the art of negotiation that his education had previously neglected.

5

Locke returned alone to Josten's just before the second hour of the afternoon with the autumn air cool against his freshly shaved face, chewing on the last of the half-dozen sweet cakes he'd picked up for lunch.

The place was in a fine state of near-pandemonium, with locksmiths performing surgery on at least three visible doors, while the customary crowd of businessfolk bustled about eating, shouting, negotiating, or simply trying to maintain airs of importance. At the same time, the ordinary and legitimate business of the Deep Roots party went on. Locke and Jean had agreed that there was no need for them to oversee every last detail of the Committee's business, lest they go mad while driving everyone around them mad into the bargain.

Unusual events and setbacks, however, were very much their business, and Locke hadn't taken five steps past the front doors before a small pack of Nikoros' messengers and assistants descended on him waving scraps of paper. Locke flipped through them as he walked through the crowd and made his way up toward the party's private gallery.

Constables had detained several important party supporters for public drunkenness. A district organizer had dumped his life's savings into a bag and fled the city just before dawn for reasons unknown. A candidate for the seat in the Isas Vadrasta was going to fight a duel tomorrow, and there was no quality replacement if he ended up full of holes. Locke sighed. Casualty reports, by all the gods, like some captain on a battlefield! Sabetha's hand could be in any of it, or none of it. No doubt the lists of complications would only get longer as the weeks wore on.

'Here's Master Lazari now,' said Jean as Locke ascended the final step to the private gallery. Jean and Nikoros were standing before a group of eight men. Most of them looked capable to Locke's eye – city bruisers, obvious ex-constables, and a few with the deep tans and weather-worn faces of caravan guards. They all nodded or muttered greetings.

'We've got a lead on some women, too,' said Jean, whispering into Locke's ear. 'Bodyguards. Nikoros found them; he'll bring them in tomorrow.'

'Good,' said Locke. He waved the slips of paper at Jean. 'Seen these?'

'If those are the notes on today's pains in the ass, yes. You got anything to tell our new friends?'

'We want you content,' said Locke, addressing the men. 'We want you to feel that you're being treated fairly. If you're not, bring it to us. If anyone threatens you, or makes you an offer – you know the sort of thing I'm talking about – bring it to us. Quietly. I *guarantee* we'll come up with a better deal.'

There was no point in mentioning consequences or making threats; gods, no. Doing that in public was a sure sign of insecurity. Threats, when needed, would be a private affair. If these men had real quality they would appreciate not being treated like idiots.

'Go find Josten,' said Jean. 'Have yourselves a bite. I'll have shift assignments once you've eaten.'

As the men left the gallery, Jean turned to Locke. 'Where'd you go to get your shave, back to Lashain?'

'I didn't mean to be out so long. I, uh, just thought I'd have my driver take me around some of the Black Iris places Nikoros listed for us. See if there was anything interesting going on.'

'You were looking for her, weren't you?'

'Uh … yes. Didn't spot her on any street, though.' Locke ran a hand over his chin for the twentieth time. 'How does it look?'

'What?'

'The shave.'

'Like a shave. Fine.'

'You sure?'

'For Perelandro's sake. You got peach fuzz scraped off with a razor; you didn't commission a bust of yourself in marble.'

Locke crumpled the notes he'd been handed and put them in a coat pocket. 'Well, look, if you've got the new bruisers in hand and you've already heard the news, I'm, uh, going up to the room … to get ready.'

'You've got at least four hours before we have to leave.'

'Yeah, but if I don't start my nervous pacing now, I'll never have it all done in time.'

6

'How's it look?'

Almost precisely four hours later, Locke was standing before a full-length mirror in their suite, showing off a slight variation in the tying of his black neck-cloth.

'It looks like clothing,' said Jean, who'd been dressed for the better part of an hour and was now lounging in a high-backed chair, ominously juggling a hatchet in one hand.

'Too prissy? Too eastern?'

'You do realize you've pushed that damn thing around at least a dozen times now?'

'Just doesn't seem right.'

'You do realize that you didn't even *own* any of these outfits until yesterday? Why are you fretting about the deeper meaning of clothes that are newer than some of the crap digesting in that meagre gut of yours?'

'Because,' said Locke, 'I can't help myself, and I know I can't help myself, and it doesn't *help*, you get it?'

'I do get it,' said Jean softly. 'All too well. But I can't be of service by patting you on the back for being nervous. You've got to stick your chin out and call yourself ready sometime.'

'Nervous,' said Locke. 'I wish I was nervous! Nervous is when armed people try to kill me. This is something else. Gods, it's been five years. She could ... I just ... I don't even ...' He closed his eyes and leaned against the mirror's frame.

'You might as well practise finishing your sentences,' said Jean. 'I hear that women find it irresistible.'

'Five years,' said Locke. He looked up, and the haunted expression in the mirror seemed like a self-accusation. 'I'm going to have to tell her about Calo and Galdo.'

'She may already know.'

'I doubt it,' said Locke. 'She was playing with us this morning. I just don't think ... that she would have done so. I wouldn't have, in her place.'

'Five years apart, and you imagine that the two of you match moods so closely? Did you even do that when you were together?'

'Well—'

'You and I are *lucky to be alive* to even see her,' said Jean. 'Remember that. As for what happened while she was gone, it was as much her decision to leave as it was ours to stay.'

'I know,' said Locke. 'In my head. The message hasn't reached my gut just yet. There seems to be a tiny man in there attacking me with feathers. Now ... jewelry. I should—'

'Gods above,' said Jean, rising from his chair. 'Do you think she's going to fling herself out a window if your shoes have too many buckles?'

'Her fashion sense might have grown more extreme since we last met.'

'Quit making such a yammering twit out of yourself. Find your way to the door.'

Step by step out of the room, into the main hall, past the bar and the tables full of Nikoros' people with their lists and plans and dull assignments. Gods, he was really on his way! His knees seemed to be made of wet cotton; his pulse was like the sound of the ocean in his ears.

New solicitors watched from the Deep Roots gallery; new bruisers studied him from the front doors; new chains gleamed around the necks of all the waiters. So many cordons of security drawn tight against every possibility, and here he and Jean were planning a social call to the heart of Sabetha's power.

Out loud he would have been careful to say, "the opposition" or "his counterpart," but in the privacy of his own thoughts there was no hiding from her.

Nikoros met them and saw them to the door. 'You were right about the guards and solicitors,' he whispered. 'I do feel better!'

'Uh ... good, good,' said Locke, ashamed at his own distraction.

'Now that we have some security,' said Jean, immediately taking the weight of confidence and authority that Locke had let slip, 'it's time we started reaching out and handing our friends some difficulties of their own. Think on it for us, would you? Weaknesses we can exploit, fast and easy ones.'

'My pleasure,' said Nikoros. 'You know, two days in, this has already been more interesting than anything that happened last time. I'll wait up for you, shall I? I'd love to find out what sort of woman our, ah, opposition is.'

'So would we,' said Jean.

7

The carriage ride through the wet curtains of evening fog was no help for Locke's nerves, but as the minutes passed he mastered himself well enough, he thought, to be able to handle simple sentences and walking.

The Vel Vespala, the Evening Terrace, was one of Karthain's more fashionable quarters, its plazas dotted with taverns, chance houses, coffee bars, and bordellos. All of these places were so many blurry amber and aquamarine lights in the mist as Locke and Jean's carriage pulled up before the Sign of the Black Iris, the place Nikoros and his friends referred to as the Enemy Tavern.

'Well then,' said Locke. 'So here we—'

'I'm not taking a quarter of an hour to get out of the carriage,' said Jean. 'It's out the door on your feet or out the window on your head. Think fast.'

Locke managed the former.

The Sign of the Black Iris was a comfortably appointed place, not as large as Josten's Comprehensive but perhaps slightly more luxurious, the wood panelling a touch richer, the marble of the exterior facings a trifle shinier. No doubt the rivalry between the two inns kept the pockets of many Karthani craftsfolk admirably lined.

Locke's nervous distraction abated as his old street instincts kicked to life. The porter at the door was nothing special, but the two men at the rear of the darkened foyer were interesting. They were not at ease in their fine clothes, and what a coincidence that two lean fellows with such scars and crooked noses should be passing the time together! Muscle for sure. Sabetha, too, had set alley hounds to guard her lair.

'Ahh, sirs.' Another sort of creature entirely entered the foyer to greet them. This man was silver-haired, thin as a scabbard, with a drooping black flower pinned to the right lapel of his coat. 'Firstson Vordratha. I'm Mistress Gallante's confidential secretary. You gentlemen do move at a relaxed pace. She's been expecting the two of you for *some time* now, yes, some time indeed.'

'I would point out,' said Jean, gesturing to a mechanical clock on the foyer wall, 'that it's not yet five minutes to seven.'

'Of course. I made no reflection upon the accuracy of the clock, mmmm?' The lines at the edges of Vordratha's mouth moved up a fraction of an inch. So he was that sort of fellow, supercilious and needling, unable to resist amusing himself with lame little digs. Locke's concentration came into even sharper focus as the urge rose to slam Vordratha's head against the door. 'Come now, she wishes to see you directly. In private.'

Locke and Jean followed him up to a hallway on the second floor. They brushed past a surprising number of men and women for a direct route to a private audience … ah, but of course, they were all studying Locke and Jean while feigning indifference. Stealing a glimpse of faces and builds and manners in case the two of them ever attempted another visit without an invitation. It was flattering, really.

At the end of the hall, Vordratha held a door open. The space beyond was dim, lit by the golden glow of small lamps on a number of tables. A private dining space, with high windows looking out into the evening fog.

A woman stood alone at the far end of the room, her long hair unbound, a cascade of dark copper falling to the middle of her back. She turned slowly, and before Locke knew what was happening he and Jean were through the door, the door fell closed with a click, and Sabetha was coming toward them down the shadowed passage between the rows of lamplight.

8

She wore a velvet jacket the colour of blood, a shade darker than her hair. Her outfit had the dash of a riding habit, narrowing to emphasize her slender waist, and beneath the long dark skirt she wore seasoned leather boots. A scarf, white as dove's feathers, was wrapped tightly around her neck. Other than a single lapel iris matching that of Vordratha, she had no ornaments but contrast – the harmony of skin, scarf, hair, and coat. She'd made an artist's palette of herself, emphasizing a beauty that had bloomed in the five years they'd been apart.

Locke stepped out in front of Jean and removed his leather gloves with shaking hands. Five years of dreaming and planning for this moment deserted him in an instant, leaving him with nothing but a half-wit's hypnotized stare and the air in his throat.

'H-hello,' he said.

'Hello, Locke.'

'Yes. Sabetha. Hello. Uh.'

'Meant to say something grander and wittier, didn't you?'

'Well …' The sound of her voice, her ordinary voice, unaffected, undisguised, unaccented, was like a glass of brandy gulped on an empty stomach. 'Whatever it was it seems to have business elsewhere.'

'It'll come back to you when you least expect it.' She smiled. 'Write it down then and have it sent to me. I'll give it a favourable hearing.'

They were just a few feet apart now, and in her face he could see time's peculiar alchemy – every line was where it ought to be, but all the softness and reediness of the girl was gone. Her figure and features were fuller. Her eyes had changed, moving from a lively hazel to a truer, darker brown, a shade that was faintly reflected in her hair.

'Take my hands,' she said, and gently redirected his fingers when he tried to entwine them with hers. Palm against palm they stood while she returned his stare; her touch was soft and dry. For a moment of pure anticipation Locke thought she might pull him into an embrace, but she maintained the respectable distance between them. 'You're too gods-damned thin,' she said, losing some of her dominating composure.

'I've been ill.'

'They told me you were poisoned.'

'Who's they?'

'You *know*,' she said. 'And you've been out of the sun. Your Vadran is showing.'

'We both seem to have gone back to our roots.'

'Ah, the hair?'

'No, the backs of your *knees*. Of course the hair.'

'It's strange. I've been every shade of black, brown, and blonde these past few years, so I can disguise myself best now by going back to what's natural. Does it please you?'

'You know it distracts the hell out of me.' Locke felt himself blushing. 'Puts me at the most severe disadvantage.'

'I know,' she said, again allowing a touch of a smile. 'Perhaps I wanted us on familiar ground for the evening.'

She released his hands, gave a playful half-bow, and moved around him.

'Hello, Jean,' she said. 'You've lost at the belly and gained at the shoulders, I think.'

'Hello, Sabetha.' He extended his left hand. 'You've gained a great deal and lost nothing I can see.'

'Dear heart.' She met his hand with her own, and her eyebrows rose when he took her by the forearm and shook politely. 'What's this? Five years apart and suddenly I'm just a business associate?'

Locke bit the inside of his lip as she put her arms around Jean and set her head against the lapels of his jacket. After the tiniest pause, Jean returned the embrace, his own arms easily folding around her and overlapping in the middle of her back.

'I'll just need a moment to make sure everything's still in my pockets,' he said as they parted. She laughed.

'What, you don't think I'm serious?' Jean examined his jacket carefully. He didn't bother grinning to lighten the moment.

'Ahh,' Sabetha said, stepping away from both of them and folding her hands in front of her. 'So how long did it take you to figure it out?'

'About a minute,' said Locke.

'Not bad.'

'A minute too long. The initials on that purse were cheeky as hell. But that getup was excellent.'

'You liked it? Good. It wasn't easy, taking a few inches off my regular height.'

'One of the hardest things in false-facing,' said Locke with a nod. 'You were showing off.'

'No more than you, before we were done. Still feigning illness in public.'

'It worked,' said Locke. 'After a fashion. But you'd seen it before; surely that's why you weren't caught too off-guard.'

'That,' she said, 'and you two should remember I can still read most of your hand signals.'

Locke exchanged a glance with Jean; the fact that he hadn't been alone in neglecting this point was little comfort.

'You get that one for free,' she said.

'So why'd you do it?' said Locke.

'I wanted to see you both,' she said, glancing away. 'I found that I was impatient. But I wasn't ready for … for this, just yet.'

'We might have been a little late for this appointment if they'd thrown us in a hole,' said Jean.

'Tsk,' she said. 'You're insulting us all. As if you couldn't have clever-dicked your way clear of those imbeciles before lunch. After all, your friend Josten still has his ardent spirits license. Clearly you two haven't forgotten how to stay on your toes.'

'That was cute,' said Locke.

'As was your riposte. It's a wonder to me, how many people are so willing to believe the best of the laws that they live under.'

'They haven't had our advantages. Anyway, you shouldn't have sent a fat, good-natured fellow for that sort of work,' said Locke. 'You should have arranged to put the warrant in the hands of some shrivelled tent-peg like your Vordratha.'

'Isn't he a treasure? Such a smirking dry bitch of a man. He can't have spent more than a minute with you, and you'd crawl over broken glass to kick him in the precious bits, I'd wager.'

'Point me to the glass,' muttered Jean.

'Perhaps … once he's given me a good six weeks of work.' She tossed her hair back and matched gazes with Jean. 'Jean, may I ask you to … allow Locke and myself a few moments alone? I told Vordratha to have a chair set up just outside the door.'

'I'm not sure I'm comfortable with that.'

'Don't sit in it, then.'

Jean's only response was to clear his throat.

'May I beg to point out,' said Sabetha, 'that the last reasonable chance you had to be cautious was when you stepped out of your carriage? I could have twenty armed people crouched in the next room. If I did, why would I bother to ask for privacy?'

'Well,' said Jean with a sigh. 'I suppose I can feign civility with the best of them.'

He was gone in a moment. The door clicked shut behind him, leaving Locke and Sabetha alone with four feet of darkened floor between them.

'Have I offended him?' said Sabetha.

'No.'

'He seemed pleased to see me for a moment, and now he's sour.'

'Jean had ... Jean met someone. And lost her, in the worst way. So don't think ... it's just that he can't be terribly at ease, concerning the matters that lie between me and you.'

'What matters could you be referring to?'

'Please *don't* do that.'

'Do what?'

'Invite me to name my troubles as though they were somehow unknown to you.'

'The device you're mistaking me for is called a *mirror*, Locke. I don't reflect your feelings as well as you seem to imagine, so I'm afraid you may have to name them for everyone's benefit.'

'Five years, Sabetha! Five *years*!'

'I can count! And so what? I'm not leaping into your arms? I'm not tearing your clothes off under one of these tables? You may have noticed that I passed those five years without crawling back to Camorr in search of you. Nor did I find *you* exactly dogging my heels!'

'I meant ... I meant to—'

'You *meant*,' she said. 'There's a worthless coin, Locke. The past isn't something we can negotiate. I might not have come back for you, but you certainly didn't strike out after me.'

'There were difficulties.'

'Oh,' she said, 'so *you're* the man whose life develops complications! I've so longed to meet you; the rest of us here in this world have it much too easy, I'm afraid.'

'Calo and Galdo are dead,' said Locke.

Sabetha leaned back against the nearest table, folded her arms, and stared out the windows for some time. 'I had my suspicions,' she said at last.

'When Jean and I came alone to Karthain?'

'I passed through Camorr about a year ago,' she said. 'I thought it best not to announce myself. It's like it was in the old days, before Barsavi. Thirty capas and no Secret Peace. I heard some confusing things … You'd been cast out by Barsavi's usurper, and no one had seen you since the mess.'

'The hammer came down on everyone,' said Locke. 'Capa Raza used us, then betrayed us. We were all meant to die, but they only got the Sanzas. The Sanzas, and a younger friend … We had a new apprentice. You'd have liked him.'

'Well,' she said, 'whoever he was, you certainly did him a grand turn as a *garrista*, didn't you?'

'I'd have died, Sabetha, I'd have *died* if it would have saved them! I didn't have a fucking chance. And some help you were, wherever the hell you'd gone off to—'

'How could I stay?' she said. 'How could I help you pretend to keep house? You wanted everything the same – same glass burrow, same temple, same schemes, and now I learn that you even started taking apprentices. Boys, of course.'

'Of all the damned unfair—'

'Roots are for vegetables, Locke, not criminals. Chains had enough blind spots of his own, thank you very much. The last thing I ever could have done was prance along hand in hand to your pale imitation!

'I might have been able to live with you as a partner,' she continued. 'As priest, *garrista*, father figure, no. Not for an instant! Gods, that fucking pile of money Chains left us was the biggest curse he could have dreamed up if he'd spent his whole life planning it. I wish he'd thrown it into the sea. I wish we'd burned that temple ourselves.'

'We did burn it ourselves,' said Locke. 'And I *did* throw the money in the sea.'

'What do you mean?'

'I had the whole mess of it sunk in Camorr's Old Harbour. As Calo and Galdo's death-offering.'

'It's really all gone?'

'To the sharks and the gods, every last copper.'

'Thank you for that,' she whispered, and she reached out to set the back of her right hand against his cheek.

He took a deep, shuddering breath, reached up, and felt the heat surge in his blood when she didn't draw away from the pressure of his hand on hers.

'For losing everything?' he said.

'For the Sanzas.'

'Ah.'

'You've grown some lines since I saw you last,' she said.

'It was a bad poisoning,' said Locke. 'And it wasn't my first.'

'I can't imagine how anyone as charming and easy to get along with as yourself could ever incite someone to poison you,' she said. 'I *am* sorry about Calo and Galdo. I'm sorry I wasn't there to help. For what it's worth.'

'I suppose I'm sorry I was such a shitty *garrista*,' said Locke.

'Maybe in a better life I could have stayed to watch these lines grow on you. Perhaps put them there myself,' she said with a thin smile. 'But it's not as though I didn't arm you with the clearest possible expression of my feelings before I chose to go.'

'Frankly, sometimes, I was surprised you stayed with us as long as you did.'

'I didn't nerve myself up to leave overnight.' She lowered her hand and slipped it out of his grasp. 'When Chains died, you thought you had to preserve everything the way it had been. Freeze our lives in amber. Maybe that was your way of mourning. It couldn't be mine.'

'Well, I, uh … did trace you as far as Ashmere,' Locke said. 'I never told anyone but Jean. I had someone up there that owed me a favour. After that …'

'Come here,' she said, pulling out the nearest chair. 'Sit down. We're pacing like servants.'

'Is that the chair with the trapdoor beneath it?'

'Oh, don't be an ass. Choose any one you like.'

Locke pulled a chair away from a table on his side of the aisle and set it down next to the one Sabetha had offered. He gestured for her to go first, and when she was seated he eased into his, facing the door to the room. They were not quite facing one another, but turned inward at an angle with their knees almost touching.

'I did what I'd planned,' said Sabetha. 'I circulated in the Kingdom of the Marrows. Started in Emberlain and moved west, hitting rich bachelors and the occasional married lord with a wandering eye.'

'Did they come up with a legendary name for you?'

'I'm sure they came up with a lot of names for me,' she smirked. 'But once I was in the thick of things I decided it was better to stay anonymous than to build a myth.'

'You know I didn't start that Thorn of Camorr bullshit—'

'Peace, Locke, it wasn't a rebuke.'

'So why'd you leave the Marrows? Get bored?'

'The Marrows are getting dangerous. Emberlain means to break from the rest of them. All the cantons are buckling on their swords. It seemed a good time to be elsewhere.'

'I've been hearing this for years,' said Locke. 'Emberlain is *always* about to secede. The king is *always* about to fall over in his tracks. I even used this nonsense as the basis for a scheme. Hells, I fully expect the peace in the Marrows to outlive me.'

'Then you must be planning to die in the next month or two,' she said. 'Trust someone who's been up there, Locke. The old king is heirless and out of his wits. It's an open secret that he's ordered his privy council to choose his successor when he finally dies.'

'How does that guarantee a war?'

'It means that there are about ten noble families that would get a vote, and a hundred that wouldn't. Do you think they won't prefer to just pull steel and get to work? They'll be hip-deep in corpses once they start really trading opinions.'

'I see. So, you were dodging that, and you got a job offer for a sojourn here in Karthain?'

'I was leaving Vintila,' she said. 'One moment I was alone in my carriage; the next I was having a conversation with a Bondsmage.'

'I know what that's like.' Locke took a deep breath before asking the next question. 'And ... they told you about Jean and I before you took the job? That you'd be set against us, I mean.'

'I was told.'

'Before—'

'Yes, *before*. And I agreed to the job anyway. Do you want a moment to think very, very hard before proceeding on this point?'

'I ... You're right, I have no cause to say anything.'

'We're not enemies, Locke; we're rivals. Surely we're both accustomed to the situation. And tell me, how would you have answered if our positions were reversed?'

'If I hadn't said yes, I'd be dead.'

'Well, if I hadn't said yes, I'd still be somewhere in the Marrows with Graf kul Daros' agents one step behind me. I have to confess I didn't manage to get out with as much money or anonymity as I might have hoped. In fact, I've … understated the mess I left behind me. I'm sorry.'

'Jean and I … weren't coming off one of our more lucrative exploits, either.'

'So neither of us had any sensible reason to refuse this engagement.' Sabetha leaned forward. 'The magi offered to get me out. To erase my tracks, help me disappear in complete safety. That was their end of the bargain. And for my part, the chance to see you and Jean again was agreeable.'

'Agreeable?'

'No doubt you find it a mild term. But this conversation's too young to go back on our steps just yet. I've given you my facts; now give me yours. Tell me what happened in Camorr.'

'Ah. Well.' Locke found himself trying to scratch at the stubble that was no longer present on his chin. 'We had a scheme going. A good one, that would have added a fair sum to that pile of treasure you detested.'

'This was when the Grey King was abroad in the city?'

'Grey King, Capa Raza, same man. Yes, we were chosen for the dubious Honour of assisting the bastard in his war against the Barsavis. He had a Bondsmage working for him.'

'My … principals told me about him,' said Sabetha.

'The murdering shit-stain was no credit to your principals, whatever they think. Anyhow, he must have spied us out along with the money in our vault. I've had a long time to think about the situation, and it's the only explanation that makes sense.

'We did our job,' he continued, 'and then it turned out that the Grey King coveted our good fortune. He had a lot of bills to pay. So we got the chop. It was—'

Every fibre of his being, already unhinged by his more recent illness, revolted at the recollection of those moments drowning in a cask of warm, soupy filth.

'… it was a near thing.'

'Did any of the Barsavis survive?'

'None. Nazca was murdered to put her father's nerves on edge. With our help, the Grey King tricked Barsavi into thinking he'd avenged her. He threw a party at the Floating Grave, and that's where he and his sons were taken apart. Hell of a spectacle. Remember the Berangias sisters?'

'How could I forget?'

'They were in on it. Turns out they were actually the sisters of the Grey King. They served Barsavi all those years, waiting for the moment to strike.'

'Gods, what happened to them?'

'Jean happened.'

'And this Grey King?'

'Ah.' Locke cleared his throat. 'He was my affair. We crossed swords.'

'Now, to that I must admit some pleasant surprise,' said Sabetha, and Locke felt a fresh warmth around his heart at the sparkle of interest in her eyes. 'Did you finally start paying attention to your bladework?'

'Ah, don't be misled. I'm afraid he opened me up like a physiker. I had to trick him into letting me sheath a dagger in his back.'

'Hmmm,' she said. 'I'm pleased you killed him. Still a pity you never amended your clumsiness with long steel.'

'Well, Sabetha, unlike some, I'm afraid I've just never had it in me to instantly presume a flawless expertise in *every last sphere* of human endeavour.'

'There was nothing instant about it. You *might* have thrown yourself into training as vigourously as I did, if you hadn't lived with the expectation of having Jean Tannen at your back for the rest of your life.'

'No. Gods damn it, I would gladly listen to you berate me until the sun comes up, *but not on this subject.* Jean isn't some dog I tricked into a leash. He's my true and particular friend. He's still *your* true and particular friend, though both of you may need some time to recall it.'

'Forgive me,' she said. 'I had your best interests at heart.'

'For someone whose primary insistence in life has *always* been that she must be taken true and unalloyed, unbending to the whims of those around her, you have a curious interest in the correction of *my* condition!'

'Ouch,' she said softly.

'Fuck.' Locke slammed his fists down on his legs. 'Forgive me. I know you mean well—'

'No, you're right,' she said. 'I'm an extraordinarily accomplished hypocrite. Anything that displeased you is unsaid. Please go on with your story.'

'Ahhh … all right. Well. Not much more to say about Camorr. We took ship for Vel Virazzo the night the Grey King died. Oh! I met the Spider.'

'What? How did that happen?'

'When the Grey King business reached its conclusion, the duke's people had no choice but to get involved. After an initial misunderstanding, the Spider and I worked together. Very briefly.'

'Sweet gods, were you *pardoned* for your crimes?'

'Oh, hells, no. Once the Grey King was dead, Jean and I bolted like rabbits.'

'And did you learn the actual identity of the Spider?'

'Yes, she and I had words on several occasions.'

'So it was a woman! As I'd always thought.'

'How did you know?'

'All those years of rumours,' said Sabetha, 'and the one detail that emerged with absolute clarity from the fog was that the Spider was a man. Everyone was certain. Now, if this person could maintain total control over every other shred of their identity, why was such a fundamental truth allowed to slip? It had to be misdirection.'

'Heh. So it was.'

'And who was she, then?'

'Ahhh,' said Locke. 'I see I've got something that genuinely intrigues you. I think I'll hold onto it for a while.'

'Oh? I'll remember this, Master Lamora. On that you have my word. So you took ship. What next?'

Warmed to the subject, Locke spent about ten minutes summarizing the two years spent in and around Tal Verrar – the nature of the scheme for Requin's Sinspire, the interference of Maxilan Stragos, the time in the Ghostwinds, the battles at sea, the loss of Ezri, the loss of nearly everything.

'Incredible,' Sabetha said when he drew his story to a close. 'I'd heard about the trouble in Tal Verrar. You *caused* all that. You brought the gods-damned Archon down! You silly, stupid, lucky little wretches!'

'And for our genius, we left Tal Verrar without Jean's love, without a fortune, and without an antidote.'

'I'm sorry for all of that. Especially for Jean.'

'I'd say something comforting, like how he'll get over it in time, but I know he won't.' Locke paused, and lowered his voice. 'I know I didn't.'

'Ah,' said Sabetha. It was a completely noncommittal noise. 'And here we are, then.'

'Here we are,' said Locke. 'Storeys told.'

'I have … instructions from my principals,' she said. 'We're not forbidden from talking to one another, but in the matter of the election ... Look, we've got to fight it out to the last. Sincerely. All of our tricks, all of our skills. The consequences for holding back would be severe. So severe, I could never—'

'I understand,' he said. 'I have similar directions from my ... uh, principals.'

'Gods, I wish we could talk all night.'

'Then why don't we?'

'Because I didn't expect to get this much honesty out of you.' She rose. 'And if I don't do what I really brought you here for, I might lose my nerve.'

'Wait, what do you mean—'

She answered him by pulling him out of the chair and into her arms. Reflexively, he fought back for a moment, but the intensity of the embrace subdued him.

'I am glad you're alive,' she whispered. 'Please believe me, whatever else happens, I'm so glad to see you.'

'I can't believe I have two reasons to be grateful to the Bondsmagi,' said Locke. Gods, she was warm and strong, and her scent so instantly familiar beneath the slightest sweet-apple scent of perfume. He ran a hand through the gentle curls of her hair and sighed. 'Assholes. I'd work for free for any chance to be near you. They're offering a fortune, and I'd throw it in the Amathel for this. I—'

'Locke,' she whispered. 'Indulge me.'

'Oh?'

'Kiss me.'

'With every—'

'No, not like that. My preferred way. You know what I mean. From back when we were—'

'Ahhh,' he said, laughing. 'Your servant, madam.'

Sabetha had always had a peculiar ticklish weakness, something he'd discovered by accident when they'd first become lovers so many years before. He gently placed his left hand beneath her chin and tilted her head back, then planted his lips high up the side of her neck, beneath her ear.

The way she moved in his arms instantly folded his better judgment up and hid it away in a deep, dark place.

'So this is what you really brought me here for?'

'Keep going,' she said breathlessly, 'and we'll find out.'

He kissed her several more times, and when he felt he'd teased her enough, ran his tongue up and down those same few inches of warm skin. She actually gasped, and clutched him more tightly still.

'Oh, dear,' he said, laughing and smacking his lips. He swallowed several times to clear a curious dry taste from his tongue. 'Your perfume. I seem to have removed some of it. I hope it wasn't expensive.'

'A special formulation, just for you,' she whispered. She continued to cling to him, digging her hands into his shoulders, and for one more moment Locke was at peace with the entire world.

The numbness began at the edge of his tongue, and in a few seconds it spread, tingling, around his mouth and up to the tip of his nose.

'No,' he whispered, hit as hard by shock as he was by whatever he'd just swallowed. He tried to pull away, but she was too strong for him; his limbs were already taking on a curious foggy dissociation. 'No, no … Jnnnn … *Jnnnn!*'

'Shhhhhh,' Sabetha whispered, no longer shuddering, no longer breathless with shared anticipation. 'A special formulation. Throat and voice go first. Just relax. Jean can't hear you.'

'Whhhh … whhhhy?'

'Forgive me,' she said. She cradled him as his legs turned to jelly. She knelt slowly, bringing him down with her, laying him across her knees. 'I wasn't sure whether I'd really do it or not. If it's any consolation, your story about Tal Verrar was the convincer. You're not as good as I am, Locke, but you're too damn good to let you run around fighting fairly. I have to beat you, for both our sakes.'

'Nnngh—'

'Don't talk. Just listen; you don't have much time left. There's a second reason. I can see now how ill you've been, and how you'll have to push yourself to keep up with me. I can't let you do it, Locke. I can't watch you do it. You'll *kill* yourself trying to best me, and you can't ask me to permit that. Not when I could stop it. I once cared for you a great deal. I care for you now. Remember that.'

She kissed him gently on the forehead, and he barely felt it.

'Remember that, and forgive me.'

9

'Nnnngh,' said Locke, coming up from layers of blackness that seemed draped over him like burial shrouds. 'Nnngh – Sab … no, please!'

He gasped, with the disbelieving gratitude of someone finally fighting back to wakefulness after an interminable nightmare of suffocation. He smelled his own sweat, and the familiar odours of wet wood and fresh lake air.

His eyes slid grudgingly open. He was lying on his back in yet another ship's great cabin, this one more luxuriously appointed than any he'd ever seen, even Zamira Drakasha's. Soft orange alchemical globes cast the fixtures and finery in an inviting light. Gulls cried somewhere nearby, and the world creaked gently around him.

'Stupid, stupid, stupid,' muttered Locke, revelling in the full recovery of his powers of speech. He sat up, and instantly became aware of the fierce gnawing hunger in his belly. 'Oh, *stupid, stupid, stupid*—'

'You can't blame yourself,' said Jean.

Locke turned to see him sitting against the opposite wall on a hanging bed furnished with embroidered sheets. Jean had fresh bruises on his bare forearms and around his eyes.

'Gods,' said Locke. 'What the hell happened to you?'

'Remember how she joked about twenty armed people in the next room?' said Jean with a sigh. He set down the book he'd been reading. 'There were twenty armed people in the next room.'

'Fuck me sideways with hot peppers and a pinch of salt,' said Locke. 'How long have I been out?'

'Half a day.'

'Where are we?'

'On the Amathel, headed west. Bound for the sea.'

'Are you kidding?'

Jean pointed at something behind Locke, and Locke turned. The rear windows of the cabin, which were open to let in a view of a grey morning over blue water, were girded with a network of thick iron bars on their outer surface. The gaps in the bars were too small for even Locke to contemplate wiggling through.

'She's put us on quite a luxurious prison ship,' said Jean. 'We're the only passengers. And we're chartered for a nice, slow voyage out to sea and around the continent.'

'Are you *fucking kidding*?'

'If all goes as she planned, we'll get back to Karthain a week or two after all the votes have been counted.'

Intersect (II)
Tinder

I have to tell you, we're not terribly impressed with your boys so far.

We thought they did very well, up to their meeting with your exemplar.

It's that meeting with our exemplar that inspires a certain lack of foreboding on our part.

They'll be back soon enough.

They're headed out to sea in irons.

You know who else thought lightly of them, once? The Falconer.

Very amusing.

Interesting things are going to be happening around Lamora, my friend. Just keep your attention focused very closely on him at all times.

The Moncraine Company

I

'He's been arrested for punching a nobleman?' said Locke.

'Hauled off in irons,' said Jenora.

'Of all the gods-damned ... how bad is that here? They're not going to hang him, are they?'

'Dungeon for a year and a day,' said Alondo. 'Then he loses the offending hand.'

'I suppose Moncraine's lucky he didn't kick the fellow,' said Jean.

'Certainly, he's lucky,' said Sylvanus, looking up from his bottle. 'He's in the one place in the city where his creditors can't skin his balls and salt them! They should let us keep the hand when they chop it off ... embalm it with tar ... make a damn fine prop, especially when I play a thaumata ... thaumur ... magic person.'

'How do we get him back?' said Sabetha.

'Back?' said a woman who appeared out of the shadows behind Alondo and Jenora. Approaching middle age, she was well muscled and stout, with mahogany skin and hair grey as wood ash. 'Why would anyone want Jasmer Moncraine *back*, having so easily got rid of him? And why are there strangers in my inn-yard?'

'I imagine they're called *customers*, Auntie,' said Jenora. 'You do remember when they used to come voluntarily?'

'Yes, I'm an attentive student of ancient history,' said the older woman. 'Alizana Gloriano, proprietor and semiprofessional martyr, at your service. Are you really looking for Jasmer Moncraine?'

'He's our employer,' said Sabetha. 'Or at least he's meant to be.'

'My gods above,' said Mistress Gloriano, putting her arms around the shoulders of Alondo and Jenora. 'The *Camorri*. They're *real*!'

'We're as shocked as you, Auntie,' said Jenora.

'It's pleasant to be thought of as such freakish wonders,' said Locke, 'but we need to reach Moncraine.'

'Well then,' said Mistress Gloriano, 'all you need to do is wait for his conviction, the day after tomorrow. Then wait another year and a day, and then stand outside the Weeping Tower. He'll be the one coming out with his right hand missing.'

'What about a solicitor?'

'We don't exactly retain one,' said Alondo.

'Tell us what we *can* do, then,' said Locke. 'Can we see him?'

'Oh yes, dear boy,' said Sylvanus. 'Enquire after the nearest gentleman or lady of high birth and smash 'em across the teeth. You could end up sharing Jasmer's cell.'

'Damn it,' said Locke. 'No offence, but the four of you sound like you'd just as soon slit Moncraine's throat as give him the time of day. … *Is* there a Moncraine Company at all? Are you putting on a play this summer? Our situation requires that we be employed, so for Perelandro's sake be clear.'

'We're still a company,' said Jenora, 'though we've had some defections. Alondo, Sylvanus, and Jasmer are the remaining full players. One or two more might come back if Jasmer could show his face in public.'

'You're not an actress?' said Jean.

'Stage-mistress,' said Jenora. 'Costumes, scenery, props. If it doesn't walk around on its own legs, it's my business.'

'And assuming,' said Locke, 'that a miracle occurred, and the gods themselves transported Moncraine out of gaol, would we have work for the summer?'

'We've lost some rehearsal time,' said Sylvanus, easing himself onto his back with a sigh.

'That sounds like a hint at a *yes*,' said Locke.

'The real problem is money,' said Mistress Gloriano. 'I invested in Moncraine two years ago for my niece's sake, and he's still down to me for twelve royals. And I'm the *least* troublesome of those he's bound to—'

'Money troubles can be finessed,' said Locke.

'There's no credit to be had,' said Alondo. 'None of us can buy so much as a grain of rice on a promise. We can find scut-work to stay fed, or even do morality plays in the streets, but the company has no funds … for scribing, for costumes, masks, lights—'

'And we have no venue, nor transport to it,' said Jenora. 'There's two rooms of old props and clothes we can work with, all stored here, but we'll make a laughingstock of ourselves if we're seen hauling it around on foot.'

'More of a laughingstock,' muttered Alondo.

'We have a wagon,' said Locke. 'Give us a moment.' He pulled Jean and Sabetha away from the tattered remnants of the Moncraine Company.

'That's a lot of our money sewn up in the wagon and horses,' said Jean.

'I know,' said Locke. 'What if we sold two horses and kept the other pair?'

'Taking care of them is going to use up more time and money we hadn't planned on spending,' said Sabetha.

'Yeah,' said Locke, 'but if we can't get this troupe back to work, we might as well turn around and roll straight back to Camorr. If that's the plan, I'm sure as hell going to develop a speech impediment when we explain things to Chains.'

'Hardly our fault Moncraine punched a swell,' said Jean.

'Chains will expect more from us than a quick sniff around before we give up,' said Sabetha. 'We were sent here *expressly* to restore Moncraine's fortunes. We've got to pry him out of this mess somehow.'

'And what if we can't?' said Jean softly.

'Then at least we tried,' said Locke. 'Sabetha's right. It's one thing to go home with our options exhausted; it's another to fold at the first sign of trouble.'

'We'll need more money,' said Sabetha. 'I don't see much chance of any thoughtful schemes just yet, but pockets are pockets and purses are purses. If we—'

'No,' said Locke. 'We can't be thieves, remember? We've got more trouble than we bargained for just pretending to be actors.'

The expression on Sabetha's face was so dangerous that Locke became aware of it, like the heat from an oil lamp, before he even turned to see it. He put his hands up, palms out.

'Sabetha, I know what you're thinking ... I've been dwelling on what you said, believe me. I can't insist that you follow my orders. But I am asking you to consider my points, and let me convince you.'

Her expression softened. 'Maybe there's hope for you after all,' she said. 'So make your case.'

'We don't *know* this place,' said Locke. 'We don't know the constables, the gangs, or the hiding places. What would we think of some asshole from the outlands trying to come it the slick coat-teaser back in Camorr? We'd laugh at the yokel and watch him hang. Well, in Espara *we're* the yokels. And if we make a mistake, there's no Secret Peace to fall back on.

'It's not that we might not need to clutch and tease a bit,' he continued. 'Just not *yet*. Not until we've learned our way around.'

'I see your point,' she said. 'In fact, I'm sure you're right. Maybe I'm a little too used to the conveniences of home.'

She put out her hand, and Locke, after a moment, smiled and shook it firmly.

'Who the hell are you people,' said Jean, 'and where did you get those excellent Locke and Sabetha disguises?'

'Quit gaping, Jean. Let's move fast,' said Sabetha sweetly. 'We need horses sold, horses stabled, Moncraine freed, money changed, and rooms. And that's just off the top of my head.'

'Mistress Gloriano,' Locke yelled, turning back toward her, 'we don't mean to put you to any trouble, but we need rooms in a hurry so we can unload our wagon.'

'You're really staying, then?'

'Of course,' said Locke. 'And keep a tab separate from the rest of the company. We'll pay actual money.'

For a few days at least, he thought.

'Well,' said Mistress Gloriano, as though coming out of a trance. 'I've no shortage of rooms.'

'Giacomo,' shouted Sabetha, 'Castellano!'

Calo and Galdo came at a near-run and skidded to a halt in front of Sylvanus.

'These are the Asino brothers,' said Sabetha. 'You two, find out where Mistress Gloriano's putting us, and get our things heaved out of the wagon as quick as you can.'

'What, first we're the bloody wagon guards, now we're fuckin' stevedores?' said Calo. 'You want a foot massage and some chilled wine while you watch us work?'

'We've all got jobs,' said Sabetha, 'and if you touch my feet I'll cut your ears off. *Move!*'

The next fifteen minutes were a blur of activity for everyone except Sylvanus, for whom they were merely a blur. Jean took a moment to pitch a little tent over the prostrate actor using the wagon tarp and some sticks, and then the Gentlemen Bastards heaved their possessions into two rooms selected by Mistress Gloriano. These were fine examples of how middle age, while charming in some humans, is less endearing in wood-panel construction and unpreserved wall tapestries. The twins claimed one room, Locke and Jean the other, and Sabetha accepted Jenora's invitation to share her room down the corridor.

Once the wagon was emptied, Jean selected the less healthy pair of horses and with Jenora's aid got them stabled. Alondo claimed to have a cousin working as a hostler near the Jalaan Gate, so Jean enlisted the young actor to help walk the best two horses back to the caravan staging area for resale.

'Now,' Locke said to Mistress Gloriano, 'we need Jasmer back. For that I think we'll need a solicitor.'

'I suppose it can't be helped,' she said. 'I've given Jasmer so much slack these past few years in the hope my investment might find its way home again.'

'Let him have a bit more,' said Locke. 'We're here now, for what it's worth. And we *need* a Moncraine play. There's no work for us back home.'

'I had wondered at the nature of your devotion. Jasmer's a Syresti, you know. Capricious and moody. Barely reliable! Not an even-tempered Okanti like myself or Jenora. Let me tell you, boy, if I knew then what a hole I'd be throwing my money down—'

'Yes, I'm sure you're quite right,' said Locke in a placating tone of voice. 'But a solicitor …?'

'There is a fellow,' said Mistress Gloriano, 'back up the avenue the way you came. Stay-Awake Salvard, he's called, on account of his pec-uliar hours. He's done papers for me. I wouldn't go so far as to accuse him of being a gentleman. Works for a lot of … colourful sorts.'

'That's good,' said Locke. 'That's great. We're colourful sorts.'

2

'Etienne Delancarre Domingo Salvard,' said Sabetha, reading out loud from the lantern-lit plaque beside the building's street entrance. 'Master solicitor, bonded law-scribe, authorized notary, executor of wills and estates, Vadran translator and transcriber. Fortunes assured, justice delivered, enemies confounded. Reasonable rates.'

Locke and Sabetha alone had come on this errand, after washing the smell of the road from their more accessible parts and swapping their filthy caravan clothes for less offensive outfits. Salvard's office was perched on the edge of the increasing desolation that led to Solace

Hill, a way station between the couth and uncouth districts of the city.

The comfortless wooden furniture and empty walls inside seemed, to Locke's eye, to indicate a certain desire to avoid giving rowdy clientele any objects for vandalism. A thin man with slicked-back hair sat behind a little podium, and near the stairs on the far side of the room lounged an uncommonly large woman. Her quilted black tunic had obvious armour panels behind the facing.

'Evening,' said the thin man. 'Appointment?'

'Do we really need one?' said Sabetha. 'We're on urgent business.'

'Two coppins consultation fee,' said the thin man, 'plus one for expedited consideration.'

'We're just in from Camorr,' said Locke. 'We haven't changed our money yet.'

'Camorri barons accepted,' said the thin man. 'One for one basis, plus one for changing fee.'

Locke shook four copper coins out of his purse. The clerk inked a quill and began scrawling on a card.

'Names?'

'Verena Gallante,' said Sabetha, 'and Lucaza de Barra.'

'Camorri subjects?'

'Yes.'

The clerk set down his quill, slid open a hatch in the wall behind him, placed the card within this compartment, and turned a hand crank. A miniature dumbwaiter went up, and a minute later the muffled jingling of a bell could be heard from within the shaft.

'Weapons not allowed upstairs,' said the clerk, rapping his knuckles on the surface of his podium. 'Cheerfully guarded here. Arms out for search.'

The big woman gave them both a thorough pat-down. A garrotte or a fruit-paring blade might have slipped through, but Etienne Delancarre Domingo Salvard clearly had strong feelings about allowing anything more conveniently deadly into his presence.

'They're clean,' said the woman, with a half-smile. 'Of weapons, that is.'

'Proceed,' said the clerk, pointing to the stairs. 'Pleasant consultation.'

Stay-Awake Salvard sat behind a desk that completely bisected the floor of his office, ensuring that anyone attempting to leap at him would have one final obstacle to surmount while he escaped or armed himself. Locke wondered if it was the nature of his clients or the quality of his advice that had made him such a cautious fellow.

'Have a seat. You two are a bit young to be caught up in the grasping tentacles of the law, aren't you?' Salvard was a wiry man in his forties with a leonine mane of greying hair, swept back as though he'd just spent twenty minutes on a galloping horse. His nose was built to support the weight of optics much heavier than the dainty piece actually perched there. Two pipes rested in wooden cradles on his cluttered desk, framing him in grey pillars of aromatic smoke. 'Or is it some matter of a marriage, perhaps?'

'Certainly not,' said Sabetha. 'We have a friend in trouble.'

'Supply the details.'

'He struck a gentleman above his station,' said Sabetha.

'Is your friend taken? Or has he fled?'

'They put him in something called the Weeping Tower,' said Locke.

'Tricky. I'm afraid the weight of the law is against him, and he should expect to be trimmed like a hedge,' said Salvard. 'But these incidents can sometimes be portrayed in a sympathetic light. What else should I know?'

'He's a bit of a drunkard,' said Locke.

'Many of my clients have crawled inside a bottle for solace. It's no unusual challenge.'

'And he's a member of a night-skinned race,' said Locke. 'A black Syresti.'

'A noble people, as ancient as our own, with many admirers at court.'

'Our friend is … next to penniless.'

'Yet obviously he has allies,' said Salvard warmly, extending his arms toward Locke and Sabetha, 'who can be relied upon to take up his interests. My fee schedules are quite elastic. Anything else?'

'He's the owner and manager of a theatrical troupe.'

Salvard lost his smile. He took a long pull on his left-hand pipe, set it down, then smoked its counterpart. He alternated pipes several times, staring at Locke and Sabetha. Finally, he said, 'So, we're talking about Jasmer Moncraine, then?'

'You know him?' said Locke.

'I should have guessed his identity sooner from the particulars, save for the fact that you genuinely seemed to want him back. That put me off the true scent. What's your interest in his cause?'

'We're actors, engaged by him for the summer,' said Sabetha. 'We've only just arrived in the city.'

'My condolences. I have one piece of relevant advice.'

'Anything,' said Sabetha.

'Many men in low trades adapt to the loss of a hand and wear hooks. In Jasmer's case, his vanity will never allow it. If you're still in Espara next summer as his stump heals, get him a simple leather cap for it, and—'

'We need him back *now*,' said Sabetha. 'We need him out of custody'.'

'Well, you won't get him, not through the workings of anyone in my profession. Now, now, my dear, it pains me to see that look on your face as much as it pains me to refuse work, so let me explain. My happy fortune is your hard luck. You must have heard of Amilio Basanti.'

'Actually, no,' said Locke.

'You truly are fresh off the wagon, aren't you? Basanti is the impresario of the city's other major company of actors, the stable and successful one. In a fortnight, Demoiselle Amilyn Basanti, his youngest sister, will become Mistress Amilyn *Salvard*.'

'Oh,' said Sabetha.

'If I were to become an advocate for the very rival my future brother-by-bonding loathes so famously, well, surely you can see that the effect upon my marital relations could only be … chilling.'

'Can you recommend someone who wouldn't be at cross-purposes?' said Locke.

'There are five other solicitors-at-law in Espara,' said Salvard, 'and none of them will touch the case. You must understand, if I weren't taking a bride I'd argue it for pleasure. I *enjoy* annoying magistrates, and I handle even the lowest and most difficult clients. No offence. My peers, however, prefer to win their cases, and this one cannot be won.'

'But those excuses you just came up with—'

'Could *mitigate* the situation, perhaps. Surely you understand that those of elevated blood don't keep laws on the books that would require them to take abuse from their inferiors. I wouldn't cite law; I'd beg for mercy! I'd spin yarns about destitute friends and children. But since I'm not going to do those things, Moncraine's trial will last about as long as this conversation.'

'Do we have any other options?' said Locke.

'Apply to Basanti's troupe,' said Salvard gently. 'At the Columbine's Petal, up in Greyside. That's where they drink. I could mention you to Amilyn. They'd find work for you, even if it's just carrying spears. Don't tie yourselves to Moncraine.'

'That's kind of you,' said Sabetha, 'but if we'd wanted to be part of the scenery we could have stayed at home. In Moncraine's company we can have our pick of roles. In a settled troupe we'll be at the end of a long line.'

Salvard again smoked his pipes in alternating fashion, then rubbed his eyes. 'I suppose I can't fault ambition, even if it's bound to end in tears. But there's no way Moncraine's slipping the hook, children. Not unless one of two miracles occurs.'

'Miracles,' said Locke. 'We're in the market for those. What are they?'

'First, Countess Antonia could issue a pardon. She can do anything she pleases. But she won't save him. Moncraine's far from her good graces. Anyway, she's more interested in the advice of her wine steward than her privy council these days.'

'What else?' said Locke.

'The noble that Moncraine attacked could grant a personal pardon by declining to make a complaint before a magistrate. The case would be dismissed. However, I'm sure you can imagine how keen bluebloods are to show weakness in front of their peers.'

'Yeah,' said Locke. 'Hells. Can we even *talk* to Moncraine?'

'There I can offer some cheer,' said Salvard. 'Anyone with a blood or trade connection to a prisoner can have one audience before a trial. Claim it whenever you like, just don't try to give him anything. You'll share his sentence if you're caught.'

'An audience,' said Locke. 'Good. Uh ... where?'

'At the heart of Espara, atop the Legion Steps, look for the black stone tower with the moat and the hundred terribly serious guards. Can't miss it, even in the rain.'

3

A thousand dead soldiers loomed out of the mist beneath the gathering night as Locke and Sabetha climbed the heights of the Legion Steps.

The marble marchers, cracked and weathered from their vigil of six hundred years, wore the armour of Therin Throne legionnaires. Locke recognized the costume from paintings and manuscripts he'd seen in Camorr. He even recalled a bit of their story – that some emperor or another, dissatisfied with Espara's lack of prominent Elderglass monuments, had commissioned a work of human art to grace the centre of the city.

Each statue was said to be a likeness of an actual soldier from a then-living legion, and it was part of their melancholy fascination that they were not posed in martial triumph, but with heads down and shields slung, as they might have been seen trudging along the roads that had once knit the fallen empire together. Now they marched in place, rank on rank forever, in columns evenly spread across the two-hundred-yard arc of the stairs.

'We've got to find his accuser and arrange to have him forgiven,' said Locke.

'It's the only chance we seem to have left,' said Sabetha.

'Gods, I wish we had more money,' said Locke. 'Going visiting in society on scraps of a pittance won't be easy.'

'Tempted to go back on your plan to avoid thieving?'

'Yes,' said Locke. 'I won't do it, though.'

'Just so long as you're tempted,' she said, smiling.

'Honesty doesn't suit any of us,' said Locke.

'I know. Isn't it strange? I keep asking myself how people can stand to *live* like this.'

What Salvard had called a 'moat' around the tower of dark stone was actually more of a gaping jagged-sided pit, at least thirty feet deep, into which drainage channels were directing streams of grey water. The only way across was a covered, elevated bridge with a well-lit guard-house for a mouth. As Locke and Sabetha approached, a quartet of guards fanned out across the entrance.

Locke picked up immediately on the importance of what these guards weren't carrying. They had no batons, no polearms. Those were weapons that could be used gently if the wielder wished. These guards carried only swords, which had a more straightforward employment.

'Stand fast,' said a weathered woman, just shy of middle age, her neck and face thick with scars. All the guards had the look of hard service. The Weeping Tower was no joke, Locke realized. Trying to bribe or suborn one of these old hounds would be suicide. 'Name your business.'

'Good evening,' said Sabetha, instantly adopting a poise that was assertive but not imperious. Locke had seen her use it before. 'We're here to speak with Jasmer Moncraine.'

'Moncraine's not going to be entertaining for a long time,' said the guard. 'What does a Camorri have to say to him?'

'We're members of the Moncraine Company, and we need to make business arrangements now that he's indisposed. Our solicitor advised us that we're entitled to one audience before his trial.'

Gods, as far as Locke was concerned, watching Sabetha handle people was as good as watching any other girl in the world take off her clothes. The way she chose her words – 'entitled,' not something meeker like 'allowed.' And the specific mention of *one* audience – a signal to the guard that the rules had been researched, would be obeyed. Sabetha had asserted all their wants while giving the firmest support to the notion that she and Locke were completely enfolded in the power of the law and these guards that served it.

It turned out the woman was quite pleased to let them in. Not, of course, without an embarrassing full-body search, or their marks on parchment, or an inventory of their purses, or a forty-minute wait. But that was all for the best, Locke thought. Only prisoners were ever granted easy passage into a prison.

4

For the second time that day Locke and Sabetha found themselves in a chamber cut in half by a physical barrier, but now it was bars of black iron. The audience room of the Weeping Tower had smooth stone walls and a rough stone floor, with no windows, no decorations, no furniture. The guards locked the door behind them and remained at attention in front of it.

They were made to wait another few minutes before the door on the opposite side of the room slid open. Two more guards brought in a man, manacled at hands and feet, and clipped a chain to a bolt in the floor. They attached this to the prisoner's leg irons, giving him a range of movement that ended about two feet from the iron bars. The prisoner's guards withdrew to a position mirroring that of the ones on Locke and Sabetha's side of the room.

The man in chains was tall, with skin like polished boot leather and hair scraped down to a grey shadow. He was heavyset but not ponderous. The weight of his years and appetites seemed to have spread evenly, settled in all his joints and crevices, and there was still a hint of dangerous vitality to him. His eyes were wide and bright against the darkness of his face, and he fixed them hard on Locke and Sabetha as though blinking were somehow beneath his interest.

'An opportunity to walk down two flights of stairs and be chained up again,' he said. 'Hooray. Who the hell are you?'

'Your new actors,' said Locke. 'Your very *surprised* new actors.'

'Ahhhhhhh.' Moncraine's seamed jowls moved as though he'd tasted something unpleasant. 'Weren't there supposed to be five of you?'

'Weren't you supposed to be at liberty?' said Sabetha. 'The other three are trying to hold your troupe together at Gloriano's.'

'Too bad you didn't come sooner,' said Moncraine. 'I'm afraid there's nothing to look forward to but packing for your return. Tell your master I appreciate the gesture.'

'That's not good enough,' said Locke. 'We were sent here to go on stage. We were sent here to learn from you!'

'You want a lesson, boy? If you find yourself being born, climb back in as quick as you can, because life's a *bottomless feast of shit*.'

'We can get you out of here,' said Sabetha.

'If you cooperate,' said Locke.

'Oh, you can spring me, can you?' Moncraine knelt and ran one manacled hand across the floor. 'You have an army of about a thousand men hidden outside the city? Let me know when they're storming the tower, so I can be sure to have my breeches on.'

'You know our master,' said Locke, lowering his voice. 'You can surely guess the nature of his students.'

'I *knew* your master,' said Moncraine. 'Years ago. And I thought he was sending me actors. Is that what you are? Is that where the gods have reached down and touched your little Camorri souls, eh? Given you the gift of silver tongues?'

'We can act,' said Sabetha.

'Can you? But are you *lions*? There's no room for any but *lions* in my company!' He turned his head to the guards at his door. 'Lions, aren't we boys?'

'Only if you don't lower your fucking voice,' said one of them.

'You see? Lions! Can you roar, children?'

'On stage and off,' said Sabetha coolly.

'Hmmm. That's fascinating, because from where I'm sitting, you look about what, sixteen? Seventeen? You've certainly never been wet for anything but dreams in the night, have you? Well, you might pass onstage, love ... let your hair down and fly your tits like flags – you could certainly keep the groundlings awake. But *you*,' he said, turning

314

to Locke. 'Who are you fooling? Small-boned sparrow of a lad. Got fig seeds in your sack where men should have the full fruit, eh? Do you even shave? What the hell do you mean by coming in here and trying to shove good cheer up my ass?'

'We're your only chance to go free,' said Locke, fuming, considering saying a number of less productive things.

'Go free? Why? I like it here. I'm fed, and my creditors can't reach me for at least the next year. The state of Espara will stop at one hand. Hells, that's a bargain compared to what I might get when my markers are called in on the street.'

'What's the name of the noble you struck?' said Sabetha.

'Why do you care?' said Moncraine. 'How can it possibly be of aid to you as you SCURRY BACK WHERE YOU FUCKING CAME FROM?'

'Keep your voice down,' said one of the guards. 'Or you'll have to be carried into court tomorrow.'

'You know, that might be pleasant,' said Moncraine. 'Can we give that a try?'

'Jasmer,' said Sabetha sharply. 'Look at me, you stupid ass.'

Jasmer did indeed look at her.

'I don't care what you think of us,' she whispered. 'You know what kind of person our master is. What kind of organization we come from. And if you don't stop braying like a jackass, this is what's going to happen. We'll *leave*.'

'I love this plan,' said Moncraine. 'Take this plan *all the way!*'

'You'll spend your year and a day inside this tower. Then they'll cut your gods-damned hand off and throw you out the door. And do you know who'll be standing there? *More Camorri than you've ever seen in your fucking life*. Not just us, or the other three currently *toiling on your behalf* on the other side of this pimple of a city. I mean big, unreasonable, cross-eyed motherfuckers straight out of the wombs of hell, and they'll take you for a ride. Locked in a box, ten days, all the way to Camorr sloshing in your own piss.'

'Now wait a minute,' said Moncraine.

'You don't have any other fucking creditors, get it? We're the front of the line now. We're all you need to worry about. You made a deal with our *garrista*. You know what that word means?'

'Of course—'

'Obviously you don't! Our master sent you five of us, free and clear, ready to get your troupe back on its feet. All you had to do was teach us about your trade. You'd rather break the deal and insult a *garrista*. So, you have a comfortable year, you stupid clown. As soon as it's over you'll see us again. Come on, Lucaza.'

She turned sharply, and Locke, supporting her act wholeheartedly, favoured Moncraine with a sour smirk before he did the same.

'Wait,' Jasmer hissed.

'What's the name of the noble you struck?' Sabetha didn't give him any more time to think or plead or stew; she whirled on him just as quickly as she'd pretended to leave.

'Boulidazi,' said Moncraine. 'Baron Boulidazi of Palazzo Corsala.'

'Why did you do it?'

'I was drinking,' said Moncraine. 'He wanted … he came down to Gloriano's. He wanted to buy out my debts, install himself as the company's patron.'

'For this you punched him in the teeth?' said Locke. 'What are you going to do if we get you out of here, try to cut our hearts out?'

'Boulidazi's an ass! A stuck-up little ass! He's barely older than you, and he thinks he can buy and sell me like gods-damned furniture. A theatrical company with his name on everything, wouldn't that be sweet! It took me twenty years to build my own troupe. I won't be anyone's hired man again. I'll take the Weeping Tower to that, any day, any year.'

'How was *assaulting* him preferable to letting him save your troupe?' said Sabetha. She sounded as incredulous as Locke felt.

'He doesn't *care* about the troupe,' said Moncraine. 'He wants it mounted on his wall like a fucking hunting trophy! He wants some charity project he can dangle at whatever gilded cunt he's chasing to show what a sensitive and artistic fellow he is. I refuse to sell my good name to help rich puppies dip their wicks!'

'What good name?' said Locke. 'Even the members of your own company want to see you get eaten by a bear.'

'And I'd be glad to supply one,' said Sabetha. 'Unfortunately for everyone, we're still going to rescue you. So I want you to sit quietly in your cell and bite your tongue.'

'Tomorrow,' said Locke, 'this Baron Boulidazi will forgive your insult and decline to make charges.'

'*What?*' said Moncraine. 'Boy, listen to me. Even if Boulidazi had a thousand cocks in his breeches and you blew every last one like a flute from sunrise to sunset—'

'He'll forgive your insult,' said Sabetha through gritted teeth, 'because that is the *only possible salvation* we can arrange for you. Understand? We have no other cards to play. So this is how it'll be. Once you're out, we'll discuss what you need to get your *Republic of Thieves* back into production.'

'The trouble with this fantasy, girl, is that it requires both of us to not be mad,' said Moncraine softly.

'All it requires is that you shut up and behave,' said Sabetha. 'And my name isn't *girl*. Most times you can call me Verena Gallante. But when I'm onstage, you'll call me *Amadine*.'

'Will I?' Moncraine laughed. 'That's a presumption a few steps ahead of my grasp. You show me your mythical thread of kindness in Boulidazi. Then we'll chat on the matter of plays.'

'Go back to your cell,' said Sabetha. 'I guarantee we'll speak again tomorrow.'

5

'Even if we get him out,' said Locke, 'we'll need to put that man on a leash.'

'He's a menace to himself and the rest of us,' said Sabetha. 'When we spring him, we should crowd him. Make it clear that he's being watched and judged at all times.'

'By the way, who's Amadine?'

'The best role in *The Republic of Thieves*,' said Sabetha, grinning.

'I haven't read any of it yet.'

'You should, before all the good parts get snapped up.'

'Someone kept it to herself all the way here!'

'Moncraine's got to have more copies of it somewhere in his troupe's mess. Jenora might know. But first, we've got our miracle to deliver on.'

'Miracle indeed,' said Locke. They were moving back down the Legion Steps, through the still ranks of the marble soldiers. The drizzle had let up, but there were soft rumbles of thunder from above. 'We need to reach this Boulidazi, more or less as we are, and convince him to forgive one of the craziest assholes I've ever met for a completely unjustified drunken assault.'

'Any ideas?'

'Uh ... maybe.'

'Spit them out. I managed to shut Jasmer up long enough to make our point; I've earned my day's pay.'

'And you were a pleasure to watch, too,' said Locke. 'But then, you're always—'

'*You* do not have the time to be charming,' said Sabetha, giving him a mild punch to the shoulder. 'And I certainly don't have time to be charmed.'

'Right. Sure,' said Locke. 'We need an angle of approach. Why should he open his door for us? Hey, what if we were Camorri nobles going incognito?'

'Hiding in Espara,' she said, clearly liking the notion. 'Trouble at home?'

'Hmmm. No. No, if we're not in favour at home we can't offer him anything. We might actually be a risk to him.'

'You're right. Okay. You and I ... are cousins,' said Sabetha. 'First cousins.'

'Cousins,' said Locke. 'So many gods-damned imaginary cousins. You and I are cousins. ... If we have to show Jean and the Sanzas, they're family retainers. We are, uh, grandchildren of ... an old count that doesn't get out much.'

'Blackspear,' said Sabetha. 'Enrico Botallio, Count Blackspear. I was a scullery maid in his house a few years ago, that summer you spent on the farm.'

'A Five Towers family,' said Locke. 'Would we live in the tower ourselves?'

'Yeah, most of his family does. And he hasn't been out of the city in twenty years; he's as old as Duke Nicovante. I'll be the daughter of his oldest son ... and you're the son of his youngest. He has no other children. Oh, your father's dead, by the way. Fell off a horse two years ago.'

'Good to know. If we need any real details of the household, I'll pass the game to you whenever I can.' Locke snapped his fingers. 'We're in Espara because you want to indulge your wish to be onstage—'

'—which could never be allowed under my real name in Camorr!'

Sabetha had never finished one of his thoughts before, in the way that Jean did all the time. Locke felt a flush of warmth.

'That's great,' she went on, heedless. 'So we're incognito, but with our family's permission.'

'Thus whoever helps us makes himself a powerful and wealthy friend in Camorr.' Locke couldn't help smiling at the improbable thought that they might have found a way out after all. 'Sabetha, this is great. It's also the thinnest line of bullshit we've ever hung ourselves on.'

'And we haven't even been here a full day yet.'

'We need given names.'

'There we can be lazy. I'm Verena Botallio, you're Lucaza Botallio.'

'Hells, yes.' Locke glanced around, affirming that they were still within the limited corridor of Espara he'd managed to half familiarize himself with. 'We should head back to Gloriano's and see how they did with the horses. Then we can go visit this Boulidazi and beg him not to think too hard about where we've come from.'

6

'Alondo's cousin was as good as promised,' said Jean. He waved at a young man, a bearded and heavier version of Alondo, who was sitting against the wall at the back of Gloriano's common room, accompanied by Alondo, Sylvanus, the Sanzas, and several half-empty bottles. Nobody else new or unknown was in the room. 'He got us just over a royal apiece for the horses. All it cost us was a couple of bottles of wine. And, ah, I promised we'd give him a part in the play.'

'What?'

'No lines. He just wants to dress up and get stabbed, he says.'

'Just as long as he doesn't expect to get paid,' said Sabetha.

'Not in anything except hangovers,' said Jean. 'I do notice you haven't dragged a large Syresti impresario back with you.'

'That game's afoot,' said Locke. 'Come spill your purse. Asino brothers! On your feet a moment, we'd have a word concerning finance.'

'Oh let them stay,' said Sylvanus. 'This is the fun side of the room, and our young hostler was about to take hoof for more wine.'

'You're not finished with the three bottles you have,' said Locke.

'They're writing farewell notes to their families,' said Sylvanus. 'Their holes are already dug in the ground. Oh, I suppose I really must get up before I piss, mustn't I?' He rolled sideways in the vague direction of the door that led back to the soaked inn-yard. 'Give us a hand, hostler, give us a hand. I shall go on all fours to make use of your expertise.'

'Marvellous,' said Locke, pulling Calo and Galdo to their feet.

'Lovely. Are you two following Sylvanus down the vomit-strewn path?'

'We may be sociably fuzzed,' said Calo.

'A little blurry at the edges,' said Galdo.

'That's probably for the best. I need you to come over here and dump out your purses.'

'You need us to what now?'

'We need a flash bag,' said Sabetha.

'What the hell's a flash bag?' said Jenora, wandering by at a moment precisely calculated to overhear what the huddled Gentlemen Bastards were up to.

'Since you ask,' said Jean, 'it's a purse of coins you throw together to make it look like you're used to carrying around big fat sums.'

'Oh,' she said. 'That must be a nice thing to have.'

Using a spare table, the five Camorri dumped out their personal funds, to which Jean added the take from the horses and Locke mixed in the remnants of the purse Chains had given them. Camorri barons, tyrins, and solons clattered against Esparan fifths and coppins.

'Get all the coppers out of the pile,' said Locke. 'They're as useless as an Asino brother.'

'Suck vinegar from my ass-crack,' said Calo.

Five pairs of hands sifted through the coins, pulling coppers aside, leaving a diminished but gleaming mass in the centre.

'Copper gets split five ways so everyone's got something,' said Locke. 'Gold and silver goes in the purse.'

'Do you want Auntie to change any of that Camorri stuff for you?' said Jenora, peering over Jean's right shoulder.

'No,' said Locke. 'For the moment, it's actually a point in our favour. What's the flash count?'

'Five crowns, two tyrins,' said Sabetha. 'And two royals, one fifth.'

'That's more money than any of Auntie's customers have seen in a *long* time,' said Jenora.

'It's shy of what I want,' said Locke. 'But it might be convincing. No journeyman actor carries around a year and a half's pay.'

'Unless they're not getting paid a damn thing,' said Jenora.

'We'll deal with that tomorrow,' said Locke as he cinched the flash bag tightly closed. 'Hopefully with Moncraine listening very attentively.'

'Where are you going now?' said Jean.

'To see Moncraine's punching bag,' said Sabetha. 'And if that Syresti son of a bitch can teach us better acting than what we'll need to pull *this* off, he'll actually deserve this rescue.'

'Want an escort?' said Jean.

'Based on what you've seen tonight,' muttered Locke, 'who needs it more, Sabetha and me or the twins?'

'Good point.' Jean polished his optics against the collar of his tunic and readjusted them on his nose. 'I'll keep them out of trouble, and see if I can trick Sylvanus into sleeping indoors.'

'Where's Palazzo Corsala?' said Sabetha to Jenora.

'That's on the north side, the swell district. Can't miss it. Clean streets, beautiful houses, people like Sylvanus and Jasmer beaten on sight.'

'We'll spring for a hired coach,' said Locke. 'We won't look respectable enough without one.'

'Shall we go call on Baron Boulidazi, then?' said Sabetha.

'Yes,' said Locke. '*No*. Wait. We've forgotten one terribly important thing. Let's run back up to Stay-Awake Salvard and hope he's still feeling sympathetic.'

7

'Tradesfolk entrance is around back,' growled the tree trunk of a man who opened Boulidazi's front door. 'Tradesfolk hours are—'

'What kind of tradesman hires a coach-and-four to make his rounds?' said Locke, jerking a thumb over his shoulder. Their hired carriage was waiting beyond the rows of alchemically miniaturized olive trees that screened Boulidazi's manor from the street. The driver hadn't liked their clothes, but their silver had vouched for them quite adequately.

'Pray give your master this,' said Sabetha, holding out a small white card. This had been scrounged from the office of Stay-Awake Salvard, who had bemusedly agreed to charge them a few coppins for it and some ink.

The servant glanced at the card, glared at them, then glanced at the card again. 'Wait here,' he said, and closed the door.

Several minutes went by. The slow drip of water from the canvas awning above their head became a soft, steady drumbeat as the rain picked up again. At last, the door creaked open and a rectangle of golden light from inside the house fell over them.

'Come,' said the bulky servant. Two more men waited behind him, and for an instant Locke feared an ambush. However, these servants wielded nothing more threatening than towels, which they used to wipe Locke and Sabetha's shoes dry.

Baron Boulidazi's house was unexceptional, among those of its type that Locke had seen. It was comfortable enough, furnished to show off disposable wealth, but there was no grand and special something, no 'hall-piece' as they were often called, to evoke wonder from freshly arrived guests.

The servant took them out of the foyer, through a sitting hall, and into a warmly lit room with felt-padded walls. A blandly handsome man of about twenty, with neck-length black hair and close-set dark eyes, was leaning against a billiards table with a stick in his hands. The white card was on the table.

'The Honourable Verena Botallio and companion,' said the servant without enthusiasm. He left the room immediately.

'Of the Isla Zantara?' said Boulidazi, more warmly. 'I've just read your card. Isn't that part of the Alcegrante?'

'It is, Lord Boulidazi,' said Sabetha, giving the slight nod and half-curtsey that was usual in Camorr for an informal noble reception. 'Have you ever been there?'

'To Camorr? No, no. I've always wanted to visit, but I've never had the privilege.'

'Lord Boulidazi,' said Sabetha, 'may I present my cousin, the Honourable Lucaza Botallio?'

'Your cousin, eh?' said Boulidazi, nodding as Locke bowed his head. The Esparan lord offered his hand. As they shook, Locke noted that Boulidazi was solidly built, much the same size as Alondo's hostler cousin, and he didn't hold back the strength in his grip.

'Thank you for receiving us,' said Locke. 'We would have both sent our cards, but only Verena is carrying one, I'm afraid.'

'Oh? You weren't robbed or anything, I suppose? Is that why you've come dressed as you are? Forgive my mentioning it.'

'No, we haven't been mistreated,' said Sabetha. 'And there's nothing to forgive; we're not travelling in our usual capacity. We're incognito, with just a bodyguard and a pair of servants, though we've left them behind for the moment.'

'Incognito,' said Boulidazi. 'Are you in some sort of danger?'

'Not in the slightest,' said Sabetha with a laugh. She then turned and feigned surprise (Locke was confident that only long familiarity allowed him to spot the fact that it was a wilful change) at the sight of a sabre resting in its scabbard on a witchwood display shelf. 'Is that what I think it is?'

'What, exactly, do you think it is?' said Boulidazi, and it seemed to Locke that he was a touch more curt than before.

'Surely it's a DiVorus? The seal on the hilt—'

'It is,' said Boulidazi, instantly losing his tone of impatience. 'One of his later blades, but still—'

'I trained with a DiVorus,' said Sabetha, poising one hand above the hilt of the sabre. 'The *Voillantebona* rapier. Don't get me wrong; it wasn't mine. My instructor's. I still remember the balance, and the patterns in the steel ... your hilt looks honourably stained. I assume you practise with it?'

'Often,' said Boulidazi. 'This one's called *Drakovelus*. It's been in my family for three generations. It suits my style – not the fastest on the floor, but when I do move I can put a bit of strength behind it.'

'The sabre rewards a sturdy handler,' said Sabetha.

'We're neglecting your cousin,' said Boulidazi. 'Forgive me, Lucaza, please don't allow my enthusiasms to shove you aside from the conversation.'

'Not at all, Lord Boulidazi. I've had my years with the fencing masters, of course, but Verena's the connoisseur in the family.'

Boulidazi's heavy servant returned and whispered into the baron's ear. Locke silently counted to ten before the servant finished. The big man withdrew again, and the baron stared at Locke.

'You know, I just now recall,' he said. 'Botallio ... isn't that one of the Five Towers clans?'

'Of course,' said Sabetha.

'And yet you give your address as the Isla Zantara,' said Boulidazi.

'I'm fond of Grandfather,' said Sabetha. 'But surely you can understand how someone my age might prefer a little manor of her own.'

'And your grandfather ...' said Boulidazi expectantly.

'Don Enrico Botallio.'

'Better known as Count Blackspear?' said Boulidazi, still cautiously.

'Verena's father is Blackspear's eldest son,' said Locke. 'I'm the son of his youngest.'

'Oh? I believe I might have heard something of your father, Lucaza,' said the baron. 'I do hope that he's well?'

Locke felt a surge of relief that they'd pretended to be from a family Sabetha had knowledge of. Boulidazi obviously had access to some sort of directory of Camorri peers. Locke allowed himself to look crest-fallen for just an instant, and then put on an obviously forced smile.

'I'm sorry,' he said, 'but I must inform you that my father died several years ago.'

'Oh,' said Boulidazi, visibly relaxing. 'Forgive me. I must have been thinking of someone else. But why didn't the pair of you simply give the name of the count when you—'

'Noble cousin,' said Sabetha, shifting instantly into her excellent Throne Therin, 'the name of Blackspear commands instant attention in Camorr, but surely you wouldn't think us so vulgar as to try and awe you with it in Espara, as the freshest of acquaintances, as guests in your house?'

'Oh – vulgar, oh *no*, never!' said Boulidazi in the same language. Anyone of breeding was expected to endure years of tutelage in it, and he'd clearly done his time in the purgatory of conjugation and tenses. 'I didn't mean that I expected anything uncouth of you!'

'Lord Boulidazi,' said Locke, returning the conversation to plain Therin, 'we're the ones who should be apologizing, for imposing ourselves upon you in our present state. We have our reasons, but you needn't regret being cautious.'

'I'm glad you understand,' said the baron. 'Tymon!'

The large servant, who must have been lurking just past the door, stepped inside.

'It's all right, Tymon,' said the baron. 'I think our guests will be staying for a while. Let's have some chairs.'

'Of course, my lord,' said the servant, relaxing out of his cold and intimidating aspect as easily as removing a hat.

'I hope you don't mind if we talk in here,' said Boulidazi. 'My parents ... well, it was just last year. I can't really think of the study as *my* room quite yet.'

'I know how it is,' said Locke. 'You inherit the memories of a house as well as its stones. I didn't touch anything in my father's library for months.'

'I suppose I should call you Don and Dona Botallio, then?' said the baron.

'Only if you want to flatter us,' said Locke with a smile.

'While Grandfather still holds the title,' said Sabetha, 'my father, as direct heir, is called Don. But since we're two steps removed, we are, at present, just a pair of *Honourables*.'

Tymon returned, along with the shoe-towellers, and three high-backed chairs were set down next to the billiards table.

Boulidazi seemed reasonably convinced of their authenticity now, and Locke felt a pang of mingled awe and anxiety. Here was a lord of the city, capable of putting them in prison (or worse) with a word, opening to their false-facing like any common shopkeeper, guard, or functionary. Chains was right. Their training *had* given them a remarkable freedom of action.

Still, it seemed wise to seal the affair as tightly as possible.

'Gods above,' said Locke. 'What a boor I've been! Lord Boulidazi, forgive me. Is it usual in Espara to give a consideration to house servants – *damn!*'

Locke pulled out his purse and made what he thought was an excellent show of stumbling toward the withdrawing Tymon. He fell against the billiards table, and a stream of clinking gold and silver just happened to scatter across the felt surface.

'Are you all right?' The baron was at Locke's side in an instant, helping him up, and Locke was satisfied that Boulidazi had a full view of the coins.

'Fine, thank you. I'm such a clumsy ass. You can see all the grace in the family wound up on Verena's side.' Locke swept the coins back into the purse. 'Sorry about your game.'

'It was just a solitary diversion,' said Boulidazi, as he helped Sabetha into a chair. 'And yes, on holidays, we do give gratuities to the help, but there's a little ceremony and some temple nonsense. You needn't worry about it.'

'Well, we're obliged to you,' said Locke, relieved that he could escape without surrendering any of the flash bag funds. All Boulidazi had to do was *believe* that money was no real object to them.

'Now,' said Sabetha, 'I suppose you'd like to find out why we've come to you.'

'Of course,' said Boulidazi. 'But first, why not tell me what it would please you to be called, if not Dona Botallio?'

'That's easy,' said Sabetha, flashing a smile that hit Locke like a boot to the chest even though he wasn't positioned to catch its full effect. 'You should call me Verena.'

'Verena,' said the baron. 'Then I beg that you'll call me Gennaro, and let no more "Lord Boulidazis" clutter the air between us.'

'With pleasure,' said Sabetha.

'Gennaro,' said Locke, 'we're here to discuss the situation of a man named Jasmer Moncraine.'

'What?'

'To put it even more plainly,' said Sabetha, 'we've come to ask that you decline to state your charges against him.'

'You want me to *forgive* him?'

'Or appear to,' said Sabetha sweetly.

'That arrogant pissant struck me before witnesses,' said Boulidazi. 'With the *back* of his hand! You can't expect me to believe that a *Camorri* would bear such a thing, were either of you in my place!'

'If I had nothing to win by a display of mercy,' said Locke, 'I'd have whipped the stupid bastard's face into bloody mince. And if none of us stood to gain right now, I'd go to court with you merely for the pleasure of hearing the sentence read.'

'We're not strangers to Moncraine,' said Sabetha. 'We've been to see him at the Weeping Tower—'

'Why?'

'Please,' said Sabetha, 'just listen. We know what a fool he is. We're not here to discuss the brighter facets of his character, because we know he doesn't have any, and we're not asking for mercy for its own sake. We'd like to propose a mutually profitable arrangement.'

'How could I possibly profit,' said Boulidazi, 'by accepting disgrace in front of the entire city?'

'First, tell us: Were you serious about wanting to fund Moncraine's troupe and buy out his debts?' said Locke.

'I was,' said the baron. 'I certainly was, until he decided to thank me by lunging at me like an ape.'

'Why did you make the offer?'

'I grew up attending his plays,' said Boulidazi. 'Mother loved the theatre. Moncraine really used to be something, back before … well, years ago.'

'And you wanted to be a patron,' said Locke.

'All my family money is sitting safe in vaults, gathering dust and shitting interest. I thought I'd do something meaningful for a change. Pick Moncraine up, run things properly, associate my name with something.' Boulidazi drummed his fingers against one arm of his chair. 'What the hell can Moncraine possibly mean to you?'

'I came here to be part of his troupe for the summer,' said Sabetha. 'I, ah, I have a certain inclination. It's awkward to talk about myself, though. Lucaza, would you?'

'Of course,' said Locke. 'Cousin Verena has always loved the theatre, as much of it as she could get in Camorr. Grandfather's hired players a dozen times for her. But she's always wanted to be *on* stage. To act. And that's just not done.'

'If I'd taken up alchemy,' said Sabetha, 'or gardening, or painting, or investment, that'd be fine. I could even ride off to war, if we had ever had any. But noble heirs don't go onstage, not in Camorr.'

'Not if they want to inherit,' said Locke. 'And Grandfather won't be with us forever. After him it's Uncle, and after Uncle it's Verena.'

'Countess Blackspear, eh?' said Boulidazi.

'Whether or not we keep Blackspear is up to the duke; the Five Towers are his to dispose of. But our lands wouldn't go anywhere. If Blackspear was rescinded, I'd be countess of the old family estates.'

'So you've come here posing as an actress to avoid a scandal in Camorr.'

'You understand perfectly,' said Sabetha. 'Verena Gallante can have a summer or two onstage in Espara, and then Verena Botallio can go back to being respectable back home. That's the bargain I struck with Father, also provided Lucaza and a few trusted men came along to keep an eye on me.'

'And that's the understanding we had with Moncraine,' said Locke. 'We'd furnish several actors, and he'd make use of us in a play. Imagine our surprise when we arrived this afternoon to discover the situation.'

'Imagine my surprise when Moncraine attacked me!' said Boulidazi. 'You're putting me between two fires, my friends. I can protect my dignity according to the laws and customs of Espara, or I can grant this request, to which I would normally be very happily disposed. I can't do both.'

'If you withdrew from chastising Moncraine out of cowardice or indifference,' said Sabetha, 'then I agree, your behaviour would be improper. But what if your peers could see that you had forgiven him for the sake of a greater design?'

'Mercy,' said Locke, bringing his hands slowly together as though squeezing his words into one mass as he spoke them, 'ambition, artistry, and good old-fashioned financial sense. All at once.'

'Moncraine wants nothing to do with me,' said Boulidazi, 'and I'm pleased to return the sentiment. Let the bastard rot for a year and a day. Maybe he'll grow some discretion when he loses his hand.'

'I don't have a year and a day, Gennaro,' said Sabetha.

'Then why not see Basanti? He's the success. Built his own theatre, even. I'm sure he'd put you onstage in a heartbeat. You're certainly, uh…'

'Yes?'

'You'd certainly have a great many eyes following you attentively, if you'll pardon my boldness.'

'Pardon gladly extended. But if Basanti's really the thing, why didn't you approach him about a partnership rather than Moncraine?'

'Basanti has no need of a bandage on his finances. Besides, there's nothing to *build* where he's concerned. It's hard to take credit for something already achieved.'

'Believe it or not, we feel much the same about Moncraine,' said Sabetha. 'He's a means to an end. Forgive him. Let him go free, and I guarantee he'll accept your patronage.'

'What makes you assume I'm still willing to offer it?'

'Come now, Gennaro,' said Sabetha, deepening her voice a little, adopting a slightly teasing tone. 'Don't punish *yourself* for Moncraine's stupidity. Your plan was a good one.'

'If you help us in this,' said Locke, 'you'll have him entirely in your power. Financial debt and moral debt, and you'll have us to keep him in line.'

'The Moncraine-Boulidazi Company,' said Sabetha.

'Or the Boulidazi-Moncraine Company,' said Locke.

'I'll look weak,' said the baron, but his voice had the wavering quality of a man nearly ready to go over the edge of the precipice they were nudging him toward.

'You'll look *clever*,' Locke said. 'Hells, you'll look like you might have planned the whole thing all along to stir up notice!'

'That's *marvellous*!' said Sabetha. 'At the end of the summer, after we've whipped satisfaction out of Moncraine, you let slip that the whole affair was just a ploy for attention. That's the payoff for a little bit of pain in court tomorrow! Basanti will be forgotten in a moment, and all the city's admiration will settle on what you've done.'

'You'll look like a bloody *genius*,' said Locke, immensely pleased with himself.

'The Boulidazi-Moncraine company,' said the baron. 'It does have a certain ... weight. A certain noble ring to it.'

'Help me have a season or two in the lights,' said Sabetha. 'Then bring the company touring to Camorr. We'll introduce you to Grand-father, all the counts and countesses, the duke ...'

'They could play all the Five Towers in turn,' said Locke. 'The roof-top gardens. Verena and I would have to disappear as actors, of course, but we'd be delighted to attend the shows as your hosts.'

'Isn't that worth temporary inconvenience?' said Sabetha with a smile that could have coaxed steam out of ice.

'I will require ... a moment to reflect,' said Boulidazi.

'Shall we leave you alone?' said Sabetha, rising partway from her chair.

'Yes, for but a moment. Tymon will fetch you anything you desire in the reception hall.'

Locke rose as well, but Boulidazi held up a hand.

'Not you, Lucaza, if you please. I'd appreciate a word.'

Locke sank back into his chair, stole a brief glance at Sabetha, and caught the slightest hint of a nod from her. She withdrew the way she and Locke had come.

'Lucaza,' said the baron, leaning forward and lowering his voice, 'I hope that I might be forgiven this liberty; I know that Camorri are not to be trifled with in matters touching family honour, and I mean no offence.'

'Truly, Gennaro, we've asked for a favour tomorrow in exchange for promises that will take months or years to fully play out. I doubt you could find two people in Espara more difficult to offend than Verena or myself at this moment.'

'You're both so well spoken,' said Boulidazi. 'I can see why you'd want to dabble on the stage. But now let me have your confidence. Your cousin ... has an aspect that *blossoms* upon consideration. When she entered this room she was merely pretty, but after watching her, listening to her ... I feel as though the air has been taken straight out of my lungs.'

Locke felt as though the air had been taken straight out of *his* lungs.

'Tell me, please,' said Boulidazi, clearly noticing the change in Locke's demeanour as Locke fought for self-control. 'Does she really love the theatre? And bladework?'

'She, uh, lives for them,' said Locke.

'Are you betrothed to her?'

Locke was overwhelmed by a flurry of immediate reactions; the urge to stand up, say yes, slap Boulidazi across the face, grab him by his hair and dig wide furrows in the felt of his billiards table using his teeth … Then came the secondary calculations like a bucket of cold water: Boulidazi would kill him, Sabetha would gladly help, the intrusion of his personal jealousy into his professional character would doom the Gentlemen Bastards to utter failure.

'No,' he said, almost calmly, 'no, I've been meant for someone else … since I was barely old enough to walk. We'll wed when she comes of age.'

'And Verena?' said Boulidazi.

(Another less than helpful flash from Locke's imagination, protesting what his higher reasoning knew to be unavoidable. Jean Tannen smashing in through a back door, hoisting Boulidazi over his head, slamming him down across the billiards table … Why were all his fantasies so calamitous for that table, which had done him no injury? And gods damn it anyway, it was never going to happen!)

'Unattached,' said Locke, hating the word even as he brought it forth. 'Father and Grandfather have always felt that Verena … is a fruit best left hanging, uh, until they know how she might be most advantageously … plucked.'

'Thank you,' said the baron. 'Thank you! That's … welcome news. I hope you won't think of me as, as grasping beyond my station, Lucaza. I come from a long and honourable line. I hold several estates with secure incomes. I've much to offer by way of … of a match.'

'I'm sure you do,' said Locke slowly. 'Were she pleased, and with Count Blackspear's consent.'

'Yes, yes. With the family's blessing … and were she pleased.' Boulidazi ran a hand through his hair and made nervous, meaningless adjustments to his white silk neck-cloth. 'I'll do it, Lucaza. I'll forgive Moncraine, and trust you to keep him under my thumb. I'll provide whatever you need to settle his debts and tame his troupe. All I ask …'

'Yes?'

'Help me,' said Boulidazi. 'Help me show Verena my quality. My honourable intentions. Teach me how I might better please her. Advise her favourably on my behalf.'

'If Moncraine goes free …'

'He will,' said Boulidazi. 'He won't be at the Weeping Tower a moment longer than he has to be.'

'Then I am your man,' said Locke softly, fighting back further visions of Gennaro Boulidazi spitting up fragments of his billiards table. 'I am *for you*, my friend.'

CHAPTER SEVEN
The Five-Year Game: Countermove

'What the hell's the matter with us, Jean?' Locke rubbed his eyes and noticed certain discomforts in his gut and around his ankles, in that order. 'She's rolled us up like a couple of old tents. And what the fuck are these things on my legs?'

Just above his feet, his thin, pale ankles were encircled by bands of iron. The manacles were loose enough to let blood flow, but weighed about five pounds apiece.

'I imagine they're to discourage us from swimming,' said Jean. 'Aren't they thoughtful? They match your eyes.'

'The bars across the windows aren't enough, eh? Gods above, my stomach feels like it's trying to eat the rest of me.'

Locke made a more thorough examination of their surroundings. Cushions, shelves, silks, and lanterns – the cabin was fit for the duke of Camorr. There was even a little rack of books and scrolls next to Jean.

'Look what she left sitting out for us,' said Jean. He tossed Locke the leather-bound book he'd been reading. It was an aged quarto with gold leaf alchemically embossed into three lines on the cover:

THE REPUBLIC OF THIEVES
A TRUE AND TRAGIC HISTORY
CAELLIUS LUCARNO

'Ohhh,' said Locke softly, setting the book aside. 'That beauty has a bitch streak as wide as ten rivers.'

'How'd she drug you?' said Jean.

'Quite embarrassingly.'

There was a knock at the cabin door. It opened a moment later, and down the steps came a spry, long-legged fellow with the tan of many active years sunk into his lean features.

'Hello, boys,' said the stranger. He had a faint Verrari accent. 'Welcome aboard the *Volantyne's Resolve*. Solus Volantyne, at your service. And I do mean that! You boys are our first and only business on this trip.'

'Whatever you're being paid,' said Locke, 'we can double it if you turn this ship around right now.'

'Our mutual friend told me that was probably the first thing you'd say, Master Lazari.'

Locke cracked his knuckles and glared. He had to give Sabetha credit for at least preserving their false identities, but he didn't *want* to have any kind thoughts toward her at the moment.

'I'm inclined to agree with her suggestion,' continued Volantyne, 'that I'm rather more likely to enjoy success and fair compensation in partnership with the woman who's still at liberty, rather than the two men she brought to me in chains.'

'We can triple her payment,' said Locke.

'A man who'd trade a sure fortune for the promises of an angry prisoner is far too stupid to be the captain of his own ship,' said Volantyne.

'Well, hells,' said Locke. 'If you won't turn coat, can you at least get me some ship's biscuit or something?'

'Our mutual friend said that food would be the second thing on your mind.' Volantyne folded his arms and smiled. 'But we're not eating ship's biscuit on this leg of the trip. We're eating fresh-baked pepper bread, and goose stuffed with honey-glazed olives, and boiled lake frogs in brandy and cream.'

'I got hit on the head somehow,' said Locke. 'This is the stupidest dream I've had in years, isn't it?'

'No dream, my friend. We've been set up with a cook so good I'd fuck him six days a week just to keep him aboard, if only I liked men. But he's another gift paid for by our mutual friend. Come on deck and let me explain the conditions of your passage. You lucky, lucky sons of bitches!'

On deck, Locke could see that the *Volantyne's Resolve* was a two-masted brig with her rigging in good order; her sails were neither straight from the yard nor frayed to threads. About two dozen men and women had been formed up to watch Locke and Jean emerge from the great cabin. Most of them had the tan, rangy look of sailors, but a few of the heavier ones, big-boned land animals for sure, looked like freshly hired muscle.

'This is the easiest cruise we've ever been given,' said Volantyne. 'We're headed west, up the Cavendria and out to sea. We'll have an autumn excursion for a month, then we'll turn round and take it slow and easy back to Karthain. You gentlemen will enjoy a luxurious cabin, books to read, fine meals. The wines we've laid in for the voyage will make you think you're royalty. All this, on one condition only – good behaviour.'

'I can pay,' said Locke, raising his voice to a shout, 'three times what each of you is receiving now! You would have it merely for getting us back to Karthain! Two days' work, rather than two months!'

'Now, sir,' said Volantyne, looking cross for the first time, 'that's not good behaviour at all. Any further talk in that vein will get you sent down to the hold. There's two ways to make this trip – with free limbs and full stomachs, or cinched up tight in darkness, let out once a day to eat and piss. I'm to take the tenderest care with your lives, but your liberty can go straight overboard if you give us trouble.'

'What about these things around our ankles?' said Locke.

'Shields from temptation,' said Volantyne.

'Gah,' Locke muttered. 'Also, where's this food—'

'Sirs, the thousand apologies,' cried a man in a stained brown robe who came stumbling up from below via the main deck hatch. He was pale, with greyish-blond hair, and carried a silver tray set with a plain iron tureen and several loaves of bread. 'I have the foods!'

'This famous cook of yours is a *Vadran*?' said Jean.

'Yes, I *know*,' said Volantyne, 'but you must trust me. Adalric was trained in Talisham, and he knows his business.'

'The oysters, in sauce from ale has I boiled,' said the cook.

He held the tray out to Locke, and the scents of fresh food were as good as a fist to the jaw.

'Um, discussion of the situation,' said Locke, 'can recommence in about half an hour.'

'So long as you quit trying to bribe my crew, you may speak as you please, honoured passengers,' said Volantyne.

2

As the first day passed, and the second, it became clear that their situation was both the most comfortable and the most vexing imprisonment Locke could have imagined.

Their meals were plentiful and magnificent, the wine better even than promised, the ale fresh and sweet, and their requests were taken up without hesitation or complaint.

'These bastards have made their fortunes on this venture,' said Jean, over the remnants of lunch on the second day. 'Isn't that right, ship-mates? It's the only possible explanation for our treatment. A pile of gold in every pocket.'

Every meal was eaten in the presence of at least four attendants, silent and polite and utterly vigilant. Every knife and fork was counted, every scrap and bone was collected. Locke could have palmed any number of useful items, but there was no point to it, not until the other difficulties of their situation could be surmounted.

Their bedding was turned out and replaced each day, and they were kept on deck while it happened. Locke could see just enough of the activity within the cabin to depress his spirits. All of their books were given a shake, their chests were opened and searched, their hammocks scoured, the floor planks examined in minute detail. By the time they were let back in, everything was restored to its proper place and the cabin was as fresh as if it had never been used, but it was useless to hide anything.

They were searched several times each day, and weren't even per-mitted to wear shoes. The only extraneous object they possessed, in fact, was Jean's tightly bound lock of Ezri's hair. Locke was surprised to see it on the morning of their third day.

'I had a few words with Sabetha, after her people finally knocked me down.' Jean lay in his hammock, idly turning the hair over and over in his hands. 'She said that some courtesies were not to be refused.'

'Did she say anything else? About me, or for me?'

'I think she's said everything she means to say, Locke. This ship's as good as a farewell note.'

'She must have given Volantyne and his crew ten pages of directions concerning us.'

'Even their little boat is lashed tighter than usual, as though some god might reach down and snatch it off the deck,' said Jean casually.

'Oh really?' Locke slipped out of his hammock, crept over to Jean's side of the cabin, and lowered his voice. 'On the larboard side of the main deck? You think we could make something of it?'

'We'd never have time to hoist it properly. But if we could weaken the ropes, and if the deck was pitching ...'

'Shit,' said Locke. 'Once we hit the Cavendria, we'll be steady as a cup of tea until we're out the other side. How many of our friends do you figure we could handle at once?'

'How many could *I* handle at once? Let's be pragmatic and say three.

I'm pretty sure I could club the whole crew down one or two at a time if nobody raised an alarm, but you've seen their habits. They never work alone. I'm not sure the brute force approach will get us very far.'

'You know, it certainly would be nice to receive an unannounced visit from our benefactor Patience,' said Locke. 'Or anyone associated with her. Right about now. Or … now!'

'I think we're on our own,' said Jean. 'I'm sure someone or some-*thing* is watching us, but Sabetha put us here. It seems within the rules as Patience explained them.'

'I wonder if *her* Bondsmagi would be so sporting.'

'Well, there is a bright side. We're eating well enough. You're not looking like such a wrenched-out noodle anymore.'

'That's great, Jean. I'm not just exiled; I'm being plumped up for slaughter. Suppose there's any chance we might run into Zamira if we reach the Sea of Brass?'

'What the hell would she be doing back up here so soon after everything that happened?' Jean yawned and stretched. 'The *Poison Orchid*'s as likely to come over the horizon and save us as I am to give birth to a live albatross.'

'It was just an idle thought,' said Locke. 'A damned pleasing idle thought. So, I suppose we pray for heavy weather.'

'And worry about cutting some ropes,' said Jean. 'Ideas?'

'I could have a makeshift knife on an hour's notice. So long as I knew it would be used before they turned our cabin over the next day.'

'Good. And what about our ankle manacles? You've always been better with that sort of thing than I have.'

'The mechanisms are delicate. I could come up with bone splinters small enough to fit, but those are brittle. One snap and they'd jam up the locks for good.'

'Then we might just have to bear them until we can hit land,' said Jean. 'Well, first things first. We need to be within reasonable distance of a beach, and we need a rolling deck, and we need to not be tied up in the hold when our chance comes.'

3

The sky turned grey again that night, and ominous clouds boiled on the horizons, but the gentle rolling of the Amathel barely tilted the deck of the *Resolve* in one direction or another. Locke spent several hours leaning against the main deck rails, feigning placidity, straining secretly for any glimpse of a bolt of lightning or an oncoming thunderhead. The only lights to be seen, however, were the ghostly flickerings from within the black depths of the lake, twinkling like constellations of fire.

Their progress was slow. The strange autumn winds were against them much of the time, and with no mages to shape the weather to their taste, they had to move by tack after long, slow tack to the southwest. Volantyne and his crew seemed to care not a whit. Whether they sailed half the world or half a mile, their pay would be the same.

On the night of their fourth day, Locke caught flashes of whitish yellow illuminating the southern horizon, but his excitement died when he realized that he was looking at Lashain.

On the fifth day they picked up speed, and the capricious winds grew stronger. The whole sky bruised over with promising clouds, and just after noon the first drops of cool rain began to fall. Locke and Jean retreated to their cabin, trying to look innocent. They buried themselves in books and idle conversation, glancing out the cabin window every few moments, watching in mutual satisfaction as the troughs between the waves deepened and the strands of foam thickened at their crests.

At the third hour of the afternoon, with the rain steady and the lake rolling at four or five feet, Adalric came to their door to receive instructions for dinner.

'Perhaps the soup of the veal, masters?'

'By all means,' said Locke. If any chance to escape was coming, he wanted to face it with at least one more of the Vadran prodigy's feasts shoved down his gullet.

'And how about chicken?' said Jean.

'I'll do one the murder right away.'

'Dessert too,' said Locke. 'Let's have a big one tonight. Storms make me hungry.'

'I have a cake of the honey and ginger,' said Adalric.

'Good man,' said Jean. 'And let's have some wine. Two bottles of sparkling apple, eh?'

'Two bottles,' said the cook. 'I has it brung to you.'

'Decent fellow, for all that he tramples the language,' said Locke when the door had closed behind the cook. 'I hate to take advantage of him.'

337

'He won't miss us if we slip away,' said Jean. 'He's got the whole crew to appreciate him. You know what sort of slop they'd be gagging down if he wasn't aboard.'

Locke went on deck a few minutes later, letting the rain soak him as he stood by the foremast, feigning indifference as the deck rolled slowly from side to side. It was a gentle motion as yet, but if the weather continued to pick up it was a very promising trend indeed.

'Master Lazari!' Solus Volantyne came down from the quarter-deck, oilcloak fluttering. 'Surely you'd be more comfortable in your cabin?'

'Perhaps our mutual friend neglected to tell you, Captain Volantyne, that Master Callas and myself have been at sea. Compared to what we endured down in the Ghostwinds, this is invigourating.'

'I do know something of your history, Lazari, but I'm also charged with your safety.'

'Well, until someone takes these damned bracelets off my ankles I can't exactly swim to land, can I?'

'And what if you catch cold?'

'With Adalric aboard? He must have possets that would drive back death itself.'

'Will you at least consent to an oilcloak, so you look like less of a crazy landsman?'

'That'd be fine.'

Volantyne summoned a sailor with a spare cloak, and Locke resumed talking as he fastened it over his shoulders. 'Now, pardon my ignorance, but where the hell are we, anyway?'

'Forty miles due west of Lashain, give or take a hair in any direction.'

'Ah. I thought I spotted the city last night.'

'We're not making good westward progress. If I had a schedule to keep I'd be in a black mood, but thanks to you, we're in no hurry, are we?'

'Quite. Are those heavier storms to the south?'

'That shadow? That's a lee shore, Master Lazari. A damned lee shore. We're eight or nine miles off the southern coast of the Amathel, and fighting to get no closer. If we can punch through this mess and claw another twenty or thirty miles west-nor'west, we should be clear straight to the Cavendria, and from there it's like a wading pond all the way to the Sea of Brass.'

338

'Well, that's good to hear,' said Locke. 'Rest assured, I've got absolutely no interest in drowning.'

4

Dinner was excellent and productive. Four of Volantyne's sailors watched from the corners of the cabin while Locke and Jean packed away soup, chicken, bread, cake, and sparkling apple wine. Just after opening the second bottle, however, Locke signalled Jean that he was about to have a clumsy moment.

Timing himself to the sway of the ship, Locke swept the new bottle off the table. It landed awkwardly and broke open, spilling cold frothing wine across his bare feet. Realizing that the bottle hadn't shattered into the selection of knife-like shards he'd hoped for, he managed to drop his wineglass as well, with more satisfactory results.

'Ah, shit, that was good stuff,' he said loudly, slipping off his chair and crouching above the mess. He waved his hands over it, as though unsure of what to do, and in an instant a long, sturdy piece of glass was shifted from his palm to his tunic-sleeve. It was delicate work; a red stain beneath the cloth would surely draw attention.

'Don't,' said one of the sailors, waving for one of his companions to go on deck. 'Don't touch anything. We'll get it for you.'

Locke put his hands up and took several careful steps back.

'I'd call for more wine,' said Jean, hoisting his own glass teasingly, 'but it's possible you've had enough.'

'That was the motion of the ship,' said Locke.

The missing guard returned with a brush and a metal pan. He quickly swept up all the fragments.

'We'll scrub the deck when we give the cabin a turn tomorrow, sir,' said one of the sailors.

'At least it smells nice,' said Locke.

The guards didn't search him. Locke admired the deepening darkness through the cabin window and allowed himself the luxury of a faint smirk.

When the remains of dinner were cleared (every knife and fork and spoon accounted for) and the cabin was his and Jean's again, Locke carefully drew out the shard of glass and set it on the table.

'Doesn't look like much,' said Jean.

'It needs some binding,' said Locke. 'And I know just where to get it.'

While Jean leaned against the cabin door, Locke used the glass shard to carefully worry the inside front cover of the copy of *The Republic of Thieves*. After a few minutes of slicing and peeling, he produced an irregular patch of the binding leather and a quantity of the cord that had gone into the spine of the volume. He nestled the glass fragment inside the leather and wrapped it tightly around the edges, creating something like a tiny handsaw. The leather-bound side could be safely nestled against the palm of a hand, and the cutting edge of the shard could be worked against whatever needed slicing.

'Now,' said Locke softly, holding his handiwork up to the lantern-light and examining it with a mixture of pride and trepidation, 'shall we take a turn on deck and enjoy the weather?'

The weather had worsened agreeably to a hard-driving autumn rain. The Amathel was whipped up to waves of six or seven feet, and lightning flashed behind the ever-moving clouds.

Locke and Jean, both wearing oilcloaks, settled down against the inner side of the jolly boat lashed upside-down to the main deck. It was about fifteen feet long, of the sort usually hung at a ship's stern. Locke supposed that the urgent need to put the iron bars around the windows of the great cabin had forced the crew to shift the boat. It was secured to the deck via lines and ring-bolts; nothing that a crew of sailors couldn't deal with in just a few minutes, but if he and Jean tried to free the boat conventionally it would take far too long to escape notice. Cutting was the answer – weaken the critical lines, wait for a fortuitous roll of the ship, heave the jolly boat loose, and then somehow join it after it pitched over the side.

Jean sat placidly while Locke worked with the all-important glass shard – five minutes, ten minutes, twenty minutes. Locke's oilcloak was a blessing, making it possible to conceal the activity, but the need to hold the arm and shoulder still put all the burden on wrist and forearm. Locke worked until he ached, then carefully passed the shard to Jean.

'You two seem strangely heedless of the weather,' shouted Volantyne, moving past with a lantern. He studied them, his eyes flicking here and there for anything out of place. Eventually he relaxed, and Locke's heart resumed its usual duties.

'We're still warm from dinner, Captain,' said Jean. 'And we've lived through storms on the Sea of Brass. This is a fine diversion from the monotony of our cabin.'

340

'Monotony, perhaps, but also security. You may remain for now, so long as you continue to stay out of the way. We'll have business with the sails soon enough. If we find ourselves much closer to shore, I shall require you to go below.'

'Having problems?' said Locke.

'Damned nuisance of a wind from the north and the northwest – seems to veer however's least convenient. We're five miles off the beach where we should be ten.'

'We are your most loyal and devoted articles of ballast, Captain,' said Locke. 'Let us digest a bit longer and maybe we'll scuttle back inside.'

As soon as Volantyne stepped away, Locke felt Jean get back to work.

'We don't have much time,' muttered Jean. 'And one or two uncut lines are as good as twenty; some things don't break for any man's strength.'

'I've done some real damage to my side,' said Locke. 'All we can do is keep it up as long as possible.'

The minutes passed; sailors came and went on deck, checking for faults everywhere but directly behind the two men working desperately to cause one. The ship rolled steadily from side to side, lightning flared on every horizon, and Locke found himself growing more and more tense as the minutes passed. If this failed, he had no doubt that Volantyne's threat to seal them up in one of the holds would be carried out immediately.

'Oh, hells,' muttered Jean. 'Feel that?'

'Feel what? Oh, damn.' The ship had tilted to starboard, and the weight of the jolly boat was pressing more firmly against Locke's back and shoulders. The lines holding it down were starting to give way sooner than he'd expected. 'What the hell do we do now?'

'Hold on,' muttered Jean. The ship tilted to larboard, and there was the faintest scraping noise against the deck. Locke prayed that the tumult of the weather would drown it out for anyone not sitting directly against the boat.

Like a pendulum, the ship swung to starboard again, and this time the scraping noise rose to a screech. The press against Locke's back became ominous, and something snapped loudly just behind him.

'Shit,' whispered Jean, 'up and over!'

The two Gentlemen Bastards turned and scrambled over the back of the jolly boat at the moment its restraints completely gave way. Locke and Jean rolled off the boat with an embarrassing want of smoothness, landed hard, and the jolly boat took off across the deck, screeching and sliding toward the starboard rail.

'Ha-ha!' Locke yelled, unable to contain himself. 'We're off!'

The jolly boat slammed against the starboard rail and came to a dead stop.

'Balls,' said Locke, not quite as loudly. An instant later, the ship heeled to larboard, and Locke realized that he and Jean were directly in the only path the jolly boat could take when it slid back down the tilting deck. He gave Jean a hard shove to the left, and rolled clear the other way. A moment later the boat scraped and scudded across the deck between them, gathering momentum as it went. Locke turned, certain that it should go over the side this time—

With a creaking thump, the boat landed hard against the larboard rail. Although the rail bent, it didn't give way completely, and the upside-down boat remained very much out of the water.

'Perelandro's dangling cock!' Locke yelled, lurching to his feet.

'*What the hells do you two think you're doing?*' Solus Volantyne came leaping adroitly across the main deck, lantern still in hand.

'Your boat's come free! Help us!' yelled Jean. A moment later he seemed to think better of subterfuge, walloped Volantyne across the jaw with a right hook, and grabbed the lantern as the captain went down.

'Jean! Behind you!' Locke yelled, dodging the boat for a second time as the deck tilted yet again.

A crewman had come up behind Jean with a belaying pin in hand. Jean sidestepped the man's first attack and cracked the lantern across the top of his head. Glass shattered, and glowing white alchemical slime sprayed across the poor fellow from forehead to waist. It was generally harmless stuff, but nothing you wanted in your eyes. Moaning and glowing like a ghost out of some fairy story, the man fell against the foremast.

In front of Locke, the jolly boat slid to starboard, hit the rail at speed, crashed through with a terrible splintering noise, and went over the side.

'Thank the gods,' Locke muttered as he ran to the gap in the rail just in time to see the boat plunge bow-first into the water, like an arrowhead, and get immediately swallowed beneath a crashing wave. 'Oh, *COME ON!*'

'Jump,' hollered Jean, ducking a swing from a crewman who came at him with an oar. Jean slammed two punches into the unfortunate sailor's ribs, and the man did a convincing imitation of a marionette with its strings cut. 'Get the hell in the water!'

'The boat sank!' Locke cried, scanning the darkness in vain for a glimpse of it. Whistles were sounding from the quarterdeck and from within the ship. The whole crew would be roused against them presently. 'I don't see it!'

'Can't hear you. Jump!' Jean dashed across the deck and gave Locke a well-meaning shove through the gap in the railing. There was no time to do anything but gasp in a surprised breath; Locke's oilcloth fluttered around him as he fell like a wounded bat into the dark water of the Amathel.

The cold hit like a shock. He whirled within the churning blackness, fighting against his cloak and the weight of his ankle manacles. They weren't dragging him straight down, but they would sharply increase the rate at which he would exhaust himself by kicking to keep his head up.

His face broke the surface; he choked in a breath of air and freshwater spray. The *Volantyne's Resolve* loomed over him like a monstrous shadow, lit by the shuddering light of a dozen jumping, bobbing lanterns. A familiar dark shape detached itself from some sort of fight against the near rail, and fell toward the water.

'Jean,' Locke sputtered, 'there's no—'

The lost boat resurfaced like a broaching shark, spat up in a gushing white torrent. Jean landed on it facefirst with a ghastly thump and splashed heavily into the water beside it.

'Jean,' Locke screamed, grabbing hold of one of the jolly boat's gunwales and desperately scanning the water for any sign of his friend. The bigger man had already sunk beneath the surface. A wave crashed over Locke's head and tore at his hold on the boat. He spat water and searched desperately … there! A dim shape drifted six or seven feet beneath Locke's toes, lit from below by an eerie blue-white light. Locke dove just as another breaking wave hammered the boat.

Locke grabbed Jean by the collar and felt cold dismay at the feeble response. For a moment it seemed that the two of them hung suspended in a grey netherworld between lurching wave tops and ghostly light, and Locke suddenly realized the source of the illumination around them. Not lightning or lanterns, but the unknown fires that burned at the very bottom of the Amathel.

Glimpsed underwater, they lost their comforting jewel-like character, and seemed to roil and pulse and blur. They stung Locke's eyes, and his skin crawled with the unreasonable, instinctive sensation that something utterly hostile was nearby – nearby and drawing closer. He hooked his hands under Jean's arms and kicked mightily, heaving the two of them back toward the surface and the storm.

He scraped his cheek against the jolly boat as he came up, sucked in a deep breath, and heaved at Jean again to get the larger man's head above water. The cold was like a physical pressure, numbing Locke's fingers and slowly turning his limbs to lead.

'Come back to me, Jean,' Locke spat. 'I know your brains are jarred, but Crooked Warden, come back!' He yanked at Jean, holding on to the gunwale of the wave-tossed boat with his other hand, and for all his pains succeeded only in nearly capsizing it again. 'Shit!'

Locke needed to get in first, but if he let Jean go Jean would probably sink again. He spotted the rowing lock, the u-shaped piece of cast iron set into the gunwale to hold an oar. It had been smashed by the boat's slides across the deck, but it might serve a new purpose. Locke seized Jean's oilcloak and twisted one end into a crude knot around the bent rowing lock, so that Jean hung from the boat by his neck and chest. Not a sensible way to leave him, but it would keep him from drifting away while Locke got aboard.

A fresh wave knocked the side of the boat against Locke's head. Black spots danced before his eyes, but the pain goaded him to furious action. He plunged into the blackness beneath the boat, then clawed his way up to the gunwale on the opposite side. Another wave struck, and out of its froth Locke scrabbled and strained until he was over the edge. He bounced painfully off a rowing bench and flopped into the ankle-deep water sloshing around the bottom.

Locke reached over the side and grabbed Jean. His heaving was desperate, unbalanced, and useless. The little boat bobbled and shook with every effort, rising and falling on the waves like a piston in some nightmarish machine. At last Locke's wits punched through the walls of his exhaustion and panic. He turned Jean sideways and hauled him in a foot and an arm at a time, using his oilcloak for added leverage. Once he was safely in, the bigger man coughed and mumbled and flopped around.

'Oh, I hate the Eldren, Jean,' Locke gasped as they lay in the bottom of the tossing boat, lashed by waves and rain. 'I hate 'em. I hate whatever they did, I hate the shit they left behind, I hate the way none of their mysteries ever turn out to be pleasant and fucking good-neighbourly!'

'Pretty lights,' muttered Jean.

'Yeah, pretty lights,' Locke spat. 'Friendly sailors, the Amathel has it all.'

Locke nudged Jean aside and sat up. They were bobbing around like a wine cork in a cauldron set to boil, but now that their weight was in the centre of the little boat, it seemed better able to bear the tossing. They had drifted astern and inshore of the *Volantyne's Resolve*, which was now more than fifty yards away. Confused shouts could be heard, but the ship didn't seem to be putting about to come after them. Locke could only hope that Jean's cold-cocking of Volantyne would prevent the rest of the crew from getting things together until it was too late.

'Holy hells,' said Jean, 'how'd I geddhere?'

'Never mind that. You see any oars?'

'Uh, I thing I bead the crap out of the guy that had them.' Jean reached up and gingerly prodded his face. 'Aw, gods, I thing I broge my node again!'

'You used it to break your fall when you hit the boat.'

'Is thad whad hid me?'

'Yeah, scared me shitless.'

'You saved me!'

'It's my turn every couple of years,' said Locke with a thin smile.

'Thang you.'

'All I did was save my own ass four or five times down the line,' said Locke. 'And cut you in on a hell of a landing. If the waves keep taking us south, we should hit the beach in just a few miles, but without any oars to keep ourselves under control, it might be a hard way to leave the water.'

The waves did their part, bearing their little boat south at a frightful clip, and when the beach finally came into sight their arrival went as hard as Locke had guessed. The Amathel flung them against the black volcanic sand like some monster vomiting up a plaything that had outlasted its interest.

5

The coastal road west of Lashain was called the Darksands Stretch, and it was a lonely place to be travelling this windy autumn

345

morning. A single coach, pulled by a team of eight horses, trundled along the centuries-old stones raising spurts of wet gravel in its wake rather than the clouds of dust more common in drier seasons.

The secure coach service from Salon Corbeau and points farther south was for rich travellers unable to bear the thought of setting foot aboard a ship. With iron-bound doors, shuttered windows, and interior locks, the carriage was a little fortress for passengers afraid of highwaymen.

The driver wore an armoured doublet, as did the guard that sat beside him atop the carriage, cradling a crossbow that looked as though it could put a hole the size of a temple window into whatever it was loosed at.

'Hey there!' cried a thin man beside the road. He wore an oilcloak flung back from his shoulders, and there was a larger man on the ground beside him. 'Help us, please!'

Ordinarily, the driver would have whipped his team forward and raced past anyone attempting to stop them, but everything seemed wrong for an ambush. The ground here was flat for hundreds of yards around, and if these men were decoys, they couldn't have any allies within half a mile. And their aspect seemed genuinely bedraggled: no armour, no weapons, none of the cocksure bravado of the true marauder. The driver pulled on the reins.

'What do you think you're doing?' said the crossbowman.

'Don't get your cock tied in a knot,' said the driver. 'You're here to watch my back, aren't you? Stranger! What goes?'

'Shipwreck,' cried the thin man. He was scruffy-looking, of middle height, with light brown hair pulled loosely back at the neck. 'Last night. We got washed ashore.'

'What ship?'

'*Volantyne's Resolve*, out of Karthain.'

'Is your friend hurt?'

'He's out cold. Are you bound for Lashain?'

'Aye, twenty-six miles by road. Be there tomorrow. What would you have of us?'

'Carry us, on horses or on your tailboard. Our master's syndicate has a shipping agent in Lashain. He can pay for your trouble.'

'Driver,' came a sharp, reedy voice from within the carriage, 'it's not my business to supply rescue to those witless enough to meet disaster

346

on the Amathel, of all places. Pray for their good health if you must, but move on.'

'Sir,' said the driver, 'the fellow on the ground looks in a bad way. His nose is as purple as grapes.'

'That's not my concern.'

'There are certain rules,' said the driver, 'to how we behave out here, sir, and I'm sorry to have to refuse your command, but we'll be on our way again soon.'

'I won't pay to feed them! And I won't pay for the time we're losing by sitting here!'

'Sorry again, sir. It's got to be done.'

'You're right,' said the crossbowman with a sigh. 'These fellows ain't no highwaymen.'

The driver and the guard climbed down from their seat and walked over to where Locke stood over Jean.

'If you could just help me haul him to his feet,' said Locke to the crossbowman, 'we can try and bring him around.'

'Beg pardon, stranger,' said the crossbowman, 'it's plain foolishness to set a loaded piece down. Takes nothing to set one off by accident. One nudge from a false step—'

'Well, just point it away from us,' muttered the driver.

'Are you drunk? This one time in Tamalek I saw a fellow set a crossbow down for just a—'

'I'm sure you're right,' said the driver testily. 'Never, ever set that weapon down for as long as you live. You might accidentally hit some fellow in Tamalek.'

The guard sputtered, sighed, and carefully pointed the weapon at a patch of roadside sand. There was a loud, flat *crack*, and the quarrel was safely embedded in the ground up to its feathers.

Thus, it was accomplished. Jean miraculously returned to life, and with a few quick swings of his fists he eloquently convinced the two guards to lie down and be unconscious for a while.

'I am really, *really* sorry about this,' said Locke. 'And you should know, that's not how it normally goes with us.'

'Well, how now, tenderhearts?' shouted the man within the carriage. 'Shows what you know, eh? If you had any gods-damned brains you'd be inside one of these things, not driving it!'

'They can't hear you,' said Locke.

'Marauders! Sons of filth! Motherless bastards!' The man inside the box cackled. 'It's all one to me, though. You can't break in here. Steal whatever you like from my gutless hirelings, *sirrahs*, but you'll not have anything of mine!'

'Gods above,' said Locke. 'Listen up, you heartless fucking weasel. Your fortress has wheels on it. About a mile to the east there are cliffs above the Amathel. We'll unhitch you there and give your box a good shove over the edge.'

'I don't believe you!'

'Then you'd better practise flying.' Locke hopped up into the driver's seat and took the reins. 'Come on, let's take shit-sauce here for the shortest trip of his life.'

Jean climbed up beside Locke. Locke urged the well-trained horses forward, and the coach began to roll.

'Now wait a minute,' their suddenly unwilling passenger bellowed. 'Stop, stop, stop!'

Locke let him scream for about a hundred yards before he slowed the team back down.

'If you want to live,' said Locke, 'go ahead and open the—'

The door banged open. The man who came out was about sixty, short and oval-bellied, with the eyes of a startled rabbit. His hat and dressing gown were crimson silk studded with gold buttons. Locke jumped down and glowered at him.

'Take that ludicrous thing off,' he growled.

The man quickly stripped to his undertunic. Locke gathered his finery, which reeked of sweat, and threw it into the carriage.

'Where's the food and water?'

The man pointed to a storage compartment built into the outside rear of the carriage, just above the tailboard. Locke opened it, selected a few things for himself, then threw some of the neatly wrapped ration packages onto the dirt beside the road.

'Go wake your friends up and enjoy the walk,' said Locke as he climbed back up beside Jean. 'Shouldn't be more than a day or so until you reach the outer hamlets of Lashain. Or maybe someone will come along and take pity on you.'

'You bastards,' shouted the de-robed, de-carriaged man. 'Thieving bastards! You'll hang for this! I'll see it done!'

'That's a remote possibility,' said Locke. 'But you know what's a certainty? Next fire I need to start, I'm using your clothes to do it, asshole.'

He gave a cheery wave, and then the armoured coach service was gathering speed along the road, bound not for Lashain but Karthain, the long way around the Amathel.

Aurin And Amadine

I

'Why in all the hells do you take this abuse?' said Jean as he and Jenora sat together over coffee the second morning after the arrival of the Gentlemen Bastards in Espara. 'Dealing with Moncraine, the debts, the bullshit—'

'Those of us left are the stakeholders,' said Jenora. 'We own shares in the common property, and shares of the profits, when those miraculously appear. Some of us saved for years to make these investments. If we walk away from Moncraine, we forfeit everything.'

'Ah.'

'Look at Alondo. He had a wild night at cards and he used the take to buy his claim in the troupe. That was three years ago. We were doing *Ten Honest Turncoats* then, and *A Thousand Swords for Therim Pel* and *The All-Murderers Ball*. A dozen full productions a year, masques for Countess Antonia, festival plays, and we were touring out west, where the countryside's not the gods-damned waste it is between here and Camorr. I mean, we had *prospects*; we weren't out of our minds.'

'I never said you were.'

'It's mostly hired players and the short-timers that evapourated on us. They don't have any anchors except a weekly wage, and they can make that with Basanti. Hell, they'll happily take less from him, because at least they're sure to play.'

'What happened?'

'I don't know,' she said, staring into her mug as though it might conceal new answers. 'I guess sometimes there's just a darkness in someone. You *hope* it'll go away.'

'Moncraine, you mean.'

'If you could have seen him back in those days, I think you'd understand. You know about the Forty Corpses?'

'Um ... if I say no, do I become the forty-first?'

'If I killed people, glass-eyes, Moncraine wouldn't have lived long enough to be arrested. The Forty Corpses is what we call the forty famous plays that survived the fall of the empire. The big ones by all the famous Throne Therins ... Lucarno, Viscora, that bunch.'

'Oh,' said Jean.

'They're called corpses because they haven't changed for four or five centuries. I mean, we love them, most of them, but they do *moulder* a bit. They get recited like temple ritual, dry and lifeless. Except, when Moncraine was on, when Moncraine was good, he made the corpses *jump out of their graves.* It was like he was a spark and the whole troupe would catch fire from it. And when you've seen that, when you've been a part of it ... I tell you, Jovanno, you'd put up with nearly anything if only you could have it again.'

'I am returned,' boomed a voice from the inn-yard door, 'from the exile to which my pride had sentenced me!'

'Oh, gods below, you people actually did it,' said Jenora, leaping out of her chair. A man entered the common room, a big dark Syresti in dirty clothing, and cried out when he saw her.

'Jenora, my dusky vision, I knew that I could—'

Whatever he'd known was lost as Jenora's open palm slammed into his cheek. Jean blinked; her arm had been a pale brown arc. He made a mental note that she was quick when angered.

'Jasmer,' she hollered, 'you stupid, stubborn, bottle-sucking, lard-witted *fuck!* You nearly ruined us! It wasn't your damn pride that put you in gaol, it was your fists!'

'Peace, Jenora,' muttered Moncraine. 'Ow. I was sort of quoting a play.'

'*Aiiiiiaahhhhhhhh!*' screamed Mistress Gloriano, rushing in from a side hall. 'I don't believe it! The Camorri got you out! And it's more than you deserve, you lousy wretch! You lousy Syresti drunkard!'

'All's well, Auntie, I've already hit him for both of us,' said Jenora.

'Oh, hell's hungry kittens,' muttered Sylvanus, wandering in behind Mistress Gloriano. His bloodshot eyes and sleep-swept hair gave him the look of a man who'd been caught in a windstorm. 'I see the guards at the Weeping Tower can be bribed after all.'

'Good morning to you too, Andrassus,' said Moncraine. 'It warms ⦁ the deep crevices of my heart to hear so many possible explanations for my release *except* the thought that I might be innocent.'

'You're as innocent as we convinced Boulidazi to pretend you are,' said Sabetha, entering from the street. She and Locke had left early that morning to hover around the Weeping Tower, ready to snatch Moncraine up as soon as he was released following his appearance in court.

'He did say some unexpected and handsome things,' said Moncraine.

'You going to call the meeting to order,' said Sabetha, 'or should I?'

'I can break the news, gir – Verena. Thank you kindly.' Moncraine cleared his throat. 'A moment of your time, gentlemen and ladies of the Moncraine Company. And you as well, Andrassus. And our, uh, benefactor and patient creditor, Mistress Gloriano. There are some … changes in the offing.'

'Sweet gods,' said Sylvanus, 'you coal-skinned, life-ruining bastard, are you actually suggesting that gainful employment is about to get its hands around our throats again?'

'Sylvanus, I love you as I love my own Syresti blood,' said Moncraine, 'but shut your dribbling booze-hole. And yes, Espara will have its production of the Moncraine Company's *The Republic of Thieves.*'

Sabetha coughed.

'I am compelled, however, to accept certain arrangements,' continued Moncraine. 'Lord Boulidazi's agreed to reconsider my, er, refusal of his patronage offer. Once Salvard has the papers ready, we're the Moncraine-Boulidazi Company.'

'A patron,' said Mistress Gloriano in disbelief. 'Does this mean we might get paid back for our—'

'Yes,' said Locke, strolling in from the inn-yard with several purses in his hands. 'And here's yours.'

'Gandolo's privates, boy!' She caught the jingling bag Locke threw at her. 'I simply don't believe it.'

'Your countinghouse will believe it for you,' said Locke. 'That's twelve royals to square you. Lord Boulidazi is buying out Master Moncraine's debts to relieve him of the suffering brought on by their contemplation.'

'To wind a cord about my legs so he can fly me like a kite,' said Moncraine through gritted teeth.

'To keep you from getting knifed in a gods-damned alley!' said Sabetha.

'Not that this isn't miraculous,' said Jenora, 'but those of us with shares in the company have precedence over any arrangement Boulidazi might have proposed. Noble or not, we have papers he can't just piss on.'

'I realize that,' said Locke. 'We're not here to pry your shares out from under you. Boulidazi is giving Moncraine the funds he needs as an advance against Moncraine's future share of the company's profits. Your interest is protected.'

'That's as may be,' said Jenora, 'but if this company is back on a paying basis, I want another set of eyes on the books. No offence, Jasmer, but strange things can happen to profits before they reach the stakeholders.'

'The one for figures is Jovanno,' said Locke. 'He's a genius with them.'

'Hey, thanks for volunteering me,' said Jean. 'I was wondering when I could stop doing interesting things and go bury myself in account ledgers.'

'I meant it as a compliment! Besides, given a choice, would you rather trust me, or the Asinos—'

'Dammit,' Jean growled. 'I'll see to the books.'

'Master Moncraine,' said Locke, 'this, by the way, is my cousin, Jovanno de Barra.'

'The third of the mysterious Camorri,' said Jasmer. 'And where are four and five?'

'The Asino brothers are still asleep,' said Jean. 'And when they wake I expect they'll be hungover. They crossed bottles with that *thing*.' He gestured at Sylvanus. 'It was all I could do to keep them alive.'

'Well then,' said Moncraine, 'let us yet be merciful. I'm for a bath and fresh clothes. Someone hunt down Alondo, and we'll have our proper meeting about the play after luncheon. How's that sound?'

'Moncraine!' The street door burst inward, propelled by a kick from an unpleasant-looking man. His expensive clothes were stained with wine, sauces, and ominous dark patches that had nothing to do with food. Half a dozen men and women followed him into the room, clearly assorted species of leg-breakers. The Right People of Espara were on the scene.

'Oh, good morning, Shepherd. Can I offer you some refresh—'

'Moncraine,' said the man called Shepherd, 'you sack of dried-up whores' cunt leather! Did you stop at a countinghouse after your escape from the Weeping Tower?'

'I haven't had time. But—'

'At some point, Moncraine, compound interest becomes less

interesting to my boss than shoving you up a dead horse's ass and sinking you in a fucking *swamp.*'

'Excuse me,' said Locke, meekly.

'Oh, I'm sorry, I didn't realize it was the Children's Festival this week,' said Shepherd. 'You looking for an ass-kicking or what?'

'Can I ask how much Master Moncraine owes your boss?'

'Eighteen royals, four fifths, thirty-six coppins, accurate to this very hour.'

'Thought so. There's nineteen in this bag,' said Locke, holding out a leather purse. 'From Moncraine, of course. He just likes to draw these things out, you know. For dramatic effect.'

'This a fucking joke?'

'Nineteen royals,' said Locke. 'No joke.'

Shepherd slipped the purse open, ran his fingers through the coins inside, and gave a startled grunt.

'Strange days are upon us.' He snapped the purse shut. 'Signs and wonders. Jasmer Moncraine has paid a debt. I'd say my fucking prayers tonight, I would.'

'Are we square?' said Moncraine.

'Square?' said Shepherd. 'Yeah, *this* matter's closed. But don't come crawling back for more, Moncraine. Not for a few months, at least. Let the boss forget what a degenerate ass-chancre you are.'

'Sure,' said Moncraine. 'Just as you say.'

'Of course, if you had any brains at all you'd never risk the chance of seeing me again.' Shepherd sketched a salute in the air, turned, and left along with his crew of thugs, most of whom looked disappointed.

'A word,' said Moncraine, leading Locke off to one side of the room. 'While I'm pleased as a baby on a breast to have that weight lifted, I begin to wonder if I'm meant to be nothing but a mute witness to my own affairs from now on.'

'If you'd had *your* way you'd be starting your real prison sentence today,' said Locke. 'You can't blame us for wanting to keep you out of further trouble.'

'I'm not pleased to be treated like I can't handle simple business. Give me the purses you have left, and I'll dispense with my own debts.'

'The tailor, the bootmaker, the scrivener, and the actors that left for Basanti's company? We can hunt them down ourselves, thank you.'

'They're not your accounts to close, boy!'

'And this isn't your money to hold,' said Locke.

'Jasmer,' said Sabetha, coming up behind them with Jean in tow, 'I'd hate to think that you were trying to corner and intimidate one of us privately.'

'We were merely discussing how I might take responsibility for my own shortcomings,' said Moncraine.

'You can hold to the deal,' said Sabetha. 'And remember who got you out of the Weeping Tower, and brought in our new patron. Your job is to give us a play. Where that's concerned, we're your subjects, but where your safety is concerned, you're *ours*.'

'Well,' said Moncraine, 'don't I feel enfolded in the bosom of love itself.'

'Just try not to screw anything else up,' said Sabetha. 'It won't be that hard a life.'

'I'll go have my bath, then,' said Moncraine. 'Would the three of you care to watch, to make sure I don't drown myself?'

'If you did that,' said Locke, 'you'd never have the satisfaction of bossing us around on stage.'

'True enough.' Moncraine scratched at his dark grey stubble. 'See you after luncheon, then. Oh, since these are matters relating to the play ... Lucaza, get a dozen chairs from the common room and set them out in the inn-yard. Verena, dig through the common property to find all the copies of *The Republic of Thieves* we have. Jenora can lend you a hand.'

'Of course,' said Sabetha.

'Good. Now, if I'm wanted for any further business, I'll be in my room with no clothes on.'

2

Just before noon the sun passed behind a thick bank of clouds, and its brain-poaching heat was cut to a more bearable lazy warmth. The mud of the inn-yard, late resting place of the very pickled Sylvanus Olivios Andrassus, had dried to a soft crust beneath the feet of the excited and bewildered Moncraine-Boulidazi Company.

All five Gentlemen Bastards had seats, though Calo and Galdo, with dark patches under their eyes, pointedly refused to sit together and so bookended Locke, Jean, and Sabetha.

Alondo flipped idly through a torn and stained copy of *The Republic of Thieves*. Each volume in the little stack of scripts found by Sabetha was a different size, and no two had been copied in the same hand. Some were marked MONCRAINE COMPANY or SCRIBED FOR J. MONCRAINE, while others were the ex-property of other troupes. One even bore the legend BASANTI on its back cover.

Sylvanus, sober, or at least not actively imbibing, sat next to Jenora. Alondo's cousin stood against a wall, arms folded.

This, then, was the complete roster of the company. Locke sighed.

'Hello again.' Moncraine appeared, looking almost respectable in a quilted grey doublet and black breeches. 'Now, let us discover together which of history's mighty entities are sitting with us, and which ones we shall have to beg, borrow, or steal. *You!*'

'Me, sir?' said Alondo's cousin.

'Yes. Who in all the hells are you? Are you a Camorri?'

'Oh, gods above, no, sir. I'm Alondo's cousin.'

'Got a name?'

'Djunkhar Kurlin. Everyone calls me Donker.'

'Bad fucking luck. You an actor?'

'No, sir, a hostler.'

'What do you mean by spying on my company's meeting like this?'

'I just want to get killed onstage, sir.'

'Fuck the stage. Come here and I'll grant your wish right now.'

'He means,' said Jean, 'that we promised him a bit part in exchange for helping us sell off some surplus horseflesh.'

'Oh,' said Moncraine. 'An *enthusiast*. I'd be very pleased to help you die on stage. Stay on my good side and it can even be pretend.'

'Uh, thank you, sir.'

'Now,' said Moncraine. 'We need ourselves an *Aurin*. Aurin is a young man of Therim Pel, basically good-hearted, unsure of himself. He's *also* the only son and heir to the emperor. Looks like we've got a surplus of young men, so you can all fight it out over the next few days. And we'll need an Amadine—'

'Hey,' said Calo. 'Sorry to interrupt. I was just wondering, before we all get measured for codpieces or whatever, where the hell are we supposed to be giving this play? I hear this Basanti has a theatre of his own. What do we have?'

'You're one of the Asino brothers, right?' said Moncraine.

'Giacomo Asino.'

'Well, being from Camorr, Giacomo, you probably don't know about the Old Pearl. It's a public theatre, built by some count—'

'Poldaris the Just,' muttered Sylvanus.

'Built by Poldaris the Just,' said Moncraine, 'as his perpetual legacy to the people of Espara. Big stone amphitheatre, about two hundred years old.'

'One hundred and eighty-eight,' said Sylvanus.

'Apologies, Sylvanus, unlike you I wasn't there. So you see, Giacomo, we can use it, as long as we pay a little fee to the countess' envoy of ceremonies.'

'If it's such a fine place, why did Basanti build his own?'

'The Old Pearl is perfectly adequate,' said Moncraine. 'Basanti built to flatter his self-regard, not fatten his pocketbook.'

'Because businessmen like to spend lots of money to replace perfectly adequate structures they can use for nearly nothing, right?'

'Look, boy,' said Moncraine, 'it wouldn't matter if Basanti's new theatre turned dog turds into platinum, while merely setting foot inside the Old Pearl gave people leprosy. The Old Pearl's it. There's no time or money for anything else.'

'Does it?' said Calo. 'Give people leprosy, I mean?'

'Go lick the stage and find out. Now, let's talk about Amadine. Amadine is a thief in a time of peace and abundance. Therim Pel has grown a crop of bandits in the ancient catacombs beneath the city. They mock the customs of the upright people, of the emperor and his nobles. Some of them even call their little world a republic. Amadine is their leader.'

'You should be our Amadine, Jasmer,' said Sylvanus. 'Think of the pretty skirts Jenora could sew for you!'

'Verena's our Amadine,' said Moncraine. 'There's a certain deficiency of breasts in the company, and while yours may be larger than hers, Sylvanus, I doubt as many people would pay to see them. No, since our former Amadine abandoned us ... she'll do.'

Sabetha gave a slight, satisfied nod.

'Now, everyone take a copy of the lines. Have them out for consultation. A troupe learns a play like we all learn to screw, stumbling and jostling until everything's finally in the right place.'

Locke felt his cheeks warm a bit, though the sun was still hidden away behind the high wall of summer clouds.

'So, Aurin falls for Amadine, and they have lots of problems, and it's all very *romantic* and *tragic* and the audience gives us ever so much money to see it,' said Moncraine. 'But to get there we've got to sharpen

357

things to a fine point … slash some dead weight from the text. I'll give you full cuts later, but for now I think we can discard all the bits with Marolus the courtier. And we'll cut Avunculo and Twitch, the comic relief thieves, for a certainty.'

'Aye, a certainty,' said Sylvanus, 'and what a bold decision that is, given that our Marolus, Avunculo and Twitch all ran across town chasing Basanti's coin when you took up lèse-majesté as a new hobby.'

'Thank you, Andrassus,' said Moncraine. 'You'll have many weeks to belittle my every choice; don't spend yourself in one afternoon. Now you, Asino—'

'Castellano,' said Galdo, yawning.

'Castellano. Stand up. Wait, you can read, can't you? You can all *read*, I assume?'

'Reading, is that where you draw pictures with chalk or where you bang a stick on a drum?' said Galdo. 'I get confused.'

'The first thing that happens,' said Moncraine with a scowl, 'the first character the audience meets, is the Chorus. Out comes the Chorus – give us his lines, Castellano.'

'Um,' said Galdo, staring down at his little book.

'What the fuck's the *matter* with you, boy?' shouted Moncraine. 'Who says "um" when they've got the script in their hands? If you say "um" in front of five hundred people, I guarantee that some unwashed, wine-sucking cow down in the penny pit will throw something at you. They wait on any excuse.'

'Sorry,' said Galdo. He cleared his throat, and read:

'You see us wrong, who see with your eyes,
And hear nothing true, though straining your ears.
What thieves of wonder are these poor senses, whispering:
This stage is wood, these men are dust—
And dust their deeds, these centuries gone.'

'No,' said Jasmer.

'What do you mean, "no"?'

'You're reciting, not orating. The Chorus is a character. The Chorus, in his own mind, is flesh and blood. He's not reading lines out of a little book. He's on a mission.'

'If you say so,' said Galdo.

'Sit down,' said Moncraine. 'Other Asino, stand up. Can you do better than your brother?'

'Just ask the girls he's been with,' said Calo.

'Give us a Chorus.'

Calo stood up, straightened his back, puffed out his chest, and began to read loudly, clearly, emphasizing words that Galdo had read flatly:

'You see us *wrong*, who see with your eyes,
And hear *nothing true*, though straining your ears.
What *thieves* of *wonder* are these poor senses, whispering—'

'Enough,' said Jasmer. 'Better. You're giving it rhythm, stressing the right words, orating with some little competence. But you're still just reciting the words as though they were ritual in a book.'

'They are just words in a book,' said Calo.

'They are a man's words!' said Moncraine. 'They are a *man's* words. Not some dull formula. Put *flesh and blood* behind them, else why should anyone pay to see on stage what they could read quietly for themselves?'

'Because they can't fuckin' read?' said Galdo.

'Stand up again, Castellano. No, no, Giacomo, don't sit down. I want you both for this. I'll show you my point so that even Camorri dullards can take it to heart. Castellano, go over to your brother. Keep your script in hand. You are *angry* with your brother, Castellano! Angry at what a dunce he is. He doesn't understand these lines. So now you will show him!' Moncraine steadily raised his voice. 'Correct him! Perform them to him as though he is an IDIOT!'

'You see us *wrong*, who see with your *eyes*!' said Galdo. He gestured disdainfully at his own face with his free hand, and took two threatening steps closer to Calo. 'And hear us not at all, though straining your *ears!*'

He reached out and snapped a finger against one of Calo's ears. The long-haired twin recoiled, and Galdo moved aggressively toward him once again.

'What *thieves* of *wonder* are these poor senses,' said Galdo, all but hissing with disdain, '*whispering*: this stage is wood, these men are dust, and dust their deeds and thousand … dust their ducks … aw, shit, lost myself, sorry.'

'It's all right,' said Moncraine. 'You had something there, didn't you?'

'That was fun,' said Galdo. 'I think I see what you mean.'

359

'Words are dead until you give them a *context*,' said Moncraine. 'Until you put a character behind them, and give him a reason to speak them in a certain fashion.'

'Can I do it back to him like he's the stupid one?' said Calo.

'No. I've made my point,' said Moncraine. 'You Camorri do have a certain poise and inventiveness. I just need to awaken you to its proper employment. Now, what's our Chorus doing here?'

'He's pleading,' said Jean.

'*Pleading.* Yes. Exactly. First thing, out comes the Chorus to plead to the crowd. The hot, sweaty, drunk, and sceptical crowd. *Listen up*, you unworthy fucking mongrels! Look, there's a *play* going on, right in front of you! Shut up and give it the attention it deserves!'

Moncraine changed his voice and poise in an instant. Without so much as a glance at the script, he spoke:

'What *thieves* of *wonder* are these poor senses, whispering:
This stage is wood, these men are dust—
And dust their deeds, these centuries gone.
For us it is not so.
See *now*, and conjure with present vigour,
A *happy* empire! Her foes sleep in ruins of cold ambitions,
And take for law the merest whim of all-conquering *Salerius*
Second of that name, and most *imperial* to bear it!
His youth spent in dreary march and stern discipline
Wherein he met the proudest neighbours of his empire—
With trampled fields for his court, red swords for ambassadors,
And granted, to each in turn, his attention most humbling.
Now all who would not bow are hewn at the feet
to better help them kneel.'

Moncraine cleared his throat. 'There. I have had my plea. I have taken command, shut those slack jaws, turned those gimlet eyes to the stage. I am midwife to wonders. With their attention snared, I give them history. We are back in the time of the Therin Throne, of Salerius II. An emperor who went out and kicked some ass. Just as we shall, perhaps excepting Sylvanus.'

Sylvanus rose and tossed his copy of the script aside. Jenora managed to catch it before it hit the ground.

'Chorus, you call yourself,' he said. 'You've the presence of a mouse fart in a high wind. Stand aside, and try not to catch fire if I shed sparks of genius.'

If Locke had been impressed by the change in Moncraine's demeanour, he was astounded by the change in Sylvanus. The old man's perpetually sour, unfocused, liquor-addled disposition vanished, and without warning he was speaking clearly, invitingly, charmingly:

> 'From war long waged comes peace well lived,
> And now, twenty years of blessed interval has set
> A final laurel, light upon the brow of bold, deserving Salerius!
> Yet heavy sits this peace upon his only son and heir.
> Where once the lion roared, now dies the faintest echo of warlike
>   times,
> All eyes turn upon the cub, and all men wait
> to behold the wrath and majesty
> that must spring from such mighty paternity!
> Alas, the father, in sparing not the foes of his youth
> Has left the son no foe for his inheritance.
> Citizens, friends, dutiful and imperial—
> Now give us precious indulgence,
> see past this fragile artifice!
> Let willing hearts rule dullard eyes and ears,
> And of this stage you shall make the empire;
> From the dust of an undone age hear living words,
> on the breath of living men!
> Defy the limitations of our poor pretending,
> And with us, jointly, devise and receive
> the tale of Aurin, son and inheritor of old Salerius.
> And if it be true that sorrow is wisdom's seed
> Learn now why never a wiser man was emperor made.'

'Well remembered, I'll give you that,' said Moncraine. 'But then, anything more than three lines is well remembered, where you're concerned.'

'It's as fresh now as the last time we did it,' said Sylvanus. 'Fifteen years ago.'

'That's you and I that would make a fair Chorus,' sighed Moncraine. 'But we need a Salerius, and we need a magician to advise him and do all the threatening parts, or else the plot goes pear-shaped.'

'I'll be the Chorus!' said Galdo. 'I can do this. Wake everyone up at the beginning, then sit back and watch the rest of you in the play. That sounds like a damn good job.'

'The hell you'll do it,' said Calo. 'You and that shaved head, you look like a vulture's cock. This job calls for some elegance.'

'You see us wrong,' said Galdo, 'who are about to get your *fuckin' ass kicked*!'

'Shut up, idiots.' Moncraine glowered at the twins until they settled down. 'It would be to our advantage to leave Sylvanus and myself free for other parts, so yes, one of you may have the Chorus. But you won't scrap for it in the dirt; you'll both learn the part and strive to better one another in it. I don't have to make a final decision for some time.'

'And what does the loser get?' said Calo.

'The loser will understudy the winner, in case the winner should be carried off by wild hounds. And don't worry; there'll be other parts to fill.

'Now,' said Moncraine. 'Let's break ourselves up and put Alondo and our other Camorri through some paces, to see where their alleged strengths lie.'

3

The sun moved its way and the clouds moved theirs. Before another hour passed the inn-yard was once again in the full light and heat of day. Moncraine donned a broad-brimmed hat, but otherwise seemed heedless of the temperature. Sylvanus and Jenora clung to the inn walls, while Sabetha and the boys darted in and out of cover as they were required to play scenes.

'Our young prince Aurin lives in his father's shadow,' said Moncraine.

'He's probably glad to be out of the gods-damned sun, then!' panted Galdo.

'There's no glory to be had because Salerius II already went out and had it,' continued Moncraine. 'No wars to fight, no lands to claim, and it's still an emperor or two to go before the Vadrans are going to start kicking things over up north. As if that wasn't bad enough, Aurin has a best friend named Ferrin. Ferrin's even hungrier for glory than Aurin is, and he won't shut up about it. Let's do … Act one, scene two. Alondo, you do Aurin, and let's have Jovanno give us a Ferrin.'

Alondo leaned back lazily in a chair. Jean approached him, reading from his copy of the script:

> 'What's this, lazy lion cub?
> The sands of the morning are half run from the glass!
> There's nothing in your bed 'tis worth such fascination.
> The sun rules the sky, your father his kingdom,
> And you rule a chamber ten paces by ten!'

Alondo laughed, and answered:

> 'Why be an emperor's son, if I must rise
> as though to reap the fields?
> What profit, then, in my paternity?
> What man lives, who, more than I,
> has rightful claim to leisure?'

'He that has *given* you leisure,' said Jean. 'Having carved it like rare meat from the bones of his enemies.'

'Enough,' said Moncraine. 'Less *reciting*, Jovanno. Less *formula*.'

'Uh, sure,' said Jean, obviously feeling out of his depth. 'Whatever you say.'

'Alondo, take over Ferrin. Lucaza, let's have you see what you can make of Aurin.'

Locke had to admit to himself that Jean was the least comfortable of the five of them with what was going on. Although he was always eager to play a role in any crooked scheme that required it of him, he tended to stay within narrower bounds than Locke or Sabetha or even the Sanzas. Jean was a consummate 'straight man' – the angry body-guard, the dutiful clerk, the respectable servant. He was a solid wall for victims of their games to bounce off, but not the sort to jump back and forth rapidly between roles.

Locke set these thoughts aside, and tried to imagine himself as Aurin. He recalled his own lack of sweet humour each time he was yanked from sleep early, most frequently because of some Sanza mis-chief. The memory served him well, and he spoke:

> 'Would you instruct me in the love of my own father?
> You push presumption to its limits, Ferrin.

Had I wished to wake to scorn and remonstration,
I would have married by now.'

Alondo assumed a more energetic persona, more confident and forceful in speech:

'Fairly spoken, O prince, O majesty! I cry mercy.
I did not come to rudely trample dozy dreams,
Nor correct you in honouring our lord, your father.
Your perfect love for him is reckoned of a measure
With your devotion to warm, soft beds
And therefore lies beyond all question.'

'Were you *not* the great friend of my youth,' said Locke, deciding a laugh would be a good thing to add,

'But the unresting spirit of some foe
Slain in Father's wars,
You could scarce do me more vexation, Ferrin.
Thou art *like* a marriage,
Lacking only the pretty face and pleasant couplings—
You do so busy my mornings with rebukes
I half-forget which of us is royal.'

'Good,' said Moncraine. 'Good enough. Friendly banter, hiding something. Ferrin sees his ticket to glory lazing around, accomplishing nothing. These two need each other, and they resent it while trying to hide it behind their good cheer.'

'Moncraine, for the love of all the gods, there'll be no play to see and no parts to act if you explain everything at the first chance,' said Sylvanus.

'I don't mind,' said Alondo.

'Nor I,' said Locke. 'I think it's helping. Me, at least.'

'Moncraine would teach you to how to play every part as *Moncraine*,' chuckled Sylvanus. 'Don't forget that.'

'Not an actor that lives wouldn't make love to the sound of his own voice,' said Moncraine, 'if only he could. You're no exception, Andrassus. Now, let's find some swords. Ferrin talks Aurin into practising in the gardens, and that's where the plot winds them in its coils.'

Hours passed in sweat and toil. Back and forth in the sun they pretended to fight, with notched wooden blades musty from storage. Locke and Jean and Alondo rotated roles, and Moncraine even swapped in the Sanzas for variety, until it became a sort of whirling pantomime brawl. Stab, parry, recover, deliver lines. Parry, dodge, deliver lines, parry, deliver lines …

Sylvanus procured a bottle of wine and ended his personal drought. He shouted encouragement at the duellists all afternoon, but didn't move once from his chosen spot in the shade, near Sabetha and Jenora. As the sun drew down toward the west, Moncraine finally called a halt.

'There we are, boys, that's enough for a mild beginning.'

'Mild?' wheezed Alondo. He'd kept his composure for a respectable length of time, but wilted with the rest of them as the muttering and swordplay had drawn on.

'Aye, mild. You're out of condition, Alondo. You young pups have all the leaping about to do, and nearly all the speaking. If the audience sees you sucking air like a fish on the bottom of a boat—'

'They'll throw things, right,' said Alondo. 'I've been pelted with vegetables before.'

'Not in *my* company you haven't,' growled Moncraine. 'Right, all of you, sit down before you throw up.'

The admonition came too late for Calo, already wobbling from his hangover. He noisily lost whatever remained in his stomach in a far corner of the inn-yard.

'Music to my ears,' said Moncraine. 'See, Andrassus? So long as I can inspire that sort of reaction in our bold young lads, I believe I may claim not to have lost my touch.'

'What do you suppose for us, then?' said Sylvanus.

'The audience might notice, were the emperor of the Therin Throne such a fine rich lovely shade of brown as myself, that his son ought not be a plain pink Therin,' said Moncraine. 'And the part of the magician requires more moving about, so I'll take it. That leaves you to sit the throne.'

'I shall be imperial,' sighed Sylvanus.

'Good,' said Moncraine. 'Now, I need an ale before I'm baked like a pie.'

'Emperor, eh?' said Locke, sinking down against the wall next to Sylvanus. 'Why so glum? Sounds like a good part.'

'It is,' said Sylvanus, 'for the few lines he has. It's not the father's play, but the son's.' The old man took a swig from his bottle and made no effort to pass it around. 'I envy you little shits. I do, though no one could accuse you of any deep knowledge of the craft.'

'What's to envy?' said Alondo. 'We're out there melting in the heat while you get to sit in the shade.'

'Heh,' said Sylvanus. 'Spoken like a true lad of none and twenty years. At my age you don't *get* to sit in the shade, boy. That's where you're sent to keep out of everyone else's way.'

'You're being morose,' said Alondo. 'It's the grapes speaking, as usual.'

'This is the first bottle I've touched since my head hit the ground last night,' said Sylvanus. 'And for me, that's as sober as a babe freshly unwombed. No, gentlemen, I know a thing which you do not. Read any script in our common property and you'll find *too many* roles to which you're suited – soldiers, princes, lovers, fools. You could never play them all if you lived to twice my age, which is a frightful number.

'At twenty, you may be anything. At thirty you may do as you please. At forty, only a few doors ease shut, but fifty, ah! Here's a sting that Moncraine feels for sure. By fifty, you're becoming a perfect stranger to all those parts that once suited you like the skin of your own cock.'

Locke had no idea what to say, so he simply watched as Sylvanus finished his bottle and tossed it into the leather-hard mud of the yard.

'I used to skim these plays for all the fine young roles my ambition could bear,' he said. 'Now I look at the broken parts, the sick men, the forgotten men, and I wonder which of them will be mine. Did you not hear why I'm emperor? Because the emperor need not trouble his fat old ass to *move*. I am as much entombed as enthroned.'

Sylvanus heaved himself to his feet, joints creaking. 'I don't mean to oppress your spirits, boys. Come find me in an hour or two, and I shall be merry. Yes, I will have quite forgotten anything I've said here, I'm sure.'

After Sylvanus had gone inside, Locke rose, stretched, and followed. He had no notion of what, if anything, he should say. In one short afternoon he had grown used to the advantage of having all of his lines scribbled out for him on a piece of paper.

4

'Right,' said Jasmer, three hours into their fifth day of practise under the unfriendly sun. 'Jovanno, I'm sure you're a fine fellow, but you've got no business saying lines in front of people. I think I can beat your friends into something resembling actors, but you're as useless as gloves on a snake.'

'Uh,' said Jean, looking up from his script, 'what'd I do wrong?'

'If you had any wit for the work you'd already know,' said Jasmer. 'Go sit the fuck down and count our money or something.'

'Hang on,' said Locke, who'd been playing Aurin to Jean's Ferrin. 'You've got no business talking to Jovanno like that.'

'This is the business of the play,' said Moncraine, 'and in this realm I am all the gods on their heavenly thrones, speaking with one voice, telling him to shut up and go away.'

'Agreed, you can order him around,' said Locke. 'But mind your manners.'

'Boy, I do not have fucking time—'

'Yes you do,' said Locke. 'You *always* have the time to be polite to Jovanno, and when you don't, we will pack up and go back to Camorr! Do I make myself clear?'

'Hey,' said Jean, tugging at Locke's tunic, 'it's fine.'

'No it isn't,' said Sabetha, joining Locke and Jean in the centre of the courtyard. 'Lucaza's right, Jasmer. We'll slave for you as required, but we won't eat shit for no reason.'

'Send me back to gaol,' muttered Moncraine. 'Fuck me and send me back to gaol.'

'We shall accommodate neither request,' said Sabetha.

'I can use him,' said Jenora, appearing from the door to the inn. 'Jovanno, that is. If he's not going to be onstage he can help me manage the property and alchemy.'

'I, uh, guess I've got … no real choice?' said Jean.

'And speaking of the common property,' said Jenora, 'I've got to tell you now, the mice and red moths have been at it. All the death-masks and robes are too scrubby to use, and most of the other costumes are only fit for cutting up as pieces.'

'Well, then, do so,' said Jasmer. 'I'm busy out here turning dogshit into diamonds; it's only fair you should get to do the same in your line of work.'

'I need funds,' said Jenora, 'and we must have a sit-down, all the stakeholders, and decide where those funds are coming from, and how to address the shares of our friends that cut and ran—'

'Good gods,' said Moncraine.

'… and on what terms! And I need to hire someone who can handle a needle and thread.'

Jean raised his hand.

'You can sew?' said Jenora. 'What, mending torn tunics and so forth? I need—'

'I know hemming from pleating,' said Jean. 'And darning from shirring, and I've got the thimble-calluses to prove it.'

'I'll be damned.' Jenora grabbed Jean by the arm. 'You can't have this one back even if you decide you *do* need another actor.'

'I won't,' said Moncraine sourly.

'Are we taking a break?' said Calo, sitting down hard.

'Sure, sit on your ass, sweetheart. Those of us still in condition will play for your amusement,' said Galdo. He kicked dirt across his brother's breeches.

Calo didn't even waste time on a dirty look. He lashed out with his legs, hooked Galdo below the knees, and toppled him. Galdo rolled over on his back, clutching at his left wrist, and howled in pain.

'Oh, hell,' said Calo, jumping back to his feet. 'Is it bad? I didn't mean to, honest – GNNNAKKKH!'

This last extremely unpleasant sound was forced out of him by a kick from Galdo that terminated in Calo's groin.

'Nah, it feels fine,' said Galdo. 'Just having a bit of acting practise.'

Locke, Jean, Alondo, Jenora, and Sabetha descended on the twins, separating them before Moncraine could get involved in the melee. What followed was a pandemonium of finger-pointing and hard words in which the intelligence, birth city, artistic capacity, work habits, skin colour, dress sense, and personal honour of every participant were insulted at least once. Through it all the sun poured down relentless heat, and by the time relative order was restored Locke's head was swimming. He didn't notice that someone had come around the corner from the street until they cleared their throat loudly.

'How grand,' said the newcomer, a tall woman of about thirty. She wore a tight grey tunic and baggy trousers, and she was of mixed Therin and dark-skinned parentage, though she was lighter than Jasmer or the Gloriano women. Her black curls were cut just above her ears, and she had the sort of cool self-composure that Locke associated with Camorri *garristas*. 'Jasmer, I'm impressed, but not really in the way I expected to be.'

'Chantal,' said Moncraine, conjuring his dignity with the speed of a quick-draw artist. 'A fine afternoon to you as well, you opportunistic turncoat.'

'You were off to the Weeping Tower,' said the woman. 'I do like to eat more than once a month. I've got nothing to apologize for.'

'What's the matter, Basanti not handing out charity to any more of my strays?'

'Basanti's got work for the taking. But I heard some interesting things. Heard you'd found a patron.'

'Yes, it turns out that not all the good taste has been bred out of Espara's quality.'

'Also heard that those Camorri you promised weren't a lie after all.'

'They're all here,' said Moncraine. 'Count 'em.'

'And you're still serious about doing *The Republic of Thieves*?'

'Serious as a slit throat.'

'Is Jenora finally getting onstage?'

'Gods above, no!' said Jenora.

'Aha.' Chantal strolled toward Moncraine. 'By my count, you're short at least one woman, then.'

'What do you care if I am?'

'Look, Jasmer.' Chantal's cat-and-mouse smile vanished. 'Basanti's doing *The Wine of Womanly Reverence*, and I don't want to spend the summer giggling and flouncing as Fetching Maid Number Four. We're in a position to help one another.'

'Hmmm,' said Moncraine. 'Depends. Did you drag that husband of yours back over here as well?'

As though on cue, a brown-haired Therin man came around the corner behind Chantal. He wore an open white tunic, displaying a rugged physique decorated with dents and scars. Those and the fact that his right ear was half-missing led Locke to guess that he was either a veteran handball player or an ageing swordsman who'd seen the writing on the wall.

'Of course you did,' said Moncraine. 'Well, my new young friends, allow me to introduce you to Chantal Couza, formerly of the Moncraine Company, and her husband, Bertrand the Crowd.'

'The Crowd?' said Locke

'He hops costumes from scene to scene like nobody else,' said Alondo. 'He's half a dozen bit players in one.'

'Him I can use,' said Moncraine, 'but what makes you think I've forgiven either of you?'

'Cut the crap, Jasmer,' said Chantal. 'I want decent work. You want a happy audience.'

'Dare I ask if there will be any more reverse defections?'

'Not for a basket of rubies the size of your self-regard, Jasmer. They're more worried about being taken in as accomplices to assault and sedition than they are about losing their places in your troupe.'

'Well, I say take Bert and Chantal back,' said Alondo.

'Likewise,' said Jenora. 'We've got parts to fill, and we don't have time to be choosy. Shall I pry Sylvanus out of bed and see what he thinks?'

'No,' said Moncraine. 'He'd say yes just because he can't take his eyes off her. Fine! You're in luck, the pair of you, but it's on wages. No percentage. You know the papers. You lost that when you walked.'

'We might have to argue that,' said Chantal. 'Either way, it's worth it to avoid Fetching Maid Number Four. Believe me, I'd much rather be Amadine, Queen of the Shadows.'

'I'm ever so sorry,' said Sabetha. If the words THAT WAS A LIE had suddenly sprung up behind her in letters of fire ten feet high, the effect could scarcely have added to her tone of voice. 'That role is no longer available.'

'Are you kidding?' Chantal strode across the courtyard until she was looking down at Sabetha, who was a hand-span shorter than the older woman. 'Who are you, then?'

'Amadine,' said Sabetha coolly. 'Queen of the Shadows.'

'Bloody Camorri. You're young enough to have come out from between my legs! But not pretty enough. You can't be serious.'

'She certainly can,' said Locke. Heat and frustration mingled badly with his acute sensitivity at hearing a stranger say anything uncomplimentary about Sabetha.

'Jasmer, you're mad,' said Chantal. 'She's no Amadine. Give her Penthra, by all means, but not Amadine! What is she, sixteen? Sixteen, boy-assed and average!'

'Average?' said Locke. '*Average*? How the hell do you get around the city with two glass eyes in your gods-damned head, woman? You gotta be stu—'

Before Locke could append the second syllable of that heartfelt but unwisely chosen word, Bertrand the Crowd, true to his appearance, had one rough hand on Locke's tunic collar and was dragging him toward a rendezvous with his other fist, already drawn back. The world moved in horrifying slow motion; Locke, who was no stranger to a beating, was cursed with an uncanny ability to recognize one just before it ceased to be theoretical.

A miracle the size and shape of Jean Tannen appeared out of the corner of Locke's vision. An instant before Bertrand could throw his punch, Jean hit him shoulder-to-stomach and slammed him into the dirt.

'Bert!' shouted Chantal.

'Heavens,' said Jenora.

Locke realized he was holding something, and he glanced down to discover that Jean had somehow tossed his precious optics into his hands while separating him from Bertrand.

Jean was a round-bellied, quietly dignified boy of about sixteen. Even his current crop of carefully hoarded stubble failed to lend his aspect any real menace. Bertrand had at least a decade on him, not to mention six inches and twenty pounds, and he looked like he could tear a side of beef in half on a whim. What happened next surprised even Locke.

Punch was traded for punch. Jean and Bertrand rolled around, a furious tangle of arms and legs, swiping and swatting and straining. The advantage shifted every few seconds. Jean got his hands around Bertrand's throat, only to find the older man hammering at his ribs. Bertrand pinned Jean beneath him, yet the boy somehow kicked his legs aside and pulled him back to the ground.

'Gods above,' said Chantal, 'Stop! Stop it, already! We can talk about this!'

Jean attempted to hold an arm across Bertrand's neck, and Bertrand responded with something fast and clever that flung Jean forward over his shoulder. When he tried to press his advantage, however, Jean did something equally fast and clever that threw Bert into a wall. The two combatants wrestled again, desperately forming and breaking grips on one another, until at last Jean slipped free and rolled clear. This was a mistake; the older man used the space between them to swing a wild haymaker that clipped Jean across the chin and finally dropped him.

A moment later, Bertrand wobbled and fell on his face, just as used up as his younger antagonist.

'Chantal,' said Moncraine, 'I would have been happy to tell you that the role of Amadine was beyond negotiation, for several reasons. And hot staggering shit, you *cannot* expect me to believe that boy can do all that and work a thimble, too!'

Jenora and the Gentlemen Bastards gathered around Jean, while

Alondo, Chantal, and Moncraine saw to Bert. Both the fighters regained their senses soon enough, and were eased up into sitting positions against the inn wall.

'Optics,' coughed Jean. When Locke handed them over, he settled them carefully on his nose and sighed with relief.

'Smoke,' muttered Bertrand. Chantal handed him a sheaf of rolled tobacco and flicked a bit of twist-match to light it. Once she'd done this, Bert tore the cigar in two, lit the cold half from the red embers of the other, and passed it over to Jean. The boy nodded his thanks, and the two combatants smoked in peace for a few moments while everyone else watched, dumbfounded.

'You play handball, kid?' said Bertrand. His voice was deep, his Verrari accent thick.

'Certainly,' said Jean.

'Come play with my side on Penance Day afternoons. We play for ale money, two coppins a man to buy in.'

'Love to,' said Jean. 'Just don't take any more swings at my friends.'

'Sure, kid,' said Bertrand. He waved a finger at Locke. 'And *you* don't talk about my wife like that.'

'Then tell your wife not to insult Verena,' said Locke.

'Hey there, skinny, we both speak Therin.' Chantal poked Locke sharply in the chest. 'You got something to tell me, tell me yourself.'

'Fine,' said Locke, matching gazes with Chantal. 'Don't insult Verena—'

'Excuse me,' said Sabetha, pushing Locke aside without humour or delicacy. 'Did I turn invisible or something? I'm not hiding behind *him*, Chantal.'

Locke winced at the unkind emphasis on *him*.

'You want to fight your own fights, bitchling?' said Chantal. 'Good. Any time you want a real education, you try and throw a—'

'ENOUGH,' hollered Moncraine in a shake-the-rafters voice, pushing the two women apart. 'Gods *damn* you all for shit-witted wastrels! Bring yourselves to order or I'll go punch another nobleman, I swear it on my balls and bones!'

'Chantal, sweetness,' said Bertrand, blowing smoke, 'when *Jasmer's* the voice of reason you might have to admit it's time to calm down.'

'Verena's Amadine,' said Jasmer. 'That's the way it is! You can have Penthra or you can have Fetching Maid Number Four and shake your tits all summer for Basanti.'

Chantal glowered, then offered a hand to Sabetha. 'Peace, then. I just hope that when you're onstage the sun shines out of your backside, girl.'

Sabetha shook with Chantal. 'When I'm finished, you won't be able to imagine anyone else as Amadine ever again.'

Bertrand whistled and grinned. 'Ha! That's good. Give my wife a couple of days to grow on you, Verena. She'll make you like her.'

'I've had a lot of opportunities in my life to learn tolerance,' said Sabetha with a thin smile.

'Now, if you're Amadine,' said Bertrand, 'who's Aurin? Who gets to do all that kissing and mooning and staring, eh?'

Locke's heart seemed to skip a beat.

'That's what we were in the business of figuring out when you showed up,' said Moncraine. He rubbed his forehead and sighed. 'I suppose I might as well make my decision. I'll hedge our bets. Lucaza, you'll be Ferrin.'

'I would love to … wait, *what*?' said Locke.

'You heard me. Aurin's a role that needs more nuance. I want Alondo to handle it.'

'But—'

'That's all,' said Jasmer. 'That's it for today. No further discussion. And gods help me, I can quote the company charter as well as Jenora can. Next one of you that lays a *finger* on anyone else here gets docked. Wages, shares, work time – I don't give a damn. I'll spank you like an angry father. Now go!'

5

'Penthra,' muttered Jean, reading aloud from the script in his hands, 'a fallen noblewoman of Therim Pel. Amadine's boon companion.'

'I've read the bloody character list, Jean.' Locke and Jean sat in the corner of Mistress Gloriano's common room farthest from the bar, where Bertrand, Jasmer, Alondo, Chantal, and Sylvanus were drinking up a significant portion of the company's future profits. Dinner was just past. 'Wait, are you trying to ignore me?'

'Yes.' Jean closed his copy of the play with a sigh. 'My ribs ache, I got thrown out of the play, I'm now a bookkeeping stevedore, and you're plumbing new depths of tedium with your moping.'

'But I—'

'Seriously, if you want to kiss her onstage so badly just speak to Jasmer.'

'He doesn't want to talk about it.' Locke sipped his cup of warm dark ale, barely tasting it. 'Says it's an artistic decision and therefore not subject to debate.'

'Then talk to Alondo.'

'He acts for a living. Why would he give up the plum role?'

'I don't know, because you tricked him? Because you convinced him? Rumour has it you took some lessons in being tricky and convincing.'

'Yeah, but ... he's a decent enough fellow. It's not like yanking Jasmer around. Feels wrong.'

'Then listen here, my friend. I'm not an oracle and I'm not going to turn into one no matter how long you sit there crying in your beer. You know I used to think that the Sanzas were the biggest annoyance around? I was wrong. Until you and Sabetha get your shit together, they're the least of all possible evils.'

'She's just so gods-damned inscrutable.'

'You were talking to her before, right?'

'Yeah. It was going well. Now it's all strange.'

'Have you considered extreme, desperate measures like talking to her again?'

'Yeah, but, well ...'

'You've *yeah-but* your way to this point,' said Jean. 'You're going to *yeah-but* this mess until it's time to go home, and I don't doubt you'll *yeah-but* her out of your life. Quit circling at a distance. Go talk to her, for Preva's sake.'

'Where is she?'

'She sneaks up to the roof when the rest of us are down here making idiots of ourselves.'

'She won't ... I dunno, it's not that it's—'

'Reach between your legs,' growled Jean, 'and find some balls, or you do *not* get to speak to me on the subject of her for the rest of the summer.'

'I'm sorry,' said Locke. 'I just hate the thought of screwing things up worse than they are. You know I've got talents in that direction.'

'Ha. Indeed. Try being direct and honest. I can't give you any more specific advice. When the hell have *I* ever charmed my way under anyone's dress, hmm? All I know is that if you and Sabetha don't reach some understanding we're all going to regret it. But you most of all.'

'You're right.' Locke took a deep, steadying breath. 'You're right!'

'Pretty routinely,' sighed Jean. 'Are you going?'

'Absolutely.'

'Not with that beer, you're not. Give it over.'

Locke did so with an absentminded air, and Jean drained the cup in one gulp.

'Okay,' he said. 'Go! Before your so-called better judgment has a chance to wake back up. Wait, that's not the way up. Where the hell are you going?'

'Just back to the bar,' said Locke. 'I have a bright idea.'

6

Languid, thick-aired evening had come down on Espara, and the city lights were flicking to life beneath a sky the colour of harvest grapes. Mistress Gloriano's crooked gables concealed a little balcony, westward-facing, where two people could sit side by side, assuming they were on good terms. Locke eased the balcony hatch open carefully, peered out, and found Sabetha staring directly at him with eyebrows raised. She lowered her copy of *The Republic of Thieves*.

'Hi,' said Locke, much less confidently than he'd imagined he would as he'd climbed the little passage from the second floor. 'Can I, ah, share your balcony for a little while?'

'I was going over my part.'

'You expect me to believe you don't already have the whole thing memorized?'

It was as though she couldn't decide whether to be pleased or exasperated. Locke knew the expression well. After a moment, she set her book down and beckoned him out. He sat down cross-legged, as she was, and they faced one another.

'What's behind your back?' she said.

'A small kindness.' He showed her the wineskin and two small clay cups he'd been concealing. 'Or a bribe. Depending on how you look at it.'

'I'm not thirsty.'

'If I'd been worried about thirst, I'd have brought you water. I was worried about knives.'

'Knives?'

'Yeah, the ones you've had out for a few days now. I was hoping to sort of dull the edges.'

'Isn't that rather knavish? Plying a girl with drink?'

'In this case it's more like self-defence. And I did sort of think you might just ... like a cup of wine.'

'And then perhaps a second? And a third, and so on, until my inhibitions were sufficiently elastic?'

'I didn't deserve that.'

'Yes, well ... perhaps not.'

'Gods, I forgot that anyone who wants to be nice to *you* has to get permission in advance and wear heavy armour.' Biting his lip, Locke poured the pale wine carelessly, and slid one of the cups toward her. 'Look, you can pretend it just appeared there by magic if it makes you happy.'

'Is that Anjani orange wine?'

'If it's Anjani my ass is made of gold,' said Locke, sipping from his cup. 'But it was some kind of orange, once upon a time.'

'And what miracle are you trying to coax out of me, exactly?'

'Simple conversation? What's happened, Sabetha? We were talking, actually talking. It was ... it was really nice. And we worked well together! But now you snap for no reason. You find excuses to cut me dead. You keep throwing up these walls, and even when I climb them, I find you've dug moats on the other side—'

'You're crediting me with an extraordinary degree of industry,' she said, and Locke was delighted to see the tiniest hint of a smirk on her lips, though it vanished between breaths. 'Maybe I'm preoccupied with the play.'

'Oh look,' said Locke. 'Now the moat is full of spikes. Also, I don't believe you.'

'That's your problem.'

'What do you have to gain by not talking to me?'

'Maybe I just don't want to—'

'But you did,' said Locke. 'You did, and we were getting somewhere. Do you really want to spend the rest of our stay here doing this stupid dance back and forth? I don't.'

'It's not so much a dance, though, is it?' she said, softly.

'No,' said Locke. 'You're the one that keeps stepping back. Why?'

'It's not easy to explain.'

'If it was, an idiot like me would have figured the answer out already. Can I sit beside you?'

'*That's* putting the cart before the horse.'

'The horse is tired and needs a break. Come on, it'll make it easier to hit me if you don't like what I have to say.'

After a pause that seemed to last about ten years, she turned to look out over the city and patted the stone beside her. Locke slid over, eagerly but carefully, until his left shoulder was touching her right. The warm wind stirred around them, and Locke caught the faint scents of musk and sage oil from her hair. A thousand fluttering things burst to life in his stomach and immediately found reasons to run all over the place.

'You're trembling,' she said, actually turning to look at him.

'You're not exactly a statue yourself.'

'Are you going to try to make me not regret this, or are you just going to sit there staring?'

'I like staring at you,' said Locke, shocked and pleased at his own refusal to turn from her gaze.

'Well, I like heaving boys off rooftops. It's not a habit I get to indulge often enough.'

'That wouldn't get rid of me. I know how to land softly.'

'Gods *damn* it, Locke, if you've got something you want to say—'

'I do,' he said, steadying himself as though for the incoming swing of a wooden training baton. 'I, uh, I'm tired of talking behind my hands and dropping hints and trying to trick some sort of reaction out of you. These are my cards on the table. I think you're beautiful. I feel like I'm an idiot with dirt on his face sitting next to someone out of a painting. I think … I think I'm just plain stupid for you. I know that's not exactly sweet talk out of a play. Frankly, I'd kiss your shadow. I'd kiss dirt that had your heel print in it. I *like* feeling this way. I don't give a damn what you or anyone else thinks … this is how it feels *every time I look at you*.

'And I admire you,' he said, praying that he could blurt everything out before she interrupted him. This desperate eloquence was like an out-of-control carriage, and if it smashed to a halt it might not move again. 'I admire everything about you. Even your temper, and your moods, and the way you take gods-damned offence when I *breathe* wrong around you. I'd rather be confused about you than stone-fucking-certain about anyone else, got it? I admire the way you're good at everything you do, even when it makes me feel small enough to drown myself in this wine cup.'

'Locke—'

'I'm not done.' He held up the cup he'd used to illustrate his previous point and gulped its contents straightaway. 'The last thing.

The most important thing … it's this. I'm sorry.'

She was staring at him with an expression that made him feel like his legs were no longer touching the balcony stones beneath them.

'Sabetha, I'm sorry. You told me that you wanted something important from me, and that it wasn't a defence or a justification … so it has to be this. If I've pushed you aside, if I've taken you for granted, if I've been a bad friend and screwed up anything that you felt was rightfully yours, I apologize. I have no excuses, and I wish I could tell you how ashamed I am that you had to point that out to me.'

'Gods damn you, Locke,' she whispered. The corners of her eyes glistened.

'Twice now? Look, uh, if I said the wrong thing—'

'No,' she said, wiping at her eyes, trying but failing to do so nonchalantly. 'No, the trouble is you said the right thing.'

'Oh,' he said. His heart seemed to wobble back and forth in his chest like an improperly balanced alchemist's scale. 'You know, even for a girl, that's confusing.'

'Don't you get it? It's easy to deal with you when you're being an idiot. It's easy to push you aside when you're blind to anything outside your own skull. But when you actually pay attention, and you actually make yourself … act like an adult, I can't, I just can't seem to make myself want to keep doing it.' She grabbed her wine cup at last, gulped most of it, and laughed, almost harshly. 'I'm scared, Locke.'

'No you're not,' he said vehemently. 'Nothing scares you. You may be a lot of other things, but you're never scared.'

'Our world is this big.' She held the thumb and forefinger of her left hand up barely an inch apart. 'Just like Chains says. We live in a hole, for the gods' sake. We sleep fifteen feet apart. We've known each other more than half our lives. What have we ever seen of other men or women? I don't want … I don't want something like this to happen because it can't be helped. I don't want to be loved because it's *inevitable*.'

'Not everything that's inevitable is bad.'

'I should want someone taller,' she said. 'I should want someone better-looking, and less stubborn, and more … I don't know. But I don't. You are awkward and frustrating and peculiar, and I *like* it. I like the way you look at me. I like the way you sit and stare and ponder and worry yourself over everything. Nobody else stumbles around quite the way you do, Locke. Nobody else can … keep juggling flaming torches while the stage burns down around them like you do. I adore it. And that … that frightens me.'

'Why should it?' Locke reached out, and his heart threatened to start breaking ribs when she slipped his hand into hers. 'Why aren't you entitled to your feelings? Why can't you like whoever you want to like? Why can't you *love*—'

'I wish I knew.' Suddenly they were on their knees facing one another, hands clasped, and Sabetha's face was a map of mingled sorrow and relief. 'I wish I was like you.'

'No you don't,' he said. 'You're beautiful. And you're better at just about everything than I am.'

'I know that, stupid,' she said with a widening smile. 'But what *you* know is how to tell the whole world to fuck off. *You* would piss in Aza Guilla's eye even if it got you a million years in hell, and after a million years you'd do it *again*. That's why Calo and Galdo and Jean love you. That's why … that's why I … well, that's what I wish I knew how to do.'

'Sabetha,' said Locke. '*Not everything that's inevitable is regrettable*. It's inevitable that we breathe air, you know? I like shark meat better than squid. You like citrus wine better than red. Isn't *that* inevitable? Why the hell does it matter? We like what we like, we want what we want, and nobody needs to give us permission to feel that way!'

'See how easy it is for you to say that?'

'Sabetha, let me tell you something. You called it silly, but I *do* remember the first glimpses I ever had of you, when we both lived in Shades' Hill. I remember how you lost your hat, and I remember how your red was coming out at the roots. It struck me witless, understand? I didn't even know why, but I was *delighted*.'

'What?'

'I have been fixated on you for as long as I've had memories. I've never chased another girl, I've never even gone with the Sanzas … you know, to see the Guilded Lilies. I dream about you, and only you, and I've always dreamt about you as you really are … you know, red. Not the disguise—'

'*What?*'

'Did I say something wrong?'

'You've seen the real colour of my hair once.' She pulled her hands out of his. 'Once, when you were the next thing to a gods-damned baby, and you can't get over it, and that's supposed to flatter me?'

'Hold on, please—'

'"As I really am?" I've kept my hair dyed brown for ten years!

379

THAT'S how I really am! Gods, I am so stupid. … You're not fixated on me … you want to fuck a red-haired girl, just like every leering pervert this side of Jerem!'

'Absolutely not! I mean—'

'You know why I've been dodging slavers all my life? You know *why* Chains trusted me with a poisoned dagger when Calo and Galdo were barely allowed to carry orphan's twists? You ever hear the things they say about Therin redheads that haven't had their petals plucked?'

'Wait, wait, wait, honest, I didn't—'

'I am so, so *stupid*!' She shoved him backward, and he crushed his empty wine cup, painfully, by sitting on it.

'I should have known. I just should have known. You admire me? You respect me? Like hell. I can't believe I was going to … I just – Get *out*. Get the hell out of here.'

'Wait, please.' Locke tried to wipe away the haze suddenly stinging his eyes. 'I didn't mean—'

'Your meaning was quite plain. *Go away!*'

She threw her own empty cup at him, missing, but speeding his stumbling escape into the little passage down to the second floor. As he tried to roll awkwardly back to his feet, a pair of strong hands grabbed him from behind and hauled him up.

'Jean,' he muttered. 'Thanks, but I—'

The same hands grabbed him, spun him around, and pressed him hard against the passage wall. Locke found himself eye to eye with the new patron of the Moncraine-Boulidazi company.

'Lord Boulidazi,' Locke sputtered. 'Gennaro!'

The well-built Esparan held Locke in place with one iron forearm, and reached beneath his plain, dusty clothing with the other hand. He pulled out ten inches of steel, gleaming in the light from the open balcony door, the sort of knife crafted for arguments rather than display cases. In an instant the tip was against Locke's left cheek.

'*Cousin*,' spat Boulidazi. 'I thought I'd dress down and come see how my investment was faring. The idiots in the taproom said you might be up here. That's a *fascinating* conversation you've been having, Cousin, but it leaves me feeling like there's a few things you haven't exactly been telling me.'

The knife-tip pressed deeper into Locke's skin, and he groaned.

'Like everything,' said Boulidazi. 'Why don't we start with *everything*?'

III

FATAL HONESTY

'I never knew any more beautiful than you:
I have hunted you under my thoughts,
I have broken down under the wind
And into the roses looking for you.
I shall never find any
greater than you.'

—*Carl Sandburg* from 'The Great Hunt'

CHAPTER EIGHT
The Five-Year Game: Infinite Variation

I

'Someone's gonna recognize us,' said Locke.

'We look like hell,' said Jean, practising understatement at the master level. 'Just two more travellers covered in dust and shit.'

'Volantyne must have returned by now. Sabetha's got to have people watching the gates.' Locke tapped the side of his head. 'You and I would.'

'That's a generous appraisal of our foresight.'

It had been a hard four days back to Karthain. They'd looted the wagon and shoved it into a ravine on the second day, needing every scrap of speed they could coax out of their unyoked team. Lashain's constables were no threat, but the previous occupant of the wagon could always hire mercenaries. There was no law on the long, ancient road between city-states; a column of dust rising rapidly in the sky behind them would probably have meant someone was going to die.

Now the city, finally in sight, had taunted them for half a day with the prospect of relative safety. They'd come up the coast road from the east, through hills and terraced farming villages, their bodies thoroughly punished by the seedy emergency saddles they'd filched from the wagon.

'Maybe you're right, though,' said Jean. 'If we've got no chance of hiding ourselves, we've got to rely on speed. We get one move, maybe, before she can respond.'

'Let's go straight for her,' said Locke. His scowl shook little puffs of dust out of the creases of his road-grimed face.

'To do what?'

'Finish a conversation.'

'You in a hurry to get back to sea? I can handle a couple of her people at a time. She's got more than a couple.'

'Taken care of,' said Locke. 'I know a fellow who'll be eager to help us past the guards.'

'You do?'

'Didn't you notice that Vordratha favours tight breeches?'

'What the hell's that got to do with anything?'

'Every little detail matters,' said Locke. 'Just wait. It'll be a fun surprise.'

'Well, shit,' said Jean. 'It's not like I've done anything especially smart in months. Why start now?'

2

They slipped into traffic and the usual milling semi-confusion of customs inspectors, guards, teamsters, travellers, and horse manure. The Court of Dust, despite the general cleanliness of Karthain, could have been peeled up beneath its paving stones and set down in place of its counterpart in nearly any Therin city without arousing much notice.

Locke scanned the crowds as he and Jean were poked and prodded by bored constables. Sabetha's spotters would most likely be working in teams, one person on watch while the other was always plausibly absorbed in some trivial business. After counting five possible pairs of watchers, Locke shook his head. What was the point?

Locke felt something else unusual going on, though. A buzz of activity around the Court, beyond mundane business. He'd spent too many hours picking pockets in crowds like this not to sense that something was awry.

Jean was alert, too. 'What's the excitement?' he asked of a passing constable.

'It's the Marrows. You ain't heard?' The woman gestured toward a crowd forming around a battered statue of a Therin Throne noblewoman. 'Crier's just about to start up again.'

Locke saw that a young woman, a finger's width over four feet tall, had climbed the statue pedestal. She wore the blue coat of Karthain, and standing below her was a man in the regalia worn by herald Vidalos, tipstaff and all.

'KIND ATTENTION, citizens and friends of Karthain,' bellowed the woman. Locke was impressed; there had to be more leather lining her lungs than his saddle. 'Hear this report of the FACTS as provided and authorized by the KONSEIL! Mendacity will NOT be tolerated! Rumourmongers will be subject to INCARCERATION on the PENANCE BARGES!

'Vencezla Valgasha, king of the Seven Marrows, is DEAD! He is KNOWN to have died in the city of Vintila, SIX DAYS AGO. He died WITHOUT ISSUE and without lawful heir! A war of secession is now under way!

'The Canton of EMBERLAIN, easternmost of the Seven Marrows, has EXILED its ruling graf and declared itself to be a SOVEREIGN REPUBLIC! The Konseil of Karthain DECLINES to formally recognize Emberlain at this time, and strongly advises citizens of Karthain to AVOID all travel in the north until the situation stabilizes!'

'Holy hells,' said Locke. 'Sabetha was right! The Marrows finally busted up. Gods, what a mess that's going to be.'

'We won't be able to pull the Austershalin brandy scam again,' said Jean. 'Not for a good long while.'

'There'll be other opportunities,' said Locke wistfully. 'If it's war, desperate people are going to be moving a lot of valuable things. But come on, we've got to move ourselves.'

They spurred their tired mounts down a broad avenue to the west, over a shaking and sighing glass bridge, through the Court of the Divines with its incense haze, and onto the Evening Terrace. It seemed surreal to be back on clean streets, among lush gardens and bubbling fountains, as though Karthain were more of a recurring dream than a real place.

Outside the Sign of the Black Iris, they aroused immediate interest. At least two watchers, unmistakably real, flashed hand signs to dark shapes on roofs. A fleet-footed child darted into the alley beside Sabetha's headquarters. Locke led their bedraggled horses to a curbside spot more commonly used for carriages, and when he hopped down a cloud of road dust floated off his boots. He wobbled and nearly pitched over before seizing control of himself. His legs felt like prickly jelly. His horse, less than endeared to him, flicked its ears and snapped its teeth.

'These animals are the personal property of Verena Gallante,' Locke said to the anxious-looking footman. 'She wants them well looked after.'

'But sir, if you please—'

'I don't. Get them stabled.' Locke shoved past the man and reached for the door to the foyer, but Jean pushed his hand aside and went first.

Inside were the two alley-hounds Locke had seen last time.

'Oh, hell,' said the closest one. Jean was already inside his guard. A variety of fast, noisy, and painful things happened, none of them to Locke or Jean. As one guard hit the floor, Jean pitched his comrade facefirst through the lobby doors like a battering ram. Then the Gentlemen Bastards followed.

Here was Vordratha, impeccably dressed and with a fresh black iris pinned to his jacket, backed by four guards with truncheons in hand. Better-dressed people scattered for the doors and staircases behind them.

'Gentlemen,' said the majordomo, peering at the guard who'd just landed at his feet, 'this is a members-only establishment with firm rules against rendering the help unconscious.'

'Your game now, Lazari,' said Jean.

'Thanks.' Locke put his hands up to show they were empty. 'Please take us to Mistress Gallante immediately.'

'Now how can I do that, gentlemen, when you'll be headed out the alley door presently with bruises on your skulls?'

'We'd really like to see her.' Before the guards could crowd in, Locke moved up to Vordratha, reached down to the man's breeches, grabbed his balls through the silk, and gave them a considerable twist. '*Or* we'd like to see your physiker's face when he gets a look at the bruises from this.'

Vordratha moaned, and his face turned shades of a colour rarely seen outside of vineyards at harvest time. The guards edged forward, but Locke held up his free hand.

'Call your friends off,' said Locke. 'I'm not a strong man, but I don't have to be, do I? I'll twist this thing so tight you'll piss corkscrews for the next twenty years!'

'Do as he says, gods damn you,' gasped Vordratha.

'Simply take us to Verena,' said Locke, watching as the guards slowly backed away, 'and I'll return your valuable property to you without lasting damage.'

It was an awkward shuffle, with Vordratha stumbling backward and Locke maintaining his tight, twisted grip on the majordomo's hopes of procreation, but it did the job of keeping the guards at bay.

'Well, how now, asshole?' said Locke. 'No little quips for us? I've never steered a fellow along by his loot sack before. Sort of like steering a boat by the tiller.'

'Camorri dog ... your mother ... sucked—'

'If you finish that thought,' said Locke, 'I'll wind your precious bits tighter than a bowstring.'

Vordratha led Locke and Jean up a flight of stairs to the private dining hall where they'd met Sabetha before. The guards maintained a respectful distance, but followed en masse. Vordratha bumped the door to the hall open with his backside, and Locke saw that Sabetha was already waiting for them.

She was dressed sensibly for anything from signing papers to diving out windows, in black breeches, a short brown jacket, and riding boots. Her hair was wound around lacquered pins; doubtless they contained tricks or weapons or both. Behind her were three more guards, armed with coshes and bucklers.

'Hello again, Verena,' said Locke. 'We were in the neighbourhood and thought we'd investigate persistent rumours that Master Vordratha has no balls.'

'Isn't this a bit crude, even by your relaxed standards?' said Sabetha.

'I suppose having your boot-print embedded in my ass makes me cranky,' said Locke. 'Tell your friends to go away.'

'Oh, that sounds lovely! Shall I tie myself up for you as well?'

'We just want to talk.'

'Release Vordratha and we'll talk as long as you like.'

'The instant I release Vordratha, all hell's going to break loose. I'm not stupid. For a change.'

'I promise—'

'HA,' shouted Locke. 'Please.'

'We have no basis for trust, then.'

'*You've* given us no basis for trust. I wasn't the one—'

'This is getting personal.' Sabetha glared at him with real irritation. She was always less in control of herself when pushed, a hot anger in direct contrast to Jean's cold fury. Locke had spent years desperately straining to read her, and he saw now that she had no clever plan for ending this standoff. His own position – his safety assured only so long as he could keep a grip on another man's privates – suddenly struck him as painfully ridiculous.

'I want to speak to you,' he said, slowly. 'Nothing more. I won't harm you or try to take you from this place. I swear it absolutely on the souls of two men we both loved.'

'What could you—'

With his free hand, Locke made two of the old private signals.

Calo. Galdo.

Sabetha stared at him; then something broke behind her eyes. Relief? At any rate, she nodded.

'Everyone out,' she said. 'Nobody lays a hand on these men without my orders. Release Vordratha.'

Locke did. The majordomo slumped to the ground and curled up in a half-moon of misery. Sabetha's guards slowly backed out of the room behind her, and Jean crouched over Vordratha.

'I'll get him out of here,' he said. 'I think you two want some privacy.'

In a moment, Jean had carried the slender Vadran out the way they'd come, and Locke was once again facing Sabetha in an empty room.

'We can't just use those names as magic words every time we find ourselves at cross-purposes,' she said.

'I know. But it's not my fault I even had to—'

'Spare me.'

'NO!' Locke trembled with hunger, adrenaline, and emotion. 'I will not be shrugged off! I will not have my feelings pushed aside for the convenience of whatever pose you think you're adopting here.'

'Your *feelings*? We're in Karthain working for the Bondsmagi, damn it, we're not children fumbling around in the back of a wagon!'

'You used me.'

'And that's what we *do*,' she said. 'Both of us, professionally. I tricked you, and I meant to trick you, and I'm sorry that hurts, but this is our trade.'

'Not this. You didn't just trick me. You used the deepest feelings I have *ever* had for anyone, and you know it! You exploited a weakness that only exists when I'm around you!'

'Woman convinces man to impale himself on his own hard-on. There's a very old story! The world didn't stop just because it happened again.'

'I'm not an infant, Sabetha. I'm not talking about sex; I'm talking about trust.'

'I put you on that ship for your own gods-damned good, Locke. I knew this would happen! I didn't just need you out of the way and I wasn't just minding your health. I knew you'd beat your brains out against your stupid obsession.'

'Oh, marvellous. *Lovely* fucking plan, because I certainly didn't think about you *once* during the nine days it took to get back to Karthain.'

She had the good grace to glance away.

'What the hell is this, anyway? First you don't need to justify yourself at all, and now it was for my own *good*?' Locke, feeling hot, angrily unbuttoned the stained, oversized riding jacket he'd taken from the stolen carriage. 'And *you* are NOT a stupid obsession!'

'I'm a grown woman who's telling you we cannot wind the clock back five years just because you can't work up the courage to make a pass at someone else.'

'Courage? Who the hell do you think you are, telling me about my courage? *Courage* is what it takes to come after you! Courage is what it takes to put up with your self-righteous gods-damned martyr act!'

'You cocksure, self-entitled, swaggering little ass!'

'Tell me you never liked me,' said Locke, advancing step by step. 'Tell me you never found me worthwhile. Tell me we didn't have good years together. That's all it would take!'

'Stubborn, fixated—'

'Tell me you weren't pleased to see me!'

'… presumptuous—'

'Quit telling me things I already know!' They were suddenly less than a foot apart. 'Quit making excuses. Tell me you can't stand me. Otherwise—'

'You … you … whew, Locke, in faith, you *reek*.'

'Is that a surprise? What was I supposed to do, swim back to Karthain?'

'You were supposed to stay on the damned ship! I gave very specific directions about the availability of baths, for one thing.'

'If you wanted me to stay on the ship,' he said, '*you* should have been on it.'

'You look ridiculous.' Locke fought for self-control as Sabetha slowly ran two fingers down his left cheek. 'You look bow-legged. Gods above, did you leave *any* dust on the road after you passed?'

'You can't, can you?'

'Can't what?'

'Can't tell me to get lost. Not to my face, not now that I've called you out. You don't really want me to go away.'

'I do *not* have to explain myself by your terms!'

'Better cinch up that jacket, Sabetha, I think your conscience is showing.'

'We are servants of the Bondsmagi,' she whispered angrily. 'We came here of our own free will, and we both screwed things up badly enough that we *need* this. Our position is precarious. And if we get too friendly, at least one of us gets killed.'

'I know,' he said. 'I'm not saying we don't need to be careful. I'm just pointing out that there's nothing forbidding us from having a personal life.'

'Everything personal is business with us.' She brushed the dust from his cheek against her coat. 'And all of our damned business is personal.'

'Have dinner with me.'

'What?'

'Dinner. It's a meal. Men and women often have it together. Ask around if you don't believe me.'

'For this you twisted my majordomo's balls off?'

'You said we're not kids fumbling around in the back of a wagon, and you're right. We're in charge of our own gods-damned lives no matter how hard we've been kicked around. We can set the clock back however many years we like. It's ours to set!'

'This is crazy.'

'No. Two weeks ago I was begging to die. *That's* crazy. Two weeks ago I came this close, *this* close.' He held up a thumb and forefinger with no space at all between them. 'I hit the black wall between this life and the next, believe me. I am *through* fucking around. Maybe this is going to complicate the hell out of things. So what? You're the complication I want more than anything else. You're my *favourite* complication. No matter what sort of holes you poke in my trust.'

'You know, self-pity is the only thing that smells worse than four days of road sweat.'

'Self-pity is about the only straw left to cling to after YOU happen to a fellow,' said Locke. 'We can have this if we both want it. But *you* have to want it, too. This isn't me trying to convince you of anything, unless ...'

'Unless?'

'Unless some part of you is already convinced.'

'Dinner,' she said softly.

'And a contractual option for ... subsequent complications. At your discretion.'

She couldn't or wouldn't meet his gaze during the silence that filled the next few seconds. Locke's blood seemed to turn to gel in his veins.

'Where are we going?' she said at last.

'How the hell should I know?' Relief hit so hard he wobbled on his feet.

Sabetha's right arm darted out and caught him around the waist. They both stood staring at the point of contact for a long, frozen moment, and then she drew back again.

'Are you all right?' she said softly.

'I, uh, guess I really liked your answer. But come now, how much time have you left me to figure out where anything is in this damned city? You're morally obligated to pick the place. Tomorrow night.'

'Let it be sunset,' she said. 'Do you trust me to send a carriage?'

'Jean and I won't be together,' said Locke. 'We'll make sure of it. If I don't come back in a reasonable amount of time, you can face him, pissed off and unrestrained. How's that for a safeguard?'

'Not trouble I'd invite if I could help it.' She put her hands behind her back and regarded him appraisingly. 'What now?'

'Depends. Do I still have an inn to go home to?'

'I've left Josten alone. Mostly.'

'Well, then, I've got to go soothe my children and, uh, figure out just how the hell I'm going to beat you.'

'Cocksure, infuriating little shit,' she said, without malice.

'Arrogant bitch,' he said, grinning as he backed toward the door. 'Arrogant, stubborn, gorgeous bitch. And hey, if I catch one whiff of that perfume you were wearing last time—'

'If I catch one whiff of horses and road sweat, you're going back to sea.'

'I'll take a bath.'

'Take two. And ... I'll see you tomorrow, then.'

'You will,' said Locke.

He reached the door, crediting himself with enough wits to not turn his back on her, at least not yet. He was about to leave when another thought struck him.

'Oh, you know, we did borrow some horses to get here. We put them in a bad way. Would you mind stabling the poor things?'

'I'll clean up after you, sure. And ...'

'Yes?'

'Is Jean all right? His face—'

'He broke his nose getting off your ship. He'll be fine. You know what it takes to really slow him down. It occurs to me, though, that you still have his Wicked Sisters.'

'I'll give them back … soon.' She smiled thinly. 'They can be my hostages for *your* good behaviour.'

'If you need hostages, you could always try a gentler version of what I just did to Vord—'

'Get the fuck out of here,' she said, fighting back a laugh.

3

'So what did you get us?' said Jean.

'Uh, a dinner date,' said Locke. 'I think I should be able to discuss drawing a few sensible lines so none of us have to worry about waking up halfway to sea again.'

They'd walked out nonchalantly and claimed the first waiting carriage-for-hire, which was now rattling toward more friendly territory through the slanting late-afternoon shadows of the city's towers.

'I assume you mentioned my sisters?'

'She'll give them back if I behave.'

'Fine, then.'

Jean's voice still had an alarming nasal quality, and Locke made a mental note to have him examined by a physiker whether he liked it or not.

'You're not mad?' said Locke.

'Of course not. I presume you two idiots hinted to one another about relighting old fires?'

'That was my distinct impression.'

'Well, assuming you don't let her drug you again, I'm proud of you. I'm the last man on earth who'd discourage you from chasing the woman you adore. Believe me. See to business and then make it as personal as possible.'

'Thanks.' Locke grinned, and enjoyed a brief moment of actual relaxation, one that ended as soon as he blinked and realized that Patience was seated just across from him, lips folded into a scowl below her night-dark eyes.

'I'd say you're placing an alarming emphasis on pleasure over responsibility, wouldn't you?' she said.

'Gods above!' Locke edged away from her reflexively, and saw Jean flinch as well. 'Why couldn't you show up on the street like an ordinary person?'

'I'm no good at being an ordinary person. Your recent behaviour has been darkly amusing, but I must confess that my colleagues and I are starting to worry about the effectiveness of your overall plan of resistance. If, indeed, such a plan exists.'

'It had to be set aside for a few days,' said Locke. 'We did manage to escape *total* humiliation, no thanks to you.'

'How would you know where the thanks should fall?'

'I don't remember you offering us a spare boat and a hot meal when we were trying not to drown,' said Jean.

'Unseasonal hard winds blew you off course for most of a week, leaving you within spitting distance of shore, and you didn't stop to ponder the implications?'

'Wait,' said Locke. 'I thought you were strictly forbidden from—'

'I won't confirm or refute any conjecture,' said Patience, sounding satisfied as a cream-fed cat. 'I'm merely pointing out that your vaunted imaginations seem to be flickering rather dimly. Of course it's possible we aided you. It's possible the other side had bent the rules as well, and earned a bit of a rebuke. You'll never know for sure.'

'Damn it, Patience,' said Locke, 'you were at pains to assure us that the rules of your stupid contest are ironclad!'

'And you were at pains to insist that you didn't trust me any farther than you could throw this carriage.'

'Why the hell are you even here? Do you have some message?'

'The message is this: Mind your task, Locke Lamora. You're here to win, not to woo.'

'I'm here to do both. Carte blanche was the deal. Are you reneging?'

'I'm just relaying—'

'My disinterest in your bullshit is so tangible you could make bricks out of it. Carte blanche, yes or no?'

'Yes,' she said. 'But you should be very, very careful how long you test our forbearance. When dealing with a horse that won't make speed, one tends to apply a whip to its flanks, doesn't one?'

'You told me you people love to sit back and watch your agents run around entertaining you. So kindly sit back, shut up, and be entertained.'

'I intend to be,' she said. Between heartbeats she was gone, without so much as a rustle of fabric.

'Gods *damn* it,' said Locke. 'Tell me I wouldn't be such a tremendous pain in the ass if I had those powers.'

'You'd be worse,' sighed Jean. 'I'd have killed you myself a long time ago. And you know what else?'

'Hrrrm?'

'Patience can lick scorpions in hell. You and Sabetha take your time and sort out whatever the last five years have done to you. I'm here to mind the shop whenever you're out.'

4

'Oh, gods,' said Nikoros, who was sitting at Josten's bar behind a half-finished drink that was a bit too large and a bit too early in the day. 'Oh, thank the gods! Where have you two been?'

'On the road, dear fellow,' said Locke, seizing Nikoros around the shoulders and pulling him to his feet. Locke ground his teeth as he noticed the sharp smell of something alchemical on Nikoros' breath, and his dilated pupils, but there was no time to berate him just now. 'Engaged in terribly important secret affairs! Where do we stand?'

'We're, uh, beset by unexpected complications,' said Nikoros, bewildered. 'We're getting our *asses* kicked. The bookmakers are projecting a fourteen-seat Konseil majority for the Black—'

'That's great,' said Locke, flush with the heady exhilaration that comes from absolute freedom to bullshit absolutely. 'That's *excellent.* That's the whole point of the exercise! Master Callas and I have been making careful arrangements to create the false impression of a *total state of disarray* on our side. Get it? We've got the Black Iris right where we want them.'

'Uh ... really?' Hope brought new colour to Nikoros' face with startling speed, and Locke sighed. Between whatever he'd been drinking and the 'adjustments' of the Bondsmagi, Nikoros probably had the free will of a sponge. 'That sounds great!'

'Doesn't it?' said Locke. 'Now summon a physiker. Then grab every trustworthy dogsbody and scribe you can lay hands on and bring them up to me in the Deep Roots private gallery in five minutes. Go, go, go! Josten?'

'At your service, Master Lazari.'

'Food for five hungry fat men, in the private gallery, as soon as possible.'

'I gave some orders when I saw you walk in.'

'Bless you. Master Callas will want coffee, too. Hot enough to strip paint. Did you have any problems while we were away? Security trouble?'

'Your people caught half a dozen folks trying to break in. Sent them off with bad headaches. They also tell me we're being watched from several points around the neighbourhood.'

'We'll tend to that soon enough.' Locke beckoned for Jean to follow, and the two of them passed through the crowd of afternoon business-folk and traders, exchanging friendly nods with Deep Roots supporters barely remembered from the night of Nikoros' party. In moments they were up in the party's private gallery, temporarily alone.

'*Is* there an actual plan running around in your head?' wheezed Jean.

'Crap sparks until something catches fire.' Locke settled into a high-backed chair and brushed dust from his filthy tunic. 'Noise and action to keep Sabetha guessing while we cook up a real scheme. We start with childish pranks and escalate steadily. Gods, I wish we had some proper urchins, some Right People that knew what they were doing.'

Camorri outlaws had never thought very highly of their fraternal associates in other cities, but Karthain was the least-regarded of all. Locke hadn't once heard of a Karthani gang that had any reach, any of the savage pride or inventiveness that Camorri, Verrari, or even Lashani crews took for granted.

'It's the Presence,' said Jean. 'The Bondsmagi have these people tamed.'

Food and coffee were the first of the commanded resources to arrive. Locke scarfed down meat and bread; neither lingered long enough before his eyes or in his mouth for full identification. Jean sipped coffee and ate a roll, almost daintily, with obvious discomfort.

A few moments later, a dark-skinned woman with neat grey hair came up the stairs carrying a leather bag.

'I'm Scholar Triassa,' she said, frowning at Jean. 'And that nose tells quite a story.'

While she began her examination, tactfully saying nothing about the fact that Locke and Jean smelled like goats, Nikoros and half a dozen scribes and assistants came up the stairs.

'Good,' said Locke, gulping a last bite of food. 'It's time to give those Black Iris gits a taste of some friendly piss-artistry. Whet your quills. Scribe everything down exactly. Give your notes to Nikoros when we're finished, and he'll handle the actual work assignments.

'I want a letter drafted immediately to the chief constable of Lashain, whoever that is. Tell them that four horses stolen from an armoured carriage service bound for Lashain have been located in the stables at the Sign of the Black Iris in Karthain. Each horse has a clearly visible brand on its neck. These horses were received as stolen property and not reported to the Karthani authorities. Sign it "a friend" and get it to the very next ship crossing the Amathel with mail.'

Jean chuckled, then grunted as Scholar Triassa continued her work. Locke paced back and forth as he spoke.

'Tomorrow I'll secure an addition to party funds. I want a thousand ducats handed out to trustworthy Deep Roots members in increments of five to twenty ducats apiece. I want them all to go out this week and place bets, with anyone taking them, on the Deep Roots winning the election. I want a sudden surge of Deep Roots confidence, so the opposition can have a good hard worry about the possibility that we know something they don't.

'I want another thousand spent on cakes and wine, rigged up in baskets with green ribbons. Complimentary baskets go to the houses of tradesfolk, merchants, alchemists, scribes, physikers – anyone respectable that *isn't* already part of the Deep Roots family. Let's go wooing new voters.'

'That might, uh, cause a problem with some of the, uh, senior party members,' said Nikoros. 'Traditionally we're very choosy about new members. We have private salons, by invitation. We don't, uh, sweep the streets for recruits.'

Locke poured a mug of coffee and took a long sip. *And for those refined tastes, you idiots have been crowded out hard in the last two elections*, he thought.

'Am I in charge here, Nikoros?'

'Oh, uh, gods yes, absolutely sir. I didn't mean to imply anything other—'

'We *will* sweep the streets for recruits if it comes to that. I'll put a bag of gold in the hands of any brick-witted cross-eyed sheepfucker who can mark a parchment. Any time you want to question me, remind yourself that the opposition doesn't share your delicate gods-damned traditions. All they care about is winning.'

'Er, of course.'

'The baskets go out. No demands, no obligations, not yet. We just want people thinking kindly of us. Arm-twisting comes later.

'More quietly,' he continued, 'hunt down our party members with debts, troubles in court, that sort of thing. Give me a list of their little problems and we'll send people out to fix them. In exchange, we'll own their asses and set them toiling.

'Now, conversely. Black Iris party members with weaknesses. Debts, affairs, scandals, addictions, legal entanglements. I want that list! I want to scratch every wound, pour vinegar in every cut, pluck every low-hanging fruit. Constant, total harassment, seizing any opportunity they give us, starting before the sun rises again.'

'As you wish,' said Nikoros.

'To that end … I need a trustworthy alchemist. I need a wagon … a few dozen small animal cages … as many live snakes as we can get our hands on.'

'Live *snakes*?' said one of the scribes. 'You mean—'

'Yeah,' said Locke. 'They've got scales, they slither around – snakes. Keep up. We only want 'em if they're not venomous! That means barn serpents, brown marshies, belt snakes. Anything else you have in these parts that fits the bill. Use mercenaries, boys, girls, anyone. … Offer a suitable bounty, but keep it gods-damned quiet. I don't want word of this little project going too far. Drop the cages in the cellar and keep the snakes there until further notice. How's Master Callas' nose?'

'Badly set,' said the physiker. 'I gather from your rather forthright aroma that you gentlemen have been unable to rest for several days.'

'Woefully correct,' said Locke.

'It'll have to be rebroken. It's plain this isn't your first such injury, Master Callas, and you're developing a breathing obstruction.'

'Then do it,' said Jean.

'I'll need two cups of brandy, some assistants, and some rope.'

'No time for all that,' growled Jean, 'and I want my head clear for work. Just do it here and now.'

'Your pardon, Master Callas, but I don't relish the thought of a man your size lashing out at me—'

'Scholar,' said Locke, 'this building is more likely to collapse than my friend is to lose control of himself.'

'I'm doubling my fee,' said the woman sternly.

'And I'm tripling it,' said Jean. 'Go on, snap the damn thing to where it ought to be. I've had worse, and I've had it without warning.'

Triassa placed her hands carefully, as though Jean's head were a clay sculpture and she meant to pinch the nose off and start over. She

397

applied pressure with one smooth motion; Jean remained still but did indulge in a long, deep, appropriately theatrical groan. The sound of whatever was moving or breaking inside the nose itself made Locke shudder as though his privates had just been dipped in ice water, and a collective gasp arose from the scribes.

'Perhaps just one small brandy,' rasped Jean, barely moving his lips. Tears ran down his cheeks. Locke pointed at one of the scribes; the woman nodded and hurried out of the gallery.

Triassa deftly set Jean's nose in cream-coloured alchemical plasters and wrapped linen around his head. 'Keep this in place,' she said. 'You've danced this dance before, so don't do anything foolish. Brace your head while you sleep. Come see me tomorrow – I'm across the street.'

'Thanks,' said Jean. A moment later the helpful scribe returned with a glass of caramel-brown liquor, which Jean poured carefully down his throat.

'Well then,' said Locke. 'Now that we've all realized precisely how tough we'll *never* be, let's stand on what we have. Pass your lists to Nikoros and he'll mind the details.'

'Sirs,' said Nikoros as his hands rapidly filled with papers, 'I'm pleased to see you back and taking a more active role in our affairs, but, ah, this volume of work—'

'Don't fret, Nikoros, there's plenty of time, assuming none of us sleeps before dawn.' Locke gave Nikoros a reassuring squeeze on the arm, then lowered his voice to a private whisper. 'Also, if I catch you stuffing another speck of black alchemy down your throat, your job situation is going to be *vacant*. Understand?'

'Master Lazari, sir, what can I say? I'm ashamed … but you were gone … everything was so confused—'

'Everything is now unconfused. We're gonna have baths drawn and rejoin civilization. Get to work. Get me that list and get me that alchemist. There's two ladies in particular waiting to see what we've got up our sleeves, and it's time for things to get hectic.'

'Uh, of course, Master Lazari.'

'Nikoros!'

'Uh, yes, sir?'

'I just had a really exciting thought. Get me the list, the alchemist, and then *get me a city constable*! A well-bent one. Someone who thinks with their purse and isn't shy about it.'

'Uh, certainly, but it may take—'

'Tonight, Nikoros, tonight!'

5

Locke and Jean found steaming baths in their suite, along with more food and enough towels, body scrapers, and scented oil jars to supply a rather hygienic harem. Refreshed and repackaged in respectable outer layers, they returned to the Deep Roots private gallery to find Nikoros waiting, new papers in hand. Locke scanned them as rapidly as the crabbed handwriting would permit.

'Good, good,' he muttered. 'Debts, lots of debts. Eager little gamblers, our Black Iris friends ... Who'd be holding most of these?'

'Most of the debts that aren't between gentlefolk would involve Fifthson Lucidus, over in the Vel Verda ... Well, he owns the chance houses in the Vel Verda, but he lives somewhere on Isas Merreau.'

'Lovely,' said Locke. 'A little duke of the dice-dens. He's not a big player in either political party, is he?'

'Doesn't give a damn about the elections, as far as I know.'

'Better and better,' said Locke. 'Exactly the sort of man Master Callas and I should see in the small hours of the night, like dutiful physikers paying a house call.'

'Physikers?'

'Absolutely. We want him firmly convinced that if he disregards our advice his health is apt to suffer. Now where's my alchemist and my constable?'

'Coming, Master Lazari, coming. ...'

6

The moons were shy in just the way thieves prefer, hidden behind clouds like black wool, and the brisk south wind carried the scents of lake water and forge smoke. Banked-down furnaces were faint smudges of red and orange nestled among the shadows of the Isle of Hammers, and the view from the window of Fifthson Lucidus' third-storey bedroom captured it all nicely.

Locke took a moment to properly appreciate the tableau before he turned and woke Lucidus with a slap to the face.

'Mmmmmmph,' said the heavyset Karthani. His exclamation was muffled by Jean, who, standing behind his bed, slapped one hand over his mouth and hauled him to a sitting position with the other.

'Shhhh,' said Locke, who sat down at Lucidus' feet. He adjusted the aperture of his dark-lantern to throw a thin beam directly on the bearded and bleary-eyed fellow, whose face wore the sort of extra years that came out of a wine bottle. 'Your first thought will be to struggle, so I'd like you to think about *where* and *how deep* I can cut you while leaving you perfectly capable of conversation.'

He unsheathed a long, freshly polished steel blade, and was sure to catch the lantern light with it before he slapped Lucidus' legs with the flat of the weapon.

'Your second thought,' said Locke, who wore an improvised grey linen mask, 'will be to summon that big man who's supposed to be watching your front door. I'm afraid we've put him to sleep for a bit. So now my associate will take his hand off your mouth, and you'll mind your tone of voice.'

'Who the hell are you?' whispered Lucidus.

'*What* we are is the important thing. We're *better than you*. There's no defence you can dream up and no hole you can hide in that will keep us from doing this to you any time we please.'

'What ... what do you want?'

'Take a good look at these names.' Locke sheathed the blade and pulled out a torn sheet of parchment with a short list on it. The names had been culled from the larger list provided by Nikoros. They weren't merely opposition voters, but components of varying importance in the Black Iris political machine. 'Some of these men and women owe you money, yes?'

'Yes,' said Lucidus, squinting at the parchment. 'Yes ... most of them, in fact.'

'Good,' said Locke. 'Because you're about to have some money problems, understand? You're going to call in your markers on all of these fine citizens.'

'Wait just a – Hggggrrrrkkk—'

This last exclamation was a result of Jean reasserting his presence, without prompting from Locke, via the careful application of a fore-arm to Lucidus' windpipe.

'I'm not soliciting *opinions*,' said Locke, gesturing for Jean to ease up. 'I'm giving orders. Yank the leash on these people or bad luck follows.

Chance houses *burn down*. Nice homes like this *burn down*. The tendons in your legs get slashed. Understood?'

'Yes … yes …'

'About those money issues.' Locke held up a purse, stuffed near bursting with about ten pounds of coins, and Lucidus' eyes went wide. 'A hidden floor panel? Seriously? I was learning how to spot that sort of thing when I was six. You squeeze these people hard, get it? Collect the debts. Do your best and you'll get this purse back, plus a hundred ducats. That's nothing to scoff at, is it?'

'N-no …'

'Fuck it up,' said Locke, lowering his voice to a growl, 'and this money vanishes. Try to cross me, and I'll carve you like a festival roast. Get to work tomorrow, and don't worry about looking for us. When we want to talk again we'll find you.'

7

'Now tell us,' said Jean, staring down at a detailed map of Karthain with all of its avenues and islands, 'which districts are usually considered an absolute lock for either party?'

It was deepening evening, the day after their midnight visit to the house of Fifthson Lucidus. Locke and Jean were in the private gallery with Damned Superstition Dexa and Firstson Epitalus. Nikoros, who'd been worked like a clockwork automaton for longer than Locke had intended, had passed out in a high-backed chair. Whether it was honest fatigue or alchemically induced, Locke allowed him to snore on for the time being.

'We've got all the right places, dear boy,' said Dexa, pointing to the southeastern portion of the map. 'Isas Mellia, Thedra, and Jonquin. The Three Sisters, the old money districts. The Silverchase and Vorhala routinely come back eight-tenths Deep Roots, as well.'

'As for the opposition,' said Epitalus, 'they've got the Isle of Hammers and the surrounding neighbourhoods. Barresta, Merreau, Lacor, Agarro – shop and trade districts, you see.' Epitalus exhaled twin streams of white pipe smoke from his nostrils, and brief-lived cloud formations drifted over the illustrated city. 'New men and women. Ink still wet on the receipts for their voting privileges, eh?'

'So it's five against five,' said Locke, 'and the other nine districts are in play?'

'More or less,' said Dexa. 'Sentiment across the city—'

'Can go hang itself,' said Locke. 'Here's the basic plan, as much as I can reveal now. We keep most of our money out of the settled districts. We don't have time to turn the Black Iris strongholds, and we shouldn't have to worry about them turning ours. We'll run some misdirection and some nice childish pranks, but most of our leverage gets thrown against the nine in the balance. How busy are you two with Konseil duties?'

'Hardly busy,' said Dexa. 'We partly recess during election season. Karthain all but runs itself, barring emergencies.'

Epitalus mouthed something under his breath, and Locke was sure it was *Bless the Presence*.

'Good,' said Locke. 'I'd like you two to do me a favour. Go after some undecided voters in districts outside your own. Make personal calls. Important people, the cream of the middle bunch. I'm sure you can think of a hundred candidates. Charm us votes one by one in the districts where every one of those votes will count. Does that sound agreeable?'

'With all due respect, Master Lazari,' said Epitalus, 'that's simply not how it's done here in Karthain.'

'I doubt your counterparts in the hierarchy of the Black Iris would quibble at such a task.'

'It's simply not how things are done where folk of *substance* are concerned,' said Dexa gently, as though explaining to a very small child that fire was hot.

'We have higher expectations than the Black Iris,' said Epitalus. 'Firmer standards. We don't scuttle about courting just anyone, Master Lazari. Surely you can see that it would make us look beggarly.'

'I doubt that any of the recipients of the solicitations I propose,' said Locke, 'would be anything but deeply flattered to receive someone of your stature.'

'We don't mean them,' said Dexa. 'Rather, our fellow members of the Deep Roots. This sort of behaviour could not be countenanced—'

'I see,' said Locke. 'Never mind that these scruples have brought you embarrassing defeat in the last two elections. Never mind that you will apply your "firmer standards" to a smaller and smaller circle of associates, with ever-shrinking influence, should you blithely allow the Black Iris to best you again.'

'Now, now, dear Master Lazari,' said Dexa. 'Surely there's no cause—'

'I am charged with winning this election,' said Locke. 'To do so I will bend every custom that must be bent. If I lack your full confidence, you may have my resig—'

'Oh no,' said Epitalus, 'no, please—'

Once again Locke saw the curious working of the arts of the Bonds-magi, as the ingrained prejudices of the Karthani warred with their conditioning to see him as some sort of cross between a spymaster and a prophet. It was something behind their eyes, and though it seemed to be going his way he thought it best to lay on some sweetness for added assurance.

'I would hardly ask this of you,' he said soothingly, 'if I didn't believe that I was sending you out to certain success. Your quality and grace will knock these individuals into our camp straightaway, and since you'll be choosing them yourselves they'll bring the Deep Roots nothing but credit. Get us a hundred or so. Winning will be worth it, I assure you.'

Dexa and Epitalus acquiesced. Not energetically, to be sure, but Locke was satisfied that their nods were sincere.

'Splendid,' he said. 'Now, I've got a dinner eng – er, appointment. Business appointment. Something, ah, that could really work to our advantage. Master Callas will be here if you need anything.'

'I thought you were overdressed for a planning session,' said Dexa.

'What about poor Via Lupa?' said Epitalus.

'Hmm? Oh, Nikoros ... Let him sleep on for a bit. He'll be up to his ass in baskets and green ribbons tomorrow.'

Locke made several pointless adjustments to his dark blue coat, and brushed imaginary dust from his black silk cravat.

'And if I don't come back ...' he muttered to Jean.

'I'll knock the Sign of the Black Iris into its own foundation, and put Sabetha on a ship to Talisham.'

'Comforting,' Locke whispered. 'Right. I've got to go wait for the carriage. Pin a note to Nikoros' lapel, would you? I'm still waiting on that bloody alchemist and constable.'

8

The carriage was on time and comfortable, but Locke rode alertly, with the compartment windows open and one hand in a coat pocket.

He could have instantly conjured lockpicks, a dagger, a blackjack, or a small steel pry bar, as the situation required.

However, before any need arose for the tricks in his coat, the ride came to an end beneath a warmly lit stone tower somewhere in what Locke guessed was the Silverchase District. At least a dozen well-dressed gentlefolk were visible, seemingly at ease. A footman in a red silk coat opened the carriage door for him and bowed.

'Welcome to the Oversight, Master Lazari,' said the footman as Locke stepped onto the curb. 'Your party's already waiting, if you'll follow me.'

Allowing himself to hope that there might be an actual dinner rather than an ambush forthcoming, Locke glanced up, and was startled. Spherical brass cages anointed with alchemical lanterns circled the highest level of the tower. These were suspended by some complex mechanical apparatus and formed a sort of gleaming halo perhaps seventy feet above the ground.

As the footman led him around the tower along a hedged path, Locke heard a muted rumbling from overhead. The cage on the side directly opposite the carriage park descended smoothly and settled into a circle of pavement about five yards across. The footman seized two levers and pulled open the cage's door, revealing the luxurious interior ... and Sabetha.

She wore a buttercream gown under a jacket the colour of rich dark brandy, and her hair fell loose past her shoulders. She was seated on a cushion Jereshti-fashion, legs crossed, behind a knee-high table. Dazed by the sight of her and the strangeness of their surroundings, Locke meekly entered the cage and knelt on his own cushion. The footman resealed the door, and after a moment the cage crept upward, worked by some mechanism that was no doubt obsessively oiled in deference to the delicate ears of diners.

'If you'd wanted me to be ready earlier,' he said, 'I'd have been happy—'

'Oh, tsk. How could I be properly mysterious and alluring if I wasn't calmly waiting for you when the door opened?'

'*You* could manage it, somehow.' Locke studied the cage more closely. Although the table was ringed by gauze curtains, these were presently pulled up to the ceiling and tied in place. The cage was composed of thin bars laid in a grid with spaces about an inch on a side, through which Locke had a view of northeastern Karthain under the gold-red lines of fading sunset. 'They punish criminals back home with a contraption like this.'

'Well, in Karthain criminals pay for the privilege of being hoisted,' said Sabetha. 'I was told that the Oversight was actually inspired by the Palace of Patience. Something about how the west gentles and perfects the ways of the east.'

'I've been out here for several years, and I don't feel gentled or perfected,' said Locke.

'Indeed, you haven't even offered to pour the wine yet,' said Sabetha with mock disdain.

'Oh, damn,' said Locke, stumbling back to his feet. There was a bottle of something airing on the table next to a trio of glasses. He did his duty gracefully, filling two glasses and offering one to her with an exaggerated bow.

'Better, but you forgot some of us,' she said, pointing to the empty glass.

'Hmmm?' Proximity to Sabetha was like sand in the gears of his mind. He imagined that he could literally feel them straining to turn as he stared at the empty glass, and then came a warm rush of shame. 'Hell and castration,' he muttered as he poured again, and then: 'A glass poured to air for absent friends. May the Crooked Warden bless his crooked servants. Chains, Calo, Galdo, and Bug—'

'May they laugh forever in better worlds than this,' said Sabetha, touching Locke's glass. They both took small sips. It was a good vintage, mellow and strong, tasting of plums and bitter oranges. Locke sat on his cushion again, and they shared an awkward pause.

'Sorry,' she said. 'I didn't mean to give things a melancholy turn.'

'I know.' Locke sipped his wine again, reasoning that if it was drugged all of his hopes and assumptions were useless anyway. The miniature arsenal in his coat suddenly struck him as comical. 'So, uh, do you like the flower I brought you?'

'The invisible flower? The hypothetical flower?'

Locke arched his eyebrows and tapped the right side of his coat. Sabetha looked down, hurriedly patted her own jacket, and pulled out an unfurled stemless rose, dark purple petals limned with crimson on their tips.

'Oh, you clever little weasel,' she said. 'While you poured the wine.'

'And you were watching the bottle rather than the beau,' said Locke with a theatrical sigh. 'It's fine. My pride's had all the stiffness trampled out of it already. I hope you like the colour, though. Karthani hot-house. It had a stem, but that made it too awkward to carry or palm.'

'I don't mind at all.' She set the rose carefully in the middle of the table. 'Assuming it doesn't explode or put me to sleep or anything.'

'I've forsworn vengeance on that score,' said Locke. 'But we do need to talk about that, so we might as well get it over with.'

'What's to talk about?'

'Kidnapping,' said Locke. 'Assault. Exile. Alchemy. Dirty tricks of that nature, aimed at you or me or Jean.'

'We learned a dozen ways to incapacitate someone before we were ten,' said Sabetha. 'It's perfectly routine for us. I agreed to a truce tonight—'

'We should extend the truce permanently,' said Locke. 'Mutual immunity from direct personal attack. If we're going to have this fight, let's have it mind to mind, plan to plan, and not need to sleep under our beds because we're afraid of waking up on a ship the next day.'

'*I'm* not afraid of waking up on a ship.'

'Push your luck, gorgeous, and eventually luck pushes back. I might be dim enough to have dinner with you in a metal cage, but consider Jean. If he's free to make his own moves he'll squash your little army like boiled goose liver and you'll be on your way to Talisham in a box.'

'Fearsome as that, is he?'

'Tell me again how many people you detailed to catch him while you were busy drugging me.'

'And if the Bondsmagi interpret this as collusion—'

'It's nothing of the sort. Hell, this only increases our entertainment value for our jackass masters. They *want* us to run this affair in our accustomed style. Skulduggery, not skull-crackery. And you can't tell me it wouldn't tickle your own pride.'

'Just to be clear, you're suggesting that I should discard an approach which has already brought me one considerable success, and continue the fight at a level more suited to the restraints of your own, well, inadequacy, and I should do this because it'll make me feel the warm glow of virtue?'

'I suppose if you discard the lovely emotional resonance of my suggestion and pin me down on cold hard meaning—'

'How strange. You sound rather like a confidence trickster. But I've no objection to ending a little game while I'm one-up on you,' she said with a thin smile. 'Truce as discussed, *strictly* limited to you and Jean and myself, so we can have more time to worry about the proper contest. Will you drink to it?'

'Full glass is an empty promise,' said Locke. Their glasses rang as they brought them together, and then they both gulped their wine to the last drop.

'Doubles or dishonour,' said Sabetha, speedily refilling the wine. Again they raced one another to the bottoms of their glasses, and when they finished her laugh seemed genuine enough to make Locke feel like a fresh wind had blown across whatever was smouldering in his heart.

'You have no idea,' he said, as the warm cloud of wine-haze steadily rose from his chest to his head, 'how much aggravation I really am willing to put up with to hear that laugh again.'

'Oh, shit,' she said, rolling her eyes without banishing her smile. 'Straight from business to skirt-chasing.'

'You're the one plying me with wine!'

'Any woman of sense does prefer her men drunk and tractable.'

'And now you're speaking of me possessively. Gods, keep doing that.'

'This is a far cry from the dusty mess that stormed my inn and accused me of cruelly tugging his heartstrings.'

'You try four days in the saddle without preparation and see what kind of mood it leaves you in.'

Their conversation was interrupted as an iron plank slid out from the tower and locked into place beside their cage. A waiter appeared and opened a door in the brass gridwork, through which he made several trips to deliver fresh wine and starter courses on gilded platters.

'I hope you don't mind that I ordered for you,' said Sabetha.

'I'm at your mercy,' said Locke, whose stomach now grumbled achingly to life. Fortunately, Sabetha seemed sensitive to the awkwardness of his new appetite. She ravaged their dishes with indelicate gusto that matched his own.

There were the underwater mushrooms of the Amathel, translucent and steamed to the texture of gossamer, paired with coal-black truffles in malt and mustard sauce. There were cool buttercream cheeses and crackling, caustic golden peppers. Spicy fried bread with sweet onions was drizzled with tart yellow yoghurt, a variation on a dish Locke recognized from the cuisine of Syrune. Each of these courses was bookended with wine and more wine. Though Locke felt his own wits softening, he was heartened to see the deepening blush on Sabetha's cheeks and the way her smiles grew steadily wider and easier as the evening wore on.

Purple twilight became full dark of night, and Karthain a sea of half-shadowed shapes suspended between blackness and alchemical sparks.

The main course was a turtle crafted to life size from glazed parti-coloured breads. The top of the starchy creature's shell was paper-thin, and when punched through with a serving ladle it proved to contain a lake of turtle and oyster ragout. The turtle came under enthusiastic siege from both ends of the table.

'Have you ever had a chance to look out over the Isas Scholastica before?' said Sabetha, recovering some measure of ladylike delicacy by dabbing at her chin with a silk cloth. 'That's it down behind me, just across the canal. Isle of Scholars. Home of the magi, or so they claim.'

'Claim? No, I've never had a chance to see it. I can't see much now, between the darkness and the wine.'

'They don't seem to frown on people building towers around the edges of their little sanctuary. I've been sightseeing up a few. I say *claim* because I'm not sure I believe they all live happily together like Collegium students in rooms. I think they're all over the place ... I think the Isas Scholastica is just where they want everyone looking.'

'All those parks and buildings and so forth down there are just a sham?'

'No, I'm pretty sure they *use* the place, just not as a sole residence.' She took a final long draught of wine and pushed her glass aside. 'Though I don't believe I've ever seen one down there. Not one.'

'What, would they wear signs or something? Funny hats? They're easy enough to spot when you can see their wrists and their manners, but at a distance they must look like other people.'

'I've seen servants,' said Sabetha. 'People driving carts, offloading things, but those wouldn't be Bondsmagi, surely. I've never seen anyone strolling the Isas Scholastica at leisure, or giving orders, or simply talking to anyone else. No guards, no masters and mistresses, only servants. If they're down there, they conceal themselves. Even from eyes that are hundreds of yards away.'

'They're odd people,' said Locke, staring into the pale orange dregs of his own wine. 'And I say that as a fully qualified professional odd person of the first degree. I wish they weren't such arrogant pricks, but I suppose odd people will keep odd habits.'

'I wonder,' said Sabetha. 'Do you ... do you feel that your ... handlers have been entirely candid with you concerning their motives for this contest of theirs?'

'Hells, no,' said Locke. 'But that was an easy question. Perhaps you've not met my side of the magi family. Why, do you think that yours are—'

'I don't know,' she said quietly, staring out into the night. 'They've delivered all the tools they said they would. They seem happy with my work, and I think their promises of consequences are certainly sincere. But their secrecy, their misdirection, it's just so habitual ...'

'You're *really* not used to feeling like a piece on a game board,' said Locke.

'No,' she said, and then she brought her brief moment of wistfulness to an end by sticking her tongue out at him. 'I haven't had all the opportunities you have to get acclimatized to the sensation.'

'Oh ho! Serpent in a dress. Well, if only I wasn't too much the gentleman to flay your spirit with a witty and cutting retort, madam, you'd be ... thoroughly ... um, wittily retorted at this very instant.'

'If you were any sort of actual gentleman you'd be no fun to have dinner with.'

'You admit you're having fun?'

'I admit it's much as I feared.' She looked down at the table for a moment before continuing. 'Your presence is ... steadily less of a chore and more of a comfort.'

'Well,' said Locke, chuckling, 'aren't I always delighted to be not quite the burden you were expecting!'

'Dessert?'

'Would you forgive me if I begged off?' Locke patted his stomach, which had mercifully reached the sheer physical limit of its gluttony. 'I'm stuffed like a grain bag.'

'Good. You're still too bloody thin.'

The waiter cleared their dishes and left a slate with a folded note pinned to it. Sabetha picked it up and glanced at it idly.

'What's that?'

'Itemized bill,' she said. 'They actually bring it to the table here. It's all the rage. Lets those that can read show it off in public.'

'Strange,' said Locke. 'But that's the west for you. So what now, Mistress Gallante? A walk, a carriage ride, maybe an—'

'Now we rest on our laurels.' She rose from the table and stretched, revealing how precisely her gown and jacket were fitted to her curves. 'Look, it's not that I haven't appreciated the break, but some things … just have to go slow.'

'Slow,' said Locke, knowing he was failing miserably to conceal his disappointment. 'Of course.'

'Slow,' she repeated. 'We've got five years and more of sharp edges to file down. I might be willing to work at it, but I don't think I can do it in one night.'

'I see.'

'Oh, don't give me that drowning-puppy look.' She touched his waist and gave him a kiss on the cheek that was not quite passionate but a shade longer than merely polite. 'Let's do this again. Three nights hence. I'll pick some other interesting place.'

'Three nights hence,' said Locke, still feeling the warm press of her lips against his skin. 'Three nights. All right. Just try and stop me.'

'I can't. I seem to have promised to fight clean.' She drew a pair of leather gloves from her jacket and pulled them on.

'Can I at least walk you to your carriage?'

'Mmmmm … don't think so,' she said mischievously. 'I try to live by a cardinal rule of our shared profession, namely, "always leave a sucker wanting more."'

She reached under the table and pulled out a coil of demi-silk rope previously hidden there. Locke watched, puzzled, as she conjured a slender metal pick in her other hand and applied it to the mechanism of the waiter's door. It opened in seconds.

'Hey, wait a minute—'

'It was in case you tried anything tricky. Whether I would have used it to escape or hang you can remain an open question.'

'Are you serious?'

'I wouldn't say that,' she said with a grin. 'But I'm definitely *sincere*. Thanks for the flower. I left you a little something in exchange.'

Then she was gone. The rope was anchored to a point on the cage beneath the table; Sabetha kicked it out the door and rappelled into the night, without a harness, sliding down on the friction of boots and gloves with her gown billowing like the petals of a wind-whipped flower.

'Gods *damn*,' whispered Locke as he watched her land safely and vanish far below. After a moment her last words finally squeezed past the film of wine clinging to his brain, and he frantically patted himself down. A piece of paper was in his left jacket pocket. A note? A love letter?

He unfolded it in haste, and discovered the bill for dinner.

9

'Move! Move! For your life, move!'

Doormen scattered from a snorting pair of barely controlled horses dragging a rickety dray tended by a single wild-eyed driver. The back of the vehicle was loaded with sacks and barrels, one of which had bled an expanding trail of grey smoke all the way down the street. With a lurching crash, the dray broke a wheel against the curb and toppled, spilling its contents in a pile before the front doors of the Sign of the Black Iris.

'It's alchemy!' The driver, a slender, white-bearded fellow in a voluminous rat-chewed coat, leapt to the ground as smoke billowed past him. Sparks leapt and flickered amidst the spilled cargo, and he unyoked his frantic animals. 'Heaps of alchemy! Fetch water and sand, or run for your gods-damned lives!'

Patrons, servants, and guards poured out of the inn to investigate the commotion, only to reel back in dismay as smoke boiled past them into the building. Crackling noises rose ominously within the haze, and fires of eerie colours burst to life. The driver of the crashed dray led his horses across the street, where he found several boys in Black Iris livery watching the unfolding disaster.

'Here,' he shouted, thrusting the reins into one boy's hands. 'Watch my animals! I'll be right back!'

The bearded man scuttled across the street and into the billowing murk. Green smoke, red smoke, and mustard-yellow smoke uncoiled from the spreading fire, tendrils wafting like sinister serpents of the air. The new hazes bore nauseating odours of garlic, brimstone, and mortified flesh. The entire street side of the Sign of the Black Iris was subsumed in a picturesque alchemical nightmare.

More or less hidden in the rising smoke, through which the masked afternoon sun shone dimly bronze, the driver darted down an alley beside the inn. He threw his coat and hat behind a pile of empty crates, then yanked away his baggy trousers and boots to reveal black hose and polished shoes. The beard was the last to go. Freshly peeled like a human fruit, smooth-cheeked and well-dressed, Locke Lamora strolled casually out the end of the smoky alley and into the court behind the inn.

'Master Lazari. Good-*oof*-afternoon!'

Sabetha rolled off the lowest eave on the Sign of the Black Iris' rear side, landed hard, recovered gracefully, and offered a half-curtsey from about ten feet away. Three of her security folk followed her, landed awkwardly, and spread out in an arc around Locke. The window they'd spilled out of remained open, its shutters swaying in the soft breeze.

'Oh, hello, Mistress Gallante,' said Locke cheerfully. 'Having problems with your inn?'

'Nothing that can't be corrected with a little assistance, I'm sure.'

'I do wish I could help,' said Locke. 'I just happened to be nearby. Ahhhh! I remember now! You're having some sort of big Black Iris party meeting today, aren't you? My condolences! The smoke, the flames ... I can only imagine the consternation.'

'I'm sure you've imagined it in detail.' Sabetha moved close enough to lower her voice. 'Bearded peasant goes in one end of an alley, clean-shaven gentleman comes out the other? Really?'

'It's a classic!'

'It's got cobwebs on it. Might have fooled someone who hadn't seen you do it before. Now, do you want to come with me gracefully or on the shoulders of my friends?'

'I remind you, darling, my person is inviolate.'

'Don't call me that when we've got our working faces on. And nobody's person is getting violated. But you can't think I'm going to let you stroll away while a cart full of alchemical crap burns on my doorstep.'

'Of course I can. It's all perfectly harmless,' said Locke. 'Oh, it might smell awful, and some of it reacts badly with water, and there's just no telling what's what until you experiment, but give it a few hours, then air your inn out for a day or two. There won't be any lingering issues.'

'All the same, I think you should sit in a little room and be bored until I've got the mess under control.'

'Now, now,' said Locke, 'you must credit me with the foresight to have a backup plan in case you decided to take it like this.'

'And of course, you must expect me to have one of my own in case you wanted to play hard to get,' she said.

'Oh, *absolutely*.'

'Well.' She ran a finger lightly up and down one of the lapels of his jacket. 'I'll show you mine if you show me yours.'

'YOU! HOLD IT RIGHT THERE!'

The shout echoed down the courtyard as a trio of surcoated constables appeared out of the drifting smoke. The leader, a man with a wheat-coloured beard and the aesthetic qualities of a lard slab, touched Locke on the shoulder with a wooden baton.

'As a constable of Karthain, sir, I must formally detain you,' he said.

'How dreadful.' Locke feigned a yawn. 'What's the charge?'

'You resemble a suspect wanted for questioning in a confidential matter. You'll have to come with us.'

'Alas.' Locke allowed the constables to gather loosely around him, and doffed an imaginary hat to Sabetha as he backed away with them. 'Verena, I wish I could continue our conversation, but it seems the deficiencies of my character have become a matter of official concern. Best of luck dealing with your little … conflagration.'

Just before the smoke cloud swallowed him again, Locke rapidly gestured in code: *Looking forward to tomorrow night.*

Her response *was* a gesture, though not one originating in the private signals of the Gentlemen Bastards. Still, Locke felt reassured by the fact that she smiled as she delivered it.

The street before the Sign of the Black Iris was a reeking mess. Well-dressed men and women with black flowers pinned to their jackets sought escape, while well-meaning people with buckets of water tripped over one another and tumbled around like billiard balls. The alchemical fires burned merrily on, a partial rainbow of sorcerous lights within the miasma. Locke's "captors" walked with him for about a block before detouring into an empty, windowless court.

'*Beautifully* timed, Sergeant,' said Locke, producing three leather purses of equal size. 'Worthy of applause.'

'We take pride in the conduct of our civic duty,' said the bearded man. He and his cohorts accepted the purses with wide grins; each had earned three months' wages for the few minutes spent loitering nearby in case of Locke's need. It was downright pleasant, thought Locke, to be treading the old familiar realms of avarice after dealing with the eerie malleability of the 'adjusted' Deep Roots people.

'Now, none of that stuff is *really* dangerous, right?' said the sergeant, one bushy eyebrow raised.

'Harmless as baby spit,' said Locke. 'As long as nobody's dim enough to shove their hand into a fire.'

Satisfied, the constables took their leave. Locke had only a few minutes to wait before Jean came strolling down the avenue from the direction of the smoke, several empty sacks flung over his shoulder.

'How'd it go up top?' said Locke as the two of them fell into step together.

'Perfection and then some,' said Jean. 'They were all so distracted, bothering to sneak might have been a waste of time. That's thirty-seven snakes down the cold chimneys.'

'Magnificently childish, though I say it myself.' Locke scratched at his chin to remove a few stubborn flecks of beard adhesive. 'Hopefully that'll keep them uneasy for a few days.'

'And if she responds with more of the same?'

'I arranged to have city work gangs do some unnecessary mucking with the cobblestones around Josten's for the next few days. No carriages can get closer than twenty yards. Our friends will grumble, but that should keep loads of mischief at a distance.'

As they walked, Locke noticed for the first time that banners had started to appear, hanging from balconies and windows. Here and there were a few brave greens, but in this neighbourhood the majority were black. Citizen interest was climbing; half the allotted six weeks was nearly gone. Annoying pranks were a fine gambit, but now it was time to begin truly curbing some of Sabetha's capabilities.

'Those spies keeping watch on our place ...' said Locke. 'Fancy a little hospitality visit once the sun goes down?'

10

Their second night of upper-storey work went as smoothly as the first. They swept the block surrounding Josten's Comprehensive just after midnight, creeping silently through rooftop gardens and over well-tended slate roofs, using chimneys and parapets for cover.

Not everyone they crossed paths with was in Sabetha's pay. A drunk woman, huddled in the corner of her terrace, was sobbing over a small painting and didn't notice them slip past. Two lithe young men wrapped in one another's arms a few gardens over were similarly absorbed. Locke crept past their cast-off clothes, close enough to sift them for purses, but pangs of sympathy stilled the impulse. Doing mischief to happy lovers might invite a cruel justice to trample his own hopes.

Their first legitimate target was taken unawares, and his possessions made his job plain. He wore a mottled grey-brown cloak ideal for blending into city shadows, carried a spyglass, and the remains of a cold meal were spread beside his hiding place. In an instant, Jean flung him down on his stomach and crouched atop him, wrenching the poor fellow's arms behind his back. Locke knelt at the man's head, bemused at how familiar he and Jean were becoming with the old Threatening Voice / Silent Brawn act.

'You try to cry out,' whispered Locke, 'and we'll rip your arms off. Shove one down your throat and one up your ass so you'll look like meat on a spit. How many of you are watching Josten's?'

'I don't know,' hissed the man.

Locke gave him a shove on the back of the head, bouncing his face off the roof tiles. Hard, but not too hard.

'It's not worth it,' said Locke. 'Your employer doesn't expect life-or-death loyalty, surely. But we *will* hurt you to send a message.'

'There's one more,' spat their captive. 'One that I know of. Maybe more. Look out past this parapet. Four rows down, roof of the apothecary shop. He's there somewhere. I swear that's all I can tell you.'

'Good enough,' said Locke. He pulled his dagger and slashed the man's cloak into strips. When Sabetha's agent was gagged and thoroughly trussed, Locke gave him a pat on the back. 'Now, don't fret. Once we've finished clearing out all your friends, we'll tip one of them off and you'll be collected. Shouldn't be more than a few hours. Don't do anything stupid.'

The second agent was crouched atop the apothecary shop as indicated, but he was a touch more alert and met them with a drawn cosh. What followed was a proper scrum, with Locke clinging to the man's legs while Jean attempted to wrestle and disarm him, hampered by the need to avoid killing him. Such was the fellow's fighting spirit that they ultimately had to pummel him unconscious before they could have a word.

As they neared the end of their circuit around the neighbourhood, perhaps ten minutes later, they found a third and likely final observer, fortunately no more on guard than the first.

'All your friends are dealt with,' said Jean cheerfully as he dangled the man over the back-alley side of the building by his jacket collar. 'Trussed up like festival chickens.'

'Great gods, mate, it's nothing personal,' sobbed the man as he stared into the shadows four storeys below. 'We're just doing our bloody job!'

'Find another job,' said Locke. 'This is us being very, very cordial. Next time we catch spies lurking in this neighbourhood, we cripple them. This isn't Karthain right now, it's the sovereign state of Fuck Off and Go Home.'

'But—'

'Take a good look at that alley,' said Locke. 'Imagine what those cold, hard stones will feel like when we throw you off this roof. You come round here again, you'd best have wings. Now, your comrades are tied up in their usual spots. Fetch them and run hard.'

'Couldn't we discuss—'

'Get the dogshit out of your ears, you witless corpse-fart,' growled Jean. 'Do you want to do as you're told, or do you want to kiss that pavement?'

It turned out he wanted to do as he was told.

II

'Have you ever thought about how badly Chains fucked us all up?'

'Gods above!' Locke narrowly avoided choking on his beer. 'How tipsy are you?'

'Not at all.' Sabetha held her own glass rock-steady for several moments to support the assertion.

'I understand your frustration with the way some things played out,' said Locke. 'You *know* I listened to you.'

'I do.'

'And you know I think you had some points. But Chains was a generous man. A generous and caring man, whatever his faults.'

'That's not what I'm talking about. He wanted a family, very desperately. You've realized that?'

'Of course. I never thought of it as a defect.'

'I often think he wanted a family more than he wanted a gang.'

'Again—'

'A conscience is a dead weight in our profession.' She stared into the amber depths of her half-full glass. 'Make no mistake, he shackled each of us with one. Even Calo and Galdo, rest their souls. For all that they did most of their thinking with their cocks and the rest with their balls, even they wound up with essentially kindly dispositions. Chains got us all in the end, good and hard.'

416

Their second dinner, the night following the alchemical 'disaster' at the Sign of the Black Iris, was held aboard the *Merry Drifter*, a flat-topped dining barge complete with gardens and lacquered privacy screens. The barge had floated gently through the heart of Karthain, beneath the strange music of the Elderglass bridges, before finally laying anchor in the Amathel just off the Ponta Corbessa. As the sky had darkened and the alchemical globes flicked to life, little boats had ferried other diners to and from shore, but Locke and Sabetha had held their choice table at the barge's stern all the while.

'I can't believe I'm hearing this from someone who came out of Shades' Hill,' said Locke. 'Is that what you would have preferred? Getting beaten and starved? Maybe buggered here and there when it suited him?'

'Of course not—'

'Sabetha, you know how much I respect you, but if you can't see what a gods-damned *paradise* we lucked into when Chains picked us, you need to set that beer down this instant.'

'I don't regret the comforts or the education. He was a faultless provider. Except in one respect … he trained a gentle streak into us and let us pretend it would never cost us.'

'You think we should have been more cruel? Ready to turn on each other like sharks in blood, like every other gods-damned gang around us? I don't know what's gotten into you, but that wasn't weakness he bred into us. It was *loyalty*. And loyalty's a hell of a weapon.'

'You have the luxury of thinking so.'

'Oh, not this again. The Jean situation, right? Straight and simple, gorgeous, don't you *dare* sit there and hit me with self-righteous envy for a friendship I kept and you walked away from.'

She set her beer down and stared coldly at him. Then, just as Locke's heart started to sink in expectation of another one of their habitual misunderstandings, the chill thawed, and she attempted a smile. She whistled, mimicking the sound of an arrow in flight, and clutched at an imaginary shaft just above her heart.

'I'm sorry,' they both said, in Sanza-esque unison, and chuckled.

'You're dwelling on something,' said Locke, reaching across the table to rest his free hand on hers. 'Let it go. Just be here. Just be Sabetha, having dinner, floating on the Amathel. Let the world end at the sides of this barge.'

'I *am* dwelling on something.'

417

'Well, don't take such a poisonous view of our upbringing. Come on. We lie for a living; it's not healthy for us to lie to ourselves.'

'What do we do BUT lie to ourselves, Locke? Aren't we supposed to be rich? Aren't we supposed to be in command of our lives, free to go when and where we please, with all the honest simpletons of the world throwing coins at our feet? Here we are, halfway around the world, working for the gods-damned Bondsmagi just to stay alive.'

'You know, Jean's slapped me out of a lot of moods like the one you're in right now.' Locke took a long pull on his beer. 'You're taking the world awfully personally. Didn't Chains ever tell you about the Golden Theological Principle?'

'The what?'

'The single congruent aspect of every known religion. The one shared, universal assumption about the human condition.'

'What is it?'

'He said that life boils down to standing in line to get shit dropped on your head. Everyone's got a place in the queue, you can't get out of it, and just when you start to congratulate yourself on surviving your dose of shit, you discover that the line is actually circular.'

'I'm just old enough to find that distressingly accurate.'

'You see? It's universal,' said Locke. 'Of course, I'm a stark staring hypocrite for telling you not to take it personally. It's easy to prescribe remedies for our own weaknesses when they're comfortably ensconced in other people. What's got you dwelling on the past?'

'I don't like dancing on strings, any strings, even my own. I've been … examining some, I suppose. Trying to follow them all the way back to where they began.'

'Ah.' Locke shuffled his glass around idly. 'You're trying to reconcile your contradictory thoughts about yours truly. And you're wondering what sort of decision you'd be making without our shared history—'

'Gods *damn* it!' Sabetha punctuated this exclamation by throwing a wadded-up silk napkin at him. 'Don't do that. It makes me feel as though my thoughts are written on my forehead.'

'Come now. Fair's fair. You read *me* like a scroll.'

'I tried to get you out of the way—'

'Half-assed,' said Locke. 'Very half-assed. Admit it. You made it difficult, but some part of you *wanted* to see Jean and I get off that ship and come riding back into town.'

'I don't know. I wanted to see you, but then I wanted you gone,' said Sabetha. 'I tried to say no to dinner. I couldn't. I don't … I don't want anyone to be a *habit* for me, Locke. If I love someone, I want it to be my choice … I want it to be the right choice.'

'I never felt as though I had a choice. From the first hours I knew you. Remember when I told you, for the first time? You nearly threw me off the roof—'

'I thought you deserved it. You know, it's an opinion I return to from time to time, whether or not a roof is available.'

'You're a difficult woman, Sabetha. But then, difficult women are the only ones worth falling in love with.'

'How would *you* know? It's not like you've ever been after anyone else—'

'That part's easy. I started with the most difficult woman possible, so there was never any need to look any further.'

'You're trying to be charming.' She squeezed his hand once, then pulled away. 'I choose not to be entirely charmed, Locke Lamora.'

'Not entirely?'

'Not entirely. Not yet.'

'Well.' Locke sighed. The evening might not be ending as he'd dared to hope, but that was no reason to be less than good company. 'I suppose I still have two ambitions to mind as long as I'm in Karthain. Dessert?'

'How about a ride back to shore?'

'I've been curious about what might happen when you suggested that. Will you be leaving by catapult? Giant kite?'

'One showy exit was amusing; two would be gauche. We can't let these westerners think Camorri are entirely without a sense of restraint.'

Their ride back to shore was a flat-bottomed boat with velvet cushions, tended by an admirably mum old fellow rowing at the stern. Locke and Sabetha rode side by side in companionable silence, through waters that gleamed white and blue from the lanterns of the dining barge. The air was full of pale, fluttering streaks, pulsing like fireflies, adding their soft touches of light to the canvas of the water.

'Firelight Sovereigns,' whispered Sabetha. 'Karthani night butterflies. It's said they hatch at dusk and die with the dawn.'

'You and I are natives of the dark, too,' said Locke. 'I'm glad some of us last a bit longer.'

Two carriages waited above the quayside.

'His and hers, I presume?' said Locke.

'To bear us back to ribbons and duties and dumping carts of burning alchemy on doorsteps.' She led him to the first carriage and held the door open. 'The driver has Jean's hatchets. Safe and sound, to be handed over on arrival.'

'Thanks. So … three nights hence?' He took her hand as he placed one foot on the step, and bit the inside of his cheek to keep from grinning too broadly when she didn't draw away. 'Come on. You know you want to say yes.'

'Three nights. I'll send a carriage. However, I'm charging *you* with finding a place this time. You've roamed the city enough to have some ideas, I think.'

'Oh, I'm full of ideas.' He bowed and kissed the back of her hand, then climbed into the carriage. 'Can I offer you one last thing?'

'You can offer.' She pushed the door shut and looked in at him through the barred window.

'Quit being so hard on yourself. We are what we are; we love what we love. We don't need to justify it to anyone … not even to ourselves. I seem to remember telling you that before.'

'Thank you.' She did something to the lock on the carriage door. 'We *are* what we are. Now, listen, my driver will let you out when you're back home. Don't bother messing with the door; I had the lock mechanism sealed on the inside.'

'Wha … wait a damned minute, what are you—'

'Have a smooth ride,' she said, waving. 'And I want you to know that the bit with the snakes was pretty cute. In fact, I took pains to see that they weren't harmed, because I was certain you'd want such adorable little creatures returned to you.'

She thumped the side of the carriage twice. A panel in the cabin ceiling above Locke slid open, and as the carriage clattered across the cobbles, the rain of snakes began.

12

'Paint me a picture,' said Locke, standing in the Deep Roots private gallery two days later. Since his return from dinner with a carriage full of less-than-deadly but agitated serpents, he'd been consumed by the paper chase, poring over maps and allocating funds, checking and double-checking lists, with no chance to engage in more hands-on weasel work.

'Nikoros just went down to fetch the latest reports,' said Jean, blowing smoke from an aromatic Syresti-leaf cigar that would have cost a common labourer a day's wages. 'But our Konseil members here have been chatting their teeth out in all the better parts of town.'

'Successfully, too, I should think.' Damned Superstition Dexa took a sip from her brandy snifter and gestured at the map of Karthain with her own cigar. Asceticism was a virtue the Deep Roots party held in slight regard. 'We've squeezed a lot of promises out of Plaza Gandolo and the Palanta District. Fence-sitters, mostly. And some old friends we've brought back into the fold.'

'*Bought* back is more like it,' said Firstson Epitalus. 'Bloody ingrates.'

'What are you handing out to steady their resolve?' said Locke.

'Oh, hints about tax easements,' said Dexa. 'Everyone loves the thought of keeping a little more of their own money.'

'The Black Iris people can drop the same hints,' said Locke. 'I don't mean to tell you your business, but fuck me, if something as boring as tax easements is enough to hook votes, those people won't care which party delivers the goods. We need some impractical reasons to motivate them. Emotional reasons. That means rumourmongering. I want to rub dirt on whoever's standing for the Black Iris in those districts. Something disgusting. In fact, we'll completely avoid mud-flinging in a few other spots to make these stand out all the more. What's guaranteed to repulse the good voters of Karthain?'

'Rather depends on how much vulgarity you're willing to countenance, dear boy.' Dexa drew in a long breath of smoke while she pondered. 'Thirdson Jovindus, that's their lad for the Palanta District. He's got what you might call an open-door policy for the contents of his breeches, but he's also just dashing enough to carry it off.'

'Seconddaughter Viracois stands for them in Plaza Gandolo,' said Epitalus. 'She's clean as fresh plaster.'

'Hmmm.' Locke tapped his knuckles against the map table. 'Clean just means we can paint whatever we like on her. But let's not do it directly. Master Callas and I will arrange a crew. Scary people on a tight leash. They'll visit some of our fence-sitters in Plaza Gandolo, and they'll make threats. Vote for Viracois and the Black Iris or bad things happen to your nice homes, your pretty gardens, your expensive carriages …'

'Well, I don't mean to tell you *your* business, Master Lazari,' said Epitalus, 'but shouldn't we be frightening voters into our own corner?'

'I don't want them frightened. I want them *annoyed*. Come now, Epitalus, how would you feel if a pack of half-copper hoods barged into your foyer and tried to put a scare into you? Swells aren't used to being pushed around. They'll resent it like hell. They'll mutter about it to all their friends, and they'll be at the head of the line to vote against the Black Iris out of spite.'

'My, my,' said Epitalus. 'There may be something in that. And what about Jovindus?'

'I'll come up with something suitable for him, too. Let the pot simmer a while.' Locke tapped the side of his head. 'Where's Nikoros?'

'Coming, sirs, coming!' Long black plait bobbing behind him, Nikoros jogged up the gallery stairs and passed a set of papers to Jean. 'Fresh as the weather, all the reports you asked for, and something, ah, unfortunate—'

'Unfortunate?' Jean flipped through the papers until he found one that caught his eye. The furrows in his forehead deepened as he read, and when finished he drew Locke aside.

'What is it?'

'The official constabulary report on the arrest of Fifthson Lucidus of the Isas Merreau,' said Jean.

'*What?*'

'It says that acting on a tip from the Lashani legate, a party of constables paid Lucidus a visit and discovered a team of stolen Lashani carriage horses in his private stable, identifiable by their brands—'

'Cockless sons of Jeremite shit-jugglers!' Locke seized the report and scanned it. 'That sneaky bitch. That beautiful, sneaky bitch. She just can't let us feel good about ourselves, not even for a few days. Oh, look, out of concern for the diplomatic aspect of the situation, they're holding Lucidus in solitary confinement until after the election!'

'Indeed.'

'Some of the Black Iris chicks must have complained to their mother hen about the big bad debt collector. So much for that scheme.'

'We should come back hard and fast.'

'Agreed.' Locke closed his eyes and took several deep breaths.

'Keep pushing everyone on that list of vulnerabilities. Send courtesans and handsome lads after all the Black Iris people with wandering eyes. Make sure the gamblers get invitations to high-stakes games. Scatter temptations all around the ones with nasty habits. Pluck the weaknesses of the flesh like harp strings, all of 'em, from every direction.

'I suppose there's money in the bank itching to be spent,' sighed Jean.

'That's right. We'll spend it down to the dust under the last scrap of copper. Then we'll sweep up the dust and see what we can get for it.'

'Um, one thing more, sirs,' said Nikoros. 'Josten tells me that we've got watchers on the surrounding rooftops again.'

'Leave that with me,' said Jean. 'We gave fair warning. This time I'll make some work for the physikers.'

13

Cool grey veils of drizzle and fog draped the neighbourhood when Jean went out, an hour after midnight, to pay a call on the new neighbours. He moved up to the rooftops as slowly and cautiously as possible, using routes he'd noted on the previous excursion. In this weather there were no drunks or lovers to stumble over, and he was confident that he crept along as silently as he ever had in his life.

His first target was obvious – so obvious that Jean watched for nearly a quarter of an hour, straining his senses to spot the ambush or the trap that had to be there. The watcher sat (sat!) in a collapsible wood-and-leather chair beside a parapet, wrapped in a cloak and blanket. If not for the fact that the seated figure moved from time to time, Jean would have sworn it had to be a decoy.

The tiniest speck of light lit the shadows beside the chair, revealing a spread of gear and comforts including bottles of wine, a silk parasol, and several different spyglasses. It had to be a joke, or a trap … and yet there was simply nobody else around. He took the opening. It was child's play to sneak up behind the seated watcher and clap a hand over their mouth.

'Scream and I'll break your arms,' hissed Jean. The watcher gave a start, but it was plain in an instant that they were small-framed and weak, incapable of serious resistance. Puzzled, Jean scrabbled for the light source, which turned out to be a dark-lantern with the aperture drawn to its narrowest setting. Jean eased it open another few clicks and held it up to his captive.

Gods, it was an old woman. A very old woman, seventy or more, and it wasn't one of Sabetha's make-up jobs, either. This woman was genuinely light and frail, her face a valley of lines, one eye grey as the overcast sky. The other one, however, fixed on him with mischievous vitality.

'Oh, hello dear,' she whispered as he withdrew his hand. 'I won't be screaming, I promise. You gave me a start, though she warned me you'd be up sooner or later.'

'She?'

'My employer, dear.'

'So you admit that you're—'

'A spy. Oh yes.' The old woman chuckled. A dry and not entirely healthy sound. 'A spyfully spying spy. Settled up here all cozy to see what I can see. Which isn't much, more's the pity. That's why I've got all the lovely spyglasses. Now, what are you going to do with me, dear? Are you going to beat the hell out of me?'

'Wha ... *no!*'

'Pick me up and throw me off the roof? Tie me up and leave me here for a few hours? Kick my teeth out?'

'Gods, woman, of course not!'

'Oh, that's exactly what she told me,' beamed the old woman. 'She said you weren't the sort of fellow who'd raise his hand to a helpless old woman. Which, let's be honest, is what time has made of me.'

Jean lowered his head against the cold stone of the parapet and groaned.

'Oh, come now, son, it's not a thing to be ashamed of, having scruples.'

'Are all of her new spies as ... um ...'

'Old as myself? Oh, there's no harm in saying it. Yes, dear, you're hemmed in by old women. All of us wrapped up in our blankets, clutching our parasols. We've got apartments to use, and people to fetch us things, but we're doing the watching from now on. Unless you beat us up.'

'Come now,' said Jean. 'You know I won't.'

'Yes, I do.'

424

'I don't suppose I could ask you very politely to get down off this roof and go away?'

'Oh, gods no. Apologies, dear, but the money I'm seeing for this … well, I don't think I can live long enough for money to ever be a problem again.'

'I could make you a better deal.'

'Oh no. No, gods bless you for offering, but no. You've got your scruples, and I've got mine.'

'I could pick you up and carry you down to the street!'

'Of course you could. And then I'd kick and scream and fuss, and you'd have to deal with that somehow. And when you were done, I'd creep back up here as fast as my joints could take me, and since you won't just punch my lights out, we'd have to do it all over again.' She punctuated these words by tapping him gently on the chest with a very slender finger. 'All over again. And again. And again.'

'Well, shit.' Jean slumped against the parapet, feeling soundly embarrassed. 'Don't, uh, come crawling to us for help if you catch an ague up here or something.'

'Never fret, dear. I can assure you that we're very well looked after. Just like your inn.'

14

At the very moment Jean Tannen was discovering old women on rooftops, Nikoros via Lupa was knocking at a lamp-lit door in a misty alley behind the Avenue of the Night Singers on the Isas Vorhala. He had a warm, nervous itch in his throat – an itch he had run out of the means to assuage.

The apothecary shop of the Brothers Farager provided the alley door as a discreet courtesy for those in need at odd hours. This included customers in pursuit of substances not sanctioned by the laws of Karthain.

The burly guard behind the door, wrapped in a heavy black coat, was new to Nikoros; the fellow that had always met him before had been older and thinner. The man let him in regardless, gesturing up the narrow steps with a grunt and leaving Nikoros to find his own way to the rear office. There Thirdson Farager sat slumped behind a counter, threads of some floral smoke wrapped around him like a ghostly shawl, idly mixing powders on a measuring board.

'Nikoros,' said the alchemist, glumly. 'Thought I might see you, sooner rather than later. What's your taste?'

'You know why I'm here,' said Nikoros. Third Farager had always been the sole provider of Nikoros' dust … had led him to the stuff in the first place, in fact.

'Muse-of-Fire,' grunted Farager, setting aside the glass rod he'd been using in his work. 'Need some more lightning for those clouds in your head, eh?'

'Same as always.' Nikoros licked his lips and tried to ignore the hollow, dry sensation inside his skull. He'd meant to put off another purchase for a few days, meant to obey Lazari and Callas … but the urge had grown. An initially aimless walk had drawn him here, inevitably as water running downhill.

'Akkadris,' said Farager. 'Well, if that's what you want, let's see your coin.'

Nikoros tossed a bag of silver on the counter. No sooner had it landed than something slapped him painfully in his left side. Wincing, he turned and found that the burly door guard had crept up to the office after him, lacquered wooden baton in hand. The man's bulky black coat now hung open, revealing the light constabulary blue of the jacket beneath.

'This is disappointing, Via Lupa. You ought to know a thing or two about the laws concerning black alchemy,' said the constable with a grin. 'That's ten years in a penance barge sitting there on the counter. Confiscation of your goods. Forfeiture of licenses and citizenship. Exile, too, if you live through your ten.'

'But surely,' said Nikoros, fear clawing at his innards, 'there must be some, ah, mistake—'

'Yeah, and you're the one that made it.'

'I'm sorry,' muttered Farager, looking away. 'They got onto me last week. I had no choice. I'd be on a barge already if I hadn't agreed to help them.'

'Oh, gods, please,' whispered Nikoros.

'It was a smart arrangement,' said a woman, appearing from the door behind Farager. She wore a dark hooded cloak, the sort of thing Nikoros might have scoffed at as theatrical, any time before the Karthani constabulary had threatened to bring his life to an end. 'Thirdson Farager made one that got him off the hook. You might be able to do the same.'

The woman pushed her hood back, revealing long, dark red hair. Her eyes glittered as she began to explain to Nikoros what would be required of him.

15

Karthain was the most cultivated and manicured city Locke had ever seen, and the Vel Verda, the Green Terrace, was perhaps its most cultivated and manicured district. The manors and promenades of the Vel Verda were walled in by thick strands of poplar, olive, witchwood, pale oak, and merinshade trees, and beyond it all loomed the crumbling shadow of the city's old walls. In any other Therin city these would have been lit, manned, and obsessively repaired, but the Karthani hadn't kept theirs up for more than three centuries.

'This is a private manor, not a restaurant,' said Sabetha as Locke led her up a winding black iron staircase. 'If you've got some sort of half-witted ambush in mind, Master Lamora, I must warn you that I'll be severely disappointed ...'

'It's vacant. One of my Deep Roots ladies holds it from a dead cousin. She's been lax about selling it off since she doesn't exactly need the money, but she was happy to let me borrow it for a night.'

'Will I be getting a pile of snakes dropped on my head?'

'Ha. No, and thank you for *that*, by the way. I was ever so worried about those little fellows while they were away from me. No, Mistress of Doubts, I've brought you here to this secluded corner of the city for the nefarious purpose of cooking your dinner myself.'

They came to the second floor of the dark, undecorated manor house, and Locke slid a wooden door in the north wall open with a dramatic flourish. Thus revealed was a tiled balcony with a marble balustrade, overlooking the dark tops of countless trees swaying softly in the autumn breeze. Lanterns in semi-opaque paper hoods filled the area with mellow golden light.

'Ooh,' said Sabetha. She allowed Locke to pull out one of the chairs at the tiny round witchwood table in the centre of the balcony for her. 'Now this is more promising.'

'I didn't just choose the setting,' said Locke. 'Tonight I'm chef, sommelier, and alchemist, in one very convenient package, and of course available at a staggeringly insignificant cost if it suits the lady—'

'I'm not sure I brought any coins small enough to pay an appropriate price for you.'

'I practise selective deafness to hurtful remarks, young woman. Though I should ask, are we under observation by one of your packs of *old* women?'

'No, not here. Much as I could have used a chaperone, they're busy where they are.'

'They're damned lucky it was Jean that stumbled over them. I don't have his qualms about punching old biddies in the teeth.'

'Well, then, why haven't you vanquished them yourself?'

'Some forms of behaviour,' sighed Locke, 'simply cannot be made to look reasonable.'

'You don't say! You might have drugged them, of course.'

'Oh, yes,' said Locke. 'Throwing alchemy at old women with gods know what sorts of constitutional complaints. If I can't murder them on purpose I'd hardly let it happen by accident.'

'That thought had crossed my mind,' said Sabetha, grinning.

'Now how's your candidate for Plaza Gandolo?' said Locke. 'What's her name again … Seconddaughter Viracois? Got taken in by the constables on a pretty serious charge, I heard. Receiving stolen goods? Stolen goods from the houses of *Deep Roots supporters*? That's pretty shocking.'

'And pretty asinine,' said Sabetha, feigning a deep yawn. 'Her solicitors will have the matter cleared up in just a day or two.'

'Well, no doubt you're right not to worry. After all, you've got quite a slate of replacement candidates if she should be tied up in the courts. As thrilling a collection of ciphers and nonentities as ever stirred the voters to indifference.'

'Now Locke,' she said softly, 'you and I going on like this before the final results are tallied is like peeking at festival presents before they're opened. This isn't the game I came to play tonight.'

'Delighted to hear it! Watch, then, and be amazed as I perform the most menial portion of an amazing alchemical process and claim all the credit for myself.'

On the table stood a silver bucket-within-a-bucket, constructed so that there was an open gap of about a finger's width between the inner and outer walls. In the centre bucket, a bottle of pale orange wine stood in water.

Locke uncapped two leather-covered decanters. He poured their colourless contents into the outer channel of the chambered bucket, then juggled the empty decanters hand-to-hand a few times and bowed.

A patina of frost appeared on the outer surface of the bucket, steadily thickening into a wall of crisp white ice. Puffs of pale vapour rose from the bucket's outer channel, and a jagged crackling noise could be heard. Locke silently counted out fifteen seconds, pulled on a leather glove, and carefully tilted the bucket toward Sabetha. The wine bottle, cloudy with frost, was now immersed in slush.

'Behold! I have chilled the wine. I am the true master of the elements. Bondsmagi across the city are handing in their resignations.'

Sabetha rendered applause by tapping one finger inaudibly against the opposite palm. Locke grinned, withdrew the bottle from its semi-solid surroundings, uncorked it, and poured two glasses.

'I give you our first toast of the evening.' Locke picked up his glass and touched it gently to hers. 'To crime, confusion, and all arts insidious. To the most enchanting practitioner they've ever had.'

'That's awkward, asking me to drink to my own honour.'

'I'm sure a self-regard as robust as your own can easily bear the strain.'

They drank; the sweet orange-and-ginger wine was cold as a northern autumn. Locke poured them each a second glass.

'My turn,' said Sabetha. 'To strange little boys and impatient little girls. May their real mistakes … be gentle and far between.'

'Am I wide of the mark, or are you in a better mood than you were three nights ago?' said Locke as he finished his second drink.

'It was quite a mood, wasn't it?'

'Did you figure anything out?'

'Only that I wasn't going to find any real answers in one night of brooding. Besides, packing you off in some sort of richly deserved trap always cheers me up.'

'You might see those snakes again, madam, if you keep up that unseemly gloating. Now, I believe I promised you dinner.'

Off to one side of the balcony was a long oak table and a smouldering brazier. Locke threw more chips of aromatic wood into the brazier and gave them a stir. Pleasantly approaching the edge of muddled as the wine mounted from his mostly empty stomach, he examined the piles of ingredients and utensils he'd set out earlier. There was a tap on his shoulder.

'Now this is *not* how it's done,' said Sabetha. She'd removed her black velvet jacket, revealing a white silk undertunic and a loosely knotted scarf just slightly darker than her hair.

'I haven't even started cooking yet!'

'Where we come from we didn't cook for one another, remember? We cooked together.'

'Well—'

'Let's see what sort of mess you've got here.' She bumped him gently aside with her hip. Together they sorted out the components of the meal he'd planned – fennel fronds, onions, sliced blood oranges, pale white olives, almonds and hazel nuts, a chicken he'd plucked and dressed, and enough assorted oils to sauté anything smaller than a horse.

'How strange,' she said, 'but it looks as though you've assembled some of my favourite things.'

'My life is haunted by wild coincidences,' said Locke.

'I suppose I should admire your constancy in one respect, Locke Lamora. All these years and you're still beside yourself to tumble a redheaded girl.'

'Oh?' His grin faded, along with some of his wine-induced buoyancy. He reached out and touched a loose strand of her burnished copper hair. 'You know, if you take offence at the notion, you have a *hell* of a strange way of showing it.'

'"Confusion and all arts insidious,"' she said, glancing away.

'Did you really restore that colour just to keep me off balance? Make me easier to play games with?'

'No,' she said. 'Not entirely.'

'Not entirely.' Locke stared at her, trying to force the muscles of his face, usually so loyal and pliable, to twitch into some semblance of a smile. 'You know, I hate the way one of us can say something ... We're enjoying ourselves for the gods know how long, but one wrong word and suddenly it's like we're not even in the same room.'

'"We" is a tactful way of saying "me," isn't it?'

'Only this time,' said Locke, 'Sabetha, listen to me. You know what I'm after. My cards are on the table and always have been. Am I fixated? *Yes.* Absolutely. Am I sorry about that? *No.* I'm standing here with my intentions plain as the rising sun, waiting for you to convince *yourself*, one way or the other. And I'll wait for that. I'll wait until I'm old and bent and need help spelling my own name. But you know, if I had the luxury of any self-respect at *all* where you're concerned, I'd be insulted by the idea that I must think convincing you to spread your legs is the big endgame.'

'I'm sorry,' she said. 'I know. I do know you want more than that, and for all your faults you give more—'

'Bloody right. I mean, who knows, maybe we could sleep together *twice*.' He drew himself up, thrust out his chest, and stuck out his tongue. 'Limitless ambitions, woman! *Limitless!*'

'Oh, you bastard.' She punched him, but it was the sort of punch delivered with a warm smile. 'So, has it … well, how long has it been, for you? Since, you know—'

'You already know the answer,' said Locke. 'Very precisely. Think about the day you left. Go back two nights from that, and there you have it.'

'Not even once?'

'I guess it's fucking ridiculous, isn't it? But no. I tried. I tried to enlist some help. One of the resident cherry tops at the Guilded Lilies. Turns out a redhead's just not a redhead if she's not, you know, twice as smart as I am and three times as infuriating.'

'Three times as smart,' said Sabetha. 'Half as infuriating. And … I am sorry.'

'Don't be. It wasn't too bad.' Locke rolled an onion across the table and bounced it off a decanter of olive oil. 'She was a friend, close to Chains and me. She knew what my problem was, and that pushing it wasn't the answer. I got a massage that was worth the price of admission.'

'I suppose I should tell you … it hasn't been the same way with me, these past few years. For several reasons.'

'I see.' He felt cold knots forming in his guts, but fought the sensation down. 'I won't lie. My feelings about you are selfish as hell. I don't like to think about you with anyone else, but … I wasn't there. You're a grown woman and you didn't owe me anything. Did you expect me to be angry?'

'Yes.'

'I might have been, once. Maybe the one real advantage to getting older is that you have the time to pull your head a little bit farther out of your ass. I don't *want* to care, understand? You're here now. With luck … I really hope you'll be here later. Besides, it seems safe to assume you weren't swept off your feet by a handsome young Vadran lord with a castle or two to spare—'

'I had some comfort from it, once or twice.' She reached out and touched his arm, not softly, as though she were afraid he might suddenly decide to be elsewhere. 'And the rest of the time, it was to empty some pockets. Or a vault. You know.'

'I do indeed.' He reached out, half-consciously, and started fiddling with another onion, spinning it like a top. 'In fact, I'm steadily emptying a bank vault because of you with every passing day.'

'Good. Because I've never been what anyone would call easy, and I'm *certainly* not cheap.' She reached up and took his other arm.

'Sabetha, what—'

'I'm making a decision. Now are you going to quit playing with that fucking onion and see what happens if you kiss me, or do I have to put a sword to your neck?'

'Promise I won't wake up on a ship?'

'Disappoint me, Lamora, and I make *no* promises as to where and when you'll wake up.'

He put his hands beneath her arms, swung her off her feet, and lifted her onto the table. Laughing, she hooked her legs behind his waist and pulled him close. Her lips were warm and still carried the faint taste of ginger and oranges; he had no idea how long they kissed, arms around each other's necks, but while they did Locke completely lost track of the fact that he was even standing up.

'Whew,' Sabetha said, when they grudgingly broke apart at last. She put a finger against his lips. 'And look at that, you're still conscious. You're one and one when it comes to kissing in Karthain.'

'That's a tally I mean to improve … Sabetha? Sabetha, what is it?'

She'd gone rigid in his arms. With his head still spinning from the one-two punch of wine and woman, he slowly turned to look over his shoulder.

Patience was standing beside the little round table, dressed in a carnelian-coloured robe with a wide hood.

'Oh, come on,' Locke growled. 'Not now. Surely you have better things to do than bother us *now*.'

'Which one are you?' said Sabetha, calmly and respectfully.

'Archedama Patience. You work for my rival.'

'Patience,' said Locke, 'if this isn't important, I swear to the Crooked Warden, I'll—'

'It is important. In fact, it's critical. It's time we spoke. Since neither of you could be dissuaded from this foolishness, both of you have a right to know.'

'Both of us?' said Sabetha. 'What do we have a right to know?'

'Where Locke really comes from.' Patience gestured for the two of them to move away from the food table. 'And what Locke really is.'

Happenings In Bedchambers

I

'Honoured … cousin,' Locke hissed, 'I need …'

'Do *regale* me with your needs,' said Boulidazi.

'Air!'

'Ah.' The iron pressure against Locke's neck eased just enough to permit a breath.

'It's not what you think,' he gasped.

'Perhaps I've been an idiot,' whispered Boulidazi, 'but you'll not find me eager to resume the role.'

'Gennaro!'

Sabetha stood in the balcony door, and her tone of voice was sufficient to check a rampant horse. Boulidazi actually lowered his blade.

'Verena, I … I'm sorry, but your behaviour—'

'It's *your* behaviour that requires explanation, Cousin!'

'I've been listening to both of you—'

'You've been skulking like a thief!'

'You proclaimed love for one another! I heard your quarrel!'

Too late, Boulidazi seemed to remember that he hadn't yet professed his interest in Verena to Verena herself. Dismay spilled across his face like paint splashed across a blank canvas, and Sabetha didn't neglect the opening.

'It was an acting exercise, you lout! An improvisation! And why should it concern you, were it otherwise?'

'An … improvisation?'

'I asked Lucaza to follow my lead and improvise a scene!' She pushed Boulidazi's arm firmly away from Locke's throat. 'A scene you interrupted! We might be the ones dressed as commoners, Baron Boulidazi, but you've bested us for coarse behaviour!'

'But …'

Locke admired the ingenuity of Sabetha's ploy, but perhaps she was pushing it too far. They needed Boulidazi controlled, not crushed. It was time to resume his role as advocate. He rubbed his aching throat.

'Cousin Verena,' he coughed, 'what Gennaro means is that I told him about my own betrothal. So, when he overheard our exercise, why, he had good cause to suspect some deceit.'

'He had no cause to lay hands on your person!'

'Cousin, be sensible. We discussed this before we set out. We knew that living incognito would require us to surrender some of the dignities of our true station.'

'Yes, but—'

'Furthermore, there are no other witnesses, so I feel no need to require satisfaction.'

Locke tried to sound as natural and confident as possible, though he suspected Boulidazi would rate the prospect of a duel with him as a physical threat on par with a difficult bowel movement. The thought of alienating Verena, however ...

'I seem to have made a mistake.' Boulidazi sheathed his knife. The cold anger of moments before was put away just as thoroughly. 'Verena, I apologize for the misunderstanding. Tell me, please, how can I recover your good opinion?'

Locke blinked at the solitary direction of the apology and the rapid shift to a smooth, wheedling manner. He'd pegged Boulidazi as sincere and straightforward, even a bit of a yokel, but the Esparan had obviously relegated the 'noble' Lucaza to the role of a tool in his designs on Sabetha. That and his ease with violence hinted at dangerous depths.

'For one thing,' said Sabetha, 'you can cease this unseemly scuttling in shadows. You're a lord of Espara and the patron of this company. I'd prefer to see you come and go openly in a manner befitting your blood.'

'Of ... of course.'

'And if you want to make yourself genuinely useful, you could secure us a more appropriate rehearsal space. I'm growing tired of Mistress Gloriano's inn-yard.'

'Where would you prefer—'

'I'm told we're to use a theatre called the Old Pearl.'

'Oh. Naturally. Well, that's just a matter of a gratuity for the countess' envoy of ceremonies—'

'See to that gratuity, Baron Boulidazi,' said Sabetha, subtly softening her posture and tone of voice. 'Surely it's a matter of little consequence for you. It will be a boon to the company to be practising on our real stage as soon as possible. Do this, and I'll be pleased to call you Genn-aro again.'

'Then consider it done.' Boulidazi bowed to her with gallant over-formality, gave Locke a perfunctory clap on the shoulder, and went away in haste. His footsteps receded down the passage, and the door to the inn's second floor banged shut.

'That was close,' whispered Locke.

'Our patron is starting to assume possessive feelings toward his noble cousins,' said Sabetha. 'He's more shifty than I realized.'

'My neck agrees.' With the threat of Boulidazi temporarily quelled, Locke's thoughts returned to the conversation the baron had inter-rupted. 'And, uh, look, you and I have had—'

'Nothing,' hissed Sabetha. 'Evidently I was wrong to say what I did, and wrong to feel those things in the first place.'

'That's bullshit!' Barely feeling the ache across his throat for the new sting of her words, Locke shocked himself by grabbing her arm and pulling her back out onto the balcony. 'I tripped over something. I don't know what it is, but you *owe* me an explanation. After everything we just said to one another, I will *not* let you push me aside just because you're pitching a fit!'

'I am not pitching a fit!'

'You make the Sanzas look like bloody diplomats when you do this. I'll run after Boulidazi and pick another fight with him before I'll let this rest. What set you off?'

'You cannot be so wholly ignorant … Do you know what they pay for red-haired girls in Jerem? Do you know what they do to us if we're pristine? The Thiefmaker did – and it's so awful it was *too much for his conscience*. Understand? That ghoul would tongue-fuck a dead rat if there was silver in it for him, but selling *redheads* was too vile. He's the one that taught me to keep my hair dyed and wrapped.'

'I've heard about these things, but I never, I never thought of you—'

'First they cut,' said Sabetha. 'Right out of a girl's sex. What they call the sweetness, the little hill. You've been around Calo and Galdo long enough, you must have heard a dozen names for it. Then while the wound is gushing, they bring in the old bastard with the rotting cock or the festering sores or whatever he wants miraculously cured, and he does his business. "Blood of the blood-haired child," is what they call it.'

'Sabetha—'

436

'And then, even though *most* of the miracle is already used up, they bring in the next hundred men that want a go at the bloody hole, because it still brings good luck. In fact, it's *especially* good luck if you're the one riding her when she finally dies!'

'Gods.'

'Yes. May they all spend ten thousand years drinking salted shit in the deepest hell there is.' Sabetha slumped against the rear wall of the balcony and stared at their discarded wine cups and scripts. 'Damn. I *am* pitching a fit.'

'You have some cause!'

She gave a sharp, self-disgusted sort of laugh.

'How was *I* supposed to know all this the first time I ever laid eyes on you?' said Locke. 'I remember that first glimpse as though it happened yesterday. But that's not the only thing I think about ... if it really bothers you that much—'

'My *hair* doesn't bother me,' she said forcefully. 'It's the stupid bastards who'd put me in chains on account of that nonsense about it. I've had to mind this every day of my life since I went to Shades' Hill. Every day! All the hours I've wasted peering at my hair in a glass, slopping it with alchemy ... someday I'll be old enough that it won't matter anymore. Someday not soon enough.'

'What about before Shades' Hill?'

'Nothing before the Hill matters,' she said quietly. 'I was protected. Then I was an orphan. Leave it at that.'

'As you prefer.' Slowly, hesitantly, he leaned against the wall beside her. Stars were just beginning to pierce the bruise-coloured sky above them, and the faint, familiar whispers of evening were rising – the hum of insects, the clatter of wagons, the din of eating and laughter and argument.

'I'm sorry, Locke,' she said after a few moments had passed. 'It's stupid and unfair to be so upset with you. I've insulted you.'

'Absolutely not.' He put one hand on her arm and was encouraged to find her resuming the habit of not flinching away. 'I'm *glad* you told me. Your problems should be our problems, and your worries should be *our* worries. You realize how rarely you bother to explain yourself?'

'Now that's a load—'

'A load of straight truth! You could give inscrutability lessons to the gods-damned Eldren. You know, it's sort of frightening how you're actually starting to make sense.'

'Is that meant to be complimentary?'

'Maybe toward both of us,' said Locke. Her weather-like mood swings, the brief seasons of warmth followed by withdrawal and frustration, her urge to control everything in her life with such precision and forethought; behaviour that had mystified Locke for years suddenly had a context. 'I honestly don't care what colour your hair is as long as you're under it somewhere.'

'You forgive me for being ... unreasonable?'

'Haven't you forgiven me for the same thing?'

'We may find ourselves once again in serious danger of a happy understanding,' she said, and the way her smile reached her eyes made Locke's pulse race. Suddenly they seemed to be competing to see who could bring their lips closer to the other's without appearing to do so—

The sound of a rapid, careless tread echoed from within the passage, and they sprang apart in instinctive unison. The passage door slammed open, and Alondo Razi stumbled out, red-cheeked and sweaty.

'Alondo,' said Sabetha with plainly exaggerated sweetness, 'would you consider yourself at peace with the gods?'

'I'm sorry,' he panted, his voice slurred. 'I don't mean to barge in on you, but I can't find Jovanno. It's the Asino brothers. Need help—'

'Don't tell me they started a fight,' said Locke, straining to banish the sudden mental image of a Sanza insulting Lord Boulidazi, and all the intersections of flesh and steel that might result.

'No, gods, no! Sylvanus bet that they couldn't chug the Ash Bastard. *Nobody* can chug the Ash Bastard. So they tried, and got what was coming. Ha!'

Locke seized Alondo by the sweat-stained collar of his tunic and briefly forgot that the Esparan had half a decade of growth on him. 'Razi,' he growled, 'what the cock-blistering hell is an Ash Bastard?'

'Come down,' said the unsteady young actor. 'Best see for yourself.'

Locke and Sabetha followed him to the common room, where they found the company and the evening ale-swillers even more scattered and dissipated than usual. Calo and Galdo were lying on their sides, artfully symmetrical, in the middle of a slick black-red puddle. The smell in the air was somewhere between wet animal fur and an unwashed torture chamber, but all the non-Sanza onlookers were quivering with mirth. Mistress Gloriano was the only exception.

'I said take it out to the yard! Idiots! Pink-skinned Therin infants!' She noticed Locke and Sabetha, and encompassed them with her glower. 'What kind of fool tries the Ash Bastard indoors?'

'What the hell are you people *talking* about?' said Locke. He knelt beside Calo. The twins were alive, though they were liquored out of their wits and had clearly lost a fight with those potent joint antagonists, vomit and gravity.

'The Ash Bastard,' said Jasmer, who was leaning against a nearly comatose Sylvanus, 'is that ghastly spittoon.'

Locke glanced where Jasmer pointed, and saw a tar-coloured cask about two feet long resting sideways on the floor. The stuff spilling from it looked like campfire ashes after a hard rain.

'It's a quaint ritual of the house,' smirked Jasmer.

'Performed in the yard!' bellowed Mistress Gloriano.

'True enough. But the gist of it, dear Lucaza, is that the Bastard collects tobacco ash and spit for weeks, when people remember not to use the floor. We test the mettle of brash young pickle-wits like your friends there by challenging them to chug the Bastard, which means we fill it to the brim with a hideous black juniper wine Mistress Gloriano imports directly from hell. We swirl it around and make them drink the slurry.'

'That's idiotic,' said Sabetha, who was making sure Galdo still had a pulse.

'Completely,' laughed Jasmer. 'No one in the history of the company has ever chugged the Ash Bastard without hucking it right back up. And lo, the Bastard is victorious once again!'

'Jasmer,' said Sabetha, lowering her voice, 'not to put too fine a point on it, but we need these two unpoisoned if they're going to keep rehearsing. In fact, we need everyone! Can't you idiots dry out a bit—'

Sylvanus, though he seemed barely aware of the existence of his own face let alone the world beyond it, gave an elephantine snort.

'Green gills or no,' said Jasmer, 'the company always takes the stage, my dear. Besides, this can hardly even be called a proper debauch by our lofty standards. Your friends hold their liquor like sieves, is the problem.'

'Sorry to make this your trouble,' said Alondo, sinking into a chair, 'but we needed some help with the floor, and moving the Asinos, and we're all too blotted to be much use, and we can't find Jenora or Jovanno ... Hey, did you two see Lord Boulidazi? He was here, too!'

'We know,' said Sabetha. 'Mistress Gloriano, we need some water buckets. Lucaza, we'd better drag these two out to the yard and get to work. They'll be stuck to the floor like barnacles if we let them alone.'

'I was going to thank you again for prying me out of Boulidazi's grasp,' whispered Locke, 'but now I think I'll wait and see how the evening ends first.'

'How do you think I feel?' She squeezed his arm and flashed him a hint of a smile, like a fellow desert traveller sharing out precious water. 'Now, pick arms or legs. Let's heave this one outside.'

'Where the hell is Jovanno?' muttered Locke.

2

Jean had watched Locke ascend the stairs, skin of wine in hand, with a mix of relief and annoyance. It was past time for Locke and Sabetha to sort themselves out, or pitch themselves out of a high window. Jean's own peace of mind would be the benefactor in either case.

He closed his eyes, leaned his head back, and let the wall do the job of holding it up for a moment. What a time he must be having, when merely sitting alone and not pretending that his bruises didn't hurt felt like an immoderate indulgence.

When he opened his eyes again, Jenora was smiling at him from two feet away.

'I've found a threadbare boy!' she said. 'Let me help you back up to your room.'

'Oh, uh, my room?'

'Trust me,' she said, hauling him to his feet. 'Until the rest of the company's too drunk to move, you never want to be the first to fall asleep around 'em. Gods know what mischief you'll wake up to.'

There was a strange heat on his cheeks, like the warmth of too many ales. Jenora's hand was around his waist as though it were the most natural thing in the world, and together they made a quick exit from the common room.

'So what are you not telling me, Jovanno?' She closed the door to Locke and Jean's chamber softly, then put her arms on his shoulders.

'Not telling you?'

'Oh, come now.' Her fingers began to work the knots between his shoulder blades. 'You read, write, and figure, but scribes don't get muscles like *this* pushing quills. I know you speak Vadran as well as Therin. You can handle a needle and thread. You fought a grown man to a standstill ... not just any man, but Bert. Bert's a scrapper and a half.'

'I've had a, ah, strange education,' said Jean, feeling his wits loosening as agreeably as his muscles under Jenora's ministrations.

'You're all strange, you Camorri. And strangely educated.'

'It's nothing sinister. We're just …'

'Slumming, hmm? Isn't that what they usually call it when someone dresses down and plays beneath their station?'

'Jenora!' Jean turned around, grabbed her hands, and halted the massage. His well-soothed wits grudgingly rose to the occasion. If she'd been snooping on them a flat denial would probably be useless. 'Look, imagine whatever you like, but *please* believe me … everyone is better off just taking things at face value.'

'Is there some sort of danger in my being curious?'

'Let's just say there's absolutely no danger in *not* being curious!'

'Rest easy. It's an informed guess, Jovanno. Your cousin Lucaza, well, he seems a little surprised every time he notices that the world isn't revolving around him. And Verena, she's no scullery maid, you know? Manners, diction, learning, poise. Then there's swordsman's calluses on these hands of yours.' She ran her fingers lightly over his palms, and the sensation made Jean's blood run hot in more than one place. 'The gods put you all together from odd parts. There's a story to be told.'

'There isn't. There are so many trusts I'd be breaking … Jenora, please.'

'All right,' she said soothingly. 'I can live with a bit of mystery. Let's work on what ails you, then.'

'What ails … I don't … oh, well, ha—'

She slipped her hands under his tunic and ran them up his back, where they started to gently but firmly put his sore muscles into something resembling their proper order. This had the natural effect of bringing them together; her breasts were warm against his upper chest, and her lips were parted in a half-smile just in front of his nose.

'Heh.' She blew playfully on his optics, fogging them over. 'Not frightened of older, taller women, are you?'

'I, uh, wouldn't really know what to be frightened of.'

'Oh? So you're an untapped vintage, hmmm?'

'Jenora, I'm not used … surely you can see that I'm not thought of as, uh, you know—'

'You know what I *don't* like, Jovanno?' She moved her hands and teased the thin line of hair that ran down his stomach. 'Stupid men, weak men, illiterate men. Men who can't tell a play from a pile of kindling.'

Their lips came together, and as they kissed she slowly, deliberately guided one of his hands until it rested atop a breast. She squeezed for both of them, pushing his fingers, and Jean felt his awareness of the world narrowing to the delightful corridor of heat that seemed to be rising between them.

'Lucaza,' he whispered. 'He might—'

'I have a feeling your friends are going to be up on the roof for a very long time,' she murmured. 'Don't you?'

Soon enough, by some process halfway between legerdemain and wrestling, their clothes were off and they fell into his bed. Jean could barely tell where light skin ended and dark skin began. He lay wrapped in the taste and smell and warmth of her, with smoke-coloured hair falling around him like a teasing shroud. Jenora seemed very much at ease taking the lead, staying on top of him, alternately slowing and quickening the rhythm of their coupling. All too soon he reached the limit of his untrained endurance, and with a joyful, aching eruption there was one less mystery in Jean Tannen's life.

Exhilarated, exhausted, and pleasantly bewildered, he clung to her for some time as their heartbeats slowed from a gallop to a canter. The pains of his tussle with Bertrand the Crowd seemed a hundred years in the past.

Jenora found her jacket in the mixed scatter of their clothing, pulled out a slim wooden pipe, and tamped it full of a tobacco mixture that smelled alien and spicy to Jean. They covered the room's feeble alchemical globe and shared the pipe back and forth in the near-darkness, talking softly by the orange glow of the embers.

'So I really was your first.'

'Was it that obvious? Would you have known, even if I hadn't said?'

'Enthusiasm is the first step,' she said. 'Artfulness comes later.'

'I hope I didn't disappoint you.'

'I'm not displeased, Jovanno. Hells, having a lover that's new to the dance means you can train him properly. Give me a few nights and I'll have you whipped into proper form.'

'The Asino brothers … they always, well, they always invited me to go with them when they went out. To buy it, you know.'

'There's no shame in doing that. And there's no shame in not having done it. But those two are *hounds*, Jovanno. Any woman could smell it a mile away. Sometimes a run with the hounds is just what you're in the mood for, but in the end they'll always roll around in muck and shit on your floor.'

'Oh, they've got an endearing side,' said Jean. 'It comes out once a month, when the first moon is full. They're like backwards werewolves.'

'Well,' she said, 'when I take someone into my bed, I prefer brains and balls in more equal proportion.'

'I like the sound of that. Hey, there's a … sorry, beneath your legs, did we …?'

'Ah. My apprentice, allow me to introduce you to the concept of the wet spot.'

'Is that uncomfortable?'

'Well, it's not what I'd call ideal. Hey, what are you—'

With an enthusiastic excess of groping and giggling, he applied his strength to shifting their positions. In a few moments, he'd pushed her to the dry side of the bed and taken her former place.

'Mmmm. Jovanno, you have a gallant streak. Another smoke?'

'Absolutely.'

They were just finishing carefully lighting the second bowl when the door burst open.

'Jovanno,' shouted Locke, 'it's the Asino brothers, you wouldn't be-lieve what they *oh my gods holy shit!*'

He stared for a second or two, then whirled away and faced out into the hall.

'I'm sorry. I'm so sorry, I didn't realize—'

'The idiot twins,' said Jean, 'are they in trouble?'

'No,' said Locke, with less than believable haste. 'No, no, no. Actu-ally, it's not important at all. We've got it handled. You, uh, you just … hell, I can sleep in the common room, you two just forget I exist. Sorry. Have, uh, have a good time!'

'We are,' said Jenora, calmly exhaling a line of smoke.

'Great! Well! Excellent! Just … going now!'

'He's down off the roof a lot sooner than I would have thought,' said Jenora once the door was closed again.

'Yeah,' said Jean, frowning. 'Something must have happened. What-ever the Asinos did—'

'Your friends,' said Jenora. 'They sort of look to you to hold them together when there's trouble, don't they?'

'Well, that's a pretty flattering way of putting it, but—'

443

'Let 'em fend for themselves for a night,' she whispered. 'Now we'll have privacy. If Verena wants to sort Lucaza out she can always take him to my room.'

'She can,' said Jean. 'She sure as hell *can*. So, uh, is it too soon to start hearing about this artfulness you mentioned?'

3

'Long summer of the Therin Throne,' shouted Calo, arms outflung to encompass the inn-yard, 'ordained time for building and growing, while earth and sky are generous. These years for princely Aurin lie fallow as a field, ploughed and yet unseeded with *valourrrrrruurrrrrrgh*—'

Calo lurched to his knees and ended what had been a fine, vigourous declamation by vomiting. Locke, watching from the shade of a wall, put his hands to his forehead and groaned.

'Gods above,' said Moncraine, 'I've seen songbirds with more iron in their gullets than you Camorri. One dance with the Ash Bastard and you're acting like you've been killed in the wars. Understudy!'

Galdo, his complexion a shade green in its own right, seemed uninterested for once in making sport of Calo's discomfort. He stepped forward and placed his hands on his brother's shoulders.

'I can do it. … I'm fine …' panted Calo. He spat and wobbled to his feet.

'Like hell, idiot,' said Galdo. 'Here's a thought. Let's do it together.'

'What do you mean?'

'Toss it back and forth.' Galdo faced Moncraine, and spoke with the precise tone and volume of his twin before the stumble: 'Swords unblooded hang in scabbards unworn, and, sun-like in its dispensations, the imperial court sheds grandeur on the world.'

'Sweet summer of the Therin Throne,' said Calo, interrupting smoothly, conquering his wobbly knees and willing the hoarseness from his throat. 'Some that live as beggars within would scorn to live as dukes without, such an empire it is, and some wear stolen splendour with the dignity of right-born kings! Below the streets the skulkers, the cozeners, the vagabonds of fortune raise bold business in catacomb kingdoms unknown to honest daylight.'

'If thieves pretend to eminence,' said Galdo, 'and meet in eager regiments, defying rightful law and crown, is it not suiting to the temper of the age? So high the tides of fortune rise beneath the Therin Throne,

444

its outlaws pay tribute with matching insolence!'

'Matching insolents,' said Moncraine. 'That'd be you Asinos. Hold, everyone, hold. This is all *very* pretty. Why don't we just dispense with the notion of parts altogether? We can stand on stage in a group and chant the lines for all the roles. Hells, we can even hold hands to keep our spirits up while it rains rocks and vegetables on us.'

'I rather liked it,' said Chantal.

'As if I gave a—'

'She's right, Moncraine.' Sylvanus stirred, emerging from the shade as well as his usual torporous morning fuddle. 'How often do you see a pair of twins on stage? We should make something of it. We've got precious little spectacle as it stands.'

'When we're in want of spectacle, Andrassus, I'll start walking around without my breeches.'

'You useless Syresti coxcomb! Think on it – twins for a chorus. Something never seen before, to let the peons know they're not watching Old Father Dullard's Piss-Weak Boredom Revival, but a proper something from the Moncraine Company!'

'Actually, it's the Moncraine-Boulidazi Company these days,' said Chantal.

'Any time you want to return to being an ambulatory pair of tits, turncoat, you can mince straight back to Basanti and ask how many lusty maids are still on offer.' Locke noticed that Moncraine's shoulders sagged despite his tone of voice. However the impresario might ridicule Sylvanus, the old lush had occasional sway over him. 'Ah, gods, past the third or fourth row of groundlings, who can tell they're twins, anyway?'

'It's what they do with their voices,' said Alondo. 'You have to admit it's good, when they're not pitching vomit everywhere.'

'We've got to do something about their hair,' said Moncraine.

'Glue a wig on baldy,' said Calo.

'Hold the fop down and shave him,' muttered Galdo.

'Hats,' said Sabetha in a politely commanding tone. 'They can both wear hats. It's a question of costuming.'

'And that would require the attention of the costumers,' rumbled Moncraine. 'I'm sure they're off somewhere attending to clothes at this very instant, but whether they're taking them off or putting them on is the question.'

'Moncraine!' A stout middle-aged Therin strolled into the inn-yard.

He had no chin to speak of, and long hair so ill-kept it looked as though a brown hawk had perched on the back of his head and clung there until it died. 'Jasmer, you lucky bastard, I didn't believe 'em when they said you were off the hook. How many cocks did you have to lick to get them to slip the chains?'

'Master Calabazi,' said Moncraine, 'you know a gentleman never does his own dirty work. I simply made a lot of promises concerning your daughters. Or was it your sons? Gods know I can't tell them apart.'

'Ha! If you're a gentleman, I fart incense. But you're out, and now someone's conjured a wild fantasy about you playing the Pearl. Is this the show? A little one?'

'It's not the size, but the employment,' said Moncraine, losing some of his forced good cheer. 'Why are you bothering me?'

'Well, you know what me and my lads need.'

'Speak to Jenora; she's the woman of business.'

'Well, I thought with that fancy new owner you've got you might lay a surety—'

'*Patron*, Calabazi. We've got a noble patron, not a new owner. And you wouldn't get a surety if Emperor Salerius himself crawled out of his tomb to watch the show. You get paid when the rest of us do, on performance nights.'

'It's just that there's some, ah, uncertainty, in your situation, and we'd like something firmer than a heartfelt assurance we'll be working—'

'I was in gaol for two days, you idiot; I didn't breathe Wraithstone smoke and lose my wits. If you want the work, you can have the usual terms, and if you don't, I won't lie awake at night wondering where I'll get three or four half-wits to shovel shit!'

The two men moved chin to chin and continued arguing in low, impassioned tones. Locke gestured to Alondo, who was lounging nearby, and whispered, 'What's this?'

'It's the trenchmen, Lucaza.' Alondo yawned. 'The Countess might be pleased to hand out the Old Pearl for shows, but she doesn't pay to keep the place clean. We do. That means empty trenches for a few hundred to piss in every night, dammed up and tended by apes like Calabazi.'

'This whole thing is more complicated than I ever imagined.'

'Too true. And Jasmer hates the business side of business, you know? He negotiates like he's having his balls scraped.'

Across the inn-yard, Jasmer brought the conversation with Calabazi to a halt by raising both palms to the ugly trenchman's face and turning away.

'Master Moncraine!' shouted yet another newcomer, appearing from the direction of the stables. Moncraine whirled.

'Gods' peace, you fucking fool, can't you see I'm work – Oh, *gods*, Baron Boulidazi, I didn't recognize you! You've, ah, come in costume again.'

'Ha! I wanted to be in keeping with the spirit of our endeavours!' Boulidazi, once again dressed in a low fashion, wore a dirty broad-brimmed hat that partly concealed his features. 'And of course, to intrude as little as possible on your affairs.'

'Of course,' said Moncraine, and Locke was certain he could hear teeth grinding even from across the inn-yard.

'And who's this? Anyone important?'

'Uh, I'm Paza Calabazi, uh, sir. I handle—'

'No, not important, or you'd know it's "my lord". Go be undistinguished somewhere else.'

'Uh ... yes, my lord.'

Locke frowned as he watched Calabazi all but scuttle away. His original impression of Boulidazi seemed more naïve than ever.

'Now, Moncraine.' The young lord gave the impresario a firm slap on the back. 'I know this inn-yard has a certain unrefined charm, but I've arranged for better surroundings.'

'The Old Pearl?' Moncraine made a visible effort to swallow his resentment. 'Is it ours, my lord?'

'We can rehearse there commencing tomorrow, and we'll get two days of actual performance. The envoy of ceremonies is a family friend. I'll even post a man to make sure that you're not pestered by the Paza Calabazis of the world.'

'That's ... well, I suppose that's very generous, my lord patron. Thank you.'

'Think nothing of it. It's in my own interest, eh? Now, what's the scene?'

'Uh, there's no scene, my lord. We, ah, need a break, I think. Arguing with Calabazi—'

'Nonsense. You're no man to be tamed by a mere argument, Moncraine.' Boulidazi mimed a fist crashing into his own jaw, a gesture that made Moncraine plainly uncomfortable. 'What did you last practise?'

'Nothing of real consequence—'

'The scene, gods damn you.'

'Uh, six. Act one, scene six. We were just nailing down … nailing down the situation of the chorus.'

'"Vagabonds of fortune raise a bold business in catacomb kingdoms unknown to honest daylight,"' said Boulidazi. 'I like that one. But that means Amadine's about to come out for the first time. Surely you won't stop now.'

'Well, perhaps not—'

'Yes. Perhaps not.' Boulidazi settled into the chair that Moncraine had occasionally rested in while watching the morning's work. 'Mistress Verena, might I beg a few moments of your Queen of Shadows?'

'Why, m'lord Boulidazi, your attention is always very welcome,' said Sabetha with a perfect curtsey. Locke would have sworn he felt the blood congealing in his heart, and he fought to maintain a façade of dopish complacency.

'Thieves in place for scene six,' shouted Moncraine. Bert the Crowd hurried into the middle of the yard, and was met by Calo and Galdo, who were intended to join the spear-carriers for several mob scenes after finishing their orations. Moncraine had promised to hire a bevy of bit players to flesh out the crowds, but didn't seem to want to start paying them too early in the rehearsal process.

'Well met, my noble peers and bastards! Well met at Barefoot Court!' Chantal advanced from her side of the inn-yard, hips swaying, arms outthrust, playing to the tiny crowd. 'What stirs, you ragged suitors, to bring you hence from drink and dice and warm attentions?'

'Allegiance, fair Penthra,' said Bertrand. 'Allegiance, fair and fallen lady, for she that claims our deep regard makes those comforts seem cold distractions.'

'Valedon, you ever were a wool-tongued devil, now here's the air hung with silk. What makes the change?' Chantal touched her husband playfully on the chin.

'My mistress and yours,' said Bertrand. 'Her goodness puts a sting to my conscience. I have been remiss in my tributes, and must amend my courtesies.'

'So would we all,' said Calo. 'Penthra, let her come forth. She has sheltered us, and kindled loyal fellowship, and even such poor wretches as ourselves must make obedience.'

'We are all wretches at our ragged court, and none therefore a poorer

448

contrast.' Sabetha's voice was effortlessly regal as she glided into the scene, out of what would eventually be the shadows of the actual stage. Not even the distraction of Boulidazi could truly dampen Locke's pleasure at watching Sabetha vanish into the role she'd so coveted.

'Grace like fire's heat, I am made ashamed of my tribute,' said Calo, sinking to his knees. 'You are Amadine, called Queen Beneath the Stones, or I was never born. My gift deserves not the name, for such a beauty. It pales, and with it my pride. I beg a second chance, to steal a more worthy courtesy!'

'Indeed, his offering is slight as a passing fancy,' said Bertrand. 'Be assured of my love, bright Amadine, and take my tribute first.'

'Unkind Valedon, this is no race with lines to cross before all others. Stand easy. Surely a moment's wait can little harm your preparations.'

Bertrand bowed and took a step back.

'I am Amadine, called many things,' said Sabetha, gesturing for Calo to rise. 'There is no honour more worthy than this, your gift of friendship. I see you are new among us.'

'Many years a thief, mistress, but far too many passed before kind fortune brought me to your company. Oh, let me trade this bauble for something more fitting, or gladly hang for trying.'

'Never speak of such an evil,' said Sabetha. 'And never speak of shame, but give what you have.'

Calo pretended to hesitantly pass something over, and Sabetha mimed holding it up between thumb and forefinger.

'A speck of a silver ring,' scoffed Bertrand. 'Careworn as a scullion's hands.'

'I more proudly take a speck from a man with empty pockets,' said Sabetha, 'than riches from a man whose purse stays heavy. What good thing might not be coined from this courtesy? It shall become bread and wine, and clothing, and sharp steel. It shall harden the sinews of our fellowship, and for that I hold it dear. You are welcome to our band, brother.'

'Gods willing, I shall never leave it!'

'Gods willing.' Sabetha held out her other hand and Calo kissed it. She turned to Bert. 'Now, Valedon, let's know your heart. Some months you've spent among us, yet aloof, a proud and solitary sort.'

'Proud and solitary as yourself, artful Amadine, though I admit my poor fellowship. Here's the remedy! Oh, how I've strained my talents to produce a worthy gift!'

'A bracelet,' said Chantal as her husband pretended to display it with a flourish. 'Black sapphires set in gold.'

'As suits a queen of shadows,' said Bertrand. 'Pray it please you. I beg you wear it, even once, though you later strike it to a royal ransom of coins.'

'Great weight to grace a single wrist. Our thanks, Valedon; your obscure character is made clear. How did you come by this treasure?'

'Three days and nights of pains,' said Bertrand, 'watching a great house, until I saw my chance for the seizing.'

'Will you wear it first, to show me its workings?'

'Why, the clasp is simple, gracious Amadine. Give me your hand, I shall anoint it.'

'I would see this treasure on your wrist, ere it touches mine. Or has your deep regard run shallow?'

'This beauty is not meant for such an unworthy display!'

'Unworthy indeed.' At a gesture from Sabetha, Chantal seized Bertrand and feigned holding a blade to his neck.

'Ladies, please, how have I offended?'

'Your face is a parchment,' said Sabetha, 'with treason there written plain. You dread the bauble's touch, and the venom of its coiled needle!' She mimed snatching the bracelet and unfolding it for all to see. 'You think us dullards, that by this infant's stratagem you might have my life? My spies advised me of your falseness.'

'I swear that when I stole the bracelet, I knew not what lay within!'

'Stole? Should I not know a thief by every scar and callus of the trade? I have them all, Valedon, familiar as children. Your hands are dough and your sinews slack. This bracelet you had as a gift from your masters.'

Calo and Galdo did their best impression of a general outcry in the crowd, and seized Bertrand by the arms.

'I see now my deception was foredoomed,' he whispered. 'Clasp the bracelet to my wrist and let justice be done.'

'Hasty dispatch is mercy undeserved. You'll have your bracelet back, miscarried murderer, after reflection. Bind him! Heat a crucible, and therein cast this scorpion bauble. Past his traitor's lips, pour the molten slurry of his instrument. Aye, gild his guts with melted treasure, then leave him on the street for his masters to ponder.'

'I beg you—'

The last plea of the unfortunate Valedon was drowned out by the noise of Calo once again throwing up. Bert and Chantal hopped backward, minding their feet, while Galdo put a hand to his mouth and went pale.

'Ha,' shouted Boulidazi. 'Ha! I think one of your twins has something to feel guilty about, Moncraine.'

'Very sorry, my lord,' moaned Calo.

'Perhaps you should try living virtuously for a few days, my friends.' Boulidazi rose and stretched. 'Well done, despite the sudden ending. Indeed! Especially you ladies. By the gods, I think we've got something here. In fact, I'm going to join you at the Pearl for the rest of your rehearsals.'

The sudden pain between Locke's temples was a match for the expression on Moncraine's face.

4

'We'll find our chance to be alone,' Sabetha whispered to him more than once in the days that followed, but such chances seemed to deliberately fling themselves out of the way as the rehearsals wore on.

The Old Pearl was a testament to the generosity of the long-dead count who'd left it to the city. Though hardly a patch on the Eldren notion of longevity, the theatre had been built to be taken for granted for centuries. Its walls and raised galleries were white marble, now weathered a mellow grey, and its stage was built from alchemically lacquered hardwood that might last nearly as long.

The circular courtyard was open to the sky, and though awning poles were in place to offer potential shelter from sun and rain, the awnings themselves were absent. According to Jenora, such comforts for the groundling crowd, like sanitary ditches, were one of the 'free' theatre's hidden expenses that the countess had no interest in bearing herself.

There was no denying that the place was far more suitable than Mistress Gloriano's inn-yard. The Pearl had a surplus of dignity to lend, even to their more ragged rehearsals, and what might have seemed silly pantomime twenty feet from a stable was somehow ennobled in the shadow of silent marble galleries.

Still, every new advantage seemed to come with a complication for a sibling. Each day began too early, with hungover company members packing unfinished costumes, props, and sundries into the wagon provided by the Camorri. The walk to the Pearl was two miles, and at the close of each day's rehearsal they would have to stuff everything back into their wagon and reverse the journey. They were permitted to rehearse at the Pearl, not reside there, and the city watch would turn them out like vagabonds if they showed any sign of spending a night. Precious hours were therefore gnawed away by travel.

Although Locke and Sabetha avoided the worst of the debauches that were a nightly ritual (Mistress Gloriano, for all her loud moralizing, seemed incapable of refusing service to any drunkard who could still manage to roll a coin in her direction), there was little freedom or leisure to be found at the inn. For one thing, there was the simple press of time, and sleep was a precious commodity after long rehearsals and tedious trudging. For another, there was Boulidazi.

True to his word, the young baron became a company fixture, 'disguised' in common clothing, and while Locke went to bed each night more exhausted than he'd been since his months as a farmer, Boulidazi seemed to have the stamina of ten mules. Word got around, somehow, that the Moncraine Company had come back to life with a slumming lord at the heart of its court, so opportunists, curiosity-seekers, and unemployed actors joined the taproom mess every evening, driving Moncraine to distraction.

Boulidazi, however, was never distracted. His eyes were fixed on Sabetha.

5

'Calamaxes, old counsel,' said Sylvanus Olivios Andrassus, squatting on a folding stool in character as His Paramount Majesty Salerius II, Emperor of All Therins. 'Not a bright day passes but you find some cloud to throw before Our sun.'

'Majesty.' Jasmer sketched a bow, expressing more tolerance than awe. 'It is of sons I wish to speak. Princely Aurin has reached a hungry age, and wants employment.'

'Employment? He's heir to Our throne, that's his trade.'

'He wants distinction, Majesty. A blade unblooded and waiting to be drawn, is Aurin.'

'You take liberties, spell-sayer. Say you that birth to the blood royal sufficeth not to mark his merit?'

'Your pardon, Sovereign. By my soul, Aurin is worthy heir to worthy line. I say only that he longs to match attainment to inheritance, as the father did, and stir this stately court with new triumph.'

'He,' mused Sylvanus, 'and dear ambitious Ferrin.'

'Rightly and loyally ambitious,' said Jasmer. 'Have you not been served in your own course by friends and generals?'

'And sorcerers.'

'Majesty.'

'Well, it's no fault of Ours that foes of old are lately grown so feeble!'

'Those foes would say otherwise, Majesty. You have been the architect of their sorrows.'

'Well, well. Some serpents flatter, ere they bite. So now let's have your fangs.'

'Majesty, there is a discontent in Therim Pel that gnaws, as vermin at a house's timbers. The matter of the thieves.'

'Gods above! Have We not seen your spells in battle wrought, and men scythed dead like harvest grain? Have We not seen thunder and lightning leashed to your whim? Now you tell Us to cringe from vagabonds.'

'Not cringe, Majesty, never cringe. But attend, for here's a sickness that's catching. Word I have of gatherings in great numbers, of boldness unbecoming, of deliberate contempt for your imperial throne.'

'All thieves scorn the law, else they would not be thieves. Why cry this stale revelation?'

'Majesty, they make society beneath bright Therim Pel and name a sovereign for their counterfeit court!'

'In jest. We too much dignify this nonsense with Our consideration.'

'Majesty, please, if you suffer scorn from base pretenders, how can it not breed by example in higher stations? I grant that you may laugh in private—'

'You *grant*?'

'Pardon, Majesty. I submit. I counsel most earnestly. Rightly should you *think* this insolence trivial, but rightly for the sake of hard-won peace should you crush it in its womb! Lest it spread to those whose spirits are more matched to your own.'

'Slay wastrels now or courtiers later, you say? Who, then, would be this sovereign of thieves, and how are they grown so fearsome that your own agencies cannot weed them?'

453

'A woman, Majesty, a woman of worthy temper, whose thralls call her Queen of Shadows. She guards well against my simpler servants. One of them was slain last night and left on a street, as warning and challenge.'

'And what of spells?' Sylvanus let the word hang heavy in the air for a moment. 'By Our command, could you not slay her at leisure, swift as a cold wind?'

'By your command,' said Jasmer, grudgingly, 'she could die this instant, yet thus would I murder opportunity.'

'What, then, do you submit and counsel earnestly?'

'Let Aurin and Ferrin be your instruments, Majesty. Their faces are little-known to the lawless. Let them enter this thieves' warren, and win this woman to their confidence, and execute judgment on her.'

'The dust is not yet settled from the corpse of your former agent, and you would put my son in his place?'

'Peace, Majesty. Has not princely Aurin wondrous skill at arms? Is not Ferrin iron-strong as suits his name? I am the soul of prudence with your issue, and would set my arts and eyes upon him from afar, though he'll know it not. He could not be safer in his own chambers … and he might do much good.'

'Strange conceit, to make an emperor's son an assassin.'

'To make it known the coming lion has some fox to him, matches subtlety to strength, and dares personal return for personal insult!'

'Aurin desires this?' said Sylvanus softly.

'He burns for a test, Majesty. The gracious gods have put one before us. I would set him to it.'

'Long have you served Us, best and brightest of Our magi, sharpest wit and quickest counsel. Yet should this go bad for Aurin, know for a certainty you will share his doom, though it took all the magi of the empire to bind you.'

'Sovereign, if my counsel from its design so wretchedly strayed I would not wish to live.'

'Then make preparation to guard with watchful spell, and We shall see it done. Bring Aurin and Ferrin before Us.'

Locke crept out from the shade of the stage pillars and into the heat. The Pearl's western galleries wore shadows like masks, but the middle of the stage was at the mercy of the late-afternoon sun. Alondo came from the opposite side, met him in front of Jasmer and Sylvanus, and together they continued the scene.

454

Scene by scene, day after day, the drama unfolded in fits and starts, as though capricious gods were toying with the lives of Salerius II and his court. Skipping forward, reversing time, shifting parts and places, demanding repetition of certain moments until every participant was ready to throw punches, Jasmer Moncraine conjured the rough shape of the story and then started to carve fine.

For Locke the days became rhythmic frustration, as he and Sabetha were herded by Boulidazi, as he dutifully applied himself to becoming a character he didn't want to play. It was not unlike inhabiting a role as Chains had taught him, and in other circumstances it might have been fascinating. Yet each time he watched Alondo take Sabetha by the hand, or shoulder, or practise stage-kisses and embraces, he learned anew how slowly time could crawl when there was some misery to dwell on.

'You don't seem yourself, Lucaza,' said Boulidazi softly as the company trudged home one dusty evening. Low style or not, Boulidazi and his men never went so far as to be without horses, and the baron hopped down now, leading his animal by the bridle to walk beside Locke. 'You tripped over some lines you should have cold.'

'It's ... not the lines, my lord.' So annoyed was Locke, so tired of rehearsal and the cloudless Esparan sky, that he was confiding in Boulidazi before he could help himself. 'I expected to be Aurin.' He stretched this confidence out with a minor lie, lest Boulidazi should suspect him of desiring more proximity to Sabetha. 'I, uh, read and studied Aurin on the journey here. I practised him. He's got all the better lines. I'm just ... not at ease as Ferrin.'

'You and I share some tastes, I think,' said Boulidazi, grinning that damned insolent grin of his.

Only one that matters, thought Locke, and fought down a fresh vision of a career as a murderer of aristocrats.

'I don't think you're a Ferrin either,' Boulidazi continued. 'He should be older than Aurin, bigger, the more confident of the two. That Alondo is more suited to the part, if you'll pardon the reflection. I'm sure if he'd been offered the choice, he'd rather have your birth and money than a few more inches of height and muscle, eh?'

'Quite,' muttered Locke.

'Chin up, noble cousin. Face forward.' Boulidazi glanced casually around to ensure nobody important was within earshot. 'Luck's a changing thing. Just look at your man Jovanno, eh? Hooked that fine smoke-skin seamstress, gods know how. Hardly the sort of thing you'd want to give the family name to, but tight and wet where it counts. And she must be hot for it, sure as hell.'

'Jovanno's got some qualities that aren't plain to the eye,' said Locke, forcing a bantering tone.

'Carrying a proper sword, is he? Those well-fed types do tend to crowd their breeches, or so I hear. Well, anyway ... how's our Verena doing?'

'You can't have missed her onstage.' Indeed, she was doing well, the most effortlessly natural of the Gentlemen Bastards as a thespian and by far the most pleasing to the eye and the romantic sensitivities. Even Chantal's scepticism had given way, first to tolerance and then to open respect.

'Naturally. I meant the down hours, the nights and mornings. Surely she can't find Gloriano's quite the thing, even as a lark. Gods know I enjoy my rolling in the muck, but I don't sleep there, eh? She might well wish a respite ... even just for a night. A proper meal, a bath, silk sheets. I've many rooms at the house sitting empty. You could make the suggestion.'

'I could.'

'And I could have a word with old Moncraine about a change in roles for you.'

'Well, now, my lord, that would hardly ... that is, I'm not sure Moncraine is open to persuasion on the matter.'

'You've got some liberal notions for a Camorri, my friend. I don't persuade; I command. Except, of course, in pursuit of fair hand and heart.' Boulidazi chuckled, but turned serious in an instant. 'So you'll speak to her, then?'

'I'll do whatever can be done.' Which was nothing, Locke thought to himself, absolutely nothing. Sabetha would never let herself be procured on the sly for Boulidazi's pleasure, but the baron hardly knew that. And if he could swap Locke into the role of Aurin! A warm feeling of unexpected satisfaction grew in Locke's gut. 'Cousin Verena is very particular about her comforts, my lord. I'm sure she's quite ready to, ah, call at your house a second time.'

'You would do me such a service, Lucaza.' Boulidazi's slap on Locke's back was hard and careless, but Locke bore it like the gentle anointing of a priest. 'She needn't fear indiscretion, either coming or going. My men have handled this sort of thing before.'

No doubt, thought Locke.

<h1 style="text-align:center">6</h1>

'It's not that I mind reusing so much of your old mess,' said Jean the next morning, driving an iron needle through a pad of salvaged canvas. 'I'm just curious as to why you're so averse to pinching a little more money out of our esteemed patron for new stuff.'

'Because he'd give back two pinches for our one,' said Jenora, who was picking through a pile of seedy costume lace. The two were comfortably seated in the shade behind the Pearl's stage, surrounded by their usual jumble of clothes and props. By a process of steady cannibalism, they were turning the dusty remains of all the troupe's previous productions into suitable and perhaps even ambitious trimmings for this one. At present they were making *phantasma*.

It was traditional in Therin theatre for the players of dead characters to dress up as *phantasma*, in pale death-masks and robes, to silently haunt the rest of the production as ghostly onlookers.

'There's two sorts of patron,' she continued. 'Some rain money like festival sweets and don't mind if they lose on the deal, so long as the production goes well. They do it to impress someone, or because they can piss coins as they please. Others take what you might call a more interested position. They expect full and strict repayment.

'Now, our lord and master ain't the one who's keeping track, but some creature of his damn well is, down to the last bent copper. I've seen the papers. We can have all we like to make the production grand, sure, but if we spend past what we're apt to take in from the crowds, there won't be profits enough to cover us plain-blood sorts after Boulidazi gets his.'

'But you said you had some sort of precedence as original stakeholders—'

'Oh, we're guaranteed a cut of profits; it's just that profits have a way of magically turning into something else before that cut gets made. Boulidazi gets security on his expenses under Esparan law. The rest of us divide the leavings. So you see, if we tap our noble patron for too many pretty expensive things, we only piss our own portion away.'

'Savvy,' said Jean. Camorr lacked that particular privilege for business-minded nobles; no doubt the wealth of its lenders and money-changers gave them teeth that Espara's commoners had yet to grow. 'I can see why you're so keen to economize.'

'A bit of pain to the wrists and elbows might save us the pain of a sharp stick in the purse when this is all—'

Uncharacteristic noises from the stage snapped Jean and Jenora out of their habitual prop-making reverie. Jasmer Moncraine had stomped across the stage with Boulidazi close behind, interrupting whatever scene was being rehearsed. Jean had seen them all so many times by now he'd learned to ignore them, but there was no ignoring this.

'You've no right to interfere with my artistic decisions,' yelled Moncraine.

'None of your decisions are privileged by our arrangement, artistic or otherwise,' said Boulidazi.

'It's the damned principle of the matter—'

'Principle gets you kind words at your temple of choice, not power over me.'

'Gods damn your serpent's eyes, you up-jumped dilettante!'

'That's right.' Boulidazi stepped in close to Moncraine, making it impossible for the impresario to miss if his temper should snap again. 'Abuse me. Forget the fact that you're a nightskin peasant. Say something I can't forgive. Better yet, hit me. You'll be back at the Weeping Tower like an arrow-shot, and I'll have the company. You think you can't be replaced? You've got five scenes. I'll hire another Calamaxes away from Basanti. The play will go on without you, and you'll go on without one of your hands.'

Jasmer stood with terrible rigidity, lines and wattles of his dark face deepening as his jaw clenched harder and harder, and for a moment it seemed he was about to doom himself. At last he took a step back, exhaled sharply, and barked, 'Alondo! Lucaza!'

Locke and Alondo appeared before him with haste.

'Swap your roles,' growled Moncraine. 'Lucaza's Aurin from now on, and Alondo's got Ferrin. If you don't like it, discuss the aesthetic ramifications with our honourable gods-damned patron.'

'But we just did up the Aurin costume yesterday, sized for Alondo,' said Jenora. Moncraine whirled and stalked toward her, plainly itching to pass on some of the abuse he'd just received from Boulidazi.

'Then take a knife to it,' he shouted, 'or put Lucaza on a fucking rack and grow him four inches. I don't give a damn either way!'

Jenora and Jean both leapt up, but before either could speak Moncraine turned and stormed away. Boulidazi smirked, shook his head, and gestured for the actors to continue practising.

Eyes wide, Jean eased himself back into his seat only slowly. The baron had never before so publicly taunted or countermanded his unfortunate 'partner,' and coarse as he was Boulidazi always seemed to work to a design. What was this ploy in aid of?

'I, uh, I'm sorry about this, Alondo,' said Locke, breaking the silence before it stretched too long.

'Bah,' said the young Esparan. 'Not as though it's your fault. Jasmer tells me to play a baby rabbit, I'm a baby rabbit, you know? And I'm still in most of the best scenes anyway. If I had to go begging work from Basanti I wouldn't even have a lusty maid part waiting for me, eh?'

7

Locke and Sabetha conferred in a rare, brief moment of privacy on the changing nature of Boulidazi's expectations. Changed as they were, the Esparan baron's old habits didn't shift, and it was simply too dangerous to attempt to steal more meaningful privacy at Gloriano's Rooms. Boulidazi or one of his several associates might appear at any time, from around any corner, up or down any flight of stairs.

Still, the baron had delivered on his promise to transmute Locke's role, and had to be kept thinking that Lucaza de Barra was his earnest ally. To this end Sabetha began to play a closer and more dangerous game of flirtation with Boulidazi. While not allowing that the time was right for her to enjoy a secret sojourn under the baron's roof, she doted on him more frequently, met his eyes more often, pretended to smile at his alleged jokes. She also deployed more of her arsenal of feminine fascinations, carefully letting her smock hang an inch or two lower on her chest, trading boots for cheap slippers to display her ankles and elegantly muscled calves. These steps, coupled with the casual ease with which Jean and Jenora went off together each night, kept the twin flames of distraction and jealousy flickering lively in Locke's breast.

His new role as Aurin turned out to be no help in the matter. While it sent a thrill shuddering up and down his every nerve to be working so close to Sabetha, professing love in the marvellously lurid language of Lucarno, the hawk-eyed vigil of Boulidazi was a check on every other expression of passion. In fact, he was so careful and so chaste in his stage embraces that Moncraine, his patience burnt to ash and the ashes ground deep into the dirt of his mood, soon snapped.

'Gods' piss, you gangling twit, the love's the whole matter of the play! Who the hell wants to pay good money to see a tragic love story if the lovers handle each other like fine porcelain? Bert! Chantal! Educate this idiot.'

Husband and wife came forward eagerly upon realizing they weren't to share the rebuke. Chantal swooned into Bertrand's arms, and he turned toward Locke and Sabetha.

'Exaggerate,' he said, 'and lean. Leaning's what makes a good embrace, kid. Stage kissing you've got down. When she's in your arms, tilt her a bit. Take her off her feet. It looks good to the audience. Quickest way to show passion that even the drunks at the far back can see. Isn't that right, jewel?'

'Oh, Bert, you couldn't explain swimming to a fish. But you've always been one for *doing*, hmmm?' Giggling and poking playfully at one another, the two of them nonetheless managed to rapidly correct the flaws in Locke's pretend-girl-embracing technique. Even Moncraine grunted satisfaction, and Locke found himself suddenly able to be arm to arm, chest to chest, cheek to cheek with Sabetha without Boulidazi raising the slightest objection. Yet anyone who has ever pretend-held an intensely desirable other person will know how little it assuages the longing for genuine contact, genuine surrender, and so even this improvement was no balm to Locke's mood or desires.

Thus the situation carried on, gaining momentum like a cart nudged off the top of a hill. The crowds at Gloriano's grew larger and more boisterous. Calo and Galdo indulged their appetite for dice and cards, closely watched by the others to ensure they didn't indulge their appetite for never losing. Jean and Jenora churned out costume after costume, restored theatrical weapons to full polish, and spun minor miracles out of dusty scraps. The daily rehearsals became tighter, scripts and notes were discarded, costume and prop trials were made. At last, one evening as the bronze disk of the sun slid westward, Moncraine summoned the company to the stage.

'Can't say for sure that we're getting any better,' he growled, 'but at least we're no longer getting any worse. I think it's time we gave public notice. My lord Boulidazi, you and the stakeholders must consent.'

'I do,' said the baron. Alondo, Jenora, and Sylvanus nodded.

'Gods save us,' said Moncraine. 'What this means, dear Camorri, is that we hire our bit players and spear-carriers. Then we announce the times of our shows, and if we don't manage to put them on, we're bloody liable. To the ditch-tenders, the beer- and bread-mongers, the cushion furnishers, the envoy of ceremonies, and the countess herself, gods forbid.'

'I presume we'll need some handbills?' said Jean.

'Handbills? Who reads? Put those up in most neighbourhoods and the good citizens would use them for ass-wiping. We send criers around the poor districts, notes to the nicest. Maybe just a few handbills around the trade streets, but in the main we keep the oldest of old fashions.'

'What's that, then?' said Galdo.

8

'Are you tired of life itself?' yelled Galdo, attempting to strike the most dynamic pose possible while perched atop a weathered market stall barrel. 'Are you dull to spectacle? Are you deaf to the timeless poetry of Caellius Lucarno, master wordsmith of the Therin Throne?'

A light warm rain was pattering down around him, rippling the mud of the market square, where dozens of Esparans were hawking food, junk, or services from under tarps in various states of repair. It seemed only natural to Galdo that after endless days of merciless sun the sky should close up and start pissing the instant he went out trying to look impressive.

'Because even if you are—' said Calo, who stood on the ground beside his brother.

'Fuck off,' yelled the nearest merchant.

'EVEN IF YOU ARE,' shouted Calo, 'you will not be able to resist the romance, the excitement, the grand dazzling festival of forthright astonishments that awaits you when the Moncraine-Boulidazi Company mounts its exclusive presentation of the legendary—'

'—the daring,' shouted Galdo.

'—the bloody and heart-wrenching REPUBLIC OF THIEVES, this coming Count's Day and Penance Day—'

Galdo had to admit that the state of full sobriety, while in most considerations far less interesting than any degree of inebriation, did at least lend itself to the better employment of reflexes. The irate merchant hurled a turnip, which Calo plucked out of the air just before it struck his head. He tossed it up to Galdo, who leapt off the barrel, somersaulted in midair, caught the turnip, and landed with arms out-flung in a flourish.

'Turnips can't stop the Moncraine-Boulidazi Company!' he shouted.

'I've got potatoes too,' yelled the merchant.

'Count's Day! Penance Day! Limited engagements,' hollered Calo. 'At the Old Pearl! Don't miss the most stupendously exciting sensation that has ever graced your lives! The dead will live and breathe and speak again! True love, flashing blades, treachery of the heart, and the secrets of an imperial dynasty, all yours, but if you miss it now you miss it forever!'

Another turnip was hurled in their direction, and both twins dodged it easily.

'You missed us now and you'll miss us forever,' shouted Galdo. He turned to his brother and lowered his voice, 'All the same, we've got eight stops left. Maybe we've favoured these dullards long enough.'

'Too right,' said Calo. The twins bowed to the general indifference of the market square and hurried off into the rain. 'Where next?'

'Jalaan River Gate,' said Galdo. 'That'll be a welcoming and patient crowd for sure, fresh off the road with mud up their ass-cracks.'

'Yeah,' said Calo. 'Gods, where would this gang be without us to do all the actual miserable footwork for it?'

'We got the aptitude, we get the chores. Bright side, though, would you rather be doing the bookkeeping?'

'Fuck no. Wouldn't mind doing the bookkeeper's assistant.'

'Hey now, prior claim.'

'Oh, I know. Good on tubby for sewing her up. I was starting to worry about him,' said Calo.

'That leaves red and the genius. Still cause for worry there.'

'How hard is it to fling yourselves at one another and let all the really excited bits just sort themselves out?'

'It's not the doing, I think; it's that our beloved patron barely lets Sabetha out of his sight. Hell's own chaperon.'

'Think we should lend a hand?'

'Hey, I'll cut the prick's throat if you'll dig the hole,' said Galdo. 'But that would ruin all this dancing and singing we're doing on the company's behalf.'

'You must've kept your brains in your hair before you scraped it off, roundhead. I wasn't talking about *doing* Boulidazi. More of dropping a useful hint in Sabetha's ear.'

9

'It will be a better turnout than I expected,' said Jasmer, hunched over a cracked mug of brandy and rainwater.

'What a generous allowance.' Baron Boulidazi sat across from Moncraine at a back corner table in Mistress Gloriano's common room. 'It's better than you ever had any *right* to expect, you damned fool.'

'Very probably, my lord.'

Locke leaned against the wall nearby, listening while trying hard to look like he wasn't. He nursed a half-full cup of apple wine. It was the eve of the Count's Day performance, and by tradition the company had drunk four toasts in a row – Boulidazi first, Moncraine second, the company third, and a last cup for Morgante the City Father, a prayer for orderly streets and crowds. Fortunately, Chains had taught Locke the fine art of making half-sips look like vast friendly gulps, and without violating the spirit of the toasts he'd managed to shield his wits from their substance.

'Probably? I've stretched myself for you again, Moncraine,' said the baron, his usual easy bravado discarded. He hadn't restrained himself while toasting, and his voice was tight with concern. 'I can't just ask my friends to put in an appearance like hired clappers, for the gods' sake. Eleven gentlemen of standing with entourages. At a first performance, no less. You know they'd usually wait to hear if it's worth the bother. So it had damn well better be.'

'You know its quality. You've been on us like a bloody leech all through rehearsal.'

'I don't just need it to be good,' said Boulidazi. 'I want it smooth. Flawless. No incidents, no foul-ups, no miscues.'

'You can't escape miscues,' said Moncraine. 'If the piece is good they just flow right past; nobody gives a—'

'*I* give a damn.' Boulidazi was genuinely in his cups, Locke saw. 'This is my bloody company now, as much as it is yours, and my reputation is hanging in the wind. Fail me and you'll regret the day you first saw the sun.'

'With every will to please my gracious lord,' said Moncraine acidly, 'if it was as easy as simply *commanding* someone to get it right, there wouldn't be any bad plays. Or paintings, or songs, or—'

'Fuck up and I'll have your legs broken,' said Boulidazi. 'How's that for motivation?'

'I was already quite adequately motivated,' said Jasmer, rising to his feet. 'I believe I'll withdraw, my lord, as your heady company quite overwhelms my peasant sensibilities.'

Jasmer moved off into the crowd to mingle with Sylvanus and Chantal. The new bit players and the inn's usual crowd of wastrels and parasites were making a joyous noise unto the wine and ale jugs. Mistress Gloriano fuelled the carousing with fresh liquor like a blacksmith shovelling coal into a smelting furnace.

'Andrassus, you goat,' yelled Jasmer, 'how's tonight's wine?'

'Undistinguished,' burped Sylvanus. 'If it hasn't improved by the seventh or eighth cup I might have to resort to sterner forms of self-abuse.'

Baron Boulidazi rose unsteadily, glowering, ignoring Locke. By chance Sabetha had just come up behind him as she wound her outwardly cheerful path through the tumult, hostess-like. The cup in her hands was as artfully decorative as Locke's.

'Verena,' said the baron in a low voice, 'surely you've done your duty to the company this evening. Let me grant you some of the comforts you're used to, to rest yourself before the show. A proper hot bath, a fine bed, ice wines, perhaps even—'

'Oh, Gennaro,' she whispered, delicately removing his hand from where it had come to rest on her upper arm, then twining her fingers through his. 'You've been so thoughtful. Surely you know it's bad luck to celebrate like that before a performance, hmmm? I'll be only too happy to accept your offer *after* we've taken our last bows.'

It was just about the best possible deflection under the circumstances, thought Locke, but it was also alarming. She'd committed herself now to being alone with him, no later than the day after next, when their second show was finished. After weeks of flirtation and half-promises, Boulidazi could only respond badly to further excuses.

'Oh, let it be so,' said the baron. 'Let me take you away from these damned people and live as we should, even for a day or two. It's your company that's kept me down here incognito, not any love of correcting Moncraine. And when this is finished, I want you … that is, I want you to think on what you want next. Imagine the role you desire. I'll have Moncraine stage it for you, anything you like—'

'You do know just what to say to a lady,' said Sabetha, laying a finger over his lips and very effectively shutting him up. 'I'll reflect on your offer. On all your offers, Gennaro. I think our desires for the future may be understood to be in close agreement.'

'Are you sure,' said Boulidazi, plainly dealing with the sudden rush of blood to somewhere less conversationally useful than his brain, 'absolutely sure, that tonight you wouldn't—'

'I wouldn't,' she said, sweetly but firmly. 'We've two long days ahead of us and so much time to spend as we wish afterward. Let's not put the cart before the horse. Or should that be *stallion*, hmmmm?'

'Right,' he said. 'Right. As you … as you wish, always. And yet—'

Locke forced himself to cease listening as Boulidazi burbled a fresh stream of love-struck inanities. The baron's predictable refusal to accept Sabetha's polite-speak invitation to piss off for the evening meant that she'd be tending him until she was too tired to do anything but collapse, sour and exhausted, sometime after midnight. Every halting step Locke had taken with Sabetha, every precious moment of understanding they'd clawed out of one another was again being wasted. Locke stared fixedly at his drink, wondering if it was time to quit playacting and throw back a few.

'Ahoy there, Lucaza,' said Calo, swooping out of nowhere to seize Locke by the arms. He spoke rather loudly: 'We're short a thrower for a game of Fuck-the-Next-Fellow.'

'But I don't want to throw dice—'

'Nonsense,' said Calo, pulling him away from Sabetha and Boulidazi. 'You're just standing here mooning when you could be losing coins like a proper lad. Come, you're rolling with us.'

'But … but—'

His sputtering achieved nothing. Calo relieved him of his wine and drank it in two gulps. He then dragged Locke on a zigzag path through the crowd, down a side passage and up the narrow stairs near Sabetha and Jenora's room.

'What the hell are you—'

'Biggest favour of your life, half-wit,' said Calo. The long-haired Sanza kicked the wall, and to Locke's surprise that section of wood panelling slid backward with a click. 'Trust me. In the box.'

Calo's shove sent Locke sprawling into the confines of a hidden room, perhaps four feet high and seven feet long. A layer of blankets softened his landing, and the space was lit by the pale red glow of a tiny alchemical lamp set atop a stack of small wine casks. The secret panel slid shut behind him.

Befuddled, Locke glanced around, taking in the very few interesting features of the tiny space. 'Fucking Sanzas,' he muttered.

'I should think not,' said Sabetha an instant later as the panel snapped open again. She closed it as quickly as possible behind her and flopped down on the blankets with a relieved sigh.

'Oh gods,' said Locke, 'this was all your—'

'The twins told me about this place. Seems Mistress Gloriano's done some smuggling in her time. Calo accidentally opened it when he tripped against the wall one night.'

'What are we going to do about that damned baron?'

'Nothing,' said Sabetha. 'He doesn't exist.'

'My throat disagrees.'

She grabbed him by the tunic, and there was nothing playful or hesitant in the way she planted her lips on his neck.

'Your throat's my concern,' she whispered. 'And there's nothing outside this room. Not now, not for as long as we're in here.'

'Your absence will be as obvious to Boulidazi as if someone had stolen his breeches,' said Locke.

'Ordinarily. That's why I made sure I handed him his last drink while we were toasting.'

'You didn't!'

'I did.' Her smirk struck Locke as extremely becoming. 'Something mild, to muddle his thoughts. Soon enough he won't want to do anything except go to bed, and for once the miserable ass and I share a notion.'

'But if he—'

'I already told you he doesn't exist.' She took his head in her hands and spread her fingers through his hair. 'I'm tired of everyone else getting what they want except us. Coming and going as they please, sleeping where they please, while you and I live from interruption to interruption.' She brushed the faintest hint of a kiss against his lips, and then a longer one, and by the time she started on the third Locke was in serious danger of forgetting his own name.

'So you really did choose to be charmed at last, hmm?' he managed to whisper.

'No.' She jabbed him in the chest, playfully but firmly. 'I'm not here because you finessed me, dunce. You were right, on the roof that night.

We want what we want. We don't need to justify it. And when we can take it, we should. I want you. And I am *taking* you.'

Her next kiss told him that she meant to be finished with talking for some time.

10

Gloriano's inn-room wobbled around Gennaro Boulidazi as though mounted on an impossibly huge gimbal, and the lights and colours of the room had begun to run together like watercolours painted in the rain. The dull pressure in his skull meant he'd gone well past the horizon of smart indulgence, but how was that possible? Gloriano's swill had snuck up on him. The thought gave him more vague amusement than alarm. Very little ever alarmed him.

Verena, now, she was at least causing him consternation. The alluring bitch! Plainly she *wanted* him, but if not for the fact that she was so bloody young he would have sworn she was deliberately leading him on for frustration's sake. She had to be skittish, of course. Still a virgin. Well, he could fix that. *Gods* could he fix that.

The very thought made images of his desire swim in his head, mingling with the already muddled scene around him. Seventeen at the oldest, body tight and firm as a dancer's, with the blood of a Camorri family that went all the way back to the old empire. She was his to shape in every way. With his parents in their graves he was his own matchmaker, his own judge and counsel. If he couldn't or wouldn't seize a prize as sweet as Verena he ought to cut his balls off and let the house of Boulidazi fall! So she couldn't go onstage in Camorr? Piss on Camorr. In Espara she could do as she pleased, at least until she started bearing children.

'M'lord.' It was one of his men, hatchet-faced Brego, whispering in his ear, too respectful or scared to touch him. 'Can I fetch a carriage for you?'

''M fine,' muttered the baron, scanning the room dazedly. 'Th' gods fucking love me. Preva loves me! Just look at what she's sent me.'

Boulidazi concentrated, fighting back against the warm haze that was slowly gathering between his senses and the world around him. Drunk actors everywhere – *his* company. And there was the mouthy seamstress, the nightskin with the papers and the answer for everything. Oh, but she was tasty despite the airs she put on, no virgin and certainly no girl. Hair like curling black silk and breasts like heavy purses under that fraying bodice. Gods, yes, she'd know what to do once her legs were spread. A man could sink right in and feel at home.

That thought stirred him to arousal, a sudden exquisite pressure. He stumbled and had to push off a random inebriate to steady himself. The poor fellow toppled to the floor, dismissed from Boulidazi's mind even before he landed.

The seamstress! He needed to spend himself a bit, drain the urge just enough to restore his self-control for a couple of days. Jenora would suit that use … would probably be flattered. Boulidazi watched her closely, noted her furtive whispers to the tubby Camorri, Jovanno. For some reason she'd taken the boy to her bed. Did she have any idea who Lucaza and Verena really were? Was she trying, in her own pathetic fashion, to sleep her way to better circumstances, fucking Lucaza's man? Now that was damned amusing.

Jenora left the inn-room just a moment later, her intended arrangements for the night obviously communicated to the boy. Jovanno, however, was dicing with Alondo and those twins. So he'd be busy for a few minutes at least. Polite Jovanno, sociable Jovanno – the boy would keep their company until the round was done. Well, tonight that would cost him first pass at some quim.

Verena would never have to know. Jenora, like all of her associates, was empty-pursed and painfully aware of it. It was the easiest thing in the world to keep a penniless woman shut up.

'I need some privacy. Jus' a few minutes,' Boulidazi muttered to Brego. Then, summoning the dregs of his concentration, he put one unsteady foot in front of the other and moved toward the stairs Jenora had taken.

11

Each kiss was longer and fiercer than the last.

Locke's hands shook with the hot anxiety of impatience and inexperience. There were so many things to figure out so quickly between short, desperate breaths. It was one thing to throw a girl around in dreams, where the mind can discard the inconveniences of physical reality, but real girls have weight and mass and demands that dream girls lack. First passion is a complicated dance.

Strangely, it helped that Sabetha seemed just as impatient. She held

468

him at bay a moment while she all but tore the ribbon out of her hair, spilling it across her shoulders. She was flushed, sweaty, as awkwardly excited as he was, and through that she'd shed the imposing grace that usually made Locke feel so small and stumbling around her. *Neither* of them could be graceful at such close quarters, and Locke found that an immense relief.

The heat grew in the tiny enclosure as they wound their arms and legs together, and the shock of actually being there with her gave way at last to the explosion of pent-up longing. Their tongues met, hesitantly at first, and they shared a nervous, muffled laugh. Then they explored the new sensation together, more and more boldly. Their hands, too, seemed to come unshackled from inhibition and roamed freely.

Order and planning were forgotten. Locke found himself having done things without any realization that he'd even started them. Their clothes were shed with reckless speed, as though torn off by ghosts. It was almost like being in a fight – the same fearful exhilaration, the same sense of time disjointed into bright, hot, all-consuming flashes. His hands on her breasts … her lips against the taut muscles of his stomach … their final scramble to arrange themselves for something that neither of them understood.

Toward that *something* they fought, and fought was an apt description. However passionate they were, however deep and pure the pleasure of their connection, there was something hesitant and incomplete about their lovemaking. They were like two pieces of an unfinished craftwork, not yet trimmed and polished to slide together properly. At last, they eased apart, exhausted but not content. It was obvious to Locke that Sabetha was straining to conceal disappointment, or discomfort, or even both.

Is that it? The thought came unbidden from whatever corner of his mind was responsible for unhelpful pessimism. Was that all? *That* was the act that turned the whole world on its ear, that made men and women crazy, that bedevilled his dreams, that made hounds of the Sanza twins?

'Look,' he muttered when he'd caught his breath. He pushed himself up on his elbows. 'I, um, I'm sorry—'

Sabetha pulled him back down and held him tight, her breasts against his back. She spread her hands possessively across his chest and kissed his neck, an act that instantly disconnected him from whatever willpower he'd managed to summon.

469

'What are you apologizing for?' she whispered. 'You think that's it? You think we never get to try again?'

'Well, I just thought you'd—'

'What, banish you like a passing fancy?' Her kiss became a playful bite, and Locke yelped. 'Preva help me, I'm sweet for an idiot.'

'Did we … did I hurt you, just now?'

'I wouldn't say hurt, exactly.' She tightened her embrace reassuringly for an instant. 'It was … strange. But it wasn't *bad*.'

There was a muffled thump from one of the nearby rooms, followed by some sort of passionate outburst that quickly subsided.

'That could be us when we've rested a bit,' she said. 'Believe me, I have every intention of practising until we get this right.'

They lay there for a while, muttering sweet inanities, letting the minutes unroll in delectable languor. Sabetha's hands had just begun roaming again, testing Locke's returning ardour, when the room's secret door slid open barely an inch. Someone moved against the dim light of the hall, and Locke's heart pounded.

'Get dressed,' hissed Calo.

'What the *hell*,' said Sabetha. 'This isn't funny!'

'Damn right it's not. It's bad.'

'What can possibly—?'

'Don't ask questions. If you trust me and want to live, get your bloody clothes on. We need you both, this instant.'

Locke's relief at not seeing Boulidazi outside the little chamber was instantly squelched by the cold dead gravity of Calo's voice. A serious Sanza was one hell of an ill omen. Locke found his clothes with the most extreme haste, and still Sabetha beat him out into the hall.

12

No one else was in the hall as they emerged, though the noise of revelry continued unabated from the direction of the common room. Calo, visibly on edge, led them the short distance to Jenora's chamber door. Locke's sense of dread grew as Calo knocked softly in a three-two-one pattern.

It was Galdo who answered, ushered them in, and slammed the door shut behind them. The scene within the room made Locke's knees feel as though they'd dissolved, and he found himself grabbing Sabetha to stay upright.

470

Jenora was huddled in a corner beside an overturned cot, wide-eyed and shuddering, her tunic torn open at the neck. Jean crouched next to her, hands on her shoulders.

Gennaro Boulidazi lay crumpled against the opposite wall, his imposing frame strangely deflated, his face pale. A pair of seamstress' shears, their plain handles roughened and stained by Jenora's long hours of work, was deeply embedded in a spreading red stain on the baron's right breast.

As Locke stared in horror, Boulidazi moaned softly, shuffled his legs, and coughed more blood onto his tunic. Dull and helpless as the baron seemed, mortal as his wound had to be, for the moment he was still very much alive.

CHAPTER NINE
The Five-Year Game: Reasonable Doubt

'What Locke is,' said Sabetha, 'is the man about to cook my dinner.'

'Surely you both saw further than that,' said Patience.

'It's no affair of yours.' Sabetha slipped out of Locke's arms, dangerously tense, her air of cautious respect banished. 'Locke might answer to you, but I don't. Best think on how my principals might respond if you use your magic to keep me from dragging you out of this house.'

'Take care when throwing rules at a rule-maker, my dear,' said Patience. 'Provoke me outside the bounds of the five-year game and I'm free to respond as I will. And you are *quite* outside the bounds of the game this evening, aren't you? Because if you're not, you'd be perilously close to the one thing you both agreed—'

'Shove your *collusion* somewhere dark and painful,' said Locke, setting his hands on Sabetha's shoulders. 'You know we weren't talking business when you appeared. Only a snoop could have such flawless dramatic timing. Why the hell are you here?'

'A matter of conscience.'

'Really?' said Locke. 'Yours? You keep alluding to its existence. Somehow I'm not convinced.'

'This interruption is entirely your own fault!' The archedama stabbed a finger in Locke's direction. 'I gave you the clearest, fairest possible warning! I told you to set aside your personal business. To get to work, not to wooing. And what have you done?'

'What have we *both* done?' said Sabetha. She folded her arms, but Locke could still feel that simmering tension, as familiar to him as her voice or her scent. He tightened his grip, doubting that she had his experience with physically attacking magi. She didn't relax, but she gave his hand a brief, reassuring squeeze. 'Enlighten us, Archedama. And I do mean *us*.'

'This reckless pursuit of your old romance,' said Patience. 'Set it aside. Go back to your appointed tasks. Don't make me carry out this obligation, Sabetha. Locke is my responsibility now, and there are things about him that you don't understand. Things you don't *need* to understand, if you would only stop here.'

'Stop what? My *life*?'

'I see I'm wasting breath. Remember that I made the offer, for what it's worth.' Patience gestured casually, and the balcony doors slid shut behind her. 'Locke, you see, is unique. But I'm not merely affirming his egotism. If you would continue pursuing him you have the right to know his true nature.'

'He's no stranger to me,' said Sabetha.

'He's a stranger to everyone.' Patience fixed her disconcertingly dark eyes on Locke. 'Himself most of all.'

'Enough cryptic bullshit,' Locke growled. 'Get to the meat of whatever—'

'Twenty-three years ago,' Patience interrupted him sharply, 'the Black Whisper fell on Camorr. Hundreds died, but the quarantine and the canals saved the city. Once the plague burned itself out, you walked out of old Catchfire, recognized by no one. Home unknown, age unknown, parents and friends unknown.'

'Yes, I do bloody well remember that,' said Locke.

'Take it as evidence. Reflect on it.'

'Here's something you can reflect on, you—'

'I *know* why you have no real memories of the time before the plague.' Again Patience parried his words with her peremptory tone. 'I know why you have no recollection of your father. In fact, I know why you make up storeys about how you took the name Lamora. You tell some it came from a sausage vendor. You tell others it was a kindly old sailor.'

'You ... you told me it was a sailor,' said Sabetha.

'Look,' said Locke, a serpentine chill creeping up and down his spine, 'look, I'll explain, I just ... Patience, how the hell can you *possibly* know that?'

'Not one instance of the surname Lamora has ever been recorded in a Camorri census. Not in any century since the imperial collapse. You'll find that we had good cause to check. You brought the name with you out of Catchfire, wholly formed in your mind, though you never knew where from. I do.'

She moved toward them with that uncanny smooth glide facilitated by her elegant robe. 'I know that you have only one true and immutable memory glowing dimly in that darkness before the Catchfire plague. A memory of your mother. A memory of her trade.'

'Seamstress,' muttered Locke.

'Yes,' said Patience, gesturing toward herself. 'I have, after all, told you what my grey name was. The one I chose for myself, long before I was elevated to archedama—'

'*Seamstress*,' said Locke, 'oh, no. Oh, *fuck no. Fuck, no!* You can't be serious!'

2

She compounded his dreadful sense of shock by laughing.

'I'm serious as cold steel,' she said with a faintly catlike grin. 'You've made quite an amusing leap to the wrong conclusion, however. I assure you that the Falconer is my one and only child.'

'*Gods*,' said Locke, gasping with relief. 'So what the hell are you on about?'

'I said your memory was immutable and true. But it's nothing to do with your mother's trade. In fact, it's nothing to do with your mother at all. It's *me* you remember.'

'And how in all the hells is that even possible?'

'There was once an extraordinarily gifted mage of my order, the youngest archedon in centuries. He earned his fifth ring when he was half my present age, and took on the office of Providence. He was my mentor, my very true friend. He was also blessed in love. His wife was Karthani, a stunning woman with a kind of beauty very rare among the Therin people. They were enchanted with one another. She died … far too young.

'It was an accident,' continued Patience, hesitantly, as though it pained her to produce each word. 'A balcony collapse. I've told you that our arts have limitless capacity to cause harm, and scarcely any power to undo it. We can transmute; we can cleanse. Your poisoning was an alien condition that we could separate from your body. But against shattered bones and spilled blood, we're helpless. We are *ordinary*. Ordinary as *you*.'

She glared at Locke with something like real anger.

'Yes,' she said, more slowly. 'Ordinary as you are *right now*. The tragedy caused a terrible change in my friend. He made a grievous error of judgment.

'He became obsessed with fetching his wife *back*. Harsh experience teaches us that we cannot master death. Still, he fell into the trap of grief and self-regard. He convinced himself that such mastery was simply a matter of will and knowledge. Will that none had ever before mustered. Knowledge that none had ever revealed. He began to experiment with the most forbidden folly in all our arts – interference with the spirit after death. Transition of the spirit into new flesh. Do you know what a horror he would have conjured even if he'd been successful?'

'The gods would never allow such a thing,' whispered Locke, not sure he believed it but certain he wanted to. The image of Bug's dead black sin-graven eyes flashed in his memory.

'For once I agree with you,' said Patience wryly. 'But the gods are cruel. They don't so much forbid this ambition as punish it. Life recoils from necromancy, like the inflammation of flesh from a venomous sting. The working of it produces malaise, sickness. It can't be hidden. Eventually he was discovered, but the confrontation was badly handled. He managed to escape.'

Patience pushed her hood back. Sabetha seemed as rooted in place as Locke was, spellbound by the tale, barely breathing.

'Before his elevation to archedon, he'd used a grey name from Throne Therin. He called himself *Pel Acanthus*, White Amaranth. The unwithering flower of legend. It was only natural that after his madness and betrayal, we called him—'

'No,' whispered Locke. The strength went out of his legs. Sabetha wasn't fast enough to catch him before his knees hit the floor.

'... *Lamor Acanthus*,' said Patience. 'Black Amaranth. I see the name means something to you.'

'You can't possibly know that name,' said Locke, his voice barely a croak. Even to his ears the denial sounded pathetic and childish. 'You can't.'

'I can,' said Patience, not gently. '*Pel Acanthus* was my friend, *Lamor Acanthus* my shame. Those names mean a great deal to me. They mean even more to you because they're who you are.'

'What are you *doing* to him?' said Sabetha. Locke clung to her, shaking. His chest felt as though it was being squeezed in iron bands.

'Ending the mysteries,' said Patience, softening her tone. 'Providing the answers. This man was once *Lamor Acanthus* of Karthain, once Archedon Providence of my order. Once a mage even more powerful than myself.'

She held up her left arm and let the robe sleeve fall away to reveal her five tattooed rings.

'*I am not a gods-damned mage,*' said Locke, hoarsely.

'Not anymore,' said Patience.

'You're making this shit up!' said Locke, enunciating each word, willing them into some sort of emotional talisman. 'So you know a ... a name. I admit that I'm astonished. But I am ... I don't know how old I am, exactly, but I can't be yet thirty. *Thirty!* This man you're talking about would be older than you!'

'Originally,' said Patience. 'And in a manner of speaking you still are.'

'What the hell does that mean?'

'Twenty-three years ago, an orphan with no past appeared in the aftermath of a deadly plague. Didn't I just tell you what happens when our most forbidden art is practised? A dreadful backlash against life itself. Sickness. The Black Whisper that came out of nowhere. *Lamor Acanthus* was in Camorr, hidden away in the hovels of Catchfire. That's where you continued your studies, using the poor and the forgotten as your subjects.'

'Oh, bullshit—'

'We *know*,' said Patience. 'There was a sorcerous event in Camorr before the plague erupted. Several members of my order were near enough to feel it. When the quarantine was lifted, our people were there in force. We sifted Catchfire house by house, until we found our answer. Magical apparatus. The papers and diaries of *Lamor Acanthus*, along with his body, plainly identifiable by the tattooed rings. And so we thought the matter was ended, horribly, but ultimately for the better.

'Years passed. Then came the unpleasant business involving my son. It brought you to our attention. You and Jean were carefully examined. Particularly Jean, since our possession of his red name made things so much easier. Imagine the intensity of our surprise when he told us that his closest friend, a Camorri orphan, had confessed to the secret name of *Lamor Acanthus*.'

'You ... told Jean your true name?' said Sabetha. Locke desperately insisted to himself that he was only imagining the hurt beneath her surprise.

'I, uh, well ... shit.' His wits, smashed to paste, couldn't seem to make the heroic effort required to rouse themselves. 'I always meant to tell you. I just—'

'He told Jean *a* true name,' said Patience. 'But there's still another,

476

isn't there? You've got grey names under grey names, Locke. *Lamor Acanthus* no more gives me the key to you than Locke Lamora or Leocanto Kosta or Sebastian Lazari does. Beneath it all is another name, the one my mentor would never have shared with another mage. So I don't know what it is ... perhaps you don't even remember it. But you and I both know it's *there*.'

'I'm not what you say I am.' Locke slumped in Sabetha's arms, despondent. 'I was born in Camorr.'

'Your body was. Don't you see? *Lamor Acanthus* succeeded, after a fashion. That's why the outbreak of plague was so sudden, so virulent. You tore your own spirit from its old body. You stole a new one. A second youth, a new wealth of years to spend honing your powers. But that's not how it worked out ... Your memories were fragmented, your personality burnt away. You locked yourself into a body that didn't have the gift you used to put yourself there. It took more than twenty years for us to see both pieces of the puzzle, but surely you can't deny that they fit together smoothly.'

'I can,' said Locke. 'I sure as hell can deny it!'

'Why do you think I've confided in you?' Patience sighed with the quiet exasperation of a teacher drilling a particularly slow pupil. 'Told you what I have of magic, shown you what I have of the magi? Did you think I was just being *chatty*? Did you really believe you were so very special? I do need you in your capacity as my exemplar for the five-year game. But I also used that to justify bringing you here, to give us more time to study you. To give myself time to make this approach.'

'This is some cruel fucking game of yours,' said Locke.

'You're still one of us, after a fashion,' said Patience. 'You have obligations to us, and we to you. One of those obligations is the truth. If the two of you hadn't rekindled your private affair, I could have postponed this. As it stands, you both have the right to know, and I had the responsibility to tell you.' Patience gently touched one of Sabetha's arms. 'I know the reason, you see, why he's dreamed of redheaded women all of his—'

'Stop!' Sabetha jerked away from Patience, stood up, and backed away from Locke as well. 'I don't want to hear it! I don't want to hear anymore!'

'Don't tell me you believe her!' said Locke.

'Coincidence piles on coincidence until the evidence becomes too strong to ignore,' said Patience.

'Stuff it,' growled Sabetha. 'I don't … I don't know what the hell to think about this, Locke, I just—'

'You *do* believe it.' Shock turned in an instant to hot anger. Confused and reeling, Locke was primed to lash out at any target he could find. Before he knew what he was doing, he chose the wrong one. 'All the things we've done, all the time we've spent rebuilding this … and you believe her!'

'You told me you named yourself after a sailor,' she said, unsteadily. 'Did you believe that? Do you … believe it now? How can you be sure that you weren't just filling some hole, or having it filled by someone else's—'

'How can you even think this?' Anger flared on top of anger, hot and sharp as a knife just pulled from flame. 'You *left* me! You manipulated me, you fucking *drugged* me, and I still came back. But one story from this fucking Karthani *witch* and you're looking at me like I just fell out of the gods-damned sky! Wait, no, *shit*—'

His remorse and better judgment arrived, late as usual, like party guests riding in just after the social disaster of the season has already erupted. Sabetha's cheeks darkened, and she opened her mouth several times, but in the end she said nothing. She turned with all the awful, decisive grace of womanly anger, threw the balcony doors open with a slam, and vanished into the darkened house.

Locke stared after her, dumbfounded, dully listening to the drumbeat rhythm of the pulse in his temples. A moment later he leapt to his feet, grabbed the silver bucket containing the chilled wine, and flung it with a snarl against the oak cooking table. Ingredients flew, glass shattered, and ice and wine alike splashed into the brazier, where they raised a soft cloud of hissing steam.

'Thanks for your even-handed fucking presentation, Patience.' He kicked a fragment of broken glass and watched it skitter off the edge of the balcony. 'Thanks for all your kind efforts on my behalf, you … you—'

'My responsibility was to tell you the truth, not wrap you in swaddling clothes.' She raised her hood again, half-veiling her face in shadow. 'Nor protect you from your own badly-aimed temper. Take it from someone who was courted into a happy marriage, Master Lamora. Your style of wooing couldn't be more perfectly designed to deliver you to a solitary life.'

'Go light yourself on fire,' said Locke, suddenly regretting that he'd smashed the only bottle of liquor he'd thought to set out on the balcony.

'We'll speak more of this later,' said Patience. 'And once the election is finished, we'll discuss arrangements for the future.'

'I don't believe a thing you've said,' Locke whispered, knowing how little conviction was in his voice.

'You refused to believe that I preserved your life in Tal Verrar for reasons of conscience. Now I give you the self-interested motive you previously insisted upon, and you refuse to believe it as well. Are you really that arrogant, that logic is as optional as a fashion accessory for you? You can certainly choose to believe that we'd entrust a normal man with even the fragments of guarded truth I've shown you. Or you can open your eyes. Accept that we've given you a chance to solve the mysteries of your past. Perhaps even a chance to redeem yourself for a terrible crime. A crime whose first victim's stolen body you will wear like a mask until the day you die.'

Locke said nothing, staring at the mess he'd made of the ingredients for the feast he'd been happily planning to cook not a quarter of an hour earlier.

'Brood all you like,' said Patience. 'Sulk all night. You've an uncanny talent for it, haven't you? But in the morning, we expect that you'll be sober, and focused, and working furiously on our behalf. My more enthusiastic young peers imagine that their colourful threats to you have escaped my notice. But now I suspect you understand how little value I place on Jean Tannen for his own sake, and how ... discretionary my protection of him might be. Jean's continued safety is entirely dependent on your discipline and inspiration.'

Patience turned and slowly strolled away into the house.

'Gods save him,' she called over her shoulder.

She left Locke standing alone on the balcony, and didn't bother closing the doors behind her.

INTERSECT (III)
Spark

The old man quietly withdrew the observation spell he'd woven around Archedama Patience, the most complex work of his life, and breathed a long sigh of relief. The strain of spying, and of conveying the results of that spying in thought to his contact on the other side of the city, had tested him sorely.

This can't be true! He could feel the fury behind the thoughts that hammered him from that contact now. Archedama Foresight was powerful, and her anger came on like the pressure of a rising headache. *I've heard NOTHING of this! Have the other three gone MAD?*

Please calm down, Archedama. I've had a difficult evening. They're not mad ... but they have gone too far. You see now why I had to tell you.

How has this been concealed from me?

Patience claimed the right to examine the two Camorri after the Falconer's mutilation. I never would have known what she'd discovered if I hadn't been there in person for Jean Tannen's interrogation. We took him in Tal Verrar, months before the Falconer's friends were allowed to toy with them. Only Patience, Temperance, and myself have known what Tannen told us. That's how the secret was kept.

Lamor Acanthus returned! The matter is so huge, I can scarcely begin to ponder it. This question belongs to us all! I'll break it wide open in the Sky Chamber!

NO! The old man felt beads of sweat sliding down his cheeks and brow. The intensity of their communication was far beyond the usual light touch of mind-speech. **Patience and Temperance have too much support in the chamber. Providence will take their side in any argument. You know as well as I that the Falconer's removal leaves you short of commanding Speakers. Your followers are dedicated, but your numbers are too few**

to broach this matter without preparation.

If Lamor Acanthus removed his spirit into another body, even an ungifted body, then he achieved something no other mage in history ever has.

In disgrace and disaster!

Yes. All the more reason we must examine him collectively, research his processes exhaustively. The mind and power of one man were not enough to overcome the difficulties. But what could the minds and powers of a hundred magi do? Or all of us, all four hundred? That's how this MUST be approached!

I agree with you. I owe Patience so much; do you think I'd turn on her for anything less than a truly existential question? Please heed me, Archedama. If you bring this before the Sky Chamber without preparation it will not go well. You must attack from a position of real strength. And to do that … I daresay that we must take unprecedented measures.

Surely you can't be suggesting—

Never. No blood must be shed, at least not without provocation. But you must assert force. You must … take control of Patience and some of her supporters, for a little while. They count on the balance of power being overwhelmingly in their favour. If you demonstrate that it is otherwise, you can then introduce the question into a genuinely receptive environment. Only that can guarantee the honest discussion this situation demands.

What you suggest could still be construed as a coup.

Only a little one. The old man smiled wryly, and passed the sensation on in his thoughts. **And only for a little while. Our very future is at stake. If we let the five-year game play itself out, let Patience and her supporters stay distracted, then … then with my guidance you can move instantly, decisively. The very night it ends. If we take the other arch-magi into custody, we demonstrate power. If we then release them unharmed, we demonstrate good intentions. Then, and only then, do I believe the circumstances will be right for us to confront the mess that Patience has made, and the secrets she's unearthed.**

The night of the election, then.

Yes. The night of the election.

If you really can serve as our eyes, I promise you I'll find capable hands to do the work.

Archedama Foresight was gone from his mind without a further sentiment, as was her way. Relieved, he rubbed his hands together to calm their shaking.

It was done, then. It was as it must be, and for the good of all his kind, he reminded himself. He'd had a long and comfortable life on account of his rings. Surely if anyone could bear the strain and the burden of what was to come, it was him.

The air of the silent room suddenly seemed to chill against his skin. Coldmarrow decided that he needed a drink very, very badly.

An Inconvenient Patron

I

'Jovanno,' said Locke. 'Did you—'

'It was me,' said Jenora, hoarsely. 'He tried … he tried…'

'He tried to tear her gods-damned clothes off,' said Jean, putting his arms around Jenora. 'He was on the ground before I got here.'

'I didn't mean to hurt him, but … he's drunk,' said Jenora. 'He put his hands on my neck. He was choking me …'

Locke crouched warily over Boulidazi and slid the baron's knife from its sheath. The heaving, bleeding man made no effort to stop him. Locke had seen bloody lung-cuts before, from duels at Capa Barsavi's court. This was near-certain death, but it wouldn't be quick. Boulidazi could have the strength to do them real harm for some time yet. So why wasn't he fighting back now? His gaze was distant, his pupils unnaturally wide. Blood bubbled around the makeshift weapon still jutting from his chest, and this seemed to be causing him startled bemusement, not mortal panic.

'He's not just drunk,' said Locke. 'It must be whatever you gave him.'

'Shit,' said Sabetha, slumping against the door. 'This is all my fault.'

'The hell are you talking about?' said Jean.

'Boulidazi's drink,' said Calo. 'We put something in it. To keep him away from … Verena and Lucaza.'

'Shit,' repeated Sabetha, and the look on her face was too much for Locke to bear.

'Here now,' he said, 'half this gods-damned company has been drunk for weeks. The twins have been out of their minds on anything that comes in a bottle or a cask. When did they ever try to rape anyone?' Locke jabbed a finger at Boulidazi. 'This is *his* fucking fault, nobody else's!'

'He's right,' said Calo, setting a hand on Jenora's wrist. 'You did a Camorri thing. You did the *right* thing.'

'The *right thing*?' Jenora brushed Calo off and took Jean's hands.

'I've hung myself. I've spilled noble blood.'

'It's not murder yet,' said Galdo.

'It doesn't matter if he lives or dies,' said Jenora. 'They'll kill me for this. They'll kill as many of us as they can, but me for sure.'

'It was clear self-defence,' growled Jean. 'We'll get a dozen witnesses. We'll get the whole damn company; we'll rehearse the story perfectly—'

'And they'll kill her,' said Sabetha. 'She's right. It won't matter if we have a hundred witnesses, Jovanno. She's a nightskin commoner and we're foreign players, and now we're all party to wiping out the last heir of an Esparan noble house. If we get caught they'll grind us into paste and plough us into the fields.'

'As my brother pointed out,' said Galdo, 'we don't have a corpse yet.'

'Yes we do,' said Locke quietly. His hands moved with a decisive steadiness that surprised his head. He removed Boulidazi's dirty waist sash and gagged the baron with it. The wounded man struggled for air, but still didn't seem to grasp what was happening to him.

'Gods, what are you doing?' said Jenora.

'What's required,' said Locke, coldly exhilarated as his oldest reflexes, his Camorri instincts, shoved aside his muddled feelings of forbearance and pity. 'If he breathes a word of this to anyone we're doomed.'

'Oh, gods,' whispered Jenora.

'I'll be happy to do it,' said Jean.

'No,' said Locke. He'd demanded this necessity; Chains would expect him to not pass the burden. His hands trembled as he unbuckled the baron's thin leather belt and wound it around his hands. Then the thought of Jean, Sabetha, and the Sanzas dangling from an Esparan gibbet flashed into his mind, and his hands were as steady as temple stones. He slipped the belt over Boulidazi's neck.

'Wait!' said Sabetha. She knelt in front of Boulidazi, who must now look tragically ridiculous, Locke realized, with the shears buried in his chest, his own sash gagging him, and a slender teenager applying a belt to his windpipe. 'You can't crimp his neck.'

'Watch me,' said Locke through gritted teeth.

'A man can be stabbed for a lot of reasons,' said Sabetha. 'But if he's pricked *and* strangled, it won't look accidental.'

Her movements were tender as she grasped the shears. Her eyes were pitiless as the night ocean.

'Just hold him for me,' she whispered.

Locke unwound his hands from the belt and grabbed Boulidazi by his thick upper arms. Sabetha gave Jenora's shears a hard shove, upward and inward. Boulidazi groaned and jerked in Locke's arms, but without real force. Even at the moment of his death, he was locked away from the reality of it.

Boulidazi slumped, his legs jerking more and more feebly until at last he was still. Sabetha settled back on her knees, exhaled unsteadily, and held out her blood-slick right hand as though unsure how to clean it. Locke loosened the baron's sash and passed it to her, then eased Boulidazi's dead weight to the ground. If they could handle him carefully, Locke thought they could keep most of the blood within him, or at least upon him.

Jenora put her face against one of Jean's arms.

'Now we can make this look like anything,' said Sabetha. 'Argument, crime of passion, anything. We put him somewhere plausible and build a fable. All we've got to do is figure out what. And, ah, do it in the next couple of—'

Someone pounded on the door to the room.

Locke fought to keep control of himself; at the first noise it had felt like his skin was attempting to leap off his body. A quick glance around the room showed that nobody else had a firm grip on their nerves, either.

'M'lord Boulidazi?' The muffled voice belonged to Brego, the baron's bodyguard and errand-hound. 'M'lord, are you in there? Is all well?'

Locke stared at the door, which Sabetha had moved away from in order to finish off Boulidazi. Calo and Galdo were the closest to it, but even they were three or four paces away. The door was not bolted; if Brego decided to open it, even a crack, he'd be looking directly at Boulidazi's corpse.

2

Sabetha moved like an arrow leaving a bowstring, and the very first thing she did was tear her tunic off.

Locke's jaw hadn't finished dropping before Sabetha was at the door, landing ghost-light on her bare feet.

'Oh, Brego,' she said, panting. 'Oh, just a moment!'

485

She gestured at Boulidazi's corpse. Calo and Galdo sprang forward to help Locke, and in seconds they managed to push the baron's body under the bed. Jean slid a blanket partly over the room's alchemical lamp, dimming it. A moment later Calo, Galdo, and Locke squeezed up against the wall just behind Sabetha, out of the visual arc of the door, provided it wasn't opened all the way.

Sabetha tousled her hair with one precise head-toss, then cracked the door open to give Brego an unexpectedly fine view of a preoccupied young woman. Her tunic was pressed to her chest with one hand to cover an artful minimum of bosom.

'Why Brego,' she said, mimicking perfect breathlessness, 'you dutiful fellow, you!'

'Why, Mistress Verena, I … my lord, is he—'

'He's busy, Brego.' She giggled. 'He's *very* busy and will be that way for some time. You can wait downstairs, I think. He's in the *best* possible hands.'

She didn't give him time to say anything else, but with a lascivious little wave she slid the door shut and bolted it.

A few agonizing seconds passed, and then Locke could hear Brego's boot-steps as he moved away down the corridor. Sabetha threw her tunic back on, sank down against the door, and sighed with relief.

'We're all gonna have grey fuckin' hair by the time the sun comes up,' said Galdo. He and Calo had both been holding daggers at the ready; now they hid the slender bits of blackened steel again. The air in the room suddenly seemed dense with the smells of blood and nervous sweat.

'Can we get the hell out of here now?' said Jenora.

'Where do you want to go?' said Jean.

'Camorr!' she whispered. 'For the gods' sakes, I know you can do … something! I know you're not really just actors.'

'Calm down, Jenora.' Locke stared at one of Boulidazi's boots, sticking out incongruously from beneath the bed. 'You're not exactly inconspicuous. How would people not notice you sneaking off hours before we're supposed to deliver the play? How could we keep you hidden on the road?'

'A ship, then.'

'If you run,' said Sabetha, 'you'll tear a hole in whatever story we invent to explain what's happened. And you'll leave your aunt to take all the trouble! If we can't make the tale neat and obvious, the countess' people will be right back to rounding up scapegoats.'

'Even if you manage to make it neat and obvious,' said Jenora, 'we're all crushed. We're liable, remember? To the ditch-tenders, the confectioners, the alemongers, the cushion-renters. Without the play, we'll be so far in default to all of 'em we might as well go turn ourselves in at the Weeping Tower now.'

'What about acts of the gods?' said Calo. 'Surely you wouldn't be liable if a hurricane blew in. Or the Old Pearl collapsed.'

'Of course not,' said Jenora. 'But whatever powers you have, I doubt they extend that far.'

'Not that far, no,' said Calo. 'But the stage is made of wood.'

'A fire! Nice one!' said Galdo. 'The two of us could handle it. In, out, like shadows. Wouldn't take two hours.'

'The stage timbers are alchemically petrified,' said Jenora. 'They won't just catch fire. You'd need a dozen cartloads of wood, like engineering a bloody siege.'

'So we can't destroy the Pearl,' said Sabetha.

'And we can't run,' said Jean. 'It'd invite all kinds of trouble, and it's not likely any of us would make it home.'

'And if we stay but don't do the play, we all get thrown into chains for debt,' said Locke. 'Debt at the very least.'

'So there's only one sensible course of action,' said Sabetha.

'Grow wings?' said Calo.

'We have to pretend everything's normal.' Sabetha counted off items using her fingers as she spoke. 'We have to get Brego out of the damned building so we can have some room to move. We have to do the play—'

'You're cracked!' said Jenora.

'... and once we've done it, *then* we let the world in on the fact that Boulidazi's dead, in circumstances that don't incriminate anyone we care about.'

'What are we going to do with the son-of-a-bitch's corpse?' Galdo kicked the nearest boot for emphasis. 'You know what it'll smell like if we treat it as a keepsake until tomorrow night.'

'And it's gonna be ass-ugly,' said Calo. 'Any dullard will see the wound's not fresh.'

'*That's* where fire comes in,' said Locke. 'We can burn him! Cook him until nobody can tell whether he died an hour or a week ago.'

'How can we control it?' said Jean. 'If we burn him beyond recognition …'

'No worries.' Locke held up the knife he'd taken from Boulidazi, the same one the baron had set against his cheek. Its blade was all business, but the hilt was set with black garnets and a delicate white iron cloisonné. 'This and all his other baubles will make his identity very plain.'

'Where are we hiding it … I mean, him?' said Jenora.

'No, you mean *it*,' said Jean, smiling grimly.

'For the smell … I suppose I have pomanders and some rose dust we can douse the body with.' Jenora was still far from settled, but her resolve seemed to be strengthening. 'That should help it keep. For a day, at least.'

'Good thought,' said Calo. 'As for where, I suppose it's too easy just to keep him shoved under this bed?'

'Out of the gods-damned question!'

'We could have Sylvanus sit on it all night,' said Locke. 'He wouldn't notice a damn thing until he'd sobered up again. Alas, everyone else would. Let's hide him with the props and costumes.'

'Let's hide him *as* a prop,' said Sabetha. 'We've got a play full of corpses. Cover him in something suitable, throw a mask on him, and as far as anyone knows, he's just scenery! That way we can keep him with us—'

'… and not have to worry about anyone finding him while we're away at the Pearl!' said Locke. 'Yeah. That leaves one last problem. … He's got a pile of gentlemen and retainers expecting to share his company at the play.'

'Hate to add turds to the shit-feast,' said Calo, 'but that's *not* the last problem. What do we tell the rest of the troupe about this?'

'*Why* do we tell the rest of the troupe about this?' said Jenora.

'I'm not best pleased to say it, but we've got to bring them in,' said Sabetha. 'They'll be everywhere, in and amongst the props and costumes. If we don't have their cooperation, we're sunk.'

'How do we make them cooperate?' said Jean.

'Make them *complicit*,' said Sabetha. 'Make sure they understand it's their necks in the noose as well, because it is.'

'*Singua solus*,' said Galdo.

'Just the thing.' Sabetha put one ear against the door and listened carefully for a moment. '*Singua solus*.'

'What's that?' said Jenora.

'It's an old Camorri tradition for when a bunch of people are planning something stupid,' said Locke. 'Actually, we have a lot of traditions for that. You'll find out.'

'Giacomo, Castellano,' said Sabetha, 'how drunk are you?'

'Nowhere near drunk enough,' said Calo.

'We've been in here long enough,' said Sabetha, 'so you two get down to the common room and round up all the company members. Slap their drinks out of their hands if you have to. Get them off to bed. We need them as right and rested as possible when we spring this surprise on them.'

'Take drinks away from Jasmer and Sylvanus,' sighed Galdo. 'Right. And while we're at it, we'll run off to Karthain and learn sorcery from the—'

'Get,' said Sabetha. 'I'll peek outside first in case Brego's still lurking.'

It was another ominous sign of the depths of the waters they were swimming in that neither of the Sanzas had any further quips or complaints. Sabetha eased the door open, scanned the hallway, and nodded. The twins slipped out in a flash.

'Jenora,' said Sabetha, 'in the company's papers, do you have anything signed by Boulidazi? Anything he scrawled on?'

'Why, yes … yes.' She pointed at a leather portfolio in a far corner. 'All the papers assigning his shares in the company, and some notes of instruction. He is … *was* literate. He liked to make a show of it.'

'I know.' Sabetha snatched up the portfolio and tossed it onto the bed next to Jean and Jenora. 'Sift through it and get those papers for me. I don't have much time to practise, but I should be able to scribble something close to his hand. He's supposed to be drunk anyway. And … exhausted.'

'It seems the dead can speak,' said Locke, embarrassed he hadn't thought of forging notes from the baron himself.

'Well enough to get rid of Brego,' said Sabetha. 'And modify the baron's instructions to his household so they don't expect him until long after the play tomorrow night. Now, Jenora – are your pomanders with the other props?'

'Yes.'

'Thank the gods for small favours. All we have to do, then, is move him once and get him perfumed, and we should be safe enough until we assemble the company tomorrow.'

Locke nodded. It was three doors down to the room where the good props were being kept. Assuming Jean helped, they could heave even a sack of muscle like Boulidazi that far in seconds. But what a crucial few seconds! Locke took up a tattered blanket from the bed to use as a shroud.

Jean seemed to follow his thoughts. He hugged Jenora, and whispered something in her ear.

'No,' she said. 'No, I'll not be made a child on account of that … that fucking pig. Let me help you.' With Jean's aid, she stumbled shakily to her feet and made an effort to straighten her torn tunic.

A few moments later they made the move. Jenora led the way, with Locke and Jean hauling the shrouded corpse, and Sabetha covering the rear, light-footed and wide-eyed. The sounds of shouting and carousing echoed from the common room. Jean bore Boulidazi's weight with ease, but Locke was straining and red-faced by the time Jenora swung the prop-room door open for them.

Another instant and it was done. Locke tore the blanket from the corpse and wadded it up before it could soak up too much blood. Boulidazi lay there with the strange limpness of the freshly dead, like a sand-filled mannequin with a dumbstruck expression on its face.

'One of us has to stay,' said Locke, reluctantly. 'This is too dangerous to leave lying around unguarded. One of us has to bar the door and spend the night.'

'Look,' said Jean, 'I would, but—'

'I understand.' Locke stifled a groan as he realized there was only one candidate for the job he proposed. 'You should be with Jenora. Get out of here, both of you.'

Jean squeezed his shoulder. Jenora, carefully avoiding even brushing against the baron's corpse, reached past Locke and drew a battered alchemical globe out of a pile of cloth scraps. She shook it to kindle a dim light, then handed it to him. In a moment she and Jean were gone.

'Thank you,' whispered Sabetha. The sympathy and admiration in her eyes were too much for Locke to bear. He turned away and scowled at Boulidazi's corpse, then found himself unable to resist as Sabetha drew him back for a brief, tight embrace. She touched her lips to his for the length of a heartbeat.

'I've got notes to write,' she said, 'but you haven't escaped. This is just a postponement. We'll have another chance. *Another* another chance.'

He wanted to say something clever and reassuring, but he felt distinctly wrung dry of wit, and managed only a forlorn wave before she slid the door quietly shut. Locke bolted it with a sigh.

Finding Jenora's supply of rose dust and pomanders took only a few moments, as most of the costumes and junk in the room had been organized for easy packing. Locke gagged and stifled a sneeze as he shook a few puffs of sweet-scented alchemical powder onto the baron's body.

'Pleased with yourself now, shitbag?' Locke whispered. His anger grew, and with a snarl he kicked Boulidazi's corpse, raising another faint puff of rose dust. 'Even dead you're still fucking with my intimate affairs!'

Locke put his back to a wall and slowly sank down, feeling the strength ebb from his legs along with his fury. What a place to spend a night! A dozen *phantasma* masks stared down at him from the walls. A dozen imaginary dead forming a court for one very real corpse.

Locke closed his eyes and tried to blot the image of the death-masks from his mind. Under the cloying odour of roses, he could still make out the faintest scent of Sabetha, clinging to his lips, hair, and skin.

Groaning, he settled in for the worst night of so-called rest he'd had in years.

3

'What in all the shit-heaped hells have you yanked us out of bed for, Camorri?'

Jasmer Moncraine looked rather trampled at the tenth hour of the following morning. Sylvanus was only a certain percentage of a human being, Donker seemed to be silently praying for death, and Bert and Chantal were using one another as buttresses. Only Alondo, of all the night's ardent revellers, seemed to be mostly intact.

The company was gathered in Mistress Gloriano's largest room. The Gentlemen Bastards had spent the better part of an hour chasing wastrels, prostitutes, parasites, and curiosity-seekers out of the inn. The company's bit players had been given stern instructions to gather at the Pearl itself. With a barred door and a nearly empty building, their privacy for the next few minutes was as certain as it could be.

'Our lord and patron has done something we need to discuss,' said Sabetha. She and the other Camorri, along with Jenora, formed a wall between everyone else and the room's table. On that table rested a shrouded and scented object.

'What's he done, commanded us to pour rose dust down our tunics? Gods' privates, that's some reek,' said Moncraine.

'What we have to show you,' said Jenora, her voice quavering, 'is the most important thing in the world.'

'On your honour,' said Locke, 'on your promises to one another, on your souls, you *must* swear not to scream or shout. I'm deadly serious. Your lives are at stake.'

'Save the drama for the stage, and for after noon,' yawned Chantal. 'What's this about?'

Locke swallowed the dry air of his suddenly spitless mouth and nodded. The human wall in front of the shrouded corpse broke up; Jean and the Sanzas pushed through the company and took up a new guard position at the door. When they were in place, Locke uncovered the baron's body in one smooth motion.

There was dead, ghastly silence, an all-devouring vacuum of dread. Moncraine's face did things that Locke would have sworn were beyond the powers of even a veteran actor.

Donker stumbled into a far corner of the room, braced himself against the wall, and threw up.

'What have you done?' whispered Moncraine. 'My gods, gods of my mother, you've fucking killed us. You fucking little Camorri murderers—'

'It was an accident,' said Jenora, wringing her hands together so hard that Locke could hear her knuckles cracking.

'An *accident*? What, what, he … stabbed himself in the gods-damned heart?'

'He was drunk,' said Sabetha. 'He tried to rape Jenora, and she defended herself.'

'You *defended* yourself?' Moncraine peered slack-jawed at Jenora, as though she'd just then appeared out of thin air. 'You witless cunt, you've done for us all. You should have enjoyed it as best you could and let him stumble on his way!'

Sabetha glared, Chantal blinked as though she'd been slapped, and Jenora took an angry step forward. Curiously enough, the fist that slammed into Moncraine's jaw half a second later belonged to Sylvanus.

'You forget yourself,' the old man barked. 'You who might have killed the useless boor weeks ago, if you'd had anything but empty

492

air in your hands! You faithless fucking peacock!'

Sylvanus moved past Jasmer, who was holding a hand to his jaw and staring wide-eyed at the old man. Sylvanus gathered spit with a phlegmy rumbling noise, then spat a pinkish gob on the dead baron's breast.

'So it's our death lying here before us,' he said. 'So what? There's few advantages to being a friend of Sylvanus Olivios Andrassus, but at least there's this. If you say you had to do it, Jenora, I believe you. If you killed the miserable shit to keep your honour, I'm proud of you for it.'

Jenora seized the old man in a hug. Sylvanus sighed reflectively and patted her on the back.

'Jenora,' said Moncraine. 'I'm ... I'm sorry. Andrassus is right. I did forget myself. Gods know I've got no business talking about restraint in the face of ... provocation. But now we've got to scatter. We've got two or three hours, at best. There's hundreds of people expecting us to be at the Pearl by midafternoon.'

'I can't run,' gasped Donker, rising from his misery and wiping his mouth on a tunic sleeve. 'I can't leave Espara! This is madness! I'm not even ... let's explain ourselves, let's say it was all an accident, they'll understand!'

Locke took a deep, steadying breath. Donker was the one he'd been afraid of; with him it all came down to how much he truly cherished his cousin.

'They won't understand a damned thing,' growled Bert. 'They've got a heap of foreigners, players, and nightskins to punish at will.'

'Djunkhar, Bert's right. They don't have to *care* if anyone's innocent,' said Locke. 'So nobody's running or confessing. We have a plan, and you're all going to swear an oath by it if you want to be free and alive at the end of the day.'

'Not me. I'm leaving,' said Jasmer. 'Dressed as a priest, dressed as a horse, dressed as the fucking *countess* if I must. There's ways out of the city that aren't past guarded gates, and unless your plan involves a Bondsmage, I'm for them—'

'Then we'll have two corpses to lie about instead of one,' said Sabetha.

Calo and Galdo reached into their tunic sleeves, taking care to be as obvious as possible.

'You puppies do love to give the fucking orders,' said Moncraine.

'This is madness and fantasy! We don't play *games* with this corpse. We run from it as fast as we still can!'

'You bloody coward, Jasmer,' said Jenora. 'Give them a chance! Who pried you out of gaol?'

'The gods,' said Jasmer. 'They're all perverts and I seem to be their present amusement.'

'Enough! This is *singua solus* now,' said Locke. 'It means "one fate." Does everyone understand?'

Moncraine only glared. Chantal, Bert, and Sylvanus nodded. Donker shook his head, and Alondo spoke: 'I, uh, have to confess I don't.'

'It works like this,' said Locke. 'Everyone here is now party to murder and treason. Congratulations! There's no backing gently out of it. So we go straight on through this business with our heads held high, or we hang. We swear ourselves to the plan, we tell the exact same lies, and we take the truth to our graves.'

'And if anyone reneges,' said Sylvanus, slowly and grimly, 'should anyone think to confess after all, and trade the rest of us for some advantage, we swear to vengeance. The rest of us vow to get them, whatever it takes.'

'Mercy of the Twelve,' sobbed Donker, 'I just wanted to have some fun onstage, just once.'

'Fun must be paid for, Cousin.' Alondo took him by the shoulders and steadied him. 'It seems the price has gone up for us. Let's show the gods we've got some nerve, eh?'

'How can you be so calm?'

'I'm not. I'm too scared to piss straight,' said Alondo. 'But if the Camorri have a plan it's far more than I've got, and I'll cling to it.'

'The plan is simple,' said Sabetha, 'though it'll take some nerve. The first thing you need to realize is that we're still doing the play tonight.'

Their reactions were as Locke expected: panic, shouting, blasphemy, and threats, more panic.

'THIRTEEN GODS,' shouted Calo, silencing the tumult. 'There's one way out and no way back. If we don't go onstage like nothing's wrong, we can't escape. You're in our hands now, and we're your only chance!'

'We piss excellence and shit happy endings,' said Galdo. 'Trust us and live. Listen to Lucaza again.'

Locke spoke quickly now, succinctly, and was viciously dismissive to questions and complaints. He outlined the plan in every detail, just as they'd conjured it the night before, with a few twists he'd thought up during his long vigil. When he was finished, everyone except Sylvanus looked as though they'd aged five years.

'This is even worse than before!' said Donker.

'Unfortunately, you can see that you're indispensable,' said Locke. 'You might have signed on to get killed onstage, but you'll get killed for real if you don't play along.'

'What ... what the hell do we do with the body?' said Chantal.

'We burn it,' said Sabetha. 'Make it look like an accident. We have a plan, for after the play. We roast him just enough to hide the real cause of death, but not enough to prevent identification.'

'And the money?' said Jasmer, his voice dry and tense. 'We won't get a second show with a dead patron. Even if we're absolved from paying damages to all the vendors, we're in the hole. Deep.'

'That's my last bit of good news,' said Locke. 'We have copies of the baron's signatures, plus his signet ring. We collect all the money from the first show; then we come back here. We have you, Jasmer, sign a false receipt from the baron for everything he's owed, just as if he'd taken it first, as was his right. Verena will forge his signature. Then *he* dies in a fire, the money goes quietly into *our* pockets, and we act like we have no idea what the hell Boulidazi did with it before he died.'

'We collect the money?' said Moncraine.

'Of course,' said Locke. 'We figured Jenora could take charge of it—'

'We *can't* collect the money,' said Moncraine. 'It's one of the things Boulidazi and I were arguing about last night before he got too drunk to think! He's got someone coming in on his orders to handle all the coin!'

'What?' said Locke and Sabetha in unison.

'Just what I said, you fucking know-it-all infants. Boulidazi might be coffin meat, but he's got a hireling already assigned to collect the money for him. None of us here will be allowed to touch a copper of it!'

495

CHAPTER TEN
The Five-Year Game: Final Approaches

I

'You're as welcome as a scorpion in a nursery,' said Vordratha, meeting Locke with a glare and a wall of well-dressed toughs at his back. As was becoming routine, Locke had been halted before making it halfway across the entry hall of the Sign of the Black Iris.

'I need to see her,' panted Locke. His flight across the city had not been dignified or subtle; he'd stolen a horse to make it possible, and bluecoats were probably scouring the Vel Verda as he spoke.

'Why, you're the very last person in Karthain who'd be allowed to do so.' Vordratha's smirk split his lean face like a sword wound. 'Her orders were explicit and vehement.'

'Look, I know our last encounter was—'

'Unpleasant.' Vordratha gestured. Before Locke could turn to run, the Black Iris guards had him pinioned.

'Remember, Master Vordratha, that you'd as good as confessed your intentions to have us beaten and left in an alley,' said Locke. 'So if our conversational options were narrowed you've only yourself to blame!'

'The mistress of the house specifically desires not to see you.' Vordratha leaned in close; his breath was like a hint of old spilled wine. 'And while I am charged not to harm you, I'd argue that I'm not responsible for anything that happens between your leaving my custody and hitting the pavement.'

Vordratha's guards pushed Locke outside and heaved him in an impressive arc that terminated in a bone-jarring impact with the cobblestones. His feelings warred bitterly over his next move, pride and desire against prudence and street-reflexes, the latter winning out only when he realized how perilously close he was to carriage traffic and how many witnesses were on hand to see him get crushed by it. Groaning, he crawled back to the curb.

His stolen horse was gone, and the Black Iris stable boys leered at him knowingly. It was a long, painful walk to a neighbourhood where a coach would deign to pick him up.

'... and that's the whole gods-damned mess,' said Locke, his fingers knotted around a glass that had once contained a throat-scorching quantity of brandy. 'I found a ride, came straight back, and here we are.'

It was past midnight. Locke had returned, sequestered Jean in their suite, and with the help of large plates of food and a bottle of Josten's most expensive distilled spirits he'd unrolled the whole tale.

'Do you really need me to tell you that the bitch was lying?' said Jean.

'I know she was lying,' said Locke. 'There have to be lies mixed in somewhere. It's the parts that might be true that concern me.'

'Why not assume it was ALL lies?' Jean ran his fingers rapidly over his temples, attempting to massage away the dull pain still radiating from his plastered nose. 'Bow-to-stern bullshit! Gods dammit, this is what you and I do to people. We talk them into corners where they can't tell truth from nonsense.'

'She knows my name. My actual name. The one I—'

'Yes,' said Jean. 'And I know who told her.'

'But I only ever—'

'That's right.' Disgust burned like bile at the back of Jean's throat, and he tapped his own chest with both hands. 'They said they opened me like a book in Tal Verrar and took everything they wanted. Therefore, *I* must have given them that name. Think! The rest of Patience's story was most likely built around it.'

'That leaves the question of the third name.'

'The one Patience claims is deeper than the one you gave me? Is it even there?'

Locke rubbed his shadow-cupped eyes. 'I don't ... I don't know. It's not a name at all. Just a feeling, maybe.'

'About what I expected,' said Jean. 'Do you *really* remember ever having that feeling, before tonight? It strikes me as a ready-made bluff. I have all manner of strange unsorted feelings in my heart and head; we *all* must. She didn't give you half a particle of telling evidence! All she did was plant a doubt that you could gnaw on forever, if you let yourself.'

'If I let myself.' Locke tossed his glass aside. 'All my life I've wondered where the hell I came from. Now I've got possibilities like an arrow to the gut, and I absolutely do *not* have time to fuss over them.'

'Possibilities,' sighed Jean. 'In faith, now, even if they were true answers, would you really want this particular bunch? I realize it's easy for me to say ... knowing when and where I was born—'

'I know where I'm from,' said Locke. 'I'm from Camorr. I'm from Camorr! Even if everything she said was true, that's all I give a barrel of dry rat shit about. That and Sabetha.' Locke stood, the lines of his face grimly set. 'That, and Sabetha, and beating the hell out of her in this idiotic election. Now—'

Someone knocked at the door, loudly and urgently.

3

Locke watched as Jean unbolted it with customary caution. There stood Nikoros, unshaven, his eyes like fried eggs and hair looking as though it had been caught in the spokes of a wagon wheel. He held a piece of parchment in a shaking hand.

'This just came in,' he muttered. 'Specifically for Master Lazari, from a Black Iris courier at the AHHHHHHH—'

This exclamation erupted out of him as Locke darted forward and seized the letter. He snapped it open, noting the quick familiar strokes of Sabetha's script:

I wish I could write your name above and sign my own below, but we both know what a poor idea that would be.

I know my refusal to see you must have been painful, and for that I apologize, but I believe I was only right. My heart is sick with this strangeness and these puzzles. I can barely tame words to make whole thoughts and I suspect you could hardly be accused of being at your best, either. I don't know what I would do were you in arm's reach; what I might ask, what I might demand for comfort's sake. The only certainty is that the terms of our employment are not relaxed, and we are both in the severest danger if we tread carelessly. Were we together, at this moment, I don't imagine we could possibly tread otherwise.

I don't understand what happened this evening. I know only

498

that it scares me. It scares me that your handler, for any reason, has taken such an interest in telling us so much. It scares me that there are things in motion around you that would appear to tie us both to such secrets and obligations.

It scares me that there may be something still hidden even from yourself, some elemental part of you that might yet tumble like a broken wall, and I am haunted by the thought that when next I find you looking at me it might not be with the eyes I remember, but with those of a stranger.

Forgive me. I know that you would be made as anxious by my silence as by my honesty, and so I have chosen honesty.

I have let feelings I once thought buried come back with real power over me, and now I find myself in desperate need of detachment and clear thoughts. Please don't try to return to the Sign of the Black Iris in person. Please don't come looking for me. I need you to be my opponent now more than I need you to be my lover or even my friend. In this I speak for us both.

'Ah, damn everything,' Locke muttered, crumpling the parchment and stuffing it into a jacket pocket. 'Gods damn everything.' He collapsed back into his chair, brows knit, and let his gaze wander aimlessly over the wall. The most awkward sort of silence settled over the room, until Jean cleared his throat.

'Well, ah, Nikoros. You look like you've been thrashed by devils,' he said. 'What's going on?'

'Business, sir, business. So much of it. And I … I … forgive me, I'm going without … the substance we've discussed.'

'You're weaning yourself from that wretched dust.' Jean clapped Nikoros by the shoulders, a gesture that made the smaller man wobble like aspic. 'Good! You were murdering yourself, you know.'

'The way my head feels, I half wish I'd succeeded,' said Nikoros.

Locke's curiosity drew him back to the present, and he studied Nikoros. The Karthani was on the come-down from black alchemy for sure; Locke had seen it a hundred times. The misery would shake Nikoros for days like a cat playing with a toy. It might be wise to cut the poor fellow's duties … or even to chain him to a wall.

Hells, Locke thought, *if I get any more twisted out of my own skin they might have to shackle me next to him.*

'Lazari,' said Jean, 'now, if that letter's what I think it is … Is it, shall we say, a finality? Or just an interruption?'

'It's a knife to the guts,' said Locke. 'But I suppose … well, I suppose I can view it as more an interruption.'

'Good,' said Jean. 'Good!'

'I suppose,' muttered Locke. Then, feeling an old familiar heat stirring in his breast: 'Yes, I really do suppose! By the gods, I need noise and mischief. I need fuss and fuckery until I can't see straight! Nikoros! What have you been doing all night?'

'Uh, well, I just came back from surveying the big mess,' said Nikoros. 'Big and getting worse. Not just for us, I mean. For the whole city.'

'I'm losing my ability to tell one mess from another around here,' said Locke.

'Oh! I mean at the north gate, sirs, and the Court of Dust. All the refugees out of the north.'

'Oh. OH! Gods, the bloody war,' said Locke. 'I'd half forgotten. What kind of refugees?'

'At this point, the sort with money, mostly. The ones that fled before the fighting gets anywhere near. And their guards, servants, and the like. All stacking up at inns until they can plead for residence—'

'Refugees with money, you say,' interrupted Jean. 'Looking for new homes. Which is to say, *potential voters in need of immediate assistance.*'

'Hells yes,' shouted Locke. 'Horses, Nikoros! Three of them, now! Have a scribe and a solicitor follow us. We scoop up anyone who can pay for enfranchisement; then we find them permanent accommodations in districts where we most need the votes!'

'And they'll be Deep Roots for life,' said Jean with a grin. 'Or at least the next couple of weeks, which is all we give a damn about.'

'I, uh … I will come, sirs, I just …' Nikoros gulped and wrung his hands together. 'I need a few minutes of privacy, first, if I might. I'll, uh, meet you downstairs.'

4

The night was cool. They rode through pale wisps of fog coiling off cobblestones like unquiet spirits, past black banners and green banners fluttering limply from balconies, through stately quiet until they reached the Court of Dust. There they found the mess Nikoros had promised.

Bluecoats were out in force, and Locke saw at once how nervous they were, how unaccustomed they must be to real surprises. Wagons were lined up haphazardly, horses snorting and flicking their tails while teamsters and stable attendants haggled. Lamps were lit in every inn and tavern bordering the court; knots of conversation and argument stood out everywhere in the uneasy crowds.

'Where the hells are we meant to go, then?' shouted a long-coated carriage hand at a tired-looking hostler. His Therin was fair, but his accent was obvious. 'All these taverns are full up, now you tell me this bloody Josten's place is closed off for your damn—'

'Your pardon, my good man,' said Locke, reining in beside the fracas. 'If you have persons of quality seeking accommodations, I can be of immediate assistance.'

'Really? Who the devils might you be, then?'

'Lazari is my name. *Doctor* Sebastian Lazari.' Locke flashed a grin, then shifted to his excellent Vadran. 'Your masters or mistresses have all my sympathies for the circumstances of their displacement, but they'll soon find they're not without friends here in Karthain.'

'Oh, bless the waters deep and shallow,' answered the carriage hand in the same tongue. 'I serve the honourable Irina Varosz of Stovak. We've been five days on the road since—'

'You're all but home,' said Locke. 'Josten's is the place for you. Josten's Comprehensive. I can arrange chambers; pay no heed to what you've been told. My man Nikoros will handle the details.'

Nikoros, barely in control of his skittish horse, approached at the snap of Locke's fingers.

'I'm, uh, not entirely sure where I'm meant to put them,' he whispered.

'Use the chambers I've kept empty for security reasons,' said Locke. 'We can find other places for them after a few days. Rack your brains for anyone in the party who's got empty rooms on their hands. Hell, there's one manor up in Vel Verda that springs to mind immediately. Might as well get some joy out of the damn place.'

Jean was already off plying his own friendly Vadran to other guards, other footmen, other curious and well-dressed strangers with road dust on their cloaks. For perhaps twenty minutes he and Locke worked together smoothly, directing minor cousins of nobility and merchants of assorted quality to Nikoros and thence to Josten's and the bosom of the Deep Roots party.

There was a fresh stir at the southern edge of the Court of Dust.

Massed hooves rang on the cobbles as some two dozen men and women in black livery rode in, led by Vordratha and a few of the bravoes Locke had seen hanging around the Sign of the Black Iris.

'That's a pain in the precious bits,' muttered Locke to Nikoros. 'I was hoping for a little more time alone to make new friends. Who told these assholes to get out of bed?'

'Oh, uh, I'm sure it was only a, uh, matter of time,' coughed Nikoros.

'You're probably right.' Locke cracked his knuckles. 'Well, now we play suitors in earnest. Here come that scribe and solicitor I wanted, at least. You ride like hell back to Josten's and help him stack our friends from the north like books on shelves!'

5

It was past the ninth hour of the morning when Jean's nagging sense of duty pulled him back to the waking world, feeling like dough just barely baked long enough to resemble bread. He made his toilet indifferently, merely taming and oiling his hair before donning a fresh Morenna Sisters ensemble. Optics in place, nose plaster adjusted, he used his suite's little mirror to affirm that his powerful need for coffee was plainly visible. Alas. They'd done good work the night before, and their reward for that work would be yet more work today.

Jean pushed the door to the main suite open and found Locke perched over a writing desk, looking even more ragged than Jean felt.

'I would inquire if you'd slept,' said Jean, 'but I've learned to recognize silly questions before I ask them.'

Locke was surrounded by the detritus of personal and party business: stacks of papers in Nikoros' handwriting, small avalanches of notes and receipts spilling from leather folios, several plates of half-eaten and now desiccated biscuits, a collection of burnt-out tapers and dimly phosphorescent alchemical globes. Crumpled sheets of parchment littered the floor. Locke peered at Jean like some sort of subterranean creature roused from contemplation of secret treasures by a mortal intruder.

'I don't much feel like sleep,' he muttered. 'You can go ahead and have mine if you like.'

'If only it worked that way,' said Jean, moving to loose one of the window-shades. 'Gods, you've got these things plugged up tight enough to keep out water, let alone an autumn morning.'

'*Please* don't touch that!' Locke shook his quill, and Jean noted that it was distinctly shorter than it had been when he'd trundled off to bed. 'Open that window and I'll burst into flame.'

'What's got you so exercised?' Jean left the curtains alone and settled into a chair. 'Anything to do with the new friends we swept up last night?'

'No.' Locke did favour him with a satisfied grin. 'The count, by the way, is seventy-two eligible adults. I've got the solicitors lined up to discuss terms with them. Nice and simple. We'll take them to the relevant offices in groups, hand over a little sweetener money with the fees, and get them registered. They'll be seventy-two lawful voters by nightfall, and then we'll decide which districts to settle them in.'

'How many fresh faces did the Black Iris snatch up?'

'Half what we got.' More teeth appeared within Locke's grin. 'I've left a reception committee at the Court of Dust to keep the party rolling, and I sent out a little expedition to survey the road. The opposition will still get some, of course, but I think we can safely say that the majority of Vadran expatriate votes will be for the Deep Roots.'

'Splendid,' said Jean. 'Now what's the business that's been wearing that quill down?'

'Oh, it's, you know.' Locke gestured at the arc of crumpled parchment sheets on the floor. 'It's a letter. My letter. To, uh, her. My response. It has a few, uh, sentiments and delicacies yet to be straightened out. I suppose by "few" I mean "all of them." Say, can I ask you to undertake an embassy to the Sign of the Black Iris when it's finished?'

'Oh, absolutely,' said Jean, 'because I really was hoping to get into another punch-up with Sabetha's boys and girls as soon as possible, thanks.'

'They won't hurt you,' said Locke. 'Nor make you hurt them. It's me Vordratha's got it in for.'

'Of course I'll carry a token of your obsession into hostile territory for you,' said Jean. 'But there's one condition. Put yourself in your bed and use it for its intended purpose, right now.'

'But—'

'You've got bags under your eyes like crescent pastries,' said Jean, feeling that he was being very kind. 'You look like Nikoros, for the Crooked Warden's sake. Like you ought to be crouched in a gutter somewhere catching small animals and eating them raw. You need rest.'

'But the letter—'

'I've got a sleeping draught right here, ready to administer.' Jean curled the fingers of his right hand into a fist and shook it at Locke. 'Besides, how could a nap to clear your head do anything but improve this epistolary endeavour?'

'Hey,' said Locke, scratching his stubble absently with his quill. 'That sounds suspiciously like wisdom, damn your eyes. Why must you always flounce about being wiser than me?'

'Doesn't require much conscious effort.' Jean pointed toward Locke's room with mock paternal sternness, but Locke was already on his way, stumbling and yawning. He was snoring in moments.

Jean surveyed the wreckage of Locke's attempts at letter-writing, wondering at the contents of the crumpled sheets. He settled his left hand in a coat pocket and ran his thumb round the lock of hair concealed therein. After a moment of contemplation, he gathered the balled-up parchments, piled them in the suite's small fireplace, and set them alight with an alchemical twist-match from an ornate box on the mantel. Locke snored on.

Jean slipped out and quietly locked the door behind him.

Josten's was in a fine bustle. Well-dressed new faces were everywhere in the common room, and the babble was as much Vadran as Therin. Diligence Josten, jaunty as a general of unblooded troops, was lecturing a half-dozen staff. He clapped his hands and shooed them to their tasks as Jean approached.

'Master Callas,' said Josten, 'my procurer of strange clientele! You look like a man in search of breakfast.'

'I have only two wishes,' said Jean. 'The first is for strong coffee, and the second is for stronger coffee.'

'Behold my *jask*.' Josten pointed to an ornate, long-handled copper pot simmering on a glowing alchemical stone behind the bar counter. 'My father's *jask*, actually. Secret of the Okanti hearth. You poor bastards were still steeping your coffee in wash-tubs when we came along to rescue you.'

The coffee Josten decanted from the *jask* was capped with cinnamon-coloured foam. Jean felt less than civilized gulping it, but his wits needed the prodding, and the blend of fig and chicory flavours hit his throat in a satisfying scalding rush. The room was already looking brighter when he reached the dregs of the small cup.

'Lights the fires, doesn't it?' said Josten, smoothly refilling Jean's cup. 'I've been pouring it into Nikoros for days, poor bastard. He's, ah, lost a personal buttress, that one.'

'I know,' said Jean. 'Can't be helped.'

Josten politely refused to let Jean go about his business on a breakfast of nothing but coffee. A few minutes later, Jean climbed the stairs to the Deep Roots private section carrying a bowl heaped with freshwater anchovies, olives, seared tomatoes, hard brown cheese, and curls of bread fried with oil and onions.

Nikoros was sprawled in a padded chair, surrounded by an arc of papers and empty cups resembling the mess that had grown around Locke. His stubble looked sufficient to scrape barnacles from ship hulls, and his lids lifted over bloodshot eyes as Jean approached.

'In my dreams I sign chits and file papers,' Nikoros muttered. 'Then I awake to sign real chits and file real papers. I imagine my grave marker will be carved as a writing desk. "Here lies Nikoros Via Lupa, wifeless and heirless, but gods how he could alphabetize!"'

'We've overworked you,' said Jean. 'And you still coming down off that shit you were shoving up your nose! Hard old days. We've been thoughtless, Master Lazari and I. Here, take some breakfast.'

Nikoros was hesitant to do so at first, but his interest grew rapidly, and soon he and Jean were racing one another to finish the contents of the bowl.

'You're the sinews of this whole affair,' said Jean. 'It's not the Dexas and the Epitaluses that hold things together. Not even Lazari and me. It's been you, it is you, and it will be you, long after we're gone.'

'Long after this disaster is past us,' said Nikoros, 'and gods grant that we still have any Konseil seats at all five years from now.'

'Here, now,' said Jean. 'We're in the thick of it, no lie. You can't see the direction of the battle because you're in the mud and the mess with all the other poor bastards, but it has a direction. You must accept my assurances that I can see a little farther than you can.'

'The Black Iris,' said Nikoros, looking away from Jean, 'this time, they've … they've got … well, they have advantages. At least that's how it seems to me.'

'They have some,' said Jean with nod. 'We have others. And we've come off rather well in this new game of displaced northerners, haven't we? Six dozen fresh voters to seed wherever we need them. The Black Iris can work whatever cocksuckery they like upon us, but in the end it all comes down to names on ballots.'

'You're being poorly served by me,' said Nikoros, almost too softly to hear.

'Nonsense.' Jean raised his voice and gave Nikoros a careful, friendly squeeze on the arm. 'If you weren't meeting our expectations, don't you think we'd have packed you off somewhere out of the way?'

'Well, thank you, Master Callas.' Nikoros smiled, but it was a wan formality.

'Gods, it must be my week to be confessor to the heartsick and weary,' sighed Jean. 'You could do with a few more hours of sleep, I think. The sort not spent jammed into a chair. Off to your chambers, and don't let me see you again until—'

A woman with short curly black hair pounded up the stairs. She wore a travelling coat and mantle, as well as a courier's pouch and a sheath knife.

'Sirs,' she said, 'I'm sorry to come rushing back like this, but I didn't know where else to go.'

'This is Ven Allaine,' said Nikoros, rising. 'Ven for "Venturesome." She's one of our troubleshooters. Ven, I'm sure you know who Master Callas is.'

Jean and Allaine exchanged the quickest possible courtesies; then she continued:

'Master Via Lupa sent us out an hour before sunrise, five of us on horseback, north from the Court of Dust. We were supposed to spot Vadran swells on the road. Introduce ourselves, make our offers, get them in the bag for the Deep Roots before they even hit the city.' She pulled her leather gloves off and slapped them against her leg. 'We planned to be out until midafternoon, but just after sunup we were overridden by bluecoats, lots of them, not sparing their horses.

'They said they had an emergency directive from the Commission for Public Order. No Karthani citizens allowed more than a hundred yards north on the road, because of "unsettled conditions." They said we could either ride back under escort or walk back under arrest. So that's it, and here I am again.'

'Are you sure they were real constables?' said Jean.

'No foolery there,' said Allaine. 'They had the papers from the Commission, and I recognized a few of them.'

'You did well,' said Jean. 'If you'd tried to argue you'd probably be trudging back home under guard right now. You and your fellows get some breakfast, and leave this with us.' Jean watched

506

her depart, then turned to Nikoros. 'The Commission for Public Order?'

'A trio of Konseil members. Chosen by majority vote of the larger body. A sort of committee to run the constabulary.'

'Shit. I suppose it'd be silly of me to ask what party those three belong to.'

'It would,' said Nikoros. 'I'm sorry, sir.'

'We'll just have to continue our diplomatic efforts within the city gates,' said Jean. 'No worries. I'll send Allaine and her crew out to join that party once they've eaten. As for you: bed. Don't say anything, just go to your chambers and go to bed, or I'll throw you off this balcony. You and Master Lazari both need it. I can call the tune for this dance for a few hours.'

After Nikoros crept gratefully off to his rest, Jean sifted the papers he'd left, noting new developments as well as familiar problems. He wrote orders of his own, passed them to couriers, received routine inquiries, and drank several different varieties of coffee, all freshly boiled and scalding, while the pale fingers of autumn light from the windows swung across the room.

Just after noon, the front doors banged open. Damned Superstition Dexa and Firstson Epitalus swept through the crowd and up the stairs, trailed by an unusually large bevy of attendants. Jean set down his coffee and paperwork, then rose to greet them.

'You!' hissed Dexa as she crested the last step, striding forcefully toward Jean. 'You and Lazari have rashly placed us in a position of the most profound and untenable embarrassment!'

Jean squared his shoulders, drew in a deep breath, and spread his hands disarmingly.

'I can see we have a misunderstanding in progress,' he said. 'Well, I'm here to instruct and condole. Everyone who isn't a member of the Konseil is dismissed.'

Some of the attendants looked uncertain, but Jean took a step forward, smiling, and shooed them off, as though dealing with children. In a moment he and the two Konseillors were alone on the private balcony, and Jean's smile vanished.

'You will never again address me in that fashion,' he said, his voice low and even but not even remotely polite.

'On the contrary,' said Dexa, 'I intend to take your skin off by means of verbal vitriol. Now—'

'Damned Superstition Dexa,' said Jean, stepping in to loom over her without subtlety, 'you will lower your voice. You will not create a scene. You will not confuse and demoralize the party members below. You will not allow our opponents the satisfaction of hearing about any disarray or dissension *here!*'

She glared at him, but then, through the force of argument or sorcerous conditioning or both, she caught hold of her temper and nodded, grudgingly.

'Now,' said Jean. 'I will listen to anything, even the most vicious chastisement, so long as it is delivered quietly and we preserve our outward show of amity.'

'I'm sorry,' she said. 'You're entirely correct. But you and Lazari have loaded our credibility on a barge and sunk it in the lake with this business of collecting strays!'

'Wealthy, well-connected strays,' said Jean. 'All of whom will be grateful for their places here, and will show their gratitude by voting—'

'That's just it,' interrupted Firstson Epitalus, 'they won't. Show it to him, Dexa.'

'We were summoned to an emergency meeting of the Konseil just over an hour ago,' said Dexa, taking several folded sheets of paper out of her jacket and passing them to Jean. 'The Black Iris convened it and barely managed to scrape the letter of the law in sending out notices. They pushed an emergency directive through by simple majority vote.'

'In light of unforeseen developments,' muttered Jean out loud as he read the tightly scripted legal pronouncements, 'and the influx of desperate and diverse refugees ... steps necessary to secure the sanctity of the Karthani electoral process ... *urgently and immediately bar all such refugees from enfranchisement as voting citizens ... period of three years!* Oh, those cheeky sacks of donkey shit!'

'Quite,' said Dexa. 'Now, proceed to the fine details.'

'All constables empowered ...' Jean read, skimming irrelevancies and flourishes, '... therefore this directive shall be considered in effect ... noon! Noon today! A few damn minutes ago.'

'Yes,' said Epitalus. 'Seems it wasn't quite such an urgent and immediate need that they didn't want to be sure all of *their own* Vadran newcomers were registered first.'

'Hells,' said Jean. 'I only sent off about half a dozen of ours. We thought we'd have all day! How many new voters did they buy?'

'Our sources say forty,' said Dexa. 'So for all your galloping about in the middle of the night, you've earned us six votes and the opposition forty, and now we have six dozen of our cousins from the north to store like useless clothes! How do you propose we get rid of them?'

'I don't.'

'But that's simply—'

'We made promises to aid and shelter them in the name of the Deep Roots party,' said Jean. 'Do you know what happens when that sort of promise goes unkept? How willing do you think Karthani voters will be to put their trust in us if we're seen kicking respectable refugees back out into the cold before the eyes of the whole city?'

'Point taken,' sighed Dexa.

'If we can't use them as voters,' said Jean, 'we can still take their money in exchange for our help. And we can use them to grow sympathy. We'll circulate some exaggerations about these people being chased out of their homes. Families murdered, houses burned, inheritances usurped – all that sort of thing. We're good with storeys, Lazari and me.'

'Oh yes, quite,' said Dexa, all the fight leaving her voice at last. 'I wager you must know best, after all.'

Jean frowned. This sort of sudden lassitude had to be some sort of friction between Dexa's conditioning and her natural inclinations. Now it was time to put her and Epitalus back together.

'You wouldn't have hired us if you hadn't wanted the best in a very unusual business,' said Jean. 'Now, if you've got no further plans for the moment, I could use your advice on some of these situations around the city ...'

Actually, he hadn't needed anything of the sort, but after a few minutes of smooth fakery he found some genuine questions to apply their nattering to, and after a few more minutes he summoned a stream of coffee, brandy, and tobacco that flowed for the rest of the afternoon. Soon enough any cracks in their working façade seemed plastered over, and Jean found himself practising dipsomantic sleight-of-hand to avoid having his wits plastered over.

Around the third hour of the afternoon Locke appeared, looking significantly less close to death. He wore a fresh green-trimmed black coat and gnawed with practised un-self-consciousness at a pile of biscuits and meat balanced daintily atop a mug of coffee.

'Hello, fellow Roots,' he said around a mouthful of food. 'I've been hearing the damnedest things just now.'

Jean passed him the papers from Dexa, and explained the situation as succinctly as possible. Locke ate with dexterous voracity, so that he was dunking his last biscuit in his coffee as Jean finished his report with innocuous hand signals:

These two were upset. Fixed now. Used argument and drink. More of latter.

'Alas,' said Locke, 'it was a grand old scheme we cooked up, but all we can do now is leave flowers on the grave and move along to the next one. Our Black Iris friends seem to be either sharper or luckier than usual these past few days. Well, leave that to me. I've got to hit back.'

He drained his coffee in one long gulp, then motioned for Jean and the two Konseillors to lean in closer to him.

'Dexa,' he said quietly, 'Epitalus, you two must know all the other Konseil members fairly well. Which Black Iris Konseillor would you say has the most ... mercenary sort of self-interest? The least attachment to politics or ideology or anything beyond the feathers in their own nest?'

'The most aptly suited to bribery?' said Epitalus.

'Let's say the most open to clandestine persuasion,' said Locke, 'by means financial or otherwise.'

'It would have to be a vault-filling sort of persuasion in any case,' said Dexa. 'Rats don't tend to desert a ship that isn't sinking. Forgive that impression of the Black Iris, Master Lazari, but that's as I see it.'

'Don't worry about it,' said Locke. 'But is there anyone?'

'If I had to wager something on the question,' said Dexa, 'I'd put my money on Lovaris.'

'Secondson Lovaris,' said Epitalus, nodding. 'Also called "Perspicacity," though gods know where that came from. He's got no real politics at all, near as I can tell. He loves the sound of his own voice. Loves being one of the selected few. Thoroughly adores the opportunities for ... enrichment a Konseil seat often attracts.'

'I'm an opportunity for enrichment,' said Locke with a smile. 'I need to meet this piece of work privately, as soon as I can, and as secretly. How would you suggest I go about it?'

'Through Nikoros,' said Dexa. 'Him and his underwriting for transport syndicates. Lovaris holds part interest in a ship called the *Lady*

Emerald. If one of Nikoros' contacts carried him a sealed letter on some boring point of nautical business, you'd have his attention and you wouldn't need to fly Deep Roots colours anywhere near him.'

'That sounds damned superlative, Damned Superstition.' Locke saluted her with his empty mug. 'I have my next mission.'

6

Three days later, a lean and scruffy man in a paint-spattered tunic emerged from the misty greenways of the Mara Karthani, where hanging lanterns swayed in the rain and Therin Throne statues in crumbling alcoves gave themselves up slowly to the elements.

Abutting the centuries-old park on its eastern side was the manse of Perspicacity Lovaris, Black Iris Konseil representative for the Bursadi District. The scruffy man knocked at the tradesfolk entrance and was let in by a dark-skinned hillock of a woman, grey-haired but dangerously light on her feet. The scuffed witchwood baton swinging from the woman's belt looked as though it had met some skulls in its time.

She led the newcomer, still dripping wet, through the richly furnished passages of the house to a small, high-ceilinged chamber where warm yellow light fell like a benediction. This illumination had nothing to do with the natural sky, of course – it was an arc of alchemical lamps above stained glass engraved with common symbols of the Twelve.

The woman shoved the lean man up against one wall of the chamber, and for an instant he feared treachery. Then her strong, capable hands were sliding down his sides in a familiar fashion. Her search for weapons was thorough, but she was obviously unacquainted with the old Camorri trick of the hiltless stiletto dangled at the small of the back from a necklace chain.

Locke had no illusions of kicking down doors and leaving a swath of dead foes in his wake if complications arose, but even a nail-scraping of an arsenal was a reassuring thing to have on hand.

'He's not armed,' said the woman, smiling for the first time. 'Nor any threat if he were.'

A middle-aged Therin man with pale hair and a seamy pink face entered the room. He and the woman traded places as smoothly as stage actors, and she eased the door shut on her way out.

'You can remove that nonsense on your head,' said the man. 'At least,

I presume it's nonsense, if you're who you ought to be.'

Locke pulled off his sopping wig of black curls and his ornamental optics, thick as the bottoms of alchemists' jars. He set them down on the room's only table, which had but one chair, on Lovaris' side.

'Sebastian Lazari,' said Lovaris as he sat down with a soft grunt. 'Lashani prodigy with no genuine history in Lashain. Doctor without accreditation. Solicitor without offices or former clients.'

'The backtrail's not up to my usual standards,' said Locke. 'No loss to admit it, since I didn't do the work myself.'

'You and your bigger friend are interesting counterparts to the lovely Mistress Gallante,' said Lovaris. 'Though obviously not from the same place.'

'Obviously,' said Locke.

'I think you've come north from your usual habitations, Master Lazari. I heard rumours a few months ago, when the archon of Tal Verrar took that long fall off a narrow pedestal. Word was a few captains of intelligence managed to duck the noose and get misplaced in the shuffle.'

'My compliments,' said Locke. 'But, ah, you might as well know I didn't leave anyone behind me interested enough to chase me down, even if your … entertaining theory were to reach the proper ears.'

'Nor shall I waste my time contacting them. The election will be past before a letter could even reach Tal Verrar. No, nothing we say here will be heard by anyone else, save my forebears.' Lovaris gestured at the ornately carved nooks and drawers decorating the walls of the chamber. 'This is my family's memorial vault. Seven hundred years in Karthain. We predate the Presence. As for you, well, I've brought you here in answer to your interesting note because I wish to inconvenience you.'

'I'm sure your line hasn't survived for seven centuries by refusing to carefully examine fresh opportunities,' said Locke. 'My note asked for nothing but this meeting. You have no idea what I'm about to offer you.'

'Oh, but I do.' Lovaris smiled without showing teeth. 'You want me to consider a turn of the coat. Specifically, you want me to wait until all the votes are safely counted and I'm back in for the Black Iris. Then and only then would I announce that my conscience had forced me to join ranks with the Deep Roots. I understand you've promised to invent a convincing story, but you haven't told anyone else what it is yet.'

Locke wanted to scream. Instead he pretended to study the nails of his right hand and disguised his next deep, calming breath as a bored sigh.

'I'll have a passable excuse for you,' he said. 'And you would find the experience personally enriching.'

'So I hear,' said Lovaris. 'Ten thousand ducats in gleaming gold. I supply a chest; you fill it before my eyes. On election night, the chest is to be kept at an allegedly neutral countinghouse by an equal number of my people and yours, until I undertake my public metamorphosis. Once I do so, your people walk away and leave mine the gold.'

'Elegant, don't you think?' Locke wanted to punch the wall. This was too much. Lovaris had information from confidential conversations with Locke's half-dozen most trusted associates, information just a day or two old. Still, Locke had stayed calm through worse. 'Come now, Lovaris, we both know you're no ideologue. The whole city knows it. Nobody's going to be particularly surprised or hurt, and ten thousand ducats will buy an awful lot of *anything*.'

'Do I look like a stranger to money?' said Lovaris.

'You look like a man of a certain age,' said Locke. 'How many more pleasant and healthy years will the gods give you? How much more pleasant and healthy could they be with that extra ten thousand to ease your way?'

'There is a more practical concern,' said Lovaris. 'Accepting a bribe is technically an amputation offence, perhaps even a capital one if state interest can be invoked. Nobody pays attention to routine little exchanges, but ten thousand ducats is a very awkward mass of coin, and it doesn't fit any of the usual patterns. If I did this, I would be *hounded* by the Black Iris. I'd be the one man in Karthain to whom the bribery laws would be applied! The only place that money could vanish to is my cellars. I wouldn't be able to join it legally with my countinghouse funds for years, and that's damned inconvenient. Nor can I simply take a letter of credit, for even more obvious reasons.'

'If you can assume that I'm good for ten thousand in cold metal,' said Locke, 'why don't I leave it to you to dictate how I can best conceal the transfer of funds to you?'

'I think not.' Lovaris rose and stretched. 'The most important point to consider is that your little scheme is only worth the trouble if we Black Iris win the election by exactly one Konseil seat. If you win, you've no need to buy me at all, and if we win by two seats or more, my turning can't shift the majority. Frankly, it's all immaterial, because I don't believe you're going to win. I don't believe you're going to lose by so *little* as one seat. You're correct that I'm no slave to ideology, but it would be tedious and stupid to suddenly find myself on the side of the minority.'

'Many interesting things could happen between now and the election,' said Locke.

'A hazy platitude. You might as well be conducting your business in public squares, Lazari. I've revealed how extensive our intelligence is because I want you to understand that you're over the barrel.'

'Fair enough,' said Locke. 'This, then, is the point in the conversation where I say "twenty thousand."'

'Ten thousand would be awkward enough. You expect me to be enthusiastic about trying to hide twice as much? The money's only an enticement if it can reach my pockets invisibly, and if I'm still relevant to Karthani politics after I've earned it. No, Master Lazari, I won't pretend I'm not ultimately for sale in some fashion, but *you* are not offering any sort of price I'm looking for. Now, before I have you escorted out, do you want a moment to put your wet disguise back on? For formality's sake, if nothing else?'

7

A lean, scruffy man in a paint-stained tunic left the tradesman's entrance of the manse of Perspicacity Lovaris and hurried west, back into the cool green maze of the Mara Karthani. Subtle signs had been laid since his last passage, knots of brown cloth tied around hedge branches at knee level, and the man followed them rapidly through twistings and turnings, through brick arches hung with yellowing vines, to the statuary niche where Jean Tannen waited.

Jean, clad in a sensible hooded oilcloak, was sitting on a bench beside the likeness of some forgotten scholar-soldier of the old empire, a stern woman carved in the traditional mode, carrying the raised lantern of learning in one hand and a clutch of barbed javelins on the opposite shoulder. Jean pulled out a second oilcloak and swept it over Locke's shoulders.

'Thank you,' said Locke, pulling off his wig and optics. 'We've got a serious hole in our security. Lovaris knew I was coming.'

'Damn,' said Jean. 'Do you want me to roust those grandmothers Sabetha's got up on the rooftops after all?'

'Gods, they're harmless. Just there to taunt us. Our problem is someone inside Josten's. Lovaris had full details of my plan and my offer, things I've only mentioned to a handful of people, in privacy, in the past couple of days! Is there any place an eavesdropper could have their way with the Deep Roots private gallery?'

'I spent hours going over all the cellars, all the bolt-holes,' said Jean. 'There's nowhere close enough, not above or below. And the noise of the place ... no, I'd stake my life on it. It'd take – Well, it'd take magic.'

'Then I'm off to hunt the rat,' said Locke. 'And since my first approach bounced right off the fatuous fucker's self-satisfaction, you'll have to visit Lovaris and try our second approach.'

'Second approach, right.' Jean rose from the bench. 'You sure our budget can bear the strain?'

'It'll take us down to the dregs, and an emergency few thousand, and those donations from our Vadran refugees,' said Locke. 'But there's not much else to spend it on at this point, is there?'

'So be it,' said Jean. 'If he bites, I'll start visiting jewellers tonight. I've picked some discreet ones.'

'Good. I'd say diamonds and emeralds, mostly, but you've got a sharp eye. Trust your own discretion.'

'And we'll need a boat,' said Jean.

'Already thinking on it!' Locke tapped his own forehead. 'But let's cover first, second, third, and fourth things before we go chasing down fifths or sixths, eh?'

'Gods keep you,' said Jean. 'Don't trip over your feet on the way home. What are you going to do about our rat?'

'Well, since someone we trust is feeding my confidential instructions to Sabetha,' said Locke, 'I reckon I might feed some confidential instructions to all the people we trust.'

8

That night, as a hard rain beat down outside, Locke put his arm around Firstson Epitalus and drew the old man into a whispered conversation in the Deep Roots private gallery.

'You know more about the Isas Thedra than I do,' said Locke. 'I need a quiet, out-of-the-way place in your district to store some barrels of fire-oil. A shack, a cellar. Somewhere nobody will disturb, at least not before the election.'

'Fire-oil? What's this for, Master Lazari?'

'I'm going to see to it that our Black Iris friends have a fairly damaging fire a few nights before the election at one of their Bursadi District properties. I'll take pains to see that nobody gets hurt. I just want them to lose some papers and some comforts.'

'Capital!' Epitalus thumped his cane on the floor approvingly. 'Well, in that case, there's an outbuilding on my own estate. The old boat-house. I'm not using it at all.'

'Good. One more thing, Epitalus. This is absolutely, vitally secret. Speak of this to no one. Am I clear?'

'As an empty glass, Master Lazari.'

The reference left them both thirsty. They toasted the frustration of the Black Iris with small glasses of cinnamon lemon cordial, and then Jean reappeared from his errand, shrugging himself out of his rain-slick oilcloak. Locke waved Epitalus off, then conversed in whispers with Jean.

'We're on,' said Jean. 'I think Lovaris was perversely pleased by the idea of us doing our part tonight, in the rain.'

'Of course. He's a miserable sack of smugness. When?'

'Hour before midnight.'

'Not much time if we're going to be careful.'

'Time enough for me to arm myself with dinner and coffee,' said Jean.

'Then I'll get the things we need from our rooms,' said Locke. 'You plant yourself in front of a fire and eat – Damn, here come Dexa and Nikoros, just the people I can't miss.'

The two Gentlemen Bastards separated, Jean headed for the kitchens and Locke headed to intercept his targets and guide them up to the private gallery. He begged a moment alone with Nikoros first.

'Look, uh, Master Lazari, here's the latest reports,' said Nikoros, fumbling with his satchel as Locke pushed him toward a quiet corner. 'We had a break-in last night at Cavril's office in the Ponta Corbessa, nothing major, but I suspect they got away with some confidential minutes and voter lists. Our delegations to the temples paid for a public sacrifice for each of the Twelve. A lash and a silver compass for Morgante, a silk shroud for Aza Guilla, a dove's heart for Preva—'

'Nikoros,' said Locke, 'I'm devout. I know the usual sacrifices. Just tell me there were no complications.'

'Well, ah, the rain probably cut down on the crowds, but they all went well. The whole city knows we've done our duty to the gods and asked their blessing.'

'If nobody got struck by lightning, I'm content. Now, I need you to get something for me. A hiding place. A shack, a cellar, a hole, anything, preferably deserted or disused. Near the Vel Vespala, as close to the Sign of the Black Iris as you can safely get. Do you know any spots?'

'I, well, let me think.' Nikoros rubbed his eyes and muttered to himself. 'There's a foreclosed chandlery that doesn't have a new tenant, about three blocks from the Sign of the Black Iris. What should I do with it?'

'Just get me the place and I'll do the work,' said Locke. 'I'm going to repeat my stunt at the Enemy Tavern, smoke it up with harmless alchemy, only this time it's going to last hours and it's going to hit 'em at the worst possible time. I'll decide when that is, but I need my fire-oil and powders stored nearby. This chandlery sounds perfect.'

'As you wish, of course.'

'And Nikoros,' said Locke, 'this is the deepest, darkest sort of secret. Don't write any notes or take any minutes on it. Keep this between you and me and the gods. Absolutely nobody else. Understood?'

'Perfectly, Master Lazari.'

'Good. Off on your other business, now, and send Dexa over to me as you go.'

'Master Lazari,' she said, waving her cigar at him. 'You look busy. Can't say I disapprove. What did you want to see me about?'

'What we're going to discuss must remain absolutely confidential,' whispered Locke, leaning in so close he was immersed in tendrils of her smoke. 'You know the Isas Mellia better than anyone. I need you to find me a shack, or a cellar, a bolt-hole of just about any sort, where I can store a certain quantity of ...'

9

An hour before midnight the rain flashed down like silver harpstrings against the darkness. A lean man and a burly man stood beneath a snuffed lantern at the edge of the Mara Karthani. They watched the manse of Perspicacity Lovaris and shivered under their oilcloaks.

'There she is,' said Locke.

A heavy dark shape, sensibly dressed like themselves, emerged from the tradesfolk entrance and walked away from them, north, in the direction of the city streets.

'And if this is a trap?' said Jean.

'I took a precaution.' Locke knelt to lift a light wooden crate onto his shoulders. Jean picked up another. 'There should be a carriage running one green alchemical lamp just north of the manse. Two of our drivers and two of our guards watching for trouble. If we come running, they'll snatch us up and get us home.'

'Good thought,' said Jean. 'Assuming we can run. I hope this is the last risky stupidity we dive into before this mess is over. I'm not sure we can get much less cautious than this.'

'May the Crooked Warden bless us for keeping Him entertained,' said Locke. 'Let's go. What kind of house-breakers would we be if we didn't keep our appointment?'

10

Two more nights and the weather moderated. The sky took back its rain, and the soft brisk wind off the Amathel felt like the kiss of cool silk. Milky moonlight spilled down on the Vel Vespala as Jean Tannen approached the Sign of the Black Iris, calmly and openly.

The foyer guards, not in the market for fresh concussions, actually held the inner doors open for him. Then came Vordratha.

'One of us must be dreaming,' he said, halting Jean three paces into the lobby. 'And I'm quite certain I'm awake, so I suggest you sleepwalk your silly ass back to someplace they don't mind your smell.'

'I'm here as an ambassador,' said Jean. 'Touching on a personal matter of Mistress Gallante's. Of course I don't have an appointment, but she'll want to see me anyway.'

'I'll tell you what,' said Vordratha, 'you're free to kneel and kiss one of my boots, in which case I might possibly consider relaying your petition.'

'Friend Vordratha,' said Jean with a smile, 'in your capacity as Verena's majordomo and all-around mirthless damp prick, you deserve congratulations. In your capacity as any sort of meaningful opposition to my fists, you're half a second of easy work.'

'You're a crude bastard, Callas.'

'And you're still favouring lamentably tight breeches.' Jean feigned a yawn. 'I'll take the same two hostages my colleague did. I invite you to ponder the difference in our sizes and proportional strength of grip.'

Vordratha showed Jean to the now-familiar private dining hall, warned him that the wait might be lengthy, and slammed the door behind him.

Time passed, and Jean paced quietly, alert for trouble. He estimated it was a quarter of an hour before the door opened again and Sabetha came in.

She was dressed mostly in black, black tunic and breeches under a heavy mantled black coat with silver buttons and chasings. Her hair was loose and wind-whipped, her white scarf hanging in folds around her neck, her boots covered in fresh mud.

Not for the first time, Jean felt a strange sense of displacement as his memories of Sabetha tangled with the woman before his eyes. It was like looking at a reverse ghost, a reality somehow less tangible than the recollections five years gone. He'd lived those five years so gradually, but to his eyes she'd received them all at once, and in studying the new lines time had sketched for her he felt the faint tug of his own passing years, like a weight in his heart. How much older did he look to her?

He took a deep breath, banishing the broody thought. While Jean was often bemused by the philosophical notions that made free with his heart and head, long hours of tutelage in arms had also given him the trick of shoving such notions aside, cubbyholing them for contemplation once he'd survived his immediate responsibilities.

Sabetha pressed herself back against the door, closing it, and folded her arms.

'If this continues,' she said, 'Vordratha might become the first man in the history of the world to have himself made into a eunuch for reasons of self-defence.'

'In fairness,' said Jean, 'I can't imagine he's ever found much use for the blighted things.'

'He's a devoted father of seven.'

'You're joking!'

'I was as surprised as you. Seems he's equally dedicated to his children and his career as a professional asshole. Please don't actually hurt him again.'

'My oath to the Crooked Warden,' said Jean. He pulled an envelope from within his coat. 'Now, to why I came. This— Well, I don't want to speak for him. But you ought to know it's taken him a few nights to finish this. Much lost sleep and many false starts.'

'As it was in the beginning, I suppose.' She took the envelope with a hand that shook just enough for Jean to notice, then slipped it into her coat. 'And … is that it, then?'

Had the question sounded tired, Jean would have taken it for a dismissal, but Sabetha sounded wistful, almost hurt. He cleared his throat.

'Diplomacy and curiosity don't always mix,' he said.

'We're not strangers, Jean.'

Jean slipped off his optics and made a show of polishing them against a coat sleeve while he considered his words.

'All I can see,' he said at last, 'is two people I care for being divided and ruled by the words of a stranger. This bullshit of Patience's! I'm sorry. I didn't come to lecture you. But surely you can—'

'You delivered his letter,' said Sabetha. 'Now you're inquiring into his business. Is Jean even here right now? Jean I could speak to, but Locke's … legate to my court, that man's business is dispensed with and the door is open.'

'Again, I'm sorry.' Jean realized that their physical situation had the look and feel of a standoff; so long as they both remained on their feet informality and relaxation would be difficult to kindle. He eased himself into a chair. 'You know that I worry about him. I worry about the pair of you. And I regret that I haven't, ah, exactly paid you a social call since our return. When you first invited us here, I was a little cold.'

'You were preoccupied.'

'That's kind of you to suggest.'

'And then I dropped twenty hirelings on your head and packed you off to sea.' Sabetha sat down and crossed her legs. 'It couldn't have helped. I hope you don't think I was pleased you broke your nose.'

'You provided us with a comfortable ship,' said Jean. 'Leaving it in the middle of the night was our decision. I was annoyed at the time, but I know it was just business.'

'Maybe there's been a little too much "just business."' Sabetha fussed self-consciously with her gloves. 'I kept your hatchets as a sort of assurance, and then as a sort of joke, and then I handed them to Locke like you were some kind of … hireling. I would not have desired to give that impression.'

'Gods, Sabetha, I'm not made of porcelain! Look, we're not— We haven't been *bad* friends, merely absent ones, long apart. And if there are more difficult possible circumstances for a reunion, I'll eat my boots. Cold. With mustard.'

'Now who's being kind?' she said. 'I've missed you. Personally and professionally.'

'I've missed you,' said Jean. 'Sharp edges and all. Life was always better with you around. Everyone around you catches your light. We're doing it now, even across the city, working against you. I haven't seen him like this ... well, not for a long while. Sick with worry and totally exhilarated.'

'The conversation turns to our mutual friend again.'

'Yes. I mean— Look. Let me say this much, please.' Jean took a deep breath and pushed on before she could interrupt. 'He and I had a dangerous misunderstanding in Tal Verrar. We both looked at the same thing, and we both made bad assumptions that led us in opposite directions. We got lucky, but bad assumptions ... they're a possibility to be aware of, you see?'

'Jean.' She spoke haltingly, each word crisp and fragile. 'You must trust ... do I seem at ease to you? Do I seem wholly myself? You must trust that I have reasons, *urgent* reasons for my behaviour, and that they are as much to my grief as they are to his—'

'Stop.' Jean raised his hands placatingly. 'Sabetha, however damned foolish I think you're being, you do have a right to your own judgment. I don't like the judgment, but I'll respect the right, all the way to my grave. I've said my piece.'

'Thank you,' she said, and her smile warmed him like a fire. 'It seems you and he have both grown more diplomatic since we parted.'

'We've made second careers out of finding excuses not to murder one another. It's had a salutary effect on our manners.' Jean found his feet again and held out his hand. 'Sister Bastard, I'd like to detain you longer and make my job that much easier, but I imagine we're being watched. We can't afford to try the patience of our employers.'

'Brother Bastard.' She took his hand and squeezed it. 'I wish I didn't have to agree. Thank you for talking to me.'

'I hope we get to do it again.'

'One day at a time,' she said, softly. 'Until we find out what's waiting at the end of all this. But hope is a good word. I hope you're right. About everything.'

'Is there any message I can take back for you?'

'No,' she said. 'Whatever there is to say, I'll say it myself, in my own time.'

They embraced, and Jean swept her off her feet. She laughed, and he turned the sweep into a complete twirl that ended with her elegantly set down atop a table. He bowed.

'I return madam to the pedestal on which she usually resides.'

'You cheeky lump! And here I was almost feeling sorry about trouncing the bright red fuck out of you in the election.'

'Tsk. Whatever you are, you're not the least bit sorry,' said Jean, waving as he let himself out. 'As you said … we're not strangers.'

II

The room, so warmly lit, so invitingly decorated, felt cold after the door closed behind Jean. Strange how the empty seats and unused tables suddenly contrived to give the place the air of a deserted temple. Sabetha had never felt so isolated here before.

She leapt off the table and landed softly on the toes of her boots, scarf and coat rustling. The envelope was out of her pocket before she knew it, hands moving faster than the thoughts that usually ruled them.

'Of course I'm not alone,' she said. 'You're here.'

The room was still. The bustle of Black Iris business could be heard only faintly through the floor.

'I am a grown woman having a conversation with an envelope,' she muttered several heartbeats later.

He was there like smoke, like a ghost in the room, like a scent in her clothing. It had been so long that she had forgotten the actual scent, only that she remembered carrying it. Remembered wanting it, then not wanting it, then wanting it again despite herself.

There were two Lockes, she thought, turning the envelope back and forth in her hands. Two real Lockes under all the faces he wore in the course of his games. One of them put such a sweet sharp ache in her heart she could scarcely believe that a younger, softer Sabetha had sealed the feeling away and managed to leave. That man broke all the patterns of law and custom and dared the world to damn him for it.

The other Locke … that man was bound tight to those patterns, their absolute prisoner. He would do *thus* because *thus* was the way it always had been in Camorr, or the way it had always been for a *garrista*, or for a priest, or a Right Person, or a Gentleman Bastard. The reasons were endless, and he would cling to them viciously, thoughtlessly, tangling everyone around him into the bargain.

Even his eyes seemed different, when he was that second man. And that was a problem.

If there were two, might there not be three? Patterns behind the patterns, secrets behind the secrets, new strings to dance on, and these ones leading all the way back to the Bondsmagi of Karthain. Another Locke, unknown even to himself. What would become of the Lockes she knew if that stranger inside them was real? If he woke up?

'Which one of you wrote this?' She sniffed gently at the envelope, and the scent of it told her nothing.

Everything about the room was suddenly wrong. She didn't want to be here in this quiet citadel, this orderly heart of her temporary power. The business between her and Locke was thieves' business; she needed a thief's freedom to face it. And a thief's most comfortable roof was the night sky.

She swept an alchemical globe into her coat pocket and shook her boots off, scattering flakes of drying mud on the floor. Barefoot, she padded to one of the room's tall windows and cracked it open.

Sabetha had adjusted the lock mechanism herself and rehearsed the process of slipping out many times; she'd mentally mapped four distinct routes around and down from the roof of the Sign of the Black Iris. The stones beneath her feet were cool but not yet unbearably cold.

Up she went, night breeze stirring her hair, soft moonlight showing all her possible paths. The world of streets, alleys, horses, and lamps receded below her, and she grinned. She was fifteen again, *ten* again, hanging on ancient stones with nothing but skill between herself and the fall.

She was on the roof, quiet as a sparrow's shadow, heart pounding not with exertion but with the thrill of her own easy competence and the anxious mystery of the envelope.

Her rooftop sentry, crouched in the shadow of a tall chimney, all but exploded out of his shoes when Sabetha's hand fell lightly on his shoulder.

'Take a break,' she whispered, straining to keep the sound of her smile out of her voice. 'Get some coffee and wait below for me to come fetch you.'

'A-as you say, Mistress Gallante.' To his credit, he was tolerably silent as he moved off. Not a patch on a proper Camorri skulker, but willing to make an effort.

Sabetha settled into his spot, pulled the alchemical light from her pocket, and once again turned the envelope over and over between her fingers.

'Get on with it,' she said, knowing it was empty theatre for an audience of one. 'Get on with it.'

Minutes passed. Silver cloud-shadows moved and blended across the dark rooftops. At last she found her hands taking the initiative from heart and mind again. The seal was cracked before she knew it, the letter slipped out. The handwriting was as familiar as her own. Her teeth were suddenly chattering.

'Dammit, woman, if you're vulnerable to him it's because you wanted to let yourself be vulnerable. Get on with it.'

Dear Sabetha, she read:

I have instructed J. to put this into your hands directly and so presume to write your name, selfishly. I want to say it out loud, over and over again, but even alone in this little room I am afraid of sounding like a lunatic, afraid that you would somehow be able to sense me making a damned idiot of myself. At least, having written it, I can stare at it as long as I like. It keeps snatching my attention away. How can any other word I write expect to compete? This is going to be a long night.

I suppose it's true to the peculiar course of our courtship that so much of my courting takes the form of apologies. I like to think I have some talent for them; gods know I've had so many opportunities and reasons to practise.

Sabetha, I am sorry. I have put my recollection of everything said and done since I came to Karthain under a magnifying lens, and I realize now that when I returned after escaping from your arranged vacation, I said some things I had no right to say. I took offence at your deception. I confused the business with the personal, and piled self-righteousness high enough to scrape the ceiling. For that, and not for the first time, I am deeply ashamed. It was wrong of me to throw such a fit.

Sabetha sucked in cool air with an unseemly gasp, suddenly realizing she'd been holding her breath. What had she expected? It certainly wasn't this.

Once, you will recall, I told you that I gave you my absolute trust as my oath-sister, my friend, and my lover. Absolute trust is something that can only be given without conditions or reservations, something that can only be rescinded if it was meaningless in the first place.

I do not rescind it. I cannot rescind it.

You tricked me fairly, using something I gave you freely. I am a fool for you not merely by instinct but also by choice. I apologize now, not to beg for sympathy, but because it is an obligation of simple truth and affection I owe you before I have the right to say anything further.

I have pondered so long and furiously on Patience's claims about my past that I have become thoroughly sick of the question. Though I desperately pray for the ultimate vindication of J.'s scepticism, I must admit I have no explanation that strikes me as convincing. There are shadows in my past that my memory cannot illuminate, and if you find that disturbing, I beg you to believe that I don't blame you. Patience's story has given us both a hard shock, and how I ought to deal with it is still something of a mystery.

How you deal with it, I must and will leave to you, not out of despair or resignation but in deference to my conscience, that broken clock which I believe is now chiming one of its occasional right hours. I will not question your reasons. It is enough for you to tell me that you wish to keep this distance between us, and it will always be enough. Know that a single word will bring me running, but unless and until it pleases you to give it, I will expect nothing, force nothing, and contrive nothing contrary to your wishes.

I desire you as deeply as I ever have, but I understand that the fervour of a desire is irrelevant to its justice. I want your heart on merit, in mutual trust, or not at all, because I cannot bear to see you made uneasy by me. I have failed and disappointed you often enough before. Not for all the world would I do so again, and I leave it to you to tell me how to proceed, if and when you can, if and when you will.

Willingly and faithfully yours,
Locke Lamora

She turned the letter over, feeling ridiculous, looking for some other note or sentiment or mark. That was all there was; no pleading, no excuses, no demands or suggestions. Everything was now left to her, and that more than anything brought a tight cold pressure to her chest and left her shaking.

Failed her? She supposed that was true, if a touch ungenerous. The natural process of growing up was to stumble from failure to failure, and all the Gentlemen Bastards had been prodigies of survival, not sensitivity. But disappoint her? The trouble with the skinny, bright-eyed bastard was that he kept refusing to do so.

This letter was the work of the better Locke, the learning and giving Locke, the man who *listened* to her. Listened to her … What a banal sentiment it seemed in itself, but she'd been a woman of the world long enough to learn its rarity and desirability. It was amusing to use men like Catch-the-Duke pieces, but dupes listened with an ear for the main chance, for their own desires to be repeated back to them. After her years in the Marrows and this sojourn among the 'adjusted,' by the gods, Locke's company was more addictive than ever – a man who was proud and unpredictable and framed himself to her desires out of love and friendship, rather than her own subterfuge.

The corners of her vision misted. She rubbed the nascent tears away with her fingers, not gently, and sniffed haughtily. Gods damn this whole stupid mess! Her heart was opened again like an old wound, but what was coming next? What did the Bondsmagi mean to *happen* to that man she loved?

Was she being selfish in holding him at a distance, or was she being sensible, shielding herself against the worst that might be coming, and soon?

'Crooked Warden,' she whispered, 'if your sister Preva has any meaningful revelations that she's not using at the moment, would you let her know that I'm willing to be moved?'

Sabetha sighed. Be moved, certainly, but not *move*. Let the night be hers for a few more minutes. Let the business of the Black Iris click on like clockwork. Let the magi sit on their own thumbs and spin. She read Locke's letter again, then stared out at the city, thoughts churning.

The rooftop tapestry of moonlight and shadows and softly curling chimney smoke comforted her, but it had no answers to give.

Two nights later, Locke and Jean sat together in the Deep Roots gallery at Josten's, dining on birds-a-bed (large morsels of several kinds of fowl on flaked pastry mattresses stuffed with spiced rice and leeks, then given 'covers' of onion and sour cream sauce). To wash this down they had flagons of sharp ale and piles of the usual notes and reports, which they discussed between bites.

Less than a week remained, and the situation was spiralling appealingly out of control. Offices were being vandalized on both sides, party functionaries harassed or arrested by bluecoats on laughable pretexts, speakers and pamphleteers having shouting matches in the streets. Locke had dispatched a team of black-clad functionaries to hand out commemorative Black Iris treacle tarts in several marketplaces. The alchemical laxative mixed into the treacle was slow-acting but ultimately quite forceful, and many of the recipients had publicly expressed their lack of appreciation for the largesse of the Black Iris.

Despite this, the odds commonly given remained eleven to eight in the Black Iris' favour. However much Locke would have liked to shift this as far as possible with childish prankery, there was, realistically, nobody left in the city yet willing to accept baked sweets from a stranger.

'Oh, sirs, sirs!' Nikoros appeared, still looking like a man fresh from a sleepless week on the road. 'I have ... I am so sorry to intrude on your dinner, but I have some unfortunate news.'

'First time for everything,' said Locke lightly. 'Go on, then, shock us.'

'It's the, ah, the chandlery, Master Lazari. The one that you asked me to secure ... in the Vel Vespala, and the one where you and Master Callas packed away all the, ah, you know, alchemical items. Two hours ago, stevedores in Black Iris livery entered the place and cleaned it out. They hauled everything away on drays to a location I haven't yet discovered.'

Locke's fork hung in the air halfway to his lips. He stared at Nikoros for a second, then shared a brief, significant gaze with Jean. 'Ah, damn,' he said at last, and took his bite of chicken. 'Mmmm. Damn. That's a fairly expensive loss. And a fine trick yanked right out of my sleeve.'

'My most sincere apologies, Master Lazari.'

'Bah. It's none of your doing,' said Locke, wondering just what had made thoroughly subservient eager-puppy Nikoros, of all people, turn coat. Something to do with Akkadris withdrawal? Some failure of Bondsmagi sorcery? Poor old Falconer, tongueless and fingerless and comatose, was something of an argument against their infallibility.

'Still,' Locke continued, 'the opposition seems to have a damnable grasp of where we're hiding our good toys these days. I want you to secure us a boat.'

'Ah, a boat, Master Lazari?'

'Yes. Something respectable. A barge, maybe a small pleasure yacht if a party member has one available.'

'Very, uh, likely. May I ask to what end?'

'We took something from one of the Black Iris Konseil members,' said Jean. 'Family heirlooms of significant ... sentimental value. We'll return them after he's done us a favour.'

'And we need the items in question to be absolutely secure until after election night,' said Locke. 'I'm not sure I can trust our current bolt-holes, so let's try putting them on the water, in something that can move.'

'I'll get on it immediately,' said Nikoros.

'Good man,' said Locke, forking another bite of chicken. 'Minimal crew, trusted sorts. They won't need to know what the boat is carrying. Master Callas and I will load the items ourselves.'

Nikoros hurried away.

'I wasn't expecting it to be him,' whispered Jean.

'Nor me,' said Locke. 'And I'm dead curious to find out how she did it. But at least we know. And now we pin our hopes on the boat.'

'To the boat,' said Jean. They raised their ale flagons and drained them.

13

The night before the election, Locke leaned on a wall high atop the northernmost embankment of the Plaza Gandolo, looking out across the softly rippling water of the river and the lantern-lights running across it like a hundred splashes of colour on a drunken artist's canvas.

To his left loomed the Skyvault Span, swaying and singing suspension bridge, its four anchor towers uniquely crowned with balconies and sealed doors. Those doors were invisible from Locke's position hundreds of feet below, but he'd listened to Josten describe them not an hour before.

According to the innkeeper, the doors were as impervious to human arts as most Eldren legacies, but a team of scholars and workers had once erected a climbing scaffold and tried to study them closely.

'Hundred and fifty years ago, maybe. Eight folk went up,' Josten had muttered after looking around the bar. 'Six came down. No bodies were ever found, and none of the survivors could say what had happened. For the rest of their lives, they had dreams. *Bad* ones. They wouldn't talk about those, either, except one woman. Confessed to a priest of Sendovani before she died. Young, like all the rest. They say the magi and the Konseil suppressed the hell out of whatever that priest wrote down. So it's just as well that Elderglass doesn't need maintenance, my friend, because nobody in Karthain has climbed the Skyvault Span since.'

'Bloody charming,' muttered Locke, staring up at the elegant dark silhouettes blotting out stars and clouds. Gods, he was reciting horror storeys to himself. Hardly suave and collected behaviour. He needed to calm down, and he hadn't had the foresight to bring a quarter-cask of strong wine.

Footsteps scuffed the stones behind him, and he whirled, neither suave nor collected.

Sabetha was alone. She wore a dark scarlet jacket over choco-late-brown skirts, and her hair was tightly bound around her lacquered pins.

'You look as though you've been listening to the storeys about this bridge,' she said.

'My, ah, tavern master,' said Locke. 'When I got your note, I asked him if he knew anything about the spot you picked.'

'Seems it's not a popular corner of the district.' She smiled and moved closer. 'I thought we could do with a bit of privacy.'

'Haunted Eldren detritus does tend to secure that. Sly woman! I would have gone with something like a private chamber at a fine dining establishment, but I suppose I'm hopelessly conventional.' A carriage rattled past, onto the creaking deck of the bridge. 'What's on your mind?'

'I appreciated your letter,' she said, gliding closer with that seem-ingly effortless dancer's step that made it look as though a wind had just nudged her along. 'And I don't mean that as the usual oatmeal-tongued sort of polite acknowledgement; I *appreciated* what you said and how you said it. I'm beginning to think I might have been ... hasty in the way I treated you. When you first arrived in Karthain.'

'Well, ah, even if drugging me and putting me on a ship was something of a personal misstep, I think we can agree it was a valid approach from a professional perspective.'

'I admire that equanimity.' She was within arm's reach now, and her hands were around his waist. He couldn't have defended himself if he'd wanted to. 'I'm not ... uneasy with you, you know. It's not you, it's ...'

'I know,' said Locke. 'Believe me, I understand. You don't have to—'

She slipped her right hand up behind his neck and pulled him so close there wasn't room for a knife blade to pass between them. Next came the sort of kiss that banished the world to distant background noise and seemed to last a month.

'Well, *that* you can do,' Locke whispered at last. 'If you feel you have to. I'll, ah, grudgingly refrain from stopping you.'

'It's nearly midnight,' said Sabetha, running her fingers through his hair. 'Not much left now but the casting and counting of the ballots. Were you planning on attending the last big show at the Karthenium?'

'Can't miss it,' said Locke. 'Too many hands to hold. Yourself?'

'There are private galleries looking down on the grand hall. Once you've given all your children suitable pats on their heads, why don't you and Jean join me to watch the returns? Ask any attendant for the Sable Chamber.'

'Sable Chamber. Right. And, ah, now you seem to be wearing that "there's something amusing I'm not telling Locke" face.'

'As it happens, I did hear the most *fascinating* thing.' She took his hand and led him to the very edge of the embankment wall. 'One of my Konseil members privately complained that someone broke into his manor and, if you can believe it, stole the reliquary shelves from his ancestral chapel.'

'Some people should learn to lock their doors at night.'

'I found myself pondering the purpose of such an unorthodox acquisition,' said Sabetha. 'I concluded that it must, in all probability, be an attempt to exercise some sort of hold on a man for whom the theft of less personal trinkets would have no real meaning.'

'I'm disheartened to learn that your speculations took on such a cynical character.'

'Konseillors of Karthain shouldn't have to worry about outside influence on the eve of an election. Don't you agree? I felt compelled to make inquiries and issue instructions to the constabulary. Merely as a matter of routine civic duty, of course.'

'Everyone knows your deep attachment to the civic health of Karthain goes back quite a few minutes,' said Locke.

'There it is! Nearly on time.' Sabetha pointed down to the water, where a canopied pleasure barge emerged from under the Skyvault Span. A long black constabulary launch was lashed alongside the barge, and bluecoats with lanterns and truncheons were swarming it. 'That's the *Plain Delight*. Belongs to a friend of one of your Deep Roots Konseillors, I believe. I also believe that the reliquary shelves in its hold will be back in the hands of their proper owner before the sun comes up. Any particular comments?'

'I can neither confirm nor deny that you're a sneaky, sneaky bitch,' said Locke.

'You're my favourite audience.' Sabetha leaned in and kissed him again, then broke off with a grin. 'Sable Chamber, tomorrow evening. I can't wait to see you. And I'll have a discreet escape route prepared, since I think a lot of irate Deep Roots supporters are going to be looking for you once the ballots are counted.'

Death-Masks

I

The next sound in the room was that of Donker attempting to fling himself at the door, only to be caught and pulled back by the combined efforts of Alondo and the Sanza twins.

'Gods damn it, you brick-skulled hostler,' Jasmer growled. 'If the rest of us have to suffer through this farce, then so do you!'

'What's the name of this hireling of Boulidazi's?' said Locke.

'Nerissa Malloria,' said Jasmer. 'Used to be a lieutenant in the countess' guard. Now she's sort of a mercenary. Hard as witchwood and cold as Aza Guilla's cunt-plumbing.'

'Where's she meant to take the money after the play?' said Locke.

'The hell should I know, boy?' Jasmer ran his hands slowly over his rough stubble. 'His lordship might've been screwing me, but it wasn't the sort of affair where we had pillow talk afterward, know what I mean?'

'I'd bet my life he'd have told her to bring the money to his countinghouse,' said Jenora. 'It's at the Court of Cranes, not far from his manor.'

'No retrieving it from there,' said Sabetha. 'I'll have to work up another note in Boulidazi's hand and send her somewhere more private.'

'She will still expect to deliver the money to *him*,' yelled Moncraine. 'And she'll expect a signed receipt, and she will rather expect him to have a PULSE when he signs it!'

'Well, she's not working for the countess now,' said Sabetha. 'She's not an agent of the law. She's Boulidazi's by hire, and she'll bend to his eccentricities. All we need to do is contrive some that will make her leave the money and go away satisfied.'

'Well, Amadine, Queen of the Shadows, what do you suggest?' Jasmer waved his hands in elaborately mystical gestures. 'Magic? Pity I'm only a sorcerer onstage!'

'Enough!' shouted Locke. 'The sand is running into the bottom of our glass, and no fooling. Leave the details of the money switch to us, Jasmer. This company needs to move to the Pearl in good order, and all of you need to act as though the play is the only care you have in the world. Stout hearts and brave faces! Out!'

The Moncraine-Boulidazi Company shuffled from the room in mingled states of shock, hangover, and grim resolve. The Sanza twins followed; it had been Sabetha's suggestion that after the meeting they lurk conspicuously, leaving as few opportunities as possible for anyone to slip away.

'Any ideas toward parting this Malloria from the money?' whispered Sabetha.

'I've got one notion,' said Locke. 'But you might not appreciate it. We'd need you to play the giggling strumpet again.'

'I'd rather do that than hang!'

'Then we need to find out what the best bathhouse in the city is, and ensure that Baron Boulidazi has a reservation there after the play is finished.' Locke rubbed his eyes and sighed. 'And please remember that I did warn you. I think this is going to work, but it's not going to have more than a scrap of dignity.'

2

'Demoiselle Gallante, I don't understand!' Brego looked uncomfortable in finer-than-usual clothes, and he gestured with clenched fists as he spoke. 'Where the devils has he got off to? Why won't he simply—'

'Brego, please,' said Sabetha. 'I know where his lordship is meant to be *later*. As for the present, you know as much as I! Didn't his notes give you instructions?'

'Yes, of course they did, but I'm uneasy! I'm charged with m'lord's personal safety, and I wish that I could—'

'Brego!' Sabetha was suddenly cold and stern. 'You surprise me. If you have clear directions from the Baron Boulidazi, why are you in difficulty about following them?'

'I ... I suppose I have no, ah, difficulty, Demoiselle.'

'Good. My own duties are about to become rather overwhelming.' Sabetha kissed her fingers and touched them to Brego's cheek. 'Be a dear and look to your business. You'll see what our lord is playing at soon enough.'

The company had left the yard of Gloriano's, arrayed in some semblance of a spectacle. Three black horses had been loaned by Boulidazi, caparisoned in his family colours, red and silver. Sabetha sat the first, sidesaddle, and Chantal walked beside her holding the reins. Behind them came Andrassus tended by Donker and Moncraine tended by Alondo. The players on horseback wore their costumes, and Alondo wore a hooded mantle and a linen mask that left only his eyes bare. A cruel thing in the heat, but it couldn't be helped.

The wagon, driven by Jean and Jenora, had also been draped in red and silver and was piled high with props and clothing. At the very bottom of the pile, shrouded and well-dusted with scents and pomanders, lay the corpse of the company's patron. Galdo walked in the rear, juggling stingingly hot alchemical balls that spewed red smoke, while Locke and Bert led the column waving red pennants.

Brego hurried off to his duties as Calo, perched adroitly atop the rear of the wagon, began to shout:

> 'Invitation! Invitation!
> Hear our joyous declamation!
> The gods are kind to you today!
> Cast off your toil and see a play!'

Calo sprang backward from the cart, turned in the air, and landed on his feet, neatly taking up the juggling of the smoke balls, which Galdo passed to him without a break in their rhythm. Galdo then vaulted into Calo's spot, and proclaimed:

'At LAST, dear friends, at LAST, the Moncraine-Boulidazi company returns in triumph to the OLD PEARL! Come see! There's a place for YOU this afternoon! Don't find yourself bereft! Don't end the day mocked by your friends and turned out of your lover's bed as a simpleton! Hear the legendary Jasmer Moncraine, ESPARA'S GREATEST! LIVING! THESPIAN! See the beautiful Demoiselle Verena Gallante, THE THIEF OF EVERY HEART! Behold the luscious Chantal Couza, the woman who will MAKE YOUR DREAMS HER HOME!'

So they continued, in this vein and in close variations, as the procession wound its way through the humid streets of Espara. The sun blazed behind thinning white ramparts of cloud, promising a fantastic afternoon's light for the play, but little mercy for those who would strut the stage.

A bold green Esparan banner fluttered from the pole beside the Old Pearl, and the theatre was surrounded by noise and tumult. Alondo had explained to Locke, a few days before, how a major play attracted an ad hoc market of mountebanks, charlatans, lunatics, minstrels, and small-time merchants, though only those that made proper arrangements with the company and the envoy of ceremonies would be allowed within ten yards of the theatre walls.

'Are you smarter than my chicken?' cried a weathered, wild-haired woman holding a nonplussed bird over her head. At her feet was a wooden board covered with numbers and arcane symbols. 'Lay your bets! Test your wits against a trained fowl! One coppin a try! Are you smarter than my chicken? You might be in for a surprise!'

Alas, Locke found no time to dwell on the question. The Moncraine-Boulidazi procession had to move on. Beyond the chicken woman moved the expected beer vendors with wooden cups chained to kegs, the trenchmen with shovels and buckets, the jugglers both clumsy and talented. There were harpists, shawm-players, drummers, and fiddlers, all wearing cloth bands around their heads with pieces of paper fluttering in them, showing that they had paid the street musicians' tax. There were pot-menders, cobblers, and low tailors with their tools arrayed on cloths or folding tables.

'Sacrilege! Sacrilege! Ghost-bringers and grave-robbers! May the gods stop your voices! May the gods turn your audience from the gates!' A wiry, brown-robed man whose face and arms bore the telltale scars of self-mortification approached the procession. 'Salerius lived! Aurin and Amadine lived! You stir their unquiet spirits with your profane impersonations! You mock the dead, and their ghosts shall have their way with Espara! May the gods—'

Whatever the man desired from the gods was lost as Bertrand shoved him back into the crowd, most of whom seemed to share Bert's opinion of the denouncer; the man was not soon allowed to regain his feet, and the company passed on.

At last, behind everything, came the simple wooden fence at the ten-yard mark, patrolled by city constables with staves. Within the boundary, merchants prosperous enough to afford tents had taken places against the walls of the Old Pearl. The public gate to the theatre was guarded by a flinty woman in a bloodred gambeson and wide-brimmed hat. She kept to the shade, head constantly moving to survey the crowd, and she wore truncheon and dirk openly on her belt. The actual money-taking was being handled by a pair of burly hirelings.

Locke spotted Brego hurrying toward the woman, folded parchment clutched in his hands. Locke suppressed a smile. That would be the sealed orders from "Baron Boulidazi," the ones diverting Malloria and her weight of precious metal from the countinghouse to the bathhouse.

The company halted at the north side of the Pearl, where Moncraine's half-dozen hired players lounged under an awning. They leapt up, nearly tripping over one another in their eagerness to be seen offering assistance with the costumes and props. As Jean and Jenora handed things to them, carefully keeping them away from the wagon itself, a woman approached on foot with a pair of guards at her back.

She was young, sharp-eyed and heavy, dressed in a cream jacket and skirts trimmed with silver lace. Sun veils dangled from her fourcorn cap, and to Locke she had the air of someone used to crowds parting and doors opening before her. Jasmer and Sylvanus confirmed Locke's suspicions by climbing hastily from their horses and bowing; in an instant the entire company was doing likewise.

'Master Moncraine,' said the woman. 'Do rise. It is agreeable to see you and your company gainfully employed again, if somewhat diminished in number.'

'My lady Ezrintaim. Thank you for your sentiments,' said Jasmer, straightening up but icing his words with a thick coating of deference. 'We have every hope that our recent loss of a few supernumerary players will prove a refinement.'

'That remains to be seen. I had expected your patron to precede his company; can you tell me where the Baron Boulidazi might be found?'

'Ah, my lady, as to that, my Lord Boulidazi has not confided his present whereabouts to me. I can assure you that he does have every intention of being present, in some capacity, for the afternoon.'

'In *some* capacity?'

'My lady, if I may ... I cannot answer for him. Save to assure you, on my honour, that my lord is labouring, even now, to ensure that today is not merely memorable but, ah, singular.'

'I shall of course be watching attentively from my box,' said the woman. 'You will inform your patron that he is expected, following the performance if not before.'

'Of ... of course, my lady Ezrintaim.'

Moncraine bowed again, but the woman had already turned and started away. One of her guards snapped a silk parasol open and held it between her and the sun. Moncraine made his obeisance for another half-dozen heartbeats, then rose, stormed over to Locke, and seized him by the collar.

'As you can see,' said Moncraine, speaking directly into Locke's ear, 'Countess Antonia's envoy of ceremonies now expects a personal appearance from the very, very late Lord Boulidazi once we've taken our bows. What do you propose to do, thrust a hand up his ass and work him like a puppet?'

'You will pretend to be Lord Boulidazi,' said Locke.

'*What?*'

'I'm fucking with you! Why do you keep acting as though it's your problem? The *play* is your problem. Leave the rest to us. And take your hand off me.'

'If I end up facing the rope because of this,' said Moncraine, 'I'm going to ensure that I bring a merry fellowship along for the drop.'

Moncraine stalked off before Locke could say anything else.

'I keep asking myself,' whispered Sabetha, giving Locke's arm a squeeze, '*are* we smarter than that woman's chicken?'

'At the moment it's an open question,' said Locke.

4

Behind the stage lay a number of corridors and small offices, as well as two large preparation areas referred to as the attiring chambers. Stairs led to a cellar where hoists could be used to send players up or down through trapdoors. The air smelled of sweat, smoke, mildew, and makeup.

The attiring chambers buzzed with chatter, most of it from the hired players. Bert and Chantal looked stern but willing, Alondo had his arm around Donker's shoulders, and Sylvanus was relieving a wine bottle of its contents. The twins were robing themselves for their joint role as the Chorus; one in red with a gold-ornamented cap to represent the imperial court and the other in black with a silver-chased cap to represent the court of thieves. Jean and Jenora hung white robes and *phantasma* masks on wall hooks, there to be seized and donned in a hurry by that significant portion of the cast that wouldn't escape the play alive.

Brego and a pair of servants came to retrieve Boulidazi's horses and colours. Once they'd gone, Jean took up a post at the back door. He would keep a close watch on the wagon and its sensitive contents, darting in to help Jenora only with a few crucial or complicated operations.

'We're on at the second hour sharp,' said Moncraine. 'There's a Verrari clock behind the countess' box. When it chimes two, the flag dips. I salute the countess; then it's out with the louts to tame the groundlings. And gods, will they need taming.'

Locke could hear the murmurs, the catcalls, the shouts and jeers of the Esparans filling the earth-floored penny pit beyond the stage, as well as musicians trying to strain coins out of the crowd.

Second hour of the afternoon, thought Locke. That left about twenty minutes for dressing and thinking. The former was so much easier. His Aurin costume was brown hose, a simple white tunic, and a brown vest. He wound red cloth in a band just above his ears; this would keep the sweat out of his eyes and suggest a crown even when he wasn't wearing one. For the early scenes at the court of Salerius II, Locke would wear a red cloak over his other gear, a smaller version of the cloak that would be worn by Sylvanus at all times.

Sabetha approached, and Locke's throat tightened. Amadine's colours were those of the night, so Sabetha wore black hose and a fitted grey doublet with a plunging neckline. Her hair was coiffed, courtesy of Jenora and Chantal's expertise, threaded around silver pins and bound back with a blue cloth matching Locke's red. Her doublet gleamed with paste gems and silvery threads, and she wore two sheathed daggers at her hip.

'Luck and poise,' she whispered as she embraced him just long enough to brush a kiss against his neck.

'You outshine the sun,' he said.

'That's damned inconvenient, for a thief.' She squeezed his hands and winked.

Calo and Galdo approached.

'We were hoping for a moment,' said Galdo.

'Over by the door with Tubby,' said Calo. 'We thought a little prayer might not be out of order.'

Locke felt the sudden unwelcome tension of responsibility. This wasn't something they were asking of him as a comrade, but across the barrier even the laissez-faire priests of the Nameless Thirteenth were bound to feel from time to time. There was no refusing this. The others deserved any comfort Locke could give them.

The five Camorri gathered in a circle at the back door, hands and heads together.

'Crooked Warden,' whispered Locke, 'our, uh, our protector ... our father ... sent us here with a task. Don't let us shame ourselves. Don't let us shame him, now that we're so close to pulling it all off. Don't let us fail these people trusting us to keep them out of the noose. Thieves prosper.'

'Thieves prosper,' the others whispered.

Chantal came to summon them for Moncraine's final instructions. There was no more time for prayer or planning.

5

The green flag of Espara came halfway down the pole, then went back up. Locke, watching through a scrollwork grille, signalled to Jasmer, who squared his shoulders and walked out into the noise and the midafternoon blaze of light.

The penny pit was full, and newcomers were still shoving their way in from the gate. Attendance at plays was an inexact affair, and Nerissa Malloria and her boys would be taking coins until nearly the end of the show.

The elevated galleries were surprisingly full of swells and gentlefolk, along with their small armies of body servants, fan-wavers, dressers, and bodyguards. Countess Antonia's banner-draped box was empty, but Baroness Ezrintaim and her entourage filled the box to its left. Baron Boulidazi's promised friends and associates filled a lengthy arc of the luxury balconies, and had apparently brought more friends and associates of their own.

Jasmer walked to the centre of the stage and was joined by a man and a woman who came up from the crowd. The woman wore the robes of the order of Morgante, and carried an iron ceremonial staff. The man wore the robes of Callo Androno and bore a blessed writing quill. The gods responsible for public order and lore; these were the divinities publicly invoked before a play in any Therin city. The crowd quickly grew silent under their gaze.

'We thank the gods for their gift of this beautiful afternoon,' thundered Jasmer. 'The Moncraine-Boulidazi Company dedicates this spectacle to Antonia, Countess Espara. Long may she live and reign!'

Silence held while the priests made their gestures, then returned to the crowd. Moncraine turned and began walking back to the attiring chambers, and the crowd burst once more into babble and shouting.

Calo and Galdo went smoothly onto the stage, sweeping past Moncraine on either side of him. Locke shook with anxiety. Gods above, there were no more second chances.

'Look at these scrawny gilded peacocks!' yelled a groundling, a man whose voice carried almost as well as Jasmer's had. The penny pit roared with laughter, and Locke banged his head against the grille.

'Hey, look who it is!' shouted Galdo. 'Don't you recognize him, Brother?'

'Faith, how could I not? We were up half the night teaching new tricks to his wife!'

'Ah! Peacocks!' roared the heckler over the laughter of the folk around him. He seized the arm of a tall, bearded man beside him and raised it high. 'Ask anyone here, it's no *wife* I keep at home!'

'Now this explains much,' cried Galdo. 'The fellow is so meekly endowed we *mistook* him for a woman!'

Locke tensed. In Camorr men were coy about laying with other men, and also likely to throw punches for less. It seemed Esparans were more sanguine in both respects, though, for the heckler and his lover laughed as loud as anyone.

'I heard the strangest rumour,' yelled Calo, 'that a play was to be performed this afternoon!'

'What? Where?' said Galdo.

'Right where we're standing! A play that features lush young women and beautiful young men! I don't know, Brother … do you suppose these people have any interest in seeing such a thing?'

The groundlings roared and applauded.

'It's got love and blood and history!' shouted Galdo. 'It's got comely actors with fine voices! Oh, it's got Jasmer Moncraine, too.'

Laughter rippled across the crowd. Sylvanus, peering out his own grille nearby, chortled.

'Come with us now,' shouted the twins in unison. Then they threaded their words together, pausing and resuming by unfathomable signals, trading passages and sentences so that there were two speakers and one speaker at the same time:

'Move eight hundred years in a single breath! Give us your hearts and fancies to mould like clay, and we shall make you witnesses to murder! We shall make you attestants to true love! We shall make you privy to the secrets of emperors!

'You see us wrong, who see with your eyes, and hear nothing true, though straining your ears! What thieves of wonder are these poor senses ...'

While they declaimed, bit players in red cloaks marched silently onto the stage, wooden spears held at cross-guard. Two carried out the low bench that would serve as Sylvanus' throne.

'Defy the limitations of our poor pretending,' said the twins at last, 'and with us jointly devise and receive the tale of Aurin, son and inheritor of old Salerius! And if it be true that sorrow is wisdom's seed, learn now why never a wiser man was emperor made!'

Calo and Galdo bowed to the crowd, and withdrew with grins on their faces, chased by loud applause.

Eight hundred people watching, give or take.

Now they expected to see a prince.

Locke fought down the cold shudder that had taken root somewhere between his spine and his lungs, and wrapped himself in his red cloak. He was seized by that sharp awareness that only came when he was walking into immediate peril, and imagined that he could feel every creak of the boards beneath his boots, every drop of sweat as it rolled down his skin.

Jenora placed Locke's crown of bent wire and paste gems over his red head-cloth. Sylvanus, Jasmer, and Alondo were already in position, watching him. Locke took his place beside Alondo, and together they walked out into the white glare of day and the maw of the crowd.

6

It was almost like fighting practise, brief explosions of sweat and adrenaline followed by moments of recovery and reflection before darting into the fray again.

At first Locke felt the regard of the crowd as a hot prickling in every nerve, something at war with every self-preservation instinct he'd ever developed skulking about Camorr. Gradually he realized that at any given instant half the audience was as likely to be looking at another actor, or at some detail of the stage, or at their friends or their beer, as they were to be staring at him. This knowledge wasn't quite the same as a comforting shadow to hide in, but it was enough to let him claw his way back to a state of self-control.

'You're doing well enough,' said Alondo, slapping him on the back as they gulped lightly-wined water between scenes.

'I started weak,' said Locke. 'I feel I've got the thread now.'

'Well, that's the secret. Finish strong and they'll forgive anything that came before as the mysteries of acting. Mark how Sylvanus seems more deft with every bottle he pours into himself? Let confidence be our wine.'

'*You* don't need bracing.'

'Now there you have me wrong, Lucaza. Pretend to ease long enough and it looks the same as ease. Feels nothing like it, though, let me assure you. My digestion will be tied in knots before I'm five and twenty.'

'At least you're convinced you'll live to five and twenty!'

'Ah, now, what did I just tell you about feigning outward ease? Come, that's Valedon being hauled off to his death. We're on again.'

So the plot unwound, implacable as clockwork. Aurin and Ferrin were dispatched on their clandestine errand to infiltrate the thieves of Therim Pel, Aurin was struck dumb by his first glimpse of Amadine, and Ferrin confided his premonitions of trouble to the audience, some of whom laughed and shouted drunken advice at him.

A bit player in white robe and mask drifted into the shadows of the stage pillars, representing Valedon, first in the chorus of *phantasma*. Aurin and Ferrin set out to win the confidence of the thieves by brazenly robbing Bertrand the Crowd, who all but vanished into the role of an elderly noble. Alondo demanded Bert's purse in the over-considerate language of the court, and while the audience tittered, Bert barked, 'Who speaks these words like polished stones? Who lays his threats on silk like fragile things? You are drunks, you are gad-about boys, playing at banditry! Turn sharp and find your mothers, boys, or I'll have you over my knee to make bright cherries of your asses!'

'Heed words or steel, 'tis all the same, you have your choice but we must have your purse!' said Locke, drawing his dagger. Alondo did likewise, playing up Ferrin's discomfort. The blades were dull, but polished to a gleam, and the crowd sighed appreciatively. Bert struggled, then recoiled and unfolded a bright red cloth from his arm.

'Oh, there's a touch, bastards,' growled Bertrand, tossing a purse to the stage and going down on his knees. 'There's gentle blood you've spilled!'

'All by mischance!' cried Locke, waving his dagger at Bert's face. 'How like you now these "fragile things," old man? Faith, he cares nothing for our conversation, Cousin. He finds our remarks too cutting!'

'I have the purse,' said Alondo, glancing around frantically. 'We must away. Away or be taken!'

'And taken you shall be,' shouted Bert as Locke and Alondo scampered comically back to the attiring chambers. 'Taken in chains to a sorrowful place!'

The pace of events quickened. Aurin and Ferrin were enfolded into the confidence of Amadine's thieves, and Aurin began to make his first direct overtures to Amadine. Penthra, ever suspicious on Amadine's behalf, followed the two men and learned their true identity when they reported their progress to Calamaxes the sorcerer.

Locke watched from behind his grille as Sabetha and Chantal quarrelled about the fate of Aurin. He admired the force of Chantal's argument that he should be taken hostage or quietly slain; she and Sabetha played sharply and strongly off one another, driving the murmur and horseplay of the crowd down whenever they ruled a scene together.

Next came the confrontation between Aurin and Amadine in which the emperor's son broke and confessed his feelings. Behind them, Alondo and Chantal leaned like statues against the stage pillars, backs to one another, each staring into the crowd with dour expressions.

'You rule my heart entire! Look down at your hands, see you hold it already!' said Locke, on one knee. 'Keep it for a treasure or use it to sheathe a blade! What you require from me, so take, with all my soul I give it freely, even that soul itself!'

'You are an emperor's son!'

'I am not free to choose so much as the pin upon my cloak,' said Locke. 'I am dressed and tutored and guarded, and the way to the throne is straight with never a turning. Well, now I turn, Amadine. I am more free in your realm than in my father's, thus, I defy my father. I defy his sentence upon you. Oh, say that you will have me. Since first I beheld you, you have been my empress waking and dreaming.'

Next came the kissing, which Locke threw himself into with a heart pounding so loudly he was sure the audience would mistake it for a drum and expect more music to follow. Sabetha matched him, and in front of eight hundred strangers they shared the delicious secret that they were not stage-kissing at all. They took much longer than Jasmer's blocking had called for. The audience hooted and roared approval.

Another brief rest in the attiring chamber. Onstage, Bert as the old nobleman, wounded arm in a sling, sought audience with the emperor and complained bitterly of the lawlessness of Therim Pel's streets. Sylvanus, regal and red-cheeked, promised to loose more guards into the city.

Donker, still hooded and masked and silent, accepted a particular wrapped parcel from Jenora and quietly took it into a private office. Jean, lounging at the back door, nodded at Locke to signify that nobody had tampered with the wagon or its cargo.

Back out into the light and heat for the irresponsible revels of the thieves, Aurin and Amadine's brief moment of defiant joy while Penthra and Ferrin brooded separately behind their backs. Now Amadine grew careless and cocksure, and Ferrin begged Aurin uselessly to remember his station and his charge.

A terrible end came swiftly to this idyll, in the form of bit players dragging Chantal out of the attiring room, red cloth clutched to her breast. Penthra had gone out into Therim Pel to clear her head with minor thievery, run into the emperor's troops without warning, and come back mortally wounded.

When Chantal spoke her final line, Sabetha wailed. Then, while all the other major players stayed frozen, Chantal rose and donned her eerie, beautiful death-mask and her white robe. Penthra's shade joined that of Valedon as an onlooker.

Recrimination followed. Amadine stood aside in sorrow and shock while Ferrin, in despairing rage, first cajoled and then ordered Aurin to slay her.

'Now, Aurin, now! She stands bereft of all power! See how her curs crouch in awe. None shall impede you. A moment's work will teach your enemies fear forever.'

'I shall not teach anyone that I destroy beauty when I find it, nor betray love when I profess it,' said Locke. 'Swallow your counsel and keep it down, Ferrin. I am your prince.'

'You are no prince, save you act as one! Our sovereign majesty, your father, has charged you to execute his justice!'

'My father watered fields with the blood of armies. I will not water stones with the blood of an unarmed woman. That is execution, yes, but not justice.'

'Then stand aside and let it be done in your name.' Alondo drew his long steel, taking care to slide it hard against the scabbard for the most sinister and impressive noise possible. 'Look away, Prince. I shall swear to your father it was done by your hand.'

'Twice now, Ferrin, have you presumed upon my patience.' Locke set a hand on the hilt of his own sword. 'Never shall I stand aside, nor shall you presume again! A third time closes my heart against you and dissolves all friendship.'

'Dissolves our *intimacy*, Prince. Such is your right and power. Dissolve my friendship, you cannot. I act in this matter as a friend must. So I presume again, though it cuts my very soul, and charge you to remove yourself.'

'I loved you, Ferrin, but for love's sake I'll slay you if I must.' Locke drew his sword in a flash. 'Advance on Amadine and you are my foe.'

'You are an emperor's heir and I an emperor's servant!' cried Alondo, raising his blade to the level of Locke's. 'You can no more run from your throne than you can from the turning of the sun! It is upon you, prince! Your life ... is ... DUTY!'

'I HAVE no duty if not to her!' Locke snarled and lashed out, catching Alondo's right sleeve, as though Ferrin had not truly expected Aurin to strike. 'And you no duty if not to me!'

'I see now you are soft as the metal of your naming,' said Alondo coldly, massaging his 'wounded' arm. 'But I am the true Therin iron. I shall mourn thee. I mourn thee already, unkind friend, unnatural son! *Here's tears for our love and steel for your treachery!*'

Alondo's voice became an anguished cry as he leapt forward. The racketing beat of blade against blade echoed across the crowd; all the jokes and muttering died in an instant. Locke and Alondo had practised this dance exhaustively, giving it the motions of two men furious and beyond reason. There was no banter, no clever blade-play, just harsh speed, desperate circling, and the brutal clash of metal. The groundlings drank it in with their eyes.

Ferrin was the better, stronger fighter, and he pounded Aurin mercilessly, drawing 'blood,' driving Locke to his knees. At the most dramatically suitable moment, Ferrin drew back his arm for a killing thrust and received Aurin's instead. Alondo took the blade under his left arm, dropped his own sword, and spilled out a red cloth. His collapse to the stage was so sudden and total that even Locke flinched away in surprise. The groundlings applauded.

Locke and Sabetha held one another, perfectly still, while Alondo slowly rose and went to the rear of the stage to receive his white mask and robe.

The final scenes were upon them. The sun had moved to crown the high western wall of the theatre. Another fray and tumult; bit players in imperial red advanced their spears upon bit players in the grey and leather of thieves. Calamaxes followed, black robe flowing, red and orange pots of alchemical smoke bursting behind him to mark the use of his sorcery. At last the screams died; Amadine's subjects were wiped out. The slaughtered thieves and guardsmen rose as one, donned robes and masks, and joined the looming chorus of ghosts.

Jasmer pulled Locke and Sabetha to their feet, pushed them apart, and stood dividing them.

'The kingdom of shadows is swept away,' said Jasmer. 'His majesty, tendering your safety, bid me watch from afar and then retrieve you. I see your duty is nearly done, though it cost you a friend.'

'It has cost me far more than that,' said Locke. 'I shall not go with you, Calamaxes. Not now or ever.'

'Your life is not your own, my prince, but something held in trust for the million souls you must rule. You as heir secure their peace. You slain or lost to dalliance condemns them to mutiny and civil war. You who claim the throne are claimed by it as tightly.'

'Amadine!' said Locke.

'She must die, Aurin, and you must rule. You will find the strength to raise your sword, or I will slay her with a spell. Either way, my tale shall flatter you to your father's court, and none live to contradict me.'

Locke picked up his sword, stared at Sabetha, and cast it back down to the stage.

'You cannot ask me to do this.'

'I do not ask, but instruct,' said Jasmer with a bow. 'And if you cannot, then, the spell.'

'Hold, sorcerer!' Sabetha brushed past Jasmer and took Locke's hands. 'I see the powers that sent you before me conspired as much against your will as my realm. Take heart, my love, for you are my love and never shall I know another. Let it be a final and fatal honesty between us now. My kingdom is gone and yours remains to be inherited. Show it much kindness.'

'I shall rule without joy,' said Locke. 'All my joy lives in you, and that but shortly. After comes only duty.'

'I shall teach you something of duty, love. Here is duty to myself.' Sabetha pulled a dagger from her sleeve and held it high. 'I am Amadine, Queen of Shadows, and my fate is my own. I am no man's to damn or deliver!'

She plunged the dagger between her left arm and breast and fell forward gently, giving Locke ample time to catch her and lower her across his knees. Sobbing was easy; even the sight of Sabetha pretending to stab herself was enough to put rivers behind his eyes, and he wondered if this touch would be admired as acting. He held her tight, rocking and crying, under Jasmer's stern, still countenance.

At last, Locke released her. Sabetha rose and walked with languorous grace to the waiting line of *phantasma*, who received her like courtiers and concealed her in the most elaborate cloak and mask of all.

Locke stood and faced Jasmer, composing himself.

'When I am crowned,' he said, 'you shall be turned out of all my father's gifts, your name and issue disinherited. You shall be exiled from Therim Pel, and from my sight, wherever that sight should fall.'

'So be it, my prince.' Jasmer reached forth and lowered a gold chain of office onto Locke's shoulders, followed by his crown. 'So long as you return with me.'

'The way to the throne is straight with never a turning,' said Locke. 'Save this which I had, to my sorrow. I shall return.'

The *phantasma* parted, forming two neat ranks, revealing Sylvanus seated, unmoving, on his throne. Locke walked slowly toward him, between the rows of ghosts, with Jasmer three paces behind. Finally, Locke knelt before Sylvanus and lowered his head.

7

Uncanny silence ruled for the span of a few heartbeats. While Locke knelt in submissive tableau, the nearest two *phantasma* swept off their robes and masks to reveal themselves as Calo and Galdo of the Chorus.

They strolled to the end of the stage and spoke in unison: '*The Republic of Thieves*, a true and tragical history by Caellius Lucarno. Gods rest his soul, and let us all part as friends.'

The crowd responded with cheers and applause. Sylvanus cracked a smile and beckoned for Locke to stand. Small objects flew through the air, but they were all being thrown against the walls and galleries to either side of the stage. Gods, they'd done it! Only a satisfied audience expended their hoarded vegetables and debris away from the stage; it was the ultimate mark of respect from Therin groundlings.

Alondo and Sabetha took off their death-masks and moved to stand abreast with Locke. Together they bowed, then made way for Bert and Chantal to do the same. Next came Sylvanus and the bit players. Only Alondo remained dressed as a ghost.

Moncraine threw back his hood and took the centre of the stage. 'My gracious lords and ladies of Espara,' he proclaimed, stifling the cheering, 'gentlefolk and friends. We, the Moncraine-Boulidazi company, have obtained much benefit from the generosity of our noble patron. In fact, so passionate is my lord Boulidazi's attachment to our venture that he insisted on rendering the most direct assistance possible. It is my great honour to give you my lord and patron, the Baron Boulidazi!'

Moncraine had done his part with excellent pretence of enthusiasm. Locke licked his lips and prayed Djunkhar Kurlin had the nerve to do the same.

Donker allowed the *phantasma* cloak to fall back, revealing an expensive suit of Boulidazi's clothing, requested the previous night in one of Sabetha's forged notes. They fit Donker as though tailored to the hostler's frame. In accordance with Locke's strict instructions, Donker swaggered into Jasmer's place on the stage. Jasmer and the other members of the company bent their heads to him in unison; the bit players were taken by surprise but rapidly made their obeisance as well, and then the first dozen or so ranks of the crowd. Shouts of disbelief echoed down from the balconies where Boulidazi's friends and associates sat, followed by appreciative laughter and clapping.

Donker pointed to them and pumped his fist in the air triumphantly. Then he faced the box of Baroness Ezrintaim, extended both arms toward her, and bowed from the waist, all without removing his *phantasma* mask.

Then, just as Locke had directed, he turned and trotted back to the attiring room. As the rest of the company took a final bow together, most of the crowd seemed amused or at least bemused by what had just transpired, and then the noisy jostling for the exits began in earnest. Musicians started playing again. The company left the stage, hounded only by a few lingering drunks and those loudly begging kisses, particularly from Chantal, Sabetha, and Alondo.

Locke pushed past the bit players within the attiring chamber and cast off his wire crown. Jean held up a hand and nodded again, and a wave of relief made Locke's knees nearly turn to water. Sabetha saw it too, and clutched Locke's arm.

Donker's instructions had been to hurry into the attiring chamber and, during the brief moments the bit players remained onstage, take a running leap into the prop wagon and be concealed under a sheet by Jean. Locke knew it was tempting fate to expect Donker to lay quietly in sweltering darkness just above a corpse, but there was nothing else for it. 'Boulidazi' had to vanish like a passing breeze, as Donker couldn't unmask or even utter a single syllable without breaking the fragile illusion. Jean had been fully prepared to bash him on the head if he balked.

'Where has the baron gone?' said one of the bit players.

'My lord's friends were waiting to collect him,' said Jean. 'You can imagine how busy the baron must be tonight.'

'Now for the envoy of ceremonies,' whispered Locke to Sabetha. 'Quickly, before the wait annoys her.'

'Do you want me to come with you?'

'I think it's our best chance.' He outlined his plan, and she smiled.

'It's no dumber than anything else we've done today!'

The attiring chamber was thick with relieved and sweaty bit players, all collecting robes and masks and props under Jenora's demanding direction. There was no time for leisure; the bit players had to be paid off for their work and sent away without the usual camaraderie and drinking. The company's goods had to be packed and rolling toward the rendezvous with Nerissa Malloria before Malloria herself decamped from the Old Pearl. That was everyone else's business, though. Locke and Sabetha swiftly shed their costume weapons (it was unlawful for them to display such things offstage) and dashed for the courtyard.

Out into the sunlight again, past the dregs of the escaping groundlings, through the detritus of fruit peels and spilled beer, they ran up the stairs to the balcony sections and nearly collided with a pair of guards outside the Baroness Ezrintaim's box.

'We request an audience with the lady Ezrintaim,' said Locke, holding up the signet ring they'd taken from Boulidazi the night before. 'We come urgently, on behalf of the Baron Boulidazi.'

'The lady will not receive players in her private box,' said one of the guards. 'You must—'

549

'None of that,' came the voice of the envoy of ceremonies. 'Admit them, and see that we have privacy.'

Locke and Sabetha were allowed onto the balcony, where they found Ezrintaim at the rail, looking down at the stage and the drudges (paid for by Moncraine) sweeping the courtyard. The baroness turned, and the two Camorri bowed more deeply than required.

'Well,' said Ezrintaim, 'your noble patron does come and go rather as he pleases, doesn't he? This is the second time I've expected him and met part of his troupe instead.'

'My lord Boulidazi sends his most earnest and abject apologies, my lady, that he cannot visit you as you required,' said Locke. 'Leaving the stage just now, he stumbled and injured his ankle. Very badly. He cannot stand at the moment, let alone climb stairs. He placed his signet in our hands as his messengers, and bid us offer it if you wished to verify—'

'My, my. The Baron Boulidazi is less than careful in his habits. Do put that down, boy, I've no need to bite the baron's ring. I've seen it before. Is your lord still here?'

'Some of his friends insisted he be taken to a physiker immediately, my lady, and without causing a scene,' said Sabetha. 'My lord was in considerable pain and may not have adequately resisted their blandishments.'

'Refusing temptation isn't Lord Boulidazi's particular strength,' said Ezrintaim, staring at Sabetha more intently than Locke would have liked. 'But if he's done himself an injury I won't begrudge his friends using their brains for once.'

'He, ah, that is, *my lord* hopes that you will consent to be his guest at any convenient time following tomorrow's performance,' said Locke. This was a risky ploy if Lady Ezrintaim had any reason to find the offer insulting, but if it helped strengthen the impression that Boulidazi was presently alive and planning an active social calendar, it meant everything to their deception.

'I see.' Ezrintaim steepled her fingers before her chest. 'Well, it would be convenient, and the sooner the better. I expect you two will also be in attendance.'

'My lady,' said Locke, 'we would appear if so commanded, but we are only players in my lord Boulidazi's company, and I don't see—'

'Lucaza,' said the baroness, 'I should perhaps disabuse you of the notion that I am unaware of Lord Boulidazi's intentions toward your cousin Verena.'

'I, uh—' Locke felt much as he would have if Ezrintaim had adopted a *chasson* fighting stance and kicked him in the head.

'You know what we really are!' said Sabetha in smooth Throne Therin, saving Locke from another useless sputter.

'Countess Antonia relies on me to be something of a social arbiter as well as her envoy of ceremonies,' said Ezrintaim in the same tongue. 'Gennaro is an eligible young peer of Espara who has lost the close guidance of his elders. I prevailed upon several members of his household staff to report on his behaviour. Gennaro is, let us say, rather forthright with them concerning his desires.'

'Does our presence in Espara cause you difficulty, my lady?' said Locke, trying to force himself to be as collected as Sabetha was.

'You've been reasonably discreet, though I will say that none of you have considered the needs of the larger world around you.' She fixed her gaze on Sabetha. 'I don't necessarily believe it would do any harm to Espara to strengthen its ties with Camorr through a marriage. If, of course, that ever was your genuine intention.'

'I haven't misled Gennaro,' said Sabetha forcefully. 'He is … overbearing and presumptuous, but in all other respects he is quite acceptable. And we share a significant interest in several arts.'

'Did your family instruct you to freely choose a future husband during your sojourn in Espara, Verena? I'd find it very strange if they did. I think you've allowed yourself to forget that you are your family's to dispose of. My sources haven't reported which family that is, but I require this much honesty: Are you a member of a Five Towers clan?'

Sabetha nodded.

'Then you know very well that you serve a duke who may require your marriage elsewhere for political reasons! Even if he doesn't, you will still require Nicovante's permission to wed, much as Gennaro will need Countess Antonia's.' Ezrintaim rubbed her forehead and sighed. 'Should you ever feel any resentment that I have looked into the affairs of Lord Boulidazi's household, please do remember that I am *specifically* empowered to avoid thoughtless entanglements like the one you two and Gennaro would have concocted for all of us.'

'We didn't mean to leap into it instantly,' said Sabetha. 'We meant to take several years.'

'There, at least, you show a grain of wisdom,' said Ezrintaim. 'But patient arrangements are quickly set aside when a woman's stomach swells.'

'I can make tea with Poorwife's Solace, the same as any woman,' said

Sabetha. 'I have been thoroughly instructed in avoiding the ... imposition of a child.'

'Rest assured it *would* be an imposition,' said Ezrintaim. 'I will assume that any such occurrence, no matter what sort of accident you plead, is a deliberate attempt to secure a hasty marriage to Lord Boulidazi. I will never threaten your personal safety, but I will certainly threaten your happiness. Is that clear?'

'Absolutely, my lady,' said Sabetha.

'Good. Let us speak no more of this until we are under Lord Boulidazi's roof. Now, your company did tolerably well today. A brisk staging despite your winnowed numbers. I'll deliver a favourable report, and I expect that attendance tomorrow will benefit. Dare I assume that Lord Boulidazi has now satisfied his urge to flounce about on stage as a bit player?'

'I fear Gennaro won't be flouncing anywhere for some time,' said Sabetha. 'His attendance tomorrow will be far more conventional.'

'Also good. I suppose you're eager to return to his side.'

Sabetha nodded vigourously.

'Then do so. Please express my desire for his swift recovery. And that he might act in a more considered fashion, henceforth.'

Locke and Sabetha excused themselves, then raced back across the Old Pearl courtyard toward the attiring chambers. Locke's head swam with the realization of what a fool he'd been to neglect the possibility that the nobles of Espara might have their own sources of intelligence, their own plans and expectations. Baroness Ezrintaim was more right about one thing than she could know. He *had* arrogantly neglected the wider world in his scheming.

'I think that was the strangest damned lecture I have ever received,' he said to Sabetha.

'You too, huh?'

8

Zadrath's Hyacinth Lane Aquapyria was the most reputable bathhouse in Espara, featuring warm baths, cold baths, steam rooms, and a variety of services both openly advertised and discreetly arranged. Within its courtyard lay a tall central building fronted with decorative columns, surrounded by private outbuildings, one of which had been secured for the use of Lord Boulidazi and his entourage.

Welcome clouds were thickening overhead when the Moncraine-Boulidazi wagon pulled into the Aquapyria's court, scarcely an hour after the end of the play. Locke, Sabetha, Jasmer, Calo, and Galdo rode, and Donker still lay miserably concealed somewhere in the heart of the wagon's contents. Locke and Galdo, dressed in threadbare but serviceable footman's jackets from the company's property, leapt out, entered the reserved bathhouse, and chased out the blue-trousered, bronze-muscled attendants.

'Lord Boulidazi will be here any minute!' cried Locke, pushing the last of them out the door. 'He desires privacy! He has injured himself and is in a foul mood!'

When the courtyard was clear, Locke and Galdo helped Donker out of the wagon and into the bathhouse, taking just a few seconds to make the move. Jasmer and Sabetha followed. Calo took the wagon to the stable, there to check the horses and quite literally sit on the corpse of Boulidazi.

Each private bathhouse had a theme to its decorations, and the one secured for 'Boulidazi's' use featured toads. Silver and iron toads surmounted all the basin fixtures, and the walls were murals of toads wearing crowns and jewelry while luxuriating in hot baths. A square sunken bath of white and green tiles dominated the middle of the room; it was about three yards on a side, and its lavender-scented waters steamed. Beside it, on a low refreshment table, several requested wines and brandies had been set out with a tray of sweets and bottles of aromatic oils.

On the left-hand wall a door led into a large steam room, where water could be poured on a brazier of coals to suit the tastes of those lounging inside.

Donker instantly collapsed against a wall, shuddering and gagging. He was frightfully pale.

'Easy there, Donker.' Locke put a hand on his back. 'You've been amazing so far. You've saved everyone—'

'Don't fucking touch me,' Donker growled, gulping deep breaths and obviously straining to avoid throwing up. 'You just leave me the hell alone. This is worse than I ever dreamed.'

'Well, it's not over yet,' said Locke. 'We still need your clothes.'

Donker surrendered them clumsily. Locke pulled a dressing screen closer to the door and arranged Boulidazi's wardrobe on and around it, haphazardly. Dagger and jacket he hung from the screen. Silk tunic, boots, vest, and trousers he scattered on the floor.

Sabetha threw her own shoes and costume components on the tiles near the bath. She retained only her black hose and a dressing gown. Locke did his best to look like he wasn't staring, and she did an admirable job of pretending she wasn't encouraging him. Once the floor was in sufficient disarray, Sabetha grabbed Donker by the front of his undertunic and steered him to the steam room.

'Donker's right,' muttered Moncraine as he followed. 'This entire plan is thinner than old parchment at too many points.'

'We're not doing so badly,' said Locke. 'If we can just get past this we're safe home with the money in our hands.'

Donker, Jasmer, and Sabetha closed themselves up in the steam chamber. Locke used some of the aromatic oils to slick his hair back, and donned a pair of costume optics provided by Jenora. He positioned himself next to the door, while Galdo ate sweets and examined the wine bottles.

There was a knock at the door not two minutes later.

Instantly, Jasmer moaned in a manner that was half-pained and half-sensual. He'd been retained for this portion of the scheme for one reason – he alone had the depth and flexibility of voice to imitate Baron Boulidazi.

Locke opened the front door of the bathhouse. Nerissa Malloria stood there holding a reinforced wooden box, with one of her burly hirelings at her shoulder. The other waited with the carriage that had brought them.

'Ahhhhhhh,' cried Moncraine. 'Ahhh, gods!'

'Mistress Malloria,' said Locke, coughing into his hand. 'Please come in. My lord Boulidazi instructed us to expect you.'

'I said more wine, damn your dry balls,' shouted Jasmer. 'Where is it?'

Galdo busied himself with a wine bottle and a pair of glasses.

'Very interesting,' said Malloria, stepping over the threshold and moving carefully to avoid the clothes scattered on the floor. Her man remained outside and closed the door. 'I'm to present this to the baron and obtain his mark on a chit.'

'The, ah, baron, my master, tripped and fell after the play,' said Locke. 'He hurt his ankle quite severely. His, ah, that is, Verena … Verena Gallante is comforting him while we wait for a physiker.'

'Comforting him,' mused Malloria.

'Ahhhhhh,' moaned Jasmer, and there was a slapping noise. 'Now,

now, you can keep doing that in a moment. The wine! Fetch the damn wine!'

The door to the steam room burst open, and grey tendrils slithered out into the air of the main room. Sabetha stood there, gown in hand, topless. She pretended to notice Malloria for the first time, half screamed, and wound the dressing gown around herself in a flash. Then she closed the door to the steam room.

'Apologies,' she giggled. 'My lord Boulidazi is in need of ministration. And wine.' She snapped her fingers at Galdo, who passed over a tray with the glasses and open bottle.

'Ministration,' smirked Malloria. 'I'm sure that's just what he needs to recover from any ... infirmity.'

'Malloria! Is that Malloria?' Locke had to credit Moncraine for his impression of Boulidazi, though perhaps the impresario's resentment coloured the act with a touch too much petulance. 'Good, good! Sorry I can't receive you at the moment. Just wait a bottle or two, there's a good woman.'

Sabetha slipped back into the steam room with the wine. Muffled giggles and laughter followed.

'Don't bother with the damn glasses,' yelled Moncraine. 'Just give the bottle here. That's it. I'll put my lips on this, and as for yours ...'

Locke stood at attention against the wall, and tried to look profoundly embarrassed. Galdo hung his head and slunk back to a place on the far wall.

Jasmer's appreciative moaning drifted from the steam room for some time. Malloria's dark amusement faded into obvious irritation.

'Um,' said Locke, quietly. 'I do have my lord's signet ring ...'

Malloria raised an eyebrow at him.

'That is, he's entrusted it to me while he's ... occupied. If you wished to—'

'Why not?' she said. 'If Lord Boulidazi has no time for me, far be it from me to *presume* upon his attention.'

She set the wooden box down next to the wine and brandy bottles, then unlocked it with a key hung around her neck. She handed a piece of parchment to Locke, who examined it while heating a stick of wax over one of the room's non-alchemical lamps.

Locke inked a quill and wrote 'Received' at the bottom of the chit. He then gave the document a splash of wax and pressed Boulidazi's signet into it.

'I'll need to retrieve the box before tomorrow's performance,' she said as they waited for the signet imprint to harden.

'Come to Gloriano's Rooms any time after sunup,' said Locke. 'And, ah, my lord would wish … that is, were he not … distracted—' Locke fumbled two silver coins out of a belt pouch and passed them to her. 'Some suitable, ah, gratuity for your trouble.'

And for your silence, thought Locke. It was a safe bet that here, as in Camorr, the well-off relied on open purses to smooth over their poor behaviour. Malloria gratified him by touching the coins to her forehead in salute.

'Appreciated,' she said. 'I'll send a man for the box before noon tomorrow.'

Locke bolted the door behind her, then ran to the steam room and threw the door open. Moncraine swaggered out, drinking from the bottle of wine, followed by Sabetha in her dressing gown and Donker with a haunted expression on his face. They all gathered at the coin box and peered at the contents. Here and there a silver coin gleamed against the copper.

'That's … more money than I've ever seen,' muttered Donker. 'Must be pretty heavy.'

'Shit,' said Sabetha. 'Donker's right about that. Where are we going to hide it now that we've got it? We can't have the company members walking around with their pockets jangling. It'll contradict the story that all the money vanished with Boulidazi.'

'Maybe Mistress Gloriano can hide it,' said Donker.

'I wouldn't ask her to,' said Locke. 'Her place is going to be full of constables once we report Boulidazi's tragic fire. Some of them might take the place apart out of boredom or thoroughness.'

'I hope you're not about to suggest that we let you take it out of the city,' said Jasmer.

'Of course not,' said Locke. 'All we want is enough to let us get home. The rest is yours, if we can find some way to dole it out in portions that won't get anyone hanged.'

Moncraine braced himself against the box and stared into its depths for some time. Then he snapped his fingers and grinned.

'Salvard,' he said. 'Stay-Awake Salvard! The good solicitor. He'll hold it at his offices, no questions asked. One of his more discreet services for clients who can't or won't trust a countinghouse. There'll be a fee, of course, but what do we care? I'll take it myself.'

'And *I'll* go with,' said Galdo, folding his arms.

'Of course.' Moncraine's smile nearly reaches his ears. 'You can carry the box. And someone will need to summon a hired carriage; we can't walk across the city with the damned thing plainly visible.'

'I'll take care of that,' said Locke, moving to the front door. 'Can the rest of you clean up in here?'

'We should leave a bit of a mess,' said Sabetha, tossing a wineglass into the steaming bath. 'Pour some of these bottles into the floor drain. Whoever cleans up will be able to report that Lord Boulidazi must have had a *lot* to drink before he went off to have his … accident.'

'Lovely notion,' said Locke, elated. 'Right. Fix this place up. I'll get a carriage and tell the Aquapyria folk that Boulidazi will be here another hour or so. Let's have Calo roll off quietly, and we'll all sneak out and meet up on the next block. Then back to Gloriano's for the, ah, last scene of this production!'

Not half past the sixth hour of the evening, Calo, Locke, Sabetha, and Donker clattered in a leisurely fashion through the neighbourhoods of Espara, plainly dressed and with their theatrical property tarped over. Nobody recognized them or gave them any trouble.

At Gloriano's, they found the rest of the company safe but for many rampant cases of nerves. As per the plan, they had chased off all the would-be drinking fellows and raconteurs and parasites with the story that they wanted order and sobriety prior to the Penance Day performance, promising a huge debauch afterward. Locke grinned, and immediately huddled in a whispered conference with Jean, Jenora, Alondo, Chantal, Sylvanus, and Bert.

'We've done it!' Locke said. 'Stay-Awake Salvard will hold the money. Jasmer and Giacomo have gone off to leave it with him. You'll all have to take it slowly, bit by bit. And be sure that Donker gets a full share; he's what you might call fragile.'

'My cousin'll find his feet soon enough,' said Alondo. 'And I'll make damn sure he gets his cut.'

A general air of relief swept the room. Although Locke wasn't relishing the task of dressing Boulidazi's corpse, and he knew neither of the Gloriano women would appreciate the only obvious location for an all-consuming accidental fire, the worst was past and the rest could wait for the fall of darkness. Jenora's aunt set to work roasting long strips of marinated beef in her wood-fire hearth. Sylvanus made the acquaintance of a bottle of plonk, and the others relaxed with cups of ale.

Just after the seventh hour of the evening, Galdo burst into the room, covered in sweat and quite alone.

9

'I'm sorry,' Galdo gasped, as soon as they'd all moved to the privacy of the room where they'd unveiled Boulidazi's corpse that morning. 'I'm so sorry! He asked me to make sure the carriage was held. He sounded so damned reasonable, like *we* do, you know? He said that if he had to walk back to the inn he'd strip my hide. He took the box … about fifteen minutes later I lost patience. I went looking for him, and when I asked Salvard's clerk for Jasmer Moncraine, the man looked at me like I'd been drinking. That's when I figured it out.'

'Moncraine's taken the money and buggered us all,' whispered Alondo.

'*Beggared* us all,' said Jenora. 'I can't even … I don't know what to say. It's like all the gods are having a long hard laugh at our expense.'

Sylvanus threw his bottle to the ground and buried his face in his hands. No more eloquent commentary was possible, thought Locke, than that a situation would make Sylvanus Olivios Andrassus waste wine.

'I'm a gods-damned fool,' said Galdo. 'I should have known.'

'He's an actor,' said Sabetha. 'More's the pity, a good one.'

'Let's get after him,' said Calo. 'He can't be dumb enough to have gone to any of the landward gates, the way they're guarded! He'd be insane to put himself on the roads knowing an alarm was a few hours behind at best. So where would he go?'

'The docks,' said Chantal.

'Well, then, let's find him and cut off that damn hand he was scheduled to lose! He's a big old fellow, how hard can it be?'

'We've got no standing here,' said Locke. 'Remember? We've got no right or call to push anyone around; we are *merely actors* so long as we're in Espara.'

'And you'll never find him,' said Jenora. 'Castellano's right, Jasmer won't go by land. The docks are thick with Syresti and Okanti. He'll get out on his choice of ships and no nightskin will ever breathe a word of it to the constables. The dock workers have no cause to love the countess' servants.'

'So we just … we just let him fuck us!' said Bert. 'Is that the plan?'

'No,' said Sabetha. 'There's one thing we can do very easily. We can make it look like Jasmer Moncraine killed Lord Boulidazi.'

'I like the sound of that,' said Locke. 'It'll certainly give the story more weight than Lord Boulidazi getting drunk and setting a stable on fire.'

'A stable!' cried Jenora. 'You can't mean—'

'I'm sorry, Jenora, I know I should have said something sooner. But it's obvious. We can't burn the inn down, and we can't just have him spontaneously combust in the yard. Don't think of it as losing a stable; think of it as not letting your aunt hang.'

'Giacomo, what did you tell the carriage driver after you realized Moncraine was gone?' said Jean.

'I gave him two coppins for his trouble and told him I'd decided to stay a while,' said Galdo. 'I didn't know what to think. I just didn't want to cause a scene.'

'Well, you've saved us by keeping your head,' said Sabetha. 'Here's the new story. After the play, I went with Boulidazi to the bathhouse. Boulidazi received the money from Malloria; she'll testify to that, and she has her sealed chit to prove it. We claim that we don't know what Boulidazi did with the money; all we know is that when he came back here to have a talk with Jasmer, *he did not have it with him.*'

'Simple enough so far,' said Chantal.

'Simple is how it stays,' said Locke, looking at Sabetha. 'If I can presume … I think I know where Verena's going next. We *all* saw Boulidazi come here. We *all* saw Moncraine come here. They had a long private conversation, then an argument. They went out to the stables together for some reason.'

'A few minutes later we noticed the stables on fire,' said Sabetha. 'Boulidazi dead in the wreckage and Moncraine vanished into the night. His guilt will be clear even to a child.'

'We'll need to bring Mistress Gloriano in on this,' said Jean. 'I'm sorry, Jenora, I know we meant to keep her out of the lies, but she of all people has to tell the constables that Moncraine and Boulidazi were here tonight.'

'There's no helping it, Jovanno, you're right.' She put her arm over Jean's shoulder. 'Auntie won't be best pleased, but *I* can get her to do anything we need. Don't worry about her.'

'This is still a miserable mess,' said Chantal. 'Boulidazi's people may yet try to wring every copper they can from us. Maybe even fold the company and take its assets. Hell, that's assuming the constables don't just throw us all in the Weeping Tower as assumed accomplices.'

'I think,' said Locke, 'that we might just have a friend in a fairly high place. Or, if not a friend, someone with an abiding interest in keeping scandals as subdued as possible.'

'There's no subduing the fucking murder of an Esparan lord!' said Bert. 'Maybe you Camorri will get yourselves off the hook, but the rest of us—'

'No,' said Locke. 'We are absolutely *not* abandoning you, any of you. Haven't we done enough to convince you of our sincerity? And haven't we pulled off some amazing things together already?'

'Fair enough,' grumbled Bert.

'*Moncraine* fucked us, so we'll *all* fuck him right back,' said Locke. 'And for what he's done, let me assure you … he's made an enemy of our master back in Camorr. He must know it. He's got enough money to live on for a couple of years, but he'll never be able to stop running. As for the company … I'm sure we can convince our master to lend a hand there as well. He has resources beyond what you'd believe.'

'At this point I'd believe just about anything,' muttered Alondo.

'We'll rehearse our story together,' said Sabetha. 'Almost like a play. After sunset, we'll dress Boulidazi one last time and arrange the stable fire. Once it's roaring, members of the company *absolutely* have to be the ones to go running and fetch the constables. You all have to act surprised and shocked.'

'Shock will be easy,' said Chantal.

At that moment, there was a knock on the door. Calo eased it open, revealing Mistress Gloriano wiping greasy hands on her apron.

'Meat's done,' she said cheerfully. 'And there's good boiled rice and some apricots … what? Why are you all staring at me like that?'

'You'd better come in and shut the door, Auntie,' said Jenora. 'Meat's not the only thing we've got to cook before the night's over.'

10

'I don't believe you Camorri,' muttered Mistress Gloriano as she helped carry the shrouded corpse of Gennaro Boulidazi from the wagon to her stables just after dark. 'Assuming this would be the first time I'd ever helped make a body disappear!'

'How the hell were we to know?' grunted Locke.

'I'm in the inn trade in a low part of town, boy. I do like my orderly life, but I've had some folk die in my rooms when it really would have been more convenient for them to be found floating in the bay. So a-swimming they went.'

Mistress Gloriano had certainly been upset to learn the truth, but once she'd accepted that Lord Boulidazi had been stabbed by her niece in the middle of an attempted rape, she'd accepted the loss of her stables as a sort of vengeance.

Calo and Galdo had one end of the corpse, Locke and Gloriano the other. They heaved the heavy parcel into a pile of hay, and Gloriano shook a faint alchemical lamp to life. Jean had moved the wagon and horses to the other side of the courtyard, leaving the structure empty.

'Gods, what a smell,' coughed Galdo as they finished unwinding the dead baron. 'Reeking meat and alchemical dust!'

'He has looked prettier,' said Calo. 'Damn, he's stiff. This ought to be fun.'

The three Gentlemen Bastards wrestled with the rigor-bound body, fitting it with the jewelry, the boots, and the dagger they'd taken from it the night before.

'Seems a damn shame to waste such a fine blade,' said Galdo.

'Be an even bigger shame to waste a fine pair of Sanza twins,' whispered his brother. 'Ugh, his fingers are swelling. I need some help shoving his signet ring where it ought to be.'

Feeling like an idiot, Locke assisted as well as anyone could, until the baron's signet ring was at least plausibly close to the right place.

'Now then, boys,' said Mistress Gloriano, 'if you're quite finished decorating him, open this oil-vase for me and give him a good soak. I daresay I'm quite prepared to light a match on this motherfucker.'

A few minutes later, orange flames were roaring against the black Esparan night, and all those members of the company that hadn't run to fetch help were filling water buckets with every outward sign of haste and sincerity.

11

'This is not how I had envisioned passing the small hours of the night,' said Baroness Ezrintaim, now dressed in boots, lightweight skirt, dark jacket, and visible sword.

Locke and Sabetha, still soot-grimed from fighting the fire, stood at nervous attention in one of Mistress Gloriano's rooms, appropriated for a private talk. It was after midnight. Constables and soldiers in equal number had the place sewn up tight, and the remnants of the Moncraine-Boulidazi company under guard in the common room. Ezrintaim had been summoned by a watch commander when the identity of the charred corpse had become generally known.

Sabetha wore what Locke thought was an excellent expression of sorrow and resignation.

'Is it … are we so certain it's him?' she said. 'The body was …'

'The body was a lump of coal, girl, but we have the signet and the dagger. We know very well it's Gennaro lying out there. I realize it can't be easy for you.' Ezrintaim rubbed her eyes. 'Still, it's reality, dead under a sheet.'

'Let me help you look for Moncraine,' said Locke, who'd decided that a show of belligerence was a good contrast to Sabetha's shock. 'Me and all my men. If I find the bastard—'

'This isn't Camorr, and you are incognito,' snapped the baroness. 'You've no right to bear arms or dispense justice, and I've no inclination to give you authority I'd have to explain to someone else!'

'I'm sorry, my lady,' said Locke. 'I only meant to offer all possible assistance.'

'The best assistance will be to follow my explicit directions,' said Ezrintaim. 'Jasmer Moncraine has murdered an Esparan peer, and he is an Esparan problem to pursue. Gods and saints, this is going to be a ten-years' wonder even if it doesn't get any worse.'

She paced the room several times, staring at them.

'I expect you to leave the city,' she said at last. 'Yes, I think that would be for the best. I'll secure your safe passage out and have you placed with a caravan. You're welcome to return to Espara as your proper selves, after a few years have passed, but never again as players. Or any other low station!'

'Thank you, my lady,' said Locke.

'And what of the Moncraine-Boulidazi company?' said Sabetha.

'What do you expect, Verena? Boulidazi is dead and Moncraine might as well be. There'll be no more performances, of course. Everything with Moncraine's stink on it will need to be swept under a rug.'

'I meant the players,' said Sabetha. 'They've been … most

562

accommodating. That bastard Moncraine has put them in a very difficult position.'

'It's the difficult position of Gennaro Boulidazi that will most concern the countess,' said Ezrintaim. 'But as far as I'm concerned, Moncraine's guilt blazes to the skies. As long as their storeys are consistent and my men don't find anything interesting in this rooming house, your associates will live. But the company will be broken up, have no doubt.'

'Most will end up in chains for debt once the solicitors have finished holding their feet to the fire,' said Sabetha.

'What's it to me, my dear?'

'They have given us good service while we've been in Espara,' said Locke. 'We feel obligated to plead on their behalf.'

'I see.' Ezrintaim sighed and tapped her fingers against the hilt of her rapier. 'Well, Lord Boulidazi died without heir. No relations beyond Espara that we're bound to respect, either. So the countess will absorb his estates and his countinghouse assets. They're a pretty enough windfall. I suppose my mistress can afford to be generous. The company will *absolutely* lose its name and its present operating charter, but I believe I can intercede to shield them from anything more drastic. I do hope that will assuage your sense of obligation.'

'Entirely, my lady,' said Sabetha, bowing her head.

'Good. You've been foolish and lucky in equal measure, Verena, and I hope you'll remember that you've benefited much from a series of diplomatic courtesies extended on behalf of all Espara.'

'Within the family,' said Locke, 'we'll be absolutely forthright about your invaluable assistance. Given the chance, we shall remember you to the duke.'

'That would be a pleasing gesture,' said Ezrintaim. 'Now, do clean yourselves up and make ready to leave my city so I can begin dealing with this damnable collection of headaches.'

CHAPTER ELEVEN
The Five-Year Game: Returns

I

Dark clouds were rolling in from the north, masking the stars. The Karthenium, palace of the long-deposed dukes and duchesses of Karthain, rose above the manicured gardens and broken walls of the Casta Gravina, a dome of rippling jade Elderglass like a jewel in a setting of human stone and mortar. The late autumn wind flowed past crenellations and etchings on the face of the glass, and the eerie music of a lost race sighed into the night, its meaning unguessable.

Green and black banners fluttered at the edges of every path and courtyard, and a river of torch and lantern light flowed through the gates of the Karthenium, into the Grand Salon, where seemingly endless black iron stairs and walkways spiralled up the underside of the jade dome. Chandeliers the size of carriages blazed, tended by men and women dangling in harness from anchor points on the walkways.

The murmur of the crowd was like the wash and rumble of the sea within a coastal cave. Locke and Jean moved warily through the affair, their green ribbons no protection against being jostled by knots of conversationalists, enthusiasts, and drunks. Black Iris and Deep Roots supporters mingled freely and argued freely in a sprawling pageant of Karthain's rich and exalted.

In the centre of the Grand Salon a raised platform held a number of slate boards and nineteen black iron posts, each topped by an unlit frosted glass lamp. The stairs to the platform were guarded by blue-coats, each sweating under the added weight of a white cloak and mantle trimmed with silver ribbons.

It was the ninth hour of the evening. The last ballots had been cast hours before, and now the verified and sealed reports from each district were on their way to the Karthenium.

'Master Lazari! Master Callas!' Damned Superstition Dexa appeared, dragging a muddled platoon of attendants and sycophants in her wake. Her triple-brimmed hat was topped with a replica of one of

564

Karthain's Eldren bridges, the towers sculpted from hardened leather, each one flying a tiny green flag. Dexa smoked from a double-bowled pipe, puffing streams of grey-and-emerald smoke from her nose. 'Well, my boys, once we've gnawed all the meat off the bones of an election it all comes down to this! Count the votes, then count the tears.'

'No tears in your district,' said Locke. 'If I'm wrong I'll buy a hat like yours and eat it.'

'I'd like to see that. But I'd prefer to keep my seat.' Dexa exhaled streamers of jasmine-scented green and spicy grey past Locke. 'Will you gentlemen be near the stage? Ringside seats as the returns come in?'

'Somewhere less hectic,' said Locke. 'We'll watch from one of the private galleries, after we've had a spin around the floor. Got to make sure everyone's got their spine straight and their waistcoat buttoned.'

'Very fatherly of you. Well then, until the cat's skinned, my regards to our fellow travellers.'

True to Locke's word, he and Jean bounced around the crowd, shaking hands and patting backs, laughing at bad jokes and offering some of their own, spouting reasoned and logical-sounding analysis on demand. Most of it was bullshit fried in glibness with a side of whatever the listener yearned to hear. *What did it matter?* thought Locke. One way or another, they were vanishing from Karthain's political scene tonight and would never be held accountable.

Vast basins of punch made from pale white and bruise-purple wines were being stirred to foam by clockwork paddle mechanisms, operated by impeccably dressed children walking slowly inside gilded tread-wheels. Attractive attendants of both sexes worked behind velvet ropes to fill goblets and hand them out. Locke and Jean armed themselves with punch, along with steaming buns stuffed with brined pork and dark vinegar sauce.

Jean spotted Nikoros hovering miserably on the periphery of a pack of Deep Roots notables and pointed him out to Locke. Via Lupa had shaved, which mostly served to highlight his unhealthy pallor and the fresh lines on his visibly leaner face. Unexpected pity stung Locke's heart. Here was no triumphant traitor, but someone thoroughly roasted on the rack of misery.

Well, what was the use of being able to lie with impunity if you couldn't use it to take a weight off the shoulders of such a plainly unhappy bastard?

'Look, Nikoros,' said Locke, pressing his untouched goblet of punch into the Karthani's hand. He spoke softly, for Nikoros alone. 'I think it's time for me to say that I know what it's like, being pressed by something that rules your conscience against your will.'

'Ah, M-master Lazari, I don't ... that is, what do you mean?'

'What I'm trying to tell you,' said Locke, 'is that I know. And I have known for some time.'

'You ... know?' Nikoros' eyebrows went up so far and fast Locke was surprised not to see them go sailing off like catapult stones. 'You *knew*?'

'Of course I did,' said Locke, soothingly. 'It's my job to know things, isn't it? Only thing I couldn't figure out is what the lever was. It's obvious that you're not exactly a willing turncoat.'

'Gods! I, uh, it was my alchemist. My ... dust alchemist. Receiving it's as bad as selling it. I got caught, and this woman ... well, I eventually f-figured out who she must be. I'm sorry. She offered me a deal. Otherwise I lose everything. Ten years on a penance barge, then exile.'

'Hell of a thing,' said Locke. 'I'd try to avoid that too, if I could.'

'I'll resign after tonight,' muttered Nikoros. 'I'd wager I've, ah, done more *damage* to the Deep Roots than any committee member in our g-gods-damned history.'

'Nikoros, you haven't been listening to me,' said Locke. 'I told you I *knew*.'

'But how does that—'

'You've been my agent more than theirs. Delivering exactly what I wanted the Black Iris to hear from a source they considered impeccable.'

'But ... but I'm *certain* some of what I had to give them was ... it was real, and it was damaging to us!'

'Naturally,' said Locke. 'They wouldn't have listened to you if you hadn't delivered real goods most of the time. I wrote the real stuff off as the price of feeding them the crucial bullshit. So don't resign a damn thing. If the Black Iris lose tonight, it's because you were in a position to serve as my weapon against them. Will that help you sleep a little better at night?'

'I, uh, I hardly know what I should say.' The loosening of the lines of tension on his face was immediate and obvious.

'Don't say anything. Just drain that goblet and enjoy the show. This conversation will stay our little secret. Have a good long life, Nikoros. I doubt you'll ever see us again.'

'Unless our employers want to bring us back for the next round, five years hence,' muttered Jean as they walked away.

'Maybe if they all want to end up in a fucking coma like the shit-bucket with the bird,' said Locke.

'And not that I'm against trying to settle the poor fellow down, but how do you think Nikoros will feel about himself if the Black Iris *win*?'

'Gods dammit, I was just trying to do what I could for the wretched bastard. At least now he can believe I chose to use him as a calculated risk. Come on; let's find this Sable Chamber and get out of the public eye.'

2

Six staircases and three conversations with only partially helpful attendants later, they found Sabetha waiting for them in a balcony room overlooking the south side of the Grand Salon. Some long-dead nobleman stared eerily from a wall fresco, gazing out at a scrollworked metal screen that allowed a fine view of the crowd and the stage below.

Sabetha wore another ensemble more in the fashion of a riding outfit than a ball gown, a tight red velvet jacket with slashed sleeves over a dress of black silk panels embroidered in scarlet astronomical signs. Locke pieced them together in his head and realized she was wearing a sunrise and moonrise chart for this very day, month, and calendar year.

'Like it?' she said, spreading her arms. 'In accordance with the instructions of my principals, I did my bit to spend every last copper they gave me.'

'Dutiful to authority, that's you every time,' said Locke. She offered her hand, and he wasn't shy in kissing it. The trio made themselves comfortable at a little table provisioned with almond cakes, brandy, and four red crystal snifters. Locke took the lead and seized the bottle.

'A glass poured to air for absent friends,' he said as he filled the fourth snifter and pushed it aside. 'May the lessons they taught us give everyone a hell of a show tonight.'

'Here's to living long enough to appreciate whatever happens,' said Jean.

'Here's to politics,' said Sabetha. 'Let's never hop in bed with it again.'

They touched glasses and drank. The stuff had a pale caramel colour and washed Locke's throat with sweet, welcome heat. Not an

567

alchemical brandy, but one of the old-fashioned western styles with hints of peach and walnut woven into its vapours.

'Here comes the verdict,' said Sabetha.

Down on the floor the crowd parted for a troop of bluecoats, escorting sombrely dressed officials carrying wooden chests and huge brass speaking trumpets like blossoming tulips. These trumpets were secured to projections on the stage, and the wooden chests were set down behind them. A petite woman with thick grey curls cut short at the neck stepped up to one of the speaking trumpets.

'First Magistrate Sedelkis,' said Sabetha. 'Arbiter of the Change. Come election season, she's like a temporary fourteenth god.'

'No representative from the magi?' said Locke. 'They don't even send a plate of fruit and a kind note?'

'I understand they vouchsafe this ceremony,' said Sabetha, 'so gods help anyone who tries to adjust the tallies. But they'll never let themselves be seen.'

'Not unless they're somewhere private with a target for abuse,' said Locke.

On the platform below, some attendants unlocked the chests, while others took positions near the slate boards.

'Fellow citizens,' boomed First Magistrate Sedelkis, 'honourable Konseil members and officers of the republic, welcome. I have the honour of closing the seventy-ninth season of elections in the Republic of Karthain by reading the results into the public record. The returns by district, commencing with Isas Thedra:'

An attendant took an envelope from one of the chests. Sedelkis tore it open and pulled out a parchment embossed with seals and ribbons.

'By the count of one hundred and fifteen to sixty, Firstson Epitalus of the Deep Roots party.'

Loud applause erupted from half the population of the Grand Salon. One attendant chalked the official numbers on a board, while others lit a green-glowing candle and used a long pole to place it beneath the first frosted glass globe.

'Do you wish to concede, madam?' said Locke.

'I think that one was one of the foregone conclusions,' said Sabetha.

'Damn,' said Locke. 'She's too clever for us.'

'For the Isle of Hammers, by the count of two hundred and thirty-five to one hundred,' announced Sedelkis, 'Fourthdaughter DuLerian, for the Black Iris party.'

The attendants lit and placed another candle, one that gave off a purple-blue light so dark it was a fair approximation of black.

'Well how now?' said Sabetha, pouring a fresh round of drinks. 'Nothing pithy to say?'

'I would never dream of pithing in front of you,' said Locke.

Seven green lights and four black lights blazed by the time Sedelkis announced, 'For the Bursadi District, by the count of one hundred and forty-six to one hundred and twenty-two, Secondson Lovaris of the Black Iris party.'

Jean sighed theatrically.

'That poor man,' said Sabetha. 'So nearly victimized by unscrupulous relic thieves.'

'We rejoice at his deliverance,' said Locke.

'For the Plaza Gandolo,' boomed Sedelkis, 'by the count of eighty-one to sixty-five, Seconddaughter Viracois of the Black Iris party.'

'Oh, Perelandro's balls, we *filled her house* with stolen goods!' said Jean. 'She was charged with eleven counts of housebreak or receiving! What possible grease could you apply to that?'

'I came up with a story that Viracois was secretly sheltering a distant cousin,' said Sabetha. 'And that this cousin was severely touched in the head. Had a real mania for stealing things. Even hired an actress to play the role for a few days. I had Viracois circulate to apologize personally for the fact that her "cousin" had managed to slip away from supervision, and once all the stolen goods were identified and returned, all those sympathetic people quietly rescinded their charges. And discreetly talked to their friends and neighbours, of course.'

'Rescinded charges.' Locke shook his head. 'No bloody wonder paying off the magistrate didn't get us anything.'

'For the Isas Mellia,' announced Sedelkis, 'by the count of seventy-five to thirty-one, Damned Superstition Dexa of the Deep Roots party.'

'Didn't even bother much with that one,' said Sabetha.

'Well, you did try to bribe her cook,' said Locke. 'And her doorman. And her footmen. And her solicitor. And her carriage driver. And her tobacconist.'

'I *succeeded* in bribing the doorman,' said Sabetha. 'I just couldn't find anything constructive to do with him.'

'At least I won't have to eat a hat,' Locke whispered to Jean.

'For the Silverchase,' announced Sedelkis, 'by the count of one hundred and eight to sixty-seven, Light-of-the-Amathel Azalon of the Deep Roots party.'

That was the last green candle to be lit for a long time, however. The next three blazed black, bringing the total to nine and nine.

'It's all theatre in the end, isn't it?' said Sabetha. The brandy had brought colour to her cheeks. 'All our running around in costumes, saying our lines. Now the chorus comes out onstage to recite the moral and send the audience home.'

'Half of them are about to wish they had some fruit to throw,' said Jean.

'Shhh, here it comes,' said Sabetha.

'The final report,' announced Sedelkis, opening the envelope with a flourish. 'For the Palanta District, by the count of one hundred and seventy to one hundred and fifty-two, Thirdson Jovindus of the Black Iris party!'

The last lamp flared with dark light.

3

Consternation erupted on the floor, shouts of joy mingling with accusations, cries of disbelief, and insults.

Sabetha folded her arms, leaned back in her chair, and adopted a wide, genuine smile.

'You boys gave me a closer run than I expected,' she said. 'And I did have the advantage of getting here first.'

'That's a gracious admission,' said Jean.

'Your gimmick with Lovaris would have been magnificent fun to watch,' said Sabetha. 'I'm almost sad I had to put my foot down on it.'

'I'm not,' said Locke.

'ORDER,' cried First Magistrate Sedelkis. 'ORDER!' The cloaked bluecoats surrounding the stage drove their staves rhythmically against the ground until the crowd heeded Sedelkis.

'All districts having reported, I hereby declare these results rightful and valid. Karthain has a Konseil. Gods bless the Presence. Gods bless the Republic of Karthain!'

'First Magistrate,' came a voice from the crowd, 'I beg a moment of stage time to amend the record in one small respect.'

'Oh, what in all the hells …' said Sabetha.

The speaker was Lovaris, who separated himself from a group of happy Black Iris notables, pushed through the cordon of bluecoats around the stage, and took a place beside Sedelkis at a speaking trumpet.

'Dear friends and fellow citizens,' he said, while beckoning for one of the glass globe attendants to approach him. 'I am Secondson Lovaris, often called Perspicacity, an honour I cherish. For twenty years I have represented the Bursadi District as an enthusiastic member of the Black Iris party. However, of late, I must confess that enthusiasm has been dimmed by circumstances beyond my control. I grieve that I must discuss this in public. I grieve that I must take corrective *action* in public.'

'Is anyone else at this table hallucinating right now?' said Sabetha.

'If we are, we're sharing a lovely fever dream,' said Locke. 'Let's see how it ends!'

'I grieve, most of all,' continued Lovaris, 'that I must announce my reluctant but immediate withdrawal from the Black Iris party. I will no longer wear their symbols or attend their party functions.'

'Gods above, are you actually resigning from the Konseil?' shouted someone in the crowd.

'Of course not,' shouted Lovaris. 'I said nothing about resigning my Konseil seat! I am the Bursadi Konseillor, validly and rightfully elected, as the First Magistrate just announced.'

'Turncoat!' shouted a man that Locke recognized as Thirdson Jovindus. 'You ran under false pretences! Your election must be nullified in favour of your second!'

'We elect *men and women* in Karthain,' said Lovaris, and it was clear from his voice that he was speaking through a smirk that would have injured a lesser man with its intensity. 'Those men and women declare party affiliations only as a matter of their own convenience. I am not bound to surrender *anything*. My honourable associate should more closely examine the relevant laws. Now, allow me to finish describing the new situation!'

Lovaris took a pole from the attendant he'd beckoned, then used it to extinguish and dislodge the candle from the middle-most black globe. One blank white glass was left in the midst of nine black and nine green.

'Simply because I have left the Black Iris does not mean that I have necessarily embraced any of the positions of the Deep Roots. I am declaring myself a party of one, fully independent, a neutral balance between Karthain's traditional ideologies. I am fully willing to be convinced to any reasonable course of action in Konseil. Indeed, I remind my esteemed colleagues that my door is ever open for your approaches and entreaties. I shall very much look forward to receiving them. Good evening!'

What followed could only be described as the crescendoing cluster-fuck of the Karthani social season, as half the Konseillors of the Black Iris party, technically immune to constabulary restraint, attempted to storm the stage through a wall of bluecoats who could neither hurt them nor allow them to hurt Lovaris. First Magistrate Sedelkis demonstrated the co-equality of the Karthani judiciary by kicking a Black Iris Konseillor in the teeth, which brought even Deep Roots Konseillors into the fray to uphold the privileges of their station. Bluecoat messengers raced off to find reinforcements, while most of the noncombatant spectators refilled their goblets of punch and settled in to watch their government in action.

'I don't believe it,' said Sabetha. 'How the hell ... I've got no more succinct way to put it. *How the hell*?'

'You warned Lovaris we were coming to try and convince him to change the colour of his lapel ribbon,' said Locke. 'And you know he didn't buy that offer for an instant. He chewed on my self-respect for a while, then wiped me away like a turd.'

'But we'd already prepared a second line of attack,' said Jean, pouring himself a fresh finger of brandy. 'Ego-fodder. Something designed to appeal to his sense that he ought to be the hinge around which the rest of the world turned.'

'Catnip for an asshole,' continued Locke. 'Jean offered the second approach, on the theory that Lovaris might be more willing to parley seriously with an envoy he hadn't just pissed all over. Turned out to be a good guess.'

'And now Lovaris is the most important man in Karthain,' whispered Sabetha. 'Now any deadlock in Konseil is going to have to be resolved by his vote!'

'A possibility he found quite stimulating. The other Konseillors might detest his guts,' said Locke, 'but they *will* be at his door, hats in hand, for the next five years, or until he's assassinated. Hardly our problem either way.'

'And that's all it took? A friendly suggestion?'

'Well, obviously, he agreed to go through with it only if the numbers added up,' said Locke. 'If you'd had a wider margin of victory, he would have stayed silent. And there was one hell of a bribe to sweeten the deal.'

'He settled for twenty-five thousand ducats,' said Jean.

'How does he expect to hide it?' said Sabetha. 'The Black Iris are going to rake him over the coals! His countinghouse will be watched, his business dealings will be dissected, any fresh property that turns up will be beaten like a dusty carpet for clues!'

'Hiding it's not the issue,' said Locke, 'since you already safely delivered it to him for us.'

Sabetha stared at him for a moment, then whispered, 'The reliquary boxes!'

'I quietly boiled twenty-five thousand ducats down to precious stones, mostly emeralds and Spider's Eye Pearls,' said Jean. 'A lightweight cargo to stash in the bottom of the drawers. Your constables were much more squeamish about digging through the dust and bones of Lovaris' forebears than he was.'

'I'd thought you'd taken them to hold hostage for his cooperation,' said Sabetha.

'It was the sensible conclusion,' said Locke. 'We didn't feel comfortable hauling a fat bribe to his manor ourselves; too much of a chance someone in your pay would notice us. Maybe even someone working for his household.'

'Try about half his household,' said Sabetha. 'So you needed that treasure delivered to Lovaris, and you fed me its location on that boat … gods! How long had you known I had Nikoros under my thumb?'

'We found out nearly too late,' said Locke. 'Just about everything he gave you before the boat was legitimately at our expense.'

'Hmmm. To give him the word on the boat …' She rubbed her temples. 'Ah! That alchemical store I relieved you of in the Vel Vespala – that tip came from Nikoros. You … you must have given everyone you suspected word of some different juicy target!'

'And the target you stepped on told us who the leak was,' said Locke, grinning. 'You have it exactly.'

'You impossible assholes!' Sabetha leapt up, moved around the table, pulled Locke and Jean from their chairs, and threw an arm around each of them, laughing. 'Oh, you two are such insufferable weasely shits, it's marvellous!'

'You weren't so bad yourself,' said Jean. 'But for the grace of the gods, we might still be cruising the Amathel.'

573

'So what have we done?' said Sabetha, her voice full of honest wonderment. 'What have we *done*? I suppose I won the election, but ... I'm not sure if winning it for about thirty seconds is winning it at all.'

'Just as I'm not sure that nudging a victory into a tie is really the same as winning for our side,' said Locke. 'Nor is it quite losing. A pretty mess, isn't it? One for the drunkards and philosophers.'

'I wonder what the magi are going to say.'

'I hope they argue about it from now until the sun grows cold,' said Locke. 'We did our bit, we fought sincerely, we perverted the final results just enough to eternally confuse anyone watching – what more could they possibly want?'

'I suppose we find out now,' said Jean.

'Did ... Patience give you any instructions or hints about what to do once the ballots were counted?' said Sabetha.

'Not a word,' said Locke.

'Then why don't we all get the hell out of here and let our employers find us in their own time?' Sabetha tossed back the last of her brandy. 'I've got a safe house just off the Court of Dust. Rented it for a month, had firewood, linens, and wine laid in. I'd say it's as comfortable a place as any to rest and figure out what we're going to ... do next.' She ran her fingers lightly over Locke's left arm.

'Any plan to sneak us out of here without getting swept up in a brawl?' said Jean.

'New skins.' Sabetha produced a scalpel-thin dagger from somewhere in a jacket sleeve and used it to slit one of three paper parcels stacked beneath the chamber's unnerving fresco. 'Much as I hate to take this dress off display, I thought we'd find our exit that much easier if we dressed like the enemy.'

4

At the tenth hour of the evening, a trio of bluecoats pushed through the curious crowds at the main entrance to the Karthenium; a slender watchman and a sturdy watchman, led by a woman with sergeant's pins on her lapels. They disposed of the last few people standing in their way with a combination of shoves and ominous mutterings about official business.

Locke and Jean followed Sabetha about fifty yards west, to a branching side court where a carriage waited. The night had darkened considerably, and as he opened the carriage door Locke's eye was caught by an orange glare somewhere to the south.

'Looks like a fire,' he said. The conflagration rippled, gilding the shadowy buildings of what must have been the Palanta District with its light.

'Damned big one,' said Jean. 'I hope it's nothing to do with the election. Maybe these Karthani play harder than I ever gave them credit for.'

'Come on, you two, let's not linger long enough to get noticed by anyone who might outrank us,' said Sabetha.

They all clambered into the carriage together. The driver, obedient to whatever orders Sabetha had given her earlier, shook the reins, and they were off, leaving the results of their tampering with Karthain's electoral process behind them. Genuine bluecoats were still arriving in force, truncheons and shields drawn, as the carriage rattled over the paving stones, away from the Karthenium.

INTERSECT (IV)
Ignition

'The First Magistrate has just read the final district report,' says one of the young men, his voice dreamy, his eyes unfocused. Coldmarrow knows from long experience that the more tenuous and subtle mind-to-mind connections are the most demanding to sustain. Any damned fool can blaze their thoughts into the night for magi far and wide to receive like buzzing insects. The intelligence network now flashing thoughts across the city is straining itself to be utterly silent.

'The last district is Black Iris ...' whispers the young mage.

'Black Iris victory,' says someone else. 'By the skin of their teeth.'

'It seems that Patience's vaunted Camorri were no match for ours,' smirks Archedama Foresight. She wears a leather hood and mantle, a dark linen mask, a mail-reinforced cuirass. Like all the men and women in the second-floor solar of Coldmarrow's Palanta District house, she is dressed for a fight. 'We'll deal with them last, after all the other satisfactions of the evening have been dispensed with.'

'Necessities, let us rather say,' coughs Coldmarrow, taking deep, steady breaths to help rule his anxiety. The air is close, and it smells of all these magi, their robes and leathers, the wine on their breaths, the oils in their hair, their nervous, excited sweat.

'Why not both?' says the archedama.

'There's a disturbance at the Karthenium,' whispers the young man who has been reporting on the election. 'Someone ... Lovaris of the Bursadi District. Some sort of announcement. He may be ... ha! He may be switching sides!'

'Damn,' says Archedama Foresight. 'But it seems to me that there's no time like the present. All our targets must be absorbed in the distraction.'

'Oh, they *are*,' chuckles Coldmarrow. 'It couldn't be working better. Are your people in their proper positions?'

'All of them,' says Foresight.

'Then here's to necessity,' says Coldmarrow, his mouth suddenly dry. 'And to the future of all our kind.'

Coldmarrow speaks a word.

The word becomes fire.

A spark flashes in the dark heart of a jar of fire-oil, one of a hundred, tightly sealed, placed in the space beneath the floor of the room a month before. This jar is half-full, containing just enough air for the flame to breathe the vapours of the oil. The explosion is white-hot, shattering the clay vessels, sucking air and oil into the roaring, all-devouring blast.

Not even magi can move faster than this, or protect themselves with so little warning. The floor moves beneath Coldmarrow's feet, then comes sharp dark heat, stunning pressure, and sudden silence. Coldmarrow dies taking fourteen magi with him, including Archedama Foresight. He has no time to feel either regret or satisfaction; it will simply have to be enough.

The war lasts nine minutes. It is utterly one-sided, the only possible war magi can wage with any hope of total victory against others trained in the same traditions, to the same standards.

Archedama Foresight's people discover that their own ambush is stillborn, their positions ready-made traps. They have always been outnumbered by the larger faction of magi they derided as meek, and now those opponents apply their numbers to disproving the slander.

No quarter is given, no fair fight allowed. Strength is brought against weakness. Across rooftops, within lamp-lit gardens, inside the halls of the Isas Scholastica and the private homes of sorcerers, the assault is quick and silent and absolute.

As the tipsy, confused politicians of Karthain clamber over one another in a comical brawl at the heart of the Karthenium, seventy magi die in the dark places of the city, taking only a handful of their killers with them.

Navigator finds Patience alone in the Sky Chamber, staring at the bowl of the artificial heavens, currently mirroring the actual sky over Karthain, the rolling dark clouds summoned to lock the light of moons and stars away. Shadow has been drawn over the city like a cloak, to better hide the evidence.

'It's over,' says Patience. She speaks real words to the air; the silver threads of thought-speech have unravelled unpleasantly across Karthain; cries of pain and betrayal, cries for help that will never come, and

Patience has hardened her mind against most of the noise. 'Now we have to live with ourselves.'

'Tell our troubles to the shades of Therim Pel,' says the one-armed woman. She wipes a tear from her cheek.

'We are each one in a thousand thousand,' says Patience. 'We have destroyed some of the rarest and most precious things in the world tonight. Our distant inheritors may curse us for what we've done.'

'We already deserve their curses, Archedama.'

'So long as there's still a world *left* for them to curse us in. Come now; help me do it.'

The two women bow their heads, move their hands in perfect concert, and speak words of unweaving that tear at their throats like desert air. The beautiful conjured heavens of the Sky Chamber fade like the memory of a dream, until there is nothing but a dome of plain white stones, greyed with the patina of old smoke.

'Do you wish to see your son now?' says Navigator.

'No,' says Patience, suddenly feeling every one of her years, suddenly wishing for the touch and the laugh of a man who was taken by the Amathel half her lifetime ago. 'I'll speak to Lamora first. But for now I want to be alone for a while.'

Navigator nods and quietly withdraws, leaving Patience alone in the silent vastness of a room that will never be used again.

One final duty remains at the end of this long campaign, and Patience does not yet have the heart to face it.

Last Interlude
Thieves Prosper

I

The remains of Gennaro Boulidazi, last of his line, were taken away under his family colours. An apoplectic Brego did most of the work, after being rebuked for his panic and disbelief by Baroness Ezrintaim. She did, however, graciously assign a number of constables to serve as an honour guard.

It was the middle of the night before all the constables and soldiers decamped from within Gloriano's Rooms, chasing off the small crowd of locals and curiosity-seekers as they went. Baroness Ezrintaim left only a small guard posted outside, their orders to preserve the peace for the 'nobles' spending their last night in Espara within.

Jean and Jenora went off together early, to spend that night as they saw fit. The Sanzas, seemingly reluctant to let one another out of their sight, claimed a corner of the main room and drank with Alondo and Donker – not the boisterous drinking of celebration but the quiet ritual of people relieved to still have throats to pour their ale down.

Bert and Chantal fell asleep on one another, wrapped up together in an old cloak. Mistress Gloriano promised Locke she would wake them eventually and pack them off to a proper room. She and Sylvanus then sat together, working on a ribbon-wrapped bottle of some expensive brandy whose existence had never previously been mentioned to the thirsty ingrates pounding her bar for service.

Sabetha was clear and to the point, without words. She found Locke bound up in his thoughts in the main room and dispelled them with a hand on his shoulder. She glanced at the stairs by way of a question, and when he nodded, her smile made him feel something even the cheers of eight hundred strangers hadn't been able to.

They commandeered an empty chamber. Sabetha used the room's only chair to wedge it shut and admired her handiwork with grim satisfaction.

They were tired, the smell of smoke was nested deep in their hair,

and the last thing they needed was more sweat without a bath, but neither of them cared. They were at home in the darkness in a way that
only the survivors of places like Shades' Hill could understand, and
alive to one another's lips and hands as they had never been before.
They were still shy, still awkward and unschooled. But if their first
night together had been confusing and incomplete, their second ... ah,
their second taught them why people keep trying.

CHAPTER TWELVE
The End Of Old Dreams

I

The smell of her, the taste of her. Locke awoke in darkness, still awash in those things. His sweat, their sweat, had cooled and dried on his skin, and the bed ... he ran his hands over her side of it and found it empty, the blanket thrown back.

He remembered where he was. The upper room of Sabetha's house off the Court of Dust, the one with the expensively luxurious mattress and the Lashani silk sheets. He couldn't have been asleep for long.

There was someone in the darkness, watching him, and he knew in an instant it wasn't Sabetha, knew with every fibre of his intuition who it must be, standing by the faint grey cracks of light at the window.

'What have you done?' he whispered.

'We spoke,' said Patience. 'I showed her something.'

Soft silver light filled the room – the cold alchemical globes, in response to a mere gesture of Patience's. Locke saw her hands moving as his eyes adjusted, saw that she wore a heavy traveller's cloak with the hood thrown back.

'Where's Jean?'

'Downstairs, where you left him,' said Patience. 'He'll awaken soon. Do you want to get dressed, or are you comfortable speaking like this?'

The cold Locke felt had little to do with the mere fact that he was naked. He slid from the bed, not caring that he concealed nothing from Patience, and dressed in what he could only hope, ludicrously, was somehow an insolent fashion. He donned trousers and tunic like armour, threw a simple dark jacket on as though it could keep Patience and her words out.

Locke saw that there was something leaning against the wall behind Patience, a flat rectangular object about three feet high, covered in a grey cloth.

'She tried to write you a note,' said Patience. 'It was ... beyond her. She left half an hour ago.'

'What did you *do* to her, Patience?'

'I did *nothing*.' Her dark eyes caught him, seemed to pierce him. Those hunter's eyes. 'To my arts, Sabetha Belacoros is a puppet waiting for a hand, but it would have been meaningless, had I *done* anything. She had to choose. I gave her information that led to a choice.'

'You utter bitch—'

'I also saved your life tonight,' she said. 'For the second and last time. This is our final conversation, Locke Lamora, if that's what you still choose to call yourself. I've come to render all dues and finish my business with you.'

'Do you want to kill me yourself, at last?'

'Certainly not.'

'And … you mean to keep your word? Money and transportation to see us on our way?'

'There's no money and no transportation,' said Patience, laughing without humour. 'You'll receive nothing else from us. Your counting-house contacts will no longer recognize you, and your Deep Roots associates already think of Sebastian Lazari as a grey ghost of a memory. Wherever you gentlemen choose to go next, I suspect you have a long walk ahead of you.'

'Why are you doing this to us?' said Locke.

'The Falconer,' she said.

'So revenge was the game after all,' said Locke. 'Well, a *creature* like the Falconer deserved every second of hurt I ever gave him, and *fuck you* if you expect me to think otherwise!'

'You can't understand what you took from him,' said Patience, her words hot and thick with scorn. 'Your flesh is inert; magic is nothing more than the sound of the wind to you. You can *never* feel it, feel the words leaving you like fire, like arrows from a bowstring! To know that power welling beneath you and bearing you like a feather on a wind. You think I'm selfish for this? Cruel? It's less than you deserve! Killing him would have been mercy. I've *killed* magi. But you stole his hands and his voice. You took the tools of magic from him and smashed him like a priceless work of art. You stole his destiny. The Archedama Patience could forgive you. The mother and the mage *cannot*.'

'I refer you to my former statement,' said Locke, his voice trembling.

A heavy tread sounded on the stairs. Jean burst into the room, slamming the door aside without knocking.

'I don't understand,' he panted. 'I was just … You fucking did something to me again, didn't you?

'A brief slumber,' said Patience. 'I wanted time with Sabetha, and then with Locke. But you might as well hear everything else I have to say.'

'Where's Sabetha?' said Jean.

'Alive,' said Patience. 'And fled, of her own accord.'

'Why do I—?'

'You've got nothing more I want, Jean Tannen,' said Patience. 'Interrupt me again and Locke leaves Karthain alone.'

Jean balled his fists, but remained silent.

'I'm leaving Karthain too,' said Patience. 'Myself and all my kind. Tonight ends the last of the Five-Year Games, and our centuries of life here. Whenever the Karthani find the nerve to enter the Isas Scholastica, they'll find our buildings empty, our tunnels collapsed, our libraries and treasures vanished. We are removing all trace of ourselves from Karthain down to the dust under our beds.'

'Why on the gods' earth would you do such a thing?' said Locke.

'Karthain is the old dream,' said Patience. 'It's served its purpose. We have gathered strength, honed our skills, and collected the wealth we need to do what we must. There will be no more contracts. No more Bondsmagi. We are retiring from the public life of this world. Never again can we allow such an institution as this to arise.'

'That … that danger you spoke of?' said Locke, unnerved and startled by the magnitude of the changes Patience's words implied.

'There are things moving and dreaming in the darkness,' said Patience. 'We refuse to risk any further chance of waking them up. Yet human magic *must* survive, so we must learn how to make it as quiet as possible.'

'Why run us through this damned election?' said Locke. 'Gods, why not just put us in a room and tell us this shit and save us all so much trouble?'

'Wise members of my order a century ago,' said Patience, 'foresaw our direction beyond a shadow of a doubt. We used our contracts to enrich ourselves, but they also made us arrogant. They fuelled the impulse to dominate, to see our powers as limitless and the world as our clay.

'These wise men and women knew that a crisis would break, a time for blood, and the only way to win would be to achieve surprise. They envisioned a disruption of our ordinary lives so profound and yet so routine that it could conceal preparations for a fight when the time came. The Five-Year Games became a regular part of our society, a pageant and a release. But a few of us were always trusted with the original intention of the games, and the knowledge that we might have to employ it.'

'So it was all just … a monumental misdirection?' said Locke. 'While we danced for everyone's amusement, you sharpened your knife and stuck it in somebody's back?'

'All those magi that I once described as exceptionalists,' said Patience. 'All those brothers and sisters. I mourn them, even as I know there was no convincing them. They will stay in Karthain forever. The rest of us go on.'

'Why tell us any of this?' said Jean.

'Because I value your discomfort.' Patience smiled without warmth. 'I described the conditions of your employment very succinctly. We are not vanishing from the world, merely from the eyes of ordinary people. Share our business with anyone and you are *always* in our reach.'

'Ordinary people,' said Locke. 'Well, how ordinary am I, really? What's the truth of all the tales you spun about my past?'

'You should look at the painting I brought for Sabetha.' Patience tapped the wrapped object leaning against the wall behind her. 'I'm leaving it here, though in a day or two it will be nothing but white ash. It's the only portrait of Lamor Acanthus ever painted during his life. I ought to tell you, the likeness is impeccable.'

'A simple answer!' shouted Locke. 'What am I?'

'You're a man who doesn't get to *know* the answer,' said Patience, and now her smile was genuine. She was shaking with the obvious difficulty of containing her laughter. 'Look at you. Camorri! Confidence trickster! You think you know what *revenge* is? Well, here's mine on you. Before I was Archedama Patience, I was called Seamstress. Not because I enjoy needlework, but because I *tailor to fit.*'

Locke could only stare at her, feeling cold and hollow to the depths of his guts.

'Live a good long life without your answer,' she said. 'I think you'll find the evidence neatly balanced in either direction. Now, one thing more will I tell you, and this only because I know it will haunt and disquiet you. My son preferred to mock my premonitions, but only

584

because he didn't want to face the fact that they always have substance. I shall give you a little prophecy, Locke Lamora, as best as I have seen it.

'Three things must you take up and three things must you lose before you die: a key, a crown, a child.' Patience pushed her hood up over her head. 'You will die when a silver rain falls.'

'You're making all this shit up,' said Locke.

'I could be,' said Patience. 'I very well could be. And that's part of your punishment. Go forth now and live, Locke Lamora. Live, uncertain.'

She gestured once and was gone.

2

Jean remained at the door, staring at the grey-wrapped package. Finally, Locke worked up the nerve to seize it and tear away the cover.

It was an oil painting. Locke stared at it for some time, feeling the lines on his face draw taut as a bowstring, feeling moistness well in the corners of his eyes.

'Of course,' he said. 'Of course. Lamor Acanthus. And wife, I presume.'

He made a noise that was half dour laugh and half strangled sob, and threw the painting on the bed. The black-robed man in the portrait looked nothing like Locke; he was broad-shouldered, with the classically dark, sharp aspect of a Therin Throne patrician. The woman beside him bore the same sort of haughty glamour, down to her bones, but she was much fairer of skin.

Her thick, flowing hair was as red as fresh blood.

'I'm everything Sabetha was afraid of,' said Locke. 'Tailored to fit.'

'I'm ... I'm sorry as hell I got you into this,' said Jean.

'Shit! Don't go wobbly on me now, Jean. I was as good as dead, and the only way out of this was to go through, all the way to Patience's endgame. Now she's played it.'

'We can go after Sabetha,' said Jean. 'She's had half an hour, how far could she get?'

'I want to,' said Locke, wiping his eyes. 'Gods, I can still smell her everywhere in this room. And gods, I want her back.' He slumped onto the bed. 'But I ... I promised to trust her. I promised to ... respect her decisions, no matter how much it fucking cut me. If she has to run from this, if she has to be away from me, then for as long as she needs,

I'll … I'll accept it. If she wants to find me again, what could stop her?'

Jean put his hands on Locke's shoulders and bowed his head in thought.

'You're gonna be fucking *miserable* to live with for a couple of weeks,' he said at last.

'Probably,' said Locke with a rueful chuckle. 'I'm sorry.'

'Well, we should case this place and pack everything useful we can lay our hands on,' said Jean. 'Clothes, food, tools. We don't have to go after Sabetha, but we'd best have our asses on the road before the sun peeks over the horizon.'

'Why?'

'Karthain hasn't kept up an army or maintained its walls for *three hundred years*,' said Jean. 'In a few hours, it's going to wake up to discover that the only thing keeping it protected from the world at large has vanished during the night. Do you want to be here when *that* mess breaks wide open?'

'Oh, shit. Good point.'

Locke stood up and looked around the room one last time.

'Key, crown, child,' he muttered. 'Well, fuck you, Patience. Three things must you kiss before I let you spook me for good. My boots, my balls, and my ass.'

Locke pulled his boots on and followed Jean down the stairs, impatient to have Karthain at his back and slowly sinking into the horizon.

EPILOGUE
Wings

1

The boy is six. He stares at the Amathel, breathes the lake air, the wholesome scents of life and freshness. He stares at the glinting lights, the jewels in the blackness, the secrets of the Eldren scattered in the depths. The dock folk claim that fishermen in the water at night have been driven mad by the lights, have dived down toward them, pulling frantically, as if toward the surface, until they drowned. Or vanished.

The boy is not afraid of the lights. The boy has power the dock folk can only guess at. He feels a pressure in his temples when he stares out across the waters. He hears something lower and lovelier than the steady wash of the waves and the cries of the birds. The power of the hidden things calls to the power of the boy.

The boy knows the Amathel took his father. He has been told this, but he remembers nothing. He was too young. There is no memory to mourn. The lake of jewels means only life, beauty, soothing familiarity.

All these things. And the power that waits for his power to match it. To *reveal* it.

2

The boy is four, the boy is ten, the man is twenty. His body shifts in this place. Sometimes he is whole, sometimes he is pleased, sometimes his memories are bright and vivid as paintings glowing with the fire of the gods in every speck of pigment.

Sometimes he speaks in a rich rolling voice. Sometimes he moves his hands and feels the fingers there, feels them brushing over surfaces and picking things up. He does not know why this pleases him, why he feels something like the hot pressure of tears behind his eyes, why the joy is so bittersweet.

Sometimes he walks in a fog. His thoughts are wrapped in dull cotton. Sometimes he is on a street, and he is confused. He is bound with rope, throbbing with pain, his hands and his mouth caked with blood. His own blood. The rain comes down and men are staring at him, studying him, afraid.

Sometimes he is gazing out across the Amathel, feeling the life of the bird for the first time. A gull, an elegant white thing, wheeling in tight circles. The boy feels its needs, its hunger, the elegant simplicity of the thing at the *centre of it all*. The boy visualizes this as a wheel, a piece of clockwork, a logic circle turning without friction or remorse. Strike, eat, live on the wind. *Strike, eat, live on the wind.*

The boy moves his fingers to call up his untutored power. He reaches out and takes the life of the bird like a humming thread in the hands that nobody else can see, the hands of power his mother has taught him to use.

The bird is startled.

Its wings fold awkwardly. It plummets twenty feet and bounces hard off a rock, then plops into the water, fluttering and squawking agitatedly, lucky its wings aren't broken.

The boy needs practise.

3

The boy is ten. The boy has run across the hills and forests north of Karthain all night with blood in his mouth. The boy has crouched in the centre of a web, still as stone, with venom in his fangs and the faintest sensation of movement rippling across his fur, the air currents of prey fluttering ever closer. The boy has swept high into the sky, chased the sun, learned to strike, eat, and live on the wind.

'You must not,' his mother insists. His mother is powerful, his mother is teaching him her gifts, but she will not let him teach her his own.

'It is not highly thought of, among our kind,' she says. 'You are a man! You will think as a man! There's no room for a man in those tiny minds.'

'I share,' said the boy. 'I command. I don't feel small. If they really are tiny, perhaps I make them big whenever I go inside!'

'You will grow more and more sensitive,' says his mother. 'You will tie yourself more and more tightly to them, do you understand? Their lives will become yours, their feelings yours. If they are hurt, you will share all their pain. If they are killed ... you may be lost as well.'

The boy doesn't understand. His mother tells him these things as though there were no compensations. The boy knows that he is alone, among all the magi his mother has presented him to, in his willingness to share the lives of animals.

There is no dissuading the boy. He has tasted life without regrets, life without remorse, life lived on the wind. It is what he is; he returns to himself after each communion feeling that part of the wild has come with him, to live inside him.

His mother could make him stop. Even at ten, the boy knows what she holds over him, burns with shame at it. But she will not use it. She lectures and begs and threatens, but she will not speak the thing that would lock his will in an iron strongbox.

She cannot, or will not, but it doesn't make the boy forgive her. He casts his awareness into hidden places for owls, ravens, hawks. He hurls himself into the sky carrying anger from the ground, and hot blood runs on his talons. He soars to forget he has legs. He kills to forget he has rules and expectations. He never shares this experience with anyone else. He goes alone to the woods, and dead songbirds fall like rain. When he is shamed in his studies or rebuked for his attitude, he remembers the blood on his talons, and he endures with a smile.

4

The boy is gone, the man is twenty-five, the man is ... lost.

Sometimes he is in the dead grey place. His legs refuse to move. His hands feel like crippled lumps. His tongue throbs with a phantom pain, an electric tingle. He is trapped on a bed as though nailed to it. He cannot remember how he came to be in this place. He sobs, panics, tries to claw his way to freedom with his missing fingers.

Only the smell of the lake relaxes him, the cool fresh scent of the water, the occasional piquancy of dead fish or gull shit. When the wind blows these things to him he can bear the confusion and the torture of the dead place.

When the wind is wrong the shadows around him pour something cold and bitter down his throat, and he goes into the darkness cursing them wordlessly.

5

The lake air blows through the dead place. He takes it in as though no other air will sustain him. It is night; the darkness is offset by the light of a single lamp. Everything is strange; he feels a buoyant force inside his chest, something rising through him like bubbles in a spring. The room is clarifying, as though layer after layer of gauze is being removed from his face.

The light stings his eyes; the new clarity is unnerving. There are shadows moving near the light, two of them.

The man tries to speak, and a strangled wet moan startles him. It takes a moment to realize that the noise is his own, that his tongue is a scrap of cauterized stump.

His hands! He remembers Camorr, remembers steel coming down, remembers the shared pain of Vestris' last moments washing over him in unbearable waves. He remembers Locke Lamora and Jean Tannen. He remembers Luciano Anatolius.

He is the Falconer, and the air in the room is heavy with the smell of the Amathel. He is alive and back in Karthain.

How long? He feels stiff, light, weak. Significant weight has vanished from his body. Has it been weeks, months?

Nearly three years, whispers a soft voice in his head. A familiar voice. A hated voice.

'Mnnnnghr,' he rasps, the best he can do. The frustration comes on like a physical weight. He can sense the currents of magic in the room, feel the strength of his mother nearby, but his tools are missing. The power is there to be wielded, but his will slides from it like sand off smooth glass.

I'll take care of it for both of us.

Cold fingers of force slide across his mind, and the impotence, blessedly, is lifted. He feels the words as he crafts them, feels them going out to her, mind to mind, his first orderly communication in … three *years?*

THREE YEARS!

As I said.

Camorr …

Yes, the Anatolius contract.

How badly was I injured? What did they do to me?

Not enough to cause your present condition.

The Falconer ponders the import of these words, flips desperately through his memories like the pages of a book.

A dreamsteel model of a city. Its towers falling into flat silvery nothingness.

Archedama Patience, in the Sky Chamber, warning him that he is headed into danger.

Steel rising and falling. Cauterizing heat, white bolts of pain in his mind unlike anything he has ever imagined. Vestris, dead. Before the blade can come for his tongue he tries to work the spell of pain-deadening, the old familiar technique, but on the other side of it ... not welcome relief. Fog, madness, prison.

Now see it all.

Patience speaks a word, and something comes loose in his mind. A patina cracks over an old memory, revealing the truth within the shell.

Archedama Patience. The night of his departure, a brief private audience. She warns him again. Again, he scoffs at the transparency of her ploys. She speaks another word, then, and the word is urgent and irresistible. The word is his name, his true name, uttered as the cornerstone of a spell. He is bound to it, then made to forget.

You ... you did it.

A subtle compulsion. A trap. An irrevocable order sleeping in his mind until the next time he used the art of deadening pain.

YOU did this to me. ...

You did it to yourself.

YOU DID THIS TO ME!

I gave you the chance to avoid it.

NO. THE CHANCE TO SHOW MY THROAT.

Your arrogance again. Can't you see that you were a problem in want of a solution?

AND YOUR SOLUTION ... ASSASSINATION. FAR FROM HOME.

I suppose that's the only honest way to look at it.

I'M YOUR GODS-DAMNED SON!

I wear five rings. You put yourself on the wrong side of them.

Well. He forces himself to lower his mental voice, to think coolly. There must be danger here. Why is she telling him this, revealing all after three years? **You certainly fucked things up, didn't you?**

All I could foresee was that you were headed into serious pain. Therefore I assumed that you would be in extreme danger ... that you would do the obvious thing.

Paralyze myself, you mean! And then it would all be over.

Except your opponents were ... scrupulous.

Ah. Is this what scrupulous treatment feels like? Lucky, lucky me.

I told you, it's not what I wanted!

You and your gods-damned prescience. Your snide little hints. The way you tried to control everyone around you with them. What good was it, if you couldn't even see THIS coming at us? Tell me, Mother, have you ever managed to have a vision of your OWN future?

No.

Well, that must be pleasant for you. To be the only real person in your whole damned world, and all the rest of us puppets for your private stage. How does it feel NOW?

'It's over,' says Patience, switching to actual speech. She is beside his bed now, looking down at him. 'All of it. Your associates are dead. Archedama Foresight is dead.'

How?

'Irrelevant. You are the sole survivor of your faction. All questions between us have been settled. We're leaving Karthain, entering the time of quiet as planned. You are my final item of business before I go.'

Come to kill me last? Come to bring an end to three years of cowardice?

'Part of me wishes you were dead,' she said. 'Wishes you'd died cleanly, as you would have had you been healthy and abroad in Karthain tonight. I can't imagine wanting to live on in your ... condition. And I will end your suffering, if it's what you desire. But I felt that I had to ask. I owe you at least this much.'

She points to the other figure in the room, a burly man, balding, with a black moustache that droops to the collar of his brown tunic. There are no rings visible on either of his wrists.

'This is Eganis, your caretaker.' She offers images and impressions, revealing to the Falconer how it has been for three years.

Eganis moving him, rolling him from side to side, turning him to avoid weeping bedsores.

Eganis feeding him, gruel and pap and milk.

Eganis emptying his chamber pot.

Eganis walking him, leading the doddering Falconer by a length of leather around his neck.

A mage of Karthain ... leashed ...

It was necessary to preserve your health.

Like a dog ...

It was necessary!

LIKE A GODS-DAMNED DOG!

You're the one who always sought to know the spirits of animals more intimately.

He sends no words, but an unrelieved outpouring of hatred so hot and acidic he sees her stagger before she can manage to gird her mind against it.

'You'll understand when you calm down,' she says. 'I'll leave this house and funds for Eganis to draw on. Without hands or voice, you're now effectively one of the ungifted, and you will never see any of us again. If you can find some reason to live, you are invited to do so. If you find the thought unpalatable, then I will ... I will end the matter quickly and painlessly.'

I will accept nothing more from you for so long as I live. Not this house. Not Eganis. Not charity. Certainly not death.

'On your own head be it,' she mutters. 'Eganis will stay. You're a mute invalid with three rings tattooed on your wrist, and Karthain could soon be a very ... interesting place for you.'

There's no hell for you deep enough to suit my tastes, Mother.

Your ambitions and your researches were a threat to every living being on this world. Consider that, when you cry your tears.

Your TIMIDITY! In the face of the secrets waiting to be unlocked everywhere the Eldren set foot, you want us to stay ignorant and helpless ... well, to hell with you. All the real power of the human race is squandered on people like you ... the wilfully small. You and all your fellow punchlines to Karthain's worst joke. Five rings! Five prisoner's shackles!

You would have been free to stick your hand into fire, if only the rest of us wouldn't have to burn with you. Good-bye, Falconer.

She departs, and the spell of thought-shaping crumbles in her absence. He is alone and voiceless with Eganis. The man looks at the Falconer, then slightly away, as though uncomfortable at seeing him with his eyes open.

'If you ever find the burden of your new life … too overwhelming,' the man mutters, 'I am instructed … to offer you mercy. I have powders that can be taken in wine.'

The Falconer glares at the man until he shrugs and leaves the room.

6

Now the Falconer notices the autumn cold. He feels it like an ache in his too-thin body. Disgusted, he rolls to his left and attempts to stand on his own two feet.

Success, but only just. Gods, he moves like a man of ninety! His hips ache and his legs seem too stick-thin to bear him, but they do, awkwardly. The Falconer chortles disgustedly at the creaky hop that passes for his walk.

There is nothing useful in this prisoner's chamber. A bed, a chair, a lamp, a chamber pot. The next room is larger, furnished with a library of several dozen volumes and a small basin. The Falconer hops wistfully to the basin, knowing what he'll see there. Dreamsteel is ubiquitous in mage households, a decoration and an amusement. The pool is inert to him, dead as water, and the frustration makes him shudder so hard he nearly falls over.

Lip trembling, he prods the silver pool with the remnants of his right hand. He needs fingers, flexible fingers! Then this steel could take any shape required at the press of a thought. When he was five, he could move the metal with a wave of his hands and a single word. Fresh heat rises in his cheeks, and for an instant he hates what he has become so fiercely he actually considers the powders offered by the caretaker.

The surface of the dreamsteel ripples in a place where he isn't touching it.

The Falconer leaps back, heart hammering, piteously loud in his weak chest. Gods! If his eyes are tricking him … if he *didn't* actually see that, he tells himself he'll *demand* the powders. His teeth are rattling from excitement as he bends back over the basin. He touches the severed stumps of his fingers to the liquid and stares at it, mustering all of his willpower from its long slumber, all of his fury, all of his inhumanly honed focus and desire. Beads of sweat pour down his forehead.

594

He shudders with a yearning so profound his breath comes in gasps.

Hair-thin strands of dreamsteel creep onto the stump of his right index finger. Then thick drops, then a tangible curving line. He feels power like a vibration along the silver edge. His grip on the energy of sorcery. His focus. Hot tears drench his cheeks, and his chest heaves like a bellows.

In a minute, he has crafted a single silvery finger, and the process gains speed. With one finger to direct the currents of magic, it is easy to craft a second, even easier to craft a third. Before he can believe it, the Falconer is staring in awestruck joy at a half-metal hand, held together by the trivial flexions of his will – four silver fingers and a silver thumb.

His wail of relief and joy is so loud and undignified that Eganis comes running from below. The man's eyes widen.

'What the hell do you think you're doing?'

There's no need for the old device, the playing of a silver thread back and forth. The Falconer's hand will now do the job itself. He flexes his mirror-skinned fingers, makes a brush-off gesture toward Eganis, and the caretaker falls gasping to his knees.

The Falconer has power, but it is weak and vague. He needs a voice. *Some* magic only makes him more desperately thirsty to have it *all* back. Thirsty! The very idea ... and yet, why not? What can caution possibly do for him now? He takes the dreamsteel basin in his new hand and tilts it into his mouth; the metal is cool and strangely salty. It pools beneath the stump of his tongue, slides in tendrils down his gullet, and there he holds it, shapes it, not as a tongue but as a thin resonant surface, vibrating half with sound and half with magic.

Eerie noises like hissing laughter fill the room as he fights to master the dreamsteel, to align it perfectly, to gild his throat.

'EGANIS,' he booms at last. The voice is cold, the words like metal grates sliding shut. 'So, you would have offered me mercy, Eganis? YOU ... offer ME mercy?'

'Please,' the caretaker coughs, 'I meant you no harm! I've taken care of you!'

'I refused you as a gift.' The Falconer seizes the basin and hurls it at Eganis, spilling the remaining dreamsteel over him. 'My mother should have sent you away.'

He moves his silver hand and speaks in his silver voice. The dreamsteel comes alive and crawls over Eganis, rolling toward his neck.

'No! Please, I can serve you!'

'You will serve me. As proof of concept.'

The Falconer makes a fist, and the loose dreamsteel flows into Eganis' ears. Parallel red lines pour out beneath the silver ones, and then become rivers. Eganis screams. He clutches the top of his head, and there is a sound like wheat husks cracking. The skull shatters. A wave of silver fountains out behind hot blood and wet brains.

The results hit the floor in many different parts of the room. The Falconer calls the loose dreamsteel back to him, forming a necklace with it. He'll need to secure more, somehow, to craft another functional hand. Still, what he has should be more than enough to give him back his wild sky.

7

There is a narrow window beside the bookshelf. A gesture from the Falconer and the glass becomes sand, sliding out of the frame, blowing away into the blackly overcast night. Another gesture and the frame hinges rust; the Falconer pulls it out of the wall and lets it clatter to the floor.

He sees that he is somewhere in the Ponta Corbessa, just a block or two north of the docks. He sends his awareness forth, softly and subtly, well aware that none of the magi still abroad in the city will show him an instant's mercy if he is located. It takes only moments to find what he wants, one of the fan-tailed carrion crows of the North Amathel, sly sociable birds with sharp eyes, sharp beaks, and sharp talons.

The Falconer takes the first crow gently and launches it into the night, using a slim thread of awareness, suppressing his delight at the sensation of soaring. A moment or two reaffirms his affinity for the work, and he extends his control to the half-dozen other crows roosting nearby.

The Falconer's purloined murder circles over the Ponta Corbessa, hunting both for other crows and a glimpse of a certain cloaked woman. She must still be somewhere in Karthain, and he'll know her at any distance, so long as she isn't hidden away under a deep spell.

Seven crows becomes thirty. The Falconer directs them with the precision of a dancing master, sending more and more of his awareness out into the feathered cloud, seeing not through individual pairs of eyes but as a thrilling gestalt, a whirling composite of dark streets, rooftops, rattling carriages, and hurrying people.

Thirty crows becomes sixty. Sixty becomes ninety. They unwind in orderly spirals, north and west, search tirelessly.

It doesn't take long to find her, at the western edge of the Ponta Corbessa. She is walking alone, toward some rendezvous, and the Falconer recognizes her beyond all possibility of doubt. Blood calls to blood.

His flights of crows, black against the black sky, converge and circle silently, three hundred feet up. In moments he has gathered one hundred and fifty, the most living creatures of any sort he has ever controlled at once. His mind is on fire with the thrill of power; now he has to be quick and certain, before Patience can bring her formidable skills into play, before any other magi can notice what's going on.

One crow flutters and falls out of the night. The rest follow a heartbeat later.

Patience is on the pavement beside a warehouse, just passing under a swaying orange alchemical lamp. The first crow shoots past her hood from behind, brushing it, squawing and cawing all the way.

She whirls to see where it came from. The next dozen birds fly directly into her face.

Eyes, nose, cheeks, lips – there is no time to be merciful. The ball of sorcery-maddened crows pecks and claws at anything soft, anything vulnerable. Patience barely has time to scream before she is blind and on her back, flailing as more crows pour out of the sky like a black cloud given flesh.

She remembers her sorcery, and half manages a spell. A dozen birds flash into cinders, but a dozen more take their place, seeking neck and forehead, wrists and fingers. The Falconer presses Patience down to the pavement, the writhing flock a pure extension of his will, a crushing dark hand. Grinning madly, he channels a thought-sending to her, hurling his sigil against her shattered mental defences, and then:

Is this weakness, Mother?

You never understood my talents.

The truth is, they never made me weak.

THE TRUTH IS THAT THEY GAVE ME WINGS.

The beaks and claws of the carrion birds are driven by human intelligence; in moments they have opened Patience's wrists, pulped her hands, peeled the skin from her neck, torn out her eyes and tongue. She is helpless long before she dies.

The Falconer disperses his clouds of winged minions and sags against the window frame, gasping for breath. He has expended so much of himself … He needs food. He must tear the house apart for anything useful. He needs clothing, money, boots … He must be away as soon as he's eaten, away from this nest of his enemies, away to re-cover himself.

'The time of quiet, Mother?' He hums the words softly to himself, savouring the eerie sensation of the dreamsteel vibrating in his throat. 'Oh, I think the last fucking thing your friends are going to enjoy is a *time of quiet.*'

Hobbling uneasily, laughing to himself, he moves carefully down the stairs. First food, then clothes. Then to gather strength for the work ahead.

The long, bloody work ahead.

AFTERWORD

I'm grateful to Simon Spanton for recommending Antony Sher's autobiographical *The Year of the King*, a book which didn't so much directly influence *The Republic of Thieves* as whet my appetite to portray the players of the Moncraine Company from several angles I hadn't previously considered. I hope that I may plead to enthusiasts of the theatre, as I did to enthusiasts of all things nautical with *Red Seas Under Red Skies*, to remember that I have not sought to accurately re-create any particular tradition of troupe or performance from our own world, but to arrange selected elements of those traditions in a shape I found amusing.

I'm grateful again to Simon Spanton and Anne Groell for their long-suffering patience and support during a troublesome time; to my brilliant Sarah, who found something broken and helped put it back together; to Lou Anders, Jonathan Strahan, and Gareth-Michael Skarka, who coaxed work out of me when I badly needed to feel capable of it, and lastly to that person whose long correspondence kept me crawling forward in hope during the lowest, darkest point of my life: Thank you.

This concludes the third volume in the Gentleman Bastard sequence, which will continue with *The Thorn of Emberlain*.

SL

New Richmond, Wisconsin, 2008 – Brookfield, Massachusetts, 2013